BAD PENNY

I was in disgrace, held tight over Vicky's lap with my bum showing, naked and vulnerable to the punishment that was about to be inflicted on me. She raised a knee, lifting my poor bottom so that my cheeks opened. The shame was unbearable, as I knew my sex would be showing in every detail of pink fleshy folds and hairy lips, as well as the centre of my bottom, the wrinkled pinkish-brown hole of my anus. I thought nothing could be worse, and then she started to spank me.

BAD PENNY

Penny Birch

I would like to dedicate this collection of stories to the naughtiest of my playmates, who know exactly who they are . . .

This book is a work of fiction.
In real life, make sure you practise safe sex.

First published in 1999 by
Nexus
Thames Wharf Studios
Rainville Road
London W6 9HT

Typeset by TW Typesetting, Plymouth, Devon

Printed and bound by
Cox & Wyman Ltd, Reading, Berks

ISBN 0 352 33335 9

Contents

1

Opening the Garden

From the very first, my sexual fantasies always revolved around being helpless: powerless to prevent something rude being done to me. I also liked the idea of being put in an awkward, embarrassing sexual situation through no fault of my own. I had been brought up quite strictly, and having such naughty ideas made me guilty and ashamed; yet that very guilt and shame served as a spur to my excitement.

So when the other girls were drooling over the latest boy-wonder pop star, I'd be thinking about how it would feel to tear my skirt on a barbed-wire fence and have to walk home in my panties. I used to lie awake at night and play with my pussy while I thought about such things, although I was still a virgin and hadn't so much as touched a man's cock. Nor had I managed to reach orgasm, mainly because my worry about being caught masturbating never allowed me to really relax. The one about tearing my skirt off was typical of my fantasies, an imaginary scene in which my body was accidentally exposed and then taken advantage of by some great, brainless oaf of a man. The men were always like that in my imagination: huge, shambling brutes driven by lust they were quite incapable of controlling. Their cocks would be monstrous things, like small logs, gnarled and veined and capable of producing prodigious amounts of come.

Of course, this was all fantasy. The only time I'd even seen a cock was when my cousin Kate let me watch her pull her boyfriend off in the back of his car. I'd been terrified, but also fascinated, by the way it swelled to erection and then spurted come all over her hand when he came. The experience fired my imagination, but unfortunately imagination was as far as it went. Being small, quiet and studious, the sort of boys I attracted were the exact opposite of the men of my fantasies. Without exception they were gentle, considerate, insecure, shy, nice ... and totally devoid of sex appeal. I didn't want a box of chocolates and a peck on the lips from a polite young gentleman. I wanted my blouse ripped open and my panties torn off by a man who could no more resist me than he could resist his own heartbeat.

To make matters worse, there was Kate. We were cousins and the best of friends, yet she had everything to attract the sort of man I wanted: a C-cup bra, for one thing. Inevitably I got left with the wet ones and, just to add extra frustration, Kate's rejects and exes would often confide their passion for her to me.

I finally broke my duck during a summer holiday, as I suppose so many people do. My mother and her sister had been taking a cottage in the Channel Islands every year since before we were born, and it had become a sort of tradition for both families. Kate and I knew all the locals and the other regular holiday-makers and, looking back on it, the social set-up was insular to the point of being incestuous. Everybody knew more or less how they related to everyone else, and God help the girl who fancied a boy who wasn't regarded as one of the attractive ones.

Kate, inevitably, was Little Miss Popular, and was regarded by the boys as *the* catch. Despite being a bit of a loner and getting teased for studying and reading more than was felt to be normal, I was by no means unpopular. This was mainly because boys tended to see me as a way of getting to Kate, but I put up with it and enjoyed myself most of the time. That year I had no boyfriend, as usual, while Kate was going out with a tall, swarthy lad called Carl.

Carl was a fisherman and about as close to rough trade

as anyone on the island, which excited the disapproval of our parents and made Kate fancy him all the more. I didn't really like him, as he was too laddish, yet I had to admit he had a certain appeal, and I was more than a little jealous of Kate. He worked with his father, and their main income came from lobster, langouste and crab. He used to be out all day and then meet us at one of the island's many bars, where he and Kate would snog and fondle the evening away while I sat and talked to his friends.

It was one such evening that sparked off my experience. Carl and three of his friends came into the bar, laughing and joking. Kate asked what was up as they sat down with us. Carl was grinning from ear to ear as he pulled Kate towards him with the characteristic roughness that always made me jealous.

'You know that bloke Ryan?' Carl asked.

Kate nodded. From the point of view of our social set, Ryan was the least desirable boy of all. Tall, red-haired, gangly and unable to dance; to even speak to him was to risk ostracisation. Personally I felt rather sorry for him, and was sure that whatever story Carl had to tell was not going to be to the unfortunate Ryan's advantage. I was right.

Carl described how he and his father had been lifting pots in one of the tiny bays beneath the cliffs to the south of the island. They had had the engine off and put the anchor down while they lunched. When they had finished, it had only been necessary to let out a little more chain to let the current take the boat on to the next pot. As they had drifted past an outcrop of rock they had come in sight of a gully that had previously been hidden. Ryan had been in the gully, stark naked, with his erect cock in his hand, masturbating.

'. . . you should have seen the fucker,' Carl finished. 'He had his eyes closed, his hand's going up and down like a fucking piston, his great hairy sac's going from side to side . . . fuck me, I thought he was going to explode. Then the old man calls out and asks him if he's having a good one. Fuck, you should have seen him move when he saw us.'

The story was greeted with more laughter from Carl's friends, even though it was probably the third or fourth time they'd heard it. Kate laughed too, mixing her giggles with a suitably ladylike measure of disgust. I smiled and grimaced at the appropriate places but my emotions were very different. For a start, I felt sorry for Ryan, whose life would now be unbearable. I also felt only some of the disgust that I was trying so hard to register in my expression. What he'd been doing struck me not only as a dirty act that only boys who were unable to get girlfriends did, but as something primitively masculine, something that he had done because he was unable to restrain his lust.

I didn't stay out late that evening, but excused myself on the grounds of feeling tired and walked back to town. It was dark and I was slightly drunk, with the unlit road barely discernible between the banks on either side. I could see were I was going, just, yet the darkness made me feel pleasantly detached. I wasn't really tired, but had wanted to let my mind run on the thought of Ryan masturbating without the distracting din of music and loud voices.

Knowing that I would see the headlights of any cars long before they got to me, I slipped my hand down the front of my jeans and began to stroke myself through my panties. My pussy was damp and felt wonderfully soft and sexy under my fingers. In my mind I was imagining Ryan's body, pale and sinewy with his swollen erection in his hands and his balls swaying beneath the shaft as he pulled at himself. Carl had said Ryan's balls had been large and covered with red hair, his cock long, white and with a red tip, a description that was supposed to shock and disgust us. It did shock me, but mainly because I wanted so badly to have seen it. My emotions were an odd mixture of shame and sexual need, and only the horror of chancing being caught in much the same way Ryan had been prevented me from going into the hedge and playing with myself.

When I got back I lay in bed, wide awake with my nightie up and my panties pushed down to my thighs so that I could pull them up quickly if anyone came in. I tried to bring myself off, rubbing at my clit with the little

4

circular motions that always seemed to give the best sensation. Twice a really strange feeling crept up on me and I thought I was going to come, but all the time I was straining my ears for the sound of Kate's key in the front door. We shared a room and, despite our intimacy, I did not want to be caught by her. There was the feeling of shame at what I was doing and what I was thinking of as well, which made it even harder to concentrate.

Kate didn't get back until nearly three, yet I was still wide awake. She was absolutely glowing, and told me how she and Carl had driven out to one of the old quarries at the eastern end of the island and had sex in the cab of his pick-up. She had pulled her top up so that he could play with her boobs and had even sucked his cock. She was immensely proud of herself and I was glad for her, but also jealous and even more turned on than before. There I'd been, lying in bed desperately attempting to make myself come, while Kate had been having sex with the big, rough Carl.

Nobody saw anything of Ryan for about a week after that, and it began to be rumoured that he had left the island out of sheer embarrassment. Finally, the following weekend, he was spotted fishing on a particularly lonely piece of the shore. This led to a whole series of new jokes about his masturbatory habits, which I joined in with, despite having very different thoughts in my head.

The place where he had been seen was called Val de Fret, an old French name typical of the islands. It was a rocky cove at the bottom of a couple of hundred feet of cliff, and if it was a pig of a place to get to, then that was presumably why he had chosen it. On that Saturday night, Kate and Carl went even further. They had gone out to the quarry as before, only this time, after she had sucked him hard, they had gone all the way. She had knelt for him in the back of the pick-up, topless and with her jeans and panties down. He had played with her tits while he rode her and came all over her bare bottom. The description made me jealous and also painfully turned on. It had been in the doggy position too, with her bum exposed to him, an idea which I found deliciously rude and incredibly sexy.

The next day was Sunday, and I managed to evade everybody after breakfast and made my way out along the cliff path. My route was rather aimless, but I knew exactly where I was going to end up. Sure enough, half-an-hour's walk found me on the cliff top that overlooked the Val de Fret. I was telling myself that I didn't want to find Ryan, but of course I did. He was there, too, sitting on a rock and just watching the waves. I was completely incapable of doing what I wanted, which was to find the way down and ask if he'd like –

Well, to be honest, I didn't really know. I wanted him to be the instigator, to make me do something really dirty, like strip and pose in rude positions for him to come over. I didn't want to have to ask, nor to get into the sort of half-embarrassed relationship that would lead to the clumsy gropes and fumbles that formed the extent of my experience of sex. Given that he knew the state of his reputation on the island, he was in fact highly unlikely to make an advance on me at all, as he would only know me as the best friend of the ever-popular Kate. I also felt more than a little ashamed of my own emotions.

As I stood at the top of the cliff, feeling frustrated and annoyed with myself for my lack of courage, I decided that the least I could do was to climb down. I eventually found a suitable-looking place and began my descent, only to be brought up short by a drop of around six feet where the vegetation ended and the bare rock began. It was vertical and, while there appeared to be toe-holds, I didn't trust myself to climb down. Feeling very pathetic, I sat down where I was sure he couldn't see me and tried to think what to do. I was feeling pretty silly, and almost started back, but decided to at least try and get a better view of him. A little way above me was one of the German bunkers with which the Channel Islands are dotted. It looked as if its observation port had been designed to overlook the Val de Fret. As the thing was solid concrete about three feet thick, with only a narrow observation slit, I knew that once inside I would be invisible, yet could watch to my heart's content.

It smelt faintly musty inside, and I had to traverse an almost completely dark room to get where I wanted. It was worth it though, because the observation slit gave me a view of the entire bay, including Ryan. He was walking around the bay, leaping from boulder to boulder and occasionally glancing out to sea. He seemed strangely furtive, considering he was fully dressed and had a perfect right to be there, and I began to wonder, and hope, that he might be thinking of playing with himself. I felt a little scared, but also thrilled by the knowledge that, while I could see him clearly, he couldn't see me at all.

He inspected the sea-cave at the very apex of the bay, but quickly came out. Again he glanced out to sea, and I became doubly sure that he was up to something. He continued to search, clearly looking for somewhere private but with no luck. Finally he disappeared from view, directly underneath me. I began to feel more nervous, wondering if he might choose my bunker as a good place to masturbate. Of course, it was exactly what I wanted, in my fantasies: but now that it stood a chance of becoming reality, I began to feel scared.

I had made up my mind to go when I heard the crunch of a boot on the gravel outside. It could only be him, and I was stuck, and faced with the embarrassment of being caught spying. I stayed still, thinking frantically of what to say. He didn't come into my room, though; and, after a couple more noises, there was silence. Finally I decided that he had gone and plucked up the courage to leave. I moved quietly across the darkened room, then into the lighter one, only to stop short.

A short stair led from one wall, up to what had presumably once been some sort of gun emplacement. Ryan was standing in it, his lower half visible and his shoulders and torso out of my view. He was also massaging his crotch.

I almost ran – but of course, from where he was, he could see all round. All round, that was, except for the interior of the bunker. Rooted to the spot, I watched as he stroked and squeezed at the bulge in his trousers. I knew my mouth was open and there was a lump in my throat the size of a football. Still I didn't run, because, when it came down to it, I needed to watch so badly.

His gentle massaging was making his cock grow, and I could see its outline inside his jeans. After a while he put his hand to his fly and drew the zip down, then undid the button and let his jeans drop. He had boxer shorts on underneath; his half-erect cock was even more conspicuous inside them. I felt myself start to shake as he took hold of his boxers and pushed them slowly down, revealing a brush of ginger pubic hair. Then his cock flopped over the top and I nearly gave myself away, just managing to stifle my gasp at the exposure of a man's penis just feet away from me. He pushed the shorts down a bit further, exposing balls every bit as large and hairy as Carl had described.

He started to masturbate, stroking his cock until it was standing upright and the head was completely out of the foreskin. It seemed much bigger than the only other erection I had seen, paler, fleshier and somehow more vital. Now that it was stiff he began to pull up and down, holding it around the shaft and tugging. I was entranced, scared and disgusted, imagining the thing being pushed into my vagina as I lay on my back with my legs open or knelt with every rude detail of my sex on display for him.

I did register that something had changed, but only too late did I realise what it was, and what that meant. Even as I realised that I could hear the sound of a boat's engine, he was ducking down into the emplacement and then he was staring me straight in the face.

Our eyes met and then I turned mine down, aware that I was blushing furiously and completely lost for anything to say. Then I panicked and ran, only to stop at the entrance, realising that if I came out of the bunker, then whoever was in the boat would see me, and in all probability see me with Ryan.

I heard him swear behind me and then ask me to stop, which I did, drawn by the tone of his voice, which was not aggressive at all, but tired and pleading. I turned back into the bunker, finding him in the act of pulling his jeans and boxers up.

'Penny, isn't it?' he said, then continued when I nodded. 'Look, Penny, I know you think I'm a jerk and everything, but –'

'That's not true,' I interrupted. 'I . . . oh, I don't know, but I don't think you're a jerk.'

'No?' he queried. 'Even . . . I mean . . .'

He broke off, no more sure of what to say than I was. I wanted to do something, say something, but I could feel the moment slipping away and knew that, if I didn't act then, there would be no second opportunity. For all my mixed feelings, I just had to do it.

'I . . . Could I watch?' I stammered, hardly able to believe what I was saying.

'Do you really want to?' he asked, his voice full of doubt.

I nodded.

'You're taking the piss,' he said, suddenly aggressive. 'If . . .'

'No, no, I mean it,' I answered. 'Please?'

He looked at me very steadily. I could feel my lower lip trembling and possibly that's what decided him, because his expression changed from annoyance to a pleased yet rather crafty look.

'OK,' he said evenly.

I bit my lip as his hand went to his trousers once more. He was still looking at me, ready for any sign that my interest wasn't genuine. I swallowed as his cock came on view again, now limp. He sat back on the lowest of the emplacement steps, the light from the door giving me a good view of his cock and balls as he opened his legs. He took his cock in his hand and began to stroke, using the other to cup his balls and massage them gently. I could feel the dampness between my legs as his cock stiffened, the head emerging from the foreskin as he rolled it down. He opened his legs further, giving me a full view of his cock and balls, a sight that had me blushing.

9

'You are pretty, Penny,' he said as he began to pull at his now hard shaft.

'Thanks,' I murmured, sensing the rising excitement in his voice.

I was getting really turned on, my qualms forgotten in the heat of the moment. He really began to show off, stroking the shaft of his cock, putting his fingers around the base to show me how long it was, holding it out towards me. I was mesmerised, really excited and yet needing to be led if we were to go any further.

'The amount of times I've wanked over you, Penny,' he sighed, 'and you're here, watching me do it.'

'Really?' I asked. 'Over me?'

'Yeah,' he said. 'I've watched you walk on the beach, with that lovely round bum spilling out of that blue bikini you wear.'

I giggled, delighted by his arousal. He was now pulling up and down fast, his qualms forgotten as he got more excited. What he was saying was so dirty, so improper, so unlike the way anybody had spoken to me before.

'And your sweet tits,' he continued. 'Come on, Penny, show me them, give me something to wank over.'

I hesitated, and could feel myself blushing. The others were right – he was a dirty bastard – but I still found myself wanting to do it.

'Come on, Penny,' he repeated, 'show me those pretty tits.'

My hands went to my top. He watched me as I shrugged it off, his eyes locked on my body and his hand jerking frantically up and down his penis. I took hold of my bra, hesitated again and then pulled it sharply up over my breasts, leaving it like that.

'Now your jeans, Penny,' he demanded. 'Come on, strip for me.'

I undid my fly button, my fingers shaking violently. I wasn't sure if I wanted to do it, yet he was getting frantic.

'I'm coming, Penny, turn round and ease them down over your bum. Come on, darling, do it,' he said hoarsely.

'You're really dirty,' I said, but I turned to show my rear.

'Stick it out,' he gasped, 'and pull your knickers down too – please, Penny, please.'

I let my jeans drop and stuck my bottom out but didn't pull my pants down, feeling shy and at once attracted and repelled by the dirtiness of what he was saying.

'Show me your cunt. Show me your arsehole,' he gasped.

I hesitated only an instant and then tugged the back of my panties down, calling him a dirty bastard as I pulled open my bum-cheeks. I was genuinely cross with what he was making me do, but too turned on to refuse him.

'You filthy, dirty . . .' I said, but it was really to excuse my own behaviour.

I was looking over my shoulder, watching the ecstasy on his face as his eyes locked on my pussy and bottom-hole. Then he was getting to his feet, his hand jerking frantically at his erection.

I squealed in protest, but too late, as a jet of sperm erupted from his cock and splashed across my naked bum.

'Dirty bastard!' I squeaked, jumping up in alarm.

I could feel it on my pussy-lips and between my bum-cheeks, and knew my panties and jeans would be soiled. My feelings of repulsion were genuine, yet deeper down I was in ecstasy over what he had done, and what I had done, pulling my pants down for a boy, showing him my rudest and most intimate parts and letting him come over them. I was grimacing as I felt the sperm squelch between my bottom-cheeks, feeling utterly ashamed of what I'd done, feeling I ought to be punished. I knew, though, that if he'd just taken it a bit slower, if he'd been more commanding than demanding, treated me as I liked to be treated in my fantasies, then he could easily have had his cock in my mouth, even taken my virginity.

I didn't regret what I had done with Ryan, but nor did it progress to anything more. Afterwards both of us dressed in silence and parted company with only a rather formal goodbye. Neither of us spoke about it to anyone either and life went on much as before. True, I had possibly made the mistake of romanticising him just because he was a loner,

11

when in truth he was both naturally antisocial and a bit of a bastard. That made no difference to my feelings about what we'd done, though, and if I felt rather guilty and ashamed, then that would have been true with anyone, not just Ryan.

What did disturb me was the way that the experience did nothing to resolve my confusion about my sexuality. In fact, it made it worse. One of my feelings after the incident with Ryan had been the need to be punished for it. I knew how, as well: over someone's knee with my panties pulled down and my bum bouncing to hard slaps from a powerful hand. It would be punishment, and I'd feel genuinely sorry afterwards, yet the idea was immensely sexy. I used to fantasise about it being done in public, with a note pinned up detailing my disgusting sin. More confusing and shameful still was the knowledge that of all the people who I wanted to do it, one was an undoubted favourite: my closest friend, another girl and my cousin – Kate.

2

Pretty in Pink

My cousin Kate got married on a glorious summer's day. The ceremony was held at a beautiful old church in rural Berkshire and the reception at their house nearby. I was chief bridesmaid, and decked out in a gown of coral-pink silk which everybody complimented me on but which made me feel like a little girl. This was partly because the other bridesmaid was Kate's little sister, Susan, a gawky, rebellious eleven-year-old. Mainly it was because Kate was getting married and I was still a virgin, and an innocent one at that.

The most I had done was let some pervert pull himself off over my bare bottom while I held my cheeks apart to show him my bumhole. The experience had enriched my fantasies no end, increasing my desire to be humiliated and controlled and adding a disturbing need to be given physical punishment, preferably by Kate. From the point of view of boyfriends, it had done me no good at all, making what was available even less tempting than previously. There had been a couple of rather weird encounters but, by Kate's standards, I was a complete innocent. I had also just about started to accept that other women's bodies excited me. Kate knew too, all of it, and while she had just giggled at my suggestion that she might like to spank me, she had been trying to find me boyfriends ever since. I hadn't fancied one of them.

Then she had met Toby, a brash money-broker with a huge income, a fancy car and the outlook on life of a pig.

13

Not a sweet, plump little piglet either, but a gorging, rutting great boar. With her pretty face, brown curls and magnificent figure, she made the perfect trophy for him and, after just over a year together, he had asked her to marry him. Both her parents and mine had put up resistance, but not much, and so it was that I found myself as her bridesmaid.

People often describe brides as looking radiant. Ravishing was a better description of Kate, with her trim waist and her big boobs threatening to spill out of her bodice. I had helped dress her and had become more than a little turned on by the process. Judging by the way she had giggled, so had she, or maybe it had just been the thought of what Toby would do to her later. In any case, the dress was magnificent, sumptuous, yet elegant in pure white silk, which was a bit cheeky as even by my reckoning Kate had given seven men the pleasure of her pussy.

The ceremony went without a hitch, and things were still running smoothly by the time the reception got to the dancing and chatting stage. There had been champagne for toasts, and wine with lunch, then more champagne, and I was more than a little tipsy. Kate and Toby were going to Mauritius for their honeymoon, and didn't have to leave until quite late, which meant that they were in no hurry. I danced with Toby, as was my duty. I like big, strong men, and for all I found him unbearably brash I had to admit that it was nice being in his arms. What did give me a shock was when he suddenly let a hand slip down from my waist and took a handful of my bottom through my dress. I squeaked, but there was nothing I could do about it without making a scene and so I let him have a good feel. With the press of people around us, nobody could see, yet I felt really guilty as he fondled my bottom, especially as it was turning me on. He then bent down, and I thought he was going to kiss me, which really would have caused a scene, but instead he whispered in my ear.

'Katie says you're a virgin,' he said quietly.

I must have gone scarlet, and I certainly didn't know what to say, but he did.

14

'Come with me,' he continued, taking me by the hand. 'Kate and I have got a little surprise for you.'

I had no idea what he was talking about, and resisted his pull until Kate appeared by my side. She had a bottle of champagne in her hand and a distinctly mischievous look in her eye. I had no idea what they were up to and was still flustered by the discovery that Kate had told him one of my most intimate secrets.

'What are you doing?' I giggled as they guided me gently but firmly towards the exit of the marquee.

'Shh, we've got a pressie for you,' Kate replied.

I still had no idea what she was talking about, but let them steer me out of the marquee and out on to the lawn. It was warm outside, and bathed in yellow sunlight that stung my eyes after the cool, softly illuminated interior of the marquee. One or two people were in the garden, including Susan, who was sitting on a swing with her knees together and her feet apart, sipping orange juice. She was already as tall as me, and seeing her sitting there looking so girlish made me feel really small. I had often baby-sat Susan, yet at the reception a lot of people had treated us much the same. I was a woman, she was a little girl, and it had really stung, especially as I had to admit that in our fluffy pink dresses we didn't look all that different.

Kate had taken my other hand, and put her champagne bottle to my lips as we walked. Some went in my mouth, but more splashed down my bodice, making me giggle at the feel of cold liquid between my breasts. We went into the house and upstairs. Kate looked out of the window as we reached the landing.

'Clear,' she said, nodding to Toby.

'What are you doing?' I asked as she opened the bathroom door and he hustled me inside.

'Like I said, we've got a pressie for you,' she replied. 'Come on, Toby, we'd better be quick; get it out.'

'Hey!' I protested as, to my horror, Toby put his hand to his zip.

'Don't be prissy, Penny,' Kate said, putting her arm around Toby's waist. 'Sit down on the loo.'

15

I sat, dizzy with drink and the excitement of the day, watching as Kate's brand new husband dropped his dress trousers and then pulled his cock and balls over the top of his briefs. I gasped, making him laugh. Without preamble he moved forward, parting his legs and bending his knees a bit so that his cock was thrust right in my face.

'Here's a lollipop for you,' he joked. 'Man flavour.'

'Katie!' I protested, looking at the big, flaccid cock in front of me.

'Go on, Penny, suck him,' Kate said, sliding her hand under his balls and lifting her lewd, fleshy handful.

His cock touched my nose and I shrank back, but only a little. I could smell his cock, an urgent male scent that had me instantly on heat. Kate was stroking him, making his cock swell with blood, right in front of my face. It looked utterly obscene, a fat, pink worm writhing in my cousin's hand on its bed of hairy ball-sac.

'Taste it, Penny,' Kate urged. 'It's for you, specially.'

Well, it was her wedding day and she was offering me her husband because she thought I wasn't getting my share of cock. It was utterly humiliating, but also completely irresistible. I paused, my lower lip trembling as I thought of what I was about to do, then I opened my mouth.

Toby moved a little forward, his cock bending as it pushed against my chin. I hesitated, mouth open willingly but not sure if I could actually do something as dirty as sucking Toby's cock. Then Kate let go of his balls and just popped it in. I squeaked in protest, only to have her stroke my chin, making me swallow and close my mouth on the intruding cock. It was a shabby trick, but I was sucking and, now that it was in, it wasn't so bad at all.

Toby took me by the back of the head and pulled me into him, making me gag as his rapidly swelling cock touched the back of my throat. He was half stiff and tasted salty and strongly male against my tongue. I put my hands up and took hold of him around his legs. He had started to slide his cock in and out of my mouth, and I responded, taking over the motion as he came to full erection. The shaft felt rubbery between my lips and I could feel the head of his cock in my throat, bulbous and fat. I was in ecstasy, and wanting to play with myself.

'Is the lollipop nice?' Toby asked, leering down at me as I sucked eagerly on his erection.

I nodded around my mouthful, not wanting to let it out.

'Sexy little bint, isn't she?' Toby addressed Kate. 'But I think it's cunt time, or I'll come in her mouth. You know I'm going to fuck you, don't you, Penny?'

'Don't be crude, Toby,' Kate admonished. 'Say pussy and be gentle with her, too.'

I didn't much care: cunt or pussy, I was about to have my virginity taken and, whatever they called it, it was mine and about to be filled with the fat penis that was currently in my mouth. I had already guessed that that was what they had in store for me. I thought of being fucked on the bathroom floor by Toby, who would then swan off on honeymoon with Kate, leaving me with my vagina full of his semen. His cock was rock-hard in my mouth, ready for me to get down on the floor, spread my knees, pull off my pants and let him in. I would have done it, but they had something even more humiliating in store for me.

'We better hurry,' Kate said, glancing nervously out of the window. 'Let him go, Penny, you slut.'

I reluctantly released Toby's cock from my mouth, but only because I knew it was going somewhere even better. I thought it might hurt, as Kate had said it did when she lost her own virginity, but I really wanted to be deflowered, then and there. As Toby pulled back, I began to slip to the floor, only to have him take me by the arms and manhandle me around. I wasn't sure what he was doing at first, but then realised. I was going to be fucked doggy fashion, bent over the toilet.

As Toby put me in position, I saw that Kate was pulling up the front of her dress, bunching the petticoats under her arm until the front of her panties showed. They were white silk, caught between her plump pussy-lips and damp where her juice had started to run. I looked up into her face as I took a grip on the toilet bowl, finding her mouth a little open and her eyes wide. She blew me a kiss as she slipped

17

a hand down the front of her panties, and then Toby was lifting my pretty pink dress.

I was shaking as he did it, lifting it up on to my back. My petticoats followed, exposing my panties. Kate had begun to masturbate, her eyes glued to her husband's erection and my bum.

'Nice arse,' Toby breathed, putting a hand out to stroke the back of my panties. 'Sorry, but I've got to do this.'

I didn't know what he meant, as he was about to fill my pussy and that was nothing to be sorry about. Then he was pulling me up and opening the toilet seat. I stared in horrified fascination at the open bowl as he took me by the hair and pushed my face down into it.

'Oh, Toby,' Kate sighed. 'Flush her, then fuck her, you dirty bastard.'

I had never been so humiliated in my life, nor so excited. My face was inches from the water, and Toby was pulling my panties down, exposing my buttocks, my anus and then my vagina, which was his to enter.

His hand was still in my hair as he came round to get to the chain. I was whimpering, absolutely ready for it with my eyes tight shut and my head well down into the bowl. Suddenly my head was pulled back and his cock was being pushed at my face. I opened my mouth just in time to have it filled with his erection. Behind him I could see Kate, now masturbating openly with her panties pushed down around her thighs and a finger buried in between her pussy-lips.

Toby groaned and his cock jerked. Suddenly my mouth was full of something salty and I realised that he had come in it. There was plenty of it, too, squeezing out around my lips and dribbling down my chin as he pushed hard into me.

'Toby!' Kate exclaimed.

'Don't worry, I can still fuck her,' Toby gasped. 'You know me.'

He pushed my face back down the toilet, actually into the water. My mouth was full of his come, which was really slimy, yet to open my mouth was to get a drink of toilet water. I braced myself for the indignity of being flushed, only to be brought up short by a knock on the door.

'Kate?' a voice demanded. 'Your cab's here.'

'Shit!' Kate exclaimed, Toby hastily letting go of my head.

It was Kate's mother. If we had bluffed it out we could have got away with it. I might have hidden in the shower cubicle, or maybe squeezed into the linen basket, even climbed out of the window. As it was, Kate had to swear and my aunt's voice changed from placid to questioning and slightly angry.

'Who's in there, Kate?' she demanded.

I was still scrabbling my panties up as Toby reached for the lock. Kate was moderately decent, but my face was covered in come.

'Stop!' I squealed as Toby turned the key, but it was too late.

'Penny?' Kate's mother asked, then the door was open.

'Auntie Elaine, hi,' I managed weakly as I found myself looking into her astonished face. I saw her glance at the blatant bulge in Toby's trousers, then her look turned to absolute outrage as she focused on my face.

I suppose, from Toby's point of view, he acted pretty coolly. He nodded politely to his mother-in-law, took Kate's hand and left the room. As he was an enormous oaf, there was nothing that she could do to stop him going, which of course only made her more annoyed. It also left me to face the full force of her temper, yet what happened next came as a complete shock.

Without saying a word, she marched forward and slammed the toilet seat down, then grabbed my arm.

'Hey! No!' I squealed as I realised her intention. She was going to spank me.

I was off balance, and came down hard over her lap. Before I could do anything about it, my arm had been twisted into my back.

'No, auntie, you can't – not at my age!' I yelled, heedless of who might hear. 'Auntie! No!'

'You think you're too old for a spanking, do you?' she snapped. 'Well, you're not, you dirty, filthy, little tramp!'

'No!' I squealed, but it was no good; my arm was

19

trapped in the small of my back and she was stronger than me, anyway.

'I'm going to spank you and I'm going to spank you bare,' she announced, starting to pull up my dress.

I begged, pleaded, cajoled and threatened, but to no avail as my lovely pink dress was lifted over my bottom. To make it worse, I could see my reflection in the mirror opposite. My aunt was seated on the toilet, a stern unyielding expression on her face. My dress was up, my pink silk slippers and white stockings showing, one little tit peeping over the top of my bodice, my face spattered with Toby's sperm. I shut my eyes, then opened them again, unable to resist watching myself being prepared for a spanking.

She raised my petticoats one by one, until there was a froth of pink and white around my middle and over my aunt's legs. My pink panties were taut over my bottom, which looked embarrassingly plump thrust up over my aunt's lap. They were quite big, but I had pulled them up too fast and a good slice of my bum was bulging out of each frilly leg-hole. Elaine turned to look at my bottom, obviously deciding whether my pants needed to come down. It was the first sign of hesitancy she had shown, prompting me to renew my pleas for mercy.

'Not on the bare bottom, Auntie Elaine, please!' I appealed.

'Stop mewling,' she snapped, and put her hand to the waistband of my panties. 'Why should I leave your pants up?'

'Because it's humiliating to have a bare bottom!' I protested.

'All the more reason they should come down, then,' she answered and started to do it.

I watched in horror as my aunt pulled down my knickers. So many times I had imagined this scene. Me bent over someone's lap, my panties on show while they lectured me, then my panties being taken down, slowly, to make me really feel the indignity of having my bum bared for punishment. Now it was for real, and it was ten times more humiliating than I could ever have imagined, especially when it was my aunt who was doing it.

She settled my panties around my thighs, leaving my bottom looking pink and vulnerable in the mirror. I could see both cheeks, looking pouted and chubby because of the way my bottom was thrust up. A little puff of black hair was visible, poking out from between my thighs, and I knew that to her the rear of my pussy, and worse, my anus, would be on show.

'I hope you feel ashamed of yourself,' she said, raising her hand over my unprotected bum.

I did, but I only managed a whimper in response, then her hand came down, planting a stinging slap on my naked cheeks. I squeaked and kicked, only to have my arm twisted more tightly still into my back even as the second smack fell. I saw my bottom bounce in the mirror, the flesh wobbling under the impact of the slap, then again, and again. I made no effort to restrain myself, but kicked and squealed and mewled as the merciless slaps rained down on my bottom. I was tossing my head from side to side as well, not just from the pain but to try and get rid of the feelings that were building up inside me. I shut my eyes to get rid of the appalling sight of myself being spanked across my aunt's lap, but it was no good – it was arousing, desperately arousing.

It also hurt, and only when I started to sob did she finally push me off her lap. I mumbled an apology, but she simply stormed from the room, leaving me red-bottomed and blubbering on the floor. Only when I heard the back door slam below me did I have the sense to get up and cover myself, stroking my burning behind before I pulled my knickers up. When my dress had fallen back into place and I had returned my left breast to my bodice, I began to calm down.

I went to the window, squeezing my bottom through my dress, still snivelling a little and feeling thoroughly sorry for myself. Outside, Elaine was walking purposefully down the garden, only to slow and take a glass of champagne from a waiter. She was obviously not going straight to my mother, at least not yet. Remembering the bottle Kate had had, I turned to find it, draining the last few inches straight into my mouth.

My head was spinning, and not just from the drink. I had really been put through it, coaxed into sucking cock, almost fucked, and with my head down a toilet! Then I'd been spanked, spanked like a naughty little girl without a thought for my modesty, spanked with my bottom bare and my mouth full of sperm.

A shiver went right through me. I had never yet reached a climax, yet my pussy had never felt so swollen and wet, nor my nipples so stiff. I badly wanted to try and come, and was sure I could, if only I could find somewhere private to concentrate.

I couldn't help a little smile as I realised that, actually, I had the perfect opportunity. I'd just been spanked, and left on the floor in tears with my bum bare and red. I knew my aunt. Once her initial fury had subsided, she would feel sorry for punishing me. With luck she would keep it to herself, and she would certainly leave me some time to compose myself and dry my tears. She'd expect me to run up to my room in a tantrum and not come down until I was ready. Only if my absence became prolonged would she come and investigate.

Sure that I had at least half an hour of peace, I made my way quickly up the stairs, feeling both guilty and naughty. I knew that playing with myself over the thought of being spanked by my aunt was a shocking thing to do, but I just couldn't help it.

Inside the room I quickly locked the door behind me. I stood with my back to the mirror and lifted my dress and petticoats with trembling fingers. As my panties came on show, I stuck my bottom out, stretching the pink cotton taut across my bulging cheeks. Reddened flesh showed around the frilly leg-holes, evidence that I had been spanked. Breathing hard, I pulled them up tight between my cheeks, so my bottom spilt out to either side, red and sore. The flesh was covered in little goose-pimples, with the flush of punishment deepest where my cheeks turn down to my thighs. I'm only a size eight, and my waist is twenty inches or so, yet I've always felt that in comparison my bottom is embarrassingly fat. It certainly looked it then, the red cheeks plump and meaty. I'd been spanked well, even my thighs showing some red patches.

Holding my panties up tight felt lovely, with the cotton pulled hard against my wet pussy. I wanted to see more, though, and so began to peel them down, knowing that the rude display I was giving was just what my aunt had seen. With my knickers at the level of my stocking tops, I was completely exposed. The rear of my pussy showed, the lips pouted and furry, the centre pink and wet with my juice. I was so wet that it was dribbling down my thighs, while my vagina looked as if it could have taken Toby's cock with ease.

I wished it had, and wondered if there wasn't something I could substitute for it while I masturbated. My hairbrush handle was a possibility, but above my pussy my anus was showing, a puckered brown hole in a nest of hair, tempting me.

I couldn't help it. I popped my finger into my mouth and sucked it, then, reaching behind me, I put the digit to my bottom-hole and eased it in. It was slimy with my pussy-juice, and my finger went in easily, first to one joint, then to another. Feeling utterly filthy, I watched myself finger my bottom, my pleasure rising with the rude, wet feeling.

Moving forward, I bent over the bed, craning to see over my shoulder as I spread my thighs. My bottom was framed in a froth of material: pink dress, white petticoats, pink panties, white stockings. The freshly spanked cheeks showed red and sore, my hairy pussy and bottom-crease open between them, my vagina wet and ready, my anus with a finger stuck obscenely up it.

Stretching, I managed to reach my hairbrush, then watched as I slid it up my pussy. It went in easily and I started to pump at both holes, quickly making myself breathless with pleasure. Reaching out again, I got hold of my toothbrush and substituted it for the finger in my bottom. Everything showed in the mirror, and I looked so rude: well-smacked bum stuck out, panties down and both my holes full.

I clenched my muscles to keep the probes inside me and put my hand back between my legs. Two fingers spread my pussy open, revealing my clit and making my rear view even ruder. I started to rub, my eyes intent on the mirror. I tried to think of how it would have felt to have Toby's cock in my vagina instead of a hairbrush, but couldn't focus. Instead my thoughts drifted to how my punishment could have been made worse. I could have had things pushed up my pussy and bum for a start, after I'd been thoroughly spanked. I could have been made to strip too, and kneel while I was lectured, with perhaps a narrow shampoo bottle in my vagina. Kate had some that were just right, and I was sure that that was what she used them for. My anus would be harder to fill comfortably, but there had been a vase of flowers on the windowsill, pretty meadow-blossoms. Having a big daisy protruding from my bumhole would have really taught me my place. I could have had my face pushed in the toilet as well, preferably after I'd peed in it . . .

That was too much. I felt the muscles of my vagina and anus start to spasm around their loads; my pussy was on fire and I thought for a moment that I was going to wet myself. I screamed, knowing I was coming and amazed by just how good it was. Again and again it hit me, the toothbrush squeezing out of my anus with the contractions while I pumped at myself with the hairbrush. I know I screamed out loud, and called Kate's name, because at the end it had been her I was imagining tormenting me and not her mother.

Finally it subsided and I sank to the floor in a sweaty, juice-smeared mess. My pussy and anus felt sore and I was incredibly ashamed of myself for being so dirty, yet I had come – and if that was what it felt like and if being dirty was what it took to get there, then I knew I wouldn't be a good girl for long.

3

Chocolate Surprise

When I went up to university, everything changed. Well, almost everything. Most importantly, I found myself in an environment where intelligence was actually respected. At school I had been nicknamed 'Little Miss Smarty-Pants' and, while my teachers had been impressed, my fellow pupils had regarded me as an impossible swot. At university I was among equals – well, actually, I was still better than most and, by the end of my first term, my tutors were already suggesting that an academic career might be an idea. Socially, things were also looking up. I had no shortage of friends and was never short of something to do.

My room was in the Kennet Building, a large student hall. The warden was the ageing and amiable Professor Ruskin, a noted archaeologist and a man so far removed from the real world that it seemed extraordinary to me that he had been put in charge of over two hundred first-year students. We came and went when we pleased, ate what we pleased and slept with whoever we pleased.

Only I didn't. The one thing that hadn't changed was my sex life. I got plenty of offers but, as always, not from the men who attracted me. An evening at the model railway club followed by a clumsy grope in a doorway was not my idea of fun, and there were plenty of gorgeous, boisterous, extrovert girls to take up the attentions of all the big, rough, masculine types who I fancied. My needs had also become stronger, more focused and harder to satisfy. Ever since nearly losing my virginity to Toby and getting an impromptu spanking from my aunt, my need for punishment and sexual humiliation had grown. I didn't just want rough sex, but to be tied and beaten first.

Unfortunately such pleasures seemed impossible to get. On one of the rare occasions I accepted a date and actually felt turned on at the end, I asked the man to turn me over his knee and spank me, only to be told that he had too much respect for me. I'd begged, and the bastard had given me a lecture on how I should empower myself and take control of my body instead of surrendering it to men. What the arrogant, self-satisfied moron didn't understand was that I didn't want to take control. I wanted to be bullied and spanked and made to suck his cock and take rear entry. I was left with a wet pussy and a lump of cold anger in my throat.

To make matters worse, and not for the first time, many of the men I liked looked on me as a friend. They'd come in late to my room, not to shag me senseless over my desk, but to tell me how understanding I was. That would be after three hours of telling me about their difficulties with some girl, as often as not my neighbour, Tiffany Bell, an oversexed American exchange student.

Tiffany was truly gorgeous, and she knew it. She looked the classic image of an American cheerleader: big, busty, blonde and, above all, wholesome. The men absolutely drooled over her. Personally, I hated her. She had all the attributes that made Kate so attractive – looks, sex appeal and confidence – but, where Kate always worshipped her men, Tiffany expected worship. She got it, too, and used to treat her admirers like dirt.

She had no shortage of them, but there was one that she took particular pleasure in tormenting. This was Aran Ray, a big, powerfully built black guy who rowed number seven in the university boat. A biochemist, like me, he was bright by any standards, and also socially popular. I'm not at all sure why Tiffany singled him out, but it was as if she was determined to make him grovel to her just for the pleasure of denying him.

For most of the term she teased him, flirting and then pulling back, letting him think she was interested, only to go off with another man. Only after he had won his place in the boat did she take him to bed, by which time he must have been fit to burst. Being next door, I had to listen to them shagging. I could make out some of the things they said, as well: not clearly, but well enough to drive me to distraction. I had been trying to write an essay, but ended up with my skirt up and my hand down my panties as I masturbated over the thought of what they were doing. After a mediocre orgasm, I felt distinctly lonely and left out, falling asleep while they were still at it.

The following evening, I was sitting alone with a cup of coffee when I heard someone knock at her door. I sighed, resigning myself to another disturbed night, and wondering if I would be able to resist playing with myself while he humped her. She answered her door, and I heard her voice quite clearly in the passage. Rather than enthusiastic and sexy, which was her normal tone, she sounded surprised and rather annoyed.

'What's the matter?' he asked.

'Just leave, OK?' she answered.

'But I thought we . . .' he said, sounding hurt.

'I know what you thought,' she replied aggressively, 'and I can tell you this, it's not going to happen again.'

Somebody turned a tap on and their voices became indistinct. I'd heard her give other men the same treatment, but was still a bit surprised. He was, after all, now a recognised athlete, and being his girlfriend should have carried all the prestige she wanted. Evidently she felt that turning him down after one night would make her look even more impressive. Her attitude struck me as completely unreasonable. She clearly saw sex with him as a sort of trophy, which was bad enough, yet I felt that at the least she could have rejected him politely.

'Come on, Tiffy, it wasn't so bad,' he was pleading as their voices became distinct again.

'Just take your dirty chocolates and fuck off!' she screamed and, a second later, the door slammed.

He knocked again but she didn't answer, leaving him standing in the passage. I felt really sorry for him, and we got on well enough in the labs, so I opened the door. He was standing outside her room with a big box of chocolates in his hand, looking crestfallen.

'Hi, Aran, are you OK?' I asked.

'Yeah,' he sighed.

'I heard,' I said. 'Come inside and have a coffee.'

Of course, Tiffany could hear all of this, just as I could hear her. As she barely condescended to speak to me anyway, I didn't really care. She had talked to me in the first week, put me down as socially unimportant and pretty well ignored me ever since.

'Thanks,' he answered, treating me to a big grin and coming into my room.

Just having him there was enough to excite me. He was huge, well over six foot and very powerfully built. There was something about his hands in particular, enormous yet long-fingered and sensitive-looking. His skin was wonderful, too, dark and glossy and smooth. I could have melted on the spot and wouldn't have minded acting as substitute for Tiffany in the least.

I let him have my chair, made the coffee and passed it to him, then sat at his feet, all of it calculated to make me seem helpful and willing. Of course, it was a waste of time. All he wanted to talk about was Tiffany, and how much he yearned for her and how wonderful she was. He was genuinely down, almost in tears, otherwise I think I'd have thrown him out from sheer frustration.

By one o'clock, my eyelids were beginning to drop. We had eaten most of his chocolates, and he was still going on about Tiffany. I really couldn't take it any more, but nor could I bring myself to get rid of him. Just as long as he was there, I felt that maybe something would happen, although I was far from bold enough to ask a straight question. He just kept talking about Tiffany and, by two o'clock, I'd had enough.

'Look, Aran,' I said, instead of replying to yet another request for my advice on how he should get around

Tiffany, 'I'm dropping. I know it's Saturday tomorrow, but I still need some sleep.'

'I understand,' he answered, 'but ... No, I can't ask that.'

'What?' I demanded, perking up a little in the hope that he might want something sexual.

'No,' he went on, 'it wouldn't be right, but ...'

He had trailed off, smiling and giving a little shrug which made him seem vulnerable for all his size.

'Tell me, Aran,' I said, very softly.

'I ... I just wondered if you'd let me hold you,' he answered. 'I'm sorry, but I feel really down and ...'

'Of course you can give me a cuddle,' I answered.

'I mean, through the night,' he went on. 'Just a hug. You can trust me, I promise.'

I sincerely hoped I couldn't, but managed a coy look before answering. 'OK, I suppose so,' I said, trying to be calm but with my blood hammering through me.

I made a very big deal of washing and undressing, pretending to be coy, but making sure he got plenty of glimpses of my tits and a good view of my panties. Normally I go to bed in just knickers and a T-shirt, but now what I wore was really important. I had some bright yellow pyjamas with cartoon animals on them, a present from a well-meaning uncle. I normally didn't wear them because they were so girly, but now that was how I wanted to feel.

Putting them on also gave me the chance to turn my back and, ever so demurely, pull down my panties to make sure he had a chance to see my bare bottom. When I turned round, he was in just his boxer shorts, a sight that had me trembling inside and desperately trying not to stare. I got into bed and held the clothes down for him. He slipped in beside me and, for the first time in my life, I had a man in bed with me. He was warm, his muscles hard against my soft flesh, his male scent making me feel open and in need of him.

I wanted him to take me into his massive arms and kiss me, letting me melt into him. The shame of knowing that

I was only a substitute for Tiffany was getting to me, too, making me feel small and bringing out all my fantasies of just being taken and used just because I was female and the man couldn't resist it. I really wanted to surrender my virginity, preferably with him mounted on me from the rear with my girlish pyjamas pulled down and my bottom spread for him.

He did nothing of the sort, just taking my hand and quickly falling asleep. I had never been so frustrated, and lay still for what seemed like hours, curled up and wishing that he'd just turn round and fuck me without even bothering to ask.

I must have gone to sleep eventually, because the next thing I remember is waking up with the first pale light of dawn seeping into the room. It took me a moment to remember what was going on, and then my frustration returned with a vengeance. He had turned at some point in the night, and I was in his lap with my bottom pressed against his crotch. He was still asleep, with one arm thrown over my waist and the other under my head so that he was holding me. That was bad enough, but far worse was the feel of his cock pressed against the tuck of my bottom through just two layers of material. I could feel it between my cheeks, a thick shaft that scared me yet made me want it inside me very badly indeed. I moved, trying to dislodge his penis from between my buttocks but only succeeding in rubbing it against myself.

He groaned quietly in his sleep and then, very gently, began to rub his cock against me. The action was unconscious, a simple response to having a soft, girlish bottom squeezed against his crotch. He was probably dreaming about the wretched Tiffany, but the sensation had me gritting my teeth in frustration. His cock grew as he rubbed, and the rubbing became more conscious, until I realised that he was at least half-awake. He may have thought I was fast asleep, and just been having a sneaky rub against my bottom. Then again he may have intended to wake me like that and then take advantage of me in my sleepy state.

Either way, his prick was quickly a hard shaft of solid meat, pressed in between the cheeks of my bottom and only a movement away from the entrance to my virgin pussy. I was sighing – gently, yet enough for him to hear. Then his big arms tightened around me and I knew he was going to do it. He held me helpless with his left arm, leaving me no chance of escape – not that I wanted it. With his right, he pushed down the front of his boxers, so that his bare cock was against the seat of my pyjamas. I groaned aloud as he began to rub again, all pretence now abandoned as he excited himself against my bottom. I stuck it out, eager for his cock.

He put his hand to my pyjamas, pushing them down over my bottom, baring me for entry. I thought the moment had come, and braced myself for the stab of pain Kate had told me to expect. Instead, he settled his cock back between my now naked bum-cheeks and once more began to rub.

His arm moved and his weight shifted as he reached back for something. I assumed he was after a condom, and stayed still, just pushing my bum out a little more to let him rub more easily. For a moment he was fiddling with something, presumably rolling the condom down on to his cock, one-handed. His left arm was still around me, holding me firmly in place, which felt so good. He also had one powerful leg curled over mine, effectively trapping me in his embrace. Desperately wanting him inside me, I reached back and pulled open my bottom-cheeks, giving easy access to my bare pussy. I felt really wonderful. I was holding my vagina open so that a man could enter me, finally surrendering my virginity, and to what a man!

Something touched between my thighs and I gasped, expecting to be filled on the instant. It was his hand, and then something moist and warm was being pressed between my cheeks. It was one of the chocolates he had bought for Tiffany, which he was presumably now going to lick from my pussy before having me. It was an exquisite humiliation, that a present that had been intended for another girl should end up smeared on my vagina. He had

31

missed, though, and was squashing it not against my pussy, but a little further back, against my bumhole.

'Not there!' I giggled as what I think must have been a bit of crystallised fruit was pushed into my anus.

He said nothing, but tightened his grip and once more began to rub his cock up and down between my buttocks. This time he had the molten chocolate to grease me with – the cream centre as well, as I think he'd chosen a rose cream. It felt even better, sliding up and down between my cheeks as I obligingly held them apart. He kept touching my anus, which I wasn't sure he should be doing if he was going to fuck me, but I've always liked my bottom-hole touched and it felt too nice to stop. Then I felt his hand go down to his cock and knew that he was going to put it in me.

'Please, Aran, now,' I begged, expecting some pain as I pulled myself open as far as I could with his leg locking mine in place.

The head of his cock nudged against my anus, making an obscene squelching noise that made me giggle again.

'Not there, Aran,' I urged. 'Forward a bit.'

He took no notice, pressing harder until my bumhole began to open under the pressure.

'Aran! Wrong hole!' I squeaked in protest.

But it was too late. He had me completely helpless, his leg and arm trapping my body. I let go of my bottom but the head was wedged half into my anus, hurting my virgin ring as he tried to bugger me.

'Ow! Aran!' I squealed.

'Relax, girl, it'll go in easy,' he said.

I knew it would, or at least fairly easily. I had masturbated with a hairbrush handle up my bottom before, and even managed to insert one of those small ladies' deodorant cans, when I was in a particularly dirty mood one wet afternoon. It wasn't even that I didn't want it; many of my fantasies involving being buggered. I would just have liked to lose my virginity before taking a cock up my bum.

'Aran, please do it in my pussy,' I moaned. 'At least first!'

32

'Too late, I'd be dirty,' he said, wedging his cock another fraction of an inch into my straining anus.

'Aran!' I whined.

'Come on, Penny, let it slip in,' he said soothingly. 'You'll take it, easy.'

I just groaned, resigning myself to buggery. As soon as I relaxed it slid a little further up, rewarding me with a sudden, sharp pain.

'Ow! Aran!' I protested. 'Slowly!'

He laughed, sensing that my plea for him to go slowly was an admission that I didn't really mind.

'Oh, that's good,' he said, easing his erection deeper with another push. 'Come on, Pen, stick your buns out.'

I obliged, still not entirely happy about having a penis forced into my rectum but resigned to it. It did feel gorgeous, and that was what made me stick my bottom out and lose my last chance of preserving at least my self-respect while I was buggered. It felt so rude with a cock up my bottom, and it was beginning to give me a wonderful, breathless sensation that I knew would get better once he was right in.

'OK,' I moaned, 'put it up then.'

I stuck my bottom into his lap and he took me by the hips. We were both grunting as he worked his cock home, each push sliding perhaps another quarter inch into my rectum. Finally, it was all the way in and, I had to admit, it was bliss. I could feel my anus straining around his erection, the flesh working in and out as he began to pump. His pubic hair was rubbing between my bum-cheeks, which were slimy with melted chocolate and rose cream. My pyjama trousers were only a little way down, and I knew the mess would get all over them, and the sheet, and everything, because I could feel it squelching in my pussy and knew that I would have to play with myself while Aran gave me anal sex. I was groaning and panting anyway, so there was no point in pretending I wasn't having fun.

'Let me get at my pussy,' I pleaded.

'Hot bitch,' he answered, but relaxed his leg so that I could lift my thigh and get a hand to my pussy.

33

I found my clit and began to rub, barely in control from the feeling of the cock in my bottom. He was pushing harder, and it had started to hurt a bit, making me grunt and squeal in the most unladylike manner imaginable. I didn't feel like a lady, though; I felt like a dirty slut for letting a man use me up the bottom. He had called me a hot bitch, which made me sound really dirty and vulgar. I really am like that underneath, but I knew that I could seem a bit prissy on the outside, and it was so nice to be doing something so dirty at last and really revelling in the experience. Despite that, I felt ashamed of myself, especially as I had surrendered with so little fuss.

He was getting faster, buggering me with little shoves of his hips that pulled my bumhole in and out and did incredible things to my insides. I matched the rhythm of my rubs to his pushes, moving my finger across my clit from side to side. I could feel the damp chocolate all over my hand and in between my pussy-lips and could feel it oozing around my bumhole as his cock moved.

'Hold me,' I begged, keen to feel the power of his arms and once more have the sensation of being unable to get away.

His arms went round me, pushed hard against my breasts and over my tummy, locking my own arms in place. His leg tightened around mine, squeezing my hand between my thighs. I thrust my bottom out as far as it would go, pushed harder on my clit and let my mind run on what was being done to me. He hadn't given me a lot of choice, but I knew he'd have stopped if I'd really complained. In my fantasy, he'd given me none at all. He would have rubbed his prick on my bum, felt turned on, pulled down my pyjamas and buggered me without so much as a word. I'd have been helpless, grunting and squealing my pleasure out as he used me up my virgin bottom. He wouldn't have a condom either. His prick would be naked up my bum, jerking as it came, slamming home in my rectum without a thought for my pain, exploding inside me, filling me with sperm and leaving me in a pool of chocolate and spunk.

I came, screaming and clutching at my pussy, bucking my hips and writhing my bottom on the hard rod that was pushed well into my back passage. He gripped hard, restraining my squirms, making me feel pathetic in his grip as I screamed and whimpered out my lust. He had already started to push harder while I was coming, increasing my ecstasy. As my orgasm subsided, he took hold of my hips again and really began to slam into me.

That hurt, and I was really squealing as he built towards his own orgasm. I couldn't talk, but only squeal and pant as he rammed his cock home in my behind. Then suddenly he was ripping down the bedclothes to expose our bodies. He pushed me forward, giving himself a view of my bare, chocolate-smeared bum and his erection protruding from my anus. His hand tightened in the flesh of my hips and he grunted, calling me a dirty bitch once more as he came up my bottom.

I was sobbing and whimpering on the bed, my anus a ring of fire around his shaft. He pulled out slowly, holding the condom on with his fingers. He slapped my bottom playfully, just once, and then rolled over and put his feet on the ground.

'You've got a nice bum, Penny,' he said gloatingly, feeling my naked bottom in a possessive manner.

'You're a bastard, Aran,' I managed.

'Good, though, wasn't it?' he said.

'Yes, I suppose so,' I admitted, rolling on to my front.

He continued to feel my bottom, rubbing the chocolate into my cheeks. I looked down, finding my bed absolutely filthy with brown and pink goo.

'How am I going to get this clean?' I asked, realising that I was faced with an embarrassing trip to the hall laundry unbearably embarrassing, in fact. I simply couldn't face it.

He just laughed and walked over to my sink to clean himself up. I stayed face down on the bed, naked and not caring that my legs, back and bottom were all covered in goo. I'd been buggered: tricked into expecting a fuck and then buggered. I'd been willing to give my virginity up and he'd put it up my bum. True, he didn't know I was a virgin, but the whole thing was still ever so humiliating.

When he'd gone, I masturbated – not once, but three times. He hadn't been in the least sympathetic about the mess we'd made, which I thought was a bit much after I'd been so nice to him about Tiffany. Despite that, there was something about the state I was in that made it irresistible. When he first left, I was in a flap because of the mess but, before I actually did anything about it, the urge to take another, slower orgasm had become overwhelming.

I locked the door and stripped, bundling my dirty pyjamas into the sink. Then I sat on my bed, opened my thighs and started to stroke my pussy. After a bit, I put my chocolate-flavoured fingers in my mouth, sucking and then going back to masturbating. My bottom-hole stung, not really painfully, but enough to keep me constantly aware of it. Aran had come into my room and buggered me. He'd tricked me into bed and then, when I'd offered him my pussy, he'd fucked my bottom instead. I reached down between my cheeks, touching the smarting flesh of my anus, thinking of how mercilessly hard he'd used me. It had hurt so much; the pain in my bottom had been like fire, but he'd just kept on until he came inside me, up my back passage.

I moaned in pleasure, the little sound reminding me of how I'd screamed at orgasm. It had been early, but my neighbours might well have heard; and if they had then they'd have known I was having sex. That would be the end of me as poor, innocent little Penny. I'd called out in helpless ecstasy during the night from a man's cock inside me, just like Tiffany did so often, and my other neighbour, Emma, not infrequently.

One finger was well up my bottom, my other hand rubbing my clit with the same side-to-side motions I'd used earlier. In front of me were the chocolates, still open, the brown humps of their tops peeping out of their little holes. I took one, a coffee cream, and popped it into my mouth. Next to its place was a mint ball, a big, round one. It was too tempting. I took the mint ball out, and, feeling deliciously dirty, pushed it into my aching bottom-hole. It hurt a bit going in, just like his cock had, and was then lost inside me.

I lay back, rubbing gently at my clit until the coffee cream in my mouth had melted to a rich, thick paste. My hand went to my mouth, extracting the chocolate. My eyes were shut in pleasure as I slapped it on my pussy and rubbed it in, deliberately smearing it all over my pubes and up my thighs. Both my hands were covered in chocolate as I put them to my breasts, cupping them, rubbing them and giving both a liberal coating of sweet brown goo. It felt truly gorgeous as I massaged it into my breasts, then my belly, then lifted my bottom to squeeze my cheeks and make sure they were really covered in it. I did my face last, rubbing at my pussy until I could feel my orgasm coming, then pulling away and dirtying my face. With my whole body dirty, I reached forward and grabbed three more chocolates, stuffing two in my mouth and the last in my pussy.

My hands went back between my legs, one finger probing my anus and tickling the sore flesh, another going to my clit for the final burst. As I opened my bumhole the mint cream began to ooze out, melted and sticky. I could feel the one I'd put in my vagina, still hard but moving as my body heat began to melt it. I slid a finger deep into my anus as I started to come, remembering Aran's cock and wondering what he'd think if he could see me in the state I was in. My orgasm peaked, subsided, peaked again and then dropped away, leaving me panting and happy on the bed.

I did feel a bit guilty about what I'd done, but more concerned for the mess I'd made. There was chocolate all over the bottom sheet and all over me. It was still early, and there was a fair chance I could get to the showers unobserved. Taking great care not to soil anything else, I washed my hands at the sink and tiptoed across the room. For once I was grateful for the paper-thin walls and bad acoustics of the hall. I couldn't hear anybody moving, so poked my head out and made a dash for the showers. I made it and, after a long session with a bar of soap and a scrubbing brush, I was clean and pink again.

Another quick streak and I was back in my room, mercifully undetected. The instant I came in the smell of chocolate hit me, and I realised that I had a lot of cleaning up to do. I didn't dare use the hall laundry, but there was a public one not too far away that would be safe. After drying myself and opening the window, I bundled the sheet into a ball and put it and my pyjamas into a plastic bag.

I was stark naked and constantly aware of the ache between my bottom-cheeks. It actually made me walk a bit strangely, which really brought home the implications of having been buggered. People use the word to describe something that no longer works, something which has been used too much, or misused. That was how I felt: misused, like a broken toy. As if having had a cock pushed up my bottom made me unfit for polite company. Of course, it was nonsense, because nobody else need know and physically I'd be fine, just as soon as the persistent throbbing ache in my anus went away. The idea of being good for nothing because I'd accepted buggery really got to me, though, a purely mental thrill that combined with my mild pain to make me desperate to come yet again.

I did it on my knees, overwhelmed by the whole concept, masturbating with my face to the carpet and my bare bottom stuck up in the air. It felt appropriate to be naked, as if it was no longer suitable for me to dress, as if I needed to be marked as a slut. I started to fantasise over how it would feel to be made to go naked for having done it. I'd be sent to a seedy tattoo parlour and have the word 'SLUT' put across my bottom, indelibly. Women would turn their noses up at me in the street, or laugh at me. Men would use me at their leisure, tipping me over any time they felt like sliding an erection up my bottom, which I would have to keep permanently greased and ready. I came again, very quickly, and went back to cleaning up, feeling rather ashamed of myself for my dirty fantasy but rather proud of myself for coming three times in as many hours.

I made four in the end. When I was dressed and ready

to go, the whole experience just got too much for me. I pulled down my jeans and panties and did it standing by my door. I didn't fantasise, but thought of Aran and the way he'd made me feel so fragile and helpless, of the chocolate and the sticky mess I'd covered myself in, of the way I'd been tricked into surrendering my bottom-hole to his cock, but most of all of the fact that, even though I'd been taken so rudely, I was still a virgin.

After my fourth orgasm, my pussy was as sore as my bottom and I forced myself to get on with it. I was pretty sure the laundrette I wanted opened on Saturdays and that my behaviour, or at least the details of it, would go undetected. Tiffany had gone out at some point between my third and fourth orgasms, and I had heard nothing whatever from Emma's room. She had a boyfriend in another hall, and might well have been out, which meant that Tiffany alone might guess more than the fact that I had had a man in my room. She, of course, would know that it had been Aran, but I didn't really care.

As I walked up the road, trying to look nonchalant, I started to wonder why Tiffany had been so aggressive to Aran. She was a bit of a bitch, but not normally that bad. Perhaps he had tried to give her the same treatment he had given me, a chocolate-smeared cock up the bottom. I couldn't see Tiffany accepting it – she was far too clean-cut – yet the idea amused me just because I knew how outraged she'd have been at the mere suggestion.

I reached the laundrette and went inside. There was a group of machines at the far end which were screened off, allowing an extra little bit of privacy. I decided to use one and, as I stepped around the screen, I realised that I wasn't the only one who'd had a chocolate surprise. She might have had second thoughts about it, but she'd done it. Tiffany was standing by a machine, a brown-stained sheet already in it while she inspected a heavily soiled nightie with a frown of consternation.

4

Purity

By the Easter term of my first year at university, I was beginning to acquire a quite unfair reputation as a bluestocking. After my brief and unsuccessful relationship with Aran Ray, I hadn't been out with anyone at all. Aran was a successful rower and considered among the most attractive men in the university, yet he and I had lasted under a week and then ended it with a very public argument in the hall canteen. I'd completely lost my temper, which is rare for me, and called him a variety of unflattering things before telling him to get stuffed. Possibly other men reasoned that, if I could treat the wonderful Aran Ray like that, then I was unlikely to be sympathetic to them, or possibly they just thought I was a bitch.

What they didn't know was that Aran's idea of sex was to lubricate my bottom and bugger me. He liked me on all fours and had a thing about making a mess of my body first, generally with chocolate. I loved the idea of a big, strong man pushing his cock into my greasy bottom-hole, but he had two major faults. First, he always got carried away and hurt me before he came; and second, he just wasn't interested in pussy. He also left me in a filthy mess more often than not and never helped me clean up, but I would have put up with that. It was his refusal to compromise that I couldn't stand, especially as I badly wanted to be fucked and he wouldn't do it.

That was the mainstay of our argument, but the

hundred-odd people who were listening got quite the wrong impression. Possibly I would have benefited from being even more graphic in my description of his shortcomings, because I quickly discovered that I had created the impression of being a virgin and wanting to stay that way. I was a virgin, but the last thing I wanted was to stay that way. That had been towards the end of the winter term, but it wasn't until two weeks into the following term that I realised how bad – or good, I suppose I should say – my reputation was.

I was in the library, immersed in the latest *Journal of Genetics,* when I felt a gentle tap on my shoulder. I looked around to see a woman who I knew faintly as either Rachel or Raquel.

'L P at five-thirty, my room, Bourne Hall, fifty-seven,' she said, and winked, leaving me completely mystified.

She turned away as if she had just imparted some deep secret. When she had tapped me on the shoulder, my immediate assumption was that she was going to ask to read the journal after me. She was a second year and a botanist, and the only thing we had in common to my knowledge was the same plant genetics tutor. As to what 'L P' was, I had no idea whatever. If it was a departmental discussion group or something, then she had no reason to be so shifty. In fact, I could think of no reason for her to be shifty at all, unless . . .

Gay and lesbian societies were quite open in the university, yet neither were entirely de-stigmatised. Possibly Rachel, or Raquel, was a lesbian and wanted to sound me out. L P might well stand for Lesbian something or other, although nothing that I could think of. The main lesbian society was PURLS, a somewhat unfortunate acronym which I knew provided the lesser minds of the rowing club with endless trivial amusement. PURLS was pretty militant, and possibly L P was a more restrained splinter group.

I was intrigued in any case. I didn't see myself as a lesbian, and certainly not of the type who ran PURLS. On the other hand, I had long before come to terms with the fact that my cousin Kate attracted me sexually, and I couldn't deny finding other women's bodies intriguing. Female bottoms in particular got to me, their shape being somehow so much more satisfying than the male equivalent.

Raquel, or possibly Rachel, was tall and perhaps a little severe-looking, but that wasn't a problem for me. I'd always imagined Kate punishing me, and Rachel had her height, if not her beauty. Rachel wore long dresses, too, and kept her hair up in a bun, a style also followed by Kate's mother, who really had spanked me. It was easy to imagine her ordering me sternly to bend over her knee for punishment, or perhaps making me kneel in front of her to kiss her shoes . . .

I shook myself, forcing my attention back to the *Journal of Genetics* to stop myself having to run to the loos to masturbate.

I had to attend the meeting, I was far too curious not to. Bourne Hall was no great distance from my own hall of residence and fifty-seven proved to be a corner room with a view over the river. I wasn't too concerned with the view, because all my attention was taken up by the company. There were seven women in the room, and they were unified by a certain look. None of them could have been called pretty, but it wasn't that there was anything physically wrong with them. It was rather that they affected a rather dowdy, perhaps even austere, appearance. I was in my usual jeans and T-shirt, with my hair in a bright red scrunchie, but suddenly felt as if I'd walked into a vicar's drawing room in my bra and panties.

'Hi, Raquel,' I announced myself rather uncertainly.

'It's Rachel, Penny,' she replied, 'but welcome anyway. Do sit down.'

I nodded to the others as Rachel introduced me. I didn't recognise any of them but they all looked to be stern, rather serious young women. As I took my seat, a rather good description of their manner occurred to me – strict but fair – rather in the style of old-fashioned English girls' school teachers. It was a description that appealed directly to my sexual fantasies, although the prospect of actually becoming involved with such a group was more than a little daunting. I had never yet touched another woman sexually, and the idea made me feel a little ashamed of myself, yet it was undoubtedly appealing.

'I think everybody's here,' Rachel said, 'so now perhaps I should explain our aims to the newcomers and give them a particular welcome – Faith, Clara and Penny.'

She nodded to me and two of the other girls, both of whom looked more at home in the company than I did.

'As you know,' she continued, 'we are a branch of the League of Purity . . .'

My fairy-tale castle of imaginary pleasures collapsed on the instant. They were no clandestine society of old-fashioned lesbians, but the local representatives of the League of Purity. I'd heard of them, vaguely, but only knew that they took vows to remain chaste until married, or some such pointless rubbish.

As Rachel wittered on, all I could do was sit there and wish I had the guts to get up and tell them that not only had I been buggered and sucked men's cocks, but that I had enjoyed every second of it. Of course, I didn't, and could only sit there politely while she talked about God and our moral duty and treating our bodies as temples and so on and so on. Like so many organisations based on religion, their creed had been constructed by extracting the bits they wanted from Christian ethics and dumping the rest. Having been a confirmed atheist since the age of twelve, I was less than impressed. I also felt really hurt. Rachel had singled me out as a potential new member, and had not even troubled to sound me out on my principles first.

Looking around the room, I realised how other people saw me, or at least how Rachel obviously did. I had always seen myself as cheerful, impish, perhaps a little coquettish, maybe even impudently sexy: certainly dainty and undoubtedly feminine. The last time I could remember feeling as bad was when I'd been judged last in a sandcastle competition at the age of about five, and I was close to tears by the time Rachel asked if anybody had any questions.

It went on a little longer and finished with some dreadful hymn. I was keen to leave as soon as politely possible, but was cornered by Rachel before I could escape.

'Penny,' she began, taking me confidentially by the elbow, 'might I offer a little advice, from an elder sister as it were?'

'OK,' I answered, although it wasn't what I was thinking.

'I know that you are with us in your heart,' she began, 'as I heard what you said to that dreadful man, Aran Ray. Yet I do feel that you might dress a little more demurely . . .'

She trailed off and gave me a nod that was both knowing and somehow commanding, as if she had set me back on the right path with a kindly word. I thanked her and left, walking back towards Kennet Hall, where my room was. I was in a black mood, but what Rachel had said at the end had actually cheered me up a bit. Her remark about Aran gave me an inkling of why she had singled me out, and her comments on my dress made me think that there was hope for me yet.

When I got back to the hall I stood in front of my mirror, trying to see myself as another person might see me. Try as I might, I couldn't see myself as one of them, and it wasn't just my clothes. Facially, I did look impish: cheeky with a smile, sulky with a frown. The red scrunchie holding my long dark hair in a pony-tail looked sweet, too, or at least I thought it did. As far as my clothes were concerned, they struck me as entirely practical. It was true that the outlines of my nipples showed through my T-shirt; but with small, high breasts, a bra is seldom necessary.

That cheered me up a little, but I still went to bed in a bad mood which was made worse by the sounds of my neighbour, Tiffany Bell, being humped by her latest conquest.

* * *

I have never been a great one for standing up to people, barring the occasional loss of temper, and so felt under pressure from the League of Purity when most women would have found no difficulty in telling them to get lost. Their aim was to have a hundred members by the end of term, at which time some self-satisfied prig would be coming from the parent society in the US and everyone would take the oath of chastity. As they only had a dozen members between the male and female branches, this meant that they were pretty keen to hang on to the ones they'd got. I generally managed to avoid them but still got dragged along to another meeting, after which I had the bad luck to bump into Tiffany Bell. We didn't get on anyway, and she took great delight in the discovery that I was supposedly involved with the League. The information was round the hall in no time, with much the same effect as if someone had welded me into a chastity belt.

I pretty much despaired, concentrating on my work and assuming the social situation would work out in due course. Nothing changed much for two weeks and then Rachel visited me again to bully me into going to a lecture on pornography, or rather, against pornography. She explained that the speaker was terribly important in the anti-pornography campaign and that it was vital to get him a good audience. I couldn't see why, but still let her dragoon me into it, even promising to wear a dress. After all, there was always the chance that he would bring some samples.

Of course, he didn't, but just talked about how awful it was for anyone to see sexual images, particularly of women. I suppose in his way he was a good speaker – at least, he certainly had conviction. On the other hand, his arguments were thin and circular. What he called facts were dubious theories, based on bad statistics. The statistics were built around the theories, and so it went, round and round. I quickly switched off, finding more interest in the cracks in the lecture theatre ceiling.

It was when he started talking about peoples' need to free themselves from what he called the trap of immorality that he got my interest back. The idea seemed to be for those who had used pornography to admit to it so that others could keep an eye on them. For their own good, of course, not at all to enable the watchers to feel superior. He then asked the audience if any of its members would like to unburden themselves of their past sins. I was immediately both horrified and fascinated. The audience had greeted his talk with murmurs of self-righteous approval while he had demonstrated how pornography was supposed to cause everything from divorce to murder. Now he was asking people to stand up and admit to reading it, or 'using it', as he put it. The thought scared me, even though it was nothing to do with me. I prefer my own imagination and had never bought a pornographic magazine in my life. Still, I could imagine the equivalent if he had asked women who masturbated to stand up and admit it.

I would have stayed firmly in my seat, and that was exactly what the audience did, all except one. I had turned to look around the hall, as had everybody else, each secretly hoping that some fool would admit to the unspeakable sin of enjoying looking at naked girls. He was near the back, a tall sandy-haired young man in rather old-fashioned clothes. He was white in the face, but he had his hand up. Everybody was staring at him as if he had just admitted to genocide with a side order of cannibalism.

Personally I was disgusted: not with him, but with the whole self-satisfied, pompous travesty. I could see why the speaker was popular, though. Both he and the audience were clearly getting enormous enjoyment from the poor man's discomfort. I couldn't decide whether the man was brave or stupid, but I felt immensely sorry for him in either case. The lecturer then told him to stand up and explain himself. That was too much for me. I simply wasn't prepared to be part of the hypocrisy of what they were doing. I got up and walked out, hearing the poor man admit to having had some magazines at school as I left.

I was really shaking as I came out. The theatre was one of a number opening off a central foyer, in which there was a hot drinks machine. I made for it, desperately in need of something to calm my nerves. For some reason, I felt a deep empathy with the sandy-haired man. The rest of the audience seemed really bloodthirsty to me. My fingers were trembling as I dialled for a large cocoa, which I had just picked up when the lecture theatre door banged. I jumped, spilling my cocoa and looking round nervously. I know it's ridiculous, but at that instant I expected to find a baying mob coming towards me, intent on lynching anybody who wasn't one of them. Instead it was the sandy-haired man, and he was in a worse state than I was.

He was in tears and his jaw was shaking, his face set in an expression of absolute misery. He was walking fast and heading for the main doors, casting me only a brief and embarrassed glance.

'Are you all right?' I asked, which was a silly question as he obviously wasn't, but he must have heard the sympathy in my voice because he stopped.

He didn't say anything, but shook his head. I could see the tears on his cheeks and felt even more desperately sorry for him than I had before.

'Come and have a cocoa,' I suggested.

He nodded and gave me a weak smile, coming over to the machine. He was shaking so badly that he couldn't get the money into the slot and I had to help him. I wanted to hold him and stroke his hair but contented myself with putting a hand on his shoulder.

'They'll be out soon,' I pointed out as he made for a row of seats. 'Let's go upstairs.'

Upstairs was a gallery that looked down on the foyer and which was ringed with big soft seats. I took his arm as we walked up.

'Why did you walk out?' he asked at the top of the steps.

'I couldn't stand it any more,' I replied. 'They're so smug, so self-righteous, and I felt really sorry for you.'

He didn't answer, but sipped his cocoa and, after a bit, let his breath out as if in relief at having escaped. We stood in silence for a while, looking down at the foyer, until I finally plucked up the courage to ask what I wanted to know.

'Why did you do it?' I queried.

'I . . . I don't know,' he answered. 'He made me feel really guilty, as if I'd done something really dreadful.'

'What, read a couple of girlie magazines?' I answered, unable to keep a slight giggle out of my voice.

He didn't answer, but sat down on one of the seats, leaning forward with his cocoa in both hands. I sat down next to him, feeling somewhat conspiratorial and not a little naughty. The very act of walking out had been in defiance of Rachel, and now I was sitting with a man who she undoubtedly considered wicked in the extreme. The gallery was dim, lit only by the lights in the foyer, which added to the atmosphere of doing something I shouldn't. He was attractive, and I felt a bond between us in our mutual lack of supposed virtue. I was intrigued too, and wondering if I hadn't found a man to my taste.

'So what did you tell them?' I asked after a moment.

'That I used to keep two porn mags at the bottom of my tuck-box at school,' he admitted, obviously sensing my sympathy.

'And then?' I questioned.

'He asked me if I . . . if I used to use them. That's what he said; it was obvious what he meant, and everyone was looking at me, and I just couldn't handle it. I ran out.'

'So, did you?' I asked.

He looked at me suspiciously, presumably wondering why I, who had after all been at the meeting, was asking the question not in a demanding or accusing tone, but in a mischievous one. He obviously felt pretty guilty about reading pornography, but to me it was no big deal. At my school, obviously unlike his, it was considered perfectly normal for boys to drool over pictures of naked girls, and presumably toss off over them in private. Kate used to reckon that boys who read porn mags were likely to be better in bed, simply because they'd have picked up a few useful tips.

'You can tell me,' I continued when he didn't answer.

I was beginning to feel smutty, really for the first time since I'd finished with Aran Ray. It was how mixing with

48

Kate and her friends had always made me feel: sexual, aware of myself as an animal, a female animal with female needs. I put my hand on his leg, feeling solid muscle. He was tall and looked fit, making his shyness and insecurity seem out of place. For the first time, I felt that I had met someone who would be physically able to dominate me with ease, yet who might really empathise with me. Not only that, but if he spent his time wanking off over dirty pictures, then he might just be as dirty-minded as me; maybe he even liked to spank girls.

'Please,' I insisted, stroking his leg.

'Yes,' he admitted quietly.

'Tell me,' I breathed.

'You're not going to suddenly yell rape or something, are you?' he asked.

I shook my head. My fingers were trembling on his thigh, and I was wondering if I dared move a little further up, towards his crotch. A strong feeling of expectation was building up inside me, yet I felt less than entirely sure of myself, and while it seemed that something was going to happen, I didn't really want to lead.

'I . . . I mean, tell you what?' he said uncertainly.

'What do you like to see?' I asked. 'Especially?'

'You'll just think I'm a pervert,' he said uncertainly.

'I promise I won't,' I assured him.

'Girls . . . girls in their knickers,' he stammered.

'And nothing else?' I queried.

'Well, maybe,' he answered, 'or maybe just showing them, as if by accident or to tease . . . Look, you just think I'm a pervert, don't you?'

'No, no,' I insisted, 'I want you to tell me. After all that rubbish he was spouting, I just want to hear that girls are sexy, that I'm sexy . . .'

'You are,' he put in, 'you're really sweet.'

'Thanks,' I answered. 'Now go on like you were before. Tell me what sort of panties you like.'

I may have been inexperienced, but I knew enough from Kate to know that one of the best ways to seduce a man was to get into a dirty conversation. It was turning me on,

49

too. The idea of girls showing their panties really appealed to me, although in my fantasies mine were always put on show to humiliate me or shown off because I'd torn my skirt or something. Another thing about panties is that they represent a girl's last barrier to a cock or a smacking hand, and I'd always found the idea of having my knickers pulled down particularly exciting.

'White are best,' he said, 'and quite big, and tight . . .'

'What about pretty colours, like pale blue or pink?' I asked.

'They're nice,' he answered. 'Anything, as long as it doesn't look deliberately tarty. My favourite picture shows a girl bending over a gate, and this farmer's lifted her skirt to show her knickers to his friends, but she hasn't realised. It's only a cartoon, but it's so sexy. Her knickers are pink and really tight, and her bottom looks so firm and full . . .'

'Mine are pink,' I said. 'Would you like to see me like that?'

He nodded and swallowed hard. I was really turned on, imagining the girl he'd described and thinking how humiliating it would be to be caught like that, and then when I protested they'd just laugh at me, take my precious panties down and give me a good spanking to teach me a lesson. Maybe it was because I'd seen him really broken down, or maybe because I was so turned on, but I felt I could ask.

'Go on, then,' I urged.

'What?' he queried.

'Make me show my panties,' I told him.

'Here?' he demanded.

'We'll hear anyone coming,' I pointed out, 'but let's go in by the canteen, just in case.'

I took his hand and pulled him after me, feeling thoroughly mischievous. The area we went to was a square enclave and mainly blocked from view by a pillar. It was for students to get snack lunches but the little canteen was shut, leaving us a quiet space illuminated only by the street lights outside.

I felt great. Downstairs they were still ranting away

about the evils of pornography and sex in general. I was upstairs and about to show my panties to a handsome young man. It was all so deliciously rude, and I was giggling as we made for the bit with the best light.

'What's your name, by the way?' he asked, sitting down by the wall.

'Penny,' I replied. 'Penny Birch, and yours?'

'Alexander Shaw,' he told me.

'Well, Alexander,' I replied, deliberately imitating Rachel's voice. 'Now that we've been formally introduced, I suppose it's acceptable to flirt with you.'

He may not have realised who I was imitating, but he laughed anyway.

'It is quite unsuitable,' I said pompously, continuing the game, 'for a woman to dress in a fashion that either highlights her figure or risks being sexually provocative. Above all, she should never show her underwear. This position, for instance, is quite indecorous.'

I turned and pulled up my dress, showing my legs and then the seat of my panties. As I looked back over my shoulder, I found him transfixed, his eyes glued to my bottom and legs. He looked really excited, and it was because of me. It felt really good, bending over to show my panties, an act which Rachel would have found unspeakably rude.

'That's nice,' he breathed.

'Especially offensive to propriety,' I continued, sticking my bottom out, 'is any display that in any way suggests that the woman is sexually available.'

I wiggled my bottom, watching him. His hand was near his crotch, but not actually on it. I stayed in position, bent forward so that my skirt rested in the small of my back. My bottom was stuck right out, my panties taut across my cheeks. My pulse was fast and my breathing was deep, too, as if I needed to take in extra air.

'Should you see a woman in such a pose,' I went on, elaborating the game, 'it would not be inappropriate to punish her. A spanking might be considered suitable.'

That was it; I'd been teasing, playful, yet I'd said what I really wanted.

'Would you let me?' he asked quietly.

My heart leapt as he said it. I'd done it; I'd found someone who wanted to smack my bottom!

'You wouldn't!' I teased.

He grinned, and not shyly either.

'No, sir, please!' I squeaked as he got up. 'Not that!'

'I'm afraid that it is my duty,' he said sternly.

'No,' I whimpered, 'please, no, sir, not a spanking!'

He approached me, slowly, and then took me gently around the waist. I closed my eyes in bliss, concentrating on the feel of his strong arm as it circled my waist. We'd been playing, an erotic game, but still play. Now we weren't. He was going to spank me for real. It would really sting, really make me blush and kick and squeak. I sighed as his hand touched my bottom through my panties. It began to move, firmly and in little circles.

'Come on, punish me,' I breathed.

His hand left my bottom and then came down across my cheeks, quite hard. I gave a little gasp, revelling in the sensation of it as another smack fell on the seat of my panties. I was bent over with my dress pulled up, being spanked purely because it excited him to punish me. My bottom was warming under the smacks too, and the heat went to my pussy.

He tightened his grip and started to spank harder, making me feel helpless. I started to kick a bit with each slap, wondering if he still needed prompting to take my panties down. A sudden flurry of sharp smacks had me squeaking and gasping and I realised that he almost certainly didn't.

'I'm going to pull your knickers down, Penny,' he said.

I just sighed. His hand went to my waistband and down they came, slowly, peeled down to expose my hot bottom to his gaze. The way he did it was really lecherous, and very different from the pre-emptory, matter-of-fact way my aunt had pulled my panties down the last time I'd been spanked. She'd done it because she didn't see why they should stay up, although she was certainly aware that it shamed me to have my bottom stripped as if my exposure were of no importance. Alex obviously regarded it as very important, peeling them down and breathing heavily as my bare bum came on show. I sighed deeply as he settled them around my thighs, opening my legs in completely willing surrender.

I was open in front of him, wet, vulnerable and eager, my pussy gaping, my bumhole showing, my reddened bottom stuck up, naked. He began to caress me, fondling my bottom like a prize peach and giving the occasional little slap to make my cheeks bounce. There was something really lewd about the way he did it, moulding and squeezing my flesh, pulling my cheeks open so that he could get a sneaky peep at my bottom-hole.

'I want to see you kick again,' he said, his voice thick with lust.

He took me back around the waist, much harder, and really began to beat me. The smacks were hard, and given with the flat of his hand across the tuck of my bottom so that each sent a shock straight to my pussy. It hurt, too, and I was quickly kicking as much as he could have wanted, my legs going up and down and my bottom bucking under the pain. I was squealing too, trying to keep quiet but not really succeeding.

When he finally stopped, it was all I could do to slump over the table. I felt genuinely punished and sorry for myself, but also in ecstasy, having been given a good, hard, male spanking for the first time.

He went back to exploring me, now touching my body with a prurient interest that I can only describe as molestation. Not that I minded, but it made me feel really defiled to have my bum-cheeks pulled apart and my anus inspected in minute detail from a distance of a few inches. He paid no attention to my boobs at all, but was completely absorbed in my naked, red bottom and the rear of my pussy. I took a grip on the far side of the table and clung on, hoping that, when he'd taken in every detail of my sex, he'd just fuck me out of hand.

'You're so lovely, Penny,' he breathed.

'You can touch,' I assured him. 'Anywhere.'

'Even . . .?' he said hesitantly.

'Yes,' I answered, although unsure if he meant my pussy or anus.

An instant later fingers touched my vagina and the very centre of my bumhole simultaneously. If his gaze had been intrusive, then once he'd been given permission to touch it was worse. A finger slid up my vagina, another probed my anus.

'Not pussy and bum with the same finger,' I told him.

'Right,' he replied and slid his fingers further in.

He put another in my pussy and started to wiggle all three inside me. The intrusive, prying quality of his exploration was really getting to me, but when he started to move them I really let go, panting and sighing and just purring from the feel of such intimate indignity. I was so wet that I could feel my own juice on the insides of my thighs where my panties were touching. He seemed content with just molesting me, but he was only using one hand, and I could guess what he was up to with the other. I was enjoying being felt, but he was getting quite frantic and maybe was just going to come while he fondled me. I was sure it would be easy to enter me, yet there was still a little scared voice in the back of my head telling me not to let him. Then I remembered Rachel and the League of Purity and how much I hated their cold, disapproving attitude to life.

'Put it inside,' I begged, my voice urgent yet small in my own ears.

'May I really?' he asked as if in disbelief.

'Yes, please do it,' I begged, determined to let him have me before I got second thoughts.

'Oh, thank you,' he sighed as he took his fingers out of me.

Even as I felt something firm touch my vulva I realised that he too must have been virgin, for all his height and looks. Then my vagina was opening under the pressure of his cock and I wasn't thinking of anything except the fact that I was being entered. There was no pain; it just slid inside me, filling me with a blissful, soothing sensation that just made me want to close my eyes and purr.

I was lost, bent over with a freshly smacked bottom and a penis inside me, absolutely in heaven. He did it slowly at first, as if unsure, then sped up and started to groan and grunt. I realised he was going to come, as he was riding me with the same frantic urgency that Aran had always shown just before orgasm. It had hurt in my bottom; though in my pussy it was bliss and had me panting and groaning without restraint. He hadn't been in me two minutes, though, and I wanted more . . .

Only I didn't get it. At that instant, just as he started to come, the lights flooded on. I opened my eyes to find myself looking straight at Rachel and the speaker from the meeting. Her mouth was open, and I'll never forget the look on her face if I live to be a hundred.

'Penny!' she gasped.

As if that wasn't bad enough, Alex was at the point of no return, actually coming as the lights went on. He pulled sharply back, spraying my reddened bottom-cheeks with sperm and treating them all to a fine view of his erection at the very point of orgasm. Rachel screamed, the speaker was trying to find words but couldn't. I just smiled.

5

Hothouse Peaches

There had always been something sexual between my cousin Kate and I. Not that it had ever amounted to much: just hugs and kisses that were perhaps more intimate than was normal between close friends. There had also been her desire to have me lose my virginity, and to watch it happen. She had been seriously turned on by it, playing with herself while her brand new husband prepared to enter me. Unfortunately that had been the moment that Kate's mother Elaine, my aunt, chose to turn up. They had made a hasty retreat; I'd been spanked.

I hadn't seen Kate since, but the memory of that spanking was still hot in my mind. It had turned me on so much that I'd given myself an orgasm afterwards – my first – yet in my fantasy it had been Kate and not her mother who had me across her knee as I squealed and kicked my way through the punishment. I'd always liked the idea, and had actually suggested it to Kate before that, but she'd just giggled.

Since then a lot had happened to me. I'd gone up to university, done well enough to give my confidence a serious boost and had two serious relationships. The first had been with Aran Ray, a magnificently athletic black man who was obsessed with my bottom. He had buggered me, really roughly. I hadn't minded until I found out that he was uninterested in anything else. Then there had been Alex, who was obsessed with me full stop and with whom I was still going out. He had taken my virginity; indeed, we had traded virginities. We had been experimenting enthusiastically ever since, and, nearly a year after I had seen Kate, my sexual experience and confidence had improved a thousandfold.

Kate, sadly, had not had such a good time of it. Her husband, Toby, had proved to be the bastard everybody except Kate thought he was in the first place. They had parted after less than a year, and I had promised to come and stay with her to console her. Her mother was in the Channel Islands, as was mine, which left Kate and me alone in the house in Berkshire. Aunt Elaine didn't know that the marriage had failed, and it was this, more than the actual break-up, that was worrying Kate. From the point of view of Toby, she was simply glad to be away from him, and if her pride had taken a knock, then she could hardly be described as distraught.

As soon as I took her in my arms to hug her, I knew that I wanted her, completely. I was prepared to try as well, although typically I lacked the guts to simply proposition her. Instead I suggested a swim in a nearby quarry in which we had frequently played as children. This was a lonely, disused gravel pit surrounded by a high bank and filled with clear, cool water. I knew we'd strip to swim, and I knew we'd play about in the water, from which I had a pretty strong hope of sex.

It was a wicked little plot, and it began beautifully. Kate was keen on the idea of visiting the quarry, and there was never any question of bothering with swimsuits. We'd always bathed naked there, and if we were now grown women, then we'd never been seen by anybody, either. I watched her undress with a delicious thrill of anticipation running right through me. She had always been gorgeous, with a full, ultra-fcminine body that had made the boys' tongues hang out. Now she was even nicer. She was perhaps half a stone heavier than a year before, but tauter and firmer. She still had a trace of puppy fat on her tummy and bottom, which I found adorable, and from her tumble of brown curls to her magnificent legs, she was just pure sex.

I felt tiny and girlish by comparison, as I always had, but

from the effect I had on Alex and from Aran's almost demented lust for my bottom, I knew that, for all my small size, I didn't lack appeal. Kate seemed to think so too, complimenting me on my waist with a look that just had to be more than aesthetic appreciation.

'You do have rather a fat bottom, though,' she teased, which was cheeky, considering the size of hers.

If I'd had any guts, I'd have grabbed her then and started a play fight. We'd have been naked in the grass and the hot sun, and that would surely have been that. Instead, I hesitated a moment too long and let her get into the water ahead of me. The sexual tension was there, though, and I was sure that it was just a matter of getting to grips. The water was warm at the surface but cool deeper down, which made my nipples stiff and tingly. Kate's were the same, little dark buds sticking out from her magnificent boobs and tempting me to touch, to kiss and to suck.

I swam towards her, my stomach knotted with tension and a need that entirely destroyed my reserve. She smiled at me, mischievous and uncertain. We touched, the flesh of her flanks cool and yielding under my fingers. Her mouth was a little open, her eyes wide and full of desire.

Something caught my eye, a movement. I looked around to see a man standing among the scrub at the lip of the quarry, watching us. As soon as he noticed my attention he ran, but it had completely shattered the moment. The magic of the place, built up since I'd been about four, died on the instant.

I was furious, and far more upset than I had any right to be, considering he had had as much right to be there as we did. It had happened at the worst possible moment, though. A little earlier and it would only have been an annoying interruption. Later and, while it would have been embarrassing, the bond of intimacy between us would have been established. As it was, we both knew something had been about to happen and that was what made it really difficult. Afterward, we were nervous with each other, really for the first time ever. I felt stupid for having tried, but still wanted to, desperately.

We had lunch at a pub and then went back to the house. The day was sultry, with just the faintest of breezes stirring the big copper beeches that surrounded the house. I have always loved trees and woods and the country in general, and found the peaceful, timeless air of the place soothing. Yet it added another dimension to my need for Kate. To play with her, naked and uninhibited in the warm sunlight on the lawn, would be an experience so sweet, so exquisite, that the thought had me near to tears.

Unable to stay with Kate, I went upstairs, feeling confused and desperately in need of her. Now that our moment in the quarry had been broken, I wasn't at all sure how she'd react, yet I had to do something or I'd go mad. I decided to masturbate over her and then take a more detached look at things once I'd calmed down a little. I undressed slowly, letting my clothes fall away until I was once more naked, then stretched out on the bed. I started to think about Kate, trying to concentrate on the fantasy and ignore her very near presence. It was impossible as, for all my excitement, I was in no state to masturbate successfully.

For a while I watched dust motes dance in the yellow sunlight, then got up and went over to the window. Below me the garden was a maze of old brick walls and hedges, half overgrown, the wrought iron rusting and the white paintwork peeled and cracked. A walled area, once the kitchen garden, was directly below me, with a long, ornate hothouse of ironwork and green encrusted glass to one side.

I could just make out the outline of someone in the greenhouse, and knew that it could only be Kate. Suddenly, the urge to go to her became overwhelming. Even if she slapped me and screamed at me, I had to try. Quickly pulling on shorts and a T-shirt, I made my way downstairs and out into the garden. The kitchen garden was separated from the main area by a high wall of crumbling red brick, and the little arch that led into it was half choked with bindweed. I pushed through, finding myself beside the greenhouse.

I could see part of Kate's white dress through the dirty panes, but something prevented me from calling out or tapping on the glass. She was standing with her back to me, eating a peach. The peach tree, which had been allowed to run riot and had taken over the greenhouse, surrounded her on all sides, creating a shaded space lit yellow and pale green through the dirty glass. To her side was a broad wooden shelf stacked with trays of peaches, many of them beginning to soften and brown.

Watching Kate as she ate, I admired the riot of brown curls that fell to her waist and the way her softly rounded contours showed where the dress touched her. The outline of her body was just visible through the light fabric, the side of one full breast showing as a curve of shade, with paler crescents where her waist broadened to her hips. I could also make out the deeper white where her panties were strained against her dress by her lush bottom. I thought of how white her skin was, and how she had stripped in front of me without a second thought.

She turned sideways and settled her bottom against the shelf, her eyes closed in bliss as a dribble of peach juice ran down her chin and on to the front of her dress. I could make out the dark circles of her nipples, slightly stiff and making little bulges in the white cotton. Her left hand was resting lightly on her belly and, as I watched, she began to make little circular motions, stroking the slight bulge of her stomach. Then her hand moved higher, touching a breast and pinching the nipple lightly between two fingers. She took another bite of the peach, splashing juice down her front so that a strip of her dress clung to her skin, showing the small depression of her belly button.

I settled back against the mass of foliage and big white flowers, my own hand going to the V of my shorts, where I could feel the swell of my pussy-lips under the tight denim. I watched, mesmerised, stroking myself as Kate put her hand between her legs and bunched her dress up with her fingers. The white V of her panties came into view and she slipped her fingers under the elastic and began to knead, ever so slowly.

My breathing had quickened and the material of my shorts had begun to get damp where my fingers were pressing it in between my pussy-lips. I wanted Kate so badly, far too badly to resist; I made my way quickly around the side of the greenhouse, and ducked low, so as not to startle her. I was praying that she wouldn't reject me as I slipped my sandals off, so that my feet would make no noise on the gravel of the greenhouse floor. I pushed the foliage that obscured the open door aside, sure that she would hear me, yet desperate for the first thing she felt to be my mouth on hers. As I came to a place where I could see her clearly, I paused, my tummy fluttering with the uncertainty of what I was about to do.

She was now masturbating freely, her panties pushed down around the top of her thighs and the thick, dark bush of her pubic hair showing. She had two fingers holding her pussy-lips apart as she rubbed at her clit and I could see the swollen pink flesh of the centre of her vulva. Her eyes were still tight shut, and I wondered if she was thinking of me. Taking a deep breath, I stepped forward and put my arms around her. Even as her body tensed in alarm I kissed her, full on the mouth. She opened her eyes sharply.

'Penny!' she protested, pulling back.

'Don't be shy, Kate, please?' I responded, keeping my arms around her.

She looked full into my eyes for a moment, her lips slightly parted in uncertainty.

'Please, Kate,' I pleaded, 'I was watching you, and . . . and I've always wanted this.'

She stayed still, saying nothing but with the tip of her tongue just showing at the side of her mouth as she wet her lips. She seemed to reach a decision and her arms came around me and pulled me in to her. Then she was kissing me and breaking off to whisper to me, urgent, passionate words that made me realise that she must have felt the same frustration as I had. Suddenly, everything was all right and we were trying to get at each other with a frantic passion born of long denial. She pulled my top up over my breasts, her teeth finding a nipple as her hands went lower. One moment her fingers were working desperately at my belt and the next my shorts were down and I could feel the air on my naked bottom. My mouth found hers and opened, our tongues touching as she cupped my buttocks, opening my cheeks, twice touching my anus and then penetrating it as she gave a sigh of total abandonment deep in her throat.

I let my own hand slip down to her bottom and we began to explore each other as we kissed. She pulled her finger out and began to stroke my cheeks, pulling me tight into her with the other arm. I put an arm out to steady myself and found my hand resting on something soft and furry, a peach. A deliciously naughty idea came into my head and, using my other hand, I began to inch her dress up at the back until she in turn had her bottom bare. I pulled her pants back up and held them open by the elastic at the back; they were quite big, covering her well-fleshed bottom almost completely. I was still kissing her as I put the overripe fruit to the small of her back and squashed it so that the juice ran down her knickers and in between her buttocks. She purred as I dropped the crushed peach down the back of her panties. I let the waistband go with a smack and pulped the peach on to her bottom. As the juice soaked through the flimsy cotton of her panties, I felt her shiver in my arms.

A delicious feeling of being in control came over me as I took another peach and squished it down her knickers, along with the first. It was a new sensation for me, and one I liked. Kate pushed her bottom out to meet the pressure from my hands as I rubbed the peach in and purred as my lips touched the side of her neck. I took a peach in each hand and reached up under her dress to squash them against her heavy breasts, then cupped one in each hand and began to tease her nipples with my thumbs. The sticky juice was all over her front, mingled with bits of peach flesh and skin. She leant back, allowing me to work on her as I pleased. I let the juice-soaked front of her dress fall against her breasts so that her nipples showed, swollen and dark through the sodden fabric. She sighed, then abruptly pulled the dress up over her chest, letting her breasts fall loose with the juice running down between them and over her belly.

Her pussy had not had its share of peach, and I determined to remedy that quickly. I selected a particularly ripe fruit and held it up to her face. She giggled as I pulled open the front of her panties and popped it in, then crushed it with my hand. It burst with a delightful squelch, staining her knickers and running down the insides of her thighs. I slid a hand in to retrieve the stone, then let my fingers slip between her pussy-lips as my mouth found a sticky nipple. The peach flesh tasted sweet and rich, perhaps even a little rotten as I picked bits off her boobs with my teeth. There were runnels of it on her belly, which I lapped up, moving slowly downwards over the soft swell of her flesh. Her tummy button was full of juice, which I licked up, then traced a line of kisses down to her pubic hair and the top of her panties.

I hesitated, savouring the moment, then tugged down her panties and buried my face in her pussy, getting a mouthful of peach pulp as my tongue searched for her clit. The taste of peach was thick in my mouth and mingled with the taste of Kate. I lapped at her clit, delighting in her urgent moans and the soft, compelling pressure as she put a hand to the back of my head. Her thigh muscles quickly began to tense around my face, signalling the onset of orgasm. I slid a hand between her legs and felt for her vagina. My thumb slid inside her as my middle finger burrowed deeper, finding the tight knot of her anus and pushing inside. Her hand locked in my hair and she pushed my face hard into her. My tongue was working frantically on her clit and her groans were becoming deeper and more urgent still. I felt the muscles of her vagina and anus start to pulse and she screamed, her hand twisting hard in my hair as she came with my face pushed so hard into her pussy that I couldn't breathe.

As I pulled slowly back I was smiling, blissfully happy and well aware that it was now my turn. I looked up, finding her beautiful body smeared with dark yellow peach pulp and bits of golden-pink skin from the neck down. Her knickers were sodden and dripping with juice. The white summer dress was a filthy tangle on the ground, dust and bits of leaf and peach adhering to the wet cotton. I reached out and took hold of her panties, wanting her bare. She made no protest as I pulled them down and off, leaving her gloriously naked.

'Me please, Katie,' I said, putting my paws up under my chin to imitate a puppy begging.

She smiled, a mischievous grin, and pointed to my shorts. I let them slip to the ground and stepped out of them, suddenly finding my breathing coming deep and my pulse hammering. There was something commanding about her now, something deliciously commanding. Without warning, she reached out and took me by the hair, pulling me abruptly forward and over the shelf. I realised what she intended an instant before it happened and opened my mouth to catch my breath, only to have it filled with gooey peach as my face was pushed into the tray.

I wriggled and squirmed, pretending to struggle but at the same time lifting my bottom in the hope that Kate would smack it. I was sure she would and, just as I had expected, her palm came down hard, full across the cheeks of my bum. It stung and made me jump, but she held me firmly in place, planting another hard smack and then going to work in earnest, spanking me while I wiggled and danced in my exquisite pain. My face was covered in peach flesh, Kate pushing it back in each time I came up for air, and I could picture my bottom going pink, then red as the stinging slaps covered every square inch of my cheeks.

Finally I could take no more and begged her to stop, which she did after one final hard slap on the plumpest part of my bottom. I felt no urge to move, but lay whimpering with my face in the remains of the peaches. My bottom felt warm and tingly and I was acutely aware of my exposed position, T-shirt up around my neck, little breasts dangling naked, bare scarlet bottom raised high, legs open and my pussy completely vulnerable to Kate.

'Lick me,' I begged.

She didn't reply, but traced a long line down my back with a fingernail and then moved round to kneel behind me. I couldn't see her, and there was an agonising moment of suspense before I felt her tongue touch the smarting surface of my freshly spanked bottom. It felt cool and wet against my hot flesh, dabbing at my cheeks, then moving into the centre, touching within an inch of my anus and finally finding my pussy. For a moment she teased, flicking her tongue on my pussy-lips, only to suddenly bury her face in my rear and start licking my clit. I groaned and pushed my bottom into her face, instantly in ecstasy and knowing that I would come without difficulty. Spanking always helps me to come, but even with Alex I'd never known such a quick hit of pleasure – and, goodness knows, he used to spank me and lick me often enough. Maybe it was because Kate was a girl and had her own pussy, but she seemed to know just what to do. I came in her face, calling out her name as my orgasm hit me and her tongue pressed hard on my button.

When I had finished I turned and we drew together, cuddling blissfully into each other's arms. Our bodies were wet with peach juice and sweat and she felt warm and soft in my arms as I kissed her and squeezed her. We stayed like that for a long time, just cuddling, which was something that Alex never really did. Finally we pulled apart and looked at each other, then simultaneously burst out laughing at the state of our hopelessly peach-sodden clothes and hair. I turned to show her my still-smarting bottom and gave her a look of mock reproach.

'I've wanted to do that for ages!' she said brightly.

'And I've wanted you to do it for ages,' I admitted. 'Thank you, it was lovely.'

She didn't reply, but looked shyly at the ground and flicked her foot at a piece of peach flesh.

'I . . . I'm really glad you came to me,' she said at length. 'I can't remember the time when I didn't want to do that, but I never dared.'

'Me, too,' I responded and held out my arms for her.

6

Teenage Reprieve

My first year at university changed my life completely. I was still technically a teenager, yet with my new-found intellectual confidence and my relationship with Alex Shaw, all the insecurities and uncertainties of adolescence had gone. Or, at least, I thought they had. It wasn't for another five years that I discovered otherwise.

The Channel Island holidays that had been so much a part of my life from my earliest childhood had come to a stop when I had gone to university. In the summer after my first year, I spent most of my time with Alex and hadn't joined my mother and aunt on holiday. After that the habit lapsed, and when my mother finally gave up on the grounds that the place was just too crowded, that appeared to be the end of it. Only when I was a first-year PhD student and had come to think of myself as a confident, modern young woman, did I go back.

It happened as a result of the collapse of my relationship with Alex. We'd been together over five years and had really got rather bogged down. He still had the smutty, schoolboy-like lust for me that had appealed so much at first, yet, for all the time we'd been together, he still wasn't as cuddly and loving as I felt I needed.

We had organised a trip to the Loire Valley together, camping and visiting the great châteaus and vineyards. The idea was to revitalise our relationship, but unfortunately it didn't work, making things worse instead of better. It came to a head one night in a campsite outside Chinon, and the next morning we went our separate ways without a word.

Fortunately, my parents had been generous and I had enough money to see myself safely back to England. More than enough, in fact, and so I decided to take it slowly. I was feeling confused, but actually quite happy and liberated, and so decided on a tour of Brittany and Normandy. This was great fun, and included a couple of worthwhile sexual encounters as well. The first of these was hitching a lift and ending up being fucked in the cab of a lorry by the huge, hairy French driver. There was something primevally lustful about the way he mounted me and just fucked and fucked until I was sore. The second was getting drunk in a café in Cherbourg and ending up in bed with a French girl and her lover. We put on a show for him, stripping and playing with each other's breasts. Just as we were climbing into a sixty-nine, the door burst open and her husband came in.

That left me on the streets of Cherbourg at two in the morning, drunk, horny and without the foggiest idea what to do. Most of my stuff was in the auberge I'd booked into before getting drunk, and that was firmly closed up for the night. I didn't dare wake the fiery old matron who ran it, although the idea did give me a rather nice fantasy about being put over her knee and spanked for being a drunken slut. It was warm enough, so I began to walk the streets, ending up down at the harbour. I sat down on a bench to watch the gentle waves lap at the quay, feeling more free than I ever had before. All I had was a light dress and my bag. In the hurry to escape what looked like blowing up into a nasty fight, I'd left my panties on the floor and was completely bare under my dress.

My bench was set back into a dark recess and I was completely alone, so I pulled my dress up and began to play with myself: just gently, not really intending to come but just for the soothing pleasure of stroking my pussy. I started to think about the girl I'd been going to lick. I hadn't even known her name, but we'd been intending to lick each other to orgasm in front of her lover. Just knowing that I'd have done it felt so dirty, and I was much too drunk to feel any guilt at all. My thoughts went back to my cousin Kate and my first lesbian experience, wallowing together in a mess of peach pulp and bringing each other to orgasm. Twice at university I'd ended up in bed with other girls, always drunk and always guilty and ashamed in the morning. Not that it stopped me going back for more.

It was noticing that one of the boats in the harbour had a Guernsey registration that turned my thoughts further back still, to the Channel Island holidays of my childhood and teenage years. I hadn't made a very good teenager, lacking the qualities needed in such a restrictive, structured social environment. This had been especially true on the Channel Islands, where my experience with the perverse Ryan had been my only really worthwhile sexual experience. At the time I'd felt used and had been rather shocked. Now it would have been different. I'd have given him a long, slow striptease, allowing him to concentrate on my bottom, which was what he liked best. I would have pretended to be coy, getting him more and more wound up but making sure we fucked and ended up with his cock deep up my bumhole.

Looking at the boat, I began to think of the rough, manly fishermen I'd known. None had ever shown much interest in me, preferring Kate's more opulent curves and extrovert character. Her boyfriend Carl had been the best of them: big, strong, swarthy and lusty, not unlike the lorry driver who'd fucked me the week before. The boat in front of me was not his father's, or I think I'd have borrowed a rowing boat and gone out to it. As it was, the proximity of the island started to tempt me and I began to wonder about going there.

There was no reason why not. I was completely free, with no obligation to be anywhere or to see anyone for over a month. My mother would be cross when she heard I'd been wandering around France on my own instead of coming straight home, but that was something I could handle when the time came. Nothing was stopping me and, by the time I had soothed myself into a light sleep, I was on a full-blown nostalgia trip for my teenage years.

The next morning I retrieved my bags from the hotel, showered and breakfasted. The big Frenchwoman was a bit sniffy with me, but unfortunately didn't whip me over her knee for a panties-down spanking, contenting herself with a remark I didn't understand as I left. I was determined on the course of action I had decided on the previous night and made straight for the airport.

The journey is so short that the planes barely get to a cruising altitude before coming down again, and before noon I was looking out of my window at the fields and cliffs of the island I was so familiar with. I could even make out the Val de Fret, and the German bunker in which I had had my encounter with Ryan. I felt so nostalgic for it all that there were tears in my eyes, with all the bad times forgotten and all the good enhanced a thousandfold.

One sniff of the air as I stepped from the plane and everything changed. It was a hot day, with a light breeze blowing the smell of the sea over the tarmac. Everything came rushing back with a force that made me feel weak. All my sorrows and insecurities returned, as strong as ever, and I almost booked a ticket for Eastleigh and left without ever stepping outside the airport terminal.

I've always had a streak of stubbornness, and that was what made me pick up my bags and start for town, not really sure where I was going, but determined to at least try and lay the ghost that had sprung on me with such unexpected force. Just walking into town was an extraordinary experience; I recognised every field and building, yet felt strangely detached, as if I were walking though a scene from a film. I booked into a tiny hotel-cum-pub just off the square and went into the bar for a badly needed glass of orange juice.

That was the moment that I really felt as if I'd stepped back in time. It was a bar that my parents had favoured for pre-lunch drinks, and six years might as well not have happened. The bar was the same; several of the customers were the same; even the barmaid was the same. She was Linda, a pretty local girl who I mainly remembered for always being jealous of Kate.

'Hi, Penny, you've cut your hair!' were her first words.

I hadn't seen her in six years and the first thing she did was comment on my haircut. It had been long then, but I'd had it cut into a short bob when I'd first started with Alex, some five years before.

'Hi, Linda,' I answered. 'An orange juice please, pure.'

She poured my drink and we began to chat, pretty inconsequentially, but more and more about the island and old friends. Some things had changed, but not much, and to all intents and purposes life was much as I remembered it. I didn't let it show, but her reminiscences did nothing for my self-confidence. It had nose-dived, the moment I'd smelt the air of the island, and had been in free fall ever since. University, my PhD work, Alex – even events in France the previous night suddenly seemed like things that had happened to someone else. Little, shy Penny who never went out with anybody couldn't possibly have done anything as outrageous as have sex with a French couple and get thrown out of the house by an enraged husband.

If there's one thing I pride myself on, it's knowing when my emotions are leading me and remaining aware of reality. Even when drunk or in the throes of orgasm, there's always a little piece of my mind that stays detached and observant. Now it was telling me that I had a stark choice: either leave or do something that would lay the ghost of my teenage years completely.

It was Linda who decided my choice.

'Are you coming to the Barn tonight?' she asked cheerfully.

The Barn was the scene of Kate's greatest triumphs and my greatest failures. It had always been very much the place to be for the more trendy teenagers, and many, many times Kate had been chased by all the best men in the place while I'd had to put up with the attentions of every sort of man except what I wanted. If I could go there and have a good time of it, then I knew it would all be OK.

'Sure,' I answered.

Logically, I knew that I would be able to hold my own. I'd developed a lot in six years and was also no longer in

Kate's shadow. Emotionally, it was a very different matter, and there was a horrible queasy feeling in my stomach as I walked into the Barn that night. Like everything else, it had hardly changed; indeed, the only obvious difference was that many of the people who'd been too young to go when I'd last been there now made up a fair proportion of the crowd.

Still feeling rather delicate after the previous night's excesses, I ordered orange juice and propped myself up at the end of the bar, waiting to be recognised. There were a fair number of familiar faces there but, unlike Linda, none of them had immediately recognised me. Even when Carl appeared and I smiled right at him, I only got a smile back: just that, not a flicker of recognition.

I was surprised, and not a little put out, as Linda's reaction had shown that my appearance couldn't have changed all that dramatically. Surely they couldn't have been so unaware of me that when I reappeared I was effectively a stranger?

I began to feel really sorry for myself and was wishing I had stayed in France, when someone tapped me on the shoulder. I turned to find Carl looking at me.

'You're Penny, aren't you?' he asked.

'Yes, you remember me,' I replied.

'Sure I do,' he answered. 'You're Katie's little friend.'

I nodded, although less than flattered by being described as Kate's 'little friend', especially as I'm actually a month older than Kate.

'Is Katie around?' he asked hopefully.

'No, she's married now,' I answered, not at all surprised that his first interest was in Kate.

'What?' he demanded: 'Not to that ponce Toby?'

'Yes and no,' I replied, thinking that Carl was the only person on the world who could consider the brash, very obviously male Toby a 'ponce'. Toby had come to the island with Kate before their marriage, much to Carl's disgust.

'How's that?' he queried, his Neanderthal brows knitting in perplexity.

71

'She married Toby,' I explained, 'but they didn't even last a year. He turned out to be a complete bastard.'

'Did he?' Carl asked.

'Yes,' I pointed out patiently, 'so Kate left him and they got divorced.'

'So she's not married?' he demanded.

'Hang on, hang on,' I continued, 'I haven't finished. She met this guy called Jeremy and married him as soon as the divorce came through. He's an advertising executive, they live in Sonning Common and have two daughters, Pippa and Jemima.'

'Oh . . . right,' he answered and then stopped and looked around the room before turning to me with what I suppose was supposed to be a winning smile but was in fact an extremely dirty leer.

'What about you, then?' he asked.

It couldn't have been more obvious if he'd flopped his cock out and asked if I fancied a suck. I played along, though, giving him a potted history of my last five years and accepting his offer to join his friends. I wasn't entirely flattered but was telling myself that his response was typical and at least pleasantly virile. I was also wondering why he had looked round the room before issuing his invitation. Possibly he'd been checking for anything better in the way of talent, or possibly he'd been making sure whoever his current girlfriend was wasn't around.

'Look what I've found,' he addressed his mates as we approached the table.

They greeted me cheerfully, and I had to explain why I wasn't with Kate again. There were five of them and no girls, for some reason, and they seemed more than happy to pay court to me once they were sure Kate wasn't around. It is nice being the centre of attention of five men, but in this case it was rather like being the lone female in a pen of rutting boars – the lone female pig, that is. Not that I minded, as I've always liked to think of male sexuality in terms of something primitive and uncontrolled.

Carl and his friends were certainly primitive and hardly controlled, but I made a big effort to be sweet and giggled in all the right places instead of making the sarcastic remarks that came to mind. I was very aware that I was playing a game and acting a part designed to produce a particular result. It was something that I could never have done as a teenager and, as the evening went on, my confidence gradually returned. The feeling of *déjà vu* didn't go away, though, but became stronger, until it really felt like six years had never happened.

They were trying to get me drunk and I let them, accepting half-pints of cider and then several glasses of gin and lime. They also kept testing me, making little comments to see if I would be shocked and giving half-joking suggestions. I played along, pacing my drinking as best I could and very aware of their games. Thus, when Carl's friend Gary played an old trick on me, I knew exactly what was going on.

He was standing up with a pint in either hand after returning from the bar with part of a round. He could perfectly well have put them down, but instead he asked me to get his money out of the pocket of his baggy jeans so that he could go and pay. I knew what was coming, as I'd seen it done to Kate and other girls. I plunged my hand down into his pocket to find not money, but a fat, half-erect penis.

The girl is supposed to scream, jerk her hand back and go into a fit of giggles. Yet she has touched his cock and the boys' theory is that, once a girl has touched a man's cock, she's likely to want more. I knew what was coming and, instead of jerking my hand away, I took a firm grip on his cock and began to tug at it.

Only when it was fully erect and the head was poking out of his pocket did I let him go. He sat down hastily, blowing his breath out and looking at me in wide-eyed astonishment. I smiled and winked.

Their attitude changed after that. Before, they'd been teasing and tempting, hoping to get me drunk enough to perhaps give one of them a blow-job, but not really expecting anything. My behaviour with Gary made them realise that there was a very real chance of a lot more, although they were evidently surprised that the shy, skinny girl they'd really only known as Kate's friend had changed so much. The truth was that I hadn't really changed at all, not deep down. What had changed was my confidence.

I could have left then and the ghost would have been laid, but I had the very real chance of sex with one or more of them and was keen to get it. Even though I like to think of myself as liberated, I must admit to allowing social pressures to affect me. At university, I wouldn't have considered going off with five men at once, simply because my life would have been unbearable afterwards. It had been bad enough when Alex and I had been caught fucking over a table in the lecture theatre canteen, but at least it had been one-to-one.

Now it was different. I could do as I liked and leave the island the next day. If people wanted to talk, then they could. It would make no difference to me. It was going to happen, too; it was approaching closing time and there was an urgency and expectancy in their manner. Each was doing his best to get close to me, hoping to be the one I chose. Gary had put his arm around me, but I had put mine around Carl, refusing to show any favours. I knew what I wanted, and I knew they were capable of it. It was just a question of playing my cards right.

Shortly before closing time, I got up for a visit to the loo, intending to relieve myself and tidy up. When I came out of the cubicle, it was to find Linda propped up on the sinks, obviously waiting for me.

'Hi, Linda,' I greeted her cheerfully.

'Penny, Penny, we've got to talk,' she hissed, grabbing my arm urgently.

'What's the matter?' I questioned her.

'You know what that lot want, don't you?' she asked in a loud whisper.

'Sex, I imagine,' I told her.

'More than that,' she hissed conspiratorially. 'They'll take you out by the lighthouse and gang-bang you!'

'Are you sure?' I asked hopefully, remembering that the quarry where Carl had always taken Kate for sex was out by the lighthouse.

'Yes,' she insisted. 'They did it to Becky!'

'Don't worry about me,' I assured her. 'I can look after myself.'

'I'm coming with you,' she said, sounding concerned.

'I'm all right,' I insisted. 'Look, Linda, I'm not a baby. I know what they're after. If you want to come and join in, fine; otherwise, leave me to it.'

She stopped, looking at me uncertainly. I could read her like a book. She wanted to do it but, unlike me, she had all the complicated social pressures of the island to worry about. I knew who Becky was as well, a big, bouncy girl with a tumble of auburn curls and a cheeky smile. I could easily see her letting herself go and knew that Linda was wondering if she dared do the same. My reaction may have surprised her, and perhaps it made her feel more daring, because she suddenly nodded and smiled. I took her hand and we walked out of the loo together. Her hand felt soft and feminine in mine and, as we approached the men's table, a dirty little thought was starting to come into my head. Would they appreciate a girly show, and would Linda let me?

'Linda's coming with us,' I announced as I sat down boldly on Carl's lap.

What they'd have done was offer me a lift to town and then suggest going the long way. I'd be across their laps in the back, and probably being snogged and felt up by whoever I'd chosen. They'd have stopped and the lucky one would have suggested a walk, which would have ended in the quarry where I'd have been coaxed into going as far as possible, probably ending up on my back with him humping merrily away for the best part of two minutes before coming inside me. He'd have suggested that it wasn't fair to leave his mates with raging erections, and they'd have had me, one by one, either in my pussy or my mouth.

My boldness caused Carl to raise his shaggy eyebrows, but Gary's face dropped. It was only then that I remembered that he was Linda's brother. The others – Pete, Lewis and Saul – just looked shifty, as if they'd been somehow caught out.

The Barn was noisy and crowded, yet a lot of people turned to look as we left and I could almost feel the rumours starting. I didn't care, and I had decided that Linda would just have to look after herself.

Lewis got into the driver's seat, which I was grateful for as he was the most bulky of them and probably the least pissed. Seeing no reason to pretend innocence, I leant forward to him and suggested the lighthouse route myself. Someone took hold of my bottom and gave it a firm squeeze, his hand enclosing the whole of one cheek.

I sat back, finding myself on Carl's lap. He kept his big hand under my bottom and used the other to feel my breasts, quite casually, having a thoroughly good grope. Linda was beside me, seated on both Pete and Saul, Gary in the front. There was a lot of laughter and giggling as we drove out to the end of the island and, by the time we had parked in the entrance to the quarry, Linda had her top off and my dress was up around my waist. Gary had cheered up when he realised that his sister wasn't going to spoil the party, and was first out of the car.

We tumbled out of the car, staggering down to the flat, grassy quarry floor. There were hands on my bottom as we walked, feeling and exploring. It was almost dark, although the beam from the lighthouse would sweep across above us every so often, throwing back a weird grey-white light from the face of the quarry. They pulled my dress off without waiting to ask, then my panties, laying me down on the grass, naked except for my sandals. I saw Linda's bra being pulled off as she struggled to get her jeans down, then it went dark again and someone had put a half-stiff cock in my hand.

I pulled at it and then put it in my mouth, sucking eagerly without the slightest idea whose it was. The next passage of the lighthouse beam revealed Carl kneeling over me with a grin of triumph on his face. I took him deeper, delighted to be sucking on his erection. Of all Kate's boyfriends, he was the one who'd most strongly affected me, her favourite and the one who'd made me so jealous, so often. Now I had his cock in my mouth and he'd shortly be mounting me.

76

He wouldn't be the first, though. Gary had me by the ankles and was pulling my legs up and apart. A flash of the lighthouse beam showed me his erection rearing up out of his jeans, rock-solid and ready for my vagina. It went dark again and he was on me, then in me and riding me. I closed my eyes in bliss, sucking on Carl while Gary fucked me. I could hear Linda's squeals of joy behind me; then she shut up – presumably because one of the others had put his cock in her mouth.

Gary came in me and was replaced by Carl, while Saul came over to give me something to suck. With each passage of the light I could see Linda, rolled up on her back with her legs right up to her boobs. Pete was on top of her, humping away while she sucked on Lewis' cock. Her breasts looked lovely and big, squashed out under her knees, and I had a strong urge to play with her – only the boys had no intention of letting us go.

It was like being gang-raped by a tribe of baboons on amphetamines – not that I'd know, but still. Once they'd got going there was no stopping them, and Linda and I got used and used and used. They didn't even bother to undress, although she and I had been stripped naked. Instead, they just had their cocks sticking out of their trousers: which, as far as they were concerned, was all they needed. There was nothing perverse about them, either. It was strictly pussies and mouths and, while my tits got a fair share of attention, I wasn't buggered, or spanked, or made to humiliate myself at all. I didn't mind too much, though, because their sheer animal lust made up for it.

I know all five of them fucked me at least once and everyone took his turn in my mouth as well. Saul took his first orgasm all over my face, which was really messy and turned me on no end. With the strange light and the passion of it all, it's hard to be sure what happened, but I'm sure they all came at least twice, which is pretty good going for men, even virile young men. I actually think Gary may have fucked Linda, or at least put his cock in her mouth, although I can't be sure. If he did, then she made no complaint.

Eventually they wore themselves out, Saul coming in Linda and then Carl in me for I think his third orgasm. I was sweaty, sore and covered in sperm, lying naked on the grass. Linda was beside me, in no better a state. Saul had fucked her doggy fashion, and she had stayed kneeling, her bottom stuck up temptingly. I hadn't come, as not one of them had bothered to give me even a token lick. I didn't think she had either, and was wondering if she'd like to exchange favours.

She rolled to her side and stuck her tongue out at me in a gesture of happy exhaustion. I smiled back and held my hand out, finding hers as the light vanished. We drew together, kissing in the dark, her mouth full of the same salty, male taste as my own. I wasn't surprised that one of them had come in her mouth, and nor did I care as our arms went around each other. We snogged and cuddled, aware of the show we were putting on for the boys. I was wondering if it would get them going again – which would be fine, as long as they didn't separate Linda and me. Her body was wonderfully resilient, slick with sweat and sperm and ever so warm and alive. Our sex was perhaps a little clumsy and a little drunken, but it lacked nothing in passion. My fingers found her pussy as we clung together with our breasts touching. She sighed as I started to masturbate her, finding her clit and rubbing it. Then her hand came down between my legs and a finger slid into my pussy. We masturbated together, oblivious to everything else except each other, finally coming together with our fingers on each other's pussies and our tongues entwined in a mess of the boys' sperm.

We lay together for a long time, cuddling and occasionally kissing each other gently. There was no sign of the boys, but I thought nothing of it as I still wanted to explore Linda. She made no objection as I began to fondle her bottom and I let my hands slide down between her lush cheeks to find her anus. She just sighed and cuddled me more closely, kissing my nose as if to assure me that she had no objection to the intimacy of what I was doing. I began to tickle her bottom-hole, very gently, making her groan with pleasure. I was beginning to wonder if the boys would like to watch me spank her when I was startled by the sound of the car's engine and flooded with light from its headlights.

We came apart, vaguely aware of their laughter above the sound of the engine. I could barely see in the glare but managed a protest that was just met with more laughter. Then they began to drive off. Linda got to her feet and shouted something to Gary, but it made no difference. One of them waved something out of the window and I realised that he had my panties. I looked around, finding to my horror that they had taken all my clothes, and Linda's, leaving only our handbags.

I shouted after them but was left watching as they drove off. We stood in disbelief, watching the car's lights fade away and then vanish. We'd let them have us, surrendering ourselves to them only for them to play a stupid, childish trick, leaving us naked and filthy three miles from town. I felt utterly used, yet had the consolation of having laid my ghost with a vengeance.

7

Tweezers

I had gone over to the archaeology building because they have one of those snack dispensers that operate by an ingenious mechanism involving retracting steel coils and dish out a good twenty different snacks into the bargain. It was only as I stood waiting my turn that my eyes drifted to the board listing the staff and I noticed the name of Professor Ruskin.

Ruskin had been the warden of my hall when I was a first year. We had got on well at the time, but I had imagined him long retired and decided to pay him a visit while I was in the building.

His room turned out to be on the top floor of a curious annexe built on top of Egyptology and reached by an iron walkway that connected the two buildings. It was typical of the older parts of the university: iron beams and brick painted in dull cream and set with numerous high windows and apparently purposeless niches. The landing at the top of the stairs smelt of dust and age. Of the three doors opening off it, two were labelled as stores and the third had the professor's name painted on a wooden plaque.

I knocked, only half expecting a response. There was an indistinct sound from within, so I tried the door anyway, opening it to find the professor seated at a desk with his back to me. He was stooped over his desk, studying something with a hand lens and making notes at the same time. His unkempt hair was its normal shoulder-length tangle yet even whiter than I remembered it. It made him look like Einstein, and I had always been sure he cultivated the image on purpose.

'Hello, Professor,' I ventured when he made no move to turn around.

He gave a little start at what was obviously an unexpected interruption to his train of thought and turned to look at me. For a moment, he merely looked puzzled and then his face brightened in recognition.

'Ah, Penny,' he greeted me. 'I am so glad to see you. Tell me, do you shave your pubic hair?'

'Er, sorry?' I replied, taken aback at his question. The way it had been asked was typical of him, scientifically curious but quite innocent of any intention to offend, and it was impossible to be annoyed at what would have been an unreasonably personal question from most people.

'I do apologise,' he continued. 'Perhaps I should explain. I have been studying a remarkable example of *charta Claudia* that was found plastered into the wall of a villa that's being excavated down near Silchester. Generally such things prove to be legal or religious documents, but this is very different. It is a record of the plucking of a slave girl's *mons veneris*: hair by hair, apparently. What I am unable to ascertain is whether the account is an accurate description of a real event or mere wishful thinking.'

'Wouldn't it take an awfully long time?' I asked, glancing at the ancient sheets of discoloured papyrus sandwiched into their protective plastic casings. It was a deep brown, almost black, the cramped writing a series of barely visible marks in a hardly darker shade.

'My thought exactly,' he replied. 'Which is why I had hoped to test the process. Where, though, would I find a volunteer? Students are so precious these days that one daren't even ask, you know. No spirit of enquiry; not a bit of it.'

He turned back to his desk, shaking his head sadly at the state of modern students, though I found it hard to believe that a girl in the fifties or sixties would have been any more willing to have her pubic hairs plucked out one by one than her modern counterpart. I found myself amused by the professor's dilemma. He quite plainly had a genuine interest in completing his bizarre experiment; to his remote, academic mind the idea was no different than wanting to run a test to see if some feat of athletics or construction that the ancients claimed was feasible. That it was a sexual act, and a pretty perverse one at that, evidently only filled him with regret that such a trivial and transient thing as current moral standards should prevent him from asking for a volunteer. A picture came to my mind of him pinning up a notice in the common room among the notices of coming lectures, sporting events and suchlike. The whole scenario was absurd, but also quite rude and sent a wicked thrill right down my spine.

'I don't shave, actually,' I said, without giving myself a chance to reflect and not sure if I was teasing him or actually prepared to go through with it.

'Splendid,' he said. 'But are you quite sure you can spare the time?'

It was his reply that decided me. The idea that I might find the idea improper never entered his head; he was simply concerned that by assisting him I would be delaying my own work.

'I'm waiting for something to be published, so there's not much on,' I answered. 'But perhaps we should lock the door?'

'The door? Ah, yes, I see; explanations might prove difficult.'

I waited while he crossed the room and let the catch into place on the door. He was smiling enthusiastically, obviously delighted by my acquiescence, but with an attitude of boyish mischievousness rather than sexual expectation. Deciding to bare myself in preparation, I struggled my pants off under my dress and laid them over the back of a chair. He sat down again, not troubling to watch but running the tip of his pencil over his notes.

'Ah, yes, here we are,' he was saying as I leant over his shoulder to read the translation. ' "The girl Lunula . . ." meaning "small moon", a pet name, I imagine, ". . . who was noted for her copious growth of black hair", hm, perhaps if you could . . .'

I lifted the front of my dress to show him my own thick, dark pussy fur.

'Yes, that is, I think, a reasonable match to the description. Hm, yes, "growing so richly as to obscure the anus . . ." '

I hesitated only a moment, then turned around and pulled my dress up over my bottom, opening my cheeks so that he could see my hole. I could feel myself blushing furiously, but the embarrassment was mingled with an exhibitionist thrill. Bending over, holding my bum-cheeks wide apart to allow the inspection of my bottom, is the most immodest and revealing pose imaginable; yet, when he spoke, his voice was calm and matter-of-fact.

'Hm, unfortunately there is only a little hair around your anus; indeed, it is clearly visible, though the inner curve of the nates is by no means hairless. We should allow perhaps five per cent.'

Looking back over my shoulder, I could see him inspecting my bottom, his left hand cupping his chin and his right holding his pencil by the tip. He moved the pencil forward and I felt the rubber on the end tap against the super-sensitive flesh of my anal ring and trace a slow line up the curve of the inside of one cheek.

'Yes, I think five per cent,' he repeated as he turned back to the table. 'A reasonable estimate, given that we know nothing of Lunula's actual size in comparison to yours. Now, let me see . . .'

'OK?' I asked, as I was still holding my obscene pose.

'Eh? Oh, yes, yes, thank you.'

I let go of my bottom-cheeks and wiggled so that my skirt fell back in place. Acutely conscious that I was bare underneath, I took a spare chair and pulled it up so that I could see his translation.

'The next part is not particularly relevant,' he continued. 'Hm, ". . . a wet day in summer . . .", "A tunic so short as to show her buttocks when she bent to serve . . .", "laughing and . . ." a word I do not recognise, but it seems she was not averse to their attentions. I am not clear on the next bit, as there appears to be some sort of play on words, something to do with jealousy. In any case, someone called Galeria, possibly the wife of the author, suggested the diversion of plucking the girl's pudenda naked. Hm, "... lying on a ..." I've no idea what that is, but presumably a piece of furniture, "... with her ankles and arms tied beneath to prevent her closing her legs or guarding herself." '

'It may have been a bench of some sort,' I suggested. 'A narrow, horizontal surface in any case. I can see that the instinct to protect the area would be very strong; perhaps I should be tied in the same way.'

'Yes,' he replied, without the slightest trace of irony, 'that would be sensible. We must reproduce the original conditions as accurately as possible. Perhaps if you were to sit on the work bench with your back to the wall?'

'That should work,' I said as I climbed on to the bench and turned round, lifting my skirt so that my bare bottom sat on the hard, wooden surface. I sat cross-legged while he rummaged through his drawers, eventually producing a spool of pink binding tape. I turned and held my crossed wrists behind my back while he fastened them securely, and then wriggled back round before spreading my legs as wide as they would go. He tied pink tape to my left ankle and looped it around one of the bench supports, repeating the process on the other side so that I was obliged to keep my legs apart. I could feel my pulse quickening and my breathing getting deeper, but did my best not to display my reactions. Despite my best efforts, I couldn't resist a shiver as he took hold of the piece of skirt that was all that hid my vagina and lifted it quite casually, tucking it into my waistband so that my whole pubic area was bare. Tied helpless with my pussy on show – and I knew it would be moist and open – I felt ready for the process to begin and was steeling myself for the touch of his fingers in my hair. Instead, he returned to his seat and took up the manuscript again, not so much as bothering to glance in my direction until he had found his place.

'It appears they used some form of tweezers,' he said after studying the document in silence for a while. 'Made of bone, apparently. I imagine that a pair of Spencer Wells forceps will provide us with an adequate alternative. I'm sure I have some, somewhere.'

My sense of anticipation rose to an almost unbearable peak while he pottered around the room, searching for the instrument that was going to be used on me. I wanted to beg him to get started and point out that, however cool and detached he might feel, being half naked and in bondage was having a hell of an effect on me. I shut my eyes and tried to think sobering thoughts and had succeeded in relaxing myself considerably when I was brought back sharply to reality by the cold touch of steel on my belly.

'They were in the drawer right underneath you all the time,' he chuckled, amused at his own forgetfulness. 'Right, let's begin, then. Just let me set the tape recorder up.'

I let out a little sob as he went back across the room for the machine, setting it running and taking up the forceps. The muscles of my vagina tensed involuntarily as he approached me, clicking the forceps together like a child with a favourite toy. Then he stopped.

'Oh, the clock, of course; how stupid of me,' he said, glancing around the room.

I only just managed to choke down a scream of frustration, but fortunately the large stop-clock was on a shelf and he had soon readied it on the bench next to my right thigh.

This time it was for real and I watched in fascination as he closed the forceps on a hair that stuck out somewhat from my nest of curls and pulled at it, making the skin rise in a little dimple. I was shivering and my nervousness was making the muscles around my vagina contract in little starts.

He gave a sudden tug, pulling the hair from its roots and drawing a squeak from me at the sudden sharp pain. The anticipation was actually a lot worse than the pain and the next few hairs came out easily as he worked along the top edge of my pubic triangle, quickly settling down to a rhythm as he became used to the task.

I can only liken the feeling to having one's pussy attacked by a nestful of baby scorpions – not that I've ever had that experience. Each tiny pin-prick of pain came so close on the heels of the last that I could never quite get my breath and was soon panting like a dog. He took no notice of my state but continued to pluck, gradually exposing an area of flesh with the tortured hair follicles standing up in angry red goose-pimples.

'Ten minutes,' he remarked to the tape recorder in a detached manner. 'Note the not inconsiderable swelling of the *labia majora* and that the vagina has begun to moisten, a bead of white fluid forming at the entrance. This demonstrates arousal in the subject, which is confirmed by heavy, irregular breathing and muscular contractions.'

I had no idea that ten minutes had gone by, though I was fully aware that I was aroused and that my pussy was beginning to swell and juice. The sensation of pain in my mound had become the centre of everything, made worse by the slow, methodical nature of the torment and the total inattention to my vulva.

'Twenty minutes,' he said. 'The entire vulva is now swollen and moist, the vagina slightly open and sufficient fluid has been released to dampen the perineum and run down to the anus. Contractions are more regular and the subject is beginning to push her hips forward rather than pull away from the forceps.'

It was only when he said it that I realised I had been pushing my pussy out in a half-conscious desire to be brought off, which wouldn't have taken more than a few careful touches to my clit. I rejected the idea of asking him to bring me to orgasm, sure that if I waited long enough I would get there anyway and that the result would be really special.

'Thirty minutes,' he said. 'There is little change in the appearance of the vagina, though the opening is now clearly visible. I would surmise that a plateau of sexual excitement has been reached. Penny?'

'Yes,' I managed in between breaths. He was right: if anything, I had come down a bit from my earlier state and was in a sort of sexual trance, quite happy to be lying back with my legs spread. Indeed, I couldn't imagine being in any other position. I knew I wasn't going to come, but no longer cared, any more than I cared about my blatantly intimate display, both physical and mental.

'Some fifteen per cent of the area is now bare,' he continued. 'It is my intention to continue plucking the *mons veneris* before proceeding to the *labia majora.*'

Fifteen per cent! I realised that this was going to be a very long haul and lay back with my eyes shut, relaxing as best I could against the surface of the hard, wooden work bench.

Three whole hours passed, though it didn't seem anything like as long in my mist of pain and pleasure. His voice brought me round and I leant forward to look at myself. My pubic mound was as bald as a plucked chicken and very red, my whole pussy was throbbing and I could feel a cold, wet patch under my bottom. I saw that he was untying my ankles.

'Are you finished?' I asked weakly.

'Very nearly,' he replied, 'it only remains to do the anal area, for which Lunula was turned on to her front, and I feel we should follow the procedure. When I have untied your legs, perhaps you could adopt a kneeling posture.'

'OK,' I managed, waiting until I was free before turning carefully over, my hands still strapped up behind my back. The cool air made the skin of my bottom prickle where it was wet with sweat and juice. Placing my knees wide apart and dipping my back so that my bottom was wide open, I knew he'd have the best possible access to my anus and the hairy area around it.

'Splendid,' I heard him mutter and then there was a sharp twinge of pain as a hair was pulled out. 'Three hours and ten minutes. The subject is now in a kneeling position to allow access to the hair on the inner surface of her nates. The anus is notably distended and undergoing slow, rhythmic contractions, indicative of a state of extreme sexual arousal.'

The new position and his casual, impersonal remarks

were too much. I thought of my bumhole pulsing in my ecstasy, pink and swollen and stuck out as if expecting something up it. I needed to be touched, or at least to be able to rub myself against something, and I didn't give a damn about how rude an exhibition I made of myself.

'It is interesting,' the professor remarked, 'that by this stage Lunula had been begging to be helped to orgasm for some time, whereas you. . .'

'Do me too, then,' I pleaded. 'Put something against my pussy so I can rub myself.'

'I think not,' he continued. 'They denied her request, and I feel we should mimic conditions as closely as possible.'

'Please!' I whimpered.

He didn't trouble to reply, tugging another of my anal hairs free. As he rested his hand in between my bottom-cheeks to enable him to stretch taut an area of skin for depilation, I managed to rub my anus against his flesh. For a moment, I thought I was going to come, then his voice broke the moment.

'Don't wriggle so, Penny,' he admonished in a quiet, steady voice, utterly unsuited to a man who has just had a girl try and bring herself off by rubbing her bottom-hole against his hand. 'Nearly finished.'

I was panting like a dog as he continued plucking me, my bottom-crease now throbbing with the same fiery pain as my pussy.

'There we are,' he was saying and I realised that it was over. 'They then took turns to have intercourse with her. I really do not think that would be suitable, but perhaps I can help you to an orgasm? I have a tall specimen jar here that might prove efficacious.'

I begged for it, completing my humiliation by asking for something up my bottom as well.

'Certainly,' he replied merrily. 'The handle of this seeker should do. Pop, in it goes.'

My bottom-hole stretched to accommodate the rounded wooden handle, and as I felt the cool glass of the jar push against my clitoris, I immediately began to rub against it, moving my hips in what I was only too aware must be an utterly abandoned display. I came within moments, screaming my orgasm without thought to who might hear, coming again and then subsiding in a sweaty, itchy mess on the bench.

'Most interesting,' the professor was saying as he obligingly extracted the seeker from my bottom. 'Three hours and thirty-five minutes. I shall, of course, include your name when I publish my results.'

8

Smut

I had been woken by the sound of rain flurries on the window but, by the time I had finished breakfast, it was clear, with that lovely fresh feeling that only comes after summer rain. Not to have gone out would have been a sin, so I threw on a baggy T-shirt and a pair of tatty jeans and left the house. I had no particular destination in mind, but headed in the general direction of the downs, choosing a likely-looking footpath that ran between high hedges of blackthorn and scrub hazel.

I was in the most cheerful of moods. I was in love. For nearly two months I had been in a full-blown lesbian relationship with Amber Oakley. She was everything I needed in a lover: warm, sensitive, imaginative, cuddly and, above all, as dirty-minded as I was. She also kept me physically well disciplined without ever trying to actually control my life, which was wonderful. Regular, unashamed spankings were now a part of my daily life, not to mention the cane, the riding whip and several other implements ideal for application to bad girls' bottoms.

She had also introduced me to a wide variety of exquisite sexual deviations and several friends with similar tastes. There were Ginny and Michael Scott, and Ginny's brother Matthew, who had introduced me to the delights of being a pony-girl, an exquisite fantasy involving being harnessed and treated like a pony. Amber had been at school with Ginny, and both were tall, strong girls with opulent figures who found my own small size and fragility particularly appealing. There was also Matthew's fiancée, Catharine King, a vivacious redhead with whom I got on very well indeed. Amber's friends Anderson and Vicky completed the group, both tall, dark and similar enough to have been brother and sister. All summer we had been indulging ourselves in each other, and for the first time in my life I felt that I really belonged.

I had given up my flat when I moved in with Amber, but was spending a weekend house-sitting for Ginny and Michael. This gave me three days of total peace before my last week at Amber's and then the start of term and the run up to the completion of my PhD, and I was intent on relaxing as much as possible. Being deep in Wiltshire, there was endless opportunity for walking miles with my head in the clouds, just thinking and feeling happy.

I had walked perhaps a mile without seeing a single person when my attention was drawn by a scatter of torn paper strewn across the path ahead. This rather broke my mood, and my first feeling was of annoyance at whoever had littered the place, then distaste as I saw that the pieces of paper were the shredded remains of a pornographic magazine. It wasn't the display of naked female bodies that I disliked, but the way in which it was done. The material was incredibly vulgar, without the slightest attempt at art or subtlety. Breasts were thrust out, thighs spread to expose gaping vaginas, buttocks held apart and anuses stretched open. The occasional scrap of cheap, brightly coloured underwear only accentuated the coarseness of it. Every bit was sodden with the night's rain, adding a final sordid touch.

I hurried past, wondering whether such crude images were really what men wanted of the female form and at a deeper level what impulse had made the owner of the magazine tear it into shreds on a country footpath. Feelings of guilt after masturbation seemed the most likely explanation, which led my chain of thought to the possibility – no, the very strong probability – that whoever had torn the magazine up had been masturbating in the little copse that bordered the footpath. The idea sent a shiver down my spine; even as I walked past, there might be some man just yards away pulling at his cock as he stared at crude, dirty pictures of naked girls. Of course, it had to be a man; women just don't do that sort of thing. He'd be young, inexperienced, perhaps a sixth-form boy at one of the nearby public schools – but no, more likely a dirty old man, thick-set and greying, spittle running down his chin as he imagined fantasies that were unobtainable in his home life.

Maybe he'd be thinking about how he'd like to spank the girls' bottoms: over his knee with their silly nylon underwear pulled down before he fucked them doggy fashion, on their knees in the leaf mould and soil of the copse floor. If he saw me walking past, would he transfer his fantasies to me? Watching my bare breasts move under my top, or the way my bottom pushed out my jeans? Perhaps he'd imagine me masturbating in his place, legs wide, pink pussy glistening in the sunlight as I came over the sight of his erection.

It was when my chain of thought reached that point that I realised that I was going to have to do it. I felt both naughty and guilty as I turned and walked back along the path, certain despite all reason that anybody who saw me would know exactly what was going through my mind. By the time I got to the sodden remains of the magazine, my heart was in my mouth. I stopped, listening and glancing nervously up and down the path before hurriedly gathering up some of the pictures and scampering into the shelter of the hedge.

My heart was beating fast, and a sensible voice in my head was telling me to stop being so silly, drop the revolting pictures and walk away. Another part of me wanted to masturbate very badly indeed, and I knew that even if I gave in to common sense and abandoned my plans I would be back again for my smutty pictures within minutes. My mind made up, I walked into the copse, looking for a place that allowed the comfort and privacy I would need to reach orgasm. I like to masturbate with both hands, starting with the left on my pussy while I explore my body and finally using the middle finger of my right hand to rub myself while I hold my lips apart. The ground was soaking, and if I lay down I would get a dirty bottom. The idea turned me on even more, but then I would have to walk back through the village with a wet rump, which wasn't such a good idea.

Luck was with me, though, in the shape of a long-abandoned tractor, half eaten away by rust but with the plastic seat still secure, set high on the body. To sit in the seat would mean I was about three feet off the ground and really spread open, which was a lovely idea. I stood still and listened for a long moment, but heard nothing. I put the pictures on the broken dashboard, intent on a little fantasy striptease before getting down to it in earnest.

I was shivering as I returned to my dirty old man fantasy, imagining him watching as I undid my jeans and stuck my bum out, easing them down ever so slowly over my cheeks. I was glad I had chosen fancy panties that morning: tight, white and lacy at the back so my bum looked like a fat little peach encased in see-through lace. His cock would be fit to burst as I bent right over, the outline of my vulva showing through my panties as I took the jeans down to my ankles and stepped out of them. I'd have agreed that there'd be no touching, driving him to distraction as I straightened up and hooked my thumbs into the waistband of my panties, grinning cheekily over my shoulder at my imaginary voyeur, preparing to complete my exposure, lowering my panties and touching my toes so he could see absolutely everything. I knew what I looked like bent over and bare-bottomed – Amber had a set of mirrors in her dining room that was designed for exactly that. Being small and quite petite, the rear of my pussy shows completely, pouting out between my thighs like a little split fig; my bottom-hole shows, too, tight and pink in a nest of black fur.

I stood, holding my pants round my ankles with the cool air on my bare bum, feeling dirtier every moment. This would be too much for him; he'd have to come, groaning in ecstasy at my vulgar, sluttish display, white come spurting over his hand and dribbling down the sides of his erect cock.

The thought sent a shiver right through me and I was just about to sneak a finger back between my legs and put it in myself when a rustle of foliage snapped me out of my fantasy. I hastily pulled my panties back up in a flush of insecurity, only to see a jay flap away through the trees. I stood listening, but there were no more sounds and, after a while, my excitement got the better of my trepidation. I reassured myself that anyone approaching would be bound to make a lot of noise, just as I had done, and so I would always have time to make myself decent. I put my hands to my breasts and stroked the little bumps of my nipples through the cotton, as much to soothe myself as for the pleasure. The intense, delicious feeling of doing something improper returned, stronger than before; I wanted to do something dirty, something even dirtier than my little striptease or frigging over the scraps of porn.

The question was, what? I considered wetting my pants, perhaps on all fours with my bum stuck in the air or lying on my back so they got well and truly soaked, before finishing myself off with the sodden material still clinging to my skin. It would be really messy, though, and there was no way of cleaning up, so I reluctantly rejected the idea.

Tying myself up? Using my clothes, it would be easy to sit in the tractor seat and tie my ankles to the sides so that I was forced to sit with my legs wide apart. It would provide lovely orgasms, especially when my muscles tensed against the bonds. On the other hand, if someone did come, I'd be well and truly caught and my position would take a lot of explaining.

Punishing myself? With a hazel switch or some birch twigs I could whip my bottom up to a good rosy pink. It would be nice and I tried a couple of experimental smacks with my hand, tugging my panties tight up my bottom to get at the bare flesh. My bum tingled pleasantly, but I knew I wouldn't be able to get the full thrill of chastisement without someone else to take control and so abandoned that idea as well. Besides, when I told Amber what I had done, she was bound to want to take her cane to my bum and it would be a shame to spoil the target for her.

Thinking of Amber reminded me of something I had done shortly before meeting her. After I'd accidentally come across Ginny and Michael playing pony-girl games in a wood, I'd masturbated and had used an immature maize cob as an improvised dildo. The feel of it had been exquisite and it was just possible something similar might be available now. As I had walked up the footpath, there had been a field of maize before the copse, maize that should have knobbly little cobs just right for pushing into girls' holes. I reached for my jeans, then decided against it and instead peeled my top off, determined to do it in just panties, socks and trainers.

The copse was bordered by a rusting iron fence. Sure enough, the maize field was there, separated from the copse by a couple of yards of earth, or rather of glutinous brown mud. I climbed over the fence, feeling very exposed in the alley of clear ground between the two banks of greenery. My fingers were trembling as I pulled off a cob and peeled away the fibrous leaves encasing the fruit. It was the palest yellow, the size of a large carrot and had a hard, bumpy texture, just right to use on my clit.

I stood up and pulled my panties down, carefully pulling the leg-holes over my muddy trainers and hanging them on the fence, then stretching luxuriously naked in the sunlight. There was a strong temptation to sit down in the mud, to feel it squelch up my bottom and rub handfuls over my boobs. Maybe just a little bit, I reasoned – after all, it would soon dry and wouldn't show through my jeans. Before I could change my mind, I squatted down, waited for a delicious moment of suspense and then sat my bare bottom squarely down in the thick brown goo. It was cool and felt lovely as I took two handfuls and smeared it over my breasts, rubbing my nipples until they protruded pink and hard through the muck. I leant forward on all fours, picking two ears of corn and rocking back to squat on my heels as I peeled them. The smaller went up my bottom, the mud lubricating my anus as it stretched to accommodate the thick cob. The other was for wanking with, and I still wanted my smutty pictures to come over, so I stood up and climbed gingerly back over the fence. Walking back to the tractor, I swung my hips deliberately, thinking how rude I must look with the cob sticking out from between my bum-cheeks, obviously up my bottom-hole.

I took my place in the seat, tipped back so the penetration of both my holes would be visible to an imagined onlooker. The larger cob slid up my vagina easily and I left it there while I arranged the pictures across the rusting dashboard until I had as dirty a show of bum and tit as any dirty old man could want. Right in front of me was a fleshy blonde, face heavy with bright red lipstick and blue eye-shadow, tarty blue knickers pulled aside to show her shaven quim and wrinkled bumhole.

I sat back and pulled the cob out of my pussy with a sticky plop, my eyes locking with hers as I began to rub, wondering how I myself would look in such a sordid pose, imagining my dirty old man staring at my filthy, mud-smeared body, taut anus full of one maize cob, another being rubbed frantically on my clit as my vaginal muscles began to contract in orgasm. My eyesight fogged and I'm sure I screamed at least once as I came again and again, ending up limp and panting in my seat, utterly drained and in absolute bliss.

As I had suspected, it didn't take long for the mud to dry, especially when I had scraped the worst of it off, and I was soon looking respectable. I then went to the field to retrieve my panties, which were of course still draped over the fence. Only they weren't – they'd gone.

9

Lace, China and the Cane

Some people are just born lucky. One such was Anderson
Croom, whose parents had left him a beautiful house in
Surrey and enough money to leave him in comfort, if not
quite luxury, for life. He was also tall, handsome and well
formed. The combination of wealth and looks would make
most men unbearably smug and arrogant. Anderson was
neither, instead going through life with a boyish innocence
and an unquenchable cheerfulness. I liked him from the
first time we met and became closer with time.

He didn't have to work, but spent his time collecting
things, studying forensic science as a hobby and indulging
his passion for unusual sexual practices. That was where I
came in, because he and his girlfriend, Vicky Belstone, were
close friends of Amber's. Anderson brought the same boyish
enthusiasm to sex as he did to life as a whole, revelling in
physical pleasure and with an awareness of sexual subtleties
second only to Amber's. He took a particular delight in
things considered especially rude, as I do myself. His special
joy was buggering girls and making them come while he was
inside them. Even Amber occasionally submitted to his cock
up her bottom, which was an extraordinary thing for her.

Vicky was the ideal partner for him: nearly six feet tall,
lithe and strong with a combination of a dirty mind and a
sensible outlook. Had it not been for her, I feel sure that
Anderson would have managed to get locked up for
something, as he was always ready to take risks; in fact, he
thoroughly enjoyed doing so.

Their house was a great rambling red-brick structure built at the end of the last century. It was hidden in thick woods at the bottom of a valley, with the River Wey flowing through the garden. There was no better site for misbehaviour, and he and Vicky took every opportunity of indulging themselves, not infrequently with Amber and me.

Like Amber, Anderson was a fanatic for organising and making things, also for collecting unusual erotic adjuncts. It was a rumour that a junk shop somewhere in Addington had a stock of genuine malacca canes that left Vicky and I sitting at their house while he and Amber went to London on what was in all probability a wild-goose chase. As both Vicky and I knew whose bottoms the canes would be tested on if they were successful, there was a distinct atmosphere of anticipation as we sat at the kitchen table and ate ham and French bread together.

Not surprisingly, the conversation had turned to caning, a subject with which both of us were pretty familiar. I find something exquisite about the cane as an implement of punishment. It's very formal, and somehow very English. It also hurts and a good caning will leave precise red lines that last for a couple of weeks. Amber caned me regularly, and I found that having my bottom marked with a set of tramlines is a wonderful reminder of being under discipline. Also, after a good caning, the thoughts of the submissive sex that I crave are never far under. All I need to do is catch sight of my well-beaten bottom in the mirror or to feel the dull ache of the marks, and in my mind I'm back over Amber's study table with my naked bottom raised for punishment. Cane marks look pretty, too, whereas most implements just leave shapeless blotches.

It looked pretty well inevitable that Vicky and I were going to end up punishing each other before the afternoon was out, and so I was surprised when she suggested spending the time looking through the attic.

'He's got some great stuff,' she explained, 'going right back to when the house was built. It was his great-grandfather's originally, or maybe even his great-great-grandfather's.'

'What sort of stuff?' I asked.

'Clothes mainly, dresses and some underwear, which is really cute. There are those big drawers which split open at the back and all sorts.'

'Sounds fun,' I agreed, remembering how much Amber liked me in Victorian underwear and how pleased she'd be to come back and find Vicky and me in costume. 'Can we try some on?'

'Sure,' she answered. 'That's exactly what I had in mind.'

I followed her up the stairs with my sense of sexual anticipation growing. She was in jeans and, as we went, I found myself admiring her muscular but very feminine bottom and wondering what the afternoon would bring. One of Vicky's strong points was that she was always very aware of her playmate's mental state, and this was my first chance to experience it on a one-to-one basis. I also knew we'd get punished when the others got home, which made me feel pleasantly naughty as she pulled down the ladder to the attic.

Inside, it smelt of dust and age, a curious aroma born of products that really aren't used much any more, like mothballs and camphor. I wouldn't say it was a sexy smell, but it certainly added to the atmosphere, and made things seem less ordinary, which is always nice for sex games.

There was lots of other stuff as well as the clothes, from furniture like a great gilded mirror, through paraphernalia like a globe that still marked the British empire in red, to a wooden chest entirely full of toy cars. Vicky was pretty familiar with things and showed me a few choice objects before we got to the clothes. These were wonderful, a great range of both male and female wear dating from between about 1890 and the beginning of the Second World War. Some of the silk had perished, but the tougher fabrics were still sound, packed in between layers of special paper and heavily mothballed.

Vicky's height made it a bit difficult for her, being tall even by modern standards, but someone, presumably Anderson's grandfather, had once had a governess who must have looked truly terrifying. The dress was in black bombazine, and as heavy as perhaps a dozen modern dresses. It was laced and flounced and decorated with jet beads, every detail being black except for a thin trim of ivory lace around the high-necked collar and the cuffs. Just looking at it made me feel deliciously small and submissive and the idea of being spanked over Vicky's lap while she wore it was far too good to resist.

She didn't take much convincing, either, and we decided to play at governess and charge in a very definitely adult game that was sure to focus on the chastisement of my bottom. Of course, if Vicky was going to be the governess, then I would need something suitably girly to complement her. Being five foot three, I made an ideal charge, and we had soon found the sweetest Alice-in-Wonderland type dress, which I simply couldn't resist.

'Where shall we play?' I asked as Vicky rummaged out a selection of petticoats, drawers, chemises and even two corsets.

'In the bedroom you and Amber use,' she answered. 'It used to be the nursery.'

'Is that why there are bars on the windows?' I asked.

'Yes,' she replied, 'though Anderson decided to keep them for a very different reason than safety, as you well know.'

I did. On a previous visit Amber had made me strip and tied my wrists to the bars before tickling me into a frenzy with a peacock feather. She'd then caned me and let Anderson fuck me while I was still tied up. The feel of his hair rubbing on my freshly punished bottom had given me a delicious blend of pleasure and pain that had combined beautifully with the mental torment of being tied and teased before being entered. Vicky had watched, and helped Amber bring me off afterwards.

Anderson liked antiques and there was little modern about the room, which I could see was going to be close to ideal. I climbed down and caught the clothes as Vicky dropped them through the hatch, then took them down the passage as she busied herself with closing the attic up. As

I turned, I saw that she had collected something else, which she had concealed under a petticoat. She also favoured me with a wicked grin as she pushed the ladder up.

We took our time changing, stripping and washing first, then helping each other with the garments. Vicky chose a pair of voluminous drawers in heavy linen as her foundation garment. These were bulky, heavily trimmed with lace to below her knees, and opened among a gathering of material at the back. This served to accentuate the size of her bottom, which could be exposed by pulling the back open. Despite covering far more than any modern garment, they seemed delightfully naughty and I took great pleasure in pulling them open and kissing Vicky's bottom through the gap.

She put a chemise on next, a delicate garment of loose, light cotton which fitted snugly over her apple-like breasts and laced across them. This left her boobs twin globes of pink flesh in nests of lace and criss-cross strapping, which looked irresistibly sweet, especially as her nipples showed through the thin cotton and pushed it up into little humps as they stiffened under my caresses. I only stopped because I wanted to prolong our pleasure, leaving the delights of Vicky's breasts so that she could help me with my underwear.

I had chosen a combination chemise and drawers, which fitted well but was just pleasantly tight across my bottom. Rather than being open at the back, these allowed access by a panel which could be unbuttoned to bare the wearer's bottom, either for ablutionary purposes or for punishment. I had chosen it because I really liked the idea of feeling the buttons popped open one by one while I was held helpless over her lap. I've always loved the moment of exposure before punishment, even if it's just my bikini bottoms being tweaked down when I'd been showing most of my bottom anyway. With the panel-backed combinations, the sensation would be more exquisite by far.

We put petticoats on over our foundation garments, three each so that our hips appeared to flare in a wonderfully exaggerated fashion. Vicky then produced

101

some tights which we cut down to make knee-length stockings and tied in place with lengths of ribbon. Our corsets followed, although they had become a trifle fragile with age and it was impossible to lace each other up as tightly as we might have liked. To remedy this, we bandaged our tummies and eventually managed to get my waist down to an impressive eighteen inches and Vicky's to twenty, which was perhaps even more extreme given her height.

The feeling of restriction was intensely erotic, although I imagine a lot of that was the unfamiliarity of the clothes and the erotic associations that we ourselves invested in them. My dress was butter yellow and lacy, and had the sweetest little pinny and mob cap to go with it. Once I had got into it, I felt fully in role as a Victorian girl, demure yet cheeky, alarmed by the thought of showing so much as her ankles, yet constantly aware of the threat of bare-bottomed discipline should she stray. I realised that I was probably exaggerating my role, but didn't care, intent instead on getting the most out of my fantasy.

Vicky had looked sweet in her underwear, like those wonderful old French photographs of partially naked Parisian *demimondaines*. The black dress transformed her completely, into a tyrannical, stern governess, who looked as if she would administer a dozen strokes of the cane to her charges' squirming bottoms as soon as look at them. I put her long black hair into a severe bun to complete the image, resulting in a look that had me weak at the knees.

We stood looking at each other for a long while, each allowing our respective fantasies to come to maturity. For me, I was Miss Penelope, a well-brought-up young lady with just enough of the rebel in her to ensure that she got into trouble. I would be with my governess, of whose control I was immensely resentful, considering myself far too grown up to need supervision. My imaginary parents would take a very different view, considering me considerably less cultured than I should be and in need of frequent discipline to keep me on the straight and narrow. They would have given my governess complete authority over me, including the imposition of physical discipline whenever and however she felt I needed it. Punishing me was a task she would take to with an attitude of self-righteousness, based on her certain knowledge that it would do me good. Despite her very real belief that she was dishing out no more than justice, she would take a deep and abiding pleasure in inflicting pain and humiliation on me in her efforts to turn me into a well-brought-up young lady.

As Vicky was in the dominant role, it would be up to her to control the run of our play, yet I knew I could rely on her to ensure that I didn't escape my just desserts. I wasn't sure quite how she saw my role, and wouldn't ask until it was over and we were lying in each other's arms with our clothing in erotic disarray.

She tilted her delicate chin up a fraction of an inch and I hung my head in response. It had begun.

'You are a wilful, stubborn girl, Penelope,' she began. 'Now will you confess to your sin?'

'It was another and not I, Miss Victoria,' I replied.

'Nonsense, as well you know,' she snapped. 'And you shall address me as Miss Belstone, child.'

'Yes, Miss Belstone,' I responded meekly, 'yet it was not I.'

'A liar as well as a thief,' she said. 'Yet there is a cure for such ills, which I intend to apply should you fail to confess.'

'No, Miss Belstone!'

'Then confess.'

'Oh . . . oh, very well . . . I took a slice of apple pie from the kitchen and I am truly sorry and I shall never do it again, but please, please do not chastise me; I could not bear the indignity, nor the pain.'

'You shall have both, and in full measure. You are a liar and a thief and thus require correction. Were I not to do it, I would be failing in my duty, both to your parents and to yourself.'

'No, Miss Belstone, please! I couldn't bear it!'

'Nonsense, girl; you have borne it before and I have little

doubt you shall bear it again, both from myself and, when you marry, from your husband, should he deem it necessary.'

'Please!'

'Remember, Penelope, spare the rod and spoil the child. It is just and necessary and for your own good. Now come across my knee and it will all be over in a trice.'

'No, Miss Belstone, I cannot bear it! For I know you will shame me and lay bare my most intimate part . . .'

'Certainly I shall. Is there any reason why I should not?'

'Yes, indeed. I am a young lady. Such conduct would be quite improper!'

'Your modesty? A young lady? You have been a naughty girl and, until you are corrected, you have forfeited the right to modesty. As for being a young lady, young ladies do not steal; neither do they lie. Besides, I alone will see, which is no cause for shame, save that which you should rightly feel for your behaviour. Now will you do as you are told?'

'No, Miss Belstone, I really cannot bear a spanking . . .'

She grabbed me and there was a brief struggle, which I lost. In no time she had me across her knee, with my arm twisted up hard into the small of my back. All my pleas, all my kicks and struggles, had gone for nothing, I was bum up and about to be punished. I felt a sharp pang of humiliation as she began to lift my skirts: first my pretty yellow dress, then my petticoats, one by one, until only my combinations covered my seat, and those were stretched taut across the bulging cheeks of my bottom. I began to shiver as she started on the buttons that were all that separated me from the final disgrace of having my precious bottom exposed. Each popped open under her fingers, exposing a little more flesh. I could feel the flap falling aside as my bum-cheeks came on show, but she kept the top one done up, sparing me the indignity of the exposure of the centre of my bottom. Or so I thought but, when she had finished with the others, she calmly undid it, allowing the flap to fall away and bare my poor bottom completely.

I was in disgrace, held tight over her lap with my bum

showing, naked and vulnerable to the punishment that was about to be inflicted on me. She raised a knee, lifting my poor bottom so that my cheeks opened. The shame was unbearable, as I knew my sex would be showing in every detail of pink fleshy folds and hairy lips, as well as the centre of my bottom, the wrinkled pinkish-brown hole of my anus. I thought nothing could be worse, and then she started to spank me.

Her blood was up and she was merciless, her cruel hand smacking down hard across my poor, naked bottom. I squeaked from the first slap and was quickly kicking and wriggling over her lap without the slightest thought for my dignity. I knew I would look a truly wretched sight, with my skirts up, my combinations open and my naked bottom dancing to her smacks. It stung crazily, and I was squealing and begging for her to stop, only for her to redouble the force of her blows. When she had finished with my bottom, she turned her attention to my thighs, slapping each and then finishing with a blistering set right across the fattest part of my rear end. Then it stopped as suddenly as it had begun, and I was left snivelling and sobbing over her lap, limp and beaten, feeling genuinely contrite.

'You may rise,' she said in a voice that was unyieldingly stern yet sympathetic.

I got up, rather awkwardly, and let my skirts fall over my bottom, which was throbbing with pain and undoubtedly red all over.

'Had you been honest in the first instance,' she said, looking me directly in the eye, 'that would have sufficed.'

I hung my head, unable to meet her gaze.

'As it is,' she continued, 'I feel obliged to take sterner measures, and this time I strongly recommend accepting your just desserts with an attitude of proper penitence.'

'Yes, Miss Belstone,' I said feebly.

'However,' she went on, 'it would not do to have you disgrace yourself during punishment. Take the chamber pot from under the bed and use it as you need.'

'In front of you, Miss Belstone?'

'Certainly; I wish to see that you have done what is necessary.'

'Yes, Miss Belstone,' I answered and got to my knees to look under the bed.

The chamber pot was the last thing she had brought down from the attic, and which she had concealed from me. It was under the bed, a big china vessel sturdy enough to be sat on. I pulled it out and set it on the floor in front of her, then lifted my skirts. It was quite difficult to get access to my pussy without risking wetting my clothes, but I managed by pulling the flap of my combinations through my legs and holding it up while I squatted over the chamber pot. The position was incredibly rude, leaving my pussy gaping wide in front of her and my sore bottom sticking out as if I was expecting something up it.

She watched me fill the pot with an expression of haughty disgust, then passed me a tissue. I dabbed at my pussy gently, dropping the tissue below me and then rising. The chamber pot was nearly half full of pale gold pee, and I pushed it under the bed, my mind full of shame, humiliation, thoughts of my spanking and the emotions that came from those feelings.

'Touch your toes,' she ordered brusquely.

I obeyed, and once more had to suffer the indignity of having my skirts lifted and my bottom laid bare. She then swept out of the room, leaving me in that thoroughly undignified position while I pondered the next phase of my punishment. It was obvious that she was going to beat me, and I had little doubt what she'd do it with, either. I was proved right moments later as she came back into the room holding a deep brown cane made of dragon grass, the heaviest and hardest of any cane type except malacca.

She went behind me, so that all I could see was my upturned skirts and the lace trim of my petticoats. It's bad enough being caned anyway, but not being able to see the person who's doing the punishment makes it a lot worse. All I could do was stay still, trembling in anticipation of my beating.

'I feel that twelve strokes will serve to do justice,' she

remarked coldly, 'and that another twelve in addition should be sufficient to remind you of your manners.'

I winced, knowing that twenty-four strokes would leave my already sore bottom a burning ball of pain, with twenty-four sets of tramlines criss-crossing my skin. I was shivering as she took hold of my skirts and pushed my back down to force me to open my bottom. I braced myself, only to have the first stroke whistle through the air just inches from my quivering flesh. I bucked involuntarily, my heart leaping at the expected stroke. She gave a small, amused sound and then brought the cane down hard across my naked bottom without the slightest warning.

Not surprisingly I jumped and yelled, only to be told not to be a baby. I could feel tears of humiliation starting in my eyes as she pressed down on the small of my back again, forcing me to stick my bum out for the next stroke. It came, planting a line of fire across my unfortunate buttocks and making me squeal again.

'And what do you say?' she demanded.

'Thank you, Miss Belstone,' I gasped.

'And how many strokes was that?' she added.

'Two, Miss Belstone.'

She made me count out every stroke, one by one, which I managed although my whole body was shaking with reaction, and my eyes were nearly blind with tears. Then I had to thank her for punishing me, an additional humiliation. For this I had to kneel and kiss the cane that had just been used to thrash me. My bottom was burning and my breath was coming in little gasps as I put my lips to the hard rod. Obliging a punished girl to kiss the implement that had been used on her bottom is an exquisite ritual, and is usually the final torment before playmates revert to more conventional sex.

I thought that she was going to break role, or at least partially, putting my head under her skirts and opening her drawers so that I could lick her to orgasm while I knelt with my burning bottom pushed out behind me. I hung my head, waiting for her orders. Instead she stood still, flexing the wicked cane thoughtfully.

'I wonder,' she said pensively. 'I wonder whether you have truly learnt your lesson.'

'I have, Miss Belstone,' I replied. 'I will never be naughty again, truly. I . . .'

'Speak when you are spoken to,' she snapped.

I shut up, waiting meekly for whatever she had in mind.

'No,' she continued, 'I do not feel that you have entirely learnt your lesson. This is hardly the first time I have been forced to spank you, nor yet to apply the cane. Come here, you little brat, and I shall truly teach you respect.'

She leant down and took me by the hair through my mob cap, gripping hard. I squeaked in alarm, wondering what she was going to do to me; then, as she sank to her knees, I realised her intentions.

'Miss Belstone!' I protested.

'Do not think to call out,' she told me, drawing out the full chamber pot from under the bed. 'For we are alone. Likewise, do not think to run and tell tales, for everyone knows you are a liar and it is I who shall be believed.'

'No, Miss Belstone,' I pleaded shrilly. 'No!'

She ignored my protests, dragging me towards the chamber pot by my hair. She was strong, and I could do nothing as my face was brought closer and closer to the pot. She pulled off my mob cap and twisted her hand hard into my hair, leaving my head bare so that I would get the full benefit of what was about to be done to me. I was shaking violently as she pulled my face over the pot and held it there, inches above what I'd done in it.

'And in it goes,' she said with a cruel delight.

She pushed my head down, right into the chamber pot, forcing my face into my own pee. I went under and then it was in my mouth and up my nose, in my hair and all over my face. It was too much; reaching back, I delved into my skirts and found my pussy, pulling the flap forward to get at myself and beginning to masturbate frantically. She kept my face under until I was desperate to breathe, then pulled my head back to leave me gagging and spluttering, my face and hair dripping and filthy.

My face went back in the pot as I started to come. I

swallowed some of my pee and then choked on the bit of tissue I had used to dry myself. I was unable to keep my mouth shut as I came; indeed, I didn't want to but was revelling in the taste of my own pee and humiliation of having my face in it. The orgasm was brilliant, a frantic, out-of-control peak that left me weak and shivering. Vicky kept my face well in the chamber pot until I had finished coming, let me take a breath and then dipped my face in it one more time out of pure sadism.

'Vicky!' I heard from behind me as my pee once more bubbled into my mouth.

Vicky let go and I knelt up, but of course I couldn't open my eyes.

'You dirty little sluts!' I heard Amber's voice.

'You can't leave them for a minute,' Anderson put in. 'We should have chained them up in the cellar.'

'Yes, we should,' Amber agreed. 'Vicky, take Penny and wash her face, then Anderson and I will interview you in his study.'

Of course she was playing, just as we had been, but there was at least a hint of real decision in her voice, although not anger. Vicky led me to the bathroom and bathed my face in cold water so that I could open my eyes. We were giggling together as we went downstairs, thoroughly pleased with ourselves and more than ready to accommodate whatever Amber and Anderson could come up with.

The study door was shut and, when we knocked, we were told to wait outside, for all the world like schoolgirls outside the headmistress's study. We put our backs to the wall and waited, feeling the thrill of trepidation at what was coming. My bottom was one great bruise and I knew that Amber would spare me further punishment. Unless, of course, she chose to cane my thighs, which was not at all impossible. The prospect was actually quite frightening as, while a caning on the bottom gives both mental and physical pleasure, having my thighs caned produces pleasure only in its mental aspect. I determined to let her anyway, and not use my stop word as to let Vicky have her full pleasure of me and then deny Amber would hardly have been fair.

As it was, I was wrong. After a while, Amber called out, an imperious summons that brooked no refusal. Vicky and I trooped into the study and went to stand in front of the desk with our heads hung in shame. Anderson was seated behind the desk with Amber standing at his side, one hand on his chair.

'We have decided,' he said after a pause to allow us to get thoroughly scared, 'to make the punishment fit the crime. Penny, turn around and pull up your skirts.'

I obeyed, displaying my naked bottom to them through the hole of the still undone combinations. Anderson steepled his fingers, admiring my bottom with a detached expression.

'Twenty-four, I make it,' he declared, and I realised that he had been counting the tramlines on my buttocks.

'I agree,' Amber added. 'Twenty-four strokes applied after a hand spanking and then her face pushed into the contents of her own chamber pot: quite disgusting.'

'Absolutely disgusting,' Anderson agreed. 'Yet, Victoria, I am sure you'll agree that justice demands that you take the same punishment.'

'Yes, sir,' Vicky answered meekly.

'Good, I'm glad you agree,' he continued, 'because that is what is going to happen. Fetch the pot, but do not empty it.'

'Sir?' she queried.

'We feel,' Amber explained, 'that for true justice to be done, your punishment should be slightly in excess of that which you inflicted on poor Penny. Therefore we will allow your fluids to mingle and trust that the knowledge adds to your chagrin.'

'It will, miss,' Vicky answered and scampered from the room.

I waited for them to punish me and was a little surprised when nothing happened. Vicky returned quickly, placed the chamber pot to one side and returned to her place in front of the desk. She had her hands folded in her lap, and I could see that she was trembling.

'It so happens,' Anderson said coolly, 'that by good

fortune we managed to purchase no less than six fine malacca canes, still wrapped in the original oil paper from which they were despatched from the factory at some time prior to the last war. We intend to test one on you but, as we are such nice, kindly people, we will let you have a nice warm-up spanking first.'

Vicky said nothing but made a little whimpering sound in her throat.

'Come across my knee,' Amber said benevolently.

Vicky didn't hesitate, waiting until Amber had seated herself comfortably on a suitable chair and then draping herself elegantly over my mistress's lap. Amber took her arm and twisted it into the small of her back, just as Vicky had done to me. I watched in rapture as her skirts came up. For all Amber and Anderson's clothing, I was still enjoying my Victorian fantasy and was thinking of Vicky as my stern and unyielding governess, about to be put through the unendurably humiliating experience of taking a spanking from my mother while I watched.

The black bombazine skirt came up and was piled on to Vicky's back. Her underskirt followed; then the three petticoats, one by one. I could hear her breathing as Amber opened her drawers, and knew exactly how she felt. Not that I had a trace of sympathy. I was a malicious little brat and took nothing but pleasure in the exposure and punishment of my governess.

Vicky's bottom came bare, the pert, muscular buttocks thrust high and open, her pussy peeping out sweetly from between her thighs and her anus a dimple of darker flesh in the softly furred valley between her open buttocks. Amber started to smack her, gently at first, with her fingertips, but becoming more severe as Vicky's bottom began to warm. She took it better than I had, I'll give her that, but then just about everybody does. Her bottom was quickly red and she was absolutely purring with pleasure, which made it a bit difficult to think of her as chastened and sorrowful.

She played her part well, though, thanking Amber and kissing her shoes ever so sweetly. Anderson told her curtly to bend over the desk, which she did, with her reddened bottom stuck up ready for the cane.

They got one of the malaccas out, a beautiful but terrifying object with a crook handle and nodes along its length at a spacing of perhaps three to four inches. It looked really wicked, but no more so than Amber and Anderson's smiles. Vicky looked round, her lower lip stuck out and trembling as she saw what was about to be used on her bottom. The dragon cane she'd taken to me was no instrument for novices, yet it paled in comparison to the cane that Anderson was now handling with all the delight of a schoolboy who has discovered a particularly fine new conker.

I was profoundly grateful that it wasn't about to be used on me, or at least not on this occasion. I knew I'd enjoy it when it happened, but that didn't stop me being scared of it. Nor did it Vicky, who was trembling so hard that the flesh of her bottom was wobbling ever so prettily.

'Ladies first,' Anderson said, offering the cane to Amber.

'Not at all,' she insisted. 'She's your tart, you should beat her first.'

'Thank you,' Anderson replied and gave Amber a polite inclination of his head.

He came round to where he could get at Vicky, gave a couple of experimental strokes through the air to get the feel of the cane and then brought it down hard across his girlfriend's bare bottom. She yelped and jumped, not surprisingly, but counted the stroke off and once more stuck her bottom out.

I watched her being beaten with a curious mixture of delight and trepidation. It takes a lot to really get to her, at least by my standards but, by the time Anderson had given her his twelve strokes of the malacca, she was sobbing and squirming over the table, wriggling her bum around and pushing it out in the most wanton display. I could see the white juice on her pussy and knew that she was getting very, very high on her punishment. It must have hurt crazily, though, because her bottom was a mass of wide, dark tramlines that made the ones on my bum look really rather mild. I knew that in due course I was going to get the same, which was what balanced my pleasure in watching her punished with concern.

Amber took over, adding to the mess Anderson had made of Vicky's bottom and also giving her three across her thighs. These were delivered through the cotton and lace of Vicky's fancy drawers, yet made her yell more than any of the ones put across her bum. By the end she was in a real state, breathing hard and with a trickle of white juice running from her pussy down into her pubic hair. I love the sight of a girl's pussy from the rear, especially when she's really excited, and Vicky was. I had more or less abandoned my Victorian fantasy and wanted to lick her from behind, which would have been a most unsuitable act for a well-brought-up young lady to perform on her governess.

'Good,' Amber announced, placing the malacca cane on the desk and standing back a pace. 'Now you may use your potty.'

Vicky turned her a truly wonderful look, full of pleasure and shame, pain and longing. I watched as she pulled up her skirts and split her drawers wide, then lowered her bottom delicately on to the chamber pot. Her eyes closed in bliss as she started to pee, the golden liquid gushing out from her pussy and splashing into the bowl. Her mouth opened and she gave a deep sigh of contentment. We had played before, but I had never seen her in such a state of rapture before the actual moment of orgasm.

She was destined to have her face pushed in it, but I knew she'd never get that far when she cut her stream off and put her hands to her pussy. We let her do it, not wanting to interfere if she had reached the point where she could no longer resist coming and aware that there would always be another opportunity for completing her punishment.

She was sat on the potty with her dress right up and her legs wide, showing us every detail of her pussy as she rubbed gently at her clit. Her face was set in an expression of serene pleasure. She began to lose it as she started to come, her mouth opening wider and her eyes coming open to look down at her pussy. She pressed her skirts back and leant forward so that she could see, and then, as she started to come, pee erupted from around her frantically rubbing finger. It sprayed everywhere, all over her dress and her thighs, wetting the carpet and spattering the front of the desk. I'd never before seen a girl pee and orgasm simultaneously and watched in open-mouthed delight as Vicky climaxed as she squatted over the chamber pot. She was breathing fast and making little whimpering noises, then gasping out her pleasure as her pee continued to squirt out.

My eyes had been riveted on Vicky but, as her orgasm subsided, I saw that Anderson had his cock out and was nursing an erection. He glanced at Amber and she came around the desk, tugging at her belt buckle as she went. I watched as her jeans came down over her magnificent bottom, her panties going with them. She bent forward, presenting Anderson with her rear for him to enter the vagina or anus as he pleased. He stood up with his cock in his hand but, instead of going to Amber, he took Vicky by the head and thrust his cock into her mouth. She closed her eyes and sucked willingly, then opened them in alarm as he pulled out and began to push her head down.

She scrambled back from the chamber pot. I could see the contents, evidence of just how bad she'd been. She groaned aloud as he pushed her head down and then unceremoniously stuffed her face into it. I hadn't expected him to do it to her just after she'd come, but she'd put up no resistance and I was delighted that he had.

'Right,' he said sternly, 'keep your face in your mess while Amber and I enjoy ourselves. Penny, lift her skirts and clean her up, with your tongue.'

I was shivering again as I pulled Vicky's skirts up over her well-whipped bottom. I pulled the drawers apart and exposed her, swallowing as I saw her wet pussy and the brownish dimple of her bumhole. Anderson was watching me, and Amber was leaning around as well, only Vicky couldn't watch me, and that was because she had her face in the contents of her potty.

I stuck my tongue out and leant forward, applying it to Vicky's anus. As I began to lick her bottom, Anderson moved towards the delightful female who was offering herself so submissively, bum up over his study desk. I knew that there was no other man to whom she would make such a present of herself, but then Anderson was born lucky.

10

The Puppy Girl

I threw the journal down on top of the heavy cloth-bound book of which it contained a synopsis. It was finally complete, nearly five years of work compressed into a few pages of highly detailed information, every detail of which was now stamped on my mind. Over the past week I had read and re-read it innumerable times, spending the rest of my time wandering around the department looking lost. I stared out of the window for a few minutes and was just reaching for my thesis again when someone knocked on the door, opening it without waiting for my response. The head of an ancient porter appeared around the door, then his hand as he dropped an envelope on the bench.

'Post for you, Dr Birch,' he announced and disappeared as abruptly as he had arrived.

I smiled, despite myself; for five years, the old man had never condescended to do more than grunt in my direction, only referring to me as Miss Birch when addressing a member of the academic staff. Now that I had my doctorate, he was suddenly all politeness and respect. The envelope had been expensive once but was now dog-eared and covered in mud. It proved to be an invitation from a private laboratory in north Devon, containing a couple of paragraphs of praise and comment on my work on genetic sequencing and an invitation to visit a research institute. It was from a Dr Hetherington, a name that meant nothing to me. This was surprising and a little irritating as I had thought I knew everyone within my field, so I sought out my supervisor, or rather ex-supervisor.

He turned out to have gone to the refectory, where I found him wolfing curry and rice and discussing gastropod polymorphism with the ancient Professor Watts. When I finally managed to introduce the name of Dr Hetherington into the conversation, it was Professor Watts who replied.

'Hetherington? Fine brain, mad as a hatter.'

'Did you know him then?' I asked.

'Certainly, did his doctor's with me. Surely you remember him, Laurence?'

My ex-supervisor shook his head.

'Couple of years before your time, then. Must remember the scandal though. '62 it was, or '63. Caught in the woods with an undergraduate. Pretty little thing, she was. Had her on a dog lead; hm, sorry, Penny.'

'Don't mind me,' I insisted. 'I had a letter from him this morning inviting me to go down and look at his research establishment near Crediton.'

'Good heavens, I had no idea he was still working. Still, he was a genetics man.'

'I think I'll accept, then,' I put in. 'It sounds fascinating.'

'Certainly mysterious, but watch your step; he's a most peculiar fellow.'

'Oh, I can look after myself,' I replied airily.

A week later, I took a train to Exeter and was collected by Dr Hetherington's assistant, a young woman named Helen. She greeted me warmly, taking the hand I offered but leaving me with a strange impression that she would rather not have shaken it, but licked it instead. This was obviously ludicrous, so I declined her offer to carry my case and followed her to the car. One other thing struck me about her: although it was a warm day, she wore a heavy overcoat. She was extraordinarily energetic, one moment walking ahead of me, the next behind, and keeping up a constant flow of questions about my research, interspersed with comments about her own. Apparently, Dr Hetherington had been working on inter-specific genetic transfer for years. She had joined him a year ago, shortly after the publication of my first paper on gene

117

sequencing. It was my paper that had enabled them to make a crucial breakthrough, a breakthrough that she refused to discuss until we arrived.

I would like to think that I am not entirely stupid and, by the time we had turned off the A30 and were winding our way through the woody hills to the north-east of Dartmoor, I had put two and two together and reached a conclusion so extraordinary that for a moment I doubted my own reasoning. There was something else as well. Since I had been living with Amber I had learnt a lot about reading the signs of sexual excitement in other women and, unless I was very much mistaken, Helen was showing all the right signs, and in a way that could only mean one thing: a desire for domination.

A couple more miles passed and I had decided what to do. Possibly I was about to make a prime fool of myself, but it was a risk I was prepared to take.

'Stop the car,' I ordered as we came in sight of a lay-by next to a small wood.

She obeyed, looking at me rather uncertainly.

'Don't worry,' I continued. 'Just step out of the car and go a little way into the wood.'

'OK,' she replied, her voice trembling as she looked nervously around.

I followed her into the shade of a thick stand of holly.

'Now open your coat,' I said, keeping my voice gentle but firm. 'Then your top.'

Her fingers were trembling as she undid her coat buttons one by one and then started on those of her blouse, keeping the coat close enough to cover her chest. I found myself biting my lip as I caught a glimpse of creamy white flesh. The next moment, my jaw had dropped and, despite my suspicions and my attempt to remain cool, I realised that I was gaping like an idiot.

Helen had pulled her blouse wide open, exposing small, neat breasts, each one just full enough to fill a cupped hand. Only I couldn't have done it; I didn't have enough hands. There were three pairs, one above the other, each identical and set at an even distance apart.

'My own developmental sequence and morphology, canid location sequencing,' she said quietly. 'It only took six months. Would you like to touch them?'

I stepped forward, entranced by her. Reaching out, I took the lowest pair of breasts in my hands, exploring their soft, rounded shape and trailing my thumb over the nipples so that they became stiff. I could feel her trembling as I moved to the second pair and stood closer so that I could kiss her, first on the neck and then on her mouth. I wanted to bury my face in her breasts, suck and fondle each one, in awe as much as in ecstasy, but I resisted the urge, sure that there was a better route to follow.

'Be my puppy-dog,' I said, doing my best to sound commanding but feeling as if I was pleading.

She looked into my eyes, her own very wide and moist and I knew that I had struck exactly the right chord. She dropped to all fours, never taking her eyes off mine, and knelt, waiting for praise or rebuke, a stroke or a smack, whatever I cared to give.

'I think you need a little walk,' I said and strode off into the wood, ordering her to heel and completely ignoring her difficulties with holly leaves and sticks. After about fifty yards, I felt secure enough and seated myself on a convenient beech trunk.

'You wanted to lick my hand at the station, didn't you?' I asked as she reached me and sprawled out at my feet. 'No, don't respond. I know you wanted to, so now I'm going to beat you for it, not really because you deserve it, but because I want to and because I can. First, I think we'd better have those clothes off. Whoever heard of a puppy in a coat or jeans?'

I pulled her clothes off, taking plenty of opportunity to stroke her wonderful breasts and exploring her without the slightest thought for where she might or might not want to be touched. She looked exquisite naked, her body soft and vulnerable in her kneeling position, her breasts dangling like teats under her chest. I was desperate for my own pleasure but held back, determined not to show my feelings.

She knelt, presenting her bottom for punishment, trembling in apprehension of what I might do but accepting my choice. I decided to make her wait and to amuse myself with her for a bit.

'Roll,' I ordered and watched her turn on her back, apparently oblivious to the display she was making of her open vagina.

'Now come to me and beg.'

She crawled over, squatting down with her hands tucked up like paws under her chin. I placed a foot between her legs, the curve of my boot running from the soft swell of her bottom to her tummy. I let her rub herself against me for an instant and then pushed. She fell back in the leaf mould, her big eyes looking hurt as she curled on to her side, tender bottom stuck out towards me. I picked up a long beech twig, watching her eyes follow my movement as I raised it over my head.

She squealed as the stick came down on her buttocks, leaving a crooked red line across the white skin. One was enough; she began to whimper and I took mercy on her, sliding one hand between her legs to cup her pubic mound, the ball of my thumb spreading her sex-lips and my other hand exploring her multiple breasts. She came fast, pressing herself frantically against my hand so that she was doing all the work.

It was just too much. I stood back, almost tearing my knickers in my haste to get them down then kicking them to one side as I sat back on the beech trunk and pulled my skirt up to show her my pussy.

'Lick,' I ordered unnecessarily as she scrambled over and buried her face between my open thighs. I felt dizzy with pleasure, the canopy of leaves spinning over my head as her tongue worked at me, making me tense a little bit, then harder and finally bringing me to a peak that made me scream as her front teeth nipped at my clit.

For a long while I sat on the log, saying nothing, Helen kneeling in front of me with a coy smile on her face, making no move to dress or cover herself and still clearly my puppy-dog. I gave her a kiss and took a final squeeze of her middle left breast.

'You may get dressed,' I said. 'At least for now.'

She got to her feet and began to brush the leaves and bits of twig from her body, then started to dress.

'By the way,' I asked, bending to retrieve my knickers, 'I understand the physical change, but what about your behaviour? Is it psychosomatic?'

'Not at all, or at least not in my case,' she replied, reverting to the sharp young scientist as easily as she had left. 'The truth is, I've always had puppy-dog fantasies; that's why I chose what I did. I could as easily have had tortoiseshell fur or a real pony-tail.'

'And what does Dr Hetherington think?' I asked, recalling the reason he had had to leave the university.

'Oh, he knows all about it, believe me,' she replied mischievously. 'He probably won't let me eat out of my special bowl for a week when he finds out what we did.'

We walked back to the car and twenty minutes later arrived at the lonely farmhouse that held Dr Hetherington's laboratory. The man himself greeted us at the front door. He was tall and silver-haired, with a humorous face and an expression that gave only a hint of the fierce intelligence that it concealed. He wore loose trousers under a standard white lab coat, his hands thrust deep into the pockets. He noticed immediately that Helen's coat was open and made the correct deductions, or at least some of them, and he gave us a knowing smile.

'Ah, Dr Hetherington,' I greeted him. 'I am astonished by your brilliance, but I feel I must question your ethics. Was it right to allow Helen to risk the first trial of such an elaborate technique?'

'Helen? The first?' he replied. 'Not at all, Dr Birch, not at all. No, no, the first trial was an equine developmental sequence, Persheron Cart Horse, as it happens. Would you like to see?'

Dr Hetherington reached for the buttons of his lab coat.

11

New-Age Rough

'You must go and talk to her,' my mother said, spearing a runner bean with her fork in a deliberate manner. 'She'll listen to you.'

'But . . .' I began.

'Don't quibble, Penny,' she retorted in her 'no-nonsense' voice. It was a tone I could remember from my earliest childhood and I knew that there was no point in arguing.

'Oh, all right,' I sighed, giving in to the inevitable. 'But how am I supposed to find them?'

She started to explain that it should be simple to find a London bus with a psychedelic paint-job in the mere few hundred square miles of the West Country. I filled my mouth with chicken and bread sauce to avoid having to reply and switched off. It was one of those awkward family discussions. Kate's little sister, Susan, had taken it into her head to shack up with some ageing hippie and was travelling around southern England in his clapped-out bus. Inevitably, both Kate's mum and my own, sisters with a similarly tough and old-fashioned outlook on life, disapproved. We all knew she wouldn't take any notice of Kate, so it was me they expected to go and talk her out of what they saw as a foolish liaison. 'You are the sensible one,' my mother had explained. 'Katie's so woolly-minded and Elaine and I are really too old for this sort of thing.'

What made it worse was that, although nothing had been said, I was sure Kate and my closeness hadn't gone entirely unnoticed. It was typical of my mother that while her daughter and niece having had sex together was '... one of those things that shouldn't be mentioned ...', another niece being in an open relationship with an older man, and a hippie at that, was '... quite simply beyond the pail ...'.

'... you can start in Blandford Forum, that's where her postcard came from,' my mother was finishing, 'and don't put so much in your mouth. Really, Penny, your manners are dreadful.'

I grimaced and loaded my fork with a rebelliously large roast potato.

My intention was to drive around Dorset for a few days, visit Lulworth Cove and perhaps the fossiliferous strata at Lyme Regis and then return to report that I had been unable to find them. Fate was not keen to let me have things so easily. As I was threading my way through the small roads to the south of Salisbury Plain, I passed a long-abandoned chalk quarry and there, making an extraordinary contrast with the dirty white quarry and the bright green vegetation, was a London bus, an undoubtedly psychedelic London bus.

I stopped the car and reversed back to where I could see the bus. It had to be the one: luminous yellow, fuschia pink and lime green were the predominant colours, painted in swirls, crazy zigzags and concentric rings. Someone had been painting big turquoise flowers but had given up, and an open tin of paint stood on the ground by a front wheel. I parked and walked into the quarry. The last time I had seen Susan, she had been a gawky schoolgirl, already taller than me, but with all the sex appeal of a stick of celery, and that was the picture of her that was in my mind. Neville, the boyfriend, I imagined as a sort of cross between John Lennon and a tramp: lanky, stooped, bespectacled and with matted hair hanging to his knees.

It was getting late, and clouds were blowing in from the west, plunging the quarry into an eerie half-light. The lower deck of the bus was dark, the upper illuminated, and I was on the point of calling out when I was taken by a sudden fit of shyness. I hadn't really thought out what I was going to say, or even what my intentions were. I certainly had no intention of trying to persuade Susan to drop him, especially as it would have been terribly hypocritical of me when I was having occasional sex with her big sister.

I paused in indecision, then, displaying an example of displacement reaction that would have had my old ethology tutor reaching for his notebook, I decided to climb on to the lowest ledge of the quarry-side and sneak a look through the windows. It was a bit of a scramble, but I got up and turned to look back at the bus from the concealment of a convenient stand of scrub willow. My viewpoint was excellent, and it was some view. A man, presumably Neville, was standing with his back to me, his trousers around his knees and his meaty buttocks moving rhythmically as he pushed himself into a slim young woman who was bent over the seat in front of him. She had a little leather collar around her neck, but was otherwise stark naked, her round, muscular little bum bouncing to his thrusts, her eyes tight shut and her mouth wide in breathless ecstasy. It was Susan, quite clearly Susan, despite her hair having been shaved at the sides and sprayed into irregular scarlet spikes.

I stood gaping in amazement, my eyes riveted to the obscene movement of Neville's backside as he fucked the girl I used to baby-sit a few short years before. She was twenty now, I reminded myself, and there was nothing immature about the little boobs dangling from her chest or her neat but womanly bottom and long, shapely thighs. Neville was a worse shock. I had expected someone with some mystique or charisma, but he was a short, fat man of perhaps fifty-five with long, straggling hair sprouting around a bald patch and a hairy, overweight backside. It seemed extraordinary that such a pretty, lithe young girl should offer herself so rudely to this dirty old man. A final touch of debasement was added by the contrast of her total nakedness and his state of partial undress, his woolly jumper pulled up over his beer belly and his greyish underpants and threadbare longjohns pushed down over his buttocks, just enough to give comfortable access to his cock.

His pushes became faster, then stopped as he came to a shuddering climax, making her squeal so loudly that I heard her. He rested for an instant before pulling out of her and sitting down heavily on a seat. She turned to the side and, just for an instant, I could see full between her bum-cheeks, her pussy neat and pink but her anus a dark spot, gaping black and wide. My mouth dropped open even further – he hadn't been fucking her; his prick had been up her bottom. I'd watched her get buggered and she'd obviously been enjoying it.

It took me a moment to pull myself together enough to think clearly, but as I started back down the slope my mind was nonetheless a confusing welter of thoughts. Ignoring the uncomfortable and slightly humiliating dampness in my knickers, I was torn between distaste at Susan being involved in a relationship that involved being bum-shagged by an ageing hippie and my feelings that she was entitled to make her own choices and it was none of my business to interfere.

Not that I'm one to talk, in any case. More than a few men have put their cocks up my bottom, and generally at my instigation. I love that really dirty, breathless feeling of having my anus invaded by a nice, fat cock, preferably with my face pushed into a bed, several pillows under my tummy to keep my bum up and the man in a welter of guilty ecstasy as he rides my bottom. Somehow it didn't seem the same for little Susan to be doing it, especially with such an obvious dirty old man.

I resolved to talk to them and, after waiting five minutes for them to rearrange themselves I poked my head through the curtain that shielded the entrance to the bus and called upstairs.

My shout was followed by a clatter of activity and Neville's head being thrust down the stairway. His expression was wary, even aggressive, for an instant, and then melted to surprise at the sight of me. As I was wrapped in a heavy polo-necked jumper several sizes too large, I must have been about as threatening as a slightly damp teddy-bear.

Ten minutes later, I was relaxing on a bus seat, stretched out with a beer in one hand while I took a long draw on the outsize joint that Neville had made for us. Susan was in a manic state, one moment walking up and down the aisle and pushing herself up on the seat handles so that her feet left the ground, the next sitting on Neville's lap or by his side as she stroked him. She had thrown on a long T-shirt, but still had her little dog collar with the ring at the front. I could see that she was naked underneath the top, as occasionally the neck would slip down to uncover a pert breast or the cloth would catch between the cheeks of her trim little bum. He was calmer, sitting back and smoking and talking, his easy and unpretentious manner making me warm to him. After a while, I began to see why Susan liked him. The relationship still seemed incongruous, but my mind kept going back to the way he'd been using her up her bottom just a few minutes before.

I'm not totally immune to dirty old man fantasies myself. I'd occasionally frigged off over fantasies of being had by a tramp, a game-keeper or whatever, usually in country settings and once or twice imagining their cocks up my bum instead of in my pussy or mouth. Still, I'd never been tempted to put such dirty ideas into practice. True, I'd once sucked a much older man's cock after a party. He had been perhaps in his late fifties, but very attractive and hardly counted as a dirty old man. Also Amber had let her godfather fuck me, but that didn't really count. All the men who'd buggered me had been young and good-looking ... well, reasonably so anyway ... OK, so there was the Czech guy who'd been maybe forty, but that had been different ... OK, so I'm a slut and I like it, but Neville really was the limit. Or was he?

As we talked and became more relaxed, I began to wonder how it would feel to take Neville's cock, which had looked pretty skinny. Really dirty, was the answer. It would be humiliating, really humiliating. If there's one thing I can't resist, it's sexual humiliation, under the right conditions, and the current situation was becoming more and more right. Of course, the real question was whether they'd mind me joining in; but, from Susan's state of manic excitement and constant references to sex, I guessed that she wouldn't be entirely averse.

I began to think about it more seriously, imagining the shame of confessing I was willing, my pants being pulled down, having my bottom-cheeks pulled open, letting him lubricate my anus ...

'You caught us at it,' Susan giggled, breaking into my reverie.

'I know,' I replied, now sure that they wouldn't be offended.

'How?' Susan asked.

'I'm afraid I peeped,' I replied. 'I wanted to be sure someone was there, and ...'

I stopped as Susan was blushing and giggling, her head slightly down so that her eyelids half hid her big, grey eyes. Neville just grinned, clearly pleased with himself.

'So you saw what ...' she started and then stopped when I nodded.

'You wouldn't tell anyone, would you?' Susan asked.

'Don't be silly,' I reassured her, and then, before I could think twice, I added, 'it really turned me on, actually.'

Susan smiled at me and put a finger in her mouth, as if uncertain of what to say. For a moment we were silent, the smoke floating in banners in the warm evening air.

'I thought I'd left enough time for you to sort yourselves out,' I said. 'Sorry if you hadn't finished.'

'I hadn't, well, you know, I wanted to come ...'

'Oh, sorry ...'

There was another moment of silence, this one slightly awkward while Susan fiddled with the hem of her T-shirt.

'Penny,' she spoke quietly, 'would you mind if I gave ... I mean if I, um, played with myself now ... 'cause I feel really horny.'

'Susan ...' Neville broke in.

'No, no, go ahead,' I replied quickly, expecting her to go downstairs to masturbate. 'I don't mind at all.'

'No, I mean while you both watch,' she stammered.

She had curled her legs up and was holding the T-shirt down over her knees, apparently oblivious to the fact that her position left her pussy showing, the swollen outer labia pouting from between her thighs with a glimpse of darker, moist pink between them. The sight sent a little shiver through me and I found myself swallowing in sudden excitement.

Susan lifted her T-shirt, knotting it around her waist and so enhancing her sweet hips and then parting her legs to expose the full expanse of her downy, black pussy fur and her round little tummy. She locked eyes with mine as her fingers went to her vagina and probed, emerging wet and glistening. I watched as she spread her pussy with her middle fingers, stretching the flesh and bringing her clit into prominence. She put the middle finger of her other hand into her mouth and began to suck it, making a sight that I found irresistibly erotic: the scarlet hair in its punk spikes, the nipples pushing up the fabric of her T-shirt, the pretty face looking coy and sweet and the long thighs wide open with the wet, pink centre of her pussy spread in blatantly rude display.

Putting the finger to her clit, she began to rub, her eyes closing in pleasure. Her thighs began to tense as she masturbated, her bottom sliding forward on the seat so that I could see the swollen pink knot of her freshly fucked anus, a dribble of white pussy juice running down to the puckered flesh and filling the opening. Her muscles began to contract and relax, the rhythm quickening as she neared orgasm. She squealed and at the last instant slid a finger below her pussy and up her bottom-hole, stabbing it well in as her ring contracted around it and then pulling it free with a sticky pop and opening her eyes to grin at us with an expression of impish delight.

'Now you,' she said, looking right at me.

Neville said nothing, but turned to me with a hopeful look on his weathered face. Susan's offer was far too good to refuse. I'd been turned on from the start and watching Susan masturbate had added to it. The effects of several beers and a joint may have also made a difference, but I doubt it.

I looked at Neville, not quite sure of myself. Susan wanted me to masturbate for them, but I was game for more.

'Do you want to?' he asked, gesturing to his crotch.

'Go on,' Susan urged breathlessly.

I nodded, swallowing as he stood and came towards me, his crotch level with my face. His hands went to his fly and I watched like a mouse enchanted by a cobra as he eased his zip down and delved inside his longjohns and pants for his prick. I reached out my hand tentatively and let him lay it on my palm, the flaccid shaft greyish-pink against my pale skin. He was circumcised, his knob fully out of a thick ring of flesh that was all that remained of his prepuce. I curled a thumb over the shaft and began to stroke gently, making it move oddly, the inside squirming under the skin as it filled with blood in response to my gentle rubbing. Susan leant forward on the seat, putting her arm around my waist and watching me caress her boyfriend's cock from a distance of inches.

'Go on,' Susan repeated, her voice quiet but insistent and excited.

I felt a lump of excitement rise in my throat, knowing she wanted me to gulp the obscene thing into my mouth so that she could watch me suck it. I hesitated for a second and then flopped it into my mouth, tasting the thick, salty, meat as my tongue enfolded the rubbery shaft. I glanced to the side to see Susan's eyes wide and moist with excitement as she watched my lips work on Neville's rapidly thickening cock. His hand cupped my head gently and he pushed his prick deep into my mouth, making me gag briefly from the feeling of his swollen knob at the back of my throat. For a while he worked me, holding me by the back of my head and using my wet mouth as a slide-box for his prick, then suddenly stopping and pulling away, probably only an instant before reaching the point of no return and filling my mouth with thick, salty come.

'Would you like to try?' he asked.

'Up my bottom?' I replied.

'Yeah,' he managed, his breath coming hoarse and fast.

'Please, Penny, I really want to see it,' Susan begged.

His cock was just in front of my face, standing proud and glistening wet with my saliva. It was quite long but not very thick, and the prospect of having it pushed up my back passage filled me with need. It just looked so deliciously obscene, stuck out of his trouser fly with bits of his underwear showing. It was too dirty to resist.

'OK,' I said after a pause, 'if Susan cuddles me while you do it.'

'Say what you want,' he asked, pleading.

'I'd like you to bugger me, please,' I replied, more than willing to play his game of talking dirty. 'I'd like you to bend me over, and pull down my panties, and lick my anus, and force your lovely cock up my bottom; then use me slowly, pushing it in and out, pulling it out so my bumhole's gaping open like Susan's was and stuffing it back up me. Then I want you to take me by the hips and bugger me properly, ramming it in and out until I'm panting like a bitch on heat. Then I'd like you to spunk up my bottom and watch it dribble out and run down my pussy . . .'

As I had been speaking, I had turned over, kneeling on the seat so that my bottom stuck up in the air, covered only by my long jumper and the plain white knickers that I had chosen that morning. Susan moved around so that my face was between her little breasts, her hands coming up under my jumper, taking a grip on the waistband of my panties and pulling them down over my bum, helping me wriggle them down and off. I rubbed my face into her chest, nipped the erect bud of a nipple through her T-shirt as she cradled my head in her arms. I pushed my bum up higher and wiggled it, signalling that I was ready and willing to have my bottom fucked.

There was an instant's pause and then Neville took hold of the hem of my jumper, pulling it tight against my flesh. The rough wool tickled my bare skin as my last vestige of modesty was eased up over my bottom and then pulled off over my head, leaving me naked. I shivered in pleasure as the cool air touched my flesh and with the knowledge that he could see the whole of my nakedness. I pulled the small of my back in and opened my legs a little more, not wanting to hide his view of my pouting pussy or the crack of my bottom. Susan pulled me further into her chest as his hands cupped my bottom-cheeks, weighing them and pulling them open. There was a pause, and I knew he would be inspecting my anus, thinking how tight it looked, wondering how it was going to feel straining around his erection when he buggered me.

Something wet touched my bottom-hole and I relaxed, letting it open to his tongue. I felt a runnel of saliva touch my pussy-lips as the firm, muscular tongue-tip explored my anus, opening and lubricating my back passage for his cock. Sighing and cuddling Susan, I pushed outwards, drawing a murmur of appreciation from him as my anus everted to accept his tongue. I imagined my bumhole as a fleshy pink flower, opening slowly in response to moisture. I had seldom felt so open and juicy, both pussy and bum, and I knew I would be ready for his cock soon when one and then two fingers were slid easily up my behind.

'Are you sure, Penny?' he asked gently.

'Yes, put it in,' I managed, gagging in my passion. 'Go on, bum-shag me, use me like you use Susan, right up my dirty little hole.'

The fingers were pulled out and I relaxed, breathing slowly and deeply, keeping my anus receptive. His thumbs gripped the inside of my cheeks, spreading the target, then I felt pressure in the centre as his round, fleshy knob touched me. I gasped as my bumhole strained to accommodate him, giving a little stab of pain as the head of his penis popped in and my anus closed around the narrow part of his shaft. I began to pant rhythmically as he forced his full length into my rectum, pulling slowly in and out to grease his shaft until I felt the coarse material of his trousers touch the tender flesh of my thighs and buttocks and knew that his erection was well and truly up my bottom.

'Hang on,' I asked, knowing that when he started to thrust it would be hard to speak coherently, 'I want your balls out so they bang against my pussy.'

'OK,' he sighed and began to wriggle his cock around inside me, keeping himself stimulated while I reached between my legs, found the opening of his fly and burrowed my hand into the slit of his longjohns and finally his underpants. His balls moved inside his thick, leathery scrotum as I scooped the sac out and nestled my pussy against it, finding that the coarse hair tickled my clit in a delightful way that made me giggle as I cuddled back into Susan, my head now slipped down to her tummy. Without warning she threw her legs up and wrapped them around my head, pushing my face into her wet pussy. I began to lick even as Neville's first real thrust caught me.

He really buggered me in earnest, gripping my hips and pushing his cock back and forth in my straining bumhole, making me pant as I licked his girlfriend's pussy. I had seen girls buggered on video, the pinky-red flesh of their bumholes stretched taut around their partner's cock shafts, the distended flesh everting each time the man pulled back. I knew my own anus would now look the same, stretched obscenely around the intruding prick as he used my bum for his pleasure.

His ball sac slapped against my empty, sodden fanny with each thrust, increasing my ecstasy but never quite bringing me off. Susan's hand locked in my hair as Neville began to pump faster, knocking the breath out of me as his hips smacked against my bare bum. My anus was on fire and I felt completely out of control, unable to do more than pant out my lust into Susan's sex, my mouthful of fleshy pussy almost suffocating me. I'd lost all track of how many times his prick had been rammed home in my bumhole when he suddenly stopped.

He began to pull it out and I guessed he was going to torment me by putting it back in. I was right. Four times he withdrew and then slid it back in. Each time my anus was left gaping, only to be filled with his erection. Each time it came out, I thought of how obscene I must look, with my bumhole open and his cock rearing above it, ready to go back up. Each penetration was pure bliss; yet, when he had pulled it out the fifth time, I was left waiting expectantly for my filling.

'Put it in; I want to come,' I pleaded, only to have his hand lock in my hair.

He took a firm grip and pulled my face off Susan's pussy.

'Oh, no,' I moaned as I realised what he intended and that I was too aroused to resist.

He jerked my head round and I found myself faced with his erection, the erection that had just been in my bottom. He didn't try and make me suck, but held me still, forcing me to make the choice.

'Oh, God, I'm going to do it,' I sighed and opened my mouth.

I began to suck, licking and slurping my mouth around a penis that had just been in my rectum. Susan was giggling and making little noises of excited disgust. Neville was breathing hard and grunting deep in his throat. It was like having all my dirtiest fantasies rolled into one, and I had to come while I was doing it. My hand went to my pussy, finding my clit, which was so hot and so sensitive that it felt as if it were burning. I concentrated on the cock in my mouth as I frigged, sucking and rubbing my tongue on the shaft, tasting his erection and my own flavour.

My orgasm hit me with incredible power, rising in my clit and going right through my body. I felt my sore, gaping bumhole contract, on nothing, then on Susan's finger. Neville pulled back, leaving me empty and resentful of being deprived of my lovely mouthful.

Susan's finger came out of my anus and into my mouth as Neville took me by the hips. I was in the middle of orgasm, my peak spoilt by Neville depriving me of his cock. As my tongue touched Susan's finger it started again, then Neville's cock was stretching my anus out, filling me, hurting me, buggering me until his balls were touching my frantically rubbing fingers.

I screamed and screamed as the full force of my

133

interrupted climax hit me, punctuating my outbursts with sucks of Susan's finger. She laughed at my shameless ecstasy, bringing my pleasure to a peak so intense that I nearly fainted. Then I was coming down and becoming more aware of the pain in my bottom-hole as Neville's pushes became frantic. He went on for what seemed like ages, until I was squealing and kicking my feet against the seat. It hurt, yet I was determined to let him have his full pleasure in return for what he had given me. Finally, his hands locked in the soft flesh of my hips; he grunted and shoved his cock in my bottom to the very hilt. I felt a wet sensation around my anus and I knew that he'd given me the final, delicious indignity and come in my rectum.

12

Peeping

As my modem chimed its way towards connection with the Internet, a sound from outside my window drew my attention. Looking down I saw a straggling group of students heading for the Union building. They were clearly headed for a party; all of them were in fancy dress, and it was their laughter that had caught my attention.

I turned back to my monitor as my link came up, intent on discovering whether any comments had yet been made on my latest paper. There was a team in the US whose research was on similar lines, and I was particularly pleased that I had published first and also keen to find out what they thought. My usual search engine came up on the screen and I tapped in my name and a few key words which I hoped would cut out a good proportion of the irrelevant websites which normally come up in a search.

My search produced fourteen responses, and all ten on the first page were university websites. Feeling pretty pleased with myself, I clicked on the first and was soon absorbed in the comments of a Dr Pearce from one of the smaller middle-American universities.

Some time later the janitor, Colin, poked his head around the door to say that he was locking up and that I would have to leave by the back door. I thanked him absently and went back to my reading. As his footsteps receded along the corridor I was left in near silence, the only noises the hum of my computer and the distant throb of the city traffic. A moment later, I heard the characteristic crash of the front doors being slammed shut and knew that Colin had left.

It was nearly midnight when I broke off to fetch a coffee and visit the loo. My footsteps rang loud in the empty building, the echoes twice making me turn to see if anybody was coming down the corridor behind me. Laughing at my own irrational nervousness, I pushed open the door to my room and returned to my desk. A couple of clicks returned me to my original search, from which I went on to the second page. Of the four remaining sites, two were alternative pages at universities which I had visited, one was in some language I didn't recognise and the last appeared completely irrelevant. Feeling a touch disappointed, I moved the cursor towards the area for disconnection, only to stop as the final address caught my eye.

The site was something called 'Peeping', which intrigued me. I clicked on it, wondering how it had come up on my search. The screen went white, then red and some text appeared in the middle. It was headed 'Peeping', as the search data had told me. Below was my name and the name of the university and department, which explained why the page had come up. At the bottom was a link which said, 'Click here to watch Penny pee, and more!'.

I moved the cursor straight to it, feeling slightly alarmed. Enough rude photos have been taken of me and I could think of more than one that showed me peeing. How any of them would have got on to the net, I had no idea, but I intended to find out. The screen went white again, then gave a message announcing that it was loading a large AVI file. I waited, fiddling nervously with my mouse and thinking about students getting access to pictures of me with my panties around my thighs.

The wretched thing was infuriatingly slow, but finally a picture appeared. At first I felt relief, as all it showed was a crescent of black against a white background. Then I realised that I was looking at the underside of a toilet seat and an instant later I appeared. I knew my mouth was open as I watched, but could only stare in horror at the screen. I appeared over the toilet, my face clearly recognisable. I turned, tugged my trousers and panties down and lowered myself on to the toilet, my naked bottom filling almost the entire screen. The picture darkened and then became brighter as the camera adjusted, showing a shockingly detailed view of the most intimate parts of my body. The soft curves of my thighs and bottom-cheeks occupied most of the screen, so close up that the texture of my skin was discernible. Every little fold and wrinkle of my pussy showed too: my pouted, hairy outer lips, my delicate inner lips protruding from between the outer, even the hood of my clitoris with the tip of the little whitish-pink button poking out underneath it. My anus was fully visible, too, a wrinkled star of pink-brown flesh, every tiny crevice visible.

Then I started to pee, a great gush of liquid squirting from my pussy while drips ran down my labia. I knew I was blushing furiously, yet couldn't stop watching, simultaneously fascinated and horrified by the site of my own pussy gushing pee into the toilet bowl. Of course I know how I pee, so I knew that the most humiliating moment of all was still to come. Sure enough, the flow of pee died to a trickle and stopped, my bottom wiggled as I shook the last drops free and then my hand appeared, clutching a piece of blue toilet paper. I put my hands to my face and watched through my fingers as I dabbed at my pussy, dropped the paper and then slid the top joint of my middle finger into my vagina.

I was squirming in shame as I watched myself pull the finger out and then put it to my clit, rubbing with little circular motions. I was praying that it wouldn't prove to be one of the few times when I had actually masturbated to orgasm on the loo, especially as when I got near orgasm I tended to slide a finger up my bottom. Fortunately it wasn't one of those occasions, but as the AVI ended I was left sitting staring at the screen, numb with shock and embarrassment. If there's one thing I know, it's my own sexuality, and it didn't surprise me that I was turned on as well. Sexual humiliation does that to me, and this was a prime example.

I suppose my feelings were especially strong because my sex life had been a bit flat recently. As so often happens in my life, all the proposals that came my way were of the 'candlelit dinner and loving relationship' type. I was still in love with Amber, but could have done with the occasional rough shag with no emotional strings. For some reason, nobody seems to make that sort of suggestion to me, or at least they hadn't since I had taken up my lecturer's post in the north Midlands. There had been one or two exotic encounters, but nothing that could be repeated and so being made use of on the Net really stirred me up, whether I liked it or not.

I sat there for a bit and then rather guiltily saved the AVI on to a floppy disc, intending to take it home and then masturbate over it at my leisure. I knew I'd have to, and knew the orgasm would be great, but that didn't in any way diminish my feelings of righteous indignation that somebody had had the sheer cheek to film me peeing and then put it on the net for public viewing!

Several questions were going through my mind: where, when and how – but, most importantly, who? I was determined to find out, although I was also aware that the one way to absolutely guarantee the maximum embarrassment was to make a complaint. As it was, there was a good chance that nobody I knew would ever access the site in question. If I complained, then it could be guaranteed that every person in the university would have accessed the site within hours of learning about it. My colleagues would make sympathetic comments, my students would snigger every time I came into a room, some wag was more than likely to take a print and put it on the notice board. No, complaining was out of the question, but revenge wasn't.

I was pretty sure I knew the answers to where and when. The film had been taken in a cubicle and really the only cubicles I ever visit are those in the department loos, specifically those reserved for female members of staff. When I had gone for a pee earlier, the loo paper had been white and recyclable, as it usually was. Blue paper was unusual, but I could vaguely remember some perhaps a month before.

How, was a trickier question, and one that particularly fascinated me. Cameras can be pretty small, but I was sure I'd have noticed one in a lavatory bowl. Besides, it was hard to see why it wouldn't be damaged by water when the loo was flushed. Fortunately, there was one way to satisfy my curiosity, assuming that the camera hadn't been removed.

As I walked down the corridor towards the relevant loo, my mind started to calm down and consider things more rationally. My initial intention had been to find how it had been done and pinch the camera. Unfortunately, if I did that, whoever was responsible would guess that they had been discovered and go to ground. Instead, I would have to investigate but do nothing that would reveal my knowledge. The loos were on the floor below, a small washroom with only two cubicles. I entered one at random, acutely aware that I might once more be presenting my bare bottom to the world. Having had the coffee I managed to pee and, as I stood up, glanced into the bowl.

Nothing seemed unusual, but the location of the camera was obvious, and very clever. Nobody, but nobody investigates the little soap cages in a public loo, and that, of course, was where the camera was hidden. Of course, I couldn't study it in detail for fear of giving myself away, but I had no doubt of my deduction. The camera was probably hidden in a waterproof casing of some kind, which had then been painted that peculiarly intense blue which toilet soap always seems to be. It was presumably activated remotely and the images captured on computer.

Given that such a small object had to have a limited broadcast range, I could be sure that the pick-up was in the department building, which narrowed my search considerably. Other than myself, there was only a handful of people who used the toilet. I felt I could safely eliminate all my female colleagues, none of whom I could conceive of doing such a thing. There were only three female graduates, and two were intense, fiercely intellectual young women who could safely be eliminated. The third was

Wendy Smith, a bright, cheerful girl who I was supervising myself. We got on well and, while there was certainly something mischievous about her, I couldn't really imagine her wanting to post an AVI of me peeing on the Internet.

That left people who weren't supposed to be in the loo, and it seemed pretty certain that it would be a male student, probably a third-year. Third-years had their own benches, powerful computers and access to all the equipment they'd need. They were also a pretty rowdy bunch and I could easily see them finding the idea of filming their female lecturers in embarrassing situations absolutely hilarious.

I left the loo with my suspicions narrowed down to about six people. Back at my flat, I put the AVI on to my hard disk. I knew that if I tried to ignore it, I wouldn't be able to get to sleep properly. I would just end up getting up in the early hours and playing it while I masturbated, so it seemed sensible to give in to the inevitable earlier rather than later. I put the AVI on repeated play and spread myself naked in my armchair, my fingers going to my pussy as I watched the image of myself peeing into the toilet bowl and felt the humiliation of knowing that the image in front of me was available to anybody with the technology to get at it. By the time I came, I had one finger in my bottom-hole and was wishing I'd done the same when I was caught on film.

It had been a long time since I felt guilty and ashamed of myself after masturbating, but that time I did, and I went to bed plotting revenge.

Not that revenge was easy. I had thought that tracking the culprit down would be simple. As a lecturer I had access to all the student computers, and it should simply have been a question of searching hard disks until I discovered some tell-tale trace that linked the user to the camera in the loo. There was nothing. One or two had bookmarked pornographic sites, but these were just collections of girls in rude poses and gave no hint of more debauched activity. Finally, I had to conclude that the students were either innocent or very, very careful.

140

Having drawn a blank, I decided to investigate from the other direction. Accessing the 'Peeping' website at home, I once more found the page inviting surfers to watch me pee and then moved up to the main page.

Half an hour later, I was sitting there with my fly undone and my hand down my panties. The owner of the site was a compulsive voyeur and a complete pervert. Everything he presented was dedicated to catching girls in awkward and compromising poses. There was a photo-gallery of girls sunbathing topless and nude; another of girls accidentally showing their panties; a third of girls undressing, seen through bedroom windows. Most of these appeared to have been collected from around the world, but not so the hidden camera movies. There were three of these, all showing girls peeing in detail that left nothing at all to the imagination. There was the one of me, another of Wendy and a third of one of the female first-years who shouldn't really have been using that loo.

I didn't approve, but I couldn't help being turned on. The photos had had me massaging my pussy through my jeans; the AVI of Wendy prompted me to unzip and slip my hand down my panties and, when I got to the one of the undergraduate, I couldn't resist wriggling my trousers and panties down and masturbating over the sight of the pee gushing from her neat little pussy.

After coming, I sat down to try and derive some useful information from the site. Whoever had planted the camera was obviously at the university, and some of the still pictures also showed local scenes. These intrigued me, as several of them had been taken from the same place and were remarkable in that the photographer had been very close to the girls and yet they had obviously had no idea of his presence. They had all been taken from a low angle, two showing views up girls' skirts, and a third a girl bending to tie her trainers in such a way that her knickers showed. My first thought was that he must have used a video camera concealed in a bag, but the angle just wasn't right. Finally, I decided that the pictures must have been taken through a small window at pavement level, or perhaps a ventilator.

In the background of all three was the upper part of a war memorial which I recognised, along with the upper stories of several buildings that also seemed familiar. Then I realised where the place was: Hulme Green, a shopping area at the junction of three roads to the south of the city. The area was well away from the university, but in a suburb that was one of the main student accommodation areas. I smiled as I sat back, now pretty sure that I would be able to work out who the Peeping Tom was.

Investigation of Hulme Green that weekend quickly bore out my theory. The photos had been taken from a broken ventilator at pavement level. Unfortunately the ventilator opened out from a semi-subterranean public lavatory, for men. This was hardly the sort of place I could hang around, let alone go into, so I bought a coffee at a nearby café and sat down to watch and think.

As I observed men's comings and goings, it quickly became apparent to me that the Hulme Green Gents was more that just a public convenience. For a start, the same men kept coming back with a frequency that suggested that either they drank by the gallon or that they had some ulterior motive. I have met enough completely open gay men to know what was going on; the place was clearly what is called a 'cottage'. The men I was watching, or at least some of them, were visiting the toilets for sex, an idea that was somehow pleasantly rude although it was sex of a type that in no way involved me.

The whole thing was becoming great fun, with the thrill of the chase blending with an erotic *frisson* and just a hint of danger. As I sat and watched, a plan started to take form in my head. By the time I had finished my second coffee, it was fully formed and, while it relied on one or two assumptions, it was also pretty well risk-free and easy enough to put into effect.

The first assumption was that the Peeping Tom was proud of what he did and wanted to share his dirty secret with others. The fact that he had posted the pictures on the Net rather proved this. The second assumption was that he'd use the place again. As I would have heard if anyone connected with the department had been arrested as a Peeping Tom, it seemed reasonable to think that he had got away with it and would be back.

It wasn't practical to stake the place out, and I had better things to do anyway, yet it struck me that if I left a message on the wall suggesting a meeting then the culprit was likely to respond. I would have to bait my hook by offering to swap pictures or something; but, once done, I could simply observe the suggested meeting place and see who came. Then I'd know who it was and could concoct a suitable revenge at leisure.

The problem was getting into the gents. Hulme Green was pretty busy and I didn't have the guts to simply stroll in, especially when there was a perfectly good ladies right beside the gents. On the other hand I am slight, short-haired and fresh-faced and was sure that, with a bit of effort, I could pass as a boy.

When I came back the next day I was armed with a black marker pen and full of a deliciously illicit thrill. After a bit of trial and error, I had managed to make myself up to look like a very effeminate fourteen-year-old boy. It wasn't the world's best disguise, but a brief test run proved that it was good enough.

Going out as a boy produced all sorts of strange feelings. For a start, I felt as if I was in a completely different world, partly because I was pretending to be something I wasn't and partly because of people's reactions. I'd read works by feminists that described going out disguised as men. The main comment had been that one is no longer looked at primarily in terms of the sexual characteristics of one's body. I found this to be true, but oddly disconcerting rather than a relief. I also found myself disagreeing with them that one gets more respect as a man. I certainly didn't, or at least not as my adolescent male alter ego. Attitudes towards me ranged from total indifference, through wariness, to a sort of carefully judged aggression, as if determined to make me accept a lower place in some imaginary pecking order. Fortunately, total indifference was by far the commonest of these and I reached Hulme Green without incident.

Being Sunday, there were fewer people about, yet going down into the gents still required a fair bit of courage. I sat on a bench eating a sandwich and watching men go in and out, screwing up my courage until I was sure that nobody else was using the loos. Twice I delayed, on some imagined pretext, but once the sandwich was finished I had no further excuse for loitering. Rising to my feet with a good-sized knot of tension in my stomach, I began to walk towards the iron gate that was the physical aspect of one of society's strongest taboos.

I swallowed as I crossed the imaginary barrier and descended the steps towards a right-angled opening that looked black and ominous. If I felt like Orpheus descending into the underworld, then it's probably mainly my overactive imagination, yet what I was doing was something perhaps more socially unacceptable than going naked in public.

As I pushed the door open, the first thing I noticed was the smell: scarcely pleasant, but intensely male. Inside were several sinks, a long porcelain trough and a row of cubicles. The function of the trough was obvious, yet its very unfamiliarity served to strengthen my feeling of being out of place.

One glance told me that the broken ventilator had to belong to the end cubicle, and a dozen quick steps took me to it. As I slid the heavy iron bolt home on the door, I once more felt secure, although in the very heart of the lion's den. Looking up, I could see the ventilator, a torn plate revealing a tiny patch of sky outside. As a peep-hole, it was ideal. Looking around, one thing that really struck me was the graffiti. The walls were covered in it: comments on football teams, boasts of sexual prowess or conquests, supposed phone numbers of willing girls, but, most of all, offers to meet for homosexual sex. The number and the urgent tone of these surprised me, suggesting a vigour to the local gay scene that I had never suspected. Further proof of this was given by a hole in the wall, the height of which made its purpose very obvious. It had been hacked through the metal wall, a fact which seemed to me to demonstrate an absolutely brutish lust for sex. The thought of meeting the man prepared to tear through a metal wall to get what he wanted both scared me and turned me on, although logically I knew that, as a girl, he probably wouldn't want me at all. Above the hole someone had written the words 'Glory Hole', making it even more obvious what it was used for.

The place had a dangerously sexual atmosphere to it, which was beginning to get to me. So were some of the comments on the wall, and I decided to make the most of what would probably be my only opportunity to read them. The one that had caught my eye was a claim that 'Sally from the chippy' gave blow jobs for five pounds. As two other men endorsed the remark, it seemed to me quite likely that she really did, and the idea of this girl having her cock-sucking ability advertised in a public lavatory affected me strongly. The very dirtiness of the idea was really exciting, and I found myself fantasising that, if I put an exhortation of my own abilities down, I'd get a line of dirty old men coming round to my flat to have their cocks sucked. They'd pay me five pounds for it, or maybe four, as I ought to undercut Sally to really show what a little slut I was.

Another piece described buggering a girl in one of the local parks. The man claimed to have had her kneeling with skirt up and her tights and panties pulled down. He had pulled her top up so that he could feel her boobs, greased his cock with Vaseline and put it up her bum when she thought she was going to be fucked. Apparently, she had struggled but quickly started to enjoy it and had let him come up her bottom. I doubted it was true, yet I'd had something not dissimilar done to me, and so perhaps it was. In any case, the very idea made me shiver and had me imagining men standing exactly where I was and masturbating over the dirty little story.

I looked away deliberately, my head spinning with dirty thoughts. To calm myself, I turned my attention to the ventilator and my purpose in being there. Even on tiptoe, I could barely reach it but, after climbing on to the loo and bracing one foot against the door, I managed a moderate view. Outside I could see a fair bit of Hulme Green and the top of the war memorial, exactly as it had been in the pictures. It was ideal for a voyeur, appearing only as a small, dark hole at pavement level, yet providing a view straight up the skirts of any girls who passed. As the view was of the area outside the gates to the ladies, it could also be guaranteed to be successful. The combination of ingenuity, determination and perversity that had been necessary to achieve views of girls' panties filled me with a similar alarm to that I had felt when viewing the glory hole. Only now it was more personal: very personal, in fact, as one of the voyeur's greatest successes was catching me peeing!

It was more than I could resist not to use the peep-hole myself. The first girl who passed was wearing jeans. I wrote my message as I waited, inviting 'Internet voyeur' to meet and adding a few flattering comments and an offer of pictures as extra bait. I got lucky on the second girl. She was a pretty blonde with a snub nose and freckles, her skirt just long enough to be modest yet show her legs to advantage. From my angle, the view was anything but modest. As she walked past, I was given a clear view of her panties, bright yellow and ridden up between the cheeks of her chubby little bottom. I climbed down, feeling turned on and a bit guilty. I knew I was going to have to masturbate, though, and sat down on the seat, only to stop dead.

Protruding from the glory hole was a large, dark, heavily hooded cock and a pair of enormous balls in a sac, richly grown with crinkly hair. I froze, staring at the thing, a big, fat, excited set of male genitals pushed out for my attention.

'Come on, boy, you know you want to do it,' a voice spoke, a whisper hoarse with urgency.

I almost ran, terrified by the knowledge of what I was supposed to do. I couldn't, though; I was rooted to the spot. I put my hand out instead, my fingers trembling and

146

my pulse hammering. Some men's cocks look nice: quite handsome, even. This one wasn't, it was ugly and also big. It was more than I could do not to touch it, stroke it, watch it thicken and stiffen in my hand, see the spunk erupt from the tip when he came. My hand closed on the grotesque thing and it squirmed in my fingers, the blood coming into the shaft as I began to pull up and down.

'Squeeze my balls; suck me,' he groaned from beyond the partition.

It was an order, and one I was powerless to resist. Leaning forward, I cupped his balls in my hand, feeling his coarse hair and the wrinkled skin of his sac. The balls moved inside, firm, egg-shaped lumps moving in my palm as I squeezed gently. His cock was coming to full erection, the head fully out of the foreskin, meaty and red. The shaft was dark, not the glossy deep brown of a black man's cock, but a dull red-brown. It was also heavily veined and bent upwards and a little sideways, a distorted thing at once virile and obscene. A hole which must once have held a piercing added a final, nasty, irresistible touch. I opened my mouth, gaping wide, feeling absolutely filthy as my lips touched it. I kissed, tasting the salt and the flavour of aroused male. Then my mouth was around it and I was sucking with a desperate eagerness that came from the sheer dirtiness of my position. I was in a male lavatory, sucking on a man's penis, a man who I had never even seen, but whose orders I had obeyed simply because I'm too much of a slut to resist. Worse still, he thought he was being sucked off by another man.

I wanted him to come in my mouth, badly. Also on my face, so that when he had I could sit back and masturbate with the taste of come in my mouth and my face and hair splashed with sperm. His cock had hardened fast, and was now fully erect, a great column of solid prick for me to suck on. I put my spare hand around the base of his shaft, masturbating him right into my mouth, desperate for my faceful of come. His balls squirmed in my hand and his groans were audible through the wall as he pushed his cock out to get it deeper into my mouth. I knew it wouldn't be

147

long when he started to grunt and pant, a noise with all the raw, male vitality I had been imagining. I pulled back as I felt his cock jerk, catching a thick jet of semen across my face and lips. I tugged hard at it; the second spurt splashed over my nose and the third right into my open mouth. Then I put his gorgeous cock back in my mouth and sucked and sucked until I'd drained him and he was beginning to go limp.

My hands were already going to my zip as I sat back, the sperm bubbling up around my lips as I prepared to frig myself into oblivion. I saw his cock pull back as I pushed aside the pair of tights that I had bundled into the front of my panties. I stopped, realising that there was a major problem. If he looked through the glory hole, he would see not a stiff pink cock and a pair of balls as he expected, but my pussy. Quickly rearranging myself, I stood up, putting my back to the glory hole.

'Don't be shy; put it through and I'll wank you.' His voice came clear through the partition.

Of course, that was one thing I was completely incapable of doing. I started to panic, pulling some paper from the roll and wiping at my face, even as I considered how best to answer.

'Come on,' he urged. 'I want to see your cock.'

I wasn't at all sure what he'd have thought if he'd discovered I didn't have one, and that he'd been sucked off by a girl, but I wasn't hanging around to find out. Wishing that I'd brought a compact with a mirror, I made a last check for stray splashes of come in my hair and bolted from the toilet. A man coming down the stairs gave me a look of surprise and then I was out and running for my car.

When I got home I masturbated until I was sore. I did it with my boy's clothes still on, kneeling over my toilet with a courgette pushed up my pussy in place of the marvellous, grotesque penis I had sucked. Of course, I knew full well that, had it gone further, it wouldn't have been my pussy that got filled and ended up greasing my bottom and wedging the courgette into my anus. I pushed it in and out as I played with my clit, reaching the most exquisite orgasm with my anus stretched wide around the intruding vegetable while I imagined that it was his cock.

I had set the meeting a week away to make sure the voyeur had a chance to read my invitation. All that week, I took care to use the female students' loos and kept an eye on the staff ones. I saw nothing suspicious and so was amazed to discover new postings when I checked the 'Peeping' website the following Saturday.

There were three, and all of them had been done in our female undergraduates' loos, the very ones I had been using to avoid being caught again. The first two were of one of the prettiest women in the second year, a slim, shy girl with long black curls who I considered exceptionally bright if rather introverted. To my surprise, the voyeur's work showed that she had her labia pierced. The third AVI was of the same girl that he had caught in the staff loos before.

What amazed me was not just his ability to avoid detection, but his ability to select the prettiest girls to film. Of course, it was possible that he just posted the best, but I doubted it. In either case, it was impossible not to feel just a little flattered when he had posted me along with Wendy and perhaps the two prettiest undergraduates in the department.

Not that that diluted my desire for revenge, and it was with considerable satisfaction that I positioned myself to watch the park on the next Sunday. I had chosen a half-collapsed brick hut as a meeting place. This was on a piece of wasteland that adjoined the park and would provide shelter for the imaginary meeting, but leave me in no doubt as to who went there. The back window of my flat overlooked it, too, which meant that I could watch in perfect safety and comfort, sitting by the window with a pair of binoculars, a cup of coffee and a sandwich.

Unfortunately, my man was too suspicious to be caught so easily. Nobody arrived at the hut when they were supposed to, yet there was a man sitting on the old bandstand and evidently intent on the hut. As he was wearing a black raincoat with the collar up and a purple woolly hat, it was impossible to see who it was.

I was faced with a frustrating dilemma. All I needed was the man's identity and I would be able to work out some fitting revenge at leisure. I couldn't simply walk past him as, if he saw me, he was bound to be suspicious. On the other hand, if I failed this time, he might well not take the bait again; besides which, I wasn't at all sure if I had the courage for a second visit to the gents at Hulme Green.

Time was passing and I needed to think fast. Deciding on a bold plan of action, I put on my heaviest overcoat, a blue one that makes me look a bit like Paddington Bear, and hurried round to the park. I was just in time, as my man was already walking away from the bandstand towards the railway arches at the far side of the park. I followed, knowing that once I had his address, it would be simple enough to find out his identity.

I hurried to follow, concerned that I might lose him in the maze of little streets beyond the railway, or that he might get on to a bus. Neither happened, and I was not at all surprised when twenty minutes later we passed the sign that announced the start of Hulme Green. He went to one of the dingiest parts of the area, a cluster of Victorian back-to-backs bordering the canal. I watched him enter the last in a row, descending a flight of steps into a basement flat. At no point had I had a chance to see his face, yet he was of middling height and stockily built, which had allowed me to eliminate just about all our male students. Of the remainder, one stood out, a rather quiet boy called Marcus who I had always suspected fancied me and I could just imagine setting up the camera system.

Sure that it was him, I walked on, intent on discovering the number of the house he had gone into. It was thirty-eight; but as I reached the low wall that cut the end of the street off from the canal I realised that I might be able to confirm my suspicions on the spot. The wall didn't meet the houses, but left a narrow gap. This was clear on the side opposite thirty-eight and I could see a skylight that evidently opened on to the basement flat. The equivalent space by thirty-eight was hidden by a decaying mattress, yet presumably had an equivalent skylight.

Thoroughly enjoying my role as detective, I pushed my way into the narrow gap and past the mattress. Marcus was about as unthreatening a person as it is possible to be, and I was even considering a direct confrontation and a bit of corporal punishment. I hadn't caned a man since I'd moved out of Amber Oakley's to take up my lecturer's post and, while I normally like to be on the receiving end, this seemed a perfect opportunity to get back in trim.

I settled by the skylight and peered down into the basement. The window was half-hidden by a drape on the inside, yet I could make out the lower part of a swivel chair and a piece of desk. Someone was seated at the chair, only visible from the waist down, but presumably Marcus. I made myself as comfortable as possible, hoping that he would come further into view and allow me to make sure of my identification before I confronted him.

He didn't but, from his movements, it was clear that he was seated at a computer and operating the mouse and a keyboard. Knowing that he could well stay in that position for hours, I began to rise, only to stop as his hand went to his crotch and he began to stroke himself through his jeans. Well, if he could film me peeing, I could certainly watch him masturbate – and then catch him red-handed.

I was grinning to myself as he slipped a hand down his trousers and began to knead his genitals. He was obviously watching something smutty on the screen, possibly even the AVI of me on the loo. For a long while, he kept his hand down his jeans, his cock stiffening to become a hard ridge under the cloth with his hand moving up and down the length in a lazy rowing motion. I was riveted, and looking forward to the moment he took it out.

Finally, he pulled his hand free and began to undo his fly, opening the button and drawing the zip down with a haste that marked his increasing excitement. I watched in rapture as his other hand came into view and he pushed his jeans down, exposing tight blue underpants absolutely bulging with cock and balls. He settled his jeans around his thighs, which I could see were solid with muscle, then tweaked open the front of his pants to pull out his balls and erection.

I gasped. His cock was thick and dark red-brown, the head a reddish pink, the shaft curved up and a bit to the side, the foreskin heavy and uneven. I had seen his cock before; indeed, I had sucked it. I stayed staring in surprise, realising that what I was seeing meant that innocent young Marcus was not only bisexual but an out-and-out pervert. When I'd sucked him, I'd been thinking of him as a mature, confident, strong gay man, highly sexed and dominant. Now I was confused by what seemed a contradiction between what I knew of Marcus and his gross and apparently insatiable sexual appetite.

He was tugging hard at his cock now, left-handed while he used his right to control the mouse. If I was going to confront him, now was the time, yet he had managed to bring out both the dominant and submissive elements of my sexuality, which made me unsettled. The sight of him pulling at his fat, ugly cock produced an even more primitive desire in me. I was so wet between my legs that my jeans were damp, and I urgently needed his cock inside me.

I walked quickly to his door, determined to do it before common sense got the better of me. I knew logically that I had a strong hold on him and that, outside of his sex life, he was a quiet, polite young man. Emotionally I could only see him as the sort of unbalanced animal who was likely to fuck me on the doorstep if I disturbed him in such an aroused condition.

The bell rang and, after just the sort of pause you'd expect from someone caught in the middle of having a wank, I heard footsteps approaching the door. I folded my arms and put on my most poised and dominant expression, determined to carry it off by sheer willpower.

The door opened and my resolve vanished on the instant. It wasn't the mild, timid Marcus who stood at the door, but Colin, the department janitor. He was similar in

152

build to Marcus, but there the resemblance ended. A rather curt, short-tempered man of indeterminate age, he was just the sort who triggered the dirty-old-man fantasies I occasionally like to come over, as indeed he had. Of course, I would never have dreamt of actually having sex with him in reality. Only I had: I'd sucked his cock through a glory hole in Hulme Green public lavatories.

'Dr Birch?' he asked, sounding puzzled as to why a junior lecturer should be calling on him on a Sunday afternoon.

But we both knew. If he had the intelligence to operate a website, he clearly wasn't as dim as people thought him. The difference was that, while I knew that he was a dirty bastard, he had no idea about me. At least I thought he didn't.

Even as I struggled for something to say, his expression of surprise turned to a dirty grin. He reached out and took my arm and I let him draw me into the flat, unresisting. I knew what was coming, even as he started to fumble at the peg fastenings of my coat. I helped him, popping open the pegs as I wondered why he was so certain that he could just have me on the spot.

'You dirty bitch,' he drawled as my coat came open. 'I've watched you wank, but I never thought you'd come and get some.'

Then I knew. Of course he'd watched me come. I'd done it in the staff loos more than once. He had just kept the rudest film for his own viewing.

'How did you find out it was me?' he demanded as he started to push me to the floor.

I didn't answer and he didn't press the point. He was hitching my skirt up, then I was on my back and his hands were fumbling at my panties. I lifted my bottom so that he could pull them off, opening my thighs even as he started on my blouse buttons. I lay passively as he opened them and pulled my bra up to get at my breasts. He began to fondle them with one hand, the other going to his trousers. I sighed as my nipples popped up under his rough fingers, revelling in his delight in my body, in his sheer lust for me.

His gross cock burst from his fly as he scrabbled round beside me, his balls following and the whole lot being pushed in my face as he took me by the hair. I let him put his balls in my mouth, then his cock, sucking eagerly just as I had done in the Hulme Green lavatory. I put my fingers to my pussy and began to frig, opening the hole that was about to be invaded by his cock. I was panting as he pulled away, climbing over my leg and mounting me without further preamble.

Then he was in me and I was being fucked on the floor, hard and fast as I lay in my undignified position with my tits bare and my panties discarded on the floor beside me. Soon I was gasping and grunting without restraint, begging for his cock deeper in me with my legs curled up and his fingers locked hard in the soft flesh of my thighs.

I really thought he was going to come, but without warning he pulled back and took me by the hips, turning me bum up without difficulty. For a moment I thought he was going to bugger me and was about to demand lubricant and a condom when his cock bumped once against my pussy and was rammed up me from the rear. He did it hard, making me grunt as my breath was knocked out. My coat was wrenched up, then my skirt.

'You've got a lovely arse, you fucking little slut,' he gasped, taking me by the hips and starting to hump me with even more vigour than before.

I didn't reply. It was all I could do to breathe, with him ramming his prick in and out of my pussy. I was thinking of my position too, kneeling on the floor with my coat thrown up over my head and my bottom spread in front of me. He'd be able to see my bumhole, watch his cock glide in and out of my sodden pussy, smell my excitement. I put my face to the floor and my hands back between my legs, finding my pussy and starting to masturbate, spreading my thighs open to be sure he knew what I was doing.

'You're nothing but a fucking little tart, aren't you?' he spat.

I groaned my agreement and then grunted as he planted a hard slap on my bottom. It stung, and made me feel even more at his mercy. He could beat me, bugger me -- anything, just as long as it kept up my feeling of being used roughly and without thought for my dignity. He slapped me again and I started to come, clawing at my pussy, and squealing as he rammed his cock into me. My mouth was open against the floor, my fingers wet with my own juice, the muscles of my vagina and anus starting to spasm, my whole being centred on the cock inside me and my clit. My climax hit me and I screamed, getting another hard slap on my bum in answer.

As my orgasm died away, rose again and then began to fade in earnest, he was calling me a tart, a slut and a whore as he rode me. Then he was out, his cock rubbing between my bottom-cheeks, then his hand. He groaned and I felt the head of his cock pressed down between my cheeks to touch my anus. I was still whimpering with the aftershock of my orgasm as his sperm splashed in between my buttocks, wetting my pussy and bumhole, only to be rubbed in as he finished himself off over me.

Well, it was a choice of talking things out with him or walking home with my panties sodden with sperm and pussy juice, so I chose to talk to him. I really had to, anyway, and in a way there's no better time for honesty than immediately after sex.

Given his character, I expected him to be fairly obdurate, or even try to blackmail me. He had the power to make my life unbearable at the university and, while I could easily have had him sacked, he had judged correctly that I wouldn't risk the exposure.

As it was, his attitude was very different. He'd planted the camera mainly for the thrill of voyeurism and watching women do something usually too intimate even for their partners to see. He'd also done it because he resented the staff's attitude to him, and that was also why he'd posted the pictures on the web. When he'd filmed me masturbating on the loo, he'd been surprised but had realised that I was more highly sexed than my colleagues. He'd started to fantasise over me more and more but had never intended to make an advance.

Then came the bit that made me feel less than clever. He'd seen me on my first visit to Hulme Green and put two and two together. He'd then decided that I probably was beddable. Unlike me, he had had the time and patience to stake the loos out and had seen me return in my disguise. He wasn't gay at all, but had known full well who was sucking his cock through the glory hole.

After that, he had expected me to meet him at the old hut and hoped that I would surrender myself there. That had been a bit too optimistic, although in other ways he seemed to know my sexuality about as well as I did myself. He had been genuinely surprised to see me when I called at his house, but had judged correctly that all I needed was a little push and my legs would be open for him.

Perhaps it was arrogant of him to assume that I was game, but he'd been right and I suppose that, if he'd been wrong, he might have used the pictures as a lever to buy my silence.

We finally agreed that, as long as he behaved as normal in the department and took the pictures off the net, then I would come round every other weekend for sex. In return for taking the other girls' AVIs off, I agreed to the occasional after-hours blow-job in my room, just as long as nobody else was in the building.

He really knew how to push my buttons because, when we had finished talking, he pulled out his cock and told me to suck it – not asked me, but told me. I did it, although it took ages to bring him to his second orgasm of the afternoon. He then spanked me over his lap, 'to remind me of my place' as he put it, and sent me home with a sore bottom. I went with a smile, looking forward to the prospect of an indefinite supply of rough sex without any strings.

13

Golden

I thought the flat was empty when I first came in, and went straight to the bathroom to dry my hair from the light spring rain that had been falling all day. It was only as I passed the bedroom door that I realised that my guest was actually in.

This was my cousin Susan, who had come up to stay with me when she had tired of her ageing hippie boyfriend. Unable to bear her mother's delight in the failure of what had been her first heavy relationship, she had asked if she could stay with me for a while. I had agreed willingly, having really taken to her since she grew up. The fact that, on the one occasion I had visited them together, the boyfriend had buggered us both and put me through one of the most erotic and possibly the dirtiest experience of my life was seldom mentioned, but it contributed a lot to the casual intimacy that quickly grew up between us. After all, if you've licked a friend's pussy while her boyfriend buggers you, you hardly need feel concerned about anything less intimate.

I was also coming to appreciate her character. I'd always thought of her as a quiet, rather thoughtful girl who took a really wicked delight in mischief for its own sake. Mischievousness was certainly a strong part of her character, and indeed it was mainly that and the knowledge of how much it would shock her mother that had prompted her to go off with Neville the hippie. There was actually much more to her, and in many ways she was more like me than her elder sister, Kate, who was my age and with whom I'd always been much more intimate. Susan was six years my junior, and, until the incident with Neville, I'd always thought of her as a little girl. Now she definitely wasn't; we weren't lovers in the sense that Amber and I were, yet we shared a bed and sometimes our bodies without really thinking about it. I didn't feel the slightest guilt, although we were cousins; it was just that we were very close and sometimes we got a bit carried away. She also used to give me the occasional spanking when I needed it, which was really nice and did a lot to keep me happy.

I looked in, but she was so lost in a book that she had failed to notice my arrival. She was lying face down on the bed, legs kicked up and one foot bare, the discarded slipper lying on the counterpane behind her. She only had a T-shirt on, her pert bottom showing beneath the hem in careless display.

'Hi, Susan,' I ventured as she turned at the noise of the door opening. 'What are you so absorbed in?'

'Frazer,' she answered with just a hint of embarrassment.

'That's a bit heavy,' I replied. 'Which one?'

' "The Magic Art" from *The Golden Bough*,' she said, again with that catch in her voice that suggested that she hadn't really wanted to be caught reading it.

'Is that the one with all the pig spirits and symbolic virgins?'

'No, this is about pagan magic and so on; silly, I know, but I was having a bit of a nostalgia trip.'

'Tell me, then,' I asked, settling myself on the bed by her side.

'All right, but if you laugh . . .' Susan said as she rolled over and folded her hands across her tummy, giving me a shy smile before continuing. 'I was just remembering how Barbara Trowleigh and I tried to use one of the rituals to make the boys we fancied interested in us.'

I began to giggle; I couldn't help it, especially thinking of Susan's friend Barbara, a strapping, no-nonsense woman who was a broker in the City. I'd only met her once, and she was perhaps the strongest, most sensible woman I knew, making the image of her using magic rituals to pursue boys seem quite ridiculous. Susan blushed but then made a sudden grab for my waist. Almost before I could protest, she was turning me face down on the bed and straddling my back.

'I told you not to laugh!' she said as my skirt was pulled up and a firm smack planted on my bottom.

'Ow! Susan!' I protested, only to have my knickers pulled down and my bottom smacked again.

'Promise you won't laugh,' she demanded, 'or I'll use the hairbrush on you.'

'OK, I promise!' I squeaked, not at all in the mood for a bottom-blistering spanking with my long, wooden-handled hairbrush.

She gave my bottom a couple more playful slaps for good measure and then dismounted from my back, rolling once more into a comfortable position as I rearranged my dishevelled clothing.

'OK,' she said, 'it was like this. Barbara had a crush on one of the boys from the village but didn't have the guts to do anything about it. Now, we had an art teacher called Phaedra Mace who used to go around in a kaftan and wear lots of beads, and she was always going on about paganism, the earth mother and natural magic. Barbara was a great favourite of hers anyway, and so she ended up borrowing books from Miss Mace, including *The Golden Bough*, and it wasn't long before she'd decided to make a ritual doll to attract the boy and, as her best friend, I naturally got roped into it.

'Even then I felt a bit silly about it, and I think Barbara did, too, but it was fun and, what with all the Christianity that used to get rammed down our throats every day, it felt deliciously naughty to be indulging in pagan practices. First we tried the ritual of piercing the doll's heart, but of course nothing happened. It's so silly really, when you think how gorgeous Barbara is: with all that hair and her lovely round titties, I'm sure he'd have jumped at the chance of going out with her, if he'd thought for one instant that she was interested. Anyway, nothing happened, and then at one art class Miss Mace posed nude for us to draw and, when some of the girls were a bit embarrassed, we got this long lecture on how we shouldn't be ashamed of our bodies and nudity was beautiful and close to nature. She was very convincing and ended up talking some of us into posing as well – including me, actually, stark naked with a bowl of fruit in my lap.'

'Slut,' I interjected, giving her a playful slap on the thigh.

'Honestly, I never thought of it as sexual,' Susan continued, 'though, looking back, I'm sure Miss Mace fancied Barbara. Nothing ever came of it – at least, not that I know about. Anyway, deriving our inspiration from Miss Mace, various books and our own imagination, we concocted increasingly elaborate rituals, none of which worked, but by this time we were doing it as much for the fun of the thing as for the original purpose. The thrill of going naked in the woods was something else, especially as we were terrified of getting caught. We began to do slightly sexual things, like gently whip each other's bottoms with twigs. Barbara would be the priestess, and part of the ritual was for me to kiss her buttocks. I even kissed her bottom-hole once, after which we walked all the way back without saying a word to each other. That was the last time before end of term exams got in the way . . .'

Susan paused and watched with a smile as I lifted my bottom off the bed and took down my pants, rucking my skirt up so that I could touch myself. We thought nothing of masturbating in front of each other and often did it side by side while we discussed our sexual fantasies. Now I wanted to do it slowly and easily while Susan told me about what she had done with Barbara.

'Carry on,' I said. 'I just want to play with myself while I listen.'

'OK,' she said. 'Well, what with exams and sports events and so on, nothing more happened that term, but I had been invited to visit her in the holidays and so we ended up together in Dorset. We talked about what we'd done in the term, but I don't think anything would have happened if we hadn't found this special place. As it was, we were out walking one day on the cliffs and came across a landslip which had made it possible to climb down to the sea. We meant to go down to the shore, but when we scrambled down we found a sort of bowl fifty feet or so below the cliff top, full of a gooey blue-grey mud and with a single huge rock more or less in the middle. It was the perfect place for a ritual, and we decided to go across. Getting there was obviously going to involve getting pretty muddy, so we stopped to take our shoes and socks off. I was wearing a dress, but Barbara had tight jeans on and so she had to take those off too, but she didn't stop there and I remember my rising feeling of excitement and uncertainty as she stripped.'

Susan paused, watching me masturbate with no attempt at hiding her interest. My pussy was soaking, and I put the damp middle finger into Susan's mouth to show her the effect she was having on me. She sucked and then smiled at me before continuing.

'Barbara turned to me when she was naked and stretched, really luxuriously so that her boobs stuck out. She then began to tease me about being shy.

'I knew exactly what she wanted and only hesitated an instant before pulling my dress over my head. I had always felt a bit skinny and immature next to her, without much in the way of boobs, and so had always been a bit behind in stripping, but then it didn't matter a bit and I couldn't get my bra and panties off fast enough. We splashed over to the big rock, getting our legs covered in the clay, which was a lot deeper than we'd imagined. Barbara then told me to lie on the rock.

'I got up and lay down on my back, feeling a bit nervous because, even though the place was secluded, we were wide open to the sky. Anyway, Barbara started to draw patterns on my flesh, like those Celtic patterns you see sometimes in jewellery and things. She used the clay, which was cold and slimy but felt really nice, and I can remember my nipples poking up through it where she'd smeared it on my boobs. For quite a while she drew and chanted, her finger-tips working in circles and arcs across my chest and tummy and legs.

'What happened then is a bit hazy. I know I was really turned on, and didn't really understand my feelings. I suppose we were using the ritual to cover our desire for each other, giving us an excuse for what we knew was really dirty behaviour. Oh, we were close enough, and used to cuddle and things, but it was only during our rituals that we did anything that I'd think of as sex nowadays. Anyway, Barbara must have climbed up on the rock, because I remember her standing over me and holding her pussy-lips apart. I was a bit shocked; even though I'd kissed her bumhole before, there was something really blatant about the way she was standing there, squatting slightly, her pussy all pink and glistening in the sun, every detail visible.

'Then she said something like, "I'm going to have to piss all over you", or maybe, "You need me to piss all over you", which just seemed so unladylike. Then a golden stream erupted from her pussy, catching me in between my boobs and splashing all over them and on my tummy and face. I closed my eyes tight, but there was an overwhelming urge to open my mouth so that she would pee in it. She was squirming her body from side to side, playing her stream over my tits and stomach in a rough cross shape. I felt the force of the pee begin to slacken and realised that it was now or never, so I lifted my head a bit and opened my mouth, my tongue pushed out a bit in a gesture of acceptance, feeling really dirty but desperate to have my mouth filled with her pee. I felt the stream splash on my neck, then on my chin, and I knew I was really going to do it as I leant forward another inch to catch it in my mouth. Then my mouth was filling with warm, salty pee, running over at the sides and dribbling down my cheeks. She wasn't very accurate, and it splashed all over my face, forcing me to keep my eyes tight shut all the time. I swallowed my mouthful.'

'Say that bit again,' I interrupted as my orgasm started to hit me.

'OK,' Susan giggled. 'I swallowed my mouthful of pee and leant up for more. My eyes were shut, but I felt her hand take me around the back of my head and pull my face forward, then the wet, hairy flesh of her pussy was pushed against my mouth and I was given another mouthful. It went all over me, in my mouth, down my throat, over my face and in my hair until I was lying there in a pee-soaked mess and licking Barbara's pussy for all I was worth. I was playing with myself, too, and I remember swallowing a mouthful of Barbara's pee when I was actually orgasming.'

I sighed my appreciation of her story, my fingers still deep in my pussy after my orgasm. I had come while she was describing Barbara peeing in her mouth, a deliciously dirty act that appealed to me immensely.

'The next thing I remember is lying there thinking what a display I'd made of myself,' Susan was saying, 'but then Barbara was cuddling me and whispering things to me and it all seemed OK, too dirty to ever tell anyone, until now, but OK.'

'That was great,' I sighed. 'What happened after that?'

'Well, I suppose it worked, really,' she said. 'We did a few more rituals the next term, before it got too cold to play naked in the woods. She started going out with the boy she fancied, and if it wasn't the magic generated by the rituals that did it, I imagine that without them she'd never have gained the confidence in her sex appeal to flirt with him. Unfortunately, it got her expelled. She was giving him a blow-job in the swimming pool toilets when they were caught, the dirty little slut. Still, she's done pretty well for a girl thrown out of school in disgrace without finishing her exams.'

'That's true,' I agreed. 'Don't you want to come now?'

My tone was hopeful because, although I'd come, she had put me in a dirty mood. I was more than keen to play with her and her story had also reminded me of something else.

'Do you remember Kate's wedding?' I asked.

'Which one?' she replied.

'The first, to Toby,' I said. 'When you and I were bridesmaids.'

'Sure; my mum had to spank you,' Susan giggled.

'Do you know why?' I asked.

'No,' she admitted, 'but we could hear the smacks and you squealing in the garden. I thought it was really funny.'

'Bitch,' I joked, but couldn't help the flush that had risen to my cheeks. I knew it had been audible in the garden and that a good two hundred and fifty people had known that I was getting a spanking. They didn't know why, though, nor that I'd been so turned on that I'd gone upstairs, locked myself in and brought myself to my first ever orgasm.

'Go on, tell me, then,' Susan teased.

'Toby was going to fuck me,' I told her, getting a wide-eyed look of surprise in return. 'Your mum caught me with come all over my face because he wanted a suck first and came in my mouth. He'd pushed my face in the toilet bowl, too, and he was going to flush my head while he fucked me.'

'The bastard!' Susan exclaimed in awe. 'But no wonder Mummy spanked you.'

'I'm afraid I enjoyed that too,' I admitted, 'but look, do you want to come in the bathroom. We could do something really rude and I promise you a great orgasm.'

'Do you want me to do that to you, to flush you?' she asked, bright-eyed and expectant.

'Yes, please,' I answered.

'Good,' she replied, 'but I'm going to go one better and pee in the bowl first.'

She jumped up and ran into the bathroom, giggling. I followed, blushing scarlet but with a big smile on my face. In the bathroom Susan was already on the loo, with her T-shirt held up above her tummy and her knees wide apart.

'Watch,' she said and, with all of the naughty, mischievous immodesty which I like so much, began to pee in the bowl.

I watched the stream of pale gold erupt from her pussy with mounting feelings of anticipation and of submissive pleasure. I got to my knees as her stream died to a trickle. She gave a little wiggle and then stood up, grinning maliciously down at me. I sighed and shut my eyes as she took me by the scruff of my neck and pulled me forward. My face was pushed down into the toilet bowl, right down until the tip of my nose was touching the water. I could smell her pee and the rich scent of pussy.

'Drink some!' she ordered.

I lapped obediently, tasting her in the water, only to have my face pushed right into it.

'A good mouthful, and swallow!' she demanded.

I obeyed, sucking up the dirty water until my mouth was full and then swallowing. Susan laughed and made noises of disgust and delight as I did it, then pulled my head back so that it was again just above the surface.

'Now I'm going to do it, Penny!' she crowed and then I heard the chain rasp.

I heard the rush of water and then it spurted out from around the sides of the bowl, soaking my hair and face. Susan was laughing as the mixture of water and pee bubbled up around my face, in a state of absolute glee at my utter degradation. She held my face well down, ensuring that I got properly flushed and couldn't pull back. It was in my mouth and up my nose, my hair was soaked and the collar of my blouse was wet through. When it stopped, I was whimpering and snivelling in a state of submissive bliss. Susan let go but I kept my head down in the toilet bowl.

'Beat me now,' I begged, raising my bottom for punishment.

'Slut!' she exclaimed joyfully and, a moment later, brought the bath-brush down hard across my bottom.

She gave me three firm smacks and then stopped to pull my dress up and take down my panties. The sharp sting of the bath-brush on my bare flesh made me squeal, but she took no notice, laughing at me as my bottom bounced and jiggled under her slaps.

I was beaten well, ending up with a red, throbbing bottom and in a state of full-blown submissive ecstasy. I knelt back and began to strip, peeling my clothes off hurriedly until I was naked on the bathroom floor, red-bottomed and still with the taste of pee in my mouth.

We tumbled into the bath together, with Susan on top of me. Our mouths met and we shared a long kiss as my hands went around her back. I rolled my legs up and opened my thighs, so that her belly was against my pussy, firm and soft and girlish. She moved up, rubbing herself on me, spreading her pussy on to mine. I sighed as we came together, feeling her lips rub on my clit.

'Piss on me, Penny,' she breathed as our mouths broke apart.

I obliged, squeezing my bladder until my pee sprayed out over her pussy. She gave a moan of contentment as I felt the warm liquid trickle down between the cheeks of my bottom. I was lying in a pool of it as Susan began to rub more urgently, wriggling her slim hips from side to side. My mouth opened under hers once more as she started to come, squirming her body against mine for all she was worth. I held her tight as she climaxed, only stopping when her body began to go limp in my arms.

I slid my arms down between our wet bodies and once more began to masturbate, Susan sitting up to make it easier for me. I felt completely soiled, lying in a bath of my own pee with the taste of hers in my mouth. She'd flushed my head in the lavatory and then beaten me, giving me one of my very best submissive highs. Now she was watching me masturbate with her face set in a mischievous, impish grin. I locked eyes with hers as I felt my second orgasm approaching, watching her lick her lips. Then she knelt up, opening her pussy in front of me.

'I'm going to piss on your cunt when you come, Penny,' she said quietly.

'Yes, please,' I begged and, even as I said it, my climax hit me.

Her mouth opened as she squeezed, and a jet of pale golden pee erupted from her pussy to splash on mine. It was running down my finger, warm and wet, filling my vagina and trickling down to my anus. I screamed with the pleasure of it, calling out her name even as she leant forward to embrace me.

We lay together for quite a while, neither of us speaking but bonded by the delicious intimacy of having done something really dirty together. Only when it started to get cold did I reach back and turn the taps on to bathe our soiled bodies in warm water.

14

Like a Red Rag

I'd lost. I dropped my cards on the table and slumped back
into my chair in horrified disbelief mixed with a rapidly
mounting thrill of anticipation. I looked at the ring of
faces, now suddenly above my level: Vicky, holding her
winning hand and grinning smugly at my discomfort;
Anderson, feigning concern but unable to conceal his
delight; Amber, wearing an openly sadistic smirk.

I shrugged and reached for my glass, my lip trembling as
the cool wine touched it. None of them said a word. I noticed
the little bumps of Amber's nipples pushing out the material
of her blouse. They hadn't been like that a moment before.

'Well?' I finally demanded.

Vicky rose and beckoned the others. They left the room,
Amber treating me to a wicked smile, Anderson giving me
a final knowing glance over his shoulder as he pulled the
door shut. I took another sip of wine. 'To be used any way
they choose by whoever they choose,' I'd said, out of
money but confident in winning, much too confident.

I knew them – there would be no let-off. At the very least
I could expect to have to offer myself to some yokel
smelling of hay and horses. The thought sent a shiver of
anticipation right down my spine. I could only smile at my
own dirty mind. Still, I wished it had been Vicky or Amber
who had lost instead.

The morning came, eventually; the others were relaxed and
unhurried while the tension inside me grew to an

unbearable knot in my stomach. I thought of backing out, but rebelled against it. I decided that Amber wouldn't let them choose anything too dreadful, then decided that she just might. I tried to browbeat Anderson into telling me, but he just smiled and carried on buttering a piece of toast with an infuriating nonchalance. Eventually I sat down by the window, watching clouds drift across the sky and trying not to bite my fingernails.

I must have been there for half an hour when I heard the door open and turned to see Amber. She was trying to look stern and cool, but I could sense her mounting excitement. Her hand came forward, tossing something towards me, aimed deliberately at the floor instead of into my lap. I bent forward, half-intentionally going to my knees as I reached for the little puddle of scarlet cloth.

'Put them on,' she ordered.

I obeyed, sliding my own knickers down under my skirt and replacing them with the plain red cotton briefs that she had thrown me.

'Leave them there,' she said as I made to pick up my discarded panties. 'Come with me.'

I followed her out of the room, knowing that she was well aware of the effect her casual dominance was having on me. Anderson and Vicky were waiting outside, he twisting a long piece of orange baling twine around his fingers, she testing the colours of various lipsticks on the back of her hand. They fell into step beside us as Amber led the way out on to the road and presently down an overgrown public footpath. None of them spoke, only Anderson humming to himself in an infuriating way as if we were just out for an ordinary morning stroll instead of intending to put me out for some undoubtedly humiliating sexual experience.

We must have gone about two miles when Amber stopped at a decaying wooden stile where the path opened from a wood on to a field.

'Here we are,' she said. 'Perfect, isn't it?'

Vicky and Anderson nodded appreciatively, but I was simply puzzled. There was nobody in sight and the footpath we had come along had been so overgrown that I didn't imagine that it was really used at all – certainly it didn't seem to lead anywhere. Amber crossed the stile and gestured for me to follow her. As I climbed the stile, a broad panorama of fields and hedges came into view, invisible from lower down.

'Pop your panties off, Penny,' Amber said, holding her hand out for them. 'Then kneel on the stile, facing into the wood. Anderson, the twine please.'

My whole body was trembling as I levered the panties down and passed them to Amber, then knelt on the stile. The top rung was under my belly, Vicky pushing gently down on my shoulders so that my bottom stuck right up. I felt Amber's fingers as she bound my ankles and wrists, easing my knees apart and taking my arms behind my back so that I could feel the cool, rough wood against my breasts through my blouse. I wondered if they had chosen my position so that I could be fucked from the rear or in order to beat me. In either case, it seemed an odd place to choose as they could have had me just as well in the garden, which was hardly less lonely or subject to intrusion.

My eyes then lit on the thick growth that bordered the wood, and I was sure I knew what they were going to do to me. There were nettles: tall, lush, painful-looking nettles, and they were growing in abundance. That was why I was bare under my skirt. They were going to lift it and tickle me with nettles. First it would be my bum-cheeks, then my thighs and lastly all the most sensitive areas of my pussy and bottom-slit. I imagined the pain, thinking of my pussy-lips, red, swollen and throbbing.

'Please, Amber, not nettles!' I begged as she tugged the final knot into place at my bound wrists.

'Nettles?' she asked and I heard Vicky laugh. 'Who said anything about nettles?'

'But . . .' I began.

'Slut,' she replied, slapping my bottom. 'I suppose that's what I'd have got if it had been me?'

I held my peace, hoping that some day I'd have her just as helpless and that, when I did, there would be some nettles handy to use on her plump rear-end. All three of them were behind me and I could only see part of Vicky's leg. I stayed still and passive, feeling the cool air between my legs and the gentle touch of my skirt moving against my skin in the gentle breeze. Some subtle change alerted me to someone taking hold of the hem and then my skirt was hoisted rudely up over my bottom and tucked into my belt. I felt a lump rise in my throat and knew I was blushing furiously. They had to be able to see every detail of my pussy, probably even my bumhole as well. I could feel Anderson's eyes drinking in every detail, memorising every little pink fold and crevice of my sex. I must have let out a sob, because Amber came round to speak to me. For the second time, I considered backing out, then thought of all the times I had fantasised about being in just such a position and stuck my tongue out at her instead.

I was still puzzled as to my fate and watched from the corner of my eye as Amber climbed on to Anderson's shoulders so that she could reach one of the spiky pine tree branches that overhung the field. She took something red from her pocket and hung it on a branch. It was the red knickers she had made me wear. As I watched, I felt a gentle pressure on my bottom, moving in patterns, and realised that Vicky was writing something across my bum-cheeks.

'Lonely here, isn't it, Penny, sweetheart?' Amber asked mockingly. 'In fact, it might be quite a while before anyone found you by accident. On the other hand, your tarty scarlet knickers make a signal that can be seen for miles. Now, my bet is that someone will see them and come to investigate. And when they do, what will they find? They'll find you all tied and with everything showing and 'Fuck me please' written across your seat in lipstick.

'Of course, nobody might come, in which case we'll come back and untie you after lunch, or maybe tea-time, and you'll have been spared even the shame of being seen like this. More likely, it'll be an elderly lady out walking

171

her dogs, or maybe the vicar and you'll get all the shame you can handle but your poor little pussy will miss out on her helping of cock. Personally, I hope it's six or seven strapping farm lads and they take it in turns with you, but we'll see. This is your last chance to back out. No? Well, then, see you later.'

She gave my bum a parting slap before climbing the stile. Vicky kissed me while Anderson let a hand stray briefly between my legs, loitering for an instant at the mouth of my vagina as if to hint at what was to come. I watched them walk off down the path, chatting idly about this and that and not even bothering to turn to look at me. From the instant the last blue flash of Vicky's jeans vanished between the trees, I felt utterly alone and utterly vulnerable. Most of all, I wished my bottom wasn't flaunted quite so blatantly. In some ways, I hoped I was found by somebody who would want to fuck me, or at least appreciate the view. I knew my pussy was wet and ready and nothing could be worse than being found by some frightfully respectable old lady. The thought brought the blood to my cheeks again and I wriggled in my bonds, at least hoping to make the skirt fall and cover my bottom. Unfortunately, Amber had done a thorough job and it was as much as I could do to move, let alone release the knot that she had made with the tail of my skirt to hold it in place under my belt. I tried not to make too much of a display of my struggles, because inevitably they would be watching and I didn't want to give them the satisfaction of seeing me wriggle.

Kneeling helplessly in my obscene position, I was acutely aware of every little sound around me, constantly expecting footsteps behind me or to see somebody appear round the corner of the footpath in front. By twisting my neck round, I could just make out the scarlet panties where they hung, marking me for use by anybody with the curiosity to investigate. I quickly lost all track of time, and had no idea if a few minutes or perhaps an hour had passed when I became aware that I wasn't alone any more. I had heard nothing and could see nothing, my skirt and

172

various bits of stile obscuring the view behind me. Since they had left me, the only sound had been birdsong. Possibly it had changed in volume or tone, or possibly something more subtle had changed. In any case, someone was behind me, I was sure of it. They said nothing, yet I knew that they would be staring at my nakedness, feeling either revulsion or delight at the sight of my open pink pussy and the invitation to fill it that Vicky had written across my buttocks.

Then there was a sound, a brushing noise like a foot being moved in long grass. A lump rose in my throat and I began to tremble, biting my lower lip as my breathing began to come faster. Suddenly something moist touched the skin of my thigh, inches from my sex. I gasped and jumped. Someone was tracing a slow pattern up my leg with their tongue. My exclamation made them stop and there was an agonising moment of suspense while I waited. Their face was so close to me that I could feel warm breath against my pussy-lips and expected the tongue to start again, or maybe a finger to begin exploring and probing me. It was more than I could do not to squirm in my bonds as I waited for it, certain that they would want to explore my bottom-hole as well as my vagina, expecting the tight little ring to be teased open and a rough finger to be poked up me. If they did, then there was nothing I could do about it, not even if they chose to have full anal sex with me.

Nothing happened, though; the tension building inside me with the expectation. Every moment was stretched out. I wanted to scream in frustration at their silence and lack of response. The stile creaked faintly under a shift of weight and I tensed, expecting to have my pussy tongued or filled with cock at any second. Again, nothing happened; only a curious shuffling noise and a quiet grunt.

'Fuck me then, damn you!' I screamed, my nerve finally breaking. 'Just put it in, you bastard!'

There was no response. I wondered if it might not just be my friends tormenting me, when, without the slightest warning, he mounted me. One moment there was nothing, then my vagina was full of cock and his coarse pubes were rubbing against the tender skin between my bottom-cheeks. He took off at a frantic pace, thrusting deep into me, his breath coming in strange little gasps. I couldn't help moaning yet found myself cursing him for the way he was using me in between my gasps and pants. Some of his weight was on my back and I could feel the coarse wool of his clothing against the skin of my bottom and thighs.

It was over in an instant. One moment he was pumping like a madman, then he had withdrawn and something warm and damp was trickling down between my pussy-lips. He didn't say a word but just left me sobbing in helpless frustration, feeling utterly soiled but desperately needing my own orgasm.

'Bring me off, please!' I begged, ashamed of myself even as I said it.

He gave a little sound, more of a noncommittal grunt than a laugh, then nothing and I realised that he had left as casually as he had arrived.

'Damn you! Bastard! Inconsiderate sod!' I screamed.

There was no answer.

'Amber!' I called.

She didn't answer, either.

'Come on, Amber,' I pleaded, 'I know you're watching. I've been had now, so please untie me. Amber?'

My tone turned to pleading but there was still no response and I realised that, for some reason, they really weren't there. A wave of panic threatened to engulf me; then I heard a voice and, to my utter relief, saw Vicky coming around the corner.

'Sorry, Penny,' she began, her fingers going to the knots at my wrists. 'We met old Mrs Greenaway from the post office halfway back and only just managed to stop her coming here! We only meant to leave you a little while and then Amber was going to come up behind you, pretend to be someone else and fuck you with the strap-on . . .'

She had climbed on the stile to get a better view of my bonds, and coincidentally of my pussy. When she stopped talking so suddenly, I knew exactly what she was looking at. I hung my head as an intense flush of humiliation went through me.

174

'Hey!' she exclaimed, 'You've been . . .'

'Yeah,' I replied, 'used by some bastard who didn't even stop to say thank you. Please tell me it was Anderson.'

'No, Anderson was with us.'

I sighed, overwhelmed by a flood of emotions but sure of one thing. I had to come, and I had to come tied up over that stile with my bare arse in the air and my knickers dangling from the branch. Vicky was still stammering apologies and expressions of horrified amazement.

'Vicky,' I said. 'Shut up. Thank you. Now go down on my pussy and don't stop licking until I say you can.'

She stopped working at the knots. For a moment I thought she was going to turn me down, then the stile creaked as she shifted into a more comfortable position and I felt the soft, gentle touch of her tongue-tip on my clit.

15

Dairy Time

The main benefit of academic life is the intellectual reward. Next to that comes the holidays. After a year in my lectureship, I was badly in need of a break, and was greatly looking forward to the summer. Best of all, I would be staying with Amber Oakley, and while my sex life had perked up from the doldrums of my first two terms, it was not what it might be. I hadn't seen Amber at all since Easter and, as I drove south, my thoughts were fixed on the pleasures of licking pussy, cuddling boobs, girly spankings and all the clever, subtle and, above all, dirty things she liked me to do.

Sometimes a long gap without seeing someone makes it difficult to re-establish the intimacy that one had before. Amber had a very simple way of getting round this. As I bent to put my cases on the floor, she pushed me down over the bed. An instant later, she had straddled my back and was pulling my skirt up. All I could do was laugh, giggling helplessly as she exposed my seat. Of course, my panties had to come down, and I made a plainly fake show of protest as she peeled them off my bum.

The spanking was great, applied with all her skill until my bottom was warm and throbbing and I was feeling as submissive towards her and as aroused by her as I ever had. I knew what would come next, her favourite way of reaching orgasm. This consisted of sitting on my face and having me tongue her bottom-hole while she frigged herself. It felt both naughty and servile to have my tongue back up her bottom where it belonged, and I actually came before she did, with my legs apart and my panties stretched taut between my knees where she had left them. After that, we went to bed, and stayed there until morning, rising only to fetch a plate of sandwiches at some time in the early hours of the morning.

In the morning, it was as if I had never been away, except that we had plenty of news for each other and were even more tactile together than usual. The thing that particularly excited her was not one of her own fantastic erotic creations, but something that Michael and Ginny Scott had come up with. They were the couple who had introduced us, and I was fond of both of them, but particularly Ginny. She was big and blonde, and had the most magnificent chest, really the very opposite of me in looks. Sexually she was playful and liberated and enjoyed many of the same things that I did. He was tall, dark and cool, and one of the few men I felt really comfortable in front of.

Amber refused to tell me what they were up to, but hinted that it was unusual even by her standards and promised that we would drive over on the following day. I was shut in a cupboard while she called Ginny, and then taken out into the paddock for a much-needed session of pony-girl play.

She was no more informative the next day, but kept teasing me and then spanked me to shut me up, which I felt was really unfair. Of course, that's just the sort of treatment that's best for me, and it put me on a nice plateau of excitement as we drove down to Wiltshire and Ginny and Michael's cottage in Broadheath.

The thing about Ginny Scott was that she was one of those rare people who manage to reach full adulthood without having the playful, carefree side of their sexualities eroded in any way. Most people either find themselves forced to conform by their jobs or are too scared of rejection to really let themselves go. Ginny was lucky. Not only was she gorgeous but, as the daughter of a wealthy farmer, she had never really had to worry about what other people thought. The only elements of sexual repression in her life had been her school and her tyrannical elder brother. Both of these factors only seemed to have served to make her naughty as well as liberated. She had also known Amber since their school days, which must certainly have made a difference.

She greeted both Amber and me with hugs and kisses, Michael with his normal cool poise and friendly, knowing smile. The word voluptuous might have been coined for Ginny and, since I had last seen her, she had filled out even more. She was wearing a loose white blouse, tied between her breasts to leave her midriff bare. The button of her trousers was also undone, so that the whole of her soft, sweetly rounded tummy was showing. She had no bra on under her blouse, which meant that her big, pillow-like breasts were clearly outlined, with her nipples showing through and making little humps in the cotton. Her trousers were black corduroy, and so full of well-fleshed bottom, thigh and pussy that I found myself licking suddenly dry lips. I've always preferred girls to be fairly tall and well endowed, but Ginny was something else.

'Haven't you been exercising her properly?' Amber asked Michael as she cast an appraising glance over the magnificence of Ginny's figure.

'Every weekend, just about,' Michael replied. 'She runs as well as ever, although I haven't raced her for a while. No, the extra flesh has more than a little to do with our new game.'

'Oh yes?' I queried, wondering what sort of sexual depravity involved deliberately fattening a girl up.

When he said he'd been exercising her, he was referring to having her as his pony-girl, rather than having sex with her, which I'm sure he did more than just at weekends. Leastways, if I'd been him, I'd have wanted her every five minutes.

'Hm, interesting,' Amber commented, taking a pinch of Ginny's bottom between her fingers. 'Still, I take it you'll beat her for it, anyway?'

'Of course,' Michael answered.

'Any more of that and you'll be the one with a smacked bottom, Miss Amber Oakley,' Ginny retorted. 'I may be more submissive than you, but I'm bigger too, so watch out.'

'Softer too,' Amber laughed and smacked her friend's bottom.

'Anyway,' Michael said, interrupting before things got out of hand, 'we've set it all up in the park, so let's drive up after lunch and we'll show you.'

No one would tell me anything during lunch, and it quickly became plain that Amber only knew some of it. The park was what had once been Ginny's family's estate, but was now a mixture of wood and scrub with a lake at the centre. The only buildings were the ruins of the old house, the stables, a boathouse and a tiny lodge. We had played there often before, and it was a place of which both Amber and I had many fond memories.

It had changed quite a bit since I had last seen it. Michael had finally begun to have the rubble of the old house cleared and explained to us that most of his earnings were going into an attempt to make the place habitable once more. The stables were the only part of the old structure in perfect condition, stalls and so forth set around a cobbled yard. This was where they kept their pony-cart and had set up whatever device they were intending to show us.

Amber and I were told to take a leisurely walk around the park, which we did, hand in hand and talking over old memories. Although it was in fact only just over a year since I had first set foot in the place, it seemed much longer and, by the time we returned to the stables, I was in a very nostalgic mood. I was also quite aroused, having been round a track on which I had been driven as a pony-girl and seen several places that brought back memories of passionate sexual encounters.

Michael was standing outside one of the stable doors, his mouth set in a pleased smile. I could hear a strange noise, mechanical but nothing immediately recognisable. He beckoned us and we approached him.

'Ladies,' he announced with a polite bow, 'may I present to you our latest creation – the cow-girl.'

When he said that, I expected Ginny to emerge from the stable in some sort of fancy American Western outfit, all chaps and rawhide thongs. That would have been fun, but a bit of an anticlimax. As it was, when Michael threw back the door, I was left completely speechless.

Ginny was on all fours, stark naked, with her golden curls halfcovering her face and with a look that was simultaneously submissive, wanton, shame-faced and aroused. I had seen Ginny drink pee from another girl's pussy before, and she hadn't looked even slightly ashamed of herself. She did now, and I could see why.

She was attached to a milking machine.

In her kneeling position her big, dangling breasts could reasonably have been described as udders, and they had adapted the suction cups to fit her nipples. The thing was on and Ginny's breathing was coming at the same rhythm as its suction, her eyes closing in ecstasy each time it drew at her flesh. Her fat breasts moved oddly as the machine sucked at them, ripples going through the soft flesh in time to the pump. Her nipples were swollen and drawn out into the suction cups, the dark skin visible through the clear plastic. So was something else, a white fluid that squirted from what I couldn't help thinking of as her teats each time the machine sucked – milk.

'You're milking her!' Amber exclaimed. 'I knew ... but ...'

Whatever they had told her, she obviously hadn't expected the reality, any more than I had. I actually felt weak at the knees. What Ginny was having done to her was so sexy, yet so indecent, that I could only stare. It was obviously putting her in heaven as well, judging from the expression on her face. This was no example of some unfortunate girl being forced into an unspeakable perversion by some twisted male; she was loving every second of it.

The rest of the set-up was pretty good, too. The machine was powered by a small diesel engine and she was in a stall with straw on the ground, conditions no better than a real cow would have been given.

I'd always known Ginny was a dirty bitch, but this really took the prize. True, she obviously was just a little bit ashamed of herself, but from my own experience I knew that that would just make the experience all the finer. Michael, as always, was completely cool.

'Would you care for a glass?' he asked politely. 'She's producing well, today; we might get a couple of pints or even more.'

He was right; the milk could be seen running from Ginny's teats and down to a valve of some sort, then along a tube to a bucket. It was squirting in at a good rate and already looked an inch or so deep. I could smell it too, a recognisably milky smell, but not quite the same as cow's milk.

'I'd love a glass,' Amber managed. 'But how did you manage it? She's not pregnant, is she?'

'No, no,' Michael replied casually as he walked over to their car. 'We got the idea from an old wives' tale, literally. Do you remember old Mrs Burrell?'

Amber shook her head.

'No, I don't suppose you would,' he continued. 'Anyway, she used to be Ginny's nurse, and both her brothers' before that. She's pushing eighty now but, one time when Ginny visited her, she claimed that, when she was little, a local woman had been a professional wet nurse and had been able to start her milk flowing more or less to order. We were a bit sceptical, but did some research and discovered that sufficient massage sometimes causes lactation to start – if the hormonal balance is right, anyway. We both wanted to try, so we borrowed an old machine from her brothers' farm and well, there we are.'

I looked back to Ginny, who was sighing gently as she was milked and looked as if she was about ready to come. It was certainly a wonderful fantasy, and both Michael and Amber were clearly getting a big kick out of just being there while she was attached to the machine. So was I, but, being mainly submissive, I would have preferred to have been in Ginny's place, or by her side, on all fours, naked and with my own little titties being sucked. Of course, I wouldn't have been able to add to the milk, so it wouldn't ever have been quite perfect. On the other hand, a nice, dirty fantasy was beginning to form in my head, one that would let me get the most out of Ginny and Michael's extraordinarily perverse achievement.

First, however, it was only fair to help Ginny to her undoubtedly badly needed climax. I urgently wanted myself dealt with, preferably stripped and humiliated before being allowed to come, but could wait. Like so many dominant roles, for Amber, Michael and I this meant being cool while the submissive got worked up to an unbearable peak. Michael had fetched three glasses from the car, half-pint tumblers eminently suitable for drinking milk out of. I was trembling, but knew better than to show my feelings, instead treating Ginny just as if she were an actual cow and we were three dairy hands sampling her produce.

Michael dipped a glass into the bucket of Ginny-milk and passed it to Amber, then filled one for me and finally himself. My hand was shaking so hard that I nearly spilt it, but I managed to take a gulp, and let it run over my tongue and around my mouth so that I could savour it fully. It was good: rich, yet oddly sharp.

I swallowed my mouthful, watching Amber and Michael drink theirs. Both looked well pleased with themselves and were watching Ginny as they tasted her milk. Despite my own need, I decided to try and humiliate Ginny even more.

'Have you tried making cheese?' I asked.

'Not yet,' Michael replied evenly, 'although I had considered it.'

'I think it would be a bit like goat's cheese,' Amber suggested.

'Perhaps,' Michael agreed, 'or sheep's. We did run up some clotted cream, though. I made her sell it at a stall at Broadheath market, in little tubs. It was very popular, and the experience humiliated her almost as much as actually being milked in the first place.'

'Beautiful,' I said, unable to hold my poise any longer.

'Well,' Michael sighed, 'I suppose I'd better do the honours before she runs dry. She does like to come while her teats are still running. She likes it veterinary style. But I'm not being a very good host, am I? Would either of you like to do it?'

'Yes, please,' Amber asked, her voice less than entirely calm.

I heard Ginny groan, and turned my attention to her. She had turned her bottom to us and lifted it, giving a pretty display of her plump, wet pussy and the puckered ring of her anus. I was still admiring the view as Amber snapped on a rubber glove and came over. 'Veterinary style' obviously involved fisting the cow-girl and letting her bring herself off against something hard. The something hard proved to be the main tube of the milking machine, which was not only warm but vibrated.

Having occasionally taken a sneaky moment of pleasure by putting the pump hose against my pussy while I filled my car with petrol, I think I have a fair idea how Ginny felt. Twenty pounds' worth of petrol is never enough to bring me off, but I reckon that if I owned a bigger car I might have made it once or twice.

Ginny certainly had no trouble. She must have been really high on the experience of being milked, and I could just imagine how having her nipples sucked into the cups must have felt. The erotic humiliation must have been exceptional as well, perhaps stronger even than being a piggy-girl, which is my personal favourite kink of the type. Add to that the vibrating hose and having Amber's well-lubricated fist working her vagina open and it wasn't surprising that, within a minute of Amber starting, Ginny had begun to moan and push her bottom up.

Fisting is not my favourite thing, but it's certainly nice, and Amber had learnt her technique from a girl called Melody, who in turn had learnt it in San Francisco, where I'm told it's something of a fine art. Anyway, she quickly managed to burrow most of her hand into Ginny's vagina and was working it inside her and rubbing on her clit with the pump hose. Ginny was always noisy, but she really screamed this time when she came, pushing her bottom back and clutching at the straw underneath her. It lasted ages, and only when Amber made her own choice to take her hand out of her friend's pussy did Ginny finally ask to be taken out of role.

I had been standing next to Michael throughout this, and getting increasingly steamed up. So had he, although, being Mr Cool, he showed this by simply taking my wrist and putting my hand to his crotch. His cock was already out, which I hadn't noticed and, by the time Ginny came, it was stiff in my hand. I continued to nurse his erection while Amber disconnected Ginny from the milking machine.

'Go on, Michael, pop her on,' was the first thing that Ginny said, when the cups had been pulled off her nipples.

Neither of us needed any encouragement. His hand was already up my skirt, fondling my bottom through my panties. When Ginny suggested he fuck me, I simply reached up under my skirt and pulled off my panties. Michael took me by the hips, lifting me with ease. As Ginny had suggested, he simply popped me on his cock, sliding inside without difficulty. I put my hands on his shoulders to steady myself and then just relaxed into it. He held me by the bottom, with the cheeks pulled apart and a little finger just touching my anus. I was soon panting and groaning as he bounced me up and down on his erection, never losing his poise until the moment he actually came inside me. Even then he just groaned, continuing to bounce me until he had drained himself dry up my pussy.

It was all hugs and kisses and excited conversation after that. Amber wanted to milk Ginny by hand when she felt ready for another go. Ginny was all for this, loving being the centre of attention as always. My own suggestion excited her even more, and it was agreed that we'd do it that evening after dinner. I was going to be Ginny's baby.

Once I knew what I was going to get, I couldn't come down from my sexual high. My idea was really dirty, and very, very humiliating for me. It also demanded Ginny being in a dominant role, which she was keen on as, with Michael, she never really had the chance.

This was even more true after Amber had given her her hand-milking and made her drink the results herself. Watching Ginny lap her own milk out of a bucket was too much for Amber, and Michael and I watched while she poured some on to her pussy and had Ginny lick until she came. She had a long skirt of plain white wool on, underneath which she took her knickers off and then just hitched up. She looked wonderful, demure yet dirty as Ginny lapped at her milk-soaked pussy. That had me hornier than ever, and I was getting desperate for my own go.

We went back to their house after that, with both Amber and I still pantyless under our skirts. As soon as we were in the door Amber took me by the hand and pulled me upstairs to get me ready. Ginny had gone to take a quick shower, and then joined us. She dressed while I sat on the bed, choosing a plain blue skirt and a big woolly jumper. I like my partners big and strong anyway, but my small size in comparison to theirs was really highlighted by the fantasy we were about to play out. Once Ginny was dressed, we were ready. First they stripped me, pulling my clothes off without my assistance. When I was naked, Amber carried me into the bathroom and put me down in the tub. Ginny had already filled it, and checked the temperature with her elbow before I was lowered in.

Michael came up to watch me bathed, and to video my self-imposed degradation. He leant on the door frame, camera in one hand, with his face set in a cool grin. I was scrubbed down, using a stiff brush and plenty of soap. This left me pink and tingling all over, but they were far from finished. They completed the job of washing me, then they took me out of the bath, towelled me down and sat me on the bathroom chair. Ginny held my legs apart while shaving foam was rubbed in between them, over my pussy mound and down between my bum-cheeks. Amber shaved my pussy, slowly, taking care to get at every crevice and fold while Ginny held me spread and helpless. Once my pussy was smooth and bald, not to mention moist and swollen, they turned me over. Ginny held my bum-cheeks apart while Amber rubbed cream in. It stung my bumhole, but she shaved my bottom with the same thoroughness she had shown my pussy, leaving me slick and hairless down between my cheeks. Michael videoed all of this, sometimes so close up that, I knew that when it was played back, the whole screen would be filled by incredibly detailed shots of my pussy being shaved or of Amber stretching my bottom-hole out to shave around the ring.

They then washed my pussy and bum again, and rubbed soothing cream in before starting to powder me. Every inch of my body was done, from feet to face, powdered and slapped a bit to distribute the powder. Inevitably they concentrated on my more sensitive areas, especially my titties, powdering each, slapping them lightly, flicking my erect nipples until I couldn't help but start whimpering. They ignored me, just turning me over to give my bottom another dose of powder and slaps and then turning me completely upside down to show off my newly shaved underside. That was filmed, too, the girls making sure that my legs stayed well spread and repeatedly exploring my pussy and anus with their fingers, just to make sure that I was really clean. By the time they had inspected me to their satisfaction, I was limp and helpless in their arms, my breathing was coming deep and strong and my need for an orgasm had risen until it was barely tolerable.

'We should take her temperature,' Amber said decisively.

'Absolutely,' Ginny agreed. 'You get her in position; I'll find the thermometer.'

I knew they weren't going to put it in my mouth, but up my bottom. Sure enough, Amber quickly had me down across her lap and once more pulled my bum-cheeks apart. I was shivering with sexual humiliation, aware that Michael could see every detail of my freshly shaved fanny and bum. I saw Ginny hand her a tub of Vaseline and a thermometer, and a moment later I felt a well-lubricated finger invade my anus. Michael was close, filming every detail as Amber opened my bottom-hole and then slid the thermometer in. I squeezed my anus on to it, hardly able to feel the thermometer, but knowing how dirty it would look on film.

Amber held me gently over her lap with the thermometer sticking out of my bottom for three whole minutes, then pulled it out and read my temperature off as normal. Michael filmed this in detail, and then a close-up of my greasy bottom-hole, which I tightened and relaxed for him, deliberately making it pulse. I felt so rude and so helpless, completely irresponsible, yet fully aware that if I did anything really disgusting it would earn me a spanking.

'We'd better put her in a nappy,' Amber said, as if reading my thoughts.

Ginny went to the bathroom cupboard, quickly finding a big white beach towel and an over-large safety pin. Amber turned me over and sat me down on the towel, which Ginny had folded into a triangle. Working with a truly nursemaid-like efficiency, Amber pulled together the three corners and pinned them at the front, over my tummy. I put my thumb in my mouth and began to suck, adding yet another touch to my submissive bliss.

Ginny left the room briefly, and I stayed quiet until she came back. She was carrying two big pink ribbons, which they tied in my hair, making bunches at either side.

'I think she's ready,' Ginny declared, standing back to admire her handiwork.

I certainly felt ready. I was in nappies, sitting splay-legged on the floor, shaved, creamed and powdered, my hair in ribbons and my thumb in my mouth, completely theirs, and best of all, about to be breast-fed, for real.

'Doesn't she look sweet!' Amber exclaimed. 'Come on, Penny, crawl a bit, then it's feeding time.'

I rolled over obediently, crawling to show off my nappy-clad bottom and my little dangling titties. Their big bathroom mirror showed my reflection, crawling naked but for the bulge of the nappy around my hips and over my bottom, with the pink ribbons making me look really girly and pathetic. It looked so rude that it made my head swim. I was also beginning to feel not just the emotional urge, but a real need to pee, and knew that when I did I would just wet myself, filling my nappy in front of them and on film so that I could relive my humiliation later. First, I wanted to be fed.

Ginny wanted to feed me, too. When I had given them a good eyeful of me crawling around the bathroom floor in my nappy and nothing else, she picked me up and carried me through to the bedroom. I expected to be put straight to Ginny's breast, but don't suppose I should really have been surprised when she tipped me over her knee instead. She pulled my nappy down at the back, just far enough to get at my bum. Her arm went around my waist and she started to spank me, not hard, but just enough to bring the blood to my cheeks. She told me that I was a naughty girl while she did it, waiting until I started to whimper before pulling up my nappy. I felt really contrite and punished, knowing that my bottom-cheeks would have red tops and that I was now going to be given a good cuddle after my spanking.

Ginny turned me over and cradled me in her arms, hugging and whispering sorry in my ear. My head was resting against the plump softness of her huge breasts, which made me feel wonderfully protected and small. She smelt faintly of milk, too, making me all the more urgent to feed, and I began to nuzzle at her jumper. She sighed as she pulled it up. She had a maternity bra on, which she unzipped, pulling out her breasts right in my face. Her jumper was up just far enough for me to get at her nipple, as if she were embarrassed to be seen feeding me. I nuzzled again, my open mouth touching the flesh of her boob, then finding the nipple.

She pulled the jumper up a little more and I began to suckle, shutting my eyes in utter bliss as her milk began to flow into my mouth. It was warm and rich, sweet yet oddly sharp, and quite simply the most delicious thing that I had ever tasted. It had been nice drunk from a glass, but to be feeding at her breast was an experience so wonderful that I quickly had tears in my eyes. I sucked and swallowed, her nipple stiff in my mouth, the milk coming in little squirts against my tongue. She was sighing gently, as deep in as I was. I pulled her jumper up more, pushing my face into the soft, fat cushion of her boob, sucking eagerly.

My head was pillowed on her chest, her left arm supporting my back and head, her right draped over my waist. My tears were flowing freely down my cheeks as I took hold of her boob with one hand, squeezing the soft flesh into my mouth. My whole world was Ginny's body and my own, the firm nipple in my mouth, the plump breast in my face, the feel of the nappy around my hips, the desperate, urgent need to masturbate.

I slid my free hand down the front of my nappy to find my pussy. The smooth skin felt exquisitely rude and, not surprisingly, I was soaking. Ginny eased her right arm under me and I knew that she had put a hand to her own pussy. We began to masturbate together, utterly wrapped up in each other, oblivious to everything else, including the fact that we were being filmed.

'Do it in your nappy, Penny,' Ginny sighed.

I nodded around my mouthful of nipple.

'I want to come when your nappy's wet, and with your pee all over my lap,' she moaned. 'Come on, darling, do it all over me.'

My bladder was taut with pee and ready to do exactly what she wanted, yet I was in such bliss that I couldn't bear to bring it to an end so quickly. Still, my middle finger was busy with my clit and I knew I could only hold it off for so long, both orgasm and urine.

'Do it, Penny, wet your nappy for me, please!' Ginny begged.

I couldn't resist any more, and let go, the pee gushing out of my pussy, all over my hand, into my nappy and down my legs. Ginny groaned as the warm, wet pee began to trickle on to her, but, maybe because my bottom had been Vaselined, I felt something else start to happen. I clenched my anus quickly, but my orgasm was building and it was just too much. Ginny must have felt my muscles tense, because she groaned again.

'Oh, you're not, Penny,' she sighed. 'Oh, you are; yes, do it, Penny, do it in your nappy, Penny!'

Her voice had risen to a near scream and, as she started to come, I surrendered my last pretence of reserve and just did what nature wanted me to do. My bumhole opened and I was filling my nappy even as I too started to come. Ginny knew exactly what I was doing, which made me want to let go even more. I felt it squeezing out and up between my bum-cheeks as she hit her climax. She called my name, tensing underneath me even as my own muscles started to contract.

I was coming. My mouth was full of Ginny's milk, my nappy sodden with pee and full of my own dirt. There was plenty of it, and more was coming. I could feel its weight in the nappy as the pressure built up in my head until I thought it would burst. I was totally out of control, surrendered to pleasure without a thought for anything else, nor capable of controlling myself had I wanted to. I squeezed another piece out of my bottom, revelling in the sensation. Then the bubble burst and I was biting and sucking at Ginny's nipple, plunging my hand down my nappy, rubbing frantically at my clit, kicking, wriggling, pulling away from her because I just had to scream, only to fill my mouth with soft, fat breast flesh once more.

Finally it was over and I was lying limp and soiled over Ginny's lap. Someone pulled the back of my nappy down so that it was obvious what I'd done, and I remembered the video camera.

'That's a wrap,' Michael said, but his voice wasn't cool any more: it was hoarse and thick.

Then Amber was picking me up very gently and carrying me into the bathroom. My eyes were shut and, if there were tears in them, then they were tears of pure joy.

16

Boot Black

The seed for one of my most exquisite fantasies came quite
by chance as I was driving back from a conference at
Exeter University and stopped in one of the lay-bys on
Salisbury Plain. As I sat nibbling a sandwich and sipping
at a carton of milk, I decided that I needed a pee badly
enough not to want to wait until I reached the services.
Unfortunately, no sooner had I got out of the car and
selected a clump of hazel as a discreet location to relieve
myself, than another car pulled into the lay-by and
discharged a number of noisy oiks. I had been in the act of
undoing my jeans and felt myself blush as I briefly made
eye contact with one of their leering faces and caught part
of a joking remark that I was certain was directed at me.
The idea of driving on induced a pang of stubborn
resentment at their interruption of my privacy and so I
followed a track that cut twin ruts into the bone-white
chalk. It went in the direction of a large stand of scrub in
which I was sure to have privacy.

Once well hidden in the scrub, it was the work of a
moment to pop my jeans and panties down and enjoy that
glorious feeling of release that accompanies a much-needed
pee. Decent again, I set off back to the car, only to be
brought up short by the sound of raucous laughter from
the direction I was going in. My first assumption was that
the oiks had come the same way or even decided to follow
me and I felt a distinct pang of apprehension and found
myself wishing the little wood was a bit less lonely. I

moved off in the other direction, hoping to skirt the wood and so reach my car, but the snap of a twig brought me up short.

'The little shit's in 'ere somewhere,' a male voice called, coarse and unsympathetic, and my apprehension turned to outright fear. The noises seemed to be coming from all sides and I was close to panic. The dense spring foliage prevented me from seeing anything but also mercifully hid me, yet any determined searchers were sure to find me and it wasn't a risk I wanted to take. I looked up, the canopy of the little wood a blur of fresh green in uneven sunlight, and decided on my best chance. A moment later I was several feet above the ground, balanced precariously in the V of two branches and realising that the small branches that supported the denser foliage would never take my weight.

''E's in the middle bit, I reckon,' the voice sounded again. 'Bob, you get round the far side.'

'Yes, Corp,' another voice, presumably that of Bob, replied.

He? Corp? Suddenly I felt extremely silly. The oiks in the car were probably long gone, and I had blundered into some sort of army tomfoolery. I was just about to call out, now concerned with the possibility of being accidentally shot rather than raped, when there was a crack from below me. I looked down to see a man in army outfit standing beneath me and looking around in a state of alarm. Before I had a chance to say anything, two other men leapt out and grappled the first to the ground. The three were laughing, the first making half-hearted protests while the others called out for their comrades.

I decided to stay put in the hope that no one would look up, now more out of embarrassment than fear. This may sound foolish, but when I was at school and our illegal 'camp' was discovered by some of the mistresses, I had climbed a tree and escaped detection while my friends had all been caught. People just don't look up very much, at least not without reason, and so I stayed very still and watched the men below me.

As it was, they were making so much noise that, had a

rhinoceros chosen that moment to charge through the undergrowth, they would probably not have noticed. Amid laughter and cries of mock protest, the first soldier, a young blond man, was pushed on to his front and had his trousers pulled forcibly down, revealing muscular young buttocks that squirmed deliciously as he struggled to escape. Another man, not much older but with two stripes on his sleeves, produced a can of boot polish and a stiff brush, smeared the black mess liberally over his hapless companion's writhing buttocks and then rubbed it well in with the brush while the others laughed uproariously at their own humour.

They didn't take long and, when they had finished, they walked off through the woods laughing together and obviously in the best of humour. I climbed down from the tree and returned to the car, supposing I had witnessed some sort of initiation ceremony. There was no sign of the yobs, who presumably had never had the slightest intention of pursuing me. I drove on, and when I eventually got to Amber's, I gave her an only slightly abridged version of the story.

That should have been that, but the sight of the army boy getting his muscular little bum boot-blacked wouldn't go away. I masturbated over it until I was sore, first just over the memory and then over the fantasy of having it done to me.

I asked Amber to play out the fantasy, which she did with relish, first stripping me in the scullery and spanking me with the shoe brush. She then blacked my bum, rubbing it up to a glossy black ball, which she showed me in the mirror before rolling me over. She gave me a few seconds to squeal for mercy and then sat her glorious bottom squarely in my face, wriggling well in and laughing at my muffled protests. I knew exactly what she wanted, and was quickly licking her bottom-hole while she masturbated. She then made me do it to myself while I admired my bottom in the mirror. It was a great session, but it didn't really satisfy. Amber would have been hurt if I'd told her that it hadn't worked, so I was tactful and held my peace.

193

What I wanted to happen was for me to be out in the country one day, perhaps on Salisbury Plain, or Dartmoor, or any of the other places where the army train. I would be caught by a group of army boys out for a laugh. That was an essential part of the fantasy; they had to just think it was funny, something done for a bit of sport, regardless of my depth of shame and physical discomfort.

Once they caught me they'd strip me and make me suck their cocks one by one, maybe fuck me or even take me up the bum. When I was lying naked in the mud, covered in sperm and sore in both my pussy and bottom-hole, they would roll me over and black my bottom. Finally, they'd tie my hands behind my back, piss all over me and leave me there to be found in my filthy, degraded state. I'd rub myself off against a stone or something and eventually hit an orgasm that I just knew would be mind-blowing.

Of course, there was absolutely no chance whatever of it happening and, like all rape fantasies, I didn't really want it to. The problem was that, to get the best out of it, things had to be out of my control. In practice, that sort of fantasy only works when the one being molested is actually in control, at least at the start. I'd done some pretty dirty things in my time, most of them involving my own pain and humiliation, yet not once had I ever relinquished that final right to stop if I had to, or at the very least felt that I could really stop it if I wanted. Even when I'd lost my anal virginity, and the massively powerful Aran Ray had held me tight in his arms and forced his cock into my chocolate-smeared bumhole, I knew that if I'd screamed the place down he'd have stopped dead and been begging my forgiveness within seconds.

Not that my need to be boot-blacked was at all similar. Aran had been lucky that he'd found a dirty slut for a girlfriend, but if you try to bugger enough girls you'll eventually find a willing one. The boot-black fantasy was just far too specialised and, while I could meet any number of army boys, the chance of any one of them wanting to black my bum up was insignificantly small, never mind a group of them. True, they might try and chat me up but, from bitter experience, I knew that they'd all try and be nice to me and each would want me for himself, so I wouldn't even get gang-banged. Not only that, but in my fantasy the army boys were over-muscled, pea-brained Neanderthals driven entirely by testosterone. Of course, they're not really like that, or they'd never get into the army in the first place, and what I was most likely to meet was a bunch of jack-the-lad types, who really do nothing for me at all.

So I gave up, contenting myself with the fantasy and a pleasant memory of seeing the army cadet boot-blacked in the wood.

By the summer, I'd put the fantasy to the back of my mind. Amber and I, along with Vicky Belstone and her boyfriend Anderson Croom, had taken a cottage in Devon for a fortnight and I was looking forward to two weeks of good company, excellent food and even better sex. The cottage was called Manga Farm, and was well on to Dartmoor, which provided a degree of seclusion that was exactly what we wanted.

I went down ahead of the others, intending to get the cottage warm and generally sort things out. Having eventually found it, with the aid of a map and some local advice, I discovered that it was everything I could have hoped for. Tiny and set into a hillside, it contained just two bedrooms and a communal living room and kitchen. It had been renovated from little more than a ruin, and there was no other building in sight of it: just the wide open moor and a great tract of pine forest. I was delighted, and explored a little before starting to make things comfortable. Only when I opened the chest of drawers in the bedroom I had chosen for Amber and me did anything puncture my state of relaxed cheerfulness. In the top drawer, exactly in the centre of the middle compartment, was a tin of black boot-polish.

It had to be coincidence. Amber had booked the cottage by phone and, although she'd been at school only a few miles away, at the time it had only been a ruined farmhouse, so she'd never even seen it. Anderson had known about it as well, but I had no reason to think that he'd been there since we'd decided to hire it. Amber might well have told him and Vicky about my boot-black fantasy, yet I couldn't see them driving four hundred miles just to torment me. After all, if they wanted to boot-black me, they could do it at any time they wanted. I decided it probably was coincidence and that the polish must have been left by the previous occupants. I did remain suspicious, though, and it put me in a slightly nervous mood as I finished getting the cottage ready.

I masturbated over the fantasy again that night, and then slept like a log. I woke early, breakfasted and then went outside to see what the day promised. The sky was cloudless, the moor baking in the sun, a great sheet of pale yellow, dun and vivid green stretching up to the darker heather and bog of the higher hills. It was early and I was completely alone, tempting me to walk down to the river to wash. I went in naked, which was bliss, with the cold water making my skin tingle and popping my nipples out. I ran back up to the cottage naked as well, just for the devilment of it and, by the time I had dried and dressed, I was in a thoroughly naughty mood.

The others weren't due until lunch time, and so I struck out on to the high moor in order to stretch my legs and get an appetite up. The ground rose quite steeply behind the cottage, building up to a plateau of rough grass and bog pools which was the river's head. There was just me, the lonely moor and the sky. Only when I had crossed the worst of the bog to a cairn at the very peak of a hill did I see anybody else. A line of walkers were coming along the hillside below me, five of them, their details indistinct in the distance. Their path was going to intersect mine if I continued, and so I changed direction, feeling antipathetic to human company for no particular reason. I aimed for something that was marked as a 'peat cut' on the map, curious as to what it might be.

I had gone no more than five hundred yards when I realised that they had subtly changed their direction as well, so that they would again intersect my path. Assuming them to have merely found a better path, I once more changed my route. Again they changed theirs and, as they were now closer, I could make out the pattern of camouflage markings on their clothes. Remembering the boot-black, I felt a twinge of suspicion, but dismissed it. There were five of them, not three, and to guess I was going to go for a walk and then pinpoint me on the open moor would have taken a lot of organising and luck. No, they had to be real army, but they were definitely aiming to cross my path. It suddenly occurred to me that I might have strayed into an area reserved for training and that I might be due a telling-off when they came up with me. Feeling rather embarrassed, I struck off at right angles, more or less back towards the cottage. The map showed another peat cut in front of me, and I made for it, hoping that it was some sort of path.

It was an obviously man-made gash in the peat, cut right down to the bare granite below. It was a good six feet deep and hid me completely, also enabling me to walk at full speed. Of course, it also meant that I could see nothing but the banks of peat and the sky, which made me nervous, perhaps unreasonably so. I didn't fancy being ticked off by some army type and hurried on.

The peat cut ended at the top of a gully where a stream had cut into the hillside. It was quite deep, and choked with boulders and rowan trees, making hard going but good cover. I jumped to the top of a boulder and looked back, finding my view of the higher ground cut off by the bulge of the hill. I could see nobody and was breathing a sigh of relief when I caught a flash of movement at the point where the peat cut crossed the skyline.

I began to move down the gully, telling myself not to be silly but with a rising feeling of panic in my stomach and throat all the same. About halfway down, I realised my mistake. Glancing behind me, I saw two of them emerge from the peat cut and move to either side, running along the side of the valley where bog gave way to firm ground. I would be trapped in a pincer, with two ahead of me and three behind.

Several thoughts were going through my head simultaneously. It seemed most likely that they were simply going through the manoeuvre because it was the best way of catching me and that was what they were trained to do. Possibly they were treating me as part of an exercise and would be perfectly friendly when they eventually cornered me. If so, then they were going to get a piece of my mind for scaring me. Alternatively, they might be doing the same in order to tick me off for entering their training area, but the brochure for the cottage had said that red flags flew from the tors when dangerous exercises were in progress. I wasn't sure about that, but was more concerned with the small chance that their intentions might involve me more intimately. It was a small chance, but an alarming one.

Lastly, there was the possibility that it was all some fancy setup of Amber's. We'd played the game of her and others hunting me down before, and I knew that she liked the game immensely, yet I couldn't believe that she would go to such lengths just to add a little extra piquancy. In any case, there was very little I could do, as they had successfully headed me off and were coming in to trap me at the bottom of the gully.

Abandoning any pretence of indifference, I made a break to my right, up the hillside towards a straggle of rocks and gnarled rowan trees. I heard a shout behind me and saw one of them move out from the gully. I felt panic and a desperate feeling of helplessness as I began to run as hard as I could. Another voice answered the first and I risked a glimpse to my side to find the group of three already halfway between me and the gully. The last of them stumbled and I saw something that added a whole new dimension to the turmoil of my emotions.

I ran on, aiming for the boulders, my legs burning with the strain. Two of them were closing on me, the others fanning out to head me off. I made the rocks, leaping on to a big boulder only to find a large pool right in front of me. I should have just splashed into it, but I hesitated and, a moment later, a rough hand caught my arm. They'd have caught me anyway, and I'd have just got wet as well as whatever they intended for me.

Almost the instant I was caught, I knew that I was in for more than a ticking-off. The man who had got me was laughing as he twisted my arm into the small of my back. He was big, well over six foot tall and broad-shouldered, and he handled me with ease.

'Got her!' he called as he pulled my other arm back.

He held both my wrists in one massive hand, ignoring my startled squeals as he lashed them together with twine. He was tying it off when his mate arrived, an even taller man, although not quite so burly.

'Come on, stop!' I pleaded.

Neither answered, but the newcomer pulled something out of his pocket, an oily rag.

'Hey!' I protested, only to have my nose pinched and the rag stuffed into my open mouth.

It tasted disgusting, rather like rancid butter, but all I could do was make muffled squeaks as more twine was used to tie it into my mouth. Even to my own ears, I sounded pretty pathetic, and so I shut up, contenting myself with squirming as the first man hoisted me casually over his shoulder. I kicked, but then my ankles were grabbed and tied together.

After that everything seemed to go by in a blur. They took me down into a little hollow among the rocks and added a blindfold to complete my bondage. Then they put me across a rock, tore my blouse open and took down my trousers and panties. I was braless, which they commented on, laughing as my little tits swung bare beneath my chest. Having my trousers pulled down was even worse. I'd chosen white panties with a pattern of cartoon ducks that morning and they laughed even more when they saw. They twanged my knicker-elastic against my bottom, laughing uproariously at my little kicks and squeaks as my cheeks bounced in response. They found taking my panties down even funnier, commenting on how plump my bottom was for such a small woman and slapping my cheeks to make them wobble.

Their mates turned up while I was being stripped for use, and all five of them began to have a good feel, exploring me with an unrestrained relish born of the fact that there was absolutely nothing I could do about it. They felt my tits and fondled my bottom; they rubbed my pussy and pulled my bum-cheeks open to have a good look at my anus; they spat between my cheeks and on my pussy and fingered me in both holes. Lastly they stuck something up my anus and sat back to decide who was going to fuck me first.

If I struggled, I was just going to roll off the rock and hurt myself. They'd just hold me down to fuck me anyway, so all I could do was lie helpless over the rock, waiting for it. My breathing was coming hard and deep and I was full of feelings of humiliation at what was being done to me. Being spat on to lubricate me was somehow particularly shameful, even more so than having something forced up my bumhole. Yet I knew that there was much worse to come. Five men were going to fuck me, maybe even bugger me. They would come in me, and leave my pussy and anus oozing sperm, only for another cock to be rammed up into the mess.

They could have just cut the pack, but they didn't, instead prolonging my torture by playing beggar-my-neighbour, last places going to those who were out first. Two were noisy, the other three quieter as they played, slapping the cards down on a rock and cursing or laughing as their luck went one way or another. Two of the quiet ones dropped out first, then the man who had first caught me, leaving two to decide who would be the first go. The way they talked, it was as if it was first go at some sort of game, like wanting first go on a fairground stall. It wasn't a game, though, it was my body they were going to use; yet they treated my degradation as a sort of joke.

'Shit! Sloppy seconds for me,' one swore as his mate laughed in triumph.

'Shag her up the arse, then,' one of them suggested.

'I might do that,' came the reply and I found myself involuntarily clenching my bottom-hole around the thing they'd stuck up me.

'Get us ready, then,' the winner said and I heard the sound of his zip being pulled down.

I waited, trembling, while one of them sucked the winner's cock. I could hear the slurping noises and his groans. I knew his erection would be growing in the other one's mouth, swelling and hardening for my poor pussy.

'Spit on her cunt, Dave; I'm nearly hard enough,' the winner said hoarsely, after no more than a minute.

I felt the wet of the man's spit hit my pussy, right on the hole. Fingers rubbed it in and entered me, opening me for his mate's cock.

'Yeah, nice,' a voice drawled, right behind me, and then I felt him kneel over me, his legs touching mine.

I was whimpering into my gag as he pulled my buttocks apart to get at my vagina. The thing in my bumhole was pulled out and I heard it clatter among the rocks. Then the head of his cock was at my hole, opening me, then in, sliding up, pulling back and then starting a steady rhythm as he began to fuck me.

The others called encouragement as he rode me, each push slamming his hard belly against my bottom. I lay there and thought of the four to come, wondering if they'd spare my bumhole her share of cock. I actually felt strangely detached and, for all my shame at my reaction, was unable to avoid the physical pleasure of a good, hard penis filling me and working in and out. I was really beginning to give in to my pleasure, even pushing my bottom up to meet his thrusts when he suddenly pulled out and came all over my bottom and the rear of my pussy. He gave a grunt and then a long sigh, one of the others making a noise of disgust at the mess that the winner had made of me.

'Are you going to fuck her arse?' someone asked the next man in line.

'Yeah, I reckon her ring'll be nice and tight,' he answered.

I relaxed my bumhole, knowing that if a cock was going to be forced up it then it was best to make myself as easy to enter as possible. I'm quite used to taking cocks and dildos up my bum and know how to relax my sphincter, although the saliva and the object that had been in me had done a lot to help.

They went through the same process of sucking the man's cock hard, and then he mounted me. He was right up on top, over my bottom, presumably so that they could see it go in. I felt the knob against my anus and forced myself to relax. He pushed down, and my bumhole opened to take him. There was a little stab of pain as he entered me, and then it was inside me and sliding into my rectum.

Buggery has always given me a lovely breathless, out-of-control feeling, which I was getting despite the circumstances. I was soon moaning deep in my throat as he worked his cock in my back passage, unable to resist the pleasure of it. With only my nose to breathe through, I had to breathe in little sharp pants, which they seemed to find funny as well, but I was really too far gone to care.

'The bitch is loving it!' one of them exclaimed.

'Dirty tart!' another added. 'Go on, Andy, fuck her little arsehole, good and hard.'

Andy just grunted and I braced myself for the less nice part of buggery, when the man is near orgasm and really starts to thrust. It didn't come; instead, the lovely, even strokes that were drawing my distended ring in and out continued, making me sigh and purr into my gag. Then he came, pulling slowly out and tossing off right into my open bumhole. I felt his come splash on my skin and run into my anus, then squelch out as my hole closed. I groaned, wishing one of them would have the decency to play with my clit.

Of course, they didn't. The third man had been having his cock sucked while I was buggered and he lost no time in mounting me. He put it in my pussy, rather to my relief, as my anus was a little sore. He grunted like an animal as he humped me, riding my bottom with a frantic haste that suggested an inability to control his lust. Sure enough, he came almost immediately, deep in my vagina to leave me oozing sperm on to my pussy-lips and the rock beneath me.

'That was good,' he sighed, giving my bottom a parting slap. 'Hot little bitch, aren't you?'

I nodded, admitting to my pleasure because my reactions had given it away anyway. Actually, I was so high on submission and sex that I was even starting to get pleasure out of the disgusting tasting rag in my mouth. There were two to go and, if they took my gag out, I was going to beg to be allowed to masturbate in front of them, putting the final degrading touch to my submission.

The fourth mounted me after taking no more than a desultory suck. My pussy stretched wide to accommodate a cock that was the thickest yet, and had me pushing my bum up and squirming in ecstasy as it was slid in and out. I was given a long, leisurely fucking before the cock was transferred to my bumhole. It was hard to get in, despite having been entered so recently, yet I managed to accommodate it and was soon being buggered with the same slow, long strokes. It was done well, leaving me breathless and faint with reaction. The cock was pulled out at the last moment, spraying my bottom with come and leaving me juicy and open for more.

The fifth took a while to get ready, and then just took me up my bottom. Once entered it was slow, and very deep, bringing me to a new peak. It was the third up my bottom and I was pretty sore, but too high to really care. The others were calling encouragement, counting out the strokes and suggesting coming up my bottom. My rider obliged, filling me with come on the fiftieth stroke, so much of it that I could feel the pressure inside me. Then the cock was being pulling out and my anus was pulsing and oozing sperm. I could feel it running down my pussy and into my pubic hair.

'Nice,' one of them said, 'what a fucking mess. Shall we just leave the little bitch here then, so someone finds her?'

'Yeah,' another answered, 'but with her arse boot-blacked and the tent peg up her dirt-box.'

I shivered at his words. The other chorused agreement with their friend's filthy, degrading suggestion. I lay trembling over the rock as one of them retrieved the tent peg which I now knew was what had originally been used to open my bottom-hole. I couldn't help but sigh, deep in my throat, as it was pushed back into me, stretching my anus once more. I heard the click of a lid being twisted off and then it was being done to me, the thing that had been my favourite fantasy for most of that year.

Two of them did it, slapping boot polish liberally on to my buttocks as the others laughed and made coarse remarks about what they'd done to me and what a slut I was for enjoying it. I could feel the polish going on, thick and greasy, and was imagining how I'd look with my little fat bottom polished up to a glowing black and with a tent peg sprouting obscenely from my anus, or my dirt-box as one of them had called it, a really crude expression which I felt very suitable for the state I was in.

They made a thorough job of it, rubbing it well in, not just to my bum-cheeks, but down between them.

'Do her face!' someone suggested, an idea that was greeted with a chorus of laughter.

They did it, smearing the boot-black all around my mouth and over my cheeks and nose. Some got round the gag, and I could taste the horrible, bitter flavour.

'And her tits!' one of them called.

The one who was doing it stopped and transferred his attention to my dangling breasts, smearing each liberally. My nipples were already stiff, and the contact of his big, rough fingers added to my sexual reaction.

'Finish with her cunt!' a voice called.

I hung my head as a good dollop of boot-black was slapped on to my pussy, mingling with their come and my own juice. It went in my hole and all over my pubic hair, but best of all, his middle finger was rubbing right on my clit as he smeared the polish well into my pussy. I began to rub, bucking my hips urgently and praying that he'd let me come, just that and it would all be worth it.

'The slut's frigging herself on my hand!' my tormentor exclaimed.

'Dirty bitch!' I heard.

'What a tart!'

'Little whore!'

I came at that. They'd caught me, tied me and stripped me, fucked me and buggered me, filled me with sperm. They'd boot-blacked my bare bottom, my face, my tits, my pussy: yet it was me who was the bitch, the tart, the dirty, degraded little whore. His finger was working hard on my clit, bringing me to a peak that made every muscle in my body contract. I felt the plug of boot-polish squeeze out of my pussy and my anus contract hard on the intruding tent peg. Someone gave a laugh at what must have been a truly obscene sight and it hit me again. The bastard wouldn't stop rubbing and I couldn't get enough air. I experienced an extraordinary sensation as I gagged on the oily rag in my mouth as I hit yet another peak, then I was choking.

An instant later the rag was being pulled out of my mouth and a hand was slapping my back. I gasped in great lungfuls of the fresh air, dizzy with my orgasm and feeling completely soiled and abused as I sank down over the rock.

'You are a dirty bitch, Penny Birch,' someone said.

'Me?' I exclaimed, even as I was still fighting to get my breath back.

She laughed and slapped my filthy bottom.

'So when did you realise?' Amber asked as she filled my glass with wine. 'When you found the polish?'

'I wasn't sure,' I admitted. 'I couldn't believe you'd go to so much effort just to realise my fantasy.'

'Any time,' Anderson said cheerfully.

We were relaxing around the fire at Manga Farm. It had taken ages to clean me up, and afterwards they'd insisted I sit back with a drink while they did everything else. It was Anderson who had planted the polish, as he and Vicky had come down to inspect the cottage. By that time they'd had the whole plot worked out, including the collusion of the two extra men. These were Dave Symmes and Rob Kale, both old friends of Anderson and Vicky and no strangers to kinky sex. They'd stayed in a nearby hotel that night and watched me bathe naked in the river that morning from the forest. After that it had simply been a matter of outmanoeuvring me, which had been easy with five of them against just me. Finally they'd caught me and given me what they knew I wanted, with the details carefully orchestrated by Amber. They'd been ready to stop if I got in a real state, but hadn't actually been sure I had guessed it was them until I'd started to really show my pleasure.

'So when were you certain it was us?' Vicky asked.

'Quite late,' I admitted, 'but I was pretty certain when Amber stumbled and went into a kneeling position briefly. No man ever had such a well-fleshed bottom, and certainly not a fit young army boy.'

'Cheeky slut!' Amber joked.

'That's when I decided it was you,' I continued, 'but I wasn't absolutely certain until the three of you joined Rob and Dave. You were quiet, which I suppose you had to be, but it was a big giveaway.'

'That was always going to be a problem,' Vicky admitted. 'You'd have been bound to recognise our voices.'

'I was sure then,' I continued, 'and it was all just too convenient as well, with you having the big wooden tent peg and the boot polish and the twine and everything.'

'And the strap-on dildo,' Vicky added.

'Well, yes,' I said, 'but I wasn't supposed to know about that. I knew for certain before that was put in me anyway, when one of you casually sucked Rob's cock for him. I'm sure there's plenty of homosexuality in the army, but they wouldn't just suck cock as if it was no big deal at all.'

'That was me,' Vicky admitted.

'And you call me a slut!' I replied. 'At least I was bound and helpless.'

'Maybe,' she retorted, 'but I know you, Penny Birch, and if we'd just ordered you to do as you were told, you'd have been on your knees with your bum in the air soon enough.'

I shrugged, wondering what I would do if five army boys ordered me to strip for sex. Run like the blazes, I was sure of it.

17

Cocks and Hens

It had been a long day. My nine o'clock lecture had been attended by just over a dozen students, all of whom looked as if they'd rather have been in bed. After that there had been a couple of tutorials before I got down to my research, which was at that dissatisfying stage where all I could do was press on and be patient. In the afternoon I had to oversee a demonstration for a particularly obtuse group of first-year chemists who were doing genetics as a minor option. By the time I had answered the last silly question, I was ready to drop, and was less than happy when I got back to the flat to find a huge pile of post to be dealt with.

Only one letter looked personal: a big, pink envelope postmarked from Devizes. I knew it would be from my friend Ginny Scott, and left it until last as a treat. When I opened it I discovered that it wasn't from Ginny, but from her prospective sister-in-law, Catharine King, and that it was an invitation to her hen party. She was marrying Matthew Linslade, Ginny's brother, and it was at his farm that we would be meeting on a Friday three weeks away. Despite it being smack in the middle of term and over a hundred miles away in Wiltshire, it was more than I could resist. Ginny was organising the party, and I could guess that anything she put together was not to be missed. Putting my tiredness aside, I wrote to say I would be there and then retired to bed with a ham sandwich and a railway timetable.

It was unfortunate that they had put the party on a Friday. As I had to lecture on Saturday mornings, this meant getting back after the party. Driving was out of the question, and so I was faced with an interminable rail journey in the dead of night. In the circumstances, I was prepared to put up with that. I was fond of Katie King: very fond, in fact, as I had been the first woman she had had sex with. When I'd been living with Amber, Katie had asked me how it felt to be spanked. I'd shown her, and her punishment had led to some deliciously messy sex. She was only a little taller than me, but with fuller breasts and hips, bright red hair and a combination of innocence and naughtiness that echoed my own character. Not only did the party raise the prospect of playing with Katie again, but Ginny would also be there and probably Amber herself. It seemed likely that the night would end in a pile of naked, giggling girls, and I was not going to miss out for anything.

Of course, I'd forgotten that Katie had no shortage of friends who'd have been horrified at what she got up to. When I arrived at the farm, there were already over twenty women there, of whom only myself and three others knew about Katie's experiments with lesbian sex. Ginny and Amber were two of them, and the third was Vicky Belstone. I greeted them all with as much enthusiasm as I felt was safe, only to have Amber take my hand and pull me firmly in the direction of the stairs.

I knew exactly what was coming, and followed with a delicious sense of anticipation and naughtiness. We went up to Matthew's bedroom and jammed the door. An instant later we were in each other's arms, kissing and fondling with a nervous passion born of long separation and the chance that we might get caught. I wanted to be spanked, but knew that it would be too noisy and so contented myself with burying my face between her thighs and giving her a leisurely lick. She sat on the bed with her skirt up and her panties pulled aside while I knelt submissively in front of her, kissing her shoes before starting on her pussy. She came fast, and was about to return the favour when we heard someone coming. Fortunately it was Matthew, who knew about us, but it still broke the moment. We returned, giggling, to the party, which was about to move on.

Having licked Amber, I was feeling incredibly turned on and desperately needed to do something about it. Of course, it was impossible, either as we drove to Broadheath or in the restaurant we had booked. I was in a cab with Amber and Vicky on the way, and both of them kept stroking my thighs through my skirt, which made it worse. By the time we got to Broadheath, I'd have gladly done it in front of the driver and Katie's friend Pauline, who was in the front – or with them, for that matter.

The restaurant was worse still, with me again seated between Amber and Vicky and the tablecloth covering enough of our legs to allow them to torment me without attracting attention. The last thing I wanted to do was stop them, but it was driving me mad, especially when Vicky dropped a spoon and took the opportunity to put her hand up my skirt and have a feel of my pussy through my knickers.

For all their lack of real sexual openness, Katie's friends were by and large pretty good company, and the party went well. There was plenty of laughter and plenty of drink, and by the time we got to the champagne and chocolates stage my head was spinning with the effects of both as well as sex. We were in the upstairs part of a converted barn, which gave us plenty of privacy, and Ginny had already told us that she had laid on a stripper for Catharine. He was going to spank her, bare-bottomed, although she didn't know it. I was greatly looking forward to seeing her rosy pink bottom and hearing her squeals of mock outrage.

Her favourite fantasy was being given a public spanking and, while her other friends didn't know this, Ginny was counting on it being accepted because it was her hen party. We also knew that she would find it incredibly humiliating in front of her friends, and enjoy it all the more for that.

When a waiter came over and whispered to Ginny, I sat

back with my drink to enjoy what I knew was coming. Sure enough, a moment later a solidly built young man in a traffic warden's uniform appeared and tapped Katie on the shoulder. As she turned around, he started to give his spiel about having failed to pay numerous parking tickets. Of course, she realised immediately that it was her stripper and not real but, when he finished his piece with the information that he was going to have to spank her, she looked genuinely alarmed.

Not that there was much she could do about it. He was a muscular, swarthy type who obviously spent a lot of time at the gym. Poor Katie didn't have a chance; he simply picked her up, pulled her chair back and laid her across his knee. She was laughing and kicking even before he started but, with his brawny arm locked around her waist, her helplessness was genuine. Everybody was laughing and clapping as he began to plant gentle smacks across her seat, although one or two of her friends looked a bit doubtful. She protested half-heartedly until he stopped and began to pull up her skirt. Then she really started to kick and struggle, which of course she had to, in order to prevent just how much she enjoyed having her bottom smacked from becoming public knowledge.

He pulled her skirt up anyway, exposing pretty blue silk panties, loose over her bottom but with plenty of cheek spilling out at the sides. She quietened down as soon as her panties were showing, presumably because there's no point in struggling once the deed has been done. He started to spank her again, slightly harder and concentrating on the chubby crescents of bare bottom flesh that showed around her panties. As I listened to her squeaks and giggles I was wishing it was me and waiting for the delicious moment when he pulled her knickers down.

Her bum-cheeks were already quite red by the time he decided to do it. He stopped, and turned to us.

'Do you think she's sorry?' he asked. 'Or do you think she needs her pants pulled down to make her really sorry?'

'Pull them down; it'll teach her a lesson,' Ginny said coolly.

'No!' Katie squeaked as his hand went to the waistband of her fancy knickers.

'Shall I, girls?' he called out.

The answer was a chorus of demands for her panties to be pulled down. Even the quietest of her friends seemed to like the idea of her getting a bare-bottom spanking in front of them and, out of twenty-five women, only two remained silent. The rest of us were demanding that her knickers come down, and I couldn't help but wonder how many of them were secretly as excited as I was by the prospect of her lovely round bottom being stripped for a humiliating public spanking.

She fought hard to keep them up, kicking and wriggling over his knee, clutching her panties and calling us all sorts of interesting names. He just pulled her arms up into the small of her back and held both her wrists with one big hand, rendering her helpless. I love to be held like that and was even wondering what the girls would think if I asked to be given the same treatment afterwards. Because everybody was watching Katie's punishment, both Amber and Vicky had taken the chance to molest me a bit more openly. Their hands were both up my skirt, kneading my pussy and thighs, and what they were doing was barely hidden by the table.

The stripper took a firm grip on the back of Katie's panties and started to pull them down. She kicked and thrashed and swore, but down they came, exposing her lovely plump bottom with a puff of red hair showing between her thighs. He actually took them off, and dangled them tauntingly in front of her face, to her increased fury. He then started to spank her again, making her cheeks bounce and wobble, with each smack making them part to show off her pouted pussy-lips and the tight spot of her bumhole. It must have been so humiliating, showing it all in front of her friends, with her arms twisted into her back and buttocks turning pink as she was punished. I knew her fury was a fake, as it was just what I'd have done in her place; after all, if you're given a public spanking, you've at least got to pretend not to like it. The stripper knew that she would say the word 'red' if she really wanted him to stop, as Ginny had primed him. Whether Katie knew that, I wasn't at all sure, and what did surprise me was her friend's delight in her pain and humiliation.

The smacks were coming quite hard, and she was really dancing over his lap, giving an open display of vagina and anus with each slap. Amber had found my clit and was rubbing it, while Vicky was tickling the curve of my bottom with her nails. My eyes were fixed on Katie's pink, wriggling bottom and I could feel my orgasm welling up. Just as the muscles of my abdomen started to contract, he stopped spanking her and everybody burst out clapping. We had to join in or somebody would have noticed, and the abruptness of the come-down from the brink of orgasm to nothing was so severe that for a moment I felt faint.

Katie stood up slowly and made a big show of rubbing her sore bottom, only covering herself when everyone had had a good look. As she sat down again, the stripper started his routine, concentrating on Katie but making sure that all of us got a good view. He also did a lot of it standing on the table, which stopped Vicky and Amber finishing me off. I like my men big and powerful, rather than specifically muscular, yet he was good-looking and moved well, which only served to add to my sexual high. He went all the way, too, removing the ridiculous fluffy pouch that was his final garment to reveal a fair-sized cock and a pair of exceptionally hairy balls.

For a moment he stood there, naked, his genitals thrust to within a foot of Katie's face. Then he bent forward and whispered something in her ear. I saw Katie smile and throw Ginny an uncertain glance, then exchange words with her. He stood back, grinning to himself as he began to dress and, a moment later, Ginny leant across the table and put her head close to mine and Vicky's.

'He wants a suck,' she whispered, 'and Katie's up for it but doesn't want everyone to know. I'm going to say I want a breath of fresh air in a while, and she'll come outside with me. He'll be waiting in the car park. Could one of you come to help keep watch?'

'Sure,' I volunteered, before Vicky had a chance.

Ginny waited a good ten minutes after he had gone to get up, during which time I finished off the best part of a bottle of champagne. I had no intention of depriving Katie of her cock, but also had no intention of just playing lookout. The three of us walked out together, getting no more than a curious glance from her friends. Outside, the air was cool and I could feel my head swimming as Ginny and I took Katie's hands. The car park was illuminated by a single dull yellow light, and we could see the white Ford that the stripper had told us to look out for. He was leaning on the car, still dressed as a traffic warden but with a heavy overcoat over his uniform. If he was surprised to see three girls, he gave no sign of it, but smiled as we approached.

We lost no time, the stripper moving to the rear of his car and into the shelter of a mini-bus. The light was dim, but I could clearly see his cock as he pulled it clear of his fly. He took his balls out, too, and held the whole lot forward for our inspection. His cock was already half-stiff, and I guessed that he had been playing with it in the car in anticipation of Katie's mouth. Ginny sat on the bonnet of his car as Katie sank to her knees in front of him. I knew exactly how she felt: bottom warmed, well punished and more than willing to reward the man who had chastised her with oral sex. I knew Matthew liked to spank girls before having his cock sucked, because he'd done it to me. Now Katie was about to give the same treatment to a stranger, while Ginny and I watched sidelong and pretended to chat.

She had taken his cock in her hand and was stroking it, her mouth a little open in preparation for him. He was holding his coat open and watching her, waiting for the moment when she took his erection in her pretty mouth. I was tempted to try and frig off, or to get Ginny to lick me, but every car there represented a customer who might emerge from the restaurant at any time and so I didn't dare. All he had to do was close his coat, but I'd have had a lot more covering up to do.

I looked round again to find Katie sucking him. Her eyes were closed in bliss and she was rocking back and forth on her heels to allow his erection to slide in and out of her mouth. He turned to me and gave me the most wonderful look, as if daring me to be as dirty as my friend. It was more than I could resist. With a last glance in the direction of the restaurant I sank to my knees and put my face next to Katie's. I pressed my cheek to hers and put my tongue out to lick him, only to have him transfer his erection from her mouth to mine. It felt great, the swollen head taut and firm against my tongue as I sucked, his taste strong in my mouth. I sucked for a bit and then passed it back, only to find Ginny pushing in next to me, eager for her share.

We forgot all about watching as the three of us indulged ourselves with his balls and penis, licking, sucking and kissing until he began to moan. I realised that he was going to come and quickly pulled his cock from my mouth and put it to Katie's. She gaped willingly, taking it as far in as she could as he grunted and jerked. White sperm erupted from her lips and I knew that he had come in her mouth. Ginny and I began to lick at his cock and Katie's face, lapping the sperm up eagerly until our mouths were full of it. As he pulled back, with his erection already shrinking, I leant forward and opened my come-filled mouth for a long sticky kiss with both my friends. As we shared his come between us, touching tongues in the glorious, sticky goo, my need to come reached crisis point. I pulled back and wiped my mouth.

'Will you lick me, Katie?' I asked. 'Ginny can feel my bottom and . . . sorry, I don't know your name, but would you like to play with my tits while I come?'

'It's Marco,' he answered, 'and yeah, I'd love to, but someone's coming.'

We hastily rearranged ourselves, which was just as well, as the people turned out to be the party in the mini-bus behind which we were sheltering. We gave them a polite good evening as they approached and, if they were suspicious, then they didn't say anything. Unfortunately, once the mini-bus had gone, we were deprived of our best cover, besides which their appearance had broken the desperation of my need. Instead of carrying on, the three of us went back, leaving Marco to drive off, hopefully well satisfied.

My cab arrived just a few minutes later, forcing me to leave the warm, friendly atmosphere of the party and face the prospect of the long, lonely journey home. All the way to Westbury station, I sat slumped in the back of the cab, wondering faintly if the driver would swap a blow-job for a lick of my pussy but never plucking up the courage to ask.

The train was one of those late-night ones that take peculiar routes and stop at every station. My destination was Birmingham, after which I would be able to change to an express that would whisk me home. The carriage was warm and faintly damp, making me feel sleepy as I chose a set of seats on my own and slumped into one. There was a group of lads heading back from some late-night jaunt at the far end; otherwise I was alone.

I was desperately in need of an orgasm and, had it not been for the lads and the presence of an inspector, I think I would have pulled up my dress and just done it on the spot. I even considered the train loo but, even in my drunken and excited state, one glance was enough to change my mind. Instead, I just sat there, surreptitiously stroking myself through my dress and thinking about sex, and specifically men's cocks.

Articles in magazines are always going on about the size of men's cocks and whether or not it matters. It certainly does to men, whose egos are deeply affected by the size of their cocks, be they chipolatas or cucumbers. It matters to some women as well, certainly to me, but not in the conventional way. Once it's inside, length isn't all that important, although thickness is. Morphologically speaking, only the first third or so of the vaginal canal is ectodermic in derivation, so unless a man has less than about two inches, it really doesn't matter. Having said that, I certainly know it if someone bumps my cervix. What's nice about size is not the feeling when it's in, but the pleasure of looking at it, handling it, sucking it and generally giving it loving attention. From that point of view, my attitude is the bigger the better, and I would love to have one big enough to really hug and rub my whole body against.

Then again, small cocks have their uses. I love being buggered, but can't take a really big cock up my bottom at all, while even medium-sized ones tend to hurt if the man gets carried away. A nice small one goes in easily enough and gives me that lovely breathless feeling without the pain.

Appearance can be important as well. I don't think a cock could ever really be called pretty, but a really well-formed one might be considered handsome. Marco the stripper's had been like that: thick, smooth and fleshy with a round head. It had been a joy to suck and fondle, and I would have liked to spend a lot more time over it. It had also changed size a lot from limp to erect, which I like. It's nice to have a cock at least double in length as the man becomes more and more excited, and I find the sort that just spring up and stay much the same size a bit of a let-down.

Handsome cocks are nice, but there's also a certain bizarre delight in ugly ones. The janitor, Colin, with whom I had occasional rough sex at the university, was like that. His cock was big, and heavily veined, and a bit bent, and a dirty red-brown colour. Instead of repelling me, it fascinated me, and really brought out my submissive feelings. He used to hold me by the hair and make me suck him for ages, which was bliss, especially as he often spanked me first in just the way Marco had spanked Katie.

In a way, a cock is the very definition of obscenity. Even when limp, a man's penis is an extraordinarily rude object, protruding out from under his belly along with his balls and set in a nest of hair. Erect, it becomes far more so: a bloated, straining thing just aching to be put to a girl's body, be it her hands, her pussy, her tits, her mouth, her bumhole – anywhere, as long as it's sheathed in soft, female flesh. It's like that rhyme about girls being made of

216

sugar and spice and all things nice – sweet, demure, clean. Boys are made of slugs and snails and puppy dog's tails – dirty, rude and vulgar; and constantly desperate to fill the pretty, delicate girls with their obscene cocks. Only, of course, it's the girl who has been shamed when she's given in to their sordid demands and handled their cocks, or sucked them, or let them into her pussy.

I shivered at the thought, thinking of some of the men who had given me the rough, dirty sex that I crave. There had been plenty, and at that moment there wasn't one who I wouldn't have given in to. From gangly, dirty-minded Ryan who had given me my first sexual experience by coming all over my bottom while I posed for him to the over-muscled Marco whose cock I'd just helped Katie King suck, any one of them could have had me any way they wanted. I'd have gone down on them right there in the carriage, or knelt on the seat with my dress up and my panties down to let them have me from behind. If the ticket inspector came, well then, I'd just have to accommodate him as well, maybe in my mouth, or up my bottom.

The train stopped and the lads got out, tumbling noisily on to the platform. As they passed I heard one make some boastful and probably false remark about some girl. I laughed to myself. I don't really like laddish types but, at that moment, all it would have taken was one little push and I'd have let them all have me, one by one or all together.

My carriage was now empty, and my thoughts turned back to masturbation as the train picked up speed. A glance at my map showed that, while it was only a little way to the next station, there was a long gap afterwards. All I had to do was wait, then take a seat near the middle and sit so that I was shielded below the waist but could see both doors. With a hand up my dress, I would be able to get to my pussy and achieve the direct stimulation of my clit that I needed so badly. I relaxed, leaning my head against the padded seat and letting my mind drift back to thoughts of men's cocks.

I closed my eyes and let my hand stray to my belly, only

half aware of what I was doing. My flesh felt soft yet resilient through my dress, tempting me to slip my hand further down. I cupped the mound of my pussy, kneading gently, which produced a really satisfying feeling. My middle finger found the groove between my pussy-lips, taking my pleasure a step higher. I could feel the material of my dress and the panties beneath it, with warm, damp flesh underneath.

Somebody coughed, a small, diffident noise, yet enough to make me jump and send the blushes straight to my cheeks. As I opened my eyes, I found the inspector standing directly opposite me and looking at me with a curious expression.

'Do you have your ticket, miss?' he asked.

'Er . . . yes, somewhere,' I stammered, blushing furiously as I thought of him watching me play with my pussy through my dress.

As I rummaged through my bag in a desperate search for my tickets, I compounded my embarrassment by spilling some of the contents, including a packet of condoms. He said nothing, but accepted the tickets when I had finally found them and continued down the train.

When he had gone, I sat staring out into the night, feeling thoroughly embarrassed and more turned on than ever. I also felt cowardly, because I knew that, in my position, Ginny would have propositioned the guard. Amber wouldn't have been interested, but Vicky and even Katie might have had the courage to go ahead where I hadn't. I much prefer to give in, and have only really made advances when I've been pretty certain of the outcome. He'd seen me playing with myself and his expression had at least hinted at taking pleasure in what he saw, yet I hadn't had the guts to ask for what I wanted.

It was agony, knowing that at that very moment I might have been sucking on his cock while I played with myself instead of staring out of the window and feeling fit to explode. I was also exhausted, warm and drunk. I was vaguely aware of the station and the train starting again, but must have been asleep moments later.

I can't have been asleep for long, but I dreamt I was being chased by weird little goblins with cocks as long as their bodies. It faded just when they caught me and started to strip me, which was a pity, but I came round to the realisation that something was wrong. I was still in a half-dream, aware that the goblins weren't real but that something had changed. My legs felt different and, after some very hazy thought, I realised that they were bare. Somehow my dress had ridden up, and my legs were showing.

In my sleepy, drunken state, it seemed a really nice idea to just lie there with my legs bare, showing off to anyone who came past. The dress was right up, so high in fact that the front of my panties might be showing. I tried to remember if I'd pulled it up in order to masturbate, and wondered if I'd done it in my sleep. I hadn't; someone had done it to me, and that someone was watching me.

My awareness of him was definite, although it came from nothing obvious. The light patterns must have changed, and perhaps his breathing was audible, but he was certainly there. If I hadn't been so drunk, I'd have jumped up immediately. With my reactions following so far behind my mental speed, I didn't, but stayed slumped on the seat. If I appeared calm, then inside I was in utter turmoil. Someone, a stranger but probably the railway guard, had lifted my dress to look at my legs and panties. He'd seen me playing with myself and, when he found me asleep, he hadn't been able to resist molesting me.

I fought down the very real urge to sit up and scream at him to get lost. My earliest fantasy had been about men being unable to control their lust for me, and this one clearly couldn't. He'd risked his job, maybe even his freedom, just for a look at my panties. Possibly he was just too thick to consider the consequences of his actions, but I quite like the idea of men as brainless hulks driven only by lust. Whatever the case, I found his attention both frightening and thrilling and stayed put, hoping that he'd take his exploration of my body further.

We stayed still for a long time, he presumably wondering

if he dared interfere with me, me hoping that he would do exactly that. Eventually it was me who decided to do something, and I gave a sleepy moan and moved a little further down the seat, hoping to improve his view. Nothing happened for a moment and then I felt a touch on my dress, somehow guilty and uncertain as he lifted it as high as it would go. He had bared my tummy and the whole front of my panties. My legs were open and I knew my panties would be wet, which he'd be able to see.

I gave another little moan and let my left leg move, giving him a full view of my panty crotch. He moved back, evidently thinking I might wake. I could hear his breathing clearly now, hoarse, low and full of passion. Once more he approached, and I felt his hand on a breast, gentle and cautious, then firmer as his confidence built. I moaned for real as his fingers brushed my nipple through my dress. He stopped, then went on when I didn't appear to wake.

He treated himself to a really good feel of my boobs, one hand on each, stroking and fondling until my nipples were rock hard. I could feel the lace of my bra cups against my skin, further exciting me as he explored. Then one hand, his right, lifted and I heard the faint sound of a zip being pulled down. He was going to fuck me, or at least wank over my panties. I sighed and stretched, arching my back in pleasure. He didn't stop, evidently having decided that I was in a drunken stupor. He squeezed my breasts, one after the other, then took his hand away.

I could hear a slapping noise, fleshy and somehow really dirty as I knew it was made by his cock slapping against his hand as he jerked himself to full erection. The noise stopped, and then my panties were being pulled aside to expose my pussy. He was going to fuck me, and he thought I was asleep.

His body pressed down between my thighs, spreading them. His cock touched my pussy, bumping against my clit twice before finding my vagina. It slid into me really easily, the sensation of entry making me groan aloud. I didn't care if he knew I was awake any more, and he obviously didn't either, as he took hold of my legs as he began to fuck me.

The position must have been uncomfortable for him, as he was soon panting and grunting as he moved in and out with little, hard thrusts. I lay back and let him use me, sighing and moaning but with my eyes still closed. His arms were locked around my thighs and most of his body weight was resting on my hips, creating a wonderful pressure as he rode me.

He pulled out suddenly, only to wrench my panties up around my thighs, roll my legs up and enter me again. The manoeuvre pulled me forward a bit, so that his balls banged against the tuck of my bottom each time he pushed into me. I put my hands to my tits and began to feel, abandoning my pretence of sleep completely.

'You dirty bitch,' he growled, which seemed a bit unfair, as he'd mounted me without so much as a by-your-leave.

Seeing that I was awake, he pulled out again and took me by the thighs, twisting to indicate that I should turn over. I obliged, kneeling half on the seat and presenting him with my bottom. He got back up me without preamble, leaning over to take a tit in each hand. It was like he was fucking a doll, moving me for his best access, first rolled up, and now into doggy position. His weight was pressing me down into the seat, and only the tip of his cock was in me, but he didn't seem to care. He began to grunt and I knew he was going to come, only for his cock to slip out at the last instant. It bumped against my clit, then shot back up my pussy, making me gasp. He grunted, slamming hard into me, only for his cock to slip out again and slide up between my bottom-cheeks. He was coming. I could feel the wet sperm between my bum-cheeks. He rubbed his cock in it, right against my bumhole, his balls banging my empty pussy, his come squelching and oozing up between my buttocks and dripping into my panties.

And he just left me like that, kneeling on the seat with my bottom covered in spunk. I didn't care, I just wanted to come myself. I put my hand back between my legs and started to rub my clit. Only when I was on the edge of orgasm did I realise the reason for his haste. Lights were slipping by outside, then an area of sidings as I started to come. I closed my eyes and screamed out my pleasure, letting my orgasm break like a wave in my head and then quickly turning to sit my soggy bottom down on the seat.

I rearranged my dress as we drew into the station, painfully aware that my panties were still down and that I was sitting in a pool of my own juice and the guard's sperm. I was panting too, partly from my orgasm and partly from the effort of supporting most of his weight while he fucked me. The train stopped and I heard someone open a door further down my carriage. I struggled to control my breathing as a cheerful looking middle-aged woman appeared in the isle. She smiled at me and I smiled back, sure that she couldn't fail to detect the rich scent of sex.

She didn't notice, but asked politely if she could sit opposite me. I could hardly refuse, although what I really wanted to do was tidy myself up a bit and then try and sleep for the rest of the journey. Instead I had to listen politely to her chattering and hope she would get off. She didn't, and when we reached the suburbs of Birmingham I was still in the same awkward and uncomfortable state. Only then did the guard appear to check her ticket. I was thoroughly fed up, and also in two minds about the guard's behaviour. He hadn't forced me at all, and I was fairly sure that he'd have made a hasty retreat if I'd shown the least resistance. On the other hand, the only words he had spoken to me had been to call me a dirty bitch; and he had taken advantage of me. As he took her ticket he gave me a knowing leer, and that was what decided me.

'Excuse me,' I addressed the woman as I stood up and fumbled under my dress for my panties, 'but I just need to adjust myself. This gentleman raped me earlier, you see, and he left me in a bit of a mess.'

18

Black Mischief

I had lunched at the Student's Union, on the grounds that
it was cheap and filling. It was also convenient for the labs
and, as I was buried in a particularly exacting experiment,
I had no wish to waste time walking to the staff refectory.
As I was leaving, my mind was intent on my work, yet one
of the posters drew my attention. It was a drawing,
exquisitely executed and very elaborate in silver ink on
black. I paused, impressed by the skill of the artist but
taken aback by the subject. It was basically a goat's skull,
complete with horns and set about with cabbalistic
symbols and faintly Saxon scrollwork. Only when I had
finished admiring the picture did I read the poster, which
turned out to advertise a black-magic group that some
students had formed. It was called 'the Coven of the Silver
Moon', and purported to be for women only and to
involve moon worship.

I turned away, feeling both amused and slightly irritated.
I was amused because of the very absurdity of such beliefs,
and annoyed because I always liked to hope that anybody
with the intelligence to get into university ought to be at
least reasonably rational. Still, I reflected as I left the
building, it was no more absurd than many other religious
or quasi-religious groups.

That would have been that, had it not been for one of
my female students, a rather graceful girl called Ella,
turning up to a tutorial in the most outrageous outfit I had
seen in some time. It wasn't complicated, consisting of a

black cape with a lining of purple silk and high-heeled black boots. What was outrageous was that that appeared to be all she had on; when she walked in, her legs were bare to the thigh and I got a glimpse of bare tummy as well. A brief flash of a small, naked breast as she sat down confirmed my impression.

Being fairly used to students being deliberately outrageous in an attempt to shock their elders, I took little notice, and was surprised when she apologised and explained that she was going straight on to something else afterwards.

'What?' I queried, fascinated to know what sort of event required such dress at eleven o'clock in the morning.

'A ritual of the noon solstice,' she explained. 'It's out on the moors and there won't be time to change.'

'Oh, right,' I answered, remembering the poster. 'That wouldn't be anything to do with the Coven of the Silver Moon, would it?'

'That's us,' she replied cheerfully, as if admitting to membership of the debating society.

'I thought you were moon worshippers?' I queried.

'Well, yeah,' she explained, 'but we've got this guy coming up from London to do the ritual. He's really into it. He's even supposed to be able to do summonings.'

'Summonings?' I queried incredulously.

'Yes, the possession of his body by a spirit,' she answered. 'It's incredible.'

'Incredible is the word,' I replied, despairing of her gullibility. The man was obviously a fraud, and presumably got his kicks out of the adoration of credulous pagans. Possibly out of their bodies, too, I considered, glancing at my companion's outfit. She was actually one of my brighter students, which made her bizarre beliefs even more extraordinary.

I saw her the next day in the department and asked how the ritual had gone. She explained enthusiastically, describing how the man, who described himself as an Archmage, had led them in ritual dance, summoned summer spirits to him and implored them to grant a fine summer that would be beneficial to all nature.

I pointed out that different types of summer weather would in fact favour different aspects of nature, which perplexed her somewhat, although she assured me that the Archmage would have been able to explain the anomaly. He was still in the city, and she suggested I visit that evening, certain that a meeting with him would dissolve my scepticism. I agreed, keen to take a break from work and certain that he would be unable to match me in an argument.

His arguments failed to impress me so, in a sense, I was right. On the other hand, he had a glib retort for every one of my objections. My strongest point was that he was completely unable to produce any visible effect, let alone a tangible one. Unfortunately, I had to concede that my own work involved investigating things that nobody had ever actually seen as such. The fact that I was able to demonstrate the existence of an amino acid to my own satisfaction was countered by his assertion that he could demonstrate the existence of a spirit to his.

By the time I went home I was thoroughly worked up, my sole consolation being that he had been as well. I was quite pleased with myself, though, as I had held my ground as the sole sceptic in a large group of believers. I had also noted that there was a good deal of eroticism in their imagery and rituals, and was beginning to wonder if the whole thing didn't serve as a pretext for sexual behaviour that they might not otherwise have felt happy about.

That really set me thinking and, the more I thought about it, the more opportunity there seemed to be for mischief. It's not that I have anything against people with strong beliefs in things I consider obvious nonsense, but I do find it quite impossible to take them seriously. The ritual that they had been discussing, and which the Archmage claimed to have done, was one called the Summoning of the Egregore of Lilith. As far as I could remember, Lilith was an Assyrian demoness with some fairly nasty habits, yet they considered her to represent the essence of female human sexuality. The ritual involved the invocation of her egregore into the body of the priestess.

Once possessed, the priestess would indulge herself with her fellow coven members.

The ritual also involved large numbers of black candles and lots of other paraphernalia. These included whips and, to me, the whole thing looked like an excuse for some juicy sadomasochistic sex. The priestess could get high on the heavy red wine and bizarre incenses that the ritual required, then have a great time taking out her darkest fantasies on the others. Afterwards, she wouldn't have to feel guilty about making another girl lick her bottom, or whatever, because it hadn't really been her doing it, but Lilith. Nor would the others have to feel guilty, because an essential part of the ritual was submission to the will of Lilith; so, if the priestess sat on a girl's face, then she had to lick, didn't she?

I didn't believe a word of it, but the idea of being ravished on the floor by a sex-crazed priestess really appealed to me. The priestess of the Coven of the Silver Moon was a girl called Poppaea, who affected green hair and make-up and was even smaller and more lightly built than me. Ella had told me that Poppaea was a third-level initiate, which meant nothing to me but seemed to impress the others, even the Archmage. Highly initiated she might be but, compared with the women who've dominated me sexually, she really wasn't in it. Certainly she was no Amber Oakley, and I suspected that the only reason they hadn't tried the ritual was that Poppaea wasn't really cut out for it.

She was very much the driving force behind the Coven of the Silver Moon, though, and she also had a thing about me. This was mainly because she resented my imperturbable atheism, but I could tell that there was more to it. It was an odd sensation, being fancied by a female student, especially as she clearly found her emotions hard to deal with. Having been through the same myself, I was sympathetic and would have been more than happy to guide her gently into bed, had it not been for our positions. Seducing students is generally frowned upon, although not specifically forbidden. On the other hand, she was studying

226

fine art and I taught only within the natural sciences, so there was no possibility of me ever examining her. There would still have been a fair-sized scandal if we'd started a relationship, so I hung back, tempted, yet never allowing myself to lose control.

As term went by, I became better friends with them, especially Poppaea. In her, I could sense a measure of the way that I knew Amber felt about me. She was so tiny and fragile that I just wanted to cuddle her and stroke her long green hair. She also used to make little gestures that may or may not have been conscious, but which I recognised as acts of submission with a very definite erotic undertone. By the end of term, it was driving me crazy, and my resolve not to touch her was beginning to falter.

There was a full moon just before the end of term, and Poppaea, Ella and the others were intent on making it a major ritual. They were extremely keen for me to join in, and were certain that I need only experience the full intensity of the ritual to be convinced. My presence would also bring their number to thirteen, which they felt would make a big difference. Poppaea was particularly persuasive, and I eventually let myself be talked into it, but only on the condition that after the moon ritual they attempted the Summoning of the Egregore of Lilith. Poppaea's eyes lit up at the suggestion and, although she and some of the others seemed genuinely frightened by the idea, they were more than willing to go along with it. I went home that evening feeling deliciously wicked. I had no illusions whatever about my behaviour, which was devious, manipulative and thoroughly dirty. My aim was clear: to set up the most exquisite all-girl orgy and, if the others felt they needed an excuse to liberate the dark depths of their sexualities, then I was more than happy to assist. It took three orgasms before I could get to sleep that night: one over Poppaea, one over Ella and one over all twelve of them.

Poppaea was extremely careful to make sure we weren't disturbed for the ritual. She didn't reveal where it was going to happen to anybody until lunch time on the day of the full moon. Even then, she only told her second-level initiate before disappearing to set everything up. It was all very mysterious, which added to the fine head of anticipation that I had been building up for days. It was a Thursday, which meant taking a five o'clock tutorial, but by good luck this was with Ella, and we finished early and walked back to the room in which we were meeting together.

Poppaea's number two was a girl who called herself Hecate, also an art student but dark-haired and rather sultry in her looks and style. She greeted us with kisses and motioned us into the room. Everybody else was already there, except Poppaea, and it was only then that Hecate revealed that the ritual was to take place not in the city at all, but at a secret place well out on the moors. I was glad of this and also excited, as it removed my last worries of scandal and because I adore being naked outdoors.

Dusk was falling as we drove out towards the hills, and there was a rising sense of exclusivity and intimacy among us. For all my rejection of their beliefs, I could appreciate the pleasure they got in their worship and found myself drawn in by them. I could sense the sexual tension as well, in the group as a whole and between certain couples. Hecate, who was driving, seemed to have a special intimacy with a tiny, delicate girl called Delphinia, who had hair so pale that I had first thought her an albino. Ella was next to me, but was having her hair stroked by Ea, a slight red-haired girl who was perhaps the quietest of the group. One other thing was curious, although presumably coincidence: of the twelve girls in the university mini-bus, I was the fourth or fifth tallest, whereas it's rare for me not to be the smallest person in any given group.

Poppaea had chosen her site well, a clearing in a stand of oak without a house in two miles and completely hidden. When we arrived, the last light was fading from the sky and we could see the ring of candles through the trees as we drew close. Poppaea was seated on a tree trunk, stark naked but for a spray of wild flowers tangled into her hair. She looked beautiful, delicate, almost elfin, and the sight put a lump into my throat. There was a strong scent of incense in the air as well, helping to create a weird, unwordly atmosphere. I've always felt at home in woods and wild places, which Poppaea had assured me was proof of my underlying pagan nature and an important part of my femininity. Looking at her, poised and gloriously naked as she waited for us, I couldn't help but agree: at least in the sense that I had a genuine affinity with what she called the wildwood.

We undressed at the edge of the clearing, each walking towards Poppaea when she was naked. I came last, kissing her offered hand and then taking my place across the glade. Poppaea came down from her trunk and, lifting her hands so that her long green hair streamed down around her body, began to chant.

I suppose it was beautiful in a way; certainly it was very moving, yet I feel sure that the others got far more out of moon ritual than I did. To be fair to Poppaea, she had done a great job of it, creating an exquisite atmosphere and leading us in a complex ritual that was somehow more private than the most intimate sexual acts. The moon was the focus of it, and indeed the focus of the coven, also something that they felt closely linked to in the same way that I feel linked to wild places. I recognise my feelings for what they are, though, without needing to call upon mystical explanations.

If the ritual didn't move me as much as it might have done, then the same wasn't true of being in a group of thirteen naked women. We held hands most of the time, and several parts of the ritual involved more intimate contact, although never of an overtly sexual nature. Still, when it came to kissing Poppaea's belly immediately above the line of her pubic hair, which was green, it was all I could do not to bury my face in her pussy. I didn't, but returned to my place with my face flushed and butterflies in my stomach.

They then initiated me, which was an even more intimate ritual. I had to kneel to each girl in turn, offer her a libation of mead and kiss her hands, lips, breasts, belly and pussy in strict order. Twelve times I did that and, by the time it was Poppaea's turn, my head was swimming with the scent of female sex. When I kissed her breasts, I let my tongue touch each nipple, then got to my knees, kissed her sweet little tummy for the second time and put my face to her pussy. I kissed once, then again, my tongue finding her clit for just an instant, only for her to draw me gently away. I'd felt her reaction, though, and knew it was only a matter of time. The submissiveness of the ritual wasn't lost on me, and I finished by bowing my head to Poppaea's feet and kissing the ground in front of her. When I looked up into her eyes, they were bright with a glow of triumph, although where she evidently thought she had captured my faith, what she had really done was expose the absolute heart of my sexuality.

I returned to my place in a state of rapture, which I could tell was shared by the others. What I didn't share was their nervousness, both because I didn't actually believe that Poppaea was about to allow her body to be taken over by a demoness, and partly because I was no stranger to submitting my body to another's will.

Poppaea began by setting up a tripod in the middle of the circle and placing a bronze crucible on it. This she filled with a pungent oil, which she set alight. The smell was even more intoxicating than the incense, and made my head spin. She stepped back and again began to chant, an evocation to Lilith to take possession of her. This was quite long and repeated each time she reached the end, while Hecate passed a great bowl of blood-red wine to each of us in turn. Lastly she offered it to Poppaea, who lifted it to her lips and drained the contents.

Once more she began chanting, her voice becoming shrill. We joined in, using subtly different words, in which Hecate led us. Suddenly Poppaea stopped and the night was abruptly silent but for the hissing flame. She stood bolt upright, her eyes shining in the moonlight and her hair in wild disarray. As she started to speak, her voice became deep and gravelly, very different from her normal voice and hoarse with passion.

We knelt as one at her command, putting our faces in the dirt. I knew it was just an act, but I was still trembling, the more so when I peeped out to see what she was doing. She had picked up a switch from the ground and was standing over Hecate, stroking her body with the tip. Hecate was whimpering as she was touched, the long, whippy twig making a pattern down the centre of her back and then down between her open bottom-cheeks. All twelve of us were in identical positions, faces in the dirt, bottoms high, in an attitude of absolute obeisance. Poppaea moved from Hecate to Ea, teasing her neck, her back, her bottom, her thighs and lastly her pussy with the switch. Her manner was lazy, controlled, luxuriantly erotic, as she took her time with each girl. When my turn came, I lifted my bottom higher, delighting in the subtle torment as she scratched my skin and flicked the switch gently against my naked pussy-lips.

It left me trembling hard and wishing for more, but reluctant to move until ordered. Only when she had completed the ring did she sit on the trunk, open-legged with the pink flesh of her pussy showing sparkling wet in the candlelight. She beckoned Hecate, who crawled forward obediently. The expression on Poppaea's face was an exquisite blend of cruelty and lust as she took Hecate by the hair and pulled her face in between her thighs, forcing her to lick. Poppaea sighed, and then opened her eyes and beckoned to Ea. She put Ea to one breast and Sumi, a pretty Oriental, to the other, then beckoned Delphinia forward and gestured haughtily to Hecate's open bottom.

I watched in ecstasy as the delicate girl buried her face in between Hecate's cheeks and began to lick unrestrainedly at her pussy and bottom. Ella rose and came forward, moving uncertainly towards Ea. Poppaea's switch lashed out to catch Ella across the thigh, and the chastened girl sank quickly to her knees. Others moved forward, crawling, trying to get close enough to pay homage to their priestess's body. I joined in, mesmerised by Delphinia's tiny, pert bottom, which was directly in front of me, the pouted pussy-lips and the tight dark spot of her bottom-hole tempting my tongue. I drew close and kissed the tuck of her bottom, then the rear of her pussy, burrowing in to taste her. Her thigh muscles moved as I tongued her, her bottom lifting to invite more, her cheeks coming further apart as if to offer me the centre. I kissed right on Delphinia's anus and then poked my tongue out and began to lick the tight little hole.

Poppaea laughed as she watched me tongue Delphinia's bottom: a cruel, triumphant sound. An arm curled under my belly to find my pussy, the fingers probing eagerly to find the opening of my vagina. Then I was being rolled over and someone was mounting me, her mouth finding mine as my arms closed around her back. Events became blurred after that. I was in a tangle of naked limbs, fingers exploring me intimately while I did my best to return their caresses. I remember taking my turn to lick Poppaea while Hecate beat me with the switch. I remember Delphinia's sweet little face, her eyes shut as she licked my pussy. I remember being held down by three or maybe four of them as Poppaea sat her bottom on my face and ordered me to lick her anus in that same deep, gravelly voice. Finally, I remember her standing over me and laughing in absolute delight as she peed in my face.

It went on for ages, and I know I came at least twice, once under Delphinia's tongue and once under my own fingers with my face smothered in Hecate's little round breasts. Poppaea finally passed out, or at least seemed to. At the time, I was in a clinch with Ella, kissing as we worked our fingers in each other's pussies. With Poppaea out of action, their passion began to subside, although Ella and I brought each other off before collapsing in exhaustion. I lay for a long while with Ella snuggled into my arms, her head resting between my breasts as she sucked her thumb.

Hecate was the one who finally roused us and turned on an electric torch so that we could tidy up. That broke the spell, and I was amazed how shy and embarrassed some of the girls were, once they were dressed. The enthusiasm with which they'd indulged themselves told me that it had not been the first time, yet nor did they have my experience. I've introduced enough girls to the pleasures of lesbian sex to recognise the aftermath of uncertainty and guilt and, while none of the coven had the open delight of Amber Oakley or Ginny Scott, none of them had been virgin to such pleasures, either.

I'd enjoyed myself enormously anyway, and simply didn't have the heart to tell them that the experience hadn't altered my belief in the least. I was also coming to see the value of their faith, as it provided an excuse to indulge in the most exquisite pleasures and also created a deep bond between them. I was now part of that and, if I didn't actually believe, then there was no way that I was missing out on the chance of more orgies like the one we had just indulged in.

Hecate drove us back. She seemed the strongest and most controlled of the group, and was also older than anyone except me. As I came to realise while we drove back, the others regarded Poppaea with something approaching awe, and the events of the night had strengthened that feeling. They considered her to possess something deeply spiritual, almost messianic, and Hecate in particular seemed to worship her. We had revived her with what was left of the wine, and she quickly returned to her normal self, claiming to remember nothing of what had happened after she drank the libation.

I sat relaxed at the back of the mini-bus while they questioned her in hushed terms. There was a smile on my lips and I felt thoroughly happy as I thought of how jealous Amber would be when I told her. She'd undoubtedly spank me, both for making such a pig of myself and for being such a cynic. When she'd turned my bottom a dozen shades of purple, she'd make me tell her every single detail and then demand an orgasm. Her favourite technique was to sit on my face and masturbate while I licked her bottom-hole. 'Queening' was the correct term for it, and it made me feel deliciously submissive, while a good measure of her pleasure came from making me pleasure her in such a dirty and humiliating way.

233

Thinking of Amber set me on a new train of thought. She worked with leather and moulding latex and could make just about anything in the way of erotic adjuncts. She had a thing about petite girls as well, particularly myself and, while she lacked my absolute disbelief, she also felt an affinity with the outdoors.

As we drove back through the night towards the city, a wicked plan began to develop in my mind. Delphinia came to sit next to me after a while, and cuddled up against me. She was quickly asleep, but my mind was still working when we got back.

I spent the summer living with Amber, and didn't see any of the girls until the following term. Hecate had graduated and moved to London, which deprived the coven of its most organised member. Ea was made a second-level initiate, but as I was older and, frankly, much more organised, Poppaea came increasingly to rely on my back-up.

I continued to keep my involvement with them pretty quiet, but I did go to bed with Poppaea, because I simply couldn't resist it. It actually happened on the first night I was back. I had spent the previous night in bed with Amber and was feeling lonely and badly in need of someone to cuddle. I ran into her in the Union refectory, her green hair being unmistakable. I went to sit with her, we went for a drink afterwards and, from that point, there was no doubt that we'd end up in bed.

Poppaea was a sweet lover, small and gentle and very obliging. She was also surprisingly forceful, and full of dreams of fully re-establishing pagan worship in the country. Although I didn't share her beliefs, I admired her honesty and determination, and was on the point of abandoning my wicked plan when I discovered a weakness in her faith that changed my mind.

She knew full well that the trance-like state she described as possession was only achieved through her own will, and that very few people could do it. Like innumerable mystics before her, what she wanted was some form of tangible

234

proof of her beliefs yet, unlike so many mystics, she was not inclined to accept the comforting placebo of 'faith'.

After some wrestling with my conscience, but not really that much, I decided to go ahead and give Poppaea what she wanted. The only difference was that I wouldn't ever tell her the truth. Fair enough, I'm a disgraceful, scheming little brat and I need my bottom smacked, but it has been a lot of times and it never makes any difference.

I set everything up beautifully, though I say so myself. When Poppaea was in one of her most energetic moods, I pointed out to her that when I had first heard about summonings I'd thought it meant producing an actual, physical being.

'Well, it could,' she answered, 'but think of the energy you'd need to focus. Everything would have to be perfect: the place, the time, everything, and even then, I doubt it would work.'

'Couldn't we try?' I asked.

'I have,' she answered despondently, 'and we've never come close. Not even the Archmage can do it.'

'If anybody can do it, you can,' I assured her.

'It's extraordinarily hard to focus that much earth energy,' she replied. 'I know how, in theory, and of course the first question is, who do we summon?'

'I've been doing a bit of research on that,' I admitted. 'I knew how badly you wanted it, so I've tried to work something out for you, from first principles, as it were.'

'Yes?' she answered, immediately intrigued.

'As I see it,' I said, taking the final plunge, 'it's a question of facilitating whatever process is involved in the materialisation. As you say, it takes a lot of energy, whether from a physical or a metaphysical point of view. So, we ought to choose a deity closely linked to our own land and our own background. Then we select a place used by worshippers in the distant past: a stone row or circle for instance. Next, we choose a significant date and set up the ritual just so. Finally, and this is the clever bit, we offer one of our number as bait, a sort of exotic prey to draw in our intended target.'

'A sacrifice?' Poppaea demanded in astonishment.

'No,' I assured her, 'well, not really, but sort of, yes, a sexual sacrifice, perhaps.'

'How do you mean?' she queried.

'Well, to put it bluntly, you would be tied to the top of the altar with your legs spread wide.'

'To tempt the deity to enter me?'

'Exactly.'

Poppaea went quiet, but I could see that she was thrilled by the idea and more than a little doubtful.

'You're thinking of summoning Herne, aren't you?' she asked, after a long silence.

'Yes,' I answered, impressed by the way she had reached a conclusion that I'd been expecting to have to lead her to and delighted by the way she'd taken the bait.

She shivered and pulled her knees up under her chin, a mannerism she always used when thinking hard.

'Come on, Poppy,' I urged. 'We can at least try.'

She nodded and I knew I had her. Whether she really believed we could do it I'm not sure, but I knew she was thinking of how it would feel to be spread out naked on that altar stone, waiting to be entered, and she knew full well that when nothing happened, there would still be an obliging tongue to make sure she didn't go entirely unfulfilled. It was then that she gave me an unexpected surprise.

'I'd have to lead the ceremony,' she declared decisively. 'Would you go on the altar?'

I nodded and immediately knew why she couldn't resist the idea.

Autumn equinox was a Sunday and the night of the new moon, which was perfect. We'd chosen a stone circle in north Wales, which was a bit of a drive but had the advantage of remoteness and being in the middle of a gigantic forestry plantation.

I signed the mini-bus out myself, which was an advantage I had as a lecturer, and drove down on the Sunday morning. We lunched at a convenient pub and then walked out to the site, finding it satisfyingly lonely and full of atmosphere. The pines were mature, a good forty feet tall. This created a dank, dim space beneath them, which was thick with the scent of pine resin and earth. The stone circle had been left clear, an area of rough, tussocky grass with thirteen weathered standing stones set around a central block. The air was warm and still, adding a drowsy element to everything else, and I knew from that moment that, come what may, the experience was going to be very deep indeed.

The idea was to evoke the very essence of the wildwood, for which autumn was the perfect time. Poppaea had made up incense from aromatic woods and woven garlands of flowers and leaves that were deliberately chaotic and free of symmetry. Everything we were to use was either stone, wood or some other natural product. Even the candles were beeswax and, when the time came to undress, we took off everything, right down to our jewellery.

They had covered the altar stone with a bed of ferns and circled it with hemp, to which I was to be fastened. For all my knowledge of what was really going to happen and my disbelief, it was impossible not to feel affected as Poppaea and Ea led me to the altar. I was trembling, but sat down and submitted myself to them, allowing my wrists and ankles to be fixed tightly to the ring of hemp so that I was spread-eagled on the altar. My arms were thrown back above my head and my legs pulled wide to leave my vagina easily accessible. My head was back so that, unless I made a deliberate effort to look forward, all I could see was the rich blue of the evening sky. Poppaea had decided that dusk was the correct time for the ritual, it being the hour at which most predators preferred to hunt. Most sightings of Herne the Hunter were also recorded from dusk or dawn as well.

Most of the sightings also involved not just Herne, but the Wish Hunt, a pack of demonic hounds, so it was just as well that I was so firm in my atheistic convictions. The others were the exact opposite, and every one of them was nervous. To me, it was play; to them, it was serious, and it amazed me that they were willing to subject themselves to the attentions of a being best known for hunting down benighted travellers. Poppaea's logic was that we would be safe both because we were worshippers and we were female and giving ourselves willingly. Actually, it was me who was being given willingly, but they'd be there too, and naked if not actually bound.

I relaxed on my bed of fern as the ritual began, listening to Poppaea's soft, insistent chanting and watching the candlelight flicker in their faces and the trees behind. They did look enchanting, and I couldn't deny the power of the ritual, nor the effect it was having on me. They then started to prepare me, Ea and Delphinia doing most of the work while the others chanted. Being anointed with cabbalistic symbols on my face, breasts and belly was both erotic and disturbing, and left my breathing deep and my nipples sticking up. Being licked by Ea to make my pussy swell and open was bliss yet unbearably frustrating. She did it by tickling my sex-lips with the very tip of her tongue, never quite touching my clit. She would tap her tongue gently over my vagina, then move up between my labia, flicking it from side to side until she was nearly at my clit, only to stop and repeat the process. All I could do was squirm in my bonds and whimper for more, which she denied me.

Only when I was screaming in frustration did she change her tactics and give me a good slurping lick, running her whole tongue up my pussy to wet me with her saliva. As she pressed against my clit, I was begging her to take me up to orgasm, but she didn't even reply, instead rising to her feet and slipping two fingers inside me to check that I was moist enough for entry. I was, and I was also in desperate need of my orgasm.

Their chanting rose in intensity as I squirmed and writhed on top of the alter. I was wishing desperately that it was all true because, at that moment, I really did want to be made an erotic sacrifice. The whole experience was just too much, and I would have taken anything with an open, yielding submission. They could have had a goat mount me and I wouldn't have cared – anything, just as long as I was thoroughly used.

238

Poppaea set fire to the scented oil that was in a wooden bowl on the rock between my legs. It burnt greenish-yellow and threw weird shadows around the clearing, the smell rich and heady in my nostrils. I could feel the heat on my thighs and pussy, warm and sensual. Then she was putting something to my mouth, a flask of mead, from which I drank deeply. I watched as she put the flask to her own lips, swallowing, then taking a mouthful and bending to let it run from her lips on to my pussy. Each girl in turn did this, until my belly and the ferns beneath my bottom were wet and sticky with mead. Delphinia kissed me on my clitoris, which sent a shock right through me. A little more and I'd have come, but she left to return to her place.

I was ready, and Poppaea began what I knew was the final chant, her voice loud, demanding and somehow hopeful. I lay back, feeling a terrible fraud but not in the least sorry I'd done it. Just for the state they'd put me in, I'd have done it a hundred times. Poppaea switched to Gaelic, her voice rising to a scream, imploring Herne to come and ravish me where I lay tied and helplessly ready.

Then it happened. The air went misty and I became aware of a strange scent, intensely animal yet also hot, like burning leaves mixed with sweat and dung. The chanting stopped abruptly and somebody screamed. I pulled my head up to see the girls fleeing pell-mell into the trees. Coming out of the mist directly in front of me was the reason.

The first thing I saw was the great antlers, backlit against the candle glow from the mist. They sprang from a head, a grotesque thing with burning red eyes and the mixed characteristics of human, goat and deer. Shaggy fur covered the broad, muscular shoulders, only to give way to two large and undoubtedly feminine breasts. There was nothing whatever feminine about what was below. His belly was muscular and hairy, and from the base of it sprouted the most enormous penis I had ever seen. It was blatantly erect, standing close to the vertical, while it must have been over a foot in length and was thicker around than my arms. A deep red-brown in colour, the shaft was heavily veined and gnarled, like a tree trunk. The head was round and taut, a shiny red-purple bulb already oozing something white and thick. A massive scrotum hung beneath it, bulging with testicles the size of tennis balls.

He was coming towards me, the monstrous cock proud and ready for my pussy as I lay helpless with my legs tied apart and my open, wet vagina offered for entry. Everyone else had fled, leaving me to my fate. Then I realised that I was not quite alone as Poppaea came up beside me and sank to her knees next to the altar stone. I watched, unable to take my eyes away as he advanced, his erection threatening my vagina, which suddenly seemed very small and tight.

Poppaea said something in Gaelic and Herne turned, looked at her, grabbed her by the hair and thrust his penis into her mouth. She gaped, her cheeks bulging and then stretching with the effort of accommodating it. He thrust twice and then a great gush of white come exploded from around his shaft, dripping down Poppaea's chin and on to her breasts. As she sucked at him in obvious ecstasy, he turned and for a moment I saw his buttocks, which were hairless, round and as feminine as the breasts. Poppaea sucked eagerly, rubbing the sperm into her breasts and pussy as it dripped from her mouth. He finally pulled out and she put her head to the ground in utter submission as he swept the incense salver off the altar to clear his access to me.

I shut my eyes and groaned, waiting to be ravished. I sensed him mount the altar, then the fur of his legs touched my thighs and a clawed hand brushed my breast. Then something was pushing against my vagina, something huge and rubbery. I could feel his sperm oozing into my vagina as he pushed, stretching me, opening me. My teeth were gritted as my flesh stretched around the head of his cock, which must have been at least the size of my fist. For a moment, I wasn't sure I could take it; but in it went, making me gasp out loud. He was filling me, easing it slowly into my vagina, the sperm dripping out and down between my bottom-cheeks to mingle with the mead and my own juices.

He mounted me, the big breasts squashing against my little ones, warm and undoubtedly real. His fur tickled as he began to ride me with long, controlled strokes, each one of which caused an eruption of sperm into my vagina and then out to wet my thighs and bottom. All I could do was take it, sighing and panting as I was fucked. His head was against my face, the strong animal scent thick in my nostrils, one glowing eye looking right into mine.

I turned my head to find Poppaea looking on in awe. Of the others there was no sign whatever, but she was reaching out a trembling hand to stroke his back. His humping became faster and I shut my eyes, vaguely aware that she was stroking his bottom. I was almost out of my senses and was wondering how much longer I could stand it when he stopped abruptly. I opened my eyes as the vast cock was pulled from my vagina, which was left gaping, sore and oozing come. Poppaea knelt at his feet as he dismounted, only to be taken by the hair and put back to his cock.

He made her suck for perhaps a minute while my aching body shook and trembled with reaction. Then he threw her roughly over and mounted her from behind. I heard her say one word, again in Gaelic, although the pleading tone was not lost on me. Her pert buttocks were up, open and ready for entry. I saw another spurt of come erupt out over her bottom and the huge cock put to her vagina. He entered her carefully and, although she screamed when it went in, it was ecstasy more than pain. As he rode her she put her face in the dirt, babbling something I couldn't understand and clutching at the grass with her hands.

After perhaps fifty hard thrusts he suddenly pulled out and sent another jet of come over her bottom and back, soiling her hair and even hitting the ground beyond her head. She stayed down, and made no resistance as his great hairy arms lifted her with ease. She groaned and gave a little whimper, perhaps expecting to be carried off. Instead she was lowered on to me, head to tail so that her face was over my pussy and her pussy over my face. He took her head and pushed her into me, then gave her a hard slap on the bottom that sent a spray of come into my face.

She began to lick me as I raised my head, poking my tongue to get at her pretty pink pussy. I could smell her, a musky, feminine scent mixed with the stronger, animal scent of his come. The smell reminded me of leather and sweat, like the smell of a girl who has been beaten with a new leather strap. My tongue found Poppaea's clit, tasting the meaty, salt flavour of his come. It was thick, almost like honey, and spread liberally over her pussy and between her bottom-cheeks. Her own tongue was working on my clit as I lapped, Herne looming over us with his mighty arms folded across his chest.

I came first, Poppaea hitting her climax even as my thigh muscles started to contract around her face. Every muscle in my body was tense, my bottom clenching and my arms and legs straining against the rope as I climaxed, still licking desperately at Poppaea's sex. I hit a second peak, then she was pulling up from me and calling something I couldn't make out. I shut my eyes, determined to lick until she wanted me to stop, despite the pain in my neck muscles and my exhaustion. I could see her bumhole contracting rhythmically in the candlelight as she went through a long, long climax, peaking perhaps four or five times before finally subsiding on to me in a sweaty, juice-smeared heap.

My head fell back to the ferns and I closed my eyes, opening them a moment later to find that we were alone.

Amber had done me proud. I'd expected her to be pretty impressive, but she'd surpassed my most vivid imaginings. The magnificent fake Herne had fooled everyone, even Poppy while she was actually being mounted. Of course, it had been smoky and pretty dim, and she'd been taken from behind, yet she'd also sucked on Amber's splendid strap-on dildo and never realised it was not flesh. It was also just like Amber not to be able to resist the androgynous touches, leaving her breasts and buttocks bare so that she could achieve at least some physical sensation in addition to the mental pleasure of ravishing Poppaea and me. She'd done something there, too, because the fullness of both her breasts and bottom had been more like Ginny's than her own.

242

I hadn't really expected the other girls to be quite so terrified yet, when they met Poppaea and me at the mini-bus, they were all very apologetic. Ea had watched from the woods and she, even more than the others, was completely in awe of Poppaea. That was what removed any last doubts I might have had about my deception because, although Poppaea was completely exhausted, she was also absolutely glowing. The girls couldn't praise her enough and every one of them now regarded her with an admiration that was akin to worship. I got my share of praise, too, and I admit to revelling in it; yet what I really wanted to do was meet up with Amber and find out just how she had done it so well.

We were supposed to meet at my flat, for which Amber had a key. As it was, Poppaea needed a cuddle so badly that I stayed with her until dawn, only then slipping out of bed and making my way across the city in the first light of morning. Amber wasn't at my flat and, for a horrible moment, I thought she'd got fed up and gone home. Then I realised that nothing whatever had been disturbed and that nobody had been there at all.

The light on my answering machine was blinking, and I pressed the button, expecting to hear Amber saying she'd broken down somewhere between Wales and my flat. As the machine clicked and whirred I was smiling at the image of Amber calling out the RAC in her full Herne the Hunter get-up, but when the tape started it was not her voice, but Ginny's that spoke.

'Penny, hi, it's Ginny,' her voice sounded. 'I hope I've caught you in time. Look, Amber can't make it, she's had to go abroad . . .'

243

NEW BOOKS

Coming up from Nexus and Black Lace

Nexus

There are three Nexus titles published in March

The Black Widow by Lisette Ashton
March 1999   Price £5.99   ISBN: 0 352 33338 3

Spurned by her husband, and cheated of her heritage, the Black Widow feels justified in seeking revenge. Determined to lay claim to Elysian Fields, a health farm with a unique doctrine of sensual pleasure and erotic stimulation, the Black Widow wants what is rightfully hers. Indulging a new-found passion for sexual domination, she is only too pleased to deal with those that get in her way. Punishments are cruel and explicit as she forces subordinates to do her bidding. Caught in the middle of the hostile takeover, Jo Valentine finds herself entangled in the Black Widow's web. By the author of *The Black Room* and *Amazon Slave*.

The Reluctant Virgin by Kendal Grahame
March 1999   Price £5.99   ISBN: 0 352 33339 1

The beautiful Karina Devonside is due to inherit a fortune on her twenty-first birthday, but she is far from happy. Unlike her naughty best friend Sandy, she is still a virgin, and circumstances are conspiring to keep her that way. But Sandy's tales of sluttish behaviour have been driving Karina wild for too long now – who will she choose to help her sate her lust? By the author of *The Training of Fallen Angels* and *The Warrior Queen*.

Choosing Lovers for Justine by Aran Ashe
March 1999   Price £5.99   ISBN: 0 352 33351 0

Chosen to live a life according to discipline and subservience, the young Justine is introduced to a succession of lovers. Each one has favoured methods of taking pleasure from her willing body – pleasure which is often found through the demands of pain and submission. Presided over by her strict guardian Julia, we follow Justine's initiation into a world of obedience, dominated by the less than genteel ladies and gentlemen of the Edwardian well-to-do. This novel, by the author of *The Handmaidens* and *Citadel of Servitude*, is the second in a series of Nexus Classics – dedicated to putting the finest works of erotic fiction back in print.

There are three Nexus titles published in April

Displays of Innocents by Lucy Golden
April 1999   Price £5.99   ISBN: 0 352 33342 1

The twelve stories in this collection reveal the experiences of those who dare to step outside the familiar bounds of everyday life. Irene is called for an interview, but has never been examined as thoroughly as this; Gemma cannot believe the demands made by her new clients, a respectable middle-aged couple; Helen learns that the boss's wife has an intimate way of demonstrating her authority. For some, it widens their horizons; for others it is an agony never to be repeated. For all twelve, it is a tale of intense erotic power.

Disciples of Shame by Stephanie Calvin
April 1999   Price £5.99   ISBN: 0 352 33343 X

Inspired by her grandfather's memoirs, the young and beautiful Amelia decides to begin her own erotic adventures. She soon draws all around her into her schemes as they help her to act out her most lewd fantasies – among others her best friend, Alice, who loves to be told what to do, and her shy aunt, Susan, who needs to be persuaded. All her friends take part in her increasingly bizarre games, before the final, most perverse drama unfolds.

The Institute by Maria del Rey
April 1999   Price £5.99   ISBN: 0 352 33352 9

Set in a strange institute for the treatment of delinquent girls between the ages of eighteen and twenty-one, this is the story of Lucy, a naughty young woman who is sentenced to be rehabilitated. Their disciplinary methods are not what she has been led to expect, however – they are, in fact, decidedly strange. This is the third in a series of Nexus Classics – dedicated to bringing the finest works of erotic fiction to a new audience.

BLACK
lace

The Top of Her Game by Emma Holly
March 1999   Price £5.99   ISBN: 0 352 33337 5

Successful dominatrix Julia Mueller has been searching all her life for a man who is too tough to be tamed. But when she locks horns with a no-nonsense Montana rancher, will she discover the perfect balance between domination and surrender, or will her dark side win out?

Raw Silk by Lisabet Sarai
March 1999   Price £5.99   ISBN: 0 352 33336 7

When software engineer Kate O'Neil leaves her lover David to take a job in Bangkok, she becomes sexually involved with two very different men: a kinky member of the Thai aristocracy and the charismatic proprietor of a sex bar. When David arrives in Thailand, Kate realises she must choose between three very different men. She invites all three to join her in a sexual adventure that finally makes clear to her what she really wants and needs.

Stand and Deliver by Helena Ravenscroft
April 1999   Price £5.99   ISBN: 0 352 33340 5

It's the 18th century. Lydia Fitzgerald finds herself helplessly drawn to Drummond, a handsome highwayman. This occurs despite the fact that she is the ward of his brother, Valerian, who controls the Hawkesworth estate. There, Valerian and his beautiful mistress initiate Lydia's seduction and, though she is in love with Drummond, Lydia is unable to resist the experimentation they offer.

Haunted by Laura Thornton
April 1999   Price £5.99   ISBN: 0 352 33341 3

A modern-day Gothic story set in both England and New York. Sasha Hayward is an American woman whose erotic obsession with a long-dead pair of lovers leads her on a steamy and evocative search. Seeking out descendants of the enigmatic pair, Sasha consummates her obsession in a series of stangely perverse encounters related to this haunting mystery.

Nexus

NEXUS BACKLIST

All books are priced £5.99 unless another price is given. If a date is supplied, the book in question will not be available until that month in 1999.

CONTEMPORARY EROTICA

AMAZON SLAVE	Lisette Ashton		
BAD PENNY	Penny Birch		Feb
THE BLACK GARTER	Lisette Ashton		
THE BLACK WIDOW	Lisette Ashton		Mar
BOUND TO OBEY	Amanda Ware		
BRAT	Penny Birch		May
CHAINS OF SHAME	Brigitte Markham		
DARK DELIGHTS	Maria del Rey		
DARLINE DOMINANT	Tania d'Alanis		
A DEGREE OF DISCIPLINE	Zoe Templeton	£4.99	
DISCIPLES OF SHAME	Stephanie Calvin		Apr
THE DISCIPLINE OF NURSE RIDING	Yolanda Celbridge		
DISPLAYS OF INNOCENTS	Lucy Golden		Apr
EDUCATING ELLA	Stephen Ferris	£4.99	
EMMA'S SECRET DOMINATION	Hilary James	£4.99	
EXPOSING LOUISA	Jean Aveline		Jan
FAIRGROUND ATTRACTIONS	Lisette Ashton		
JULIE AT THE REFORMATORY	Angela Elgar	£4.99	
LINGERING LESSONS	Sarah Veitch		Jan
A MASTER OF DISCIPLINE	Zoe Templeton		
THE MISTRESS OF STERNWOOD GRANGE	Arabella Knight		

SAMPLERS & COLLECTIONS

EROTICON 4	Various		
THE FIESTA LETTERS	ed. Chris Lloyd	£4.99	
NEW EROTICA 4			

NEXUS CLASSICS
A new imprint dedicated to putting the finest works of erotic fiction back in print

THE IMAGE	Jean de Berg	Feb
CHOOSING LOVERS FOR JUSTINE	Aran Ashe	Mar
THE INSTITUTE	Maria del Rey	Apr
AGONY AUNT	G. C. Scott	May
THE HANDMAIDENS	Aran Ashe	Jun

Please send me the books I have ticked above.

Name ....

Address ....

....

....

.... Post code........................

Send to: Cash Sales, Nexus Books, Thames Wharf Studios, Rainville Road, London W6 9HT

Please enclose a cheque or postal order, made payable to **Nexus Books**, to the value of the books you have ordered plus postage and packing costs as follows:

UK and BFPO – £1.00 for the first book, 50p for the second book and 30p for each subsequent book to a maximum of £3.00;

Overseas (including Republic of Ireland) – £2.00 for the first book, £1.00 for the second book and 50p for each subsequent book.

If you would prefer to pay by VISA or ACCESS/MASTER-CARD, please write your card number and expiry date here:

....

Please allow up to 28 days for delivery.

Signature ....

MEDICAL
Pulse-racing passion

How To Resist The Single Dad
JC Harroway

A Date With Her Best Friend
Louisa Heaton

MILLS & BOON

HOW TO RESIST THE SINGLE DAD
© 2022 by JC Harroway
Philippine Copyright 2022
Australian Copyright 2022
New Zealand Copyright 2022

First Published 2022
First Australian Paperback Edition 2022
ISBN 978 1 867 26252 7

A DATE WITH HER BEST FRIEND
© 2022 by Louisa Heaton
Philippine Copyright 2022
Australian Copyright 2022
New Zealand Copyright 2022

First Published 2022
First Australian Paperback Edition 2022
ISBN 978 1 867 26252 7

MIX
Paper | Supporting
responsible forestry
FSC® C001695
www.fsc.org

Published by
Harlequin Mills & Boon
An imprint of Harlequin Enterprises (Australia) Pty Limited
(ABN 47 001 180 918), a subsidiary of HarperCollins
Publishers Australia Pty Limited
(ABN 36 009 913 517)
Level 13, 201 Elizabeth Street
SYDNEY NSW 2000 AUSTRALIA

Cover art used by arrangement with Harlequin Books S.A.. All rights reserved.

Printed and bound in Australia by McPherson's Printing Group

How To Resist The Single Dad
JC Harroway

MILLS & BOON

Lifelong romance addict **JC Harroway** took a break from her career as a junior doctor to raise a family and found her calling as a Harlequin author instead. She now lives in New Zealand and finds that writing feeds her very real obsession with happy endings and the endorphin rush they create. You can follow her at jcharroway.com, and on Facebook, Twitter and Instagram.

Visit the Author Profile page at
millsandboon.com.au for more titles.

Dear Reader,

Having lived in a small English village for many years, I found it enchanting to write Aaron and Stella's story in such an idyllic setting. Compared to that of the city, there is a different dynamic to the close-knit communities of rural life as shown by the medical scenarios I threw my hero and heroine into. By pushing London-loving Stella out of her comfort zone, it becomes clear that her roots are an undeniable part of her identity. I know this firsthand being born and raised in Wales and now living in New Zealand! This was also my first story with a single parent, and I loved writing the scenes featuring Charlie. Showing Aaron's character through his relationship with his son really helped me to get into my hero's head and unearth different aspirational aspects of his personality.

I hope you enjoy *How to Resist the Single Dad*.

Love

JC x

DEDICATION

To Becky, my horse-loving, Wellie-wearing,
Land Rover–driving friend.

CHAPTER ONE

WATCHING DR AARON BENNETT speak from the main lecture-theatre podium of London's City Hospital gave Stella Wright serious crush flashbacks. Of course she had fancied him. Who wouldn't? But, where her ridiculous teenage obsession had been abstract, that of the shy fourteen-year-old she'd once been, now she struggled to focus on his lecture to this year's intake of general-practitioner trainees.

Like an expensive single-malt whisky, Aaron had only improved with age. He sported a head of sandy blond hair that had the tendency to flop over his aristocratic brow. His dark-framed glasses made his bright blue eyes—ones she had once considered *dreamy*—appear more intense. He wore a fine-knit V-necked jumper over his shirt, and when he had turned his back on his audience to point at the screen, Stella had almost drooled at his toned backside. In fact, his entire look brought to mind a sexy professor fantasy that Stella should in no way indulge.

She dragged her eyes away. She was long ago done with charmers and Aaron Bennett epitomised the definition. Or at least he had during his twenties and early thirties in their Cotswold village of Abbotsford.

With a reputation as a charismatic playboy, he'd regularly blasted back into their sleepy village for a weekend of hedonistic fun, always driving a fast sports car and bringing with him a gaggle of friends looking for a wild party at the country estate his parents still ran. His notorious reputation had been the talk of the town, every eligible woman and mother alike wondering when the local heartthrob would settle down. Return home for good and take up his place in the small community.

To everyone's surprise, he eventually had.

And now, here in London—Stella's home these past nine years—he seemed somehow out of place, even though he himself had trained and worked in the capital.

Of course, she hadn't heard a word of what he'd actually said for the last five minutes since she'd first drifted off into a lust-filled daydream and then been reminded of another Cotswolds smooth-talker, one who'd done such a good job of breaking her heart, she'd sworn off relationships at the tender age of eighteen. Which was why, when he closed his laptop at the end of his lecture and said her name, Stella almost slid from her seat to disappear beneath the desk.

'Could Stella Wright please see me? Thank you.' He swept his gaze over the doctors filling the auditorium.

In case her friends were watching and wondering what she had done to upset the teacher, Stella forced her face to freeze on a benign smile, while her insides tumbled over themselves to make sense of his request. What could Aaron Bennett want with *her*? Yes, they came from the same small village, where his family descended from a long line of landed gentry. She knew all about his tragic past, which like Stella's own notoriety had no doubt been prime village-gossip fodder. But they'd never actually spoken to one another.

Fourteen- or fifteen-year-old Stella would have swooned.

It was a good thing that twenty-seven-year-old committed singleton Dr Stella Wright's swooning days were over.

As Aaron fell into conversation with one of the keener registrars, a gorgeous blonde Stella knew well enough to guess had approached him with an intelligent question that had nothing to do with his backside or dreamy eyes, Stella headed for the stairs and raked her scattered wits for something to say other than *Hi, I used to have a crush on you.*

For goodness' sake, he was one of her educational supervisors. Her past and irrelevant infatuation with Dr Delicious should serve only to remind her of the momentous reasons she'd left Abbotsford for the big-city lights of London in the first place. Why she'd followed in her sister Darcy's footsteps and moved here, reinventing herself in the process.

Heartbreak Harry, as she'd named her ex.

Stella cast a glance at Aaron. Had he remembered her from Abbotsford, heard the gossip?

Still in conversation with the blonde, he seemed completely oblivious to Stella. Perhaps he didn't know she existed. Well, that suited her just fine.

She paused halfway down the steps to reply to a group text from her GP trainee friends, who were about to scatter across the country for the final eighteen months of their training.

Clubbing tonight—last night before we all disperse.

Stella smiled, a spasm of nostalgia pinching her ribs. She was staying in London. She loved living here. The vibrancy, the constant bustle, the anonymity of being one person out of millions. But she would miss her crew. Who would go clubbing with her now? Her sister was recently all loved up, so she had no hope of dragging Darcy out on the town.

Just then her friend Tom called out from the front of the lecture theatre, where there was a bottleneck at the exit.

'Stells.' He waved, snagging her attention away from Aaron's broad shoulders. 'Pre-drinks at the pub tonight? Wear your dancing shoes.' Tom offered a playful wink, a shimmy to a tune only he could hear and left the lecture theatre.

Tom didn't do subtle. There was no way Aaron had missed their interaction.

Prickles danced over her skin, a sensation of Aaron's observation that should have been uncomfortable but instead left her wondering if he was still single or remained unattached after the death of his wife.

She looked up, sucking in a breath as her stare collided directly with his. He had been watching her, his conversation seemingly abandoned as he stared intently.

A small smile twitched her cheeks while she battled the incendiary effects of that direct eye contact. It could have only lasted a second or two, but it was long enough for Stella's pulse to skyrocket and her breath to trap under her diaphragm as if she had a stitch.

Had she imagined a tightening of his facial muscles between his brows, the thinning of his lips? Was he judging her penchant for having a good time, letting down her hair, dancing?

Clearly they had little in common beyond coming from the same village.

Stella lingered over the last few steps to the front of the auditorium, waiting for him to wind up his conversation.

The other doctor headed for the exit, leaving her and Aaron alone. The vast theatre, which could easily seat three hundred people, shrank to the size of a broom cupboard. The closer she stepped, the more attractive he became. Nerves accosted her stomach at his tall, imposing masculinity. Their differences—the age gap and the country-boy, city-girl chasm—seemed increasingly trivial.

'Dr Wright, thanks for waiting behind,' he said, his deep voice confident and full of warmth. He tossed his glasses onto the podium and held out his hand.

'No problem,' she croaked, shaking his hand firmly in order to boost her wobbling confidence. Alone with her and up close he seemed to have morphed into the hottest man she'd ever met.

With his glasses removed, his bold blue eyes

were more vibrant. His biceps and pecs were clearly demarcated beneath his jumper. His tie was ever so slightly askew, lending him a roguish, devil-may-care vibe that tied all of his attractive qualities together with a bright red bow, a combination that packed a considerable punch to Stella's poor neglected libido.

She swallowed. Time to get a grip. His hotness was completely irrelevant.

a) He had looked disapproving at her clubbing plans.

b) Despite no trace of a dad bod, Stella knew from her parents that he had a young son.

c) Perhaps the most important factor of all: Stella hadn't dated since Harry.

'I won't keep you long.' He dropped her hand.

Stella wiped her palm on her trouser leg as discreetly as possible, praying like crazy that he hadn't felt the judders zapping along her nerves as they touched. This close she could smell his aftershave, which was woodsy and fresh and made her homesick for autumn walks through the countryside and roaring fires on a cold day.

'What's this about?' she said, the flash of what looked like guilt or sympathy on his face raising her defensive hackles. Was he recalling what he knew of her from the small talk that had once circulated in Abbotsford?

She felt like a germ swimming in a petri dish.

Privacy was scarce in village life, and Stella had left the Cotswolds for university under a cloud of unjust gossip that still had the ability to make her shudder with shame. Not because the rumours had been true—beyond being young and naive and falling head over heels for the wrong man with a young son and a complicated past he'd lied about, she'd done nothing wrong. But because she couldn't for the life of herself fathom that she'd once been so gullible, so lovestruck, so pitiable.

If only she could forget the humiliation of not only having her tender teenaged heart broken for the first time, but also being unfairly vilified as some sort of Lolita-esque home-wrecker…

'I'm afraid there's an issue with your GP placement,' Aaron said without reference to Abbotsford. Perhaps he didn't recognise her after all.

Stella winced at the bedside manner of his tone. 'What issue?'

Aaron's stare roamed her face as if peeling away her layers of armour, one by one. Did he have to look at her with such…intimacy?

'I'm afraid your assigned GP, Dr Roberts at Ealing Health has suffered a serious medical emergency and will no longer be able to accommodate you at his surgery.'

Stella covered her mouth in shock. 'Is he okay?' *Poor Dr Roberts.*

'He suffered a myocardial infarction yesterday,' Aaron said, 'and underwent coronary artery stenting this morning, but obviously he isn't expected back at work for some time.'

Stella nodded, realisation dawning. She was due to start her GP placement at Ealing Health on Monday. Dr Roberts was meant to supervise her training for the next year and a half.

'So what happens now?' she asked, her skin tight with prickles. 'Presumably I'll be placed at my second-choice surgery in Hammersmith.'

'I'm afraid not.' Aaron's lips flattened, drawing Stella's gaze reluctantly from his piercing and perceptive eyes. Idly she wondered if he'd be a good kisser. He must be to have earned his reputation.

He cleared his throat, drawing Stella back to the conversation. 'They already have a GP trainee there.'

'So where exactly will I be placed?' Stella's blood started to roar in her ears. She empathised with poor Dr Roberts, she truly did, but there had to be a suitable alternative. The powers that be at the Royal College of General Practitioners must have a plan B for this kind of unfortunate eventuality.

Aaron frowned, his lips twisted with frustration, a move that did nothing to diminish his rugged good looks. 'As most of the placements have already been finalised, you've been assigned to my practice in the Cotswolds.'

Stella's mouth fell open. 'What...? But...' No. Abbotsford was a part of her previous life, a life she'd abandoned when she'd wrapped up her tattered heart, left behind tragic small-town Stella and moved permanently to London. She had abandoned the misty-eyed and gauche teenager she had been, grown up, reinvented herself. Here she was fun and free Stella with a career she adored, a buzzing social life and an enviable shoe collection to complement her party outfits.

Aaron rubbed his hand along his cleanly shaven jaw as if he was as irritated with the arrangement as she was, which inflamed her further.

'I'll go anywhere else,' she pleaded. 'There must be somewhere else.' She was being rude, but his news couldn't be any less welcome.

'I'm afraid not.' His polite smile was tight. 'But bear in mind that I didn't ask for a trainee either.'

She flushed and then qualified, 'What I mean is that I specifically requested to be assigned to a London practice. I'm more likely to receive a broad experience in the city and this is where I plan on living and working. I've no interest in a village practice.'

She had left village life behind.

At her unintentional put-down, the corners of Aaron's eyes crinkled, his irises chilling two shades icier.

He crossed his arms over that broad chest and this time her keen eyes caught a glimpse of golden chest hair behind the loosened collar of his shirt. 'That may be the case, but there is nowhere else at such short notice.' Now his expression sported as much frustration as Stella felt coiling in her stomach.

Her heart sank, the bad news in no way softened by the flare of lust running through her veins.

No, no, no. She couldn't work for her ancient crush, and she couldn't spend the next year and a half living in the village that featured at the centre of her most shameful regret.

Perfect.

Aaron's lush lips moved. Instead of imagined kisses, Stella listened as he confirmed her worst fears. 'I'm afraid, Dr Wright, that, like it or not, we're stuck with each other.'

CHAPTER TWO

AARON STAMPED HIS feet in order to drive some blood into his frigid toes and pressed the phone closer to his ear to hear over the chatter of some rowdy passers-by. The streets around City Hospital were conveniently littered with long-established aptly named pubs: The Surgeon's Arms, Nightingale Inn, and his personal favourite: The Crown and Canker. It was Friday night. Spirits were high.

'Okay, Charlie. Dad will help you build a castle in the morning, I promise,' he said to his five-year-old.

'Will you be here before breakfast, Daddy?'

'Of course I will. I promise.' He winced. A slither of that special brand of guilt reserved only for parents snaked down his spine. 'Does Grandma have our favourite cereal, the one that makes our muscles strong and our brains smart like a superhero?'

His son's boyish chuckle warmed him through,

as it never failed to do. If only it could permanently drive away the constant fear that he was making a hash of raising his son solo.

'Yes, Daddy. See you at breakfast. Goodnight. I love you.'

'I love you too, Champ.'

Aaron spoke briefly to his mother, confirming that he'd be back in Abbotsford first thing in the morning and then hung up the phone. For a handful of seconds he stared at the blank screen, paralysed by familiar remorse. He tried to minimise his nights away from Charlie. He'd made a promise to his tiny days-old son that he'd always be there for him, be both parents rolled into one, so that the boy would never want for anything. The only reason he'd taken the GP lecturing position at City Hospital was because he could make a difference, give something back to the general-practitioner training programme and limit his absence from home to one night a month.

It was silly, but to Aaron the time away seemed interminable.

He slipped his phone into his pocket, struggling with the sense of failure and regret that became heightencd whenever they were apart. But no amount of self-flagellation changed their circumstances.

It was still just the two of them. The Boys' Club.

Snapping from his trance, Aaron ducked out

of the dreary mid-November weather and inside the warmth of The Crown and Canker. The sweet smell of real ale and wood smoke accosted his nostrils and provided a sense of nostalgia akin to a comforting embrace. He cherished every moment of being a single dad, but after a long week at work, he couldn't deny himself his one vice: a pint or two of good beer in good company.

And tonight, more than ever, he wished to forget the new distraction in his life, one he certainly didn't need: Stella Wright.

He'd instantly spotted her familiar name on his list of GP trainees. The first time he'd seen her at City Hospital, back in the summer, when he'd attended his interview, he'd recognised her, despite only previously knowing her from afar. She was the kind of woman you noticed. Strikingly attractive, her kaleidoscopic green-brown eyes bright with intelligence and that ready, infectious laugh that had seemed to demand his attention. Just like today, she'd been with the tall redheaded man who'd beckoned her from the front of the lecture theatre. Was she out with him now, laughing, drinking, dancing? Clearly they were a well-matched couple.

No wonder she despised the idea of leaving London.

Sleepy Abbotsford and a hick GP like him

had little to offer a young, vibrant socialite like Stella Wright.

I'll go anywhere else.

Oh, her plea had kneed him right in the groin, because he harboured similar reluctance. The last thing he wanted was an unwilling trainee messing with his ordered existence. He had vowed, after losing his wife, Molly, only days after she'd given birth to their only child, that providing Charlie with stability and more love than he could ever need would be Aaron's number-one priority.

He sighed. There would be no avoiding the issue when she arrived in his GP practice on Monday morning. He'd have a major complication to manage, one with mesmerising hazel eyes, a captivating smile and a stimulating personality. One who unconsciously reminded him that he was more than a rural GP, a father, a son. He was also a man, a part of himself he'd sidelined for the past five years.

Fortunately for him, not only did Stella likely have a boyfriend, but Aaron had also become a pro at multitasking since Charlie's birth. If he focused on his priorities—Charlie and his work—he could keep any attraction he felt towards Stella the way it should be: irrelevant.

Dodging a raucous crowd who appeared fully committed to celebrating the start of the weekend, Aaron scanned the crowded pub. He spotted his old friend, Joe Austin and Joe's girl-friend, Darcy—who just happened to be Stel-la's sister—in a nook near one of the windows. Aaron waved, stretching above a sea of heads and weaved through the Friday night revellers, his spirits rising in the buoyant atmosphere.

This was exactly what he needed tonight. Forget Stella Wright.

He arrived at Joe and Darcy's table, his stom-ach swooping to his boots. Stella sat with them. He hadn't spied her from across the pub. Now his blood surged with adrenaline, both thrilling and dreaded.

Their eyes clashed like a high-speed colli-sion. Hers were defiant, challenging in a way that heated his blood.

'You made it,' said Joe, grinning in welcome and rising to his feet.

'Yeah, sorry I'm late.' Aaron dragged his stare away from Stella, whose lips had flattened with disapproval the minute he joined them, and greeted Darcy. 'Lovely to see you again.' He kissed Darcy's cheek.

'You remember my sister from Abbotsford, of course,' said Darcy, seemingly unaware of the frosty atmosphere surrounding him and her sister.

Aaron shrugged out of his coat. 'A little, yes.'

He offered Stella a nod of recognition and a tight smile that he hoped concealed the rush of turmoil her presence created.

Of course their age difference, he at least fourteen years her senior, meant he hadn't been familiar with Stella when they'd both lived in Abbotsford beyond knowing that she existed. He had vague memories of Darcy's younger half-siblings, of there being three Wright sisters, but then he had left home for university, become too absorbed in his own life and only returned to the village to live six years ago.

'But we met properly earlier today.' He cast another glance at Stella, finding her mouth pursed with displeasure in a way that told Aaron she hadn't been aware that he was invited this evening.

'Oh,' Darcy chuckled, glancing at Stella with mischief in her eyes. 'Did you know that she had an enormous teenage crush on you back in the day? Hanging on every word of the gossip from your famous weekend parties.'

'Oh, please.' Stella dismissed her sister with an eye roll, her expression feigning boredom. Only the flush colouring her high cheekbones gave away any discomfort.

'Is that right?' he said, disregarding the increased thrill of his pulse and the renewed rumbling of fascination this news provoked. He placed his coat on the window seat lining the ancient bay window, a spot that would position him directly opposite Stella, and smiled benignly at the woman who had all but told him earlier that his small country practice was lame.

She had certainly outgrown any interest in him.

He dragged in a strengthening breath like the ones that he had employed to help him ignore her presence in his lecture. Until her supervisor's ill-health had forced Aaron's hand, forced him to speak with her directly. Forced him to invite her to his quiet country practice where he reigned, controller of his predictably stable universe. And Charlie's.

Stella tossed her dark hair over one shoulder and turned her apathetic gaze his way. 'I didn't know you were joining us tonight…that is, joining *them*.' She pointed to her sister and Joe, who watched their stilted interaction with barely concealed amusement.

What was it about her that drew his curiosity? So she was the first woman in years to ignite a spark in his libido. That meant nothing. Even if she wasn't with the guy he'd seen her with on more than one occasion, he had his life just the way he wanted it and he wouldn't risk disruption to the status quo for something as trivial as sexual attraction. Especially not for a woman who would not only be his trainee, but who also thought his life, his practice, probably even he himself were dull and provincial.

Aaron shrugged. 'Is it a problem?' He had come here to relax, to catch up with Joe. He refused to spend the night trading gibes with Stella, even if it was the most exhilaration he'd had in ages.

She shook her head. 'I'm not staying.' As if to prove her point, she stood, scraping back her chair on the ancient floorboards. 'I'm here with people. We're going clubbing later.' She tilted her chin as if expecting some comment.

He didn't need her reminder to know that she likely viewed everything about him with derision, or that in addition to their age difference, their personalities, their interests couldn't be more different.

He hid his sigh of relief, grateful that she would soon be leaving. She looked far too sexy in her little black dress, and he wasn't used to noticing members of the opposite sex. But there was no ignoring Stella. He looked down to where her long, slender legs ended in a pair of gravity-defying heels—clearly he was a weaker man than he would have thought.

'I see you're wearing your dancing shoes.' He couldn't help but badger her, if only to keep her at a distance.

Stella nodded, defiance pursing her lush lips. 'Yes.' She gave his outfit—jeans, a navy sweater and boots—a return once-over that made his body temperature rise a few degrees.

'You're welcome to join us, if you like.' Amusement sparkled in her eyes. 'Although Darcy and Joe have declined. Fuddy-duddies.'

It was issued as a challenge, one he was only too happy to decline as Joe and Darcy merely sniggered. 'No, thanks. My clubbing days are over. But enjoy yourself. As you probably recall, there aren't any nightclubs in Abbotsford, so it's sensible to get your fix before Monday.'

Mock horror widened her eyes. 'How will I ever endure such a sleepy backwater?'

He grinned. 'Oh, we find a way to make our own fun.' Aaron looked away from the tantalising sparks of fire, for which he liked to think he could take credit. For a man who avoided complications, who relished the quiet, predictable life, he was having way too much fun sparring with this woman.

'Unfortunately for her,' he said to Joe and Darcy in explanation, 'Stella will be joining me as my trainee at the practice from next week.'

At his reminder that she'd been far from enthusiastic earlier, Stella opened her mouth as if to speak and then closed it again, her eyes narrowing.

He took advantage of her temporary speechlessness. 'Well, it looks like it's my round. Can I get anyone a drink?' With Joe and Darcy's order fresh in his mind—Stella had declined—he made his way to the bar, putting some much-needed space between them.

He'd just about reached the front of the queue when someone jostled him from behind. Aaron glanced over his shoulder at the same moment someone grabbed his arm.

'Oh, sorry.' A red-faced Stella braced her hand on his bicep while she corrected her balance. She looked none too pleased that she'd been forced to touch him rather than wobble from her heels.

Aaron took advantage of the fortuitous split second and inhaled the delicious scent of her perfume, enjoying the heat of her body so close and the blush staining her cheeks.

'Did you change your mind about the drink?' Aaron asked, glancing down to where her hand still rested on his arm. He dared not think about how long it had been since a woman had touched him; he was already ancient and out of touch in this woman's eyes.

Stella snatched her hand away. 'No, I didn't. I just came over to clarify a few things with you.'

Ah, she'd come with an agenda. Why bother if she found him so…objectionable? Perhaps he made her nervous. She certainly seemed a little jittery, her eyes darting around the pub as if seeking out an escape route.

'Oh?' He stared into those amazingly spangled eyes, feeling a little like the man he'd been at Stella's age—single but never short of the company of a beautiful and fun woman, confident that he was master of his own destiny, cramming pleasure into every second of his free time. Awareness of her warmth still invading his personal space, of the way her dress clung to her breasts and of the way she made him feel twice as alive as he'd been before she appeared in his consciousness, forced him to redirect his stare to the selection of spirit bottles behind the bar.

Off-limits, way off-limits.

She was too young for him. She would be working for him, no matter how much they both begrudged that twist of fate. And, as always, Charlie needed all of Aaron's spare energy.

'The concerns I voiced about my placement have nothing to do with you personally,' she said, a soft aggrieved huff passing her full lips. 'I hardly know you.'

Said lips were slicked with some sort of shiny gloss. Aaron couldn't help but wonder how it would taste. He needed to focus on her grievances, not indulge inappropriate fantasies.

'It's nothing to do with your practice specifically,' she continued as she did her best to keep her body as far away from his as possible in the crowded bar, a feat that involved shifting her weight from one foot to the other in time with the flow of bodies around them.

'It's not even about the lack of dancing facilities.' Her mouth twitched as she held his stare.

He dragged his eyes away from the temptation of those lips, delighted to discover her sense of humour. It only increased her attractiveness.

She sobered then. 'I had a plan. A plan that doesn't include returning to Abbotsford.'

Aaron nodded in sympathy, his mind abuzz. So it was the place that offended her, not him. But that made no sense. Her parents still lived in the village. She'd grown up there. Would it be so terrible to spend time in a place so familiar? Now he wished that he had paid more attention whenever he heard mention of the Wright family over the years. Maybe then he would understand her reluctance.

Perhaps it was related to the man he had seen her with.

He swallowed the foreign taste of jealousy, his gaze flicking to the very guy, whom Aaron had spotted in conversation with a group of late twenty-somethings at the other end of the bar.

'It's just that when you've been expecting one thing and looking forward to the next stage of your career…' she shrugged '…and then it's suddenly snatched away…'

He wasn't unfeeling. He could understand that she wanted to be close to the man if they were an item. He himself had trained in London and never imagined that he would return to Abbotsford so soon, until he'd met and fallen in love with local woman Molly.

His life had been perfect for a while. Until he'd messed it up.

'Yes,' he said, his throat raw with guilt, 'life is great for disrupting best-laid plans.' No one knew that better than him. Healthy women weren't supposed to die after giving birth to healthy babies in modern, first-world hospitals.

'Anyway,' continued Stella, 'as you pointed out, you are just as stuck with me as I am with you.'

She stared as if expecting him to wave a magic wand and reassign her to another practice. If he could do that he would have done it before even telling her of the change in placement. With his commitments to the educational-supervisor role and to his personal life, he had no desire to foster a reluctant and disappointed trainee who pushed his buttons and left him…restless.

Aaron winced. 'Yes. I apologise for the way that sounded. What I meant was that with my lecturing timetable, I had no intention of taking on a registrar this year. Although, as you yourself insinuated, my quaint country practice likely has little to teach you, anyway.'

He should stop goading her, otherwise Monday would be unbearable. They were polar opposites personality-wise, and she would clearly struggle to respect his professional opinion. It was doomed to complication, something he avoided at all costs. He'd had enough of that in his life, and he owed it to Charlie, and to Molly, to make their son's upbringing as normal and drama-free as possible.

So what the hell was he doing?

Stella narrowed her eyes as if he'd insulted her rather than voiced the facts. 'You know, until we met this afternoon, I believed the hype about you, your reputation as one of the Cotswolds' nicest and best GPs.' She fisted a hand on her hip.

'Thank you,' he deadpanned. A wave of heat and shame flooded Aaron's body. There was something about this woman that made him uncharacteristically adversarial. To make amends, first thing tomorrow, he would appeal to the powers that be to find Stella a more mutually acceptable placement.

'Look.' He adjusted his tone in surrender. 'I can understand that you don't want to be so far away from your boyfriend.' Aaron tilted his head in the guy's direction. 'Let me see what I can arrange, okay? If you really hate the idea of a rural practice in Abbotsford, I'll apply to the college to have you reassigned as soon as possible. It's not our intention to make your GP training torture, after all.' He managed his most cordial smile, dismissing the way she seemed to have awoken him as irrelevant.

'Tom's not my boyfriend.' Stella frowned.

Aaron's heartrate soared, as if one obstacle had been removed. But there were plenty more; best he remember that.

'He's just a friend,' she said, lifting her chin. 'I'm single and my preferring to stay in London has nothing to do with a man, I assure you.'

Except her emphasis, her dismissal made it sound exactly that. The knowledge he was free to find her as attractive as he liked inflamed him. This was bad, bad news. She was hard enough to ignore when he had designated her neatly out of bounds, but now that he knew they were both single, his imagination was free to wander. Right down Lust Street.

Nope, not going there. But a little harmless sparring could surely be returned to the table. He couldn't have her thinking him dull as dishwater.

'Don't be too emphatic,' he joked, his lips twitching with mischief. 'Or you'll have me wondering if your reluctance to work for me is from fear that your ancient crush will resurface.'

He needed to stop this inappropriate informality, but it had been so long since he'd even noticed members of the opposite sex, let alone wanted to talk—no, spar—with one. And he would need to employ humour and every defence known to man in order to keep her at arm's length once they were working side by side.

'I would never change my life for a relationship.' She huffed, unimpressed in a way that made him desperate to shock her and watch her reaction.

'And as for my ancient crush,' she swept her stare from his eyes to his toes and back, 'you shouldn't put too much store in what my sister says. Fifteen-year-old me was also madly in love with every member of the boy band of the moment and several cartoon characters, so don't take it too personally.'

Aaron chuckled. *Touché.*

Then she upped the ante, leaned close as if about to impart a secret. Aaron's body reacted to her proximity as if his libido was responding to a flashing green light. If it wasn't for Charlie and the fact that he'd had his chance at happiness and messed up, big time, he'd would have been seriously afraid for the week ahead.

Stella's breath tickled his neck. 'See you Monday, boss,' she whispered and sauntered off, leaving him confused, conflicted and neck deep in the delusion of possibility.

He abandoned the view of her retreat, the inevitable sinking feeling putting things back into perspective. This round, he would concede her the final word, because he and Stella could never be anything more than a fantasy.

CHAPTER THREE

MONDAY MORNING PUT paid to a weekend of repeatedly chiding herself for getting carried away and bicker-flirting with Aaron in the pub on Friday night. As penance, Stella had donned her most professional demeanour along with her thick tights, tweed skirt and cashmere jumper. She needed the armour if she was to survive working for Aaron, and, far from the sleepy rural practice she had imagined, Abbotsford Medical Centre was a busy place.

Much to Stella's disappointment, from the moment she had walked through the door, Aaron had been polite, formal and utterly appropriate in return.

No more hot looks she wasn't sure that she'd imagined but that made her flustered. No more flirtatious banter back and forth. And his gaze never once dropped below eye level, so her comfortable but flattering outfit was utterly wasted.

She sighed, watching him talk to their latest patient, a six-year-old girl named Gabby.

She had discovered that he was one of two partners at the practice, which served Abbotsford and a clutch of surrounding villages. The building itself had been refurbished since Stella had been a patient, and there was a practice nurse, a team of receptionists and two health visitors. Stella had spent the morning sitting in on his first surgery of the day, and this afternoon she would join Aaron's minor-surgery clinic.

So far, she had been pleasantly surprised by the variety of cases she'd seen. They'd referred a young woman with Wolff-Parkinson-White Syndrome to the specialist at Gloucester General Hospital for an ablation procedure, admitted an elderly farmer with an infectious flare-up of his chronic obstructive pulmonary disease and confirmed three pregnancies. Gabby was their last patient for the morning.

'Gabby, this is Dr Wright,' he said, drawing Stella into the consultation. 'She's going to have a look at your sore throat, okay?' Gabby nodded, big, tearful eyes wary.

Ignoring Aaron's imposing presence just behind her, her body's memories of his strong muscles under her hand and the warm, delicious scent of him in the pub when she'd stumbled at the crowded bar, Stella stooped to Gabby's level where the girl sat on her concerned mother's knee.

'Can I gently feel your neck and then shine a light inside your mouth?' she asked, smiling and showing Gabby the princess and dinosaur stickers stuck to her torch.

Gabby nodded and Stella checked her neck for lymphadenopathy, carefully palpating the swollen lymph nodes on both sides.

'Open wide,' she said, taking a quick look at the girl's very inflamed throat.

'So what's your differential diagnosis?' Aaron asked Stella, smiling reassurance at the girl. 'Don't worry, I'm just quizzing Dr Wright, but you are going to feel better soon.' His attention returned to the computer monitor, his hands clacking at the keyboard keys in a totally sexy way. Was it even possible to type sexily?

Aaron did.

Stella washed her hands at the sink in the corner as she reeled off her answer. 'Viral pharyngitis, Group A streptococcal infection, scarlet fever, acute rheumatic fever and infectious mononucleosis.' She shot mother and daughter a sympathetic smile, knowing that it was likely neither of them had had much sleep the night before. 'As Gabby is pyrexial with swollen and purulent tonsils and cervical lymphadenopathy, I favour streptococcus in this case.'

'Excellent,' said Aaron, his impressed smile doing silly things to her pulse. 'Gabby, Dr Wright and I are going to give you some medicine to take, which will hopefully make you feel much better. In the meantime...' he addressed the mother '...keep her fluid intake up—ice lollies work wonders—and she needs plenty of cuddles and rest.'

He glanced at Gabby. 'Would you like me to prescribe cartoons, too?'

The girl managed a nod and a shy smile and Stella joined in, a small sigh trapped in her lungs. Aaron in GP mode would lift anyone's spirits. Even she felt better in his presence and she wasn't even sick. He showed just the right blend of compassion, confidence and explanation. She could tell from his interactions with this morning's patients that he was well respected, trusted, even treasured around these parts.

It would be easier for Stella if he matched her previous impressions. Playboy Aaron she could dismiss, no matter how attractive charismatic and charming. Except he was no longer the dashing young Romeo, haring around the village in his MG convertible, a pretty date at his side.

To stop herself from drooling over Aaron dressed in crisp chinos, a checked shirt and a soft-looking blue sweater she wanted to rub her-

self all over, Stella recalled his elderly prede-
cessor from her own childhood, Dr Millar. He'd
been cut from the same cloth as Aaron, always
bearing a warm smile that never failed to make
her feel instantly reassured, a silly dad joke and
a sympathetic ear.

But just as Aaron seemed to have changed, the
Stella who had once lived, once belonged in Abbotsford had been different—trusting and hopeful on the cusp of adulthood. And then Harry had
taken her heart, promising to take tender care of
it for ever, before stomping all over the vulnerable organ and inviting the entire village to witness his handiwork. She'd gone from belonging
to both him and to Abbotsford to being adrift in
one fell swoop.

In the nine years she had lived in London, it
had been easier to stay away and pretend that she
didn't care than to return home for the weekend
with all its reminders of how naive she'd been at
eighteen. More than naive: disposable, rejected,
mocked.

To stop her destructive train of thought, she
locked her attention back on Aaron, who was collecting the prescription from the printer. She'd
quizzed her parents last night when she'd arrived in Abbotsford, learning that he was still
decidedly single, despite an almost constant cam-

paign to lure him into a relationship by the village matchmakers and every hot-blooded single woman in the region. He also sent hearts and ovaries aflutter with his fanatical devotion to his little boy.

She observed him out of the corner of her eye and exhaled a discreet sigh; his magnetism, his maturity and dependability were exhausting. She was, after all, only human.

He signed the prescription and stood, passing it over to Gabby's mum. Stella perved another glimpse of his sexy backside, which looked as good in today's chinos as it had in Friday's jeans. She decided he was too perfect. There must be a catch, not that she was worried for herself. If he kept his word and applied for her transfer, she'd soon be away from his particular brand of temptation. But the local women deserved a fighting chance at resisting him, surely.

As Gabby and her mum stood to leave, there was a tap at the door.

Karen, the practice nurse, poked her head through the opening, her face serious. 'Aaron, we've just had a walk-in. It's urgent—can you come?'

Aaron excused himself to their last patient and nodded to Stella, indicating she should follow him. They hurried to the adjacent treatment room.

Stella's adrenaline spiked. She forgot all about fancying Aaron, about being back in Abbotsford, about everything except assisting the person in need of urgent care.

Inside the treatment room, a man in his early sixties sat perched on the examination couch, his fingers curled over the edge with a white-knuckled grip.

'Keep the oxygen mask on, Stan.' Karen replaced the mask over his nose and mouth. 'He's had chest pain since he woke this morning,' said Karen. 'Oxygen sats are ninety-two per cent.'

Aaron rushed to the man's side and took his pulse.

For a split second a flash of recognition gave Stella pause—the patient was Stan Mayfield, Harry's, uncle—but one look at his grey complexion, the sweat beading over his skin and his laboured breathing and she flew into action, wheeling the ECG machine she spied in the corner of the room over to the bedside.

'Call an ambulance, please, Karen,' Aaron requested calmly, encouraging Stan to lie back on the couch while he unbuttoned his shirt. That completed, he took the stethoscope from around his neck, placed the earpieces in his ears and moved the diaphragm over Stan's chest in order to listen to the heart and lungs.

'Does the pain radiate anywhere else?' asked Stella as she stuck electrodes to Stan's sternum, left chest, wrists and ankles in order to obtain an electrical trace of the heart.

Stan nodded, his eyes wide, terrified. He held up his arm, clearly too breathless to speak but indicating that the pain was spreading down his left arm.

Stella tried to comfort him with a hand on his shoulder, compassion nudging aside her adrenaline and automatic actions.

'I'm worried that you're having a heart attack, Stan,' said Aaron, his gaze flicking up to collide with Stella's. 'Dr Wright is going to take an ECG, and I'm going to give you some aspirin and something for the pain. Remind me, are you allergic to anything?' Aaron moved to the locked drugs cabinet and inserted the key from the set he kept clipped to the belt loop of his trousers.

Stan shook his head as Karen re-entered the room. 'Ambulance on its way.'

'And the only medication you're on is the anti-hypertensive I prescribed last month, Stan, right?' Aaron confirmed.

Another nod.

Stella pressed the button to take the ECG. Her respect for Aaron flew through the roof. Could he recall the medical and drug history of each of the two thousand patients registered to the practice? He'd grown up in this village. He lived here with his family. He likely knew everyone. Stella could understand how that could be an asset.

And sometimes, as in her case, a curse.

'Some aspirin, please, Karen, and morphine,' said Aaron, leaving the drugs to the nurse and joining Stella to look at the ECG tracing the machine produced. Stella pointed to the obvious ST elevation on the electrocardiogram, indicative of cardiac ischaemia. Aaron met her stare and nodded his agreement.

Stan was indeed having a heart attack.

Karen handed over the syringe and vial of morphine, which she and Aaron checked together, while Stella inserted an intravenous cannula into the vein on the back of Stan's hand. With the painkiller administered, Stan's pallor improved, his agitation lessened and his respiratory rate dropped closer to normal.

Stella stood back, feeling suddenly out of place, out of her depth, even though she knew she could have diagnosed and treated the medical emergency independently had Aaron not been here. Her bewilderment wasn't about the medical emergency. It was the wake-up call of treating someone she knew from her past life. Her pre-London, broken Stella life. A life she never wanted to revisit, but here she was anyway.

Stan had shown no sign that he recognised Stella, but seeing him again reminded her of that deceived, guileless girl she had been. She might have reinvented herself in London, taken her heartache and pretended it didn't matter, become a carefree party girl too happy-go-lucky for relationships. But the reality was that it had hurt too much to be eighteen-year-old Stella. And back here, her worst fears solidified.

She would always be that artless version of herself in Abbotsford.

The ambulance arrived, a flurry of activity as a brief history was shared and Aaron swiftly completed the paperwork and then called ahead to the accident and emergency team to let them know to expect an acute myocardial infarction.

The drama dealt with, a wave of shivers struck Stella as the adrenaline dissipated from her system.

As if he noticed her shaken composure, Aaron took her elbow and led her to the staff room.

'Time for tea,' he said in a no-nonsense tone, ushering her inside the deserted room, which was comfortably furnished with sofas, a flashy coffee machine and a reassuring array of healthy-looking potted plants.

Aaron wouldn't have missed her freak-out. He was a smart, perceptive, intuitive doctor.

He would ask questions. If he were any other man she might offer a full explanation.

Only, to him, there was none of her ugliness that she wanted to expose.

CHAPTER FOUR

'YOU DID VERY well this morning,' Aaron said, dropping her arm and flicking on the kettle. 'Tea or coffee?' He opened a large jar and placed an assortment of biscuits on a plate and then deposited them on the coffee table in front of Stella.

Stella craved the return of his touch, his warm, capable hand giving comfort she hadn't expected, even though it was probably just his doctor's compassion on display. But ever since that very first handshake back in London she'd battled this fierce attraction.

'Tea please.' Her voice sounded embarrassingly timid. She cleared her throat and reached for a chocolate digestive, needing the blood-sugar hit after the shock of seeing someone she knew, albeit from her past, in an acute medical emergency.

Poor Stan.

Perhaps it was the realisation that if Stan still lived locally, it was likely that Harry and Angus did too. Why was that only now occurring to her? She should have asked her parents if her ex was still living in the next village. What if they walked through the door one day? What if she bumped into them around about? She was over Harry, but that didn't mean that she wanted to relive his offhand dismissal, how easily he had cast her aside.

'Are you okay?' Aaron took a seat next to her so they both faced the stunning view of the rolling hills and a scattering of honey-coloured stone cottages for which the whole area was known and adored.

Stella nodded, taking a grateful sip of her scalding tea and reasoning that, after nine years, she might not even recognise eleven-year-old Angus.

'Yes. Sorry… I just…' She took a deep breath, sifting through her emotions in order to best explain herself without giving too much away to a man who unsettled her, made her crave his approval and his touch. A man she knew instinctively that she would struggle to keep at arm's length, as she normally could with men she found attractive and compelling. Not that she had ever found a member of the opposite sex this compelling.

She met his concerned stare, her mind trying and failing to come up with a good enough excuse for her behaviour. She didn't want Aaron to think she was…unhinged or unprofessional. But nor did she want to inform or remind him of her past errors of judgement, the consequences of which had played out publicly on the Abbotsford stage.

'I understand,' he said in his reassuring voice, his eyes searching and soft. 'Seeing acute medical emergencies in the community is nothing like dealing with them in hospital, where you are part of a team and have every imaginable drug and medical device to hand. You'll get used to it. And you were still part of *our* team.' His mouth stretched into a sympathetic smile that made her feel worse.

She wanted him to look at her the way he had in the pub on Friday. With heat and speculation and challenge and clear interest.

He took a biscuit, polishing it off in two bites. How could watching a man eat a biscuit be a turn-on? A bubble of light-heartedness filled Stella's chest, a miraculous feat considering the way her emotions had to-and-froed this morning.

She shook her head to both clear the erotic image of Aaron eating a chocolate digestive and to contradict his assumption. 'It's not that… I mean, you're right; it is different.' Just not in the way he meant.

She'd visited her parents here over the years, of

course, usually for just a few days, and each time she had feared the possibility of being recognised or seeing someone she knew who was linked to her ex. But this was different. Her placement with Aaron meant living here for an extended period. No matter how much she'd tried to prepare for her return to Abbotsford, she had been unexpectedly rattled by seeing Stan.

She looked up, met Aaron's quizzical stare, her stomach churning anew. 'It's just that I know him. Well, knew him. Stan. Mr Mayfield. It was a bit of a shock, that's all, although I don't think he remembers me.'

'Oh… Well, you're not really a local any more.' His teasing smile was designed to lighten the mood, she could tell. But, overcome by being back in a place associated with her most painful and humiliating memories, Stella swallowed down the absurd urge to cry all over him and his snuggly jumper.

He sensed her distraction, his expression becoming serious. 'You know, I'm a good listener, if you wanted to talk.'

She met his calm blue eyes, her pulse pounding at the realisation that despite their differences, despite how she felt about this traineeship and working with him, she respected him as a doctor. She even respected him as a man. Having been on the receiving end of it, she tried never to indulge in gossip, but you could hardly move in Abbotsford without hearing someone compliment Aaron Bennett, awesome single dad, brilliant GP and all-round nice guy. And now that she'd spent time with him, she understood the hype.

She didn't want to confide in him, except he had that bedside manner people warmed to, drawn into a confessional aura that made you believe that your secrets would be safe in his hands.

Would he understand how simply being back here reminded Stella of her worst pain and her biggest regrets? How, after Harry's betrayal, she'd vowed that she'd get smart, be done with relationships and never make herself that vulnerable to pain again?

If he hadn't touched her arm again, she likely would have kept the lid on the most shameful time in her life. But he did touch her, his fingers flexing on her forearm as if he couldn't help himself.

'It's okay,' he said in a low, soothing tone.

Stella's body shook from the collision of panic and desire. She sighed. She did owe him some sort of explanation after he had plied her with chocolate.

He probably knew the gossip version of the scandal that had driven her so far away from home, anyway. Better that he heard her side of events rather than that of the village grapevine. Better that she explained herself rather than give him the impression that she couldn't deal with her job.

Tired of tying herself up in knots, Stella took a deep breath. 'Before I moved away, I used to date Mr Mayfield's nephew.' She searched his blue eyes to ascertain if he already knew that information, seeing only mild surprise.

He nodded for her to continue, his hand slipping from her arm, his intent gaze clear of judgement or morbid curiosity. 'I don't think I know Stan's extended family. Most of them are registered at the practice in Cheltenham, I believe.'

Relief left Stella on a long exhale that Harry and Angus were unlikely to be patients of Aaron's. She wanted to say more, but for her sanity, for her pride, she needed to steer things back onto a professional footing.

'How do you deal with it?' Stella asked, feeling marginally better for the tea and biscuit. Only now that her adrenaline had waned, she became hyper-aware of Aaron once more, his warmth next to her, the solid physical size of him, his calm, unfazed disposition. Why did all of his attributes add to his charms?

'Deal with what?' His mug, which was emblazoned with the words *My Dad is a Superhero*, made her lips twitch with an indulgent smile that tugged at her heartstrings.

She tried to imagine him as a father. He still carried that air of confidence he'd had as a young man, gadding around the village in his vintage sports car, bringing home a bevy of besotted female nurses only too willing to be the woman of the moment and causing a few rolled eyes in the post office.

'Living in such a small community,' she clarified. 'You know everyone you treat and they know you. Your past. Your mistakes.'

Stella shivered as she recalled walking into the village shop soon after the rumours of her split from Harry had begun, hurtful, soul-crushing lies that had only added to her heartbreak. Unbidden, the worst of the tittle-tattle surfaced from her darkest memories.

'Has she no shame, splitting up a young family?'

'She's very young, but then, she should have known it wouldn't last.'

'Of course he would go back to the mother of his child.'

Stella hadn't been the other woman, she'd just been deceived and double heartbroken. If only she'd had two hearts to absorb the devastating impact.

How could people believe that she'd stolen her

ex from his baby mama when the reality was the opposite, that Harry had lied to Stella and strung along both of them? She had tried to ignore the stares, the loaded silences, to enjoy her last summer at home before leaving for uni. After all, she knew the truth. Her family knew the truth. Harry knew the truth.

And that had been the worst part. The piece of Stella still in love with him had hoped, dreamed, prayed that Harry would set the record straight in the community and come to her defence.

Only he hadn't. His disloyalty had amplified the pain of his rejection.

'That's true,' Aaron said, watchful. 'But everyone makes mistakes. We're all human.' His eyes clouded, perhaps with his own memories.

Stella's human fragility had certainly taken a battering nine years ago. Confused, raw and trying her best to put on a brave face for her parents, she had left for London, where, after crying every night of Fresher's Week, she realised that she could become someone new. A clean start where she called the shots.

She had left sad Stella behind and never looked back. Until now.

'So how do you distance yourself?' she asked, keeping things work-focused. 'How do you socialise with people that you know intimately? As a doctor, you sometimes see people at their worst. How do you then make conversation in the pub as if you're just another acquaintance?' Wherever she worked as a GP she would need to master this skill. She definitely needed it here.

Aaron brushed a biscuit crumb from the leg of his chinos. 'I have a young son, Charlie, so I'm not too much of a regular at the pub.' He quirked his eyebrows, his smile, the intensity of his stare reminiscent of his playfulness on Friday. 'As you already know, my nightclub days are over.'

Stella laughed at his attempt to lighten the atmosphere.

'But you're right.' He placed his mug on the table and leaned forward, resting his elbows on his knees in the way he did when he talked to the patients. 'Being a country GP has its challenges and limitations.' He spread his hands in a gesture of vulnerability. 'I only have a few close friends that I trust with my personal stuff, together with my family. Otherwise, I try to be a private guy. Most patients respect that, even here in a small community.'

'Don't you find it…lonely? Isolating? My experience of growing up here is that everyone knows your business. I found it claustrophobic.' She needed to shut up, but he was so easy to talk to.

Recalling his sad expression earlier, Stella wondered if he was lonely personally too? Five years was a long time to be alone. She shouldn't care about his solitude, about the fact that he was probably still in love with his wife. She had no desire to think of him in any way beyond strictly professional. Except her body hadn't read that small print. It lit up when he was close, craving those casual infrequent touches or the clash of his expressive eye contact.

Stupid Stella.

It was never going to happen. She worked for him and he would consider her too young. They couldn't be more different. He was the country mouse to her town mouse. He had a son and Stella wasn't sure that she even wanted children. She certainly wasn't on the lookout for a relationship, so his loneliness or lack thereof was completely irrelevant.

Only all weekend, while she'd spent time with her sister Darcy doing some of their favourite London things as a farewell—a spot of shopping on Carnaby Street, a trip to their favourite Knightsbridge tea shop and cocktails and dinner at a funky basement club in Mayfair—she hadn't been able to stop thinking about Aaron Bennett.

The real man twice as attractive as the fantasy.

Oh, no…this was bad. Her crush had no business reawakening, especially now when it came in adult form, complete with sexy daydreams and impossible cravings.

How dared he be so sexy? So distracting? So... Aaron?

'All GPs have to be good at compartmentalising,' he said, dragging her mind from the gutter. 'Once I leave the practice, I try to forget work and switch on the other parts of myself. Charlie helps me with that. Five-year-olds need lots of attention.' He grinned in that indulgent way that told Stella he loved being a dad.

Stella's rampant imagination saw Aaron the father: playful, nurturing, patient. Why was that so unfairly arousing? And how could she switch it off? He was a dad, like Harry. Another red flag she should heed. After failing to be enough for one man, despite her bond with his son, she had no desire to find herself unfavourably compared to Charlie's mother, Aaron's wife.

He stood, collecting the mugs and loading them into the dishwasher. Break time was over and Stella needed to pull herself together and stop lusting after a man she didn't want.

'At the end of the day,' he said, his eyes haunted and vulnerable as he returned to the conversation Stella had all but forgotten, 'we all have regrets and we're all entitled to privacy. Remember that.'

He left the room, leaving Stella more conflicted than ever. What regrets was Aaron harbouring and how could she hold herself distant,

as he advised, until she could flee from both the
way he made her feel reckless with need and the
way he reminded her of her own bitter mistakes?

CHAPTER FIVE

Aaron pulled away from the kerb, all too aware of how Stella's light floral scent filled his car and his growing obsession with the way she smiled, her happiness and how she made *him* feel: as if a part of him he hadn't even realised was missing had returned and wanted to steer the ship.

Well, there was no way he would allow his libido to take charge. She was fifteen years younger than him. His trainee.

But it was more than mere attraction, as rampant as that was. As much as he respected his GP partner, Toby, Stella seemed to bring a breath of fresh air and renewed energy to the surgery, as if she'd flung open the windows to invite in the cool, autumn-scented air.

On her second day Stella had again sat in on his morning surgery, impressing him with her astute diagnostic skills and the way she questioned everything, wanting to learn as much as she could from the experience, when he knew her heart wasn't in this particular placement.

She seemed to have recovered from her minor wobble after treating someone from her past. It was only when she'd questioned him about keeping a professional distance from the patients he lived alongside that Aaron realised how out of her comfort zone she was here in what he considered a little corner of paradise, a place he was privileged to live and work. That she had rocked up anyway and was giving the job her all showed her tenacity, determination, courage.

But what had made her feel claustrophobic all those years ago and was it anything to do with this ex she had mentioned? He wished she'd opened up to him more, confessed the deeper reason she was so spooked. Yesterday he hadn't wanted to push her too hard, to pry. He'd even resisted asking his parents if they remembered Stella from nine years ago. No one liked to be the subject of gossip—he understood that on a personal level.

After Molly died he had been the talk of the town for a while. Fortunately, he had been too consumed by grief and guilt to care. He'd had Charlie to focus on.

Aaron cast a side eye at Stella, who sat in the passenger seat, reconciled that she would tell him what she wanted him to know, if and when he earned her trust.

They'd just finished a house call and were now headed back to the practice for afternoon surgery.

'I remember Mrs Taylor,' she said, glancing at him with a relaxed smile. 'She used to be a music teacher at the school, didn't she?' Her voice carried a tinge of sadness, compassion for the retired woman, who was receiving chemotherapy for stage two ovarian cancer.

'Yes. She taught me piano for a while, actually.' He smiled in her direction, reluctantly returning his eyes to the road, because the green blouse she wore today brought out the sparkle in her eyes. He didn't want to crash because he couldn't stop staring at a woman he should not be thinking about that way.

'Do you still play?' The curiosity in her gaze heated the side of his face. To look at her would be to confirm what he'd see in her expressive eyes, what he felt growing stronger within him every moment they spent together and most of the moments they were apart: a constant, undeniable lure he was struggling to keep at bay.

But fight it he must until a new placement could be found and she moved back to London.

'A little—I'm trying to teach Charlie "Twinkle, Twinkle, Little Star".'

'That's adorable.' As he caught her lips curling into that wondrous smile of hers, he recalled what he'd come to think of as their *moments*, because this felt like another one.

What the hell? He should be convincing himself that he'd been mistaken, that a woman like Stella would have no use for a man like him. Except he couldn't forget their spark of chemistry on Friday night when she'd uttered a low challenge, for his ears only.

'See you Monday, boss.'

Her proximity when she'd leaned close to taunt him had set his body aflame for the first time in years. The shock that he had seriously considered kissing her was profound enough to render him on his best behaviour since.

But then they'd shared their second moment in the staff room yesterday when she'd haltingly confided in him about her reservations about returning to Abbotsford. Their differences, their working relationship…none of it had mattered in the face of her vulnerability. He had wanted to know exactly what made her tick, to understand her fears and dreams, to be alone with her. Not as her supervisor; not as Dr Bennett. Just Aaron, a man who'd, out of nowhere, reacted to this woman and needed to sort fantasy from reality in his mind so he could return to normal.

Well, his new normal anyway, the suspended

state he'd inhabited since Charlie was born: get through each day knowing that he'd done everything he could for his son. Mostly that meant putting his own needs second, but that was a small price to pay for the mistake of his past.

Dragging his gaze from Stella's profile and from all thoughts of shared moments, he returned his thoughts to his son.

'I just need to make a brief stop to pick Charlie up from school before we head back to the surgery.' His responsibilities grounded him once more. Fatherhood had become the best role in the world. That his libido felt nineteen again paled into insignificance, especially as it was directed at this particular woman. He wasn't a teenager, or in his twenties, or even in his thirties. Stella Wright needed to remain off limits, because not only had she reawoken his sexual urges, she had also reawakened his guilt.

Aaron didn't deserve such light-hearted and frivolous feelings as lust after letting down Molly and Charlie in such a devastating way. He'd had his shot at happiness. He'd had it all and his wife, his son's mother, had died because he had been careless.

'Of course. No problem.' she said.

Normally Aaron managed to drown out his self-recriminations. But today, perhaps due to

Stella's presence, memories gripped his throat in a choke hold.

Charlie's conception had been an unplanned slip-up. He and Molly had only been married a few months, and they had both wanted to wait a couple of years to start a family. She'd just opened her interior-design shop in Cheltenham and they were enjoying married life together, decorating the run-down old farmer's cottage they'd bought, establishing Aaron's growing practice, living the life of a couple before children.

Then one giggly, wine-fuelled night, a shortage of condoms and a miscalculation of Molly's likely ovulation date had changed everything. Nature had overtaken their careful planning.

Oh, they'd both been excited about the baby after the initial shock. They'd made new plans to share the parenting responsibilities so they could still both commit to their respective careers. But with Molly's death, his guilt and shame had roared to life. Aaron should have known better. He was a doctor, for goodness' sake. He should have been more responsible. Not only had he lost the woman he loved, but also his recklessness had condemned his son to life without his wonderful, kind and funny mother. Every child deserved to know both of their parents. If he'd been more careful, if Molly had become pregnant a few years later, as they'd planned, perhaps she'd still be alive.

Oh, he understood on an intellectual level that the rare postnatal complication she had suffered had nothing to do with timing. But his wisdom didn't help. His beautiful Charlie, with his mother's energy and sense of mischief, served as a constant reminder of Aaron's deepest regret.

'Does he enjoy school?' Stella asked.

He seized the lifeline, wondering how long he had been silent.

'He loves it.' Aaron forced himself to smile, to return to the present moment. To be what he needed to be: Charlie's dad. 'Walking home has become our routine, boys' time where we chat about our day before I have to head back to work for a few hours.'

'Perks of being the boss.' Stella smiled as if infected by the image of his rapscallion son, who was active and full of probing questions. Then she quickly looked away, out of the window, her expression falling contemplative as if she had suddenly remembered that she didn't actually like children. But that couldn't be true. He'd seen her interact with a few at the practice. She was a natural.

'Yes. I'm very lucky to have a job near home where I can walk him across the fields after school.' Rather than rebel against life in Abbotsford without Molly and resent being the much talked-about widower, Aaron was endlessly thankful for this close community. They had rallied around him and his newborn son when they'd come home from the nearby hospital. Baked goods and casseroles had arrived on the doorstep with reassuring regularity. Offers of babysitting had flooded in. As Charlie grew, people delighted in seeing him out and about, always cheerful and engaging.

To Aaron it was heartening and bittersweet, as if Molly's death had made Charlie different, special somehow, when Aaron wished he could turn back time so his son had two parents.

'We're also lucky to have such supportive families near by. I'm never short of a babysitter.' He tried to repay people for their kindness and consideration by being the best GP he could be.

'So who cares for him after school?' Stella asked, her gaze wary as if she was only making polite conversation.

'My parents or Charlie's other grandparents; sometimes his aunt, Molly's sister.' Aaron had never mentioned to Molly's family that the timing of Charlie's conception hadn't been exactly planned. He didn't know what Molly had told them about her pregnancy. He was just grateful that they'd never once openly blamed him for their daughter's death.

He blamed himself enough.

'I'm glad you have help,' said Stella. 'Raising children is the hardest job in the world.' She expelled a small sigh that he wondered if she was even aware of.

She had spoken generally rather than with first-hand knowledge. As far as Aaron knew, like Stella and Darcy, the middle Wright sister, Lily, had no children.

'You're welcome to join us on our walk, if you'd like. Charlie has been asking about my new work colleague.' At the slight stiffening of her body he added, 'Or you can head back to the surgery and familiarise yourself with the cases booked for this afternoon if you prefer.'

He didn't want to force his rambunctious five-year-old on her if she only tolerated children, but nor did he want to exclude her, especially when he enjoyed every second of her company more than he should.

Stella chewed her lip, clearly dithering.

'Not fond of small children, eh…?' His stomach sank, although how Stella felt about his son didn't matter. He had avoided relationships these past five years, focused on raising Charlie. They were a two-for-the-price-of-one combination that would put many women off.

He cleared his throat, irritated by his foolish disappointment. He wasn't looking for a relationship. He and Charlie had a good thing going, a routine, stability. He wouldn't jeopardise that.

'They can be a handful,' Aaron joked, trying to lighten the atmosphere and rectify the direction of his thoughts. 'Don't worry, Charlie doesn't bite, but it's no big deal. I want you to see what life as a rural GP, something I know you don't aspire to, is like, but there's certainly no obligation on you to participate in my extra-curricular activities.'

She shook her head as if clearing a silly thought. 'No, it's not that. I like kids as much as the next person. I'd love to join you actually. I'd like to see how the school has changed since I attended, and I could do with a breath of fresh air. Aside from my parents, obviously, stunning autumnal days like this one are what I miss most about Abbotsford.'

She stared out at the view—there was one around every corner—her small smile wistful.

'Oh?' he asked, intrigued anew by her complexity. One minute she acted bored by the pace of life here—bemoaning the lack of nightlife, feeling claustrophobic—the next she seemed fully at home in the village where she'd grown up. It was almost as if she was fighting her natural inclinations, acting as if she didn't belong for some reason.

But why would she do that? Perhaps it was linked to the ex she had mentioned. But that was

a long time ago. Surely she'd fallen in and out
of love a few times since then, in her search for
Mr Right?

'I used to ride a lot as a kid and into my teens,'
she elaborated. 'I spent hours riding Gertrude,
my pony, out for a hack through these lanes and
across the fields.'

'Now, there's something you can't do in London.' He could imagine Stella ruddy-cheeked and
mud-splattered as easily as he could imagine her
in skyscraper heels dancing with her arms over
her head in some nightclub.

He swallowed at the memory of her long legs
and shapely thighs, a tight black dress... He
shouldn't be imagining her at all.

She shrugged, as if she'd merely swapped one
rush for another.

Aaron understood. He'd once been desperate to move away from the predictability and
expectations of home, to spread his wings and
experience a different way of life. But unlike
Stella, he'd always known that he would end up
back here. He'd been raised to be heir to the
Bennett estate his parents currently managed,
which comprised the manor house, farmland and
a handful of rented cottages.

'Do you ride?' Stella asked.

He shook his head. 'But Charlie is desperate for a pony, ever since he saw that animated

movie with the talking horses.' So far Aaron had managed to dodge that particular demand. He shook his head. 'Never going to happen.'

'Are you overprotective, then?' she asked, looking at him with that hint of fascination that warmed his blood and had him craving their next *moment*.

'I prefer the term vigilant.' He frowned. 'It's something I never understood about parents until I had my own tiny human to love and nurture and keep alive. You never want anything to harm them, not a scraped knee or a broken heart.'

His insecurities tightened his chest, as if he'd run too far on a frosty morning. What if he made a complete hash of parenting? What if Charlie grew up hating him for the error of judgement that had led to Molly's death? What if he lost Charlie too as suddenly and pointlessly as he'd lost Molly?

'You're right. You want the best for them, all the time.' She nodded as if she knew exactly how he felt. Again he thought Stella must have some first-hand experience.

Then as if realising she'd said too much, she mumbled, 'It certainly must be a lot of responsibility.'

'And joy. Laughter. A steep learning curve.' He hesitated for a second but then ploughed on.

'You sound as if you have experience of children beyond professional exposure.'

He wanted to understand her reticence for being here, part of the Stella puzzle that clearly brought her some sadness, and he sensed it was connected. It wasn't his place to ask any more than it was his place to wonder at the softness of her lips or the intelligent depth of her hazel eyes, but there it was all the same, like an itch he couldn't scratch.

Outside the school, Aaron parked the car and turned off the engine, aware that his breath was trapped in his chest while he waited for a clue to the parts of herself she kept well hidden.

For a second, her stare moved from his eyes, to his mouth. His mind immediately returned to thoughts of kissing her. Did she fancy him in return? Had she, late at night when sleep evaded her, imagined his touch and if they would be good together, physically?

Need roared to life, waking every cell in his body. But it went beyond lust. He liked Stella. He wanted to know her. He wanted those moments.

She drew in a breath, as if preparing to share some intimate part of herself, but at the last second, she seemed to change her mind.

'Not really,' she said.

An answer that only left him with more and more questions.

CHAPTER SIX

AARON'S HANDSOME FACE lit up as the bell rang and older children began pouring into the school yard.

'Here they come.' He jumped out of the car and strode over to the school gate, where a cluster of parents and older siblings waited. Stella exited the car too but loitered near the back of the waiting crowd, feeling as if she needed a hat and some dark glasses to conceal her identity.

Did anyone here know her? Or were the prickles of apprehension dancing over her skin merely a reaction to the fact that every moment spent with Aaron seemed to bring them closer together? Make him more relatable, more complex and more human than her stamina could endure.

As he had talked about his son, his expression and the tone of his voice, even his body language shrouded in vulnerability, she'd struggled to tear away her gaze. Stella understood his sentiments and concerns with every beat of her heart. She too had loved a little boy with the ferocity of a parent, even though they hadn't been biologically related. Aaron's clear devotion to his son had brought the feelings rushing back until she could barely breathe.

For a few indulgent but foolhardy seconds Stella welcomed the memory of that other little boy, from another time: Angus. The soft, silky tickle of his fine hair against her face, the adorable toddler scent that she loved to inhale—a combination of baby shampoo, playdough and banana—the innocence of his trusting embrace, his small arms clinging to her neck as if she'd never let him fall, hurt or even cry.

She couldn't bear to think that the toddler she'd loved as fiercely as if he were her own had pined for her, even for one second.

When Harry had abruptly called things off via a cold, unapologetic text listing the reasons she knew were lies—that she was too young for him, that he needed to put his son first and try to make it work with Angus's mum—she hoped for the two-year-old's sake that Angus hadn't missed her one jot, certainly not with the soul-wrenching grief she'd experienced for him.

With the pain fresh under her ribs, Stella willed the bittersweet memories away, blinking at the sting of tears. Angus hadn't been *her* little boy, even if, for a while, she'd felt as close to

him as she had to his father, Harry, the man she'd
fallen head over heels in love with that final year
she had lived in Abbotsford.

She cast a furtive glance around to see if any
of the locals were looking her way, but all she
saw were the large number of interested glances
cast in Aaron's direction by the mums at the gate.
One even hugged him and dragged him into her
little huddle of chatting parents with an air of
ownership that had others rolling their eyes.

Before Stella could examine the hot flush of
jealousy, there was a bustle of small people, a ca-
cophony of excited squeals and the collective triumphant waving of art in the air as the younger
classes emerged.

Aaron crouched down to the eye level of a
little boy with sandy blond hair the exact shade
of his own, a golden field of corn or the very
honey-toned stone that made this region famous.

Stella's stomach did flips at the vision. They
were so alike. And she had been correct in her
prediction that fatherhood would increase Aaron's sex appeal.

Warm currents shifted low in her belly. Aaron
the man and doctor was hot enough. The addition of his fathering skills placed him beyond
tempting, a combination potent enough to make
any red-blooded woman get in line for a shot at
bagging a hot daddy doc.

But not her. She had no intention of *bagging* anyone. If only her body understood that where Aaron was concerned.

She should have headed back to the practice. Not only would she have avoided the discomfort of wanting to tear at his clothes, but also sharing this seemingly innocent everyday moment with Aaron felt like an intrusion somehow, as if she was inappropriately elbowing her way into his life the way her accusers had claimed she'd done with Harry.

Aaron turned to seek her out, his face still wearing the indulgent smile for his son. He waved her over.

Stella tried to pull herself together as father and son spoke for a few minutes. The boy glanced in Stella's direction, thrust both his backpack and creative work at Aaron and ran off across the playground towards the rear gate of the school, which bordered rolling fields that lead to Bennett Manor.

Stella joined Aaron, her pulse tripping over itself despite her attempts to stay aloof and unaffected, to deny her attraction, which grew more and more rampant by the hour. Becoming emotionally embroiled was something she normally avoided by only casually dating. It kept her distant so that she didn't feel or grow attached. In Stella's experience, which was admittedly limited, feeling only led to pain, inexplicable rejection, isolation.

'He likes to exert his independence by racing ahead,' said Aaron in explanation as they fell into step, side by side, following behind a highly energetic Charlie.

Stella breathed a sigh of relief that Aaron hadn't made a big deal of her presence, and that Charlie hadn't peppered her with a hundred questions on who she was and why she was accompanying his father on today's walk home from school.

She certainly had no answers for the boy. This might be the stupidest thing she'd ever done. Hadn't she learned her lesson with Harry and Angus?

'He is full of beans.' She smiled despite herself. She didn't want to feel anything for Aaron or his no doubt adorable son.

Pride shone in Aaron's sexy grin. Of course, it only heightened the blue of his eyes and dimpled his cheeks. She needed a barrier to his potency, a distraction, and she needed it fast.

'Does he take after your wife?' she blurted, more as a reminder to herself that Aaron was likely still in love with Charlie's mum.

He shot her a side glance, his face falling but quickly recovering as if he was well versed in discussing his loss.

Stella winced, hating that she'd voiced the first thing that came to mind. 'I'm sorry—I heard about her death at the time, from my parents.'

A flare of shame heated her cheeks, because she knew all too well how it felt to be talked about. 'It's a small village. Like I said, everyone hears about your business, don't they?'

'I guess you're right about that,' he said. 'And thank you. Did you know Molly?'

Stella vaguely recalled a tall woman with amazing glossy brown hair and a wide, infectious smile. 'Not really. My mum liked her; said she had a great eye for interiors.'

Aaron's lips curved, a return to that smile that made him instantly approachable, engaging and oh, so kissable. So inappropriate, given he was talking about his wife, the mother of his child.

Aaron glanced at Charlie, who had his arms outstretched like an aeroplane and was swooping back and forth across the field. 'He has her zest for life and her sense of humour.'

Stella tugged her coat across her chest against the dampness of the impending dusk, which had seeped into her veins.

She had once imagined that she'd found that type of connection, lasting love with Harry. Yes, she had been young, just turned eighteen when they met. But she'd fallen hard and become starry-eyed for the slightly more mature twenty-three-year-old who had driven a battered old Land Rover and would stand in the rain waiting for her to finish stabling Gertrude just so he could give her a lift home.

He'd swept her off her daydreaming feet, and when he'd confessed that he'd had a two-year-old son she'd been excited to meet adorable Angus. They'd spent so much of Stella's after-school time together that Stella had fallen in love with both of them. Twice the risk equalled twice the pain when it had ended and she had found herself instantly excluded, alone and grieving.

Then the rumours had surfaced. The gossip. How young selfish Stella had tried to steal Harry and Angus away from his ex, a woman Stella had never met, never even thought about, because Harry had never mentioned her. When he had dumped Stella, the truth emerged, Harry cruelly confessing that he'd never stopped sleeping with Angus's mum all the time he and Stella were together, and that they wanted to give being a family another try.

Stella had felt used, stupid, immature, as if for Harry she had been nothing more than a distraction, a stopgap, a way to make Angus's mother jealous and want him back. The worst part had been that Harry had simply dropped his bombshell and moved on, reunited with his ex and picked up where they left off as if Stella had never existed. As if her deep feelings, her love, were irrelevant. As if she were a nobody.

Realising that she'd fallen silent and that Aaron was watching her, she picked up the conversation. 'It must still be hard for you at times. Does he ask about his mother?'

Aaron nodded, his eyes darkening with shadows. 'There have been one or two tricky moments. Mother's Day, birthdays, Christmas. Other children's simple curiosity, prompting Charlie to think that he's different. I struggle with that.'

Stella's sentimental soft heart clenched for Aaron and his son. Children were naturally inquisitive and quick to sense that they stood out in any way. No matter how blessed and privileged your life, human beings were designed to fear exclusion. Stella knew what it felt like to be a curiosity here. To be the recipient of pointed fingers and whispered unfair judgements.

'And of course, being a single parent, I'm paranoid that I'm doing it all wrong.' Aaron glanced her way. 'How is my dad-ranking on the village grapevine?' His mouth was tugged by that self-deprecating smile she'd come to expect as predictably as the sunrise.

She reluctantly looked away. 'I think you're doing all right. I've never heard a bad word spoken about you. And you seemed fairly popular with the village mums back there.'

He tossed his head back and laughed. 'You're not jealous, are you?'

Stella found herself grinning at the delicious sound of his glee. Then she rolled her eyes. 'As if.'

'You sound disappointed that I'm not some deplorable villain.' He waggled his eyebrows and Stella couldn't help but laugh, too. He was right. It would be easier for her wayward desire and her Aaron crush if he acted a little more despicably.

'Just because we're two very different people, who want different things, doesn't mean I don't respect you professionally,' she said.

'Well, that's a start, I guess.' His mouth twisted in a half-smile.

Stella's gaze latched on to his sensual lips, increasingly erotic images of them kissing sliding through her brain.

In lieu of an ice-cold shower, she needed an antidote to his magnetism.

'Do you mind me asking how Molly died?' She didn't want to cause him pain, but there was a professional curiosity that she knew he'd understand. And more importantly, the fact that he was likely still grieving, still in love with his wife, should help keep her rampant hormones in check.

'I don't mind,' he said, his lips pressing into a flat line. 'It was a long time ago. She went into cardiac arrest soon after delivering Charlie. She'd barely even held him.'

Shocked, Stella stopped walking.

He raised his chin as if girding himself to utter the words, his stare strained but unguarded. 'Amniotic fluid embolism.'

Stella reached for his arm the way he had comforted her yesterday, horrified for such a tragic and unfair loss. 'I'm so sorry. That's rare, isn't it?'

Aaron nodded. 'They managed to revive her, but she never regained consciousness after the arrest.' His gaze fell to her hand on his arm as if disturbed by her touch.

'That's awful. Tragic.' She dropped her grip and started walking again, putting a few feet of distance between them so that she could breathe, pull herself together and stop thinking of him in a sexual way.

Their steps synced once more. This time Stella made certain to keep her distance.

'She was transferred to ICU,' he continued as if forcing himself to continue the tale. 'She died two days later.'

Chills gripped Stella's frame, her empathy and compassion drawing her to him to a dangerous degree. She hugged her arms across her chest, floundering and, for the first time in years, fearful. For herself, for how easily she could become embroiled in her feelings where Aaron was concerned.

'I don't know what to say other than I'm sorry again.'

Aaron shrugged, but Stella saw his pain lurking behind his eyes, which seemed to display his every feeling. 'It was a horrible time, obviously, but I couldn't dwell on the tragedy, the bloody waste and unfairness of it all with Charlie to look after.'

Stella swallowed, gazed over at his profile. He glanced sideways and offered her a sad smile. 'Don't worry; we're okay. Charlie and I are a team. Boys Club.' He raised his fist and pumped the air.

She smiled, trying not to remember how she had once been a part of Harry and Angus's team. Until she hadn't. Because it had all been an illusion. A joke where only she was ignorant of the impending punchline.

'And we are lucky in so many ways,' Aaron continued. 'That's the message I try to instil in him. He has many people who love him, and he lives in a wonderful place to grow up.'

'It is that.' Stella's smile stretched, a flood of nostalgic childhood memories warming her through.

For the first time in ages Stella indulged her imagination of her own future and how it might look. She'd spent so long avoiding emotional entanglement in order to protect herself, she'd never given much thought to her desires for a family. Did she truly never want children of her own? Did her job, a job she loved, really provide enough to fulfil her? Would she always be content with big-city life, even when her friends started to settle down and perhaps move away to raise their own families?

She had once wanted all of those things until Harry had belittled and humiliated her, forcing her to change.

She became aware of Aaron's gaze.

'Earlier, you gave the impression that you might have experienced village gossip in a negative way,' he said with a compassionate smile that made her feel exposed.

'Mmm, just teenager stuff.' Stella reared back from sharing too much. She'd kind of assumed that everyone, including Aaron, knew her business. But even in the few days she'd known Aaron on a closer personal level, rather than from afar, she deduced that he wouldn't toy with her emotions. He was too kind, too upstanding, too honourable.

With a sigh she hadn't realised she'd held inside since she first drove past the *Welcome to Abbotsford* sign, she offered him half an explanation. 'I was young. Naive. The ex I told you about yesterday—stupidly I fell in love. Trusted the wrong person. Made a fool of myself.'

'None of which are crimes,' Aaron pointed out with a small frown.

'No. But sometimes guilt or innocence is irrelevant, especially when the tale is juicier when the facts are omitted. But that's ancient history.' She tried to change the subject away from her. 'I'm not a heartbroken eighteen-year-old any more.'

'So you left Abbotsford amid a cloud of rumours. I can understand how that hurt, but you should know that I've never heard any of this before. I hope that reassures you that maybe the past is where it belongs.'

Of course, respecting people's privacy was a vital part of his role as a GP, but she had come to understand that discretion and integrity were inherent facets of Aaron's personality.

'I'm sure you could ask around for all the details,' she said absent-mindedly. 'There are probably lots of people who recall the *scandal*.' She made air quotes around the last word, with bravado. The last thing she wanted was for him to see her in a negative light, not when she worked for him and when her feelings for him were so conflicted.

'If you want me to know you'll tell me.' He stepped closer so that their arms almost brushed.

Something intimate passed between them, as

if they were the only two people in the world, trading their deepest, darkest secrets. As if they could become friends.

Except friends didn't want to know how their chums looked naked.

Stella cleared her dry throat, kept her eyes front.

They approached the low stone wall that bounded the house where Aaron had grown up. Stella had only been inside once for a Christmas party where all the village children had been invited to meet Father Christmas underneath the biggest Christmas tree Stella had ever seen.

She paused at the gate, clinging to her self-imposed boundaries. 'I'll…um…wait here for you.'

Aaron turned to cast her a speculative gaze. 'Okay, although you are very welcome to meet my parents. They'll probably remember you.' He smiled so that she knew he meant because she had grown up here rather than because she was still an infamous homewrecker.

Before she could make an excuse, Charlie came running from the back of the house towards them.

'Daddy. Grandma made spaghetti for dinner, my favourite.'

As if he'd completely forgotten Stella's presence, Charlie peered up at Stella from behind his father's muscular legs.

'Who are you?' he asked in that direct way that only small children could pull off.

'My name is Stella. I work with your dad.'

I also fancy your dad something chronic.

Charlie's blue eyes widened and his chest puffed out. 'My daddy is a doctor.' He stepped from behind Aaron's legs and struck a series of martial-arts poses as if fighting an invisible villain.

Stella hid her delight behind pressed-together lips.

'Are you a doctor too?' he asked, as if remembering that she was still there, an unknown grown-up who warranted investigation.

'Yes, I am.' Stella nodded, trying to unsee the undeniable resemblance, including matching dimples when they smiled, between father and son. Despite Aaron's concerns, Charlie was clearly a confident, well-adjusted and imaginative little boy, and, as Stella had predicted, adorable.

Her heart gave an involuntary lurch that she wanted to run away from.

'Are you kissing my daddy?' Charlie asked out of nowhere, as if this was a perfectly reasonable question for a new acquaintance.

Stella flushed hot, no doubt displaying a fetching shade of beetroot red. Could they both see how much she *wanted* to kiss Aaron? How the thought endlessly occupied her fantasies?

The man in question merely emitted a low, indulgent chuckle at his son's question.

But then his eyes met hers and time seemed to stop.

He arched an eyebrow, his eyes full of challenge. This was probably the look that had once lured all those pretty nurses to succumb to his charms, leap into his sports car and attend his infamous house parties.

She looked away from Aaron's intense, very adult stare. 'Um…' *Awkward.*

'No, I'm not.' Her skin prickled, too hot, too aware, too close to the man who clearly still possessed all of the moves.

Oblivious to the stifling cloud of lust and panic engulfing Stella, Charlie continued his explanation as if for the dim-witted adults present. 'My friend Johnny said ladies and men kiss. That's how they get babies.'

Aaron's eyes once more locked with Stella's as she issued a nervous laugh. He obviously shared her mirth, his mouth twitching in that sexy way that felt like a secret, unspoken adult communication.

As if granted permission to think about exactly how adults made babies, Stella acknowledged in a rush that she absolutely wanted to have sex with him.

Oh, no, no, no.

Could Aaron tell the direction of her thoughts and how turned-on she felt?

'Johnny doesn't know everything, Champ,' said Aaron, his intense stare still holding her captive as he ruffled his son's hair. 'Why don't you say bye to Dr Stella, and you and I will talk about babies at bedtime, okay?'

'Bye, Dr Stella.' Charlie took off at the speed of light, leaving a fog of thick, cloying tension wrapped around her and Aaron. Wave after wave of exhilarating lust buffeted her poor, weak body in the silent moments that seemed to stretch for ever.

This was very bad indeed.

'Johnny knows *everything*.' Aaron raised his eyebrows. His smile was cool, relaxed, but the expression in his eyes was beyond suggestive. Carnal. Intent.

Then his gaze swept to her mouth.

Stella's pulse buzzed in her ears. Was he going to kiss her?

Did he want to have sex with her, too?

Her feet shuffled, her senses alive with anticipation that she tried to squash. What the hell was happening? She couldn't seriously be thinking about Aaron Bennett's soft-looking lips, wondering if he kissed with the same all-consuming confidence that he wore as well as the fine wool jumper moulded to his deliciously contoured chest.

Kissing Aaron was not allowed. Sex with Aaron was the worst idea she'd ever had. Even standing here in a puddle of loaded silence with him was highly reckless.

Stella laughed another nervous chuckle. 'I'll… um…wait here.' Her voice cracked.

Aaron hesitated, his body inching closer. Then he sighed. 'Give me a few minutes to get him settled.'

She nodded, resolved. 'Then we should… um…get back to work.'

Even if he didn't, she needed the reminder that they were working together, that no matter how tempted, she would never know if Aaron's kisses would be demanding and animalistic or slow and seductive.

And she was one hundred per cent okay with that.

Wasn't she…?

CHAPTER SEVEN

ON FRIDAY, AARON arrived at the village pub, the Abbotsford Arms, for the school fund-raising quiz. The Parents' Association planned to update the school playground equipment and he wanted to support the event. It had nothing at all to do with the fact that he had mentioned it to Stella in the hope that she too might come along.

As the warmth of the pub interior defrosted his cold cheeks and fingers, his gaze swept the patrons for the woman he couldn't scrub from his mind, even for a second. Because that moment by the gate had been a game changer. He could no longer deny how much he wanted her or the way she looked at him in return. With hunger.

Stella stood at the bar talking to another woman around her age. She wore skinny jeans that showed off her great legs and a chunky-knit jumper that couldn't quite hide the curves of her gorgeous breasts.

A slug of heat detonated in his chest, spreading through him as if his blood was laced with narcotics.

He paused near the door, collecting his thoughts and examining his obvious excitement. Ever since Charlie brought up kissing that day, he hadn't been able to stop imagining her lips against his, her taste, if she would make sexy whimpers in her throat as their bodies met.

Was he totally insane, or just deluded?

He scrubbed hand through his hair and tugged his scarf from his neck. He'd been quite good at this dance back in the day. Flirting, seducing, fun and frivolous sex. But what the hell was he thinking now? Aside from a couple of tame dinners that had ended with polite goodbyes, he hadn't dated since Molly's death. It had been a long time since he'd shared a proper kiss, or any other intimacy, with another woman.

He knew his abstinence wasn't entirely healthy, but he'd been so focused on raising Charlie, compensating for being his son's sole parent, that his physical needs had been the least of his priorities.

But Stella and her throaty laugh and her figure-hugging jumpers seemed to have bumped the demands of his sex drive up to the top of the list.

'You decided to come?' he said to Stella as he arrived at her side and took in her warm, soft scent. He kept his arms glued to his sides to stop himself from touching her: her elbow, her hand, that small freckle on her cheek.

Those same cheeks pinkened as if he'd caught her out, exposed how she too felt about the whole kissing plan.

'Yes.' She smiled. 'Do you know Amy? She runs the riding school.'

Pretending that he hadn't noticed the breathless quality of Stella's voice, he greeted the other woman with a warm smile.

'Of course, I recognise you now.' He'd once talked to Amy about gently introducing Charlie to riding. The kid never stopped talking about ponies and practically galloped everywhere. Aaron just hadn't plucked up the courage to take him along yet. He could almost hear Molly's reservations.

Wait until he's older...

'Amy and I were at school together,' said Stella, her tongue unconsciously swiping her bottom lip as she looked up at him with that searching stare that seemed to ask a hundred questions whenever their eyes met.

She felt it too, this continual force drawing them towards a collision, like gravity. But what should they do about it, if anything? He wasn't getting any younger and he was essentially her boss.

'Well done on dragging her back to Abbotsford,' said Amy to Aaron. 'I've just this minute persuaded her to volunteer for Ability Riding while she's here. Get this city girl back into the saddle, literally.'

Amy grinned and Stella rolled her eyes. But the glow of enthusiasm around her told him she was as delighted as her friend to be associated with horses again.

The urge to touch her, kiss her, intensified. Aaron's body was also keen to get back in the saddle, but they worked together. Even a temporary fling without emotions could complicate things.

'I'm not planning on being here that long,' Stella said with a concerned frown in Amy's direction. 'So don't rely on me long-term.' At Amy's look of surprise, she added, 'Aaron has applied for a transfer back to London for me.'

Reminded of her plans to leave as soon as possible, Aaron tried to swallow down the violent rush of disappointment that he had no right to be feeling. But it was a perfectly timed reminder that no matter how many moments they shared, no matter that he couldn't stop thinking about her, that he wanted to kiss her, touch her, hear her moans of pleasure, she would soon be out of here.

She'd made it clear from the start that this wasn't the practice, or the place for her. Only he'd started to see glimpses of how being here brought out different aspects of her personality, flashes of fond nostalgia.

No matter how well her desire to return to London fitted with his aim to stay emotionally detached, Stella has settled in well at Abbotsford Health Centre. She had a warmth, a compassion that made her an excellent GP. She knew many of the local families that his practice served. Aaron knew that, despite her time away in London and her reservations about this ancient gossip, she'd be seen as one of them if she ever decided to come home and work in the village for good.

He met Amy's eye and offered a resigned smile.

Sensing both Amy's and Aaron's confusion, Stella blurted out more of an explanation. 'It's been great to be back, actually. It's just that I've lived there for nine years. I've grown up there in many ways, and that's where I always saw myself established.'

She flashed vulnerable eyes at Amy. They were clearly good friends. Amy likely knew all about this local guy, Stella's ex.

'That's funny,' Amy said, 'because until Harry broke your heart, you always dreamed about living in a country mansion like the one in Aaron's family. You planned to keep chickens and pigs and grow vegetables, while being a doctor on the side, of course.' Amy smiled fondly.

Stella laughed, nodded and avoided looking at Aaron.

Protective urges built inside him like steam. This Harry guy was the ex associated with the rumours. What had he done to her? Was Stella still in love with him, still running away from her feelings? That would surely explain what Aaron found utterly inexplicable: why she was still single.

A stubborn lump lodged in his chest; it tasted suspiciously like jealousy.

'Would you like to join our team?' Amy asked Aaron, changing the subject. She indicated a man who waved from across at the bar. 'That's my husband, Mike, and it looks like he's found us a table.'

Aaron cast Stella a surprised look. 'You're doing the pub quiz?' He hadn't planned his own team. He knew enough people in the village to just rock up and simply join an existing group.

'Of course. I'm great at general knowledge.' She narrowed her eyes in challenge. 'Why so surprised?'

He grinned, glad she was once more flirting, joking and looking at him with heated stares. 'I thought clubbing was more your style.'

She shrugged, feigning aloofness. 'I'm a woman of many talents.'

'We need a fourth, as my sister can't make it.' Amy said, subtly edging away, drink in hand.

Aaron had all but forgotten that he and Stella weren't alone. They'd worked together all week, each day becoming more fraught with sexual awareness. He felt her interest, too. It spurred his own. But he had to be sure they were on the same page.

'I'd love to join you, thanks. If it's okay with you, Stella.' Aaron searched her eyes.

He found only mischief and sparks as she looked him over as if examining prime horse-flesh. 'Mmm...it depends. What are your strengths? Because first prize includes a spa day at Hawthorne Manor, and I'm very competitive.'

Amy chuckled and left to join her husband, leaving him and Stella alone at last.

Deciding that his life could do with a few... temporary complications, he flirted back. 'I also like to win and I have many strengths.' He stepped closer, dipped his head slightly so a flush stained her neck. 'But for the purposes of a quiz, I'm good at history, sport and medicine, of course, not that you need me for that.'

Her breathing kicked up, fast and shallow as she stared up at him. Then she recovered. 'I'm not sure I need you full stop.' She flashed a playful grin, the pulse in her throat visibly hammering away.

'Maybe not, but with you being such a city lover and me being heir to the local manor, I'm also something of an expert on country pursuits.' He let his eyes linger on her lush lips for a second longer than was polite. Away from work and the perceptive eyes of his five-year-old, he felt free to flex the flirting muscles he'd kept in check all week. He was rusty, not dead.

She laughed. 'Is that so? Yes, I recall the weekend bashes at Bennett Manor, the fields littered with wine bottles and poor deceased clay pigeons.' She sipped her drink, her gaze on him over the rim of the glass.

Heat sizzled along his nerves. If she was intent on leaving soon, she would no longer be his trainee. Clearly their age difference didn't bother her, so he shouldn't let it bother him.

'Amy and Mike will cover farming and politics,' she said returning to the matter of the quiz he'd forgotten existed. 'If I take the music and popular culture questions, I suppose you might complement us nicely.'

He grinned at her mock reluctance. 'I'm glad I can be of service.'

Taking his drink from the bar staff member, he followed her to join the rest of their team, his eyes trained away from the sway of her hips.

Sitting close to her around the small table, Aaron struggled to recall any of his general knowledge. Their thighs kept bumping and every time that happened their eyes met, zaps of awareness and small smiles uniting them. She was right; their subjects of strength couldn't be more different, but laughing, competing to be the biggest know-it-all and cheering each other on, it didn't seem to matter in the slightest. Aaron couldn't remember the last time he'd enjoyed a night out as much, and it was Stella who made all the difference.

'Yes!' she cheered as the quiz master announced that their team had won the quiz.

She jumped to her feet with her arms held triumphantly aloft. The other three of them joined her. Stella hugged Amy and Mark in congratulation and then Aaron found himself the next recipient.

Chest to chest, her arms surrounding his shoulders, he could feel the fullness of her breasts, the warmth of her as he rested his hand in the centre of her back, the excited pounding of her heart.

His senses went into overdrive as her scent bathed him.

She pulled back abruptly, laughed nervously as if she hadn't meant to include him in the celebration, had gone too far. But it was too late. His body had reacted to hers, remembered the feel of her and wanted more than a chaste hug.

When she flashed him an embarrassed smile

as they retook their seats, he saw the evidence in her eyes; she wanted him too.

Recognition that hadn't been there before filled the slim space between her body and his. Stella pretended to be unaffected but she could no longer meet his eyes and her hands were tucked under her thighs as if she didn't trust herself not to reach out.

Aaron sighed under his breath, desperate to get her alone. Perhaps he would offer to walk her home later. They needed to acknowledge this rampant chemistry before it burned out of control, before he did something stupid, before she left and he missed his chance.

'Dr Bennett, sorry to disturb you.' Someone tapped Aaron's shoulder.

He turned to see one of the village youngsters, a farmer's son called Ben. 'Can you come and check out Sam? His blood-sugar alarm keeps going off, and he's acting a little bit aggressively.'

Aaron rose to his feet immediately, tilted his head indicating that Stella should follow and strode after Ben. When he reached Sam, an eighteen-year-old diabetic well known at the practice, the teen was pale, sweat beading on his brow.

'Hey, doc,' he said, his speech slurred. The way he slumped against the shoulder of the friend sitting next to him told Aaron he was probably feeling dizzy or confused.

'Sam, have you eaten?' asked Aaron, making a quick calculation of the number of empty shot glasses littering the table and dividing it by the number present in the group.

Sam didn't answer. Instead he rummaged under his shirt to silence the alarm on his blood-sugar monitor, which was alerting him to what Aaron already knew. He was hypoglycaemic, likely a side effect of drinking spirits on an empty stomach.

He heard Stella direct Ben, the kid who had called them over, to fetch a glass of orange juice from the bar.

A girl to Sam's right answered Aaron's question. 'He hasn't eaten. We were going to get some chips later.'

'How many of those has he had?' asked Stella, indicating the shot glasses.

The girl blushed and winced, no doubt feeling somehow responsible. 'About five. It's his eighteenth birthday today.'

'It's okay. It's no one's fault,' Stella said to the girl.

She accepted the glass of juice from Ben and indicated to the others in the group, who now wore matching concerned expressions, to vacate their seats and clear a path to Sam.

While Stella encouraged Sam to sip some juice, Aaron discreetly examined the boy's blood-sugar monitor, adjusting the rate of insulin infusion.

Sam's hand shook on the glass as he sipped, now a docile lamb under Stella's care.

'I don't think he needs to go to hospital,' said Stella. 'But we should take him home.'

Sam stared up at her with grateful eyes as round as saucers.

Aaron nodded, taking in the worried expressions on the faces of his friends. 'He'll be okay, guys. But I think he's had enough partying for the night. What do you say, Sam. Time to go home?'

Sam nodded slowly, rising to his feet and taking Stella's hand to steady his balance.

'I walked here,' said Stella to Aaron, her brow pinched with concern.

'So did I.' Aaron glanced around for a friendly face who could give them a lift. 'He doesn't live far, but I don't think he should walk.'

'I'll take him. I'm the sober driver tonight,' said the girl Aaron assumed was Sam's girlfriend.

'Thanks. We'll come too,' said Aaron, 'and I'll call ahead and warn his parents to expect us.'

The journey was brief and fortunately uneventful, the silence only punctuated by Sam's repeated mumbled apologies.

'Don't worry—we've all been there,' Aaron

said, recalling what it was like to be a teenager growing up in a small village; the urge to push boundaries, experiment, party hard—all under the watchful eyes of people who knew your parents and remembered you as a baby.

'Never drink on an empty stomach,' added Stella. 'Even the pub grub at the Abbotsford Arms is better than nothing.'

She and Aaron shared a secret smile, that of two people with plenty in common, most of all an attraction it was now impossible to deny.

At Sam's address, they escorted the young man inside and spoke briefly to his parents, who were well versed in managing their son's diabetes. Aaron was strangely grateful for Stella's presence. She was young, relatable, and non-judgemental. Was it because she too understood what it was like to grow up in a rural community, where entertainment was scarce and fun was often what you made it? Or was it simply a symptom of his need to know her better?

Back outside, the night had taken on a bitter chill. Aaron turned up the collar of his coat and glanced at Stella, relieved to see her tug a woolly hat from her pocket and pull it on.

'Would you like to go back to the pub?' he asked, too restless to return now that the medical emergency was resolved. 'I'll walk you if you like.'

She shook her head, once again avoiding his eyes. 'No. I think I'll head home. It's been quite a week.'

'Never a dull moment.' He grinned. 'And you thought you'd be coming to a sleepy practice which catered only for minor farming injuries and coughs and colds.'

She laughed, rolled her eyes and bumped her shoulder into his arm. 'Point taken.'

Her touch, deliberate and playful, set his pulse racing.

Then she seemed to sober. 'Abbotsford has changed, or perhaps I've changed.' She kicked at a stone with her toe.

'Maybe both,' he said, knowing no one remained the person they were at eighteen. 'Come on, I'll walk you home.'

He took off in the direction of Stella's parents' house, which was only a few streets away. He didn't want to say goodnight just yet and she'd fallen into a pensive mood he wished he could eliminate.

'It's okay,' she said, catching up in two hurried strides. 'I don't need you to walk me home. I know the way. This isn't some dodgy end of London.'

Aaron shrugged, unperturbed. 'I'll make sure you get home safe, all the same.'

'Very old-school. Thanks.' She acquiesced, falling into step at his side, her smile returned.

'Are you suggesting I'm old?' There were still a few streetlights in this part of Abbotsford, so he could see the way her rosy cheeks matched the shade of her very kissable lips.

'Distinguished and experienced perhaps.' She cast him a thoughtful glance. 'And definitely responsible. Who'd have thought…?'

He laughed, delight bubbling up in his chest. 'You had fun tonight, despite the lack of dancing. It was good to see you enjoying the quiz.'

'I did.' She grinned, her eyes bright.

He wanted to pull her close and kiss her cold-looking lips until they warmed up. 'So, you definitely still want that transfer, huh?'

Distraction was what he needed. A reminder that, irrespective of his out-of-control attraction, she'd be leaving for London as soon as she could. Only that served to make him want her more. He wasn't looking for a relationship. It could be brief but perfect.

She nodded, but unlike all the previous times, she didn't seem quite as adamant. 'You were right—your practice is busy and varied.'

She smiled up at him in that teasing way of hers. 'You even arranged an extracurricular medical event at the pub to keep me on my toes,' she said about Sam's unfortunate hypoglycae-mic attack.

'Well, I think you've settled in very well. You're certainly a hit with our female clients.' He and his partner had often discussed the need to advertise for a female GP to join them. Why could he see Stella fill that post so effortlessly?

A dangerous vision.

'Is there no part of you glad to be back?' he asked, as desperate for her confidences as he was for her kiss.

'There is.' She sighed. 'But I also feel like I've outgrown this place. Last time I lived here I was Sam's age, devastated by my first major break-up, desperate to leave and be in a place where no one knew me.'

'So staying away was easier?'

'I guess. Of course, the last thing I want is to run into an ex who broke my heart. But I got over him a long time ago.' She raised her chin.

Aaron wondered at that. It was certainly some-thing she told herself. But who was he to judge? He still carried his own regrets of the past, un-able to let go of the responsibility he felt about his part in Molly's unplanned pregnancy.

'It's just that I built a life for myself in Lon-don,' she said wistfully. 'I left here young, naive, someone who thought she knew what love was. Then I grew up.'

Closer to her street, the lights had disappeared, so he couldn't make out her usually expressive eyes, but her body language spoke volumes—hunched shoulders, hands shoved in pockets, head dipped.

'I changed,' she said, glancing in his direction. 'I realised who I wanted to be and what I wouldn't tolerate, and London helped me do that.'

It made sense. Except he had seen how naturally she fitted in here. Was running still working for her, or just holding her back?

'I don't think a city has magical powers.' Aaron stepped closer, lowered his voice. 'I think you would have done those things anyway. You can be who you are wherever you lay down your stethoscope, Stella.'

A small frown pinched her eyebrows together as if she hadn't expected that he saw her so clearly. But she too must feel their connection.

'So you don't believe in love?' he asked, needing to understand the root of Stella's fear. 'Is that why you're still single?'

He was pushing, probing, but what if she was standing in her own way? He saw it in the pub, the change, the lowering of her guard when she hadn't been able to hide her delight at their win, but then, when he'd challenged her view of Abbotsford, she'd withdrawn, as if holding herself remote once more.

Was it just from him and their chemistry, or from this place where she'd experienced the pain of a failed relationship?

'Wow—now I see where Charlie gets his propensity for asking direct questions.' She pretended to be mildly offended but he could see that she was toying with him.

'I'm serious. You're smart. You have a good job, and you're attractive. I would have thought you'd be living with someone by now or engaged, even married.'

She stopped, stared, her eyes alight as if he'd divulged an astonishing secret. 'Attractive? You think I'm attractive, huh?'

He nodded, his feet locked in place to stop himself stepping closer. Sexy, inspiring, funny. 'Beautiful is probably more accurate.' So beautiful his chest sometimes ached when he stared at her unobserved.

That tension he'd now come to expect when she was close wrapped its tentacles around them, the air seeming to pulsate. She swallowed. She must have felt it too. But then she set off walking again, dodging him and his questions.

'I've been career-focused.' She stared down at her boots. 'I don't have time for dating. And you're single too.' She shot him an accusatory look. 'It's not a crime.'

He wanted to laugh, change the subject, allow her to make light of this. But more than that, he wanted to know her, to understand what was in her way.

'No, it's not,' he said. 'But I found love. I've been married.' His reasons for avoiding dating since were complicated.

'But you haven't been in a relationship since Charlie was born?' She glanced at him, the look in those hazel eyes of hers intrigued.

Aaron shook his head. 'As you saw on Tuesday, Charlie's a full-time job, a job I love.' He smiled as an image of Charlie laughing popped into his head. 'He's had a tough enough start in life as it is. I want him to know that he might not have a mother, but he's loved and important, the most important thing in my life. Dating would… complicate that.'

'I understand.'

'Sometimes I imagine that Molly's complications could have happened during the labour, that I might have lost Charlie too.' Now, why had he told her that? It was something he only ever allowed himself to think in the dead of night.

'I'm glad that didn't happen,' she whispered, as if sensing his vulnerability. 'And it's understandable to worry about introducing him to new people. It can be confusing for children to meet a host of prospective partners, not really knowing if they will be around long-term and what importance they hold. He's a fortunate little boy that you put his needs first. Not everyone is so conscientious.' Her mouth turned down, a painful shadow crossing her expression.

Aaron assumed that she would clam up again, but she continued.

'My ex, the one I told you about…he had a son, Angus. He was two when we got together, turned three during our year-long relationship. I spent all of my free time with them. I became very close to Angus.'

'And then…?'Aaron held his breath, an ache forming under his ribs for Stella's pain, because this was the heart of her fear, and he wanted it to have never existed, for her sake.

'And then nothing.' She kept her eyes facing forward. 'The relationship ended abruptly. One day I was collecting Angus from pre-school after I'd finished school myself, playing with him until his father arrived home, the next day I was… discarded as if I had never mattered to either of them.'

Aaron's fingers balled into fists. 'I'm sorry that happened to you, Stella.' How could her ex have been so cruel as to use her like that, throw her away like rubbish after she had given so much of herself to the relationship?

She violently shook her head, as if rejecting his empathy or willing away tears. 'The worst part was that I wasn't even given a chance to say goodbye to Angus, to explain my absence. I just hope that he forgot all about me quickly, that he didn't…pine.'

Because he couldn't stand not touching her any longer, Aaron scooped up her cold hand, tugged it, warmed her frigid fingers with his own body heat. 'You loved this little boy.'

She looked up from their clasped hands. He saw it written all over her face. This was the missing link, the child she had experienced, the reason that failed love affair had cut so deep. She had been doubly invested.

She nodded, her eyes glistening. 'I did. More than I loved his father, as it turned out.' She gave a humourless laugh. 'I worried for a long time after that Angus might have grieved for me the way I grieved for him, that he wouldn't have understood where I had gone and that it had nothing to do with my feelings for him.'

'I'm sorry that you had that experience.' No wonder she had run away emotionally when she left for university. She would have been grieving for the loss of two relationships, confused and rejected and wanting the pain to stop. It wasn't

Abbotsford that she feared. It was the pain she'd experienced here.

This Harry guy had clearly used her. Smart, emotionally astute Stella would have realised that, felt the sting of humiliation on top of her heartache.

As if collecting herself from a momentary lapse of weakness, she pulled her hand from his and shoved it inside her coat pocket. 'Well, this is me. Sorry for offloading my sob story onto you. Thanks for walking me home.'

Aaron's heart sank. Of course she would shield herself from this thing brewing between them. She'd been badly hurt. Rejected by a man like him. A man with a young son.

There was a light on in the porch of her parents' cottage, casting an orange glow that illuminated the cobblestone path and reached the small wooden gate, where they paused.

'No problem.' His voice felt thick with emotion. 'Thanks for your help with Sam. We've all been there. Hopefully his hangover tomorrow will give him plenty of time to reflect on his decision to drink on an empty stomach.'

Aaron hated the polite distance in his tone. A part of him wished he'd never discovered the depths of Stella's past heartache, wished for a return of the flirtation, the careless touches, the possibility.

But a bigger part of him wanted to hunt down this Harry fellow who had made a young, heartbroken Stella leave Abbotsford feeling as if she no longer belonged and...

No—Aaron wasn't a man of violence.

'You're welcome.' She placed one hand on the gate and looked up at him, her rapid breaths misting in the damp air as she loitered, saying goodbye but not moving inside. 'I'll...um...see you Monday morning, then.'

Still she hesitated.

Even though he told himself to proceed with caution because he didn't want to hurt her, some invisible force gripped him. Her display of vulnerability, the trust she showed him, the need to comfort her... He just couldn't stop himself.

Without questioning the danger of his action, he swooped in and pressed a chaste peck to her freezing cheek, telling her that he cared, that she hadn't deserved to be treated that way, that he valued the time she had committed to Abbotsford.

It was friendly at best. Only they weren't friends.

Although his lips had left her skin, he lingered in her personal space for a split second longer than was wise, hypnotised by the scent of her perfume. A lock of her hair tickled his cheek.

He was about to stand tall, move away—

his apology for crossing a line forming on his tongue—when she turned her face to his and their lips grazed.

It could only have been described as a kiss, no mistake. And she'd instigated it.

Fire consumed his nervous system, his body so rigid he thought he might snap and shatter like an icicle. But he wasn't letting this chance slip by without taking full advantage.

He pressed his lips back to hers, applied some pressure. His stare latched to hers, silently communicating that he'd heard her tiny gasp, that he'd take her mouth graze and raise the stakes, unleashing the desire that had been brewing inside him since he'd called her name in City Hospital's lecture theatre.

Instead of moving away or shoving him aside, Stella stepped closer, fitting into the curve of his body, which was bent over hers, a big spoon to her little spoon.

At the glow of arousal in her eyes, Aaron moved his lips against hers, parting, pursing, pressing home as if their rhythm was the most natural thing in the world.

But this was his first proper passionate kiss in five years. He was kissing Stella.

She whimpered, gripped the lapels of his coat, held him firm. He forgot about the fact that she was his trainee, that he was so much older than her, that he'd just learned what she had been through in the past, forgot everything but the sensation of kissing her and the way his body flared to life, his blood pounding, his hormones raging.

Drunk, high, dazed with desire, he wrapped one arm around her waist and cupped her cold cheek with his other hand, touching his tongue to hers, licking, tasting, deepening the kiss as if life itself depended on their connection.

Stella's fingers dug into his shoulders. Then she moved her hands to his hair, her fingers spearing through the strands and dragging him impossibly closer. Their bodies meshed together, from lips to thighs. He felt every inch of her curves, her breasts, her hips, the heat between her legs. A grunt of satisfaction ripped from his throat. He pressed her up against the gate, the barrier allowing him to grind their bodies closer. His erection surged against her hip. She bucked and writhed, massaging his length between her stomach and his, torturing him to the point of combustion.

His fingers slid under her jumper, finding the soft, warm skin of her lower back. He swallowed her moan. He worried that his hands were cold, but she gripped him tighter, urged her body closer, begging with her body language for more.

And insanely Aaron wanted to give her exactly what she craved, right here on her parents' doorstep.

With a shove and a strangled moan from Stella it was over as quickly as it had begun. Cool air bathed his lips, which were parted to drag in brain-fuelling oxygen. He looked down, confusion dousing his euphoria as if he'd fallen into a waist-high snowdrift.

Stella's eyes were huge in the dark and glazed with passion, but she slipped from his arms and fumbled with the latch of the gate at her back.

'Goodnight, Aaron.' Her eyes spoke a million words—excitement, regret, maybe even a trace of that fear she must have developed after her last run-in with a single dad from Abbotsford.

Similar emotions recoiled inside him, a rush of shocking lust he'd thought he'd never feel again predominant. He should apologise for kissing her, only he wasn't sorry. He was glad that she'd taken the kiss from a friendly goodnight peck, one they could return from, to one that would likely keep him awake all night. His only regret was that he might have misled her with his passionate response, the last thing he wanted to do.

'Goodnight, Stella,' he said, rueful that Monday morning might bring recrimination and awkwardness at work.

He should be grateful that she had withdrawn from their kiss. Aaron had Charlie to prioritise and he didn't want to hurt Stella when they had no future. He'd had his chance at happiness. Five years ago, as he'd held his days-old son in his arms, he'd made peace with the fact that he didn't deserve another shot.

Except his lips buzzed in remembrance of her kiss, already craving a replay. He waited until she was safely inside before he began the pensive walk home, the conclusion dragging at his heels: that he should keep away from Stella. For her sake.

CHAPTER EIGHT

STELLA HADN'T DREADED a Monday morning as much since she attended Abbotsford Secondary School and all she had wanted was for the weekend to last for ever so she could ride Gertrude. Oh, she was keen to get stuck into a new week at the practice, but a big part of her, the part scared of how shocking and out of control her physical reaction to Aaron had been, wanted to scuttle back to London and hide just to distance herself from the memory of that kiss at her parents' gate. Except denial wouldn't work. The details of every touch, every gasp, every sensation were seared into her brain like a mnemonic she'd had to memorise at med school in order to learn the order of the cranial nerves.

Aaron kissed with the same efficient, unflinching confidence he displayed at work and out of work. She had never wanted it to stop. Only confiding in him about Angus and then kissing him…it had been too much. Too intimate. Too dangerous.

She'd sensed that Aaron too had reservations that went deeper than having to return home for the babysitter, as if they were both wary of crossing that line that would take them from colleagues to lovers. She'd watched him walk away, peeped through her parents' porch window, still haunted and turned on by his expression of both loss and desire, which had been etched into his face as he'd said goodbye.

Stupid Stella. She'd acted on her attraction and now she had to face the consequences.

Sucking in a deep breath, she tentatively tapped on his consulting-room door. There was no avoiding him today or avoiding what she'd done, because she had spent the weekend berating herself for starting that kiss and listing the repercussions for their working relationship. If only he weren't such a good listener, so perceptive and impartial. If only she could stop wanting him with a need that bordered on obsessive.

'Come in,' he called, his voice sounding way too normal for Stella's liking.

Feeling as if her legs were boneless, she entered.

Aaron was alone.

Bad, bad news—she needed as many barriers to temptation as possible.

He looked up, removed his glasses, his smile hesitant but his eyes lighting up.

Stella swallowed past her dry throat. *Act natural.*

'Do you have a minute?' Her voice broke as she tried and failed to stave off the flush of heat that crept up her neck.

Say no. Send me away. Tell me that we made a mistake that can never happen again.

'Of course.' His open, honest smile kicked up at the corners. It had the same effect as the intense, carnal expression he'd worn on Friday night when he'd rocked the ground under her feet and kissed her as if he'd been dreaming of doing so since the first time they spoke.

'As it happens, my ten o'clock cancelled last-minute. Come in.' He stood and Stella closed the door.

With her back to him she could block out the delicious sight he made. Dressed in another fine wool jumper, this one the shade of Scottish heather on a windswept moor, he looked edible. Definitely kissable. Other things too. Tempting, sexy, but ridiculously unwise things.

She turned, cemented her feet to the floor to avoid burying her face in that jumper, inhaling his scent from the soft wool and losing herself in his proximity, masculinity and mastery as she'd done at her parents' gate.

The warm room became vacuum-like and hormone-charged. Stella struggled for breath but tried to focus on the query she had in relation to her patient rather than on the man who had the ability to make her forget all of the reasons that she didn't date. Aaron wasn't the usual type she went for: guys out for a good time without strings. He was still grieving the loss of his wife. He had Charlie to consider. He was her boss.

'I need your advice,' she said. Yes, this was better. Keep things professional, pretend that the kiss to end all kisses hadn't happened and hope that he didn't want to discuss it/fire her/prohibit a rerun.

'I've…um…seen Mrs Cavanagh this morning.' She stared at her phone, the notes she'd made blurring.

'Ah, yes, chronic pain,' said Aaron. 'Tricky case—it was a bit mean of me to give you that on your first day of working independently.' He offered her a seat and then took his own, scooting it forward until their knees almost touched as he gave her his undivided attention. He'd done the same thing many times as they discussed patients or shared the same computer, only now it felt too close. An invasion of her personal space that shredded her peace of mind.

'Not at all.' Stella's stomach turned to jelly. She'd have been happy with only a fraction of his attention; perhaps then she would have been able to think.

So why didn't she scoot her chair back?

'Her history is complex but interesting,' she said, aware of the way her lips formed words and how he watched her talk, his gaze pinging between her eyes and her mouth, as if listening but also distracted by what they'd done on Friday night.

'I saw a similar case as an in-patient at City, actually.' Slightly breathless, she wet her lips, remembering those few soul-searing moments at her parents' gate and how he had made her feel eighteen again. Only it had been better than any kiss she'd experienced back then. Now she was a woman who knew exactly what she wanted.

'Three months ago you changed her medication,' she said, forcing her thoughts away from kissing and back to Mrs Cavanagh. 'She's been in tears this morning because she feels that nothing has helped so far.'

Aaron leaned back slightly and rubbed his chin while he pondered this newest development. Stella had to blink to break the memory of his stubble-rough chin scraping her face in the cold, dark night. Of the way he had groaned with pleasure, such a sexy sound. Of the way his manly body had completely engulfed her until she had wanted to melt into him.

'Do you feel she's becoming clinically depressed?' he asked, clearly faring better than her at keeping his mind on track.

Did that mean he was done with her, with whatever this was? Maybe he'd spent the weekend reconsidering his response to her rash kiss. Maybe it was just she who craved more.

Deflated by that conclusion, Stella nodded. 'I think so. She scores highly on the depression scale and she said that she hasn't been sleeping.'

'Okay, well, she recently lost her sister, so I'm not surprised that her pain has become harder to manage.' He looked at Stella with his Dr Bennett eyes, as if he hadn't kissed her until she'd almost orgasmed on Friday. 'So, what's your management plan?'

Stella hesitated. The kiss had changed their working dynamic. Where last week she'd have been confident to express her opinions, now she felt uncertain, as if she was pushing an agenda, being somehow manipulative.

No. The patient's best interests were all she cared about. Aaron would hear out her suggestions and be objective. He, after all, had been nothing but professional since she entered his room.

Stella pushed her hair from her flushed face. 'There's a newly appointed pain specialist at City Hospital who is having some success with a combination of traditional therapies and alternative approaches, like meditation. I think a referral may be warranted, but I wanted to check what you would do in this situation.'

'I agree—a referral is appropriate.' He quirked an impressed brow that made her feel ten feet tall. 'I didn't know about the new pain clinic, so thanks for the insider knowledge. And how will you manage the depression?'

'I offered her a first-line antidepressant, but she refused. She said she'd like to get the pain under control before she considers taking *any more tablets*. I gave her some information sheets on non-pharmacological remedies, exercise, sleep hygiene, et cetera, but I think she needs more than that. I also suggested that she talk to the practice counsellor, and there are some excellent guided meditations for chronic-pain management online.'

Aaron's smile widened. 'You've done everything I would have suggested. Well done. Make the referral to the pain clinic and mention the mood disturbance in your referral letter. They will re-discuss it with her, I'm sure, as the two so often go hand in hand.'

'Thanks.' Stella stood and made for the door, elated at her clinical management plan but also strangely disappointed that Aaron hadn't ravaged her on his desk.

She needed to get a grip. He wouldn't be un-professional with a waiting room full of patients beyond the door.

She didn't get very far.

Aaron's deep voice brought her escape to a premature halt. 'I think we should talk about what happened on Friday night.'

Stella froze, turned, cast him a glance full of bravado. 'About Sam?'

Being deliberately obtuse seemed petty, but resisting him was hard enough when they dis-cussed patients. Actually talking about that mind-blowing kiss might trigger another lapse of her judgement. Things were awkward enough. She was in enough trouble, wanted him too much to trust a single idea her weak brain formulated.

Aaron stood and her belly fluttered. 'No, about us.' His voice dropped an octave, his tone husky and intimate. Stella was reminded of the way he'd uttered the word *goodnight*—full of reluc-tance. Need. Regret.

'About the kissing.' He stepped closer, his eyes moving over her face slowly, thoughtfully, pa-tiently.

Why couldn't she be as cool and collected? As mature and unaffected?

She shrugged, while her heart raced with ex-citement. 'Do we need to talk about it?'

Did she have the strength to talk about it?

She'd prefer to simply launch herself across the room at him and repeat the mistake that had ruined her for all future kisses.

He tilted his head, as if he saw straight through her protective disguise, his stare intent, ducking between her eyes and her mouth as if he remembered her taste and wanted more.

'You're right. We probably should just pretend it didn't happen.' He drew in a controlled breath that Stella wanted to disrupt. She wanted to turn him on, remind him how well they had fitted together on Friday, until he too felt conflicted and needy.

His suggestion was the sensible thing to do. The best way to resume what was left of their working relationship.

Except…

His eyes became so intense, she had to blink and break the connection. 'I don't want to hurt you, Stella.'

His honesty and integrity fanned the flames of her obsession. He was making it so hard to stay rational and detached.

'I wouldn't allow you to hurt me,' she whispered, entranced by the look in his eyes.

He raised a hand and cupped her cheek. The contact made her knees almost buckle, her body sway closer.

'I have a big problem,' he said, his voice full of gravel. 'I'm not looking for a relationship—'

'Neither am I,' she interrupted then gripped his wrist, keeping his warm palm pressed to her face. She knew what she wanted and what she didn't want. She didn't want a relationship, or to be hurt. But she sure as hell didn't want to lose his touch.

His pupils flared, the black swallowing the blue of his irises. 'But I can't help wanting you. Wanting to kiss you again. Wanting more.' His thumb swiped her bottom lip in provocation.

Oh, her too.

She sighed, closed her eyes, enjoyed the moment that felt like that weightless feeling at the top of a swing.

She opened her eyes. 'I want you too, but I'm not sure that it's wise.' The last few words came out as a whisper, totally lacking conviction. How could she be so weak? So led by her hormones? She dropped her hand from his as if to bolster her resolve.

But seriously, who cared about wisdom with chemistry this good? She'd be leaving as soon as her transfer came through. Surely she could indulge in her ultimate fantasy: one night with Aaron Bennett?

Question was: would she survive it?

His hand slid from her face and hung at his

side. 'No, it's most definitely unwise.' His lips flattened, and she wanted to snatch back her words. She wanted his touch back, his skin on hers, closeness. Combustion.

'Unless…' he said, one eyebrow quirked in suggestion.

She latched onto that portentous word. 'Unless?' The pleading sound of her voice caused a flush to her skin.

He watched her parted lips in silence for a beat or two, his features shifting through a gamut of emotions as if he too waged an internal battle of sense versus need.

'Unless we both want the same thing.'

She nodded, euphoric that they might be on the same page. 'Just sex.'

Simply saying the word clenched her stomach in anticipation, the memory of his mouth on hers, his thigh between her legs, his hardness pressing into her stomach reawakening her body's aroused reaction.

He conceded with a tilt of his head. 'No emotions. Nothing serious.'

The confirmation was all Stella required for her arguments to crumble. 'After all, I'll soon be leaving.'

'And I only have room in my life for Charlie.'

She wanted to sleep with him. Why not? Neither of them had any interest in a relationship, so they could keep feelings off the table. Her move back to London would physically distance her from any stupid ideas her body might have in craving more than one night in his bed. What was the harm? Their chemistry only grew, day by day. Soon there'd be no containing it. The sexual tension drawing them closer was almost inevitable.

They were going to happen, heaven help her.

He dipped his head, brought his mouth closer as if he could no longer hold back from kissing her, but he kept her waiting, giving her time and options she didn't want.

'Still think it's a bad idea?' His breath feathered her lips, his stare dark and seductive. That look would surely have lured many women under his spell and into his bed.

Stella's heart leapt against her ribs as she tilted her chin up, looked at him from under her lashes, her lips only inches from his. 'Probably,' she shrugged, 'and I'm done with things that are bad for me.'

Despite evidence that he still had the moves that had given him a heartthrob reputation, she could no longer fit him into the same category as her bad-boy ex just to deny how much she wanted him. Younger Aaron might have been a bit of a playboy, but mature Aaron was a community stalwart, a doting father, a diligent and compassionate GP. He was nothing like Harry, who, in starting a relationship with Stella, lying about the fact that things between him and his ex were irretrievably over, had put himself, his feelings and wants above those of both Stella and his own son.

Aaron put Charlie first.

Unable to stop herself, Stella leaned closer as if pulled by gravity, placed her palm in the centre of his chest, her fingertips flexing into his soft jumper registering the pounding of his heart.

A soft groan left him. His gaze slowly traced her features. 'The fact that you're looking at me with glazed eyes, dilated pupils and parted lips tells me that you know we will be so good together.'

The vulnerability haunting his eyes shattered the last of her crumbling resolve. She wanted him and she'd exhausted all of the excuses she used to resist.

She nodded. 'Just one night.'

He reached for her free hand, tugged it and wrapped his arm around her waist, shocking a gasp past her lips. Her breasts grazed his chest, darts of pleasure shooting along her nerves. Their eyes locked.

He dipped his head.

Her chin tilted, mouth raised, ready to surrender to his delirious kiss once more.

A shrill ring tone rent the air.

With a sigh Stella felt against her lips, Aaron dropped his forehead to hers, closed his eyes and growled in frustration.

Stella's breathing came hard. Arousal spiked her blood, its potency draining away as Aaron took the phone from his pocket. He straightened, keeping one hand on her waist, stared deep into her eyes as he answered.

'Yes, Penny,' he said to the receptionist on duty today.

Stella stood transfixed by the heat and desire and promise glimmering in his eyes. They spoke of a similar need ransacking her body, making her weak, needy, heedless of the consequences of wanting this particular man and ready to throw all caution to the wind to be with him one time.

'Your ten-fifteen is here.' Stella heard Penny's side of the conversation and took a step back. The loss of his warmth and the hard comfort of his body physically hurt. Disappointment drained her limbs of energy. She sagged, looked down at her feet and then held up her hands, palms out as she backed towards the door.

What had she been thinking? They were at work. It was mid-morning. There was a waiting room full of patients out there. She'd become al-most completely carried away. Without interruption, she'd have kissed him and done who knew what else right here in his room.

As she instructed her desperate, weak libido to get a grip, Aaron ended the call, his eyes still laser-focused on her. That look was trouble, determination and resolve clear in the jut of his jaw.

'To be continued, Stella.'

Without comment, she scarpered, too turned-on and terrified to do more than nod.

By the end of her second week, Aaron was climbing the walls with exasperation to be alone with Stella. It seemed that every member of the local community had gone down with the 'flu, the seasonal spike earlier than expected that year. They had been swamped at the surgery, working late most evenings in order to meet the increased demand for appointments.

Outside of work he'd been busy too. Charlie had extra lessons for a swimming tournament and a mid-week after-school birthday party to attend. When Molly's parents asked if they could have Charlie over to stay on Friday night so they could take him to the car-boot sale two villages over on Saturday, he'd almost wept with relief and gratitude.

His first thought: to invite Stella on a date. A casual, nothing serious date. A drink in a quiet pub out of Abbotsford where they could talk, be alone, explore each other.

He missed her open smile and her playful sense of humour. Not to mention the hot promises they had made with their eyes at the start of the week when, to his utter relief, they had laid down the ground rules for managing their chemistry. And the torture had continued. Just because they skirted big circles around each other at work, succeeded in keeping their hands off each other, it hadn't stopped them practically torching the entire practice with longing stares and knowing looks.

Aaron pulled into the stable yard of Amy's riding school and parked his car. Stella had left work earlier, saying that she was going for a ride. Some of the regular Ability Riding children had missed their class due to the 'flu also ripping through the primary school, but the horses still needed to be exercised.

Instead of bounding from the car in search of Stella, his natural inclination, he paused, gripping the steering wheel as his doubts resurfaced.

As much as he didn't want to hurt Stella, neither did he want to disrupt the sense of contentment he'd finally found for himself and Charlie. He'd been as clear as he could, and she understood that his son came first. If they kept it about sex, as Stella suggested, there could be no misguided expectations.

He snorted, shook his head. He was overthinking.

This thing with Stella had an expiry date; she would soon return to London.

Tired of tying himself up in knots, Aaron headed to the stables and called out a hello. Despite the floodlit gravel car park, the buildings seemed deserted but for the horses quietly chomping hay. Perhaps he'd missed her. She hadn't answered his earlier text, which invited her out this evening, so he'd called in at the stables on the off-chance that she hadn't yet left.

His gut tight with disappointment, Aaron headed to the staff room he knew was at the back of the property. He'd once made a call here to examine an experienced rider who'd taken a fall and had a moderate concussion.

In his haste to see Stella he rounded the corner of the building and smacked right into her. His hands gripped her shoulders, to steady both her and himself as his heart thundered in relief and excitement.

'Hi,' she said, gripping his forearms, looking up at him with that secret smile she'd worn all week. A smile for him, for them.

'Sorry about that.' He smiled, pretended to be unaware of her shudder under his touch. Otherwise he'd want to pick up where they had left off on Monday in his office and kiss her until she was breathless and clinging to him and the restless energy twisting his insides vanished.

Her hair was damp at the ends as if she'd taken a shower. She smelled like a fresh meadow. He wanted to haul her close, kiss her as if the world was ending, put that glazed look of passion on her face and give her a new association with Abbotsford, one that was all about pleasure.

Instead, he slid his hands from her shoulders, down her arms and held both of her hands. 'I texted you. I called in on the off chance that you'd still be here.'

'Sorry,' she said, squeezing his hands. 'I was in the shower. Everyone else has left for the day.' Her eyes were huge in the gloom, expressive and vulnerable and full of questions. He wanted to chase away every one of her demons. But that was a boundary he had no right in breaching, not when they'd vowed to keep this casual.

She gave him a sexy smile, her tongue touching her bottom lip as she gripped his hands tighter and stepped closer so their bodies were flush.

'What did the text say?' she asked, clearly unwilling to release his hands to check her phone.

He let go of one hand to wrap his arm around her waist and dragged her close. Her pupils dilated. 'I wondered if you would like to go for a drink. I know this lovely pub in Little Dunnop. It's quiet and has a roaring fire.'

Her face fell, a frown settling between her brows.

Aaron swallowed, wondering how he'd ruined the mood. Perhaps she was hesitant to be seen alone with him in public.

'It's a couple of villages away,' he cajoled. 'Hopefully none of my patients will be there, so we're almost guaranteed an evening free of medical drama.'

Her stare rose to his. 'It's not that.' Her teeth scraped her bottom lip, and he instinctively relaxed his hold of her, in case she felt that they were rushing into this.

'It's just that my ex is from Little Dunnop.' She lifted her hand to his chest, her fingers curling into his sweater. 'I don't want to run into him or any of his family.'

Aaron winced, gutted that he hadn't thought of that. 'Of course. I understand. We can go somewhere else.'

'Where's Charlie tonight?' she asked as she looked up at him, her gorgeous eyes pools of desire.

'He's sleeping over at his grandparents' house. They like to take him out on Saturday morning.'

'In that case, no, thanks.' She raised her face,

brushed his lips with hers, barely touching but igniting his nervous system. 'I'll give the pub a miss. Do you have a fire at your place?'

'Mmm-hmm,' he said. 'One to rival any pub's in the county.'

Desperate to ravage those tantalising lips of hers, he held back, loving the direction of this conversation.

'Do you have wine?' she asked, her index finger teasing the stubble along his jaw.

'Yes.'

'A condom machine in the bathroom?' She grinned, and he laughed at her sense of humour.

'Not exactly, but we're covered.' He wrapped both of his arms around her waist, what was left of his restraint vanishing. He hauled her into his arms, crushed her chest to his and slanted his mouth over hers at last.

Stella clung to him, parted her lips and returned his heated kiss as if they'd been kissing for years, as if they were made for kissing and nothing else, as if she'd be happy to spend the night in this very spot that smelled of sweet hay and horseflesh and kiss all night long.

When they parted briefly for air, she moaned, dropping her head back and closing her eyes. 'Invite me back to yours,' she said, her voice slurred with passion. Passion he'd inflamed.

'Whatever you say.' He speared his fingers

through her glossy hair to angle her head so he could taste the soft skin of her neck in an exploratory journey he wanted never to end.

She moaned, her eyes still closed as she slipped her hands under his sweater, her fingers digging into his back, urging his body closer.

Aaron thanked the universe for his smarts; he wasn't stupid enough to question a woman when she issued a direct order. 'Come back to mine.' He held her face, his stare glued to her, felt her small, definite nod.

He made the four-mile drive home in record time.

CHAPTER NINE

THE MINUTE AARON'S front door closed behind them, banishing the November chill from his farmhouse-style cottage, Stella spun to face him. In unison and without a second's hesitation they reached for each other, tugging off each other's coats and hats while indulging in frantic, breathless kisses. Stella had never felt a fire as intense as the one burning her alive, the urgency almost too much to bear.

How could she need him so much?

It was just sex. That was what she recited over and over. They'd agreed: one night.

With a grunt Aaron swung her around and pressed her back up against some piece of furniture in the hallway, his thigh pushing between her legs. She lost herself, her only coherent thought that she would welcome him taking her right here on the flagstone floor.

Aaron tore his lips from hers, his breath gusting as he trailed kisses over her jaw and down her neck. He groaned, his voracious mouth finding every one of her neck's erogenous zones.

'Do you want that drink?' He pulled away, and Stella almost sagged into a heap.

'Later. I want you.' She heeled off her boots, gripped the belt loops on his jeans and tugged his hips between her spread thighs.

He cupped her cheek, and then both cheeks, tilting up her chin to stare down into her eyes. 'You are so beautiful, too good to be true. I plan to distract you with so much pleasure that you won't have a chance to come to your senses.'

'I'm not going anywhere.'

'Lucky me.' Something shifted across his expression—a moment of hesitation, a flash of vulnerability she dared not analyse. 'Can you stay all night?'

'Yes.'

He smiled a dazzling smile that made Stella weak.

She tugged at his waist, bringing his mouth back to hers, until their lips fused, their tongues sweeping to meet and tangle. His fingers curled into her hair and Stella hooked her arms over his wide shoulders, clinging tight.

Aaron hoisted her from the floor. She wrapped her legs around his waist and felt his erection between her legs. He carried her across the room to a wide, comfy sofa in front of the hearth, where the fire had burned low, but still gave off an orange glow and waves of heat. Not that she needed the flames; she was on fire for this man.

Aaron sat on the sofa, lowering Stella into his lap, where she straddled his thighs and stared down at his sincere and hungry expression.

He wanted her. Aaron Bennett thought she was beautiful. This must be a dream.

And tomorrow she would need to wake up. But not yet.

She kissed his jaw, his earlobe, down his neck, as all the while she worked on his shirt buttons. When she parted the soft fabric that smelled like washing powder and Aaron, she caught her bottom lip under her teeth to halt a sigh of utter longing.

He was gorgeous under the clothes, better than she'd imagined. Every muscle of his chest and abdomen was defined. Soft golden hair nestled between his pecs and formed a trail that disappeared beneath the waistband of his jeans.

Stella ran her hands over the warm ridges and dips, learning the feel of him, the places that made his eyes darken like a stormy ocean and his hands restlessly fist her hips. She continued her exploration, and he sighed, his head falling back against the sofa.

'I haven't done this for a while,' he said, his

eyes ablaze with enough desire to assure Stella that he didn't need to worry.

'Me neither.' Stella wasn't sure that she'd ever done whatever *this* was, but she shuddered to think that it would carry that degree of significance. She couldn't allow that. It was just for tonight, except she'd never before felt this all-consuming obsession, this urgent and confusing need to both slowly study every millimetre of Aaron Bennett and to tear at him until he quenched the fire burning her to ash.

She pushed the shirt from his shoulders and popped the button on his jeans, emboldened by the bulge behind his fly. She was no longer the shy, naive Stella that had once lived here. She was Dr Stella Wright, a strong, resilient woman who created her own destiny.

'Who knew you were hiding all of this under those woolly jumpers?' she teased, sitting back on his muscular thighs.

He laughed, reaching for the hem of her own sweater. She raised it over her head, tossing it to the floor.

'The first time I saw you at the hospital when I interviewed for the lecturing post back in the summer, I almost swallowed my tongue.' He slid his warm hands along her ribs and cupped her breasts through her bra. 'You're a striking woman, but the confident way you carry yourself, your fun, self-possessed attitude… I have to admit I was a little in awe of you that day we first spoke.'

In awe of her?

'Why?' She moved her hands over the smooth skin of his shoulders, too desperate to know every inch of him to pause her exploration.

'I was so attracted to you, but figured I was too old, that you would never look at me this way.' He cupped her cheek, his thumb tracing her lips.

'I happen to find your brand of maturity and responsibility a major turn-on,' she said.

Harry had made a big deal of their few-years age gap at the end. She had always suspected that it was a coward's excuse.

A lump she didn't want to acknowledge tonight lodged in her throat. Aaron was so different from Harry. She was different too. No longer young and lovestruck.

Now she could protect herself, keep her emotions distant.

'And I was wildly attracted to you, too,' she confessed. 'I was so busy ogling you, I almost fell down the auditorium steps.'

The look of wonder and desire on his face made her whimper. Emotion she couldn't name bubbled to the surface.

'Now, stop talking,' she mumbled against his

lips. She needed to switch off her thoughts, lose herself in sensation. Tonight belonged to just the two of them, would be their secret to treasure. She'd hold it inside, never tell a soul, relive the memory.

Aaron reached around and popped the clasp of her bra, single-handed. 'Do you want to move upstairs?'

'No. Impressive bra skills, by the way.' Despite the glow of the fire at her back, which bathed Aaron's skin in golden light, Stella's skin pimpled. She wanted to joke, to banter with him to keep things light, but she was already in over her head.

'I still have some moves.' Aaron stroked her back, his fingers lazy and hypnotic where his stare clinging to hers was urgent and voracious.

She nodded, sat up and slipped first one bra strap and then the other from her shoulders and tossed it to the floor. 'Show me,' she said in a breathy voice.

His stare grew intense in that way she'd come to love this week. Every time their eyes met at work, every glance or chance encounter around the health centre, felt deliciously illicit, as if they'd orchestrated a secret rendezvous.

He tugged her waist and she sank into him, their naked torsos burning where they connected. Every inch of his skin was like hot silk. His scent engulfed her until she was certain she'd never eradicate it from her senses. Her head swam with lack of oxygen, but she couldn't tear her mouth away from his wonderful kisses, which were the sweetest, most reckless indulgence she'd ever experienced.

Only she wanted more. She wanted everything he'd give her, for one night. Then she could leave Abbotsford once more knowing that she hadn't been controlled by her fears, that he'd been right: she could be herself anywhere she chose.

His warm palms cupped her breasts, and Stella dropped her head back on a moan as he thumbed both of her nipples. Her hips rocked of their own accord, seeking out friction to help her weather the storm tossing her body. When Aaron's mouth closed over one nipple, she cried out and tangled her fingers in his hair. Nothing mattered but this one precious night. Her fears, her doubts, their pasts, and futures…all irrelevant.

Stella was vaguely aware of the removal of their remaining clothes, her attention too focused on how Aaron made her feel invincible and beautiful and desired to care about the scramble of limbs and tangle of clothes. She watched him take a condom from his wallet and cover himself, her desperation reaching dizzying heights. And then he was pushing inside her, his eyes locked with hers, his hands cupping her face as if she were a prized possession, and for all she knew the sky might be falling down.

'Stella,' he muttered, the desire in his eyes scorching her skin.

She clung to him, surrounded by his strong arms. She lost herself in returning his every kiss. When he retreated, she surged to meet him. When he gripped her hands, his fingers laced with hers, she clung tighter, surrounded his hips with her legs. When she moaned his name, he urged her on, muttering her name into her hair, the crook of her neck, her ear, his warm breath dancing over her sensitised skin, adding a cascade of shivers to the rapture already taking hold. She shattered, his name on her broken cry, her climax powerful and endless.

Aaron collapsed his weight on top of her with a groan, joining her in bliss, and Stella entered a world where reality exceeded fantasy. A world where she knew exactly what it felt like to be with Aaron Bennett.

A world that she feared was changed for ever.

Aaron drowsily stroked the length of Stella's arm, which was warm from the fire's glow where he'd banked it with fresh logs. They occupied the sofa, their limbs entwined, a blanket covering them. He wove his fingers with hers, unable to stop touching her for even a second. A fleeting rush of panic stalled his breath. What if he couldn't ever stop?

No, they'd agreed on one night. They had hours until dawn, hours until he would shrug off the role of lover he'd donned for the night and resume the most important role of his life: that of Charlie's father.

Only now that he'd met Stella, now that they had crossed that line of physical intimacy, the constant guilt he'd lived with since Molly's death roared back to life, louder than ever.

He swallowed, fighting the urge to take Stella home and retreat into himself. How could he enjoy being with her when he carried so much baggage that made him feel unworthy? There was no need to fear that he was already addicted to Stella. He couldn't allow himself such an amazing privilege. He'd had his chance at love. That was why this one night of passion was all he could justify, all he could permit.

He shifted, tightening his grip on her waist, and asked in a low voice, 'Tell me what happened to turn you against Abbotsford?' It was obviously linked to this no-good ex, the one who'd cruelly used her, lied and then cast her aside. He hated that she denied herself the place she'd grown up.

He expected her small sigh, so he feathered his lips over her bare shoulder in light kisses, letting her know that nothing she told him would matter or alter how he felt about her.

His stomach rolled at the depth of those feelings he had no right to feel. But he could push those down. He would have to. For Stella, for Charlie and for his own sanity.

She turned onto her back, her head resting on his bicep, where she was still tucked into the crook of his arm. He stroked her hair back from her face and kissed her warm cheek.

'It wasn't Abbotsford as such, just the close-knit nature of village life. Everyone knowing your business.' She sighed and Aaron pressed his lips to her temple, willing her to open up. Perhaps he could reassure her that whatever she feared no longer carried the threat she perceived.

'My break-up with Harry was all such a mess at the time. I didn't know until he texted to break things off, but he didn't stop sleeping with his ex, Angus's mum, throughout our entire relationship.'

Aaron stiffened, protective urges welling up inside him. 'He strung you along and broke up with you in a text?'

She nodded, dragging in a fortifying breath, but he saw the pain still there beneath the surface. 'I believed him when he said he loved me,' she whispered. 'He was older than me, more experienced. He was my first, you know. I trusted him.'

Aaron's muscles coiled tight with rage. 'And he betrayed all of that, after he'd allowed you to get close to his son, to care about them both.' How could someone be such a snake? How could he use a person with such a big heart as Stella? She deserved so much better.

'I was so humiliated,' she continued. 'One minute he was professing undying love and including me in his and Angus's daily lives, then all of a sudden he said it was over, that he was going back to his ex. He even had the audacity to say it was for Angus's sake. And I, in my naiveté, believed him. It wasn't until later that I realised Harry always did what was best for Harry.'

Aaron bit his lip to stop himself from asking for more details. Her pain was a gnawing rumble in his gut. But there must be more to the story for her to avoid Abbotsford, avoid people who might have known her back then.

'Then the rumours started,' she said in a whisper he might not have heard if he hadn't been so close.

He froze, his breath stalling. 'What rumours?'

'Mum came home from work one day upset. People were saying that I'd been the reason Harry and his ex had split in the first place. That I was the other woman, the kind of person who thought I could break up a lovely young family for my own selfish reasons.'

'But it wasn't true.' He knew deep down in his bones that she was incapable of selfishness.

She shook her head, but she wouldn't look at him. 'I didn't know about Angus's mother. He told me he was single. He swept me off my feet. When he confessed that he had a son with a shared custody arrangement, I was delighted, already besotted and half in love with him. I was young, stupid. I should have seen through him, realised the spin was too good to be true.'

Outraged on her behalf, Aaron snorted. 'You were young. That doesn't mean you deserved to be treated that way, that you should have been able to read his mind, or that you were in any way responsible for *his* actions.'

She nodded, her eyes sadder than ever. 'I can certainly understand that now, but at the time none of it mattered. I was lost in my grief, crying all the time. Initially I was too heartbroken to care what people thought. I missed Angus. I grieved the loss of both relationships. And then later I became paranoid and anxious, refusing to leave the house in case someone said something to me and I'd break down in the street.'

'And this… Harry. Didn't he deny the rumours, defend you, tell the truth?' What kind of a man would stand by and let an innocent woman he must have cared for a little suffer alone?

'No. That was the most humiliating part of all.

It was as if he'd vanished, leaving me to clean up his dirty work.'

He rested his forehead against her temple, breathed in her warm scent. 'I know it would have been cold comfort at the time, but you must know that he never deserved you.'

Could she possibly still be in love with this guy?

Nausea gripped his throat.

She shrugged. 'I know that now. But then I wondered if his ex was responsible for starting the rumours. Or maybe Harry himself to garner sympathy and win her back for good. I don't know. The worst part was that I was so blind to what I thought love was that I truly believed we had a future. That I would go to uni but come home every weekend to be with him and Angus. That one day I'd move back here and we would be a proper family. More fool me.'

'It wasn't your fault.' He stroked her hair, knowing that he'd lost her to her memories of the pain she'd suffered.

'They were already a family,' she continued as if she hadn't heard, 'one that didn't include me.' She met his eyes. 'I was just a discarded side-piece.'

Aaron bit back a litany of curses, seeing red on Stella's behalf. 'I'm sorry that you had that experience, that this Harry guy was too much of a coward to be honest. That he behaved so cruelly.'

She shrugged but he knew a brave face when he saw one. 'It worked out for the best. I was leaving for uni anyway. When I got to London, I kept busy as a distraction, threw myself into being a medical student, worked hard and played hard.'

She smiled her wide smile and winked at him. 'I had a blast, swapped horses for parties and clubbing during any spare time I had. London is good like that—diverting, energetic, always abuzz. Pretty soon I was too busy to even think about Harry.'

'But it stopped you visiting home.' She hadn't dated again. She wasn't over it.

Acid burned behind his sternum.

She shrugged, still holding part of herself aloof, still shielding. 'You know how demanding those years are academically. I spent most of my free time studying, with the occasional party thrown in. Plus my parents often visited London, as all three of their daughters were based there. In fact, they often talk about selling up here and relocating. I suspect they will once either of my sisters starts a family.'

Aaron's heart skipped a beat without reason. 'What about you? Don't you want children one day?' It was none of his business and he shouldn't be invested in her answer. But he cared about her. He wanted her to be happy and fulfilled.

She shook her head. 'It's not something I've really considered, probably because I haven't had a serious relationship since. I love my job. I'm still focused on my career. You know what that's like.'

Silence settled in the room, broken only by the occasional crackle from the fire. Aaron grew inexplicably restless. It shouldn't matter to him that she had no plans to settle down. But he felt as if he'd just been handed a million-pound note, only to discover it was fake.

'What about you?' she said, deflecting the heat away from herself. 'Have you thought about moving on? Getting married again?' She turned onto her stomach, dipped her gaze and toyed with his chest hair, as if she cared about his future happiness. But she was just being thoughtful. She'd just confessed her reasons to fear falling in love again. She only wanted a one-night stand and she still planned to move away, despite her success at the practice.

And her practicality suited him down to the ground. Right...?

'Not really.' Aaron stroked her back, forced his body to relax, because he did care that they had this connection she could clearly take or leave, even though he shouldn't. 'Life is so busy. Charlie takes up all of my free time. I can't imagine there would be too many women willing to settle for the very occasional date sandwiched in between school pick-up and bedtime stories.'

He felt the same as her about relationships, so why was he so...irritated to hear her voice that her intentions hadn't changed just because they'd had amazing sex?

She stroked his hair, her eyes heavy. 'I think you'd be surprised when you do decide to dip your toe back into the dating pool. I witnessed quite the hormonal kerfuffle at the school gate last week. I suspect the single ladies would be lining up to date the Cotswolds' most eligible doctor.'

He laughed at the picture she painted, but the idea made Aaron shudder. Until she'd returned to Abbotsford, he'd had no interest in the local women, in women full stop.

'I can't do it to Charlie,' he said, the old guilt crawling under his skin. 'He needs me at the moment, needs all of my attention. I have to be everything to him, Mum and Dad.'

She seemed taken aback. 'So that's it for you dating-wise? Your personal needs are irrelevant because you became a parent?'

There was no accusation in her tone, just pensive curiosity.

He shrugged, because he'd never actually

given it this much consideration. 'Maybe when he's older I'll have time to date.'

But Charlie wasn't the main reason that he kept himself emotionally unavailable. He couldn't trust that he wouldn't let someone he cared for down again in the future, that he would have to relive the pain of loss. He'd rather be alone.

'How old,' she asked, 'like eighteen? When he leaves for uni?' She chuckled softly but there was something watchful, searching in her eyes.

Why was she so interested in his dating life? Had she changed her mind about the one-night rule? Perhaps his moves weren't that rusty.

His silence was the only answer he had. He couldn't seriously contemplate inviting another woman into his and Charlie's life. What if his son formed an attachment and the relationship didn't last? Look at the way Stella had been hurt. Like her, he couldn't bear to think of poor, confused baby Angus. What if a new woman in Aaron's life resurrected all of Charlie's questions about his mother's death, issues he'd dealt with? What if he grew up to resent Aaron for his choice to move on?

He'd never do anything to risk losing his son. He didn't want Molly's death to mean nothing.

At his continued stillness, Stella stroked his cheek. 'I understand. You're the most important person in Charlie's life. Of course you want to protect him. That's as it should be.' She pressed her mouth to his, comprehension in her eyes.

Because she did understand. She'd been on the receiving end of the choices some parents made to put their own, often messed up and selfish feelings first, and she'd been hurt in the crossfire.

But right now, still rocked by their chemistry and the intimacy of having her naked in his arms, Aaron's predominant fear was for himself, for his precious status quo.

Rather than examine his feelings further, he ran with her kiss, turning it from something comforting to something carnal, his body reacting to hers, his mind forgetting all of the reasons this couldn't last beyond tonight as he covered her body with his. They still had a few hours before sunrise. The best way to combat his concerns, to forget why he couldn't date, why Stella, who shared his reservations, was perfect for now?

The distraction of pleasure.

CHAPTER TEN

By the end of a busy Wednesday the following week, Stella was enjoying an erotic daydream of Aaron as she had filled every spare moment since her amazing night his bed.

The door swung open, startling her from the emails she had read and reread at least six times. She looked up from the computer, her heart lurching with predictable arousal and excitement at the sight of Aaron.

One look at his serious expression dissolved her desire, her stomach pinching with trepidation.

'There's an emergency on Penwood Hill,' he said of the local beauty spot popular with hikers. 'Community First Responders have been called, but I'm going to assist in case they need help.'

Stella stood, adrenaline shoving her body into action. 'Can I come, too?'

Aaron nodded, his eyes, which carried the glimmer of intimacy, holding hers. 'I hoped you'd want to. Let's go.'

In Stella's mind, a hundred silent communications seemed to pass between them, things they couldn't voice aloud right now, maybe never.

Do you regret what we did?

Have you thought about me since?

Are you, like me, desperate to do it again?

But now was not the time to have any of those conversations and who knew what Aaron was thinking?

As they exited her consultation room, Aaron reached for her hand. A thrill coursed through her at his simple touch, one that had nothing to do with the adrenaline of attending a medical emergency out in the field. This rush was all about the way Aaron didn't seem to care who saw them holding hands as he led her through the surgery where staff were finishing up for the day and the last patient lingered, chatting about his arthritic knee.

Stella tried to breathe through the sensation that people were staring, judging her, gossiping. It was likely all in her head. But she didn't want the locals to think she was making a play for the village's most eligible man.

Perhaps Aaron had acted unconsciously. She should have eased her hand away—the physical side of their relationship was meant to be over. Except the last time she had felt absolutely comfortable holding a man's hand—something she didn't do when she dated casually—was with Harry.

But there was no time to overthink the gesture, or interpret it as the kind of emotional entanglement that she normally avoided. In the utility room at the rear of the practice, Aaron grabbed two high-visibility all-weather jackets from the hooks on the wall and headed out to the car park with Stella in tow.

They climbed into a four-wheel drive emblazoned with the words 'Abbotsford Medical Centre', and Aaron punched an address into the vehicle's GPS.

'Tell me what we're dealing with,' said Stella, focused on the scene they would find as she clicked her seatbelt into place.

'A day tourist has slipped and fallen running the Penwood Track. Possible tib and fib fracture.' Aaron navigated the car from the car park behind the surgery and took a left turn in the direction of the neighbouring village of Penwood.

He glanced her way, his calm-under-pressure confidence as reassuring as his open smile. 'It's complicated by the fact that his wife, who is thirty-six weeks pregnant, was waiting for him in the car. By all accounts, she tried to help him down the track, but started to have strong contractions.'

'So a double emergency?' Stella's mind raced,

running through a plan to triage both patients as soon as they reached the scene.

He nodded, his eyes narrowed with urgency. 'Don't worry.' He reached across the central console and squeezed her hand. 'We can do this. The car is equipped with everything we might need.'

At Stella's hesitant nod, he continued. 'The wife became concerned when he didn't come back from his run—he's a fell runner—within his expected time. There's no mobile reception on the track, so she rushed back to the car to sound the alarm.'

He exhaled a controlled breath, a small smile just for her on his lips. 'I told you—never a dull moment around here.'

They shared a second's eye contact that had Stella recalling every touch, every kiss, every cry of their passionate night together.

Face flushed from the erotic memories, she glanced over her shoulder to the well-stocked boot while Aaron focused on the road.

'Do we have Entonox?' she asked.

'Yes. And the community responder is there, but it's his first week without supervision, poor guy.'

Pulse racing, Stella recognised the route Aaron was taking.

'You're not going to follow the road, are you?'

she asked as they bumped over a pothole at speed, flicking up gravel.

'Yes. This is the quickest route to Penwood.' He glanced at the GPS, which wouldn't know the short cut over private land that Stella knew like the back of her hand.

She shook her head. 'No, don't go through the village. The fastest way to the start of the Penwood Track is through the Brady farm, you know, Dale Brady's land.'

'Are you sure?' He shot her a searching look before taking a bend in the lane.

'Absolutely. I used to ride that way all the time on Gertrude. The farm track is wide enough for a four-wheel drive and it cuts off the corner taken via the road. Trust me. It's quicker.'

Aaron grinned and then winked. 'Whatever you say. I do trust you. Nothing much changes around this landscape. You probably know the area better than me, as I was more about driving flashy sports cars around Cheltenham than I was about taking a horse or a Land Rover over a farm track in my youth.'

Stella pursed her lips. 'Oh, I recall. You always seemed to have a different pretty female passenger, too.'

He grinned, the moment of lightness punctuating the adrenaline rush seemingly as welcome to him as it was to Stella. He reached for her hand once more, raising it to his mouth to press a kiss across her knuckles. 'Thank you for the insider knowledge. I'm glad that you're here.'

His smile, the touch of his lips to her skin, devastated Stella, who had managed to fool herself that she could move on from their one night, but she'd been sorely deluded. Not that there was time to enjoy the shudders his touch sent through her body, or panic at her realisation that she was in deep trouble where Aaron was concerned.

He was everything she had avoided these past nine years: perfect, a man made just for Stella.

She stared out of the window to stop herself staring at him. Of course he wasn't perfect. No one was. He had as many issues, as many reasons to avoid a serious relationship as she did. She just couldn't decide if that gave her solace or left a sour taste in her mouth.

At Stella's direction, Aaron took a right turn and headed for the Brady farm.

Stella pointed out the dirt road, her stomach now churning with more than adrenaline for the medical scene awaiting them as she replayed their conversation. Aaron was right. In many ways, she too was a local. She'd grown up here, had family here, was a part of local hIstory.

A sharp pain lodged under her ribs. She hadn't realised how much she was enjoying being back in her old stomping ground. How much she'd missed riding and walking this landscape. She had been forced to become another version of herself in this place, one she didn't like: gullible, broken, grieving. Her desire to leave Abbotsford and return to London had nothing to do with the place and everything to do with her aversion to being hurt again. But seeing the village, the people, the community through Aaron's eyes, she realised that the association between place and her past that she'd made was a figment of her imagination. An unhealthy link that kept her bound in fear.

That just wouldn't do.

Before Stella could ponder this momentous realisation, they arrived at the start of the Penwood Track. The single-lane road flared into a small turning circle, which doubled as a makeshift car park for those wanting to hike the track.

Aaron pulled up behind the first responder's vehicle, which was parked next to the only other car. A heavily pregnant woman was leaning against the car, one hand braced on the open driver's side door and the other on the roof of the car.

Aaron had barely engaged the handbrake when Stella flung open the passenger door and ran towards the woman. She was clearly in the middle of a strong contraction, breathing hard through the pain but in a controlled way that told Stella she'd likely laboured before.

Aaron joined them a few seconds later, one medical backpack slung over his shoulder and another which he placed on the ground at Stella's feet. 'I'll go and assist the first responder, who is with the husband. I'll do a quick triage and then I'll come back, okay?'

Stella nodded, wishing they could stick together.

Aaron addressed the woman. 'Don't worry, Mrs Heath, the ambulance is on its way.'

Then he handed Stella a head torch and took the track at a run, disappearing from sight around the bend.

As the woman's contraction passed, Stella rested a hand on her arm. 'My name is Stella, I'm a GP from Abbotsford.' She ignored how naturally that sentence formed. 'What's your first name, Mrs Heath?'

'Abby,' the woman said, gripping Stella's hand with determination bordering on panic.

This wasn't good. Stella needed to transport Abby somewhere suitable, comfortable and clean. But she had seen that look before during her obstetric post, often when a woman was transitioning into the second stage of labour.

'Can you walk?' Stella asked, glancing over

her shoulder to where the practice vehicle was parked only five metres away.

Abby shook her head, her hand gripping Stella's in a vice, her breathing becoming deep and deliberate once more. 'Need to push,' she said, scrunching her eyes closed against the pain of another powerful contraction.

Stella soothed the woman through the worst of it, her mind spinning. Her gaze searched the track for Aaron, but of course he hadn't had enough time to find the husband, let alone return to assist Stella. She had never delivered a baby outside of a hospital before. But nature waited for no one. If baby Heath was on its way, she would have to manage with what they had to hand.

'Could you move into the back of your car?'

At Abby's uncertain nod, Stella guided her the couple of steps, opened the rear door of the car and helped lower her into a sitting position on the edge of the back seat.

Stella rummaged in the backpack, finding all of the basics, but if the baby came before the ambulance arrived she would need to be prepared.

'I need to get some more supplies,' she said to Abby. 'I have gas and air in the car. I'll be thirty seconds, okay?'

Abby nodded and Stella rushed to the four-wheel drive and flung open the boot, scooping up an armful of blankets and a cannister of Entonox. She returned to Abby, her training kicking in, using but also mitigating her own flight response.

She could do this, alone if she had to. She could help Abby. She could make a difference here. That was why she had wanted to be a GP.

As she searched the contents of the bag in the light from the torch, part of her wanted to laugh at how she'd once foolishly thought working in Abbotsford would be a dull, uneventful, snooze fest. But that had been her fear talking. Another lie she'd believed to protect herself from being as vulnerable as she had once been when she was eighteen.

'I need to push,' said Abby, gripping the driver's headrest with white-knuckle force.

Stella nodded calmly, managed a smile and saw its immediate effect on Abby's wild eyes.

She removed the packaging from a plastic mouthpiece. 'Is this your first baby?' Stella connected the mouthpiece to the cannister of Entonox.

Abby took the mouthpiece from Stella and began sucking on it as another contraction took hold.

'Second,' said Abby when she could next speak. 'The baby's coming. I can't hold on.'

'Okay. It's going to be fine.' Stella pulled on a pair of latex gloves, wishing that she had Aaron's calming presence but also confident that she had been trained for this.

'You and I are going to do this together, okay?' Stella spread a blanket under Abby's legs and another around her shoulders to ward off the cold the dusk brought. Then she eased Abby's clothing down, covering her lap with a clean towel.

'I need to examine you quickly, just to make sure the baby is head first. We'll wait until the next contraction, and I'll be as gentle as I can.'

Abby nodded, her nostrils flaring as a fresh contraction started. Stella quickly established that Abby was fully dilated and indeed in full-blown second-stage labour.

'I can feel your baby's head, Abby. Everything looks great. Are you having a boy or a girl?' She changed her gloves.

'Boy,' Abby panted.

Then there was the scrunch of gravel and an out-of-breath Aaron arrived. Stella all but sagged with relief.

With an expert eye, he took in the scene and, as Abby's contraction passed and she stopped pushing, joined them in the small space the open car door allowed.

'This is Abby and she's having a baby boy,' Stella said, grateful that they'd have the benefit of Aaron's experience and an extra pair of hands.

'Abby, I'm Dr Bennett. I've just examined your

husband and he's going to be absolutely fine. He has broken his leg, but I gave him some pain medication and he's warm and comfortable and stable. You don't need to worry about him, okay? He said he loves you and he's going to be with you as soon as help arrives to carry him down the hill.'

'The baby isn't far away,' Stella informed Aaron. 'I've checked and he's a cephalic presentation.'

'Good, well done.' Aaron reached for a pair of gloves, his stare locking with Stella's. She saw his own trace of trepidation. Like her, he was probably thinking of all the things that could go wrong with baby Heath's delivery. Was he also recalling the birth of his own son, the wonderful, much anticipated moment that had rapidly turned to every husband's worst nightmare?

She wanted to hold him, to match their physical closeness to the emotional connection she could no longer deny existed. She wanted to press her lips to the fine frown lines in the corners of his eyes until she had magically chased away any residue of his pain. Instead she smiled, hoping he could read reassurance and togetherness in her eyes in the same way she saw it beaming from his.

'We can do this,' he said, his smile stretching

for Stella, and then to Abby said, 'Everything is going to be fine.'

Stella nodded in agreement and returned all her attention to Abby.

Over the next ten minutes the three of them worked as a team, their mutual trust and respect helping ease baby boy Heath into the world. There were tears from both women as Stella placed the tiny newborn in his mother's arms for the first time.

When Stella turned her relieved smile on Aaron she saw that he too was misty-eyed.

Then tears turned to delighted laughter as Aaron and Stella hugged awkwardly over the medical paraphernalia littering the ground. Stella clung to him, breathed in his familiar scent, revelled in the masculine strength of his body, her euphoria latching on to Aaron and their growing bond.

When she pulled away to check on Abby and the baby, out of nowhere chills of doubt attacked her body. Aaron had already experienced all of this with Molly. Aaron had Charlie and wasn't looking for a relationship.

More reconciled than ever that they were right to give their fling a one-night limit, she shakily packed away the equipment, avoiding glancing at Aaron.

In the next few minutes two ambulances arrived, each unloading a stretcher. Stella shoved away her conflicting emotions—fear that she'd begun to feel closer to Aaron than was wise, and relief that she'd held something back—and helped the paramedics to load Abby and the baby into the back of the ambulance. Once connected to an oxygen saturation monitor, the baby was deemed fine and healthy.

Mr Heath was carried down the hill and placed in the second ambulance, but not before more tears all round as he was introduced to his tiny son.

The minute both ambulances headed back towards Cheltenham, Stella's arms sagged to her sides, the adrenaline that had served her well draining away to nothing. It wasn't until she was seated once more in the passenger seat of the practice four-wheel drive that the tremors began.

'That was incredible,' she said, the memory of the tiny, precious newborn's weight in her arms still fresh.

She glanced at his profile, searching for the impossible, for something she feared and craved simultaneously: that his feelings resembled hers.

All she saw were shadows.

'Thank you.' Her voice broke and her eyes burned, her jumbled emotions expanding.

Had Aaron experienced the wonder she saw on the Heaths' faces when he'd first held Charlie? How quickly had that wonder turned to horror for his wife, and how could he ever get over such a monumental loss?

'What for?' Aaron gripped her hand across the centre console and squeezed. 'You and Abby did all of the work. I'm so proud of you.'

His eyes were haunted. Stella knew him well enough to see his flicker of pain, and she couldn't help the urge to offer comfort, to gently probe and ensure the delivery hadn't brought back bittersweet memories of Charlie's birth and the subsequent trauma of Molly's death.

'Can you pull over?' Stella managed to choke out.

He did so without question, perhaps sensing the unforeseen seismic shift happening inside Stella. Her head labelled it an anticlimax, but her heart perceived a sledgehammer blow of realisation.

Her self-preservation refused to label her feelings. But watching the love and connection of the Heath family and feeling the profound connection to Aaron that went way beyond physical attraction, she knew that she wanted that for herself one day. A partner so in sync with her that they could communicate with their eyes and their smiles alone. A baby that she made with the love of her life. All these years she had told herself that she had the life she wanted, but it had all been lies. She'd been hiding, pretending that she was complete so she could armour her heart.

But sharing that experience with Aaron made her aware just how much she was short-changing herself in life, denying herself its most wondrous experiences: deep love, sharing her life with someone, creating a family of their own with that person.

Aaron turned off the engine and the car filled with silence.

She unclipped her seatbelt and turned to face him, almost deaf from the thundering of her heart. 'Are…are *you* okay?'

The sadness in his expression as he registered the unspoken question behind her question tore through her chest.

She asked it anyway, because she wanted to be there for him. 'Did it bring back memories… of Charlie's birth?'

He swallowed, his gaze shifting. 'A little. I'm just so relieved that they were both okay.' He stared out through the windscreen. Darkness had descended, giving the impression that they were wrapped in their own warm, safe cocoon.

But she couldn't trust impressions.

She ached for Aaron's loss, but at the same time crumpled a little for herself. The irony of her perfect man being in love with someone else, someone ethereal and intangible, someone Stella could never rival, roared in her head, a feral scream of the danger of letting down her guard.

As Aaron stayed silent, Stella switched subjects.

'I want to thank you for everything,' she said, a lump of longing in her throat. 'For bringing me along today. For inviting me to your practice in the first place.' She looked at her hands in her lap. 'I never said thank you for taking me on, even when I disparaged your home, your workplace, your life. But I appreciate everything you've done for me. I appreciate all the opportunities you've given me.'

I appreciate you.

Too close to tears, she couldn't bring herself to utter the last sentiment aloud. She might hurl herself into his arms in search of the heady rush and rightness she knew that she would find there.

'You're welcome.' He tilted his head and seemed to see into her soul. 'Thank *you* for suggesting that short cut and for being your wonderful self back there.' He brushed some hair back from her face. His pupils were wide, swallowing the blue she loved. 'Inviting you here was one of my smarter moves.'

'I'm glad that you did.'

'It's rewarding, isn't it? Making a difference.'

He cupped her cheek, soothing some of the turmoil she carried. 'That's what I love about this job.'

She nodded, frozen by her needs. It had been years since she'd felt a true part of this community. Aaron's patience and persistence had shown her that she could be herself, no matter where she was and be valued, be a part of something bigger than herself. That she mattered, despite the memories tangled up with this place.

And now, for the first time in years, she wanted that in her personal life as well as professionally.

They stared at each other for a handful of heartbeats.

His eyes swooped to her mouth. Tension resonated from him; he was holding back, perhaps both words and actions.

Before she could question the impulse, Stella scrambled into his lap, her knees astride his thighs, and threw her arms around his neck. She couldn't deny her feelings, which hadn't lessened despite their one night as lovers.

She craved him more than ever.

Aaron's hand settled warm and comforting in the middle of her back, his stare dark, vulnerable.

Tired of restraint, she pressed her mouth to his in a cathartic surrender. He returned her kiss with a groan of release, as if he too had held back for too long.

They had broken the rules, which, for Stella, somehow sweetened the addictive kisses.

Aaron's hand curled around the back of her neck, holding her mouth in place as she tangled her fingers into his hair, tilted his head back against the headrest. He gripped her waist, fisting her skirt as she rode his lap. His hardness pressed between her legs as he tilted his hips.

Would anything extinguish this fire scorching her alive?

'What are we doing?' he asked as she let him up for air, even as his fingers slid under the hem of her sweater to the naked skin of her back, restlessly flexing, stroking, exploring.

'I don't know.' She feathered kisses over the side of his neck so the warm scent of his body filled her nostrils from inside his collar. She couldn't make her lips leave his skin. 'Perhaps it's just the adrenaline.'

She gripped his face and stared into his eyes. 'I want you.' Over and over until she'd burned him out of her system.

He searched her stare, his eyes transparent, showing her the same needs that paralysed her. 'Me too. Ever since I woke up on Saturday morning to find you gone. I couldn't wait for the start of a new week just to see you.'

His words were beyond worrisome to the part of herself she still needed to protect, but she became distracted by pleasure as his hands skated her sides, cupped her breasts, zapping her nervous system with sparks that felt way too good to be wrong.

'This is bad,' she said as he released her from another soul-searing kiss.

'I know.' He shifted under her, his lips stretching into that sexy smile she'd come to adore. 'Which is probably why it feels so fantastic.'

She writhed in his lap, torturing them both with the friction. 'Like a compulsion. But one night was supposed to be enough.'

Perhaps her addiction, her weakness for him, was amplified because she couldn't walk away yet. Nothing else had changed. Her one relationship had ended in enough desolation to keep her single for nine years, and Aaron was still in love with his wife and devoted only to his son.

He smiled, the playful delight in his eyes lightening the mood. 'So I'm a compulsion now? That's a big step up from a crush.'

Stella rolled her eyes, laughter bubbling up from her chest.

Then he sobered, pressed his forehead to hers and exhaled his frustration. 'I have to go—I need to pick up Charlie.'

As if doused in icy water, Stella pulled away.

She'd become so carried away by her feelings for him, feelings that she'd vowed she could keep in check, that she'd forgotten his personal obligations.

'Of course.' Mortified, she shifted her weight from his thighs, preparing to retake the passenger seat.

'Wait.' He gripped her hips, stared up at her in heartfelt appeal. 'Can we see each other again? Outside of work?' He smiled, cajoling, his eyes vulnerable and hopeful, and Stella wanted to give him anything. Everything.

She swallowed hard, her throat tight with the ache to say *yes*. But, as he'd just reminded her, Aaron and Charlie were a father-and-son team.

No, Aaron wasn't Harry and Stella was no longer trusting and guileless. But normally, by this stage in a relationship—where things moved from casual towards expectant, attached, romantic—she made her excuses and called it a day.

Before she could become emotionally invested.

Perhaps it was already too late.

'Don't you have Charlie to think about?' She needed to remind herself that Aaron was a package deal, that he would always put Charlie first, and that was a good thing. Given that she had just proved that Aaron alone was temptation enough, there was no way she could risk interacting with

Charlie, who, as his father's son, was no doubt equally enchanting. Not if she hoped to keep herself distant enough so she could walk away when the time came.

He nodded, his lips pressed into a flat line. 'Yes.' Regret and realisation that she was right dawned in his eyes.

She reluctantly slid into the passenger seat. 'Let's go back to Abbotsford. It's been a long day.'

He nodded, started the car without comment and drove the four miles in silence. After all, what else was there to say?

CHAPTER ELEVEN

AARON KNEW THE invitation was unwise even as the eager words left his mouth. 'Would you like to join us for dinner?'

He and Charlie had bumped into Stella at the village shop and, try as he might, he couldn't stop himself. She carried a solitary bottle of wine and they hadn't had a moment alone together since he dropped her at home after they had delivered the Heath baby three days ago and kissed in the driver's seat like horny teenagers.

'We're having meatballs and spaghetti.' Charlie beamed, as if the menu might sway her decision. 'It's my favourite. But Dad forgot to buy the pasta sauce, didn't you, Dad?'

'I did.' Aaron met Stella's stare. He was so conflicted that he almost withdrew the invitation. But the deed was done. Charlie had recognised Stella the minute they'd walked into the tiny shop and it was only one home-cooked meal, hardly a grand seduction. It couldn't even really be called a date.

'Um…' She smiled down at Charlie. 'Do you have enough? I don't want to deprive you of your favourite meal.'

'We have lots,' Charlie said dramatically, 'but I'm only allowed three meatballs, because they are this big.' He made a circle with his thumb and forefinger and looked to Aaron for confirmation.

'We normally have leftovers, but it's no big deal,' Aaron eyed her bottle of wine, 'if you have plans.' None of his business.

Stella flushed. 'My parents are out tonight. I was going to have a glass of this and maybe make some cheese on toast.' She shrugged. 'Actually, I'd love to join you for spaghetti, now that you have the sauce.'

They shared another look that made Aaron think they were both wary of the dynamics and of sharing too much. Was Stella, like him, also running out of resolve against the temptation?

Aaron's cottage was a three-minute walk, door-to-door from the shop. Aaron quickly completed the partially prepared meal with the addition of pasta sauce, Charlie set another place at the table for Stella and she poured two glasses of wine.

'See,' said Charlie, pointing with his fork, 'I have three meatballs, and you have three meatballs.' He offered Stella his happy smile as he showed off his maths skills. 'That makes six. It's a double.'

Stella gave Charlie a high five and an impressed nod. 'You're a very smart young man.'

Aaron's heart swelled with pride as he watched Stella interact with Charlie, even as the instant and easy connection between them caused a lump to press against his lungs and restrict his breath. Just like all the other wonderful things he had learned about her, he immediately knew she would make an amazing mother if she ever chose to have children.

He had an urgent and visceral urge to lean across the table and kiss her. In fact, he hadn't stopped wanting to kiss her since that very first time their lips met.

He was so doomed…

She had been right. Delivering the Heath baby with Stella had brought up a sickening collision of his past and present. The wonder of holding his son. The love he'd felt watching Molly kiss his downy head. Then the shock and desolation of his wife, Charlie's mother, being snatched away from them both.

When Abby's baby had been safely delivered he'd clung to Stella in that moment of shared joy, wondering how he had become so desperate for her in such a short space of time.

Watching her now with his son, the answer was obvious. How could he not be utterly captivated?

'What's your favourite part of school?' she asked Charlie.

Aaron stifled a laugh, knowing exactly what his son's response would be. He often asked him that very question and usually received the same answer: lunchtime, with home time in second place.

'I like lunchtime,' said Charlie, predictably. 'Today we had veggie pizza.' He stabbed at a meatball with his fork and waggled it around like a cheerleader's pompom, his 'z's lisped adorably since he had lost his first baby tooth last week.

'Yummy—I like pizza too,' said Stella, catching Aaron's eye once more.

Acknowledgement and communication passed silently between them, as if they had been together for years and knew how the other thought.

In his fantasy, he imagined it went something like:

Stella: *Your son is adorable.*

Aaron: *You're so good with him.*

Both in unison: *It makes me want you all the more.*

But the tightening in his gut reminded him to slow down his wild imaginings. Something out of his control was happening. That he craved her company, her smiles, her sharp wit was understandable. The physical compulsions made sense. But this new longing—that the affinity they had for each other extended to Charlie in Stella's case—mystified him.

He was on dangerous ground, craving the cerebral connection as much as the physical, because Stella might have been specifically designed to his specifications.

Only she couldn't be his, just as he wasn't the man for her, neither of them wanting the emotional attachment that sometimes felt as if it was developing without their permission.

Aaron filled his mouth with food, giving himself more time to think. Except he was too out of practice to untangle his emotions, having spent years merely accepting the guilt he lived with and embracing his position.

'Pizza is my favourite,' continued Charlie, oblivious to the adult tension stealing Aaron's appetite and the fact that only half an hour ago he'd declared the same was true for meatballs and spaghetti. 'But Dad always makes the edges too brown and crispy.' His son offered a withering look that spoke of his long suffering under his father's culinary challenges. 'Johnny's mum makes nice, soft edges, like the pizza at school.'

Stella looked away from a sombre Charlie and

pressed her lips together, Aaron assumed to hold in a smile.

'Does he?' She flicked a knowing look at Aaron. 'That's not good. But I have an idea. You could help him by setting a timer on his phone that will tell him when the pizza is ready to come out of the oven. I'll show you how to do it after we eat our meatballs if you like.'

Charlie's eyes went wide, impressed, no doubt delighted that he'd have access to Aaron's phone. Like most parents Aaron constantly struggled to police screen time, but this was a practical, even educational skill, so he could hardly object.

His son's face lit up, his dreamy gaze falling on Stella in a way that meant Aaron would likely be peppered with Stella-related questions for the rest of the week.

Aaron mouthed *Thank you* to Stella and gripped his silverware tighter, fresh guilt tightening his shoulders. For everyone's sake, he couldn't let them become too close. Because Charlie had naturally warmed to Stella, as if his life lacked the influence of a sage and wise woman, even if it was simply to ward off burnt pizza in the future.

The sigh Aaron held inside settled like a stitch under his ribs. Why could he see Stella fitting into their lives like the missing piece of a jigsaw? Was his guilt over Molly, the main thing that had held him back from seriously dating all these years, getting in the way of Charlie's development? Did he need a female figure in his life? Had he prevented Charlie from building a wider circle of relationships with his overprotective fears?

Restricting his own life because he didn't deserve another chance at happiness was one thing, but limiting Charlie's life in any way was the opposite of Aaron's intention.

After dinner, while Aaron loaded the dishwasher in contemplative silence, Stella kept her promise and taught Charlie how to set the timer on his dad's phone.

'Now you can show me how good you are with your numbers,' she said, her fond smile for his son shredding Aaron.

Stella's natural affinity with children and Charlie's awe and trust forced him to admit something he hadn't wanted to explore since the night they'd spent together.

He wanted more than one night.

He probably always had, instinct and the restlessness grumbling away inside telling him this with Stella had never been casual, at least not for him.

But had her desires changed? Perhaps her declaration that she still wanted him in the car had come with the high of successfully delivering the Heath baby. And could he risk exploring this further when Charlie's happiness was at stake?

His feelings might end up putting him in an impossible position: wanting a woman who could disappear at any time and risking that Charlie's feelings might be caught in the crossfire. His son had lost enough.

Charlie let out an excited squeal, alerting Aaron to a change in topic.

'Dad, Dr Stella can ride a horse.' He jumped up on the wooden rocking horse in the corner to show off his skills to their guest. 'Have you got a real horse?' Charlie asked, eyes like saucers. 'I want a pony but Dad will only buy me this one, because it's *dangerless*.' His little shoulders sagged at his dire deprivation.

Stella shot Aaron an apologetic grimace. 'No, I don't have my own horse. They are very expensive and take a lot of looking after,' she said to Charlie. 'I'm just helping other children learn to ride.'

With the dishes done, Aaron needed to usher Charlie upstairs for a bath. Otherwise they could be here all night locked in a plead-denial cycle that they had travelled many times.

'Can you stay a while longer?' he asked Stella after Charlie had reluctantly mumbled goodnight and run upstairs making clip-clop noises. 'I won't be long getting him settled.' She seemed comfortable enough to be here, despite Charlie's energy and constant chatter. And he wanted some alone time with her, to figure out their next move, because his head was scrambled.

'Sure.' She nodded, her smile indulgent despite the lingering reticence in her eyes.

He poured her another glass of wine and took the stairs two at a time. Thirty minutes later, with Charlie bathed, put to bed and a bedtime story read, Aaron came back downstairs to find Stella sitting before the fire. She'd put on an old vinyl from the selection he'd collected over the years, and a pile of Charlie's folded clean laundry sat in the basket on the floor at her feet.

'You didn't need to do that, but thanks.' He grabbed his own wine left over from dinner and took the seat next to her on the sofa.

'Is he asleep?' she asked, tucking her knee underneath her so she faced him.

His head might be all over the place but his body had no hesitations. He took her free hand in his. 'He will be soon. He's exhausted. He didn't even ask for a second story.'

'He's adorable,' she whispered, her face catching the glow from the fire.

Aaron flexed his fingers against hers. 'Did I do the wrong thing by inviting you over?'

She smiled, shook her head, no hint of wariness in her eyes. 'Did I do the wrong thing with the timer on the phone?'

'No. You've made a fan for life.'

'You're obviously very close,' she said.

Was she thinking about her closeness to Angus? Aaron tugged her hand, pressed his lips to her temple and inhaled the scent of her hair.

'We are.' He cleared a sudden blockage in his throat. 'We've had to be.'

Stella's eyes brimmed with compassion and understanding. For the first time ever Aaron contemplated a different reality for his future. Could he try to have a relationship with someone wonderful like Stella? Someone who respected his and Charlie's relationship but also fitted in as if she had always been a vital component?

'I didn't realise that he worries about me quite so much, you know, with the pizza thing and my concerns about the riding,' Aaron said, scrubbing at his jaw as doubts rattled the convictions that had helped him to survive these past five years. How messed up was it that his young son saw through him and his attempts to provide stability. Safety. Aaron was the grown-up; worrying was supposed to be his job.

Perhaps he needed to back off. He didn't want Charlie to grow up neurotic.

'Children can be very perceptive and intuitive.' Stella stroked his arm. 'Don't beat yourself up. If your worst crime as a parent is a bit of burnt pizza, he'll be absolutely fine.'

Aaron took her hand, grateful that she understood his turmoil. 'Clearly Johnny's family set the gold standard when it comes to all things from procreation to perfect pizza.'

Stella chuckled, her fingers making a lazy path on his skin. Was she aware of how her touch inflamed him, held him captive, redefined how he saw himself? Not just as a father, but also as a man.

'You're a great dad,' she said. 'He's just trying to make sense of his world.' That she saw him so clearly was evident in her next statement. 'It doesn't mean he's lacking anything or missing out.'

Aaron looked away, that persistent trickle of shame heating his blood. Of course Charlie lacked a vital part of his life: his mother. And if anyone was at fault, it was Aaron.

'I blame myself,' he said after a pause where Stella gave him the time he needed.

'For the burnt pizza?' she asked, her small, perceptive smile telling him she was kindly offering him an out clause from exposing his deepest doubt if he needed it. Wonderful, caring woman.

'That too.' He laughed, grateful for her attempt at levity, but trusting her enough to want to voice the fear he suspected would haunt him for ever. 'But mainly for Molly.'

Her stare latched to his, unflinching. Holding. Communicating.

I'm listening.

'We hadn't planned to get pregnant with Charlie when we did,' he said. 'One night we ran out of condoms. Molly thought the ovulation maths meant we'd be okay, but I'm a doctor. I should have known better than to risk such an unreliable form of contraception.'

'You wouldn't be the first married couple to dice with the dates.'

He shrugged, futility a hollow space in his chest. 'I guess not, but usually the story has a happy outcome, as ours did for a handful of precious minutes. But a part of me can't help but wonder if things would have been different if I'd been more careful. Protected Molly better.'

'What happened to Molly wasn't your fault.' Her tone was firm. 'You know that she suffered a rare but life-threatening complication of pregnancy that could have happened at any time. It's unfair and tragic and heart-breaking.' She cupped his face, holding his gaze. 'But *not* your fault.'

At his silence she continued, 'Is that why you haven't dated anyone? Because you feel…responsible in some way, because of the timing?'

He shrugged, nodded, sighed, all his ugliness spilling out. 'Every time I look at him I wonder if I'm enough, if I'm doing a good enough job. If I can possibly be everything he needs.'

'You are,' she said without hesitation.

'I'm not so sure. I watched the way he interacted with you tonight. It was lovely to see his confidence.' He frowned. 'I thought I was protecting him—he's lost so much—but perhaps I've denied him a woman's influence in his life.'

'You're doing your best out of love, that's all any of us can do. Life isn't a one-size-fits-all, nor are there any guarantees.'

'That's true.' Stella was so easy to talk to, no doubt that was what made her a great doctor. 'Then sometimes I worry that I'm doing too much, being overprotective, like with the horse riding.'

She shook her head. 'My parents used to worry too. He's the most precious thing in the world to you. It's natural.'

He stared, awed by her calm insights and natural humanity. He couldn't become reliant on her compassion and understanding. He couldn't become reliant on her full stop. He needed to keep emotionally distant for his own sake, too.

Just because he'd glimpsed how well she would fit into their lives if she lived in Abbotsford didn't mean that he and Charlie were what she wanted. She planned to leave as soon as she could, head back to her single life in London. His life, Charlie's life was here, a place from which Stella still felt she needed to run in order to out-run herself, her past, her demons.

And he would wish her every happiness and success.

He and Charlie would be fine, but only if he stayed detached. He owed it to Charlie not to mess up again. That meant maintaining their sta-tus quo, their boys' club of two, even if he had to forgo his own needs, which right now urged him to hold her tight…indefinitely.

'I'm teaching tomorrow, at the stables,' she said. 'Why don't you bring him along after my last class for a quick ride? I promise I'll take care of him—I'll have my hands on him at all times. We have riding hats and body protectors. I'll choose our most sedate and docile pony. It will be as safe as possible.'

Her concern and reassurance overwhelmed him. He wanted to kiss her so badly he needed an instant distraction.

The song had changed to a nice, slow ballad.

'Dance with me,' he said, standing.

She frowned at his extended hand. Laughed nervously. 'Really? Here?'

He nodded, recalling a pair of high heels and little black dress fit for a chic, city nightclub.

Soon she would swap her riding boots for dancing shoes and their lives would return to being different.

'You once invited me to go dancing.'

'And you said your clubbing days were over.' She placed her hand in his, eyes alive as she met his challenge.

He pulled her to her feet and into his arms. 'Yes, but there's more than one way to take a pulse.' He caressed her inner wrist over her radial artery and then touched his fingers to her neck where her carotid beat like a drum. 'This is my kind of dance.'

Falling serious because his senses were filled with her scent and warmth, he pressed her close, one hand gripping hers and the other pressed between her shoulder blades. He caught the soft sigh leaving her lips as she looked up at him from under those long lashes.

Fighting the urge to kiss her, Aaron moved them around the space between the fire and the sofa they'd occupied. This was the way he'd held her in the early hours of Saturday morning when he had willed away the first light of dawn, knowing it would bring their intimate time to an end.

She snuggled closer, dropped her head to his shoulder, reminding him how good they'd been together, how their passion had burned out of control until their reservations and differences hadn't seemed to matter.

She'd admitted that she still wanted him. And now that he was touching her again, her heart banging against his ribs and her eyes filled with what looked like longing, Aaron struggled to find the strength to care that he was risking what he valued most: the predictable stability he'd built these past five years.

If only it was just his feelings at risk, he could live with the liability. How could he have what he wanted, more time with Stella, and protect both her and Charlie from growing too attached? His son would be ecstatic at Stella's offer to show him how to ride, but could Aaron allow it, knowing the emotional risks?

Perhaps if it was a one-off…

'I can hear your mind whirring,' she mumbled into his jumper, her hand stroking his chest.

He released the sigh, tugging at the mental knots in his head. 'I want impossible things.'

'What things?' Her finger traced his jaw.

'You.'

She smiled up at him. 'I'm right here, aren't I?'

He nodded, holding her tighter because her presence back in his arms was everything he had craved since their night together. 'I'm trying to protect everyone's feelings…yours, Charlie's.'

She nodded, her gaze softening, growing more

enticing. 'I'm a grown woman. I can protect my-self.'

Without waiting for him to process her state-ment, she reached up on tiptoe, brought her mouth within kissing distance. His lips landed, soft but urgent. She moaned, angled her head, parted her lips to deepen their kiss. He gripped her waist, slid his hands up her back and tangled his fingers in her hair, losing another chunk of his restraint.

She sighed, her whole body collapsing against his chest as if she was exhausted, like him, from fighting this connection that had gone way deeper than either of them expected.

He held her face between his palms and parted from her with a reluctant groan. 'Can you stay the night? Charlie normally sleeps in until seven.' He poured his desires and the unspoken feelings he hadn't yet deciphered into his stare.

How had he gone from content with their one night to being this heavily invested? How would he return to the way he'd been happy with his sexless existence before Stella invaded his world and showed him what was lacking?

Except it wasn't just sex. If he could never sleep with her again he'd still want to see her, to work with her and be on her quiz team. She en-riched his existence, and a part of him knew that, if life were different, she would enrich Charlie's too, teach him things that Aaron couldn't.

Her expression shifted through desire to unease. She shook her head. 'I don't want to risk confusing Charlie, but I can stay a while.' She wrapped her arms around his neck, her eyes glazed with passion.

It was a compromise with which he could live.

This time they made it to the privacy of his bedroom, which was at the other end of the landing from Charlie's room, before their passion became overwhelming and undeniable. They stripped in silence, their stares locked, as if both wary, both conscious of what was at stake but unable to fight temptation any longer.

In case this was the last time they would surrender, he commanded every kiss, his passion roaring out of control. He trailed his mouth over her neck, her collarbones, her breasts, every inch of her fragrant skin, learning all of the places that made her fist the sheets and bite her lip to hold in her moans.

Needing more of her, he abandoned her sensitive nipples, pushed her legs wide and covered her with his mouth. Her gasp broke free, her fingers tugging at his hair.

'Aaron.' She whispered his name, a raft of emotions flitting across her expression.

Aaron read every single one. He knew this

woman. He wanted to bring her pleasure, soothe her every hurt, make her promises and never let her down the way she had been in the past.

Dangerous wants.

She shattered, riding out her orgasm with her stare lost in his.

He held her in his arms, kissed her, caressed her until she grew restless and needy once more, wrapping her legs around his hips and clinging to his arms, his shoulders, his back. With protection taken care of, she welcomed him inside her body, her passionate cries smothered by their kisses.

Something cataclysmic was happening. Something he couldn't examine too closely in case it changed his life irrevocably.

Unspoken words clogged Aaron's throat. This couldn't be more than sex, no matter how it felt.

He knew that her internal struggles over their fling matched his. She'd been bitterly betrayed, robbed of her relationship with a little boy she had loved, had spent the intervening nine years protecting herself with only casual dating.

He wasn't ready to forgive himself, to lay all of himself on the line in the search for wholeness, happiness. He had nothing to offer beyond his body and this violent connection they both battled. But a part of him wanted Stella to struggle to forget everything they had shared. As he would.

'Stella.' He gripped her tighter as his body reacted on instinct, driving them hard towards the point of no return. She entwined her fingers with his, matched his every move, alongside him on this journey.

They came together, so in sync it was no use kidding himself that he'd successfully managed to keep emotions at bay.

Exhausted and elated, he dragged her close, burrowed his nose in her hair and fought the temptation to ask her to stay in Abbotsford.

When he woke an hour later the bed beside him was cold. He rummaged for his phone, his heart sinking. He found her text, the screen illuminating the dark room.

I didn't want to wake you. Had a wonderful evening.

He should be relieved that, as promised, she had been considerate of Charlie and so pragmatic that she'd slipped out into the night without disturbing him. There were no loose ends he'd need to explain to a curious five-year-old.

Instead, he was more hollow than he had been in years, as if he'd been robbed of something he hadn't realised he cherished until it was gone.

He threw his phone on the bed, the mess of convoluted feelings inside telling him it was way too late for him to emerge from this unscathed.

CHAPTER TWELVE

STELLA HAD JUST stabled all but one of the Ability Riding ponies when she heard the crunch of gravel that announced a vehicle. Her adrenaline spiked, her stomach fluttering. It was them, Aaron and Charlie.

She tucked some stray hair behind her ear and brushed the hay from her mud-splattered jodhpurs, preening for Aaron, even as she lectured herself to stay impervious. But how could she fight her deepening feelings after last night?

Their passion had moved past sex into uncharted territory for Stella as she'd clung to Aaron and sobbed out her pleasure against his sweat-slicked skin. It had been almost impossible to leave his warm bed and creep out into the night.

Almost. Because of course she'd had to leave.

She had known spending any more time with Charlie and Aaron together was a colossal risk. But she'd done it anyway, because she couldn't fight her need for Aaron any longer. Maybe inviting Charlie to ride had been one stupidity too many.

Sick to her stomach at the fear of falling for Charlie's innocent enthusiasm, wide blue eyes and wicked sense of humour, and also breathless with excitement to see his dad, she rounded the corner of the stables, seeking them out like a kid on Christmas morning.

With every step closer to the car park, she recalled Aaron's heartbreaking vulnerability when he had confessed how he blamed himself for Molly's death. It wasn't that he refused to move on, he was just stuck in limbo by his sense of guilt.

Stella had wanted to hold him and never let him go until she somehow made him believe that he didn't deserve the brutality of his own condemnation.

He was human, that was all. Everyone made mistakes.

But the very reason he had avoided dating all these years, the reason he still only wanted a casual fling—because he couldn't forgive himself—placed him out of her reach. He wasn't ready for a relationship and Stella's own state of mind—she could feel herself slipping deeper and deeper under his spell—was far too prudent to tackle that giant obstacle.

She paused, watched Aaron and Charlie cross the yard, hand in hand, while her stomach churned. It shouldn't matter to her that Aaron believed himself undeserving of a second chance at love, but her careless, weak heart lurched into her throat at the beautiful sight the two of them made. The physiological reaction, tell-tale signs of over-investment—dry mouth, sweaty palms, unable to catch a breath—could mean only one thing: she was perilously close to falling, for all of her caution and good sense.

No, no, no.

What was she doing? She might have been able to recover from dinner with Aaron and Charlie. But sharing his bed, disintegrating in his arms, her every need seemingly answered by the emotions on display in his eyes... It had been too much.

And now her head was full of...terrifying possibilities.

What if she stayed here, in Abbotsford? Could she explore this relationship with Aaron, take time to get to know Charlie, see how it evolved? That sounded like a dream, except she knew from experience that dreams could turn into nightmares. When just the sight of Aaron sent her into a spin, could she stay and risk falling in love with him, with them both?

What if it didn't work out?

They spied her and grinned, waved.

The thought of being that vulnerable, rejected person again made her want to run away. She slapped a smile on her face for the delicious duo. She couldn't let either of them down. Charlie because she had promised him this adventure, and Aaron because she had vowed to take care of his little boy.

'Stella!' Charlie tugged free of his father's handhold and ran the last few paces to her side. 'Can I see the ponies?' He jumped up and down on the spot, his wiry body struggling to contain his rapture.

Stella crouched down to Charlie's level. 'Of course. That's why you're here.'

Time to pull herself together and ignore the feelings she'd stupidly allowed to develop despite all of her warnings. But how could she stay immune to these two men? They'd wormed their way into her heart with their matching blue eyes and identical dimpled smiles and their beautifully close bond. A bond she wanted to protect as much as she needed to armour her own heart.

'But,' she said to Charlie, clearing the clog of emotion from her throat, 'the most important thing about horses, as you will know, because you're a smart lad, is that we mustn't scare them.'

Charlie nodded, his wide eyes at once solemn and attentive.

Stella stood, her gaze meeting Aaron's, and her heart clenched. This was a big step for him, trusting her with his precious son, who was his entire world.

'Hi,' she said, hot and flustered, because the look on his face said, *I'm thinking about what we did last night.*

That was when she felt Charlie's small hand slide into hers. She gripped his fingers, a giant lump in her chest at his trust, his affection almost her undoing.

'How are you?' Aaron asked, his voice low like a secret, distracting her from the tsunami of feelings that almost knocked her from her feet. 'Are you sure you're not too tired for this?'

His implication adding *after our late night.*

Stella yearned to greet him with a kiss, if only to feel lust instead of all the other emotions she couldn't switch off, but she suspected they would still be there, and probably amplified. 'I'm fine.' *On fire, but fine.*

Then she said to Charlie, 'Let's get you a safety hat and body protector. And then we'll meet Zeus.'

Aaron's eyebrows shot up. 'Zeus?'

Stella nodded, her body aching to touch him, to hold him and reassure him that she'd never let anything happen to Charlie.

'Zeus is our most heroic and kind pony,' she

said, as much to Aaron as to Charlie. 'He's special; placid and unshakable. Only very special kids get to ride Zeus.'

She touched Aaron's arm, she couldn't help herself, and shot him an encouraging smile. 'You can sit in the viewing gallery if you want. That's where the parents usually wait and watch.'

Aaron hesitated for a split second, and Stella knew he wanted to be close by in case something happened. 'Have fun.' He ruffled Charlie's hair and backed away, headed for the seating area overlooking the arena. 'I'm going to take lots of pictures so you can show Johnny on Monday.'

Charlie looked up at Stella, awaiting instructions.

Her eyes burned at the trust shown by both of them. At Charlie's innocent excitement and chatter, and Aaron's unspoken belief in her. Tender shoots of hope germinated in her chest. Could she one day be a part of their precious little team? Could she fully commit to a relationship with Aaron, stay here in Abbotsford and give them her all in a way she hadn't done for nine years?

But what if she was once again cast aside, excluded? She'd be back where she was at eighteen: running from her heartache, forced to reinvent herself in order to handle the pain, grieving and alone.

She found Charlie a riding helmet and body protector, ensuring both items fitted correctly.

'Okay,' she said to Charlie, staring into blue eyes so like Aaron's she wanted to hold him too. 'Let's go meet Zeus.'

On Charlie's third lap of the floodlit indoor arena, Aaron's heart settled back into a steady sinus rhythm, each beat forcing him to admit what persisted at the forefront of his mind: his feelings for Stella.

Being with her last night, seeing her with his son, so patient and encouraging, made him admit what was missing from Charlie's life, but more importantly from his own. Yes, he could continue to be everything to his little boy and they would muddle through together, whatever hurdles they faced in life. But he wanted more than that, and perhaps Charlie needed more too.

He wouldn't interfere with her career path, but what if Stella stayed in Abbotsford? They could date, take things as slowly as she needed.

His fingers tightened around the phone in his hand, his heart sore with the sheer volume of emotions coursing through his veins. He'd taken a hundred shots of Charlie riding Zeus, Charlie brushing Zeus, Charlie holding Stella's hand and looking up at both her and Zeus in adoration. But the email waiting in his inbox created a massive distraction to his enjoyment of watching Charlie's dream fulfilled.

Stella's transfer back to a London GP practice had come through an hour ago.

Aaron's first instinct had been to ignore it for a few days, to hide it from Stella and keep her to himself a little bit longer. Because the minute he told her, he would lose her.

But was she his to keep? How did she even feel about him? Would she ever want a proper relationship with dates and sleepovers, shared life occasions and commitment? He understood why she'd wanted to avoid that for nine years, but maybe for her, nothing had changed.

Whereas for him, he no longer recognised himself. He'd try to be okay with casual, but she had destroyed his willpower, bit by bit. Even now, expertly leading the pony by a short rein while walking alongside Charlie, her other hand reassuringly on the back of the saddle, she was still making it impossible for him to resist.

'Dad, I'm doing it, look.' Charlie beamed up at him as he passed the seating for observers on his fourth lap.

'You are awesome,' Aaron said, his gaze tracking to Stella.

Their eyes met. Aaron wanted to leap over the barrier into the arena and kiss her, hold her in his arms and beg her to stay and give them a chance at something real. A new start. A shot at taking their duo and making it a trio.

Try as he might, he couldn't see long-distance working, not with their respective work commitments and Charlie's busy schedule. But there was a growing part of Aaron willing to take the risk, if only Stella felt the same.

As she helped Charlie to dismount correctly, Aaron received a text from Molly's sister, Leah, who had arrived to collect Charlie for his swimming lesson with his cousin, a weekly commitment he and Leah took in turns. Aaron replied and made his way to the stables, his stomach in knots of anticipation.

What if Stella wanted nothing more to do with him and Charlie now that her transfer had been approved? What if she left Abbotsford, left them without a backward glance? On the flip side, could he ask her to give up her city life for a relationship with a single dad tied to a village, who had himself avoided commitment for the past five years?

Charlie was filling the pony's hay net when he arrived.

'Dad,' he said, 'can I take Zeus home? I can brush him and feed him, look.' He held up a handful of hay to prove his utter dedication.

'Zeus does a very important job here,' said Stella, rescuing Aaron from a tricky conversation. 'But, if it's okay with Dad, you can come back and ride him again. Is that a good deal?'

Charlie nodded up at Stella, instantly appeased and worryingly as enchanted with her as Aaron himself. Then he hugged her legs. 'Thanks, Dr Stella.'

She placed her hand on his back, her eyes meeting Aaron's. 'You can call me Stella.'

Bile burned his throat. She had so much power to hurt him, to hurt Charlie, even though the way she swallowed hard, clearly experiencing some strong emotion, gave Aaron hope.

'Aunt Leah is here, Champ.' Aaron hated to break up the moment, but he needed to talk to Stella alone. He should have told her about the transfer straight away. He should have sussed out her intentions for returning to London before he watched her and Charlie bond over a love of horses. Because what if their boys' club of two wasn't enough for her? She would leave and maybe take more than just a piece of Aaron with her.

They walked Charlie back to the car park together. Stella was quiet, but Charlie's horse-related chatter filled the awkward silence.

Aaron only realised he was holding her hand when they approached the car and he saw the shocked expression on Leah's face. Of course, after five years alone, his in-laws, even his own parents would be stunned that he'd met someone with whom he could see a future. He should have anticipated that and spoken to Leah and Molly's parents before inviting his sister-in-law to meet Stella. He'd been just so caught up in his concern for Charlie, so wrapped up in Stella and his awakened feelings, that he'd forgotten there were people in his life who might be momentarily taken aback by the fact that he was ready to move on.

But only before they got to know Stella, witnessed the connection the three of them shared and realised that Charlie was safe in her care.

He turned to Stella as Charlie ran ahead and threw himself at his aunt, who had exited the car to open the rear door, where Charlie's booster seat sat next to his four-year-old cousin's.

'Can you give me a second?' He squeezed her hand. He should speak to Leah before she read too much into the simple gesture. Although a part of him acknowledged that, on his side, Leah's assumptions would be correct. He cared about Stella, deeply.

She cast a quick glance at Leah over his shoulder, a frown appearing and then disappearing just as quickly. 'Of course.' She blushed, pulled her hand free of his and stepped back, putting distance between them.

He reached for her again, his hand on her arm,

because he didn't want her to leave his side. If he didn't have that email on his phone, burning a guilty hole in his pocket, he'd introduce the two women right now, be open and upfront about his feelings.

'Can I give you a ride back to the village? We need to talk.' At her hesitation, he added, 'Please, it's important.'

His emotions rioted in his chest at the doubt he saw in her eyes, the withdrawal that made his stomach churn. Perhaps she wasn't ready to hear that he'd developed feelings for her.

'Sure,' she said, sounding anything but certain. 'I'll…um…just go grab my bag.'

Heartsick, he watched her walk away. Could he ask her to stay in Abbotsford, stay at the practice, stay a part of his life when it meant asking how she felt about him, and—because they were a package deal—about Charlie?

Aaron approached Leah, catching the way her stare naturally followed Stella's path over his shoulder. Aaron turned in time to see Stella, who must have been watching their interaction, dip her head and duck around the corner to the stables.

He quickly asked his sister-in-law if she could wait at his place after taking Charlie to his swimming lesson. He was making a mess of this, but Stella took priority. He would enlighten Leah and the rest of his family about his feelings later, explain that he'd found someone important to him and he'd be exploring a relationship going forward.

If she would have him.

But he was getting dangerously ahead of himself. With Charlie's wellbeing also at stake, he should employ some caution until he knew if Stella shared his feelings. And, as Leah's surprise illustrated, Aaron came with plenty of baggage. He would probably need to reassure Stella that he was ready for a new woman in his life, that she wouldn't be competing with a ghost, that she would be welcome in his extended family too.

He followed in her footsteps, nerves eating away at his certainty. Were his feelings—the happiness he'd finally found, the happiness he had tentatively come to believe he deserved—reciprocated, or had he been kidding himself all this time?

CHAPTER THIRTEEN

STELLA SHOVED HER frigid hands into her coat
pockets as she crossed the car park at a brisk
pace, just ahead of Aaron. Scalding humiliation
eroded a cavity in her chest as the old insecurities of being talked about resurfaced. From the
look on Molly's sister's face as she'd walked hand
in hand with Aaron, a look of wariness and speculation, Stella would soon be the hot topic of conversation around the village again.

Her heart, which had been bursting with pride
for what she now thought of as *her two boys*, had
stopped dead for a few terrifying seconds as she
came to a chilling realisation.

She wasn't simply filled with pride. She was
way too heavily invested in Charlie and Aaron.
So invested that she'd actually made a promise to Charlie—to be there any time he wanted
to ride Zeus—that she'd never have made three
weeks ago.

Had she changed so completely? Committed

herself to staying in Abbotsford? Committed herself to building a relationship with both father and son? But far worse, she had started to imagine dating Aaron, perhaps becoming a part of his life, long-term. His and Charlie's.

That thought, rather than fill her with the warm and fuzzies, sent shivers through her rigid limbs. What a fool.

She climbed into the passenger seat of Aaron's car and stared out across open farmland towards the village as he rounded the vehicle and took the driver's seat. She couldn't work with him, sleep with him, spend time with him and Charlie and not want more. What if it didn't work out? The pain she experienced last time had had long-reaching consequences.

But the way her chest hurt as Aaron and Leah had talked, clearly about her, each looking over at the same moment, told her it was too late for caution. He'd excluded her, perhaps unintentionally, but it had had the same humiliating effect.

She had once again allowed herself too close to a man who didn't share her feelings.

'So...you wanted to talk,' she asked Aaron, keeping her eyes on the road ahead in case he could see the moisture stinging her eyes.

If she looked at him she'd want to beg to be a part of his little tribe. But she wasn't a member. She was superfluous.

She'd sensed the first signs of his withdrawal the minute he'd arrived at the stables today. She'd convinced herself that he was nervous about Charlie's safety. Then Molly's sister had turned up and he'd become even more of a stranger, the explanation falling into place. She was still an outsider and she'd been stupid to allow great sex with a great guy to lure her into feeling something, feeling as if she belonged with them.

From beside her, he reached for her hand. 'Are you okay?'

She nodded too vigorously, avoiding his searching stare and sliding her hand from his to press at her temple. 'I just have a slight headache.' It wasn't a complete lie.

Aaron pressed his lips together and returned both hands to the wheel while Stella recoiled further into herself. This must be worse than she'd thought. He was going to tell her they were done. That it was too confusing for Charlie or too soon for him, or that the family didn't approve.

'Okay, I'll just get straight to the point, then,' he said. 'I received an email today, from the college of GPs.'

Hope wrapped cotton wool around her heart. Maybe he wasn't calling this off. Then it was dashed. Since when had she become so needy? So dependent on him for her happiness?

'Your transfer has been approved,' he continued, his face in profile so that she had no idea how he felt about the news that took her aback. She had almost completely forgotten about the transfer. Become so wrapped up in life here, in the practice, in Aaron.

'There's a place for you at King's Park Medical Centre,' he said, his tone infuriatingly neutral. 'You can start as soon as you want.'

A chill took hold. She wanted to wrap herself in a hug.

It was time to leave, exactly what she had wanted—to return to the safety of her London life, to the risk-free version of herself, to the security of being alone. Glamorous bars, meaningless dates and a continuous source of entertainment.

She should feel elated. She could resume the life she'd planned. She could run away from the gossip that would ensue if the village found out that Stella had set her cap at Abbotsford's beloved single-dad GP. She could run away from her feelings.

So why did she no longer have the slightest clue what she wanted?

'It is still what you want, right?' he asked, glancing at her clasped hands as if he wanted to touch her again.

'Of course.' *No. Yes. I don't know any more.*

Tears throbbed at the backs of Stella's eyes. If

he touched her while she was this confused she might break down. But he didn't move.

She wouldn't cry. She. Would. Not. Cry.

He nodded, his jaw muscles bunched.

Stella looked away to stop herself from over-interpreting his expression as crestfallen. Perhaps he was simply calculating how her absence would affect the practice, reshuffling the clinics to account for the extra patients.

'I can work a week's notice, if you want.' As long as she didn't touch him again or see him outside of work, she could hold it together for one more week. Five working days. Forty long, temptation-filled hours. Couldn't she?

'I don't want to leave you and Toby in the lurch,' she added.

He frowned, as if about to decline her offer. Then he nodded. 'Only if you can, otherwise we'll manage.'

He drove in silence for a few minutes. Then he pulled up outside her parents' house, killed the engine and turned to face her so she was forced to look into his beautiful eyes.

'I'll be honest, Stella. I hoped that you'd want to stay.' The blue of his irises looked cold in the dim light of the car. She couldn't read his feelings beyond disappointment.

'I hoped you'd want to continue this.' He

pointed between them, a frown pinching his eyebrows together.

'Oh?' He meant their physical relationship, their fling, sneaking around, spending a few hours together whenever the urge overcame them and Charlie was asleep.

A lump lodged in her throat, because they had acted together to protect themselves and Charlie by keeping it casual. She should have known better. A big part of her wanted to see more of Aaron, only she'd broken her own rules and fallen in way over her head. Because now she wanted all or nothing. She couldn't be with him and not want to be a bigger part of his life, to share things with him like lazy Sunday morning walks and quiz nights at the pub. Charlie's Nativity play and Christmas morning.

She had found herself again, here with Aaron, or she had realised that she'd never lost herself in the first place, that she could belong anywhere, that it was her decision.

'Aaron... I...'

'I know,' he said, his voice flat. 'I'm a lot to take on.' Frustration gusted from him on a sigh. 'That's why we could take it slow. See what happens.'

She nodded, her heart made of ice. 'That's a lot to think about.'

She didn't want slow. She'd wasted nine years being afraid, holding back, denying herself.

But clearly Aaron needed more time to get over Molly, his grief, his regrets. He wasn't ready to find love again while he believed himself to be undeserving. Could she really stay, put everything on the line once more for a man who might decide that she wasn't what he wanted after all?

If she stayed, she'd want terrifying things, like a relationship. She hadn't had that since Harry and, given her reaction to Aaron's sister-in-law's curiosity or possessiveness—how she'd felt snubbed—she wasn't sure she was strong enough to take the chance again. Not when the stakes were so high, when she was at risk of falling in love with both Aaron and Charlie.

'I get it,' he said, defeat in his eyes. 'It's been fun, right? But it's not enough to keep you here. Those nightclubs are calling. Time to put away your wellies and dust off your dancing shoes.' There was no malice in his tone, only inevitable sadness, the reminder of their differences.

Stella curled her fingers into fists in her pockets. She wanted to deny his conclusion. To say she had changed, or that she'd never been completely content with that life, she'd just been hiding. But what was the point, if that was what he thought of her? That she'd used him while waiting to return to her real life? Perhaps he didn't know her at all. Clearly she had been the one to become over-invested yet again.

But she refused to be that vulnerable this time. She knew who she was and what she wanted and what she was prepared to tolerate. It was time for some honesty.

'You said it yourself, Aaron; you don't really need me at the practice. You never wanted me there. You have your work, the estate, Charlie, your boys' club.'

She recalled the way he'd rushed over to Leah. Had he been reassuring Molly's sister that nothing had changed in his life, in Charlie's? And if Stella was nothing to him, then why would she stay here, just to be hurt down the track?

He scrubbed his hand through his hair. 'You were the one to say there are no guarantees in life. Who knows what's around the corner? You could stick around for a while. We could try to make this work.' A hesitant smile twitched his lips, his stare softening. He cupped her cheek, the warmth of his hand burning her skin. 'Maybe I could fall in love with you, Stella. Maybe you could be a part of our boys' club one day.'

If he'd told her she meant less than nothing to him, she would have been less crushed. She'd heard half-promises before. She had been not quite good enough before. Next time she gave her all to a man, she wanted his all in return.

She dragged in a ragged breath. 'That's exactly the kind of declaration a woman wants to hear,' she muttered, her emotions strung taut like piano wire. Could he even hear himself? Only the part of her that cared more than she should understood that this was a big move for him. Starting something. Opening up his life, his son's life to another woman when his heart was still full of Molly.

But did she want to be the other woman, waiting in the wings while he made up his mind to move on from his wife? She couldn't make all of the sacrifices, hang around like a spare stethoscope while he worked on forgiving himself.

She shuddered away from his touch. 'It's not that easy for me, Aaron.'

Maybe if he had fought a bit harder for her, she might have been persuaded to stay; that was the depth of her feelings for him. But she couldn't be the cast-aside one. Not again.

'Why?' The quashed hope in his eyes knocked the breath from her lungs.

'Because I'd be the one to take all of the risk. Your life is here and it's all plotted out. Your job is here, your entire family. You're even going to inherit the manor one day. You are part of this landscape.' She flung her arms wide. 'Part of local history.'

'I can't help that.' His lips thinned.

'What if I stay and this fizzles out, or worse, fails spectacularly? You have Charlie, but I'd be left with nothing again. I'd have uprooted my life for nothing.'

As she spoke the words she realised how much a part of her wanted to be that brave. To give her whole heart to this wonderful man and his little boy, not for them, but for herself. Because she'd found something in Abbotsford she had thought was gone for ever: she'd found herself, her true self.

Aaron's jaw tightened. 'Of course. Everything you've said is true, and I understand your fears. I guess I stupidly hoped that Charlie and I might come to mean more to you than a risk that's just not worth taking.'

Pain lashed Stella so she wanted to bend double. 'Come on, Aaron, don't pretend that a relationship between us would be easy. You have Charlie to consider. He, quite rightly, needs to be your first priority. But as you said, you also have other people to consider. There's Molly's family for a start. I saw the way your sister-in-law looked at me.'

She'd seen the judgement flicker through Leah's eyes. 'How do you think they'd react to a new woman in Charlie's life?'

Aaron sighed, his body rigid. 'I would hope that they'd continue to support me the way they have since Molly died. But they aren't the issue here. You're just scared to admit that you belong here because of some historical gossip that everyone else has forgotten.'

She dropped her gaze, closed her eyes. 'Stop. We need to stop.'

Now they were simply lashing out at each other. And he was right in part; she was scared. But not all of their issues could be laid at Stella's door.

When she looked up, Aaron's eyes were cloaked in regret, but also defeat. 'I told you we were a mistake,' she whispered. 'Neither of us is ready for a relationship this…complicated.'

But oh, how she'd wanted to be ready. If only he'd given some indication that he was ready to commit to her in return, rather than the vague promise of more one day.

The look he gave her cracked Stella's heart clean in two. He gave a sad shrug. 'Perhaps you're right. I'd better let you go inside, take something for that headache.'

Every step she took away from him as she walked to the front door crushed Stella's soul a little more. Sometimes there simply wasn't a cure, a magic pill. Sometimes you had to simply bear the pain.

CHAPTER FOURTEEN

AT THE END of the following week, Stella tucked her stethoscope into her bag and scooped up the tattered fleece jacket she wore at the stables from the hook on the back of the door. She cast a final look around, checking for any personal belongings she might have left behind, only to find the consulting room at Abbotsford Medical Centre wiped clean of her presence.

Her heart clenched. It was as if she had never been here.

Would she be as easily erased from Aaron's mind? When she left for London in the morning, Stella, by contrast, would carry a giant, gaping hole in her chest.

Now that she was leaving, she finally recognised that she had fallen in love with Aaron. It was all such a big mess—they had barely spoken to each other this week—that she welcomed the space, the physical distance in order to think clearly. Because seeing him every day at work, wanting to touch him, to draw him aside and ask where they had gone so wrong, left her overwhelmed. So she had stayed silent.

Stella was about to switch off the lights and leave when she heard a noise beyond the door and froze. No one else was supposed to be in the building; it was nine pm on a Friday night.

She clutched her phone like a weapon. Medical facilities were always being burgled for drugs, although this was the Cotswolds...

Stella peered through the gap in the door to see Aaron enter from the rear of the practice. His cheeks were aglow with the cold as he shrugged off his coat and placed it over a chair in the waiting room.

Stella's knees weakened with relief and longing.

He looked up and their eyes met.

Confusion moved through his expression. 'You're here—I thought you left earlier.'

Was his voice...hopeful?

Stella nodded, reminding herself not to overinterpret anything where Aaron was concerned. She couldn't be objective. 'I did leave, but I popped back to collect my things.'

Stupid, because she had hardly moved in here at the start of her placement, unpacking the bare minimum so she could make a speedy getaway. Only now it felt as if she was leaving behind a vital piece of herself, but that was less to do with this room and more to do with the man staring at her as if they had reverted to being strangers.

'I just called in to collect something I need for a house call first thing in the morning,' he said in explanation, because awkwardness prevailed in their communications now. 'Then I was on my way round to your parents' to say goodbye.'

Stella winced, wanting to scrub the definitive word from his vocabulary. She wasn't sure she had the strength to articulate a final farewell, not after all that they had been through together.

'Well… I'll…um…get out of your way.' She returned to her consultation room, her senses on high alert as he followed her and filled the doorway.

She paused, willing him to say something that would change the inevitable. A selfish thought, because she had no solution to make things right between them.

'Charlie wrote you a goodbye card,' he said, each word a blow to her stomach. 'He made me promise that I would deliver it.' He held out the envelope with her name written in giant, uneven letters on the front.

She took it, her fingers avoiding his, and slid it into her bag. She couldn't read it until she was back in London. She wouldn't break down in front of Aaron.

'Do you have time to go for a last drink at the pub?' He offered an uncertain smile, some of the old dazzle that had helped intoxicate her flashing in his eyes.

She shook her head, too devastated with longing to speak. Why did she feel as if she were on a ledge above a canyon, about to bungee jump? Suspended in that silent moment before the fall and the screams and the terrifying exhilaration? That moment when you wished you could back up, say you had changed your mind, only it was way too late.

'Right, no.' Aaron nodded with understanding that almost made Stella cave. 'Perhaps we can catch up when I'm next at City Hospital, get a drink then.' The hope in his eyes tore gaping holes through her resistance.

No, she had to be strong, to think of her own needs. When she was ready, she deserved to be loved by a man who was all about her, all in, ready to commit. But nor could she leave Aaron thinking that he had done anything wrong. *She* had been the one to change the rules halfway through the game. She was the one who wanted the impossible, wanted more than he could give.

She loved him. If this was goodbye, she could make it genuine and heartfelt.

She stepped close, cupped his cold cheeks in her palms and held his gaze. 'I had a wonderful time here. Thank you for everything. I'll never forget my time back in Abbotsford.'

Pressure pressed down on her chest so she struggled for air. She'd always remember him and Charlie and how close they'd become in such a short period of time. Only not quite close enough.

'Stella...' He groaned her name, regret stark in his eyes. They glittered with emotions. They spoke to her so clearly that she wanted to stare into them all night until dawn.

'Shh.' She pressed her index finger to his lips.

She wasn't strong enough to hear how he wished things had worked out, or how if they had met a year or so in the future the timing might have been better for him.

For an expectant second, his gaze grew intense. Stella's heart thumped. His hands gripped her waist. She thought he intended to push her away. Instead, his stare dipped to her mouth. His fingers clenched. His body became rigid.

Static buzzed in the air, like a storm before the first crack of lightning. She couldn't stop herself. She loved him. Just one last goodbye kiss.

Her finger slid from his mouth, replaced by her lips.

As he had every other time, Aaron commanded their kiss, hauled her body close to his, giving her no room to breathe. Their tongues touched. His fingers fisted her jumper. One hand gripped her neck as if he would never let her break free.

A part of her wanted to be trapped here for ever, physically bewitched with no space for thoughts. But it wasn't enough. Not any more.

To make it last, Stella poured all of the things she was too scared to say, too scared to ask for into kissing Aaron. Their passion escalated more quickly than a dangerously irregular pulse. She wanted him, one last time. Then she would walk away without regret.

As if he'd read her mind, Aaron walked Stella backwards until her thighs hit the desk. She shoved her bag to the floor and perched on the edge, tugging his belt loops to seat his hips between her legs.

Snatching her mouth free of his desperate kisses, she fumbled with his fly. 'Hurry. I want you.'

'Stella…' He trailed kisses down her neck to her clavicle, his hands cupping her buttocks to keep her close.

She shook her head. 'Don't talk.'

She didn't want to hear the question in his tone. She had no answers.

Realising her selfishness, she looked up. 'Do you want to stop?'

He grinned, shook his head. 'Never.' And then

he was kissing her again, reminding her how good they were together, how they could shut out the rest of the world, even their own misgivings, when they touched.

Her mind shut down. All her doubts about leaving and fears if she stayed were squashed by the building compulsion. There was a fumbling free of clothes, his trousers shoved down and her skirt hiked up, and from his pocket he produced a condom.

Out of nowhere, he slowed the frantic pace, kissing her closed eyelids, her neck, the top of her breasts. 'I wish I could take you home, take our time, make it memorable.' His hands caressed her back, pressing them closer, heartbeat to heartbeat.

'Aaron,' she pleaded, because she would never forget one single moment they had shared.

He reared back so their stares locked and all pretence fell away.

She gasped at the vulnerability in his stare. She bit her lip to stop herself from confessing how she felt about him, because for a blissful second she imagined that he felt the same. That he loved her and couldn't spend one second without her, let alone the eighty miles of distance that would be their ongoing reality.

She couldn't trust her intuition. She had been

wrong, so wrong before. Seen what she wanted to see. Believed what she wanted to hear. All she could trust was how he made her feel and that would have to be enough to last her a lifetime.

She pressed her mouth to his, kissed him long and deep as she guided him to her entrance.

Fully seated, he groaned, broke free of her kiss, panted.

'Look at me,' he said as her eyes fluttered shut.

She opened them, enslaved by pleasure.

He cupped her cheek, covering her face with kisses that felt like promises. But she needed certainties.

He unbuttoned her blouse, freed her breasts from her bra and took first one and then the other nipple into his mouth. She moaned, slipping deeper and deeper as he held her with such tenderness and passion combined, her throat ached with unshed tears.

She crossed her ankles at his back. His thrusts took on more determination, and still he held her eye contact, a brand burning into her soul, permanent. Unforgettable.

Stella's orgasm stole her breath, her cries muffled against his chest, against the thudding of his heart, which seemed to say everything that she wanted to hear. Aaron crushed her in his arms as his own climax struck. It seemed that he would hold her for ever as they panted together, coming down from the high.

But she had known it would come to an end.

Aaron withdrew, disposed of the condom and then tugged her close once more, pressing a kiss to her temple and holding her there.

'Stay.' He breathed into her hair. 'I'm falling for you.'

She froze. Suspended. Waiting.

The fine wool of his sweater scratched at her cheek. She was too hot. Or too cold. She couldn't tell.

She just knew that this didn't feel right.

'Don't say that,' she whispered, sliding from the desk and rearranging her clothes.

A tension tightened his swollen mouth 'Why not? It's true.'

'Aaron, please don't.' *It's too late.* 'I'm leaving.'

His stare hardened, a muscle ticking in his jaw. 'That doesn't change how I feel.'

'So you suddenly woke up this morning, my last day in Abbotsford, and realised that maybe one day down the track you might love me, is that it?'

She picked her bag up from the floor rather than look at his hurt expression. He might have strong feelings for her—they were good together physically, mentally in sync, had heaps in common—but that didn't make it love. She'd heard those empty words before. Been manipulated and used by them. She couldn't trust words again, not that he had said those particular three.

'Does it matter when I realised how much I care about you when I never thought I'd care for anyone again?' he asked, frustration in his eyes. 'You don't want to hear it anyway. You're already out of the door.'

Stella shook her head, disbelief and confusion fuelling her flight response and knee-jerk observation. 'The timing feels a little…last-minute.'

Of course he would miss their chemistry after such a long dry spell, as she would. But she'd ruined the sex-only deal with her emotional investment. She couldn't stay, sleep with him over and over and never be certain that her feelings would be reciprocated. She needed to retreat, protect herself. Figure out where she'd gone so spectacularly wrong.

He continued to stare at her. 'You think I would manipulate you to stay with empty words?'

'I don't know.' She was losing her grip on reality. 'I understand, believe me. We have sizzling chemistry. We've just proved that it will be hard to walk away from that.'

She indicated the desk, the keyboard and mouse in disarray.

'But I have to leave. Don't you understand?'

She met his eyes, pleading with him to see her point of view. 'I was the worst version of myself here, Aaron. You brought me home and showed me that I've held on to my associations, my fears for too long. That I'm strong. That I can be strong anywhere. But I've also realised that the next time I fall in love, the next time I give my all to someone, I want all of them in return.'

She didn't add that it was too late for next time; she was already in love like never before.

He scrubbed a hand over his face, clearly confused. 'I'm not him, Stella. We can make this work. I'll be in London once a month for my teaching commitments and you can come home for the weekend. It could work. We could make it work.'

'You're right, you're not him, but it could still fail,' she pointed out. 'You know the cruel twists of life better than anyone. You need more time to heal and forgive yourself. You need to focus on Charlie. You don't need a girlfriend who hasn't had a relationship for nine years and lives miles away.'

His jaw clenched. 'So you're suddenly an expert on my needs, are you?'

Stella swallowed hard, fighting tears, because the one thing she did know was that he didn't love her, he only thought that one day he maybe could.

'No…but I understand my own. I need to think about myself. And I need to get out of here. I'm sorry.'

She made it to the car before the first tear fell.

CHAPTER FIFTEEN

AARON GRIPPED CHARLIE'S hand a little tighter on their walk home from school the following Monday. The weather was as grey and dreary as his mood, but he needed to put on a brave face for his son. He'd had lots of practice this weekend.

'So how was school today?' he asked, trying to distract them both from thoughts of Stella.

'Okay.' Charlie looked up at him with a frown. Was his misery, his heartsickness displayed all over his face? He'd relived their demise a thousand times, each time growing more certain of where he'd gone wrong.

He'd messed up. He'd spent so many years living in the past that when Stella turned his world upside down, it had taken him too long to fully let go of his fear. He loved Stella. He should have told her the moment he realised. Instead he'd tried to protect himself by easing into the confession, sussing out her feelings first, telling himself that she needed to take things slowly.

He clenched his jaw. His regrets were piled so high, he felt caged in, claustrophobic, trapped by his own stupidity. Because after everything she had been through, Stella deserved to know how he felt, even if she didn't love him in return.

'Dad…' Charlie tugged his hand.

'Mmm…'

'Johnny said that he's been to London where Dr Stella is,' continued Charlie, 'and there's a giant wheel that spins you around and around,' he made a washing-machine motion with his free arm, 'and a clock called Big Bell.'

'Big Ben,' Aaron corrected, his stomach sinking. He was never going to get away without some searching questions about Stella's relocation.

Charlie nodded, eyes wide at his father's confirmation that, once again, Johnny was the class know-it-all. 'And the Queen lives there in a gold palace. And guess what, Dad?'

'What's that, Champ?' Aaron's gut twisted into knots.

'The Queen has her own horses, hundreds of them.'

He zoned out of his son's exuberant chatter.

He should never have let Stella go. He should have chased after her sooner. By the time he had called at Stella's parents' house horribly early on Saturday morning, she had already left for London. He'd hoped to convince her that his declaration wasn't a trick to keep her here to ensure a steady supply of great sex. That he loved her. That he should have said it sooner, the minute he had started to feel it, but he'd freaked out, telling himself to go slow, that her caution was natural, expected after she had been so badly hurt in the past.

'Perhaps Stella will be able to ride one of the Queen's horses,' said Charlie. 'She likes riding horses, like me, and she went to my school when she was five. Perhaps if I ever go to London, she could help me to ride one of the Queen's horses too.'

Every mention of Stella's name was like a scalpel between the ribs. 'Maybe, although the Queen's horses have very important jobs to do. They are kind of like soldiers.'

Charlie's eyes rounded at the sheer marvellousness of that concept. 'Can we go and see them, Dad? Can we?' He jumped up and down and then galloped off yelling, 'Giddy up!'

Aaron envied his son's ability to bounce back from unmet expectations. If only he could shrug off his regrets so easily. Stella had been right about him: he had carried guilt for letting Molly and Charlie down, a form of penance for being human. But fear of commitment had gone on long enough. He would always love Molly, but he loved Stella too. And unless he showed her that he was ready to take the chance on them as a couple, a family, Stella, him and Charlie, how could he expect her to take the same risk?

His relationship with Stella had popped holes in his fear as if deflating a balloon. If he was happy, Charlie would be happy. He'd met a wonderful woman who understood his work and his life, and most importantly understood him. They shared the same dreams. Yes, they were both scared, both figuring this thing between them out. But was that reason enough to be apart?

Charlie was swinging on the gate, waiting for his father to catch up, when Aaron arrived.

'Will Dr Stella still help me ride Zeus, Dad? 'Cos I really like her and I really like Zeus.'

Aaron's throat constricted. It was time to do everything in his power to make this work. 'I'm not sure, Champ.'

Here came the question Aaron had been expecting since he told Charlie about Stella's transfer over breakfast. 'Don't you need her at your work any more?'

Yes! Of course he needed her, at work and out of work. It didn't matter where, Stella belonged with them, part of their boys' club.

Aaron hesitated. He always strove to tell Charlie the truth.

'I do need her. I need to tell her that.' And

more. He scooped Charlie up and kissed the top of his head before placing him back on his feet. 'I really like her too.'

'Then you should kiss her, Dad. Johnny says his dad kisses his mum whenever she's mad, and it makes her smile again.'

How could Charlie with his youthful wisdom and uncomplicated vision of the world show him how simple it was to follow your heart?

Aaron's own heart clenched so violently he feared that he might pass out. 'We might need to have Johnny over for tea again some time soon. Clearly I have a lot to learn from that kid. Now, enough about kisses. Let's go and see what Grandma has cooked for dinner, shall we? Because I don't know about you, but I'm starving.'

'I hope it's shepherd's pie. I had shepherd's pie for lunch and it was yum. Johnny says it's made of shepherds but I know that's not right, is it, Dad?'

'No. Johnny's wrong there.' But he certainly had a point about the kissing.

Stella sat in the crowded Southbank bar with Darcy. They'd attended the nearby winter market, and, rather than fill Stella's heart with festive cheer, as it normally would, she only felt frozen to the core.

Stella had arranged to meet her friends for

drinks and dancing in the hope that it would shock her system back to normal. Except every time the door swung open to admit a customer, her stomach swooped with dread. She no more felt like dancing than she felt like taking a plunge in the frigid Thames outside.

To distract herself from the nausea of having made the worst mistake of her life, she looked out at the lights twinkling over the river. Were they dimmer than they had been a month ago?

Everything seemed to have lost its shine.

She wanted to be back in Abbotsford, sitting in the Abbotsford Arms with Aaron in front of the roaring fire. She wanted to wake up on Saturday morning and take Charlie to the stables to see the horses. She wanted to walk across the fields holding the hands of her two boys while they talked about nothing and everything, especially what they would have for dinner.

She had finally opened the letter from Charlie that morning and sobbed her heart out. He'd done a drawing of himself seated majestically on Zeus. The caption read *This was the best day.*

And he was right. In many ways it had been the best day. She had begun to admit her love for Aaron. But it also represented the worst day ever, a day when the rot had set in, destroying all hope.

'You should have stayed,' said Darcy, her gaze sympathetic, despite the bluntness of her message.

'Not this again.' Ever since Stella had returned to the flat they'd shared and she had confessed her dalliance with Aaron, Darcy had been on a mission to point out the glaringly obvious in that way unique to sisters.

Darcy's face crumpled with compassion. 'I know it's terrifying. Believe me, I fought loving Joe with everything in me. But I was just fooling myself.'

'I don't love Aaron.' *Lie.*

Darcy ignored Stella's denial. She knew her too well. 'I understand. It's hard for you after last time. But this is different. Aaron is mature and dependable.'

'He said he was falling for me,' Stella said because she'd drunk two glasses of mulled wine and she had previously omitted that part of the tale.

Darcy's eyes lit up before Stella shook her head.

'You don't believe him,' said Darcy.

Oh, how she wanted to believe him. The need burned inside her like an ember. She shook her head, her cheeks warm with shame. 'I've heard empty words before.'

'And you want actions?' Darcy twirled the stem of her wine glass thoughtfully. 'You want him to prove his love by sky-writing it across the city? Buying you a horse? Moving himself and his son and his practice to London?'

Stella gasped, horrified by the last image. 'No. Of course not.'

The idea of Aaron and Charlie uprooting from Abbotsford was preposterous. Aaron had his job, his family obligations, and Charlie deserved the idyllic childhood both she and Aaron had had growing up in the country. They belonged in Abbotsford.

'So, what did you say?' asked Darcy. 'Did you tell him how *you* feel?'

Stella deflated, crumpling like a paper bag. 'No...' Why hadn't she? She wanted Aaron. She wanted Charlie. She should have told Aaron, fought for him, not run away. What would Charlie think about her broken promise to help him ride Zeus again?

'It sounds to me,' said Darcy, in her eldest sister tone, 'that you were both being cautious, both protecting yourselves.'

'I guess.' Why was everything so clear with a little distance? She didn't want to admit outright that Darcy was correct, but her insides were coiled tight like a spring, desperate to act. Despite all of her talk, Stella had clung to the last shreds of her fear, needing to be certain of Aaron's commitment first.

Neither of them had taken that final leap of faith.

'Of course,' continued Darcy, 'he also has Charlie to think about, so…'

'So I'm going to stop hiding here and tell him how I feel.' She stood, scraping back her stool. 'I belong in Abbotsford with them.'

Darcy grinned. 'That's a relief,' she said, tugging Stella back onto her stool. 'Because Joe has asked me to move in with him, so I'll be moving out too.'

Stella hugged Darcy, her eyes burning. 'I'm so happy for you.'

She just wanted her own happy ending too. She wanted Aaron and Charlie and spaghetti and meatballs.

She pressed a kiss to Darcy's cheek. 'You were right. I do love him. Desperately.'

'Of course you do,' murmured Darcy, squeezing her tight.

Stella laughed, swiping at her damp cheeks. 'Why are you always right?'

Darcy shrugged. 'It's a big-sister thing. Get used to it.'

'I'm leaving now.'

Darcy grabbed her arm. 'You can't drive.'

'I'll take the train.' For her men, she would walk every step back to Abbotsford if she had to, because some risks were worth taking.

CHAPTER SIXTEEN

AARON RAPPED HIS knuckles against the wooden front door, the sting from both the cold and the force of his knock. Impatience pounded at him, so he restlessly paced the front doorstep of Stella's house in London.

She wasn't home.

Frustration choked him until he wanted to punch something. He settled for another attack on the door, although he knew it was futile.

He should have called, but by the time he had fed Charlie and rushed back home for an overnight bag so the boy could stay the night with his grandparents, his desperation levels had reached boiling point. He couldn't live one second longer without Stella in his life, so he'd rushed here to confess. Face to face. Preferably lips to lips and heartbeat to heartbeat. To beg her to listen while he unreservedly poured out his feelings this time, a hundred per cent vulnerable. No more fearful, fumbling *mights*, *shoulds* or *coulds*.

Scrubbing a hand through his hair, he stepped backwards and gazed up at the windows of the house, which were shiny black rectangles of doom, mocking him and his belated declaration.

He dropped his head back in despair and sighed to the heavens. His breath misted in the cold air while he contemplated his next move and where Stella might be at this time of night. The winter chill permeated his clothing. Where he had been overheated from running here from the car, now he shuddered. Perhaps Stella had already moved on. Perhaps she was out on a date right now, trying to forget him and their connection.

He huffed, shaking his head. She could deny it all she liked, but what they had shared was real and exceptional and he planned to tell her that, date or not.

'Aaron?'

He spun to see Stella on the pavement behind him, his heart climbing into his throat.

'What are you doing here?' she said, her cheeks rosy and her beautiful eyes trying to conceal the flare of what looked like, unless he was mistaken, hope. 'Your lecture is next week. Where's Charlie?' She stepped closer, panic making her voice squeak. 'Is everything okay?'

He nodded, struck dumb by relief. Would she

worry if she didn't care? Reciprocal hope surged in his chest like the jolt from a defibrillator.

'He's fine. Everything is fine.' He trailed his eyes over her from head to toe, refamiliarising himself with her outline, her shape, her essence. Had it really only been three days? It felt as if a lifetime had passed since he'd watched her pull away from the practice on Friday night.

'Well, that's a lie actually,' he said, desperate to hold her hands but giving her the space she had said she needed. 'Not everything is fine. I need to talk to you and I'll explain.'

She nodded. 'Come in.'

He followed her up the steps and inside the house—a typical Georgian mid-terrace—his hands twitching to touch her, to pull her into his arms and never let her go again.

They took off their coats and Stella led him into the lounge. 'Have a seat,' she said, her voice high-pitched. With nerves?

He wanted to hold her, to tell her that everything would be okay. Because it would. They'd figure it all out together. But being apart just wasn't an option for him, or for Charlie.

Remembering his son, he pulled the letter from his pocket. 'I brought you this. It's from Charlie. He misses you and wants to know if you have any sway with the Queen or the Horse Guards.' His lips twitched as he handed it over, hoping that Charlie's simplistic view of the world would help Stella to see that nothing was impossible with love on your side.

With his love.

But he was getting ahead of himself.

She looked at the envelope as if it was infectious. At her desperate swallow, her rapid blinking, her choked sob, he snapped and pulled her into his arms. 'Shh,' he soothed. 'It's all going to be okay.'

'I miss him too,' she mumbled into his jumper. Then she laughed, perhaps registering his son's absurd request, finally.

Aaron cupped her cheek and wiped away a tear. 'Stella, I know that you felt you had to leave. I know that you thought I only wanted you to stay for sex. And I know I messed up. I was scared that you wouldn't share my feelings. But I want you to know regardless. I love you.'

He stared into her emotive eyes. Eyes that spoke to him, even in his dreams.

'I'm deeply in love with you.' He cupped her cheeks, swiped the pads of his thumbs over her cheekbones. 'Head over heels and every other cliché you can think of. I was scared to say it in case you could never love me back. In case you didn't want me and Charlie after what you'd been through. But even if I'm not the man for you, even if you won't ever love me back, I want you to know my feelings. Because I want you to move on from your past and be happy.'

'Aaron—'

He pressed his fingers to her lips. 'Please let me finish what I came here to say, what I should have said before you walked away. I'm yours, ready to move on, ready to give you my all. I'll make this relationship work whichever way I can. I'm fully committed to that. To us. You, me and Charlie, who by the way is desperate to see Big Ben. We'll move here permanently if it makes you feel secure about my love.'

She shook her head, tears beading on her eyelashes. 'No... I don't want that.'

Pain sliced him in two. He'd known it was risky to assume that she could love him back, but he didn't regret coming here tonight.

'I see.' He dropped his hands from her face, stepped back.

'Wait.' She lunged for him, wrapped her arms around his neck, buried her face in his jumper and squeezed him tight. 'What I mean is, I don't want you and Charlie to relocate your lives for me.'

Weak with relief that she wasn't kicking him out, that there was still some hope, he pressed a kiss to the top of her head, inhaled the scent of her hair. 'I understand. I'm a package deal. Two for the price of one.'

'I don't care about that either,' she mumbled.

'So are you just wary of falling in love, or specifically wary of loving *me*?'

She surged up and kissed him, interrupting the speech he'd prepared on the drive here after surgery. 'Aaron,' she pulled back to meet his gaze, 'I already love you. And I love Charlie. I missed my boys. I was on my way back to Abbotsford tonight to tell you.'

Everything that he needed to see shone in the depths of her eyes.

'I should have told you before I left, but I was scared.' She swallowed back emotion, breaking his heart. 'Last time love broke me. But I never loved him as much as I love you. Falling in love with you was twice as terrifying. I had so much more to lose if you decided that you didn't want me.'

'You have no idea how much I want you.' He gripped her tighter. 'I wanted you all along. I just had some stuff to work through, because I never thought I'd have a second chance. I never thought I deserved it. But Charlie and I deserve to be happy and whole. And you make us happy and whole.'

'Yes. We belong together.' Her smile glittered with happiness he wanted to put there every day for the rest of their lives.

He crushed her mouth with his, kissed her as

if he'd never have another chance. But he would. He'd take every opportunity to love this woman, to tell her how much he loved her and to show her why he would never stop.

He pulled back, out of breath. 'I want all of you though, not just the incredible sex. I want to hold your hand and sit by the fire folding laundry with you. I want your reminders on my phone—I've made pizza four times since you put that there, just to feel your presence in the house. And when Charlie is asleep, I want to hold you in my arms all night, until you feel as loved as you are.'

She laughed through happy tears.

He tilted up her face and pressed his lips to hers. She tasted like Stella, and salty tears and home. He tangled his fingers in her hair and deepened the kiss, his tongue sliding to meet hers.

'I want you, if you'll have me,' he whispered, his own eyes burning. We'll figure out the geography as long as we're together.'

She cupped his face, pushed her fingers into his hair. 'I want you too. Both of you. And I want to come home, if you'll have me back at the practice.'

'I hoped you'd say that.' He kissed her again and this time they collapsed back onto the sofa so they could do the kissing justice.

'Let's go tonight,' she said when she pulled back for air.

Aaron slid his hand under her jumper, finding the clasp of her bra and popping it open with an expert flick of the wrist. 'The morning is soon enough.'

He pressed a path of kisses down her neck. 'Charlie has a sleepover tonight. I don't want to waste precious hours driving when I could be showing you how much I love you instead.'

'I can't argue with that logic.' She sighed as he divested her of her clothes and found first one nipple and then the other with his lips.

'I must say,' she smiled down at him, her eyes glazed with pleasure, 'this declaration is much better than your previous attempt. Well done.' She gripped his neck and urged his lips back to hers.

All businesslike, he broke free, scooped her up from the sofa and headed for the stairs.

'I've had some coaching from Charlie and Johnny,' he said with a wink. And then he loved her all night long.

EPILOGUE

Three years later

STELLA WATCHED EIGHTEEN-MONTH-OLD Violet chase after eight-year-old Charlie, who had charged ahead waving a stick as if to slay the make-believe dragon inhabiting the woods. Their daughter was never far behind her big brother. She reminded Stella of herself as a child, always chasing a big sister for fear of being left behind or missing out.

But fears of that nature were in the past. She had slain her own personal dragon and joined the boys' club, which had promptly become the Bennett Club, admitting not just one, but two girls to even up the dynamic.

Aaron, walking at her side with a similarly watchful eye on their children, squeezed her hand. 'Are you nervous? About returning to work tomorrow?'

Stella smiled up at her husband, her pulse stirring at the sight of him in a chunky Aran jumper that she wanted to strip off the moment they arrived home from their walk.

Of course, that would be impossible until the kids were asleep.

'A little. I didn't think my maternity leave would last this long.' She shrugged and he wrapped his arm around her shoulders, tucking her underneath so they were as close as humanly possible and still able to walk over the rugged path through the woods.

'Well, I didn't think my parents would want to retire early from running Bennett Manor, so it's all worked out perfectly. You and I get to job share and share the childcare while we enjoy our lives together.'

He glanced ahead to where their children walked hand in hand. Then he dragged her close and kissed her under an oak tree, naked of its leaves but filled with the promise of spring.

Stella lost herself in the glide of lips, the touch of tongues, the wash of love.

Charlie was a caring big brother, always looking out for his baby sister, protecting her and standing up to any perceived injustice, which was sometimes a challenge at bedtime and during their frequent trips to the stables.

A cry split the calm. Stella and Aaron broke apart, their parental senses as alert as their doctoring ones.

'Mum…' Charlie staggered back towards them carrying his sobbing sister.

Stella's heart swelled with pride and love that Aaron and Molly's son was comfortable enough to call her Mum. It had happened naturally and at his instigation, and after the first time Stella had crept off to the bedroom to cry.

'She fell over with this in her hand.' Charlie brandished the pine cone Violet had collected at the start of their walk—they had hundreds of similar specimens at home—and carried all the way, as if it was priceless treasure.

And maybe it was priceless. Because it contained miraculous seeds capable of growing a whole new tree, in the same way that Stella, Aaron and Charlie, with the addition of Violet, had grown their precious little family.

With love.

Aaron scooped Violet into his arms and hugged Charlie with his free arm. Violet snuggled into her father's jumper in a way that Stella envied and adored in equal measure.

'Well done, Charlie.' Stella took the pine cone and acccpted a mollified, teary-cheeked Violet from Aaron. She raised her daughter's tiny hand to her mouth and kissed her palm, which bore faint pink indentations from the bumps of the pine cone.

And just like that, Violet smiled, the pain forgotten.

Having received comfort from both her parents, and before Stella could hug her properly, Violet squirmed out of her arms and went to her brother.

Charlie made soothing noises as Violet held up her hand for another kiss. He repeated the gesture and they galloped off together along the path.

Aaron sighed at her side, watching his children scamper away. Stella took his hand as they set off after the pair, her heart full of love for this man who had shown her that being vulnerable was not a weakness.

'What are you thinking?' she asked, knowing the signs of his preoccupation well.

'That I hope all of their trials and tribulations, their hurts and heartaches, are as brief and easily remedied as that.'

'They'll be fine.' Stella smiled, because her husband still worried about his parenting skills. Only now twice as much because there were two humans to love and nurture.

'Yes,' he agreed. Then, 'How can you be sure?'

'Because they'll take after you, and you are infamous around these parts for being a bit of a catch—hot dad doc and lord of the manor rolled into one spectacular package.' She pulled him close for a kiss.

'Maybe they'll take after you—wonderful mother, amazing GP, not to mention your dancing skills.' He twirled her under his arm and bent her back into a dip.

She laughed, her wellies almost slipping from under her in the mud.

'Oh, and I forgot, sexy. You are so sexy.' He wrapped his arm around her waist and hauled her close, this kiss turning X-rated.

'They'll take after us,' she said, holding his hand once more.

Aaron raised her hand to his mouth and kissed her knuckles, his eyes communicating so much love that she grew light-headed. 'I love you,' he said.

'I love you too.'

'I couldn't ask for anything more,' he said.

And then they chased after their children.

* * * * *

A Date With Her Best Friend
Louisa Heaton

MILLS & BOON

Louisa Heaton lives on Hayling Island, Hampshire, with her husband, four children and a small zoo. She has worked in various roles in the health industry—most recently four years as a Community First Responder, answering 999 calls. When not writing Louisa enjoys other creative pursuits, including reading, quilting and patchwork—usually instead of the things she *ought* to be doing!

Dear Reader,

I really wanted to write a different specialty for this book and it occurred to me that I'd never written a firefighter. Initially, my hero was the firefighter and my heroine was the paramedic. But I knew that I wanted my heroine to have grown up as a tomboy due to having three older brothers—like me! And that was when I realised I needed to swap them over. Once I did that, the plot unfolded easily.

My mother used to despair that I wouldn't play with dolls or wear pretty dresses. I remember her tutting a lot! I was much more interested in building dens with my brothers, carving our own bows and arrows, and spending hours fishing in the river.

So, in this story, I had to add a despairing mother and a father that couldn't let go of his little girl. And then I developed my hero, Tom, who could see through Cara's armour and understand the hidden woman beneath the mask. Cara and Tom's connection was a pleasure to write and I hope you enjoy their story as much as I enjoyed creating it.

Louisa xxx

DEDICATION

To my three older brothers.
Thanks for sharing all the mud and drama!

CHAPTER ONE

CARA MADDOX WAS two sets in on a five-set high-intensity weights workout when her phone went off. The scary ringtone she'd allocated to her father filled the fire station's small gym and she debated whether to ignore the call. But familial duty got the better of her and she set the weights down with a sigh.

Wiping her face with a soft towel, she accepted the video call. 'Hi, Dad.'

Her father smiled at her. 'Hello, darling, how are you doing?'

He was sitting in a comfortable leather chair, and his background told her he was in the library of Higham Manor, her childhood home. Shelves and shelves of leather-bound books behind him reached from floor to ceiling.

He peered closer, then frowned. 'You look shattered. Are you taking care of yourself?'

'I'm in the middle of a workout, Dad.' She

checked her watch to note her heart rate and then paused her workout.

'Right. Of course. Got to stay fit in your type of job, I guess.'

'That's right.'

She stiffened slightly when he mentioned her job. Felt herself instantly go on the defensive. Her father had never been a fan of her joining the fire service. If he was calling just to have another go at her about it, or to suggest she change jobs, then she'd end the call. She really didn't have any time for that kind of nonsense any more.

'What can I do for you?' Best to get right to the point.

'I was wondering if you were going to come back home at the end of the month, for your mother's party? We haven't seen you in a long time, and it would be nice to see you.'

As he finished speaking, Michaels, her dad's butler, came into view, carrying a tray with coffee and biscuits.

'You're seeing me now.'

'Come now, Cara, you know it's not the same. It's your mother's birthday. She'd want you to be there.'

'She's been dead for years, Dad. She's not going to know whether I'm there or not.'

Her father bristled, waiting for Michaels

to leave the room before he began speaking again. 'But your family will. Our friends will. The *servant*s will. What will they think?'

'It doesn't matter what they think. I don't know them. They're your friends and associates. Not mine.'

'It's her *birthday*, Cara,' her father said, as if that should be enough explanation for everything. As if that should be enough motivation to get his daughter to do everything he wanted.

She felt guilty for trying to avoid it, but she'd been to many of those evenings before. They were meant to be about her mother, but all they were was a huge chance for her father to network with his friends and/or try to fix her up with the son of one of them. There would be a speech. Her mother would get a token mention. Heartfelt but short. Everyone would raise a glass and then her father's pals would go back to whatever business deals they were arranging, exchanging cards and contacts over cigars and brandies. And the entire time Cara would stand there, feeling awkward, trying to make conversation with a Tarquin or a Theodore—people she didn't know, who were all rather surprised that she did the job that she did.

It wasn't what they expected. She was the

daughter of an earl, and they expected her to be something other than a firefighter. The patron of a charity, perhaps? Someone who had a lot of lunches with her lady friends and cared way too much about handbags and nail polish. She was Lady Cara Maddox, after all.

But Cara didn't care for titles, or expectations, nor did she have lady friends. Most of her friends were guys. Her best friend was a guy. Tom Roker. Sweet, dear Tom. Handsome Tom. Paramedic. Father to a beautiful little boy called Gage. And widower of Victoria, who'd been willowy and tall and exquisite. Preened to perfection. The kind of woman Cara's father obviously wished his daughter would be more like. The kind of woman Cara could never be, which put Tom—dear, sweet, lovable, handsome Tom—completely out of her league.

Cara had always preferred the company of men. But that was what happened when you grew up with three older brothers and didn't quite fit in with the young ladies at your posh school. You hung around at rugby and polo matches, you laughed and joked with the boys, you competed with them, wrestled with them. You got to know your brother's friends and they were mostly guys. On the odd occasion when one of her brothers had brought home a friend who was a girl, Cara had had no idea how to talk to them! They'd seemed a different breed. Alien! Not interested in the slightest in Cara's topics of conversation, such as rugby or whether they wanted to arm wrestle! Clothes and designers and parties had been completely off her radar.

'I know. You don't have to remind me. I can remember all by myself.'

Her mother's birthday had also been her death day. For many weeks Serena Maddox had lain in bed, trying vainly to fight the ravages of breast cancer that had metastasised to her lungs, liver and bones. Cara had sat by her mother's bedside in those last few days when she was mostly asleep, listening to the fluid building up in her mother's lungs and throat, sponging her dry lips as her breathing got slower and slower, and she'd held her mother's hand as she'd taken her final, agonised breath.

It was a day etched into her brain. A memory filled with so much pain and so much guilt that she had never been the daughter Serena had dreamed of. Cara had let her mother down, and her father knew that, and she hated it when he used that to his own advantage.

'Come home, Cara. Your brothers will be

here. Clark is flying in from New York next week. Cameron will arrive a few days after that,' he said.

'And Curtis?'

'In Milan, still, but he promises he'll be back for the party.'

She could hear the tone in her father's voice. The tone that said, *I'm glad my boys have flown the nest and are upholding the Maddox name, but I do wish they lived closer to home.*

Her father, Fabian Maddox, Earl of Wentwich, was a proud man, and often boasted about his three sons, but Cara knew he would prefer to have them close by, so that the Maddox men could be a force to be reckoned with. Instead they were spread out across the globe, and their father could only preen, in their absence.

Clark ran a prestigious law firm in New York, specialising in family law and pandering to the rich, Cameron was in Cape Town, South Africa, running a business that built cruise ships, and Curtis was the CEO of Maddox Hotels, whose head office was in London. But she knew they were currently constructing a new hotel in Milan, which he was overseeing.

She spoke to her brothers often, and though

she'd never felt any judgment from them, she wondered if they, too, questioned her choice in jobs.

But being a firefighter was all she'd ever wanted to do. Ever since she'd been little, when a fire had broken out in the kitchens and her family and the staff had rushed from the building, only to watch in awe as firefighters rushed *towards* the flames. They'd arrived in huge fire engines, unloading equipment and hoses, and the flames licking out of the downstairs windows had soon been transformed into thick, grey smoke, billowing up into the sky.

She'd felt a nervous excitement at seeing them, had felt herself come alive watching them. It had been a heady feeling, and one she'd wanted to chase from an early age, even telling her parents, when she was just six years old, that she was going to be a firefighter. Oh, how they'd laughed at that, and Cara had felt flummoxed and confused by it. Why was it such a funny suggestion? Why did they all keep telling her that she'd change her mind when she got older?

She sighed. If all her brothers were coming back, if they were making the effort... She'd not planned on going this year. She'd done her duty, honouring her mother's birthday over the years. She'd been ready to start missing a few. Remembering her mother in her own way instead. Laying a wreath at her grave. Saying a few words, perhaps. Just... *remembering*, without having to stand around feeling uncomfortable, with people she didn't know, in order to fulfil some duty that her father had imposed.

Thankfully, she was literally saved by the bell.

The siren blasted out through the station. 'Gotta go, Dad.'

'But you've not given me your answer!' He leaned forward in his chair, filling the screen with his face.

'Sorry! Speak later!' And she ended the video call, pulling on a navy tee shirt and trousers over her workout clothes.

When that siren sounded you dropped everything.

Including any guilt.

In fact, she was grateful for it.

The siren meant that whatever was happening with her right there and then had to be put to one side for later. It wasn't important. What was important were the people who needed help. Those trapped in cars after an accident. Those who watched their businesses and often their livelihoods burning to the ground.

Green Watch often couldn't save someone's car or house or factory, but they could try to save lives—and that siren meant someone or something needed to be saved.

And that was what Cara lived for.

Tom Roker had just finished eating his sandwich when the call came through from Control about a house fire in Wandsworth and he was asked to attend.

'Roger, Control. ETA three minutes.'

'Roger that, four, three, two. Take care.'

He started the engine of his rapid response vehicle and reversed out of his spot, switching on the blues and twos as he raced towards the destination provided by his onboard computer.

The traffic was light today. The kind of traffic he wished he had to deal with most days. People got out of the way, they pulled over in the right place, the traffic lights were kind and he got to the destination quickly. His only problem was that cars lined both sides of the street. Pedestrians, neighbours—all had stopped or come out of their homes to gawp at the flaming spectacle of a house in full flame. Two fire engines blocked the street, and he

could already see the fire crews doing their
best to tame the fire. He wondered if Cara
was on duty today?

It was a strange thing. He always hoped to
see her, and yet also feared that she would be
there. The idea of her running into a burning
building… She might get a thrill out of it, but
he didn't. Not until she was out again.

Tom sounded his horn to make people get
out of the way, so he could get closer, and in
the end managed to park behind one of the
fire engines. Behind him, a normal ambulance arrived, and by the sound of the sirens
he could hear many more emergency services
were on their way.

He looked over at the house that was burning. It was a mid-terrace house, and the two
front top windows were full of flame. It was
licking at the bricks and there were holes in
the grey slate roof through which more flame
could be seen. Maybe the fire had started on
the upper floor? On the ground floor the windows looked dark with smoke, occasionally
strobed by torchlight as the fire crew made
their way through the property, most probably looking for someone not accounted for.

His heart thudded at the thought.

People were crowding around the perimeter established by a police officer, filming

it on their phones, their faces masks of awe and fear.

A firefighter wearing a white helmet came to meet him. He realised as he got closer that it was the Chief Fire Officer of Green Watch, known simply as Hodge, so Cara was most probably here somewhere, doing her thing.

'I've got Mum and Dad out, as well as two of the kids, but we're still looking for the third child. I think we're dealing with some basic smoke inhalation for most of them, though Dad's a COPD sufferer. He's also got a decent burn on his arm and left hand. They're over there in that appliance, receiving some oxygen.'

Tom nodded. Smoke inhalation could cause all manner of problems, from the simple to the most severe. Especially if the sufferer had medical issues to deal with, like asthma or COPD—chronic obstructive pulmonary disease. A patient with a respiratory issue could crash quickly, so it was important to keep a close eye on them.

'I'll do what I can.'

'Cheers, Tom.' Hodge headed back to co-ordinate efforts.

Tom made his way to the fire engine. Liam Penny, one of Cara's crew mates, was inside monitoring his patients. 'Hey, Liam. What-cha got?'

'This is Daniel Webster and his wife Maria. The little one on her lap is Teddy and the brave girl over on your right is Amy.'

The mother removed her oxygen mask. 'Is there any word on Joey? Have they found him?'

Tom clambered in. 'They're still looking.'

'I need to be out there!' The mum tried to get up and push past him, but he managed to stop her.

'They'll come and find you if there's any news. Right now, I need you to stay here.' He replaced the oxygen mask. 'It's safer for you in here. The fire crews are doing their utmost to find him, but what I need you guys to do is try to stay calm and breathe in the oxygen for me.' He didn't need any of them running out there, getting in the way of the rescue operation. It was dangerous out there. 'I'll just put this SATs probe on your finger.'

The SATs probe measured oxygen and pulse rate. Normal oxygen levels for those without COPD were between ninety-four and ninety-eight percent. As he waited for the reading to appear, Tom used a tongue depressor and a pen light to look at the back of the dad's throat. The smoke inhalation and the COPD were more of a concern than the burn on his arm and hand and would need to take priority. He saw soot deposits. He'd need to be kept under observation in hospital for a while.

More than half of all fire deaths came from smoke inhalation. The smoke could cause inflammation of the airway and lungs, making them swell up and become blocked, and depending upon what types of gases were inhaled some of the inhalations would be toxic or poisonous. This dad was lucky he'd got out.

He began to cough, his eyes reddening and watering with the effort to try and clear his lungs, so Tom set him up with some extra oxygen and tried to coach him through his breathing. The two kids didn't look too bad. Shocked more than anything.

'Do we know yet how the fire started?' he asked Liam.

'We think it began upstairs, but the flash point… We're not sure.'

'I was burning candles,' the mum said, crying. 'And I… I think I might not have switched off my curling iron. Could that have started this? Is this my fault?' She looked at Tom in fear. Fear that he would tell her that it might be. But no one knew. Not yet.

Tom noted that her oxygen SATs weren't too bad at all. Ninety-three to ninety-four. On the lower end. 'We don't know for sure. Accidents happen all the time. You'll have to wait for the investigation results.' He moved the SATs probe from her finger to the dad's, whose laboured breathing sounded much more exhausted. He didn't like the man's colour.

At that moment a couple of paramedics arrived, dressed in their neon yellow jackets. 'Hey, Tom, what have we got?'

Relieved to have back-up, Tom handed over his patients, explaining about the dad's medical history and soot-covered throat. The paramedics offloaded the small family and escorted them to the ambulance, even though the mum kept protesting that she wasn't going to leave without knowing if Joey was okay.

Tom ached for her. But at that moment he saw a firefighter emerge from the building, carrying a dog.

'Bella! Oh, my God, Bella! How could we have forgotten about you?' The mum ran free of the paramedic and towards the Boxer dog, which was limp in the firefighter's arms.

Judging by the firefighter's walk, Tom knew it was Cara and, as always, he felt relief that she'd got through this fire okay. He knew it was her thing to run into the flames to help. It was her job, after all. But he always worried about her. She was a tough little cookie, who could hold her own, but that still didn't stop him from feeling he needed to protect her. Feelings of gratitude that she was out of the fire washed over him as usual. He wanted to see her face, but she still wore her rebreather mask.

Cara laid the dog down by the appliance and pulled off her own mask to get out some of the special equipment that he knew had been donated to them by an animal charity—a mask to fit around a dog or cat's face. He didn't realise he was holding his breath until he saw the dog trying to fight the mask and wagging its tail at its owner's approach.

'You might want to get her checked out by your vet,' Cara said as she gave the dog oxygen, pulling off her helmet and laying it on the side of the appliance.

Her hair was sweaty. Some of it was plastered to her skull, dark, as if it had been dipped in molasses, the rest was wispy and golden, almost auburn. Her hair, he often thought, was like flame itself. A mass of burning colours. Autumnal.

The first time he'd ever seen her with her hair loose and hanging down her back he'd realised he was staring, mesmerised by how beautiful it was. But that had been ages ago. In another time, it seemed. Back then…before he'd known her properly and they'd become the best friends they were now, he'd been attracted to her. How could he not have been? Cara Maddox was a stunning young woman. The sight of her had taken his breath away, but he'd been in no place back then to do anything about it. He'd been a married man. It would have been wrong.

So they'd just been associates. People who met at emergencies, until slowly they had become friends.

At that moment she met his gaze, noticing him, and her face broke into a hesitant, almost shy smile. 'Hey, Tom.' She touched her hair, as if ashamed of how it looked. As if she knew that it was sweaty and plastered to her head, that her pale skin had dark smears from the smoke upon it, that there were red marks on her face from the mask. That maybe she didn't look her best.

But to him she looked beautiful. The only problem was he couldn't tell her, in case she thought he was hitting on her.

'Hey. How was it in there?'

'Hot. Like it always is.' She laughed and unzipped her jacket a little.

'Any idea of what started it?'

'Not sure. But something upstairs in one of the bedrooms.'

One of the woman's neighbours had taken the dog, Bella, offering to look after it for the Webster family, so they could go to hospital in the ambulance and get checked out.

'How are all the patients?' Cara asked.

'Not bad. Smoke inhalation, minor burns. Dad will need an eye kept on him. He's got COPD, his SATs were low, and he has soot deposits on the back of his throat. Any sign of the missing boy?'

'House was empty apart from the dog, which I found whimpering under a bed.'

'Then where is he?' Tom frowned.

'Don't know. He could have gone out and not told anyone he was going, so they thought he was still inside.'

At that moment they became aware of a commotion amongst the crowd of onlookers. They both turned to look and noticed a young teenage boy struggling to get past the police presence.

'Mum? *Mum!*'

'Joey!'

'Mum!'

Mother and son ran into each other's arms, the mum bawling her eyes out with relief.

Tom and Cara both let out a breath, small smiles creeping onto their faces.

Cara turned to Tom. 'Happy ending in that respect.'

'Yeah... Ever feel like happy endings only happen to other people?' Tom mused.

Cara laughed. 'Oh, yeah.' She looked down at the ground, almost as if she couldn't think of what to say next. 'Are you okay?' she asked.

He shrugged. Everyone still expected him to be riddled by grief. 'Oh, you know how it is.'

She nodded. 'I do. How are things with Gage? All okay?'

'He's asking a lot of questions about his mum lately.'

'What do you tell him?'

Tom looked at the remains of the burnt house. The blackened bricks, the holey roof. Windows blown out from heat. The flames were gone and all that was left were plumes of thick, grey, swirling smoke, billowing up into the sky. Nobody had died today. Not here. And for that he was grateful.

'I tell him that she loved him very much. He doesn't understand if I tell him she got sick before she died, because he doesn't re-

member that. It happened so quickly sometimes even I struggle to understand it.'

'In those early days of Covid we all struggled to understand it. Don't be too hard on
yourself.'

Cara laid a reassuring hand on his, before
turning to look at what was happening with
her crew. She had no idea what her touch
meant to him.

'I'd better go. You going to be at The Crusader tonight?'

The Crusader was the preferred pub that all
the fire crews attended—situated, as it was,
just half a mile from their station.

'You bet. My parents have got Gage for a
sleepover, so I'm free.'

She pulled her helmet back on, and gave
him a warm smile and a wave before jogging
back to her team. He watched her go, kicking
himself for not saying anything to her.

Yet again.

The ambulance was pulling away, with the
Webster family on board, and all Tom had to
do was return to his rapid response vehicle
and write his notes on the call.

The Websters had survived this terrible
event and he was glad for them. It could have
turned out so differently. A house and pos-
sessions could be replaced. People couldn't.

He thought about his son. How did you fully explain Covid to a near four-year-old? It would get easier, he hoped, as Gage got older and could understand more, but right now all his son knew was that he was the only child at his pre-school who didn't have a mummy. There were a few who didn't have dads, but mums...

Am I enough for my son?

Could he give Gage the cuddles and hugs he needed, the way his mother would have? He hoped so. Victoria had always shown her son affection. And he missed her, too. Missed her voice. Her presence. Which was strange, considering how they'd been with each other towards the end.

They should never have got married. They should never have got carried away with the romanticism of having been together since they were so young. The signs had been there, but they'd ignored them, because Gage had been on the way and Tom had wanted to do the right thing by Victoria and his unborn child.

Gage was his utmost priority now.

He couldn't be getting carried away with how he felt about Cara. He wasn't the best partner in the world for anyone to have, quite frankly. He'd failed Victoria and he couldn't go getting involved with anyone else right now. Gage wouldn't understand that.

And Cara? She would no doubt think badly of him if he declared his feelings for her so soon after losing his wife to Covid.

As the appliance pulled back into the station, the members of Green Watch descended from the vehicle and got into cleaning and maintenance mode. After every job they checked and maintained all equipment and cleaned the appliance if they'd attended a fire.

Cara began an audit of the equipment and checked the breathing apparatus supplies. She was glad of this respite. It was always a confusing moment after seeing Tom. Her feelings for him were confusing. He was her best friend, yes. Absolutely. She would give her life for him. But if she was being honest with herself then she had to admit that deeper undercurrents ran beneath the surface. Like a riptide of attraction that she had to fight every time they were together. But she was being respectful to his late wife. Acknowledging that he'd married his childhood girlfriend and had never looked at anyone else in his life so far.

Also—and she didn't like admitting this—

she knew that she could never be as good as Victoria.

She'd known Tom when he was married to his wife. Had socialised with both of them. She'd liked Victoria. Had seen why Tom was so in love with her. She'd been funny and warm. Friendly.

Cara had met Tom just half a year before Victoria had died. Their eyes meeting over the crumpled, steaming bonnets of two cars that had been involved in a head-on collision. At first she'd been startled by her reaction to a man she'd only seen for a couple of seconds. A man she had not yet heard speak. Whose name she didn't know. A man she had not spent any time with, nor yet seen smile.

She'd watched him clamber into the rear of one of the vehicles, to maintain a C-spine in an unconscious female driver who had suffered a head injury, and for a brief moment she had just stood still, watching him, mesmerised, her eyebrows raised in surprise at how she'd been frozen into place, stunned.

Is this lust at first sight? she'd mused, before her brain had kicked in and allowed the rest of the world to re-enter her consciousness. She'd heard instructions from the Green Watch Chief Fire Officer, Hodge, on how to tackle the incident. As she'd covered the driver with a blanket, to screen her from the glass of the windshield breaking as the Jaws of Life were applied, she'd stolen another glance at the paramedic who had intrigued her at first sight.

Dark hair. Dark lashes around crystalline blue eyes. High cheekbones. A solid jawline and a mouth that looked as if it was made for sin.

Cara had had to look away from him, pulse racing, face flushing, and she'd had to concentrate on what she was doing. Once the roof of the car had been cut off, she'd worked with Tom to co-ordinate the extrication of the driver. He had C-spine control, so he'd taken charge—counting them down, telling them when to get the backboard in. She'd helped to slide the patient on, then levelled the back board and helped carry her out of the car and onto a waiting ambulance trolley.

Then she'd turned away to help with the extrication of the second driver and her passenger, who were less injured, and conscious still, but who would no doubt have horrible whiplash injuries and dislocated shoulders to endure through the next few weeks. The engine block of their vehicle had crumpled inwards, trapping the legs of the driver, but thankfully had broken no bones. She'd been extremely lucky.

With the patients off to the hospital, and the crew organised to begin clearing up the equipment, she'd heard a voice behind her.

'Thanks.'

She'd turned. It had been him. Cara had done her best to keep her breathing normal, but it had been hard when he'd placed the full force of his gaze upon her. It had done alarming things to her insides. Her heart rate had accelerated. Her blood pressure had risen. Her mouth had dried to the consistency of a desert.

'Thanks to you, too.' She'd smiled. 'A job well done.'

She'd been pretty impressed that her tongue had still worked and that she'd not stuttered or tripped over her words. Because she had never felt this before. Not even with Leo.

He'd nodded. 'Absolutely. I'm Tom. I'm new.'

He'd held out his hand for her to shake and she'd taken it, glad that he couldn't ascertain that inside she felt molten.

'Cara. Nice to meet you. You've just moved to this area?'

'To be near my wife's family.'

My wife. Ah. Of course. A man like this wouldn't be single.

Disappointment had washed over her.

'Great. Well, welcome to the area.'

He'd thanked her and then headed back to his car, and she'd watched him go like a lovesick puppy. It had been then that Reed Gower, one of her Green Watch crew mates, had sidled up beside her, draped an arm around her shoulder and said, 'You know, if this were a cartoon your eyes would be on stalks and there'd be little love hearts on the end of them.'

She'd shrugged him off, annoyed that he'd noticed. 'Don't be ridiculous! He's new—I was just introducing myself, that's all.'

Reed had laughed as he'd walked away. 'Sure you were! Keep telling yourself that.'

After that she'd done her best to try and keep things distant, but he'd kept turning up at most of their shouts and eventually, as these things happened, someone on Green Watch had invited him to join them at the pub—The Crusader.

And Tom had turned up. With his wife, Victoria, in tow.

A small part of her had hoped that his wife

would be an ugly toad, but of course she wasn't. Victoria had been tall, long-limbed, gazelle-like, with wave upon wave of shiny honey-coloured, hair. And she'd had a very worthy job—but what else could Cara have hoped for? It had turned out that Victoria was a paediatric nurse. An *angel*.

Her perfect figure and shiny white teeth had been a hit with the guys, that was for sure, and very quickly Tom and his wife had become part of their group.

Until Covid had hit.

Emergency services had been classed as essential workers, so they'd still had to work, and somehow—terribly—Victoria had got Covid. The stunning Amazon Cara had considered her to be had been struck down, her fight against the disease complicated by asthma, and Victoria had been taken into hospital and placed on a ventilator.

Cara hadn't seen much of Tom after that. Understandably, he hadn't been at any of their shouts. She'd hoped he was at home, looking after his son, and not ill with Covid himself. There had been some talk of developing a vaccine, but the government had said it was at least a year away.

And then had come the news, passed down

from someone in the ambulance crew to Blue Watch, to Green Watch. Victoria had succumbed to Covid.

She was the first person Cara had personally known who had died from the disease and it had struck her harder than she'd ever imagined. It had come close, this invisible disease, and it could be fatal.

She had only been able to imagine how Tom had felt.

She hadn't wanted him to think that she didn't care enough about him to ring. So she'd rung Tom's house, left her condolences as an answerphone message. She'd hand-delivered a card through his letterbox, called his name, but there had been no answer and nothing else she could do.

When the funeral had been announced, she hadn't been able to go. Numbers had been extremely limited. But the funeral home had offered to stream the service online, so she'd watched it that way—attended that way whilst on duty at the station, watching on a laptop. Wishing she could be there to support her good friend Tom. She'd only seen him briefly in the stream, but he'd looked pale and shattered and her heart had ached for him and Gage.

He'd been off for about a month in total. The first job she'd seen him at, she'd gone to him and wished she could wrap her arms around him tightly, hug him and hold him in her arms for ever, but due to Covid restrictions the most they'd been able to do was bump elbows.

It hadn't seemed enough. Nowhere near enough. Her heart had still ached for him.

'How are you?' she'd asked him, standing a good two metres away.

'I'm okay. Thanks for asking.'

'You and Gage doing all right? Is there anything I can do?'

He'd shaken his head. 'No. Thanks. I got your card. It meant a lot.'

'I wanted you to know you were being thought about. I couldn't come to the funeral because of the restrictions.'

'I know.'

'I watched it online.'

'You did?'

She'd nodded, smiled warmly at him. 'If you ever need anything…even if it's just someone to talk to… I want you to feel you can call me. Any time and I'll listen. Rant. Rave. I'm here for you, okay?'

She'd seen his eyes redden and water, and had been touched that her offer had affected him so. If only she'd been able to reach out to hug him!

That all felt so long ago, but it wasn't. Not really.

So, yes, her feelings for Tom ran deep. There was attraction, but there was respect for all that had gone before—and the knowledge that no matter what she felt for him she could never live up to Victoria.

Cara was everything that Victoria had not been. Cara was a good head shorter than Tom's late wife. She had thick, strong muscles, from weightlifting at the gym every day, whereas Victoria had been lithe from Pilates. Cara had tattoos around both wrists and running up her forearms. Tom's wife had had none, and her only body modification had been pierced ears. Cara considered herself to be stocky, and there was nothing she loved more than to hang out in her gym clothes, or in boots and jeans and a tee. She'd never worn a heel in her life. Had never worn a pretty dress. Cara was a tomboy, through and through. Victoria...? She'd seemed to go everywhere in long, silhouette flattering dresses, that flowed and billowed around her, as if she was some sort of ethereal nymph. Graceful and elegant. Something Cara could never hope to be.

They were chalk and cheese.

So any feelings she had for Tom could never be reciprocated.

He just wouldn't see her the way she wanted him to.

CHAPTER TWO

RAIN POURED DOWN as Cara ran from her vehicle towards The Crusader, her jacket held over her head so that she didn't get wet hair. There was nothing worse than trying to enjoy a nice drink, but having cold, wet rain, dripping down the back of her neck.

She pushed open the heavy wooden doors, decorated with multi-coloured stained-glass, inhaling the familiar scent of hops and bar food. She shook her jacket as she scanned the bar area, searching for Tom.

Most of Green Watch were already there, and had command of both the pool tables and the darts board. She spotted Tom and a couple of other paramedics sitting at the games room bar, chatting. A few colleagues turned and greeted her, asking her to join them, and to add her name to the list at the pool table as she was such a good player.

'I'll just grab a drink first, then I'll be over.'

'We'll put your name up for you.'

'Thanks.' She smiled and headed over to the bar, deliberately going to where Tom was to say hi. Her heart fluttered in anticipation. He looked up as she came over and a broad, genuine smile broke across his face, lighting up those gorgeous blue eyes of his.

'Hey…look who it is. What can I get you?'

'Just a dry white wine, please.' She gave her order to the barmaid, Kelly.

'Still raining?' Tom asked.

She nodded. 'Cats and dogs.'

Kelly placed Cara's drink on the bar and Tom handed the barmaid a note.

'You playing pool tonight?'

'Always. You?'

Tom looked over at the chalkboard on the wall to check his name. 'Looks like I'm on just before you.'

'Ah, okay… Well, I'm planning to wipe the floor with you this evening. Make up for the last time.'

He laughed. 'You're going to have to bring your A game.'

'I know no other kind.'

They clinked glasses, then both took their drinks and walked over to the high tables and stools that surrounded the pool table area, taking a place by the window, which was steamed up on the inside.

'How's that family? Have you heard any more? The Websters?' she asked.

That was the thing with her job. You could be there for people, at the worst time of a family's life, but you didn't always get to hear the end of the story.

'The kids were sent home with an aunt, I think. Mum and Dad were kept in for observation, and I think the dad might be in there for a while.'

'What about his burn? Superficial? I never got a good look at it.'

'Second degree. The plastic surgeons were going to take a look, last I heard, because of how the burn was over his arm and hand. They don't want him to lose any movement or function.'

'Good. Well, I hope they're able to move on from this. It's going to be tough, losing their home, but the most important thing is that everyone survived. Houses can be replaced. People can't.'

'I think they may have some trouble moving on, though.'

'How so?' she asked.

She saw that some of the Green Watch crew were listening in to their conversation.

'They didn't have insurance.'

'What? Oh, no!' That was awful! Without insurance, they wouldn't have any money coming in to help get them somewhere else. Or to replace furniture. 'There must be something we can do for them?'

Cara's colleague Reed stepped away from the table and said, 'We could always do a fundraiser for them? Throw a party, or something? Ask for donations?'

Cara looked to Tom. 'Maybe… Do you think we could?'

He shrugged. 'I don't see why not. It would help them out, for sure.'

She thought about it. 'What sort of fundraiser, Reed?'

He took a shot, pocketing a striped ball, lining up his white cue ball perfectly for him to take on the black and win the game.

'Let me think…' He stooped low over the table, sank the black and won the game, commiserating with his opponent. 'We could ask for donations from local businesses? Auction them off?'

'We could auction promises,' Tom said. 'I saw this show once on TV where they did that. It was quite fun. Businesses donate a meal for two, for example, or a cleaner for the day, and people just auction something they're good at.'

Cara nodded. 'Like what? I guess I could run someone through a gym training session. What about you?' she asked both Tom and Reed.

Reed smiled. 'I could auction off a kiss.' He wiggled his eyebrows suggestively, causing everyone around them to laugh.

Hodge, their chief fire officer, who'd been listening over by the darts board, called over. 'Better offer an STD testing kit for afterwards, then!'

Reed pretended to be insulted, but he was smiling. 'Hey, that's...fair.' He laughed. 'I suppose we could always do one of those naked firemen calendars?'

Cara blushed at the idea.

Tom shook his head. 'They can't wait ages to get the money. They need it quickly. Whatever we arrange, it would have to be sooner, rather than later.'

Hodge nodded, thinking. 'I like the auction of promises idea. And getting companies to maybe donate items that the Websters need.'

Cara smiled. 'What do you think, Tom?'

'I'm happy to help in any way I can. I'm sure I can get a lot of the other paramedics to join in and spread the word if we have some sort of special night planned.'

'You could be a naked gardener, Tom!' Reed called, winking at Cara.

Cara felt her cheeks flush wildly at the suggestion. Tom? *Naked?* Now, that was usually an image she tried *not* to think about. Not because she didn't think he'd look good—because there was no way Tom wasn't beautiful all over—it was just because… Well, if she started thinking that way she'd never stop. And she was always trying to be respectful. Respectful of Victoria. Of Tom's loss. Of Gage. Thinking naughty thoughts could lead them down the wrong path, and there was no way in hell she was going to stupidly jeopardise her friendship with him by blurting out that she fancied the pants off him.

She hoped Tom hadn't noted the suggestive wink Reed had sent her way. She would have to have a word with him later and tell him to back off.

Cara sipped at her wine and just smiled at Tom, shaking her head as if to say, *What is he like, eh?*

'Tom. You're up next to play.'

Tom got up to the table and started racking up the balls for the next game. She watched him, wishing she could just look at him and see him as a friend, but these feelings for Tom were getting stronger every day. She had to find a way to control them!

Just as she was wondering whether she might have to avoid him for a bit—although did absence make the heart grow fonder?—the doors to the pub opened up, bringing in a burst of rain, and cold wind, and the sudden surprising outline of her father, hunkered down under an umbrella being held by his uniformed chauffeur!

At first Cara thought she was imagining things. Her father the Earl of Wentwich in a London pub? It couldn't be. Her eyes had to be deceiving her. She even gave them a rub—only to realise as she took another sip of her wine, that her father's doppelganger was headed straight for her.

'Cara, darling!'

Her cheeks flushed and she looked about her, keen for her crewmates not to realise who this was. She'd always tried to hide the fact that she was an earl's daughter, and although Hodge knew, he respected her enough to keep her secret, as she'd requested.

She'd worked damned hard to be accepted as someone who could give as much to being a firefighter as a man and prove to her crew that she could do exactly what they could.

Run into a burning building? *Check.* Carry a one-hundred-and-seventy-pound man in a fireperson's lift? *Check.* Keep up with the drills and the work and not expect any leeway for the fact that she was a girl? *Check.*

Cara dragged hold of her father's arm and quickly steered him in the other direction. 'What are you doing here?' she asked him in harsh whispered tones.

'I wanted to make sure you're all right.'

'Of course I am! How did you even know that I was here?'

'I tracked your phone using that app thing.'

Dammit! How had she forgotten to remove that after showing him how it worked?

'Dad, you shouldn't be here.'

'Why not? I thought it was time I met your team. Or are you ashamed of me?' He lifted his chin, smiling at her.

'Of course I'm not ashamed. But there are ways and means, Dad, and this isn't one of them.'

'No?' He stepped past her and headed straight for Hodge, reaching out his hand for a handshake. 'Hello. I'm Cara's dad.'

Hodge glanced at Cara. 'Lord Wentwich! Pleasure to meet you, My Lord. You have a fine daughter.'

Her father beamed. 'I like to think so, but

I wouldn't know because I hardly ever get to see her.' he said, directing his words in her direction, eyebrow raised.

Cara swallowed hard. All her work, all that time spent proving that she was just like everyone else, was about to crumble. She could sense it happening. It happened every time someone found out about who she really was. It changed people. It changed their behaviour towards her. And she didn't want her crew joking around, bowing and scraping every time she came into the room. It was stupid, and something she'd never liked.

When Leo had found out who she was, at first he'd been impressed. And then she'd quickly discovered that he was only staying with her for the fact that he could use her money and name to get the things that he wanted. He'd never been there for her. He'd never even been *attracted* to her. Something she'd realised in the most horrendous way. The things he had said...

'We were just talking about organising an evening to help a family that lost their entire home in a fire today,' Hodge told her father.

'*Really?* How awful. Our kitchens caught fire once. Terrible thing. I can't begin to imagine how they must feel.'

'We were thinking about a fundraiser. Getting businesses to donate furniture or goods, or raffle prizes. If you know of anyone who could help us out with that we'd very much appreciate it.'

Her father nodded, clearly thinking. Then his eyes lit up brightly as a thought occurred to him, and Cara knew instinctively that she was not going to enjoy the words that came out of his mouth next.

'The problem with those sorts of evenings is that you have to have the right kind of people attending. People with lots of disposable income, who are willing to throw crazy amounts around.'

'*Dad—*'

'You could hold it at my place—Higham Manor. In fact, we're holding an event at the end of the month to celebrate Cara's mother's birthday. We could make it a fundraising event and this family…the…er…'

'The Websters.'

He smiled his thanks to Hodge. 'The Websters could attend, too. In fact, let's invite them as my special guests.'

'That's amazing, Lord Wentwich! Thank you! That will certainly help keep our costs down.'

'Don't mention it. I'm pleased to help. Let's make it a masked ball. We could have music, dancing, and then the auction fund-raiser. You'll be there, Cara. Won't you?' He faced her with a smile.

Her father knew she wouldn't be able to refuse him now. He had her snared in a corner with no way out.

She would have to go. This wasn't just about her mother any more—it was about both her families. Her blood family and the people she thought of as her *real* family. Green Watch.

And Tom.

'Of course I will,' she said through gritted teeth as she stared at her father, both hating him for pulling this trick to get what he wanted—her at Higham Manor—but also grateful to him for coming up with what had to be the best way for the Webster family to get funds for a new home.

Who was she to get in the way of a family rebuilding their lives?

Hodge, Reed, Tom and all the others beamed, but she could sense the questions from some of them, and could already see Reed and James Blake and David Garcia looking at her differently.

They'd learned something new about her tonight. That her family had a manor house. That her father had a chauffeur.

That she was *different* from them.

Tom knew about her family already. It wasn't a secret to him. But he knew how much she didn't want the others to know. She hoped he would help protect her from their probing questions once her father had returned to his chauffeur-driven car.

'So it's settled, then!' Hodge beamed. 'Cara knows the time and date—don't you, darling?'

She nodded.

'I'll get my PR man on it first thing…start working on the donors in advance and seeing what prizes we can come up with.'

Hodge nodded. 'If you need us to help, just let us know.'

Her father clapped his hand to Hodge's shoulder. 'Don't worry. I can take care of everything. You guys continue to do your important work and concentrate on saving lives. I'll do the rest.' Her father shook Hodge's hand, then turned to her and kissed her on both cheeks. 'I'll leave you to your evening, then. It's been good to see you, Cara. I can't wait to see you at the ball. I know you won't let me or your mother down.'

And then he was gone, before she could say anything, and before she could blow her top. He did this every time. Took charge. He was used to it, of course, but it was one of the main reasons why she had left home as quickly as she'd been able to—to try and forge her independence. Why she'd tried to distance herself from her father's crazy influence.

They'd all left home. Cara and her three brothers. But of course her brothers were left alone to deal with their own lives. It was different for her. It was as if her father couldn't let go and kept interfering.

'Your Ladyship!' Reed bowed. 'I never knew I was in the presence of such class!'

'Give it a rest.'

She turned away and headed for the loo. She just needed a minute to gather herself. Splash her face with cold water and adjust to the fact that now everyone knew. It would no doubt get even worse once they'd actually been to Higham Manor and seen how she'd grown up. But what could she do?

As she stared at her reflection in the mirror she tried to tell herself that maybe it was better that it was all out in the open now. She waited to feel better about it, but nothing changed. She could still feel that tight, twisted feeling in her gut, and a rage against her father she knew she ought not to have. He was her one remaining parent, and she should be grateful for him, but his tight grip on her was like a chokehold sometimes.

Cara splashed her face with cold water, patted it down with paper towels and then girded herself for heading back outside. She yanked open the door and waiting outside for her was Tom. Dear Tom. Because he knew. Knew how she must be feeling.

Why wasn't she allowed to run straight into his arms?

'Hey. Want to get out of here?' he said, looking deep into her eyes. 'I have a getaway car waiting just outside.' He smiled.

He was so sweet. So perfect.

'Thanks. But, no. I need to face it. They were going to find out sometime, right?'

He nodded.

'Besides, I promised to thrash you at pool.'

She could think of nothing better than getting into Tom's car and driving away with him somewhere. Just the two of them. Pretending time didn't exist, their lives didn't exist, and it was just the two of them in each other's company for ever. They could park somewhere nice. Eat fish and chips together and stare up at the stars, holding hands or...

No. I shouldn't think of the 'or'.

He held out his hand and she looked at it as if he was offering her poison. *Take this and you'll be mine.* She wanted to take his hand so much! She often dreamed of it. The two of them walking in a park, as if they were a couple...

Only he wasn't offering his hand in that way, was he? This wasn't romantic. This was friendship. Support.

I'm with you. You've nothing to fear with me by your side. I'll protect you from their comments.

But she also knew that some of the crew—Reed, in particular—suspected she might have feelings for Tom, and if she returned to the pool table holding his hand she'd never hear the end of it.

'I'll be fine.'

She walked past him, towards her crew, head held high. Hoping that Tom understood.

Tom dropped his hand and watched her go. He had some idea of what she was feeling. Cara had always tried to forge her way through the world on her own merits, for which he was proud of her. He knew she hated it when her father railroaded her back into the world she'd used to exist in. A world in which she'd felt stifled and from which she had rebelled.

He followed her back to the pool table. It was set up, ready for him to break. Cara waited with her cue, determinedly chalking the tip.

Tom selected one from the rack on the wall and hefted it, feeling its weight, how it felt in his hands. Happy with his selection, he took the small cube of blue chalk that Cara had put down on the side, near one of the pockets, and chalked the end before bending down and lining up his white ball. He broke up the triangle of stripes and solid balls, sending them in all directions, pocketing a solid ball and giving himself another go.

'Are you rich?' Reed was asking Cara, downing the last of his pint.

Cara shook her head. 'No, I'm not. Look, I know you must all have questions, but there's a reason I've not spoken about that part of my life, okay? I'd prefer it if you all just left it alone.'

Tom had an easy shot he could take, but a part of him wanted to annoy Reed, so he went around the table to take a more difficult shot—which meant moving Reed from his position next to Cara.

'Excuse me.'

Reed backed off and headed over to the bar to refill his glass, and Tom smiled at Cara before taking his shot and missing.

Cara smiled back at him. 'Get ready to be thrashed,' she said.

He watched her pot ball after ball. She was very good. And he admired her for rolling with the punches and not leaving the pub after her father's visit. It would have been so easy for her to grab her jacket and run, but she hadn't. She'd faced it out. And he knew it was because she felt Green Watch were like her family. The family she'd always wanted. There was no way she was going to run from them.

Cara was down to her last ball before the black, but the striped ball rattled in the corner pocket and refused to go in. 'Damn!'

Tom laughed. His turn now. He looked at the layout of the balls on the table, planning his route of play. Each ball went in, one by one, with the white ball lining up for the next shot exactly as he'd intended, until he'd potted all his solids and was left on the black. It was at a tricky angle. If he missed it he would leave the table open for Cara to win the game.

'No pressure!' Cara said teasingly.

He glanced at her, warmth filling him at the smile on her face. The way her eyes gleamed in the light. He enjoyed his time with her immensely. Hours with Cara were never wasted.

She made him feel strong again. Something he'd lost since Victoria died. Losing her had left him feeling in limbo, struggling to be everything for his son Gage. And when Gage was finally asleep in bed there was hardly any energy left for him at all. He was exhausted.

Cara was helping to carry him through his grief. Always there for him. Speaking to him on the phone, or in a text, even in the later hours of the night when he was feeling particularly alone. He owed her a great deal that he could never repay.

That said, he wasn't going to throw this game. It would insult her, for a start.

Tom lined up the shot, steadied his breathing and struck the white ball. It connected with the black. Perfect angle. And the black headed over to the bottom right corner pocket and dropped in. Game won.

'Yes!' He turned in triumph to Cara, who laughed, and he pulled her into a hug, kissing the top of her head and trying not to be affected by the way her hair smelled of flowers, or how she felt in his arms. Fighting the urge to keep her in his arms longer than he should.

I need to let her go. Others are watching.

He stepped away from her, smiling, grabbing their glasses from the table. 'Another drink?'

She shook her head, looking strange. 'Just a lemonade or something, please.'

'Okay.' And he headed to the bar, determined not to look back at her, because his body was reacting in ways that it shouldn't do with a friend.

His mind interpreted the maelstrom of thoughts and feelings he was having.

He wanted more of Cara.

Only he couldn't.

And he would need to be strong to fight the feelings that were coursing hotly through his blood and toying with his concentration.

The call had come through as *'Person trapped'.* Which could mean anything. But the address was at a children's play park.

Green Watch clambered into their appliance and set off to their destination, lights flashing to get them through the burgeoning traffic.

Cara watched the houses and cars flash by, thinking over the events of the previous night. Her father showing up, playing the magnanimous hero and helping them out of a spot by offering to have a fundraising night at Higham Manor. Revelling in his role as a saviour. It was the sort of thing that he fed off, but the part he enjoyed most was interfering in her life. Why did he do it? And so often? Cameron, Curtis and Clarke didn't have the same problem.

As they pulled up at the park they jumped out to assess the situation, and quickly discovered that the person trapped was a teenage girl who had inserted herself into a baby swing as a dare. All her friends stood around her, drinking from cans and smoking, laughing at her predicament. Clearly, they all thought it was hilarious.

Hodge took point as always, forging his way through the girl's friends to assess the situation.

'What's your name, love?'

'Sienna.'

'And how did you end up in a baby swing?'

The baby swing was suspended by two thick metal chains, but the seat itself looked to be of moulded black rubber. Flexible, somewhat, but strong, all the same. Cara knew they wouldn't want to cut the chains or the seat, causing damage to the play park and therefore a headache for the local council, so this was probably going to be a pretty easy extraction by Green Watch using a bit of muscle power.

Once Sienna had explained the dare, Hodge asked her one final question. 'And are you hurt anywhere?'

'No.' Sienna's cheeks were inflamed and red as her friends recorded the situation, no doubt to put on social media later. 'Are you gonna cut me out with the Jaws of Life?'

Hodge shook his head. 'No need for that. We just need a couple of strong arms to get you out of this pickle.' He turned and motioned to Cara and the others. 'Cara? You and Reed can lift and I'll hold the seat in place.'

'Okay.'

There was a lot of squealing from Sienna. Laughter. Complaining that they were tickling her or pinching her as they hauled her upwards so Hodge could pull downwards on the rubber seat. The chains clanked and clanged as they swung this way, then that, until eventually they freed the embarrassed teen and set her back on her feet.

'There you go,' said Hodge. 'And next time you want to play on the swings stick to the ones meant for older kids, yes?'

Sienna nodded. 'Thanks.'

They headed back to the appliance. If only all their jobs could be so easy. If only all their calls could be as simple as getting people out of sticky situations.

Perhaps Cara needed a fire crew to help her out of the situation with her dad?

Back at the station, Cara had barely got the kettle on when her mobile phone, which she'd set on silent, vibrated in her back pocket. She pulled it out and saw her dad's name. She let out a breath, not sure that she wanted to read the message. What could it be now?

Hey, Cara. Just a reminder about the fundraiser. It may be for the Webster family, but it's still your mum's evening, too, and she would have loved to see you attend dressed as a lady. It's what she would have wanted. A dress and heels, please. Have your hair done. Makeup. I'll pay. Just do her proud.

Cara stared at the phone in disbelief. He'd had to go there! Getting right to the one thing that he knew Cara felt guilty about!

Serena Maddox had *dreamed* of having a daughter after three boys. She'd loved her sons—of course she had—but she'd longed to have a daughter she could dress in pink and play dolls with, have a special bond with. And Cara disappointed her from the get-go.

She'd very much been a tomboy—playing in the mud with her brothers, going hunting, making dens, playing rough, happy in jeans, not interested in anything remotely pink, and certainly not in dolls or dresses or shoes or handbags.

She'd refused to be railroaded in such a way. It had always been a disappointment to her mother. And when her mother had died Cara had felt the guilt of never giving her what she'd wanted. Not even for one day. And that guilt had caused her to stay in her own lane even more. Because what was the point in doing anything different now? Her mum wouldn't get to see it.

She'd started going to the gym even more, working out, lifting weights. Punishing herself. She'd got tattoos. Hey, she'd already failed at pleasing her mother—why not go for it?

But it had all been grief. Just her way of coping. She wasn't that bad now—though she was still a stranger to anything other than boots or trainers. And pink? There was nothing in her life that was pink. Cara liked black and grey. Didn't own a single handbag. She would feel like a complete alien from another planet if she had to go dress-shopping. Or shoe-shopping! She'd much rather hang out at the gym. The only shops she frequented were grocery stores and bookshops.

At that moment in time, she hated her father.

So she punched in the number of the only person she knew she could talk to about this.

Tom.

He answered on the first ring. 'Hey. How are you doing?'

It was so good to hear his voice. She'd not seen him since the night at the pub and she'd missed him. Just hearing his warm voice now made her want to hug the phone tight to her ear and cry.

'Not great,' she said.

'Oh. What's up? Anything I can help with?'

'I hope so. Can I pop round later? I'd like to see you.'

There was a pause as she heard him talk to someone. Gage's voice in the background. 'Sure. I'm just getting Gage ready for bed. When is your shift over?'

'In half an hour. Can I come straight round?'

'Course you can. But Gage might be sleeping, so text me when you're here, so the doorbell doesn't wake him up.'

'Thanks, Tom.'

She ended the call, feeling a little better.

Tom always made her feel good. Always listened when she had a problem. And she thought that he got a lot out of their friendship, too. She was company for him, she thought. Female company...which he had to miss after losing Victoria, right? Someone to talk to in the evenings after Gage had gone to bed.

When she got to his house he let her in, and she went straight into his arms for a long hug. It was as if he knew she needed comfort, and for a while she just stood there, head pressed against his chest, listening to the regular, methodical beat of his heart, her eyes closed in bliss, just breathing him in. He felt so strong. So sturdy. A steady presence.

She wasn't sure how long they stood there in silence, but eventually Tom asked her if she wanted to go into the lounge and he'd make her a drink.

If she was honest, she could have stood there in his arms all night. Not talking. Not speaking to each other. Just communicating through the hug. The need to be held. To be comforted. To feel safe and loved and not judged. For there to be no demands made by either person.

'Sure. Okay.' Reluctantly, she let go of him

and followed him into the lounge, where she sat down on one of his comfy sofas.

'Tea? Coffee? Something stronger?' he asked with a smile from the kitchen doorway.

'Tea's fine, thanks.' She let out a sigh.

'Is it your dad?' he asked when the kettle was on and he'd come back to the lounge whilst waiting for it to boil.

She smiled wryly. 'Who else?'

'What's he said now?'

Cara pulled her phone from her pocket and showed Tom the text.

'Emotional blackmail. Nice.' He handed the phone back. 'What did you say to him?'

'I've not answered yet. I know he's not asking for a big thing. Wear a dress. Wear some heels. Look like a proper fricking lady for a change! But it's just the way he brought my mother into it, you know? He knows how I felt when we lost her and he's using that guilt against me.'

Tom was silent for a moment, as if searching for the right words. 'I wouldn't be happy if someone used me like that either. I'd probably not speak to that person for a while. But this is different. It's your dad. He's the only parent you've got left.'

'Yeah…'

'If you want to turn up at that evening

wearing camo paint and army fatigues, I'll back you one hundred percent…' He smiled.

Cara laughed.

'But if you do decide to give him what he wants, to get him off your back, then I'll back that decision also.'

She sighed. 'What do you think I should do?'

'It's not my decision to make. But if you do go the dress route, I'd take the opportunity to tell your father he can never use your mother against you ever again.'

'Agreed. But how would I even know how to wear heels? I'd probably break my ankle.'

'Hey, come on. It's one night. A couple of hours at the most. You run into burning buildings, Cara! The bravery that takes? I couldn't do it. But I have no doubt that you can do this.'

She looked into his eyes. Saw the warmth there. The love. The support. If he had belief in her, then maybe she should have belief in herself too.

'Okay.'

'You're going to do it?'

'I'm going to do it!'

She laughed with relief. Glad that Tom had helped her see sense. He was right. It was one night. Three hours? Four? And then it would all be over and she could tell her father that she'd done her bit and he needed to let her live her life as she pleased in future.

'Let's have biscuits with that tea,' said Tom. 'I think I have some chocolate digestives to celebrate.'

'Rock and roll.'

CHAPTER THREE

TOM HAD JUST got back into his rapid response vehicle, after treating a suspected cardiac arrest, when a call came through that there had been a multi-car pile-up on one of the main roads in Battersea. He flipped the switch for his blues and twos and told Control to show him as attending, ETA five minutes.

'Roger that. Police and fire crew are also en route.'

The streets were thick with traffic, and in some parts he had to wait as vehicles already in the jam tried to find a way to move aside, to let him through. Moments like this taught him patience. There was nothing he could do, and it was too late now to go back and try an alternative route. In front of him, drivers tooted their horns at one another, and a few wound down windows to make hand gestures to other drivers, telling them to move over a bit more. And slowly, slowly, the cars parted and created a very narrow lane for him to drive down.

He inched his way along until he was finally able to get through the lights, hit a right and drive down a road that was thankfully much clearer and traffic was flowing. This was better. But his anxiety was high. The traffic jam had caused him a significant delay and time counted. Someone could be trapped inside a vehicle, losing blood, losing precious seconds in which their lives might be saved.

But despite this he knew he had to use caution still. Every junction, every crossing, every school that he passed could be a potential site of danger for pedestrians or cyclists or other motor vehicles that simply didn't see or hear him. Despite the lights and sirens, it was amazing how many people could be in their own little world when they were out and about. It wasn't unheard of for emergency vehicles to end up in a pile-up themselves.

But he was getting closer.

Then the traffic was beginning to snarl up again, and he had to inch through, until he managed to park behind a police car that itself was parked behind a fire engine.

The street was lit with strobing red and blue lights as he grabbed his jump bag, slipped on a high vis vest and walked towards the accident.

He sucked in a breath at the sight of it.

A blue car lay on its roof, facing in the wrong direction, steam hissing out of its engine. A silver car was on the other side of it, its front crumpled in, airbags deployed. A white van was parked askew to the left of them, the driver's door hanging open, and behind them a lorry that had obviously skidded to avoid them had crossed over into the wrong lane, hitting a small red car.

He could see Hodge, striding around in his white helmet, which told him that Cara had to be on the scene somewhere. Maybe one of the team currently gathered around the blue car. All around police were trying to establish a perimeter, as nosy onlookers gathered. Some officers were comforting people kerbside. Were they drivers? Walking wounded?

Tom got Hodge's attention and the chief fire officer came over to him.

'Hey, where do you want me?'

Hodge pointed. 'The driver of the blue car needs the most attention. She's trapped inside the vehicle, unconscious, breathing sounds bad, respirations are really low. We've got her on oxygen and Cara's holding C-spine. There was a child in the back, strapped into a baby seat. We've got her out. Seems fine, just a little shaken up, but she will need a check. Driver of the white van is fine—he avoided impact, as did the lorry driver. The guy driving the silver car has whiplash, and the passengers of the red car are in shock and have a few cuts and bruises.'

'Most of them have been lucky, then?'

'If you call a car crash lucky, yeah.'

Tom hurried forward towards the blue car that was upside down on its roof. He acknowledged Cara with a quick smile. 'Morning.'

'Good morning,' she said.

'We really need to stop meeting like this.'

She smiled at him as she lay on the road on her side, her arms within the car, holding the driver's neck. 'We must.'

'Was she unconscious when you got here?' asked Tom.

'Yes.'

'And hasn't woken up?'

'No. And her breathing has been slow and erratic. I can hear a wheeze.'

Thankfully, Cara and her crew had already got the driver on oxygen. Tom reached through the broken glass and past the deflated airbag to place his stethoscope on the patient's chest.

'Agreed. I think she's asthmatic.'

He felt dread wash over him. Something he always felt now, when he had to attend to an asthmatic, since the death of his wife.

Asthma was the complication in Victoria's medical history that had led to her death from Covid at the beginning of the pandemic. Hearing this woman wheeze, seeing her pale face, reminded him of his wife's attacks.

There'd been one time when she'd totally collapsed. It had been Christmas, and they'd invited both sets of parents over to their house. Victoria had woken that morning feeling breathless. They'd argued, because Tom had said they should cancel their guests, as clearly she wasn't well, but Victoria, not willing to let people down on Christmas Day, had simply shaken her head, used her inhalers and said she'd power through. He'd helped her peel veggies and prepare the table, and then he'd set off in the car to fetch his parents, who didn't have a vehicle, leaving Victoria at home.

She'd promised, she'd stay sitting down, reading a book or watching TV, until he got back. Only when he had returned they'd walked in, full of Christmas cheer, with his parents calling out 'Merry Christmas!', only to find Victoria lying on the floor of the kitchen, face pale, wheezing terribly, close to losing consciousness.

He'd called an ambulance so fast! His parents had taken over the cooking and when Victoria had got better and was finally allowed home, they all had Christmas dinner really late that night.

Had *this* woman been suffering, but thought she was okay to drive her car? Or had the attack started in the car? Maybe even caused the crash?

Tom didn't know, but the woman's airway was his primary concern. ABC. Airway. Breathing. Circulation. Airway came first. He organised a nebuliser first.

'Let's get a cervical collar on.'

He pulled the one he had from his bag and positioned it around the woman's neck. Then he could continue with his primary survey.

Cara, now free from holding the C-spine, joined her crew to help with prepping the vehicle for extraction.

Tom could see cuts on the woman's face and arms, but had no idea if she'd sustained any broken bones, and he wouldn't know for sure until they got her free of the vehicle. He attached a SATs monitor to her, checking her oxygen levels, and then Cara was asking him to move back, so they could safely break the glass around the vehicle, ready for cutting.

He stood back, knowing he could do no more until she was free, but he was worried. Focused. He wanted her out of the vehicle so he could treat her properly, but this next bit would take some time.

Cara's crew had already stabilised the vehicle, so that it wouldn't move as they cut through the metal. They were cutting through the struts to take the stress off the roof of the car, freeing it to make it easier to free the patient.

Cara used power tools to cut through the fender and expose the door hinges, before Reed removed the doors all round. Then they cut the post above the door hinges and began using another power tool to lift the car free from the dashboard and create even more room, whilst Hodge continued to stabilise the vehicle from the rear.

All Tom could hear was the crunch of metal. He checked his watch. This was time-critical. The woman could stop breathing at any moment. Behind him, other ambulances had arrived and were checking the walking wounded, so he could retain his focus on the asthmatic patient.

He wondered what her name was. Where

she was going. What she'd thought her day would involve when she'd set off this morning. Had it just been another day? Who did she have worrying about her?

Cara's crew had secured the vehicle once more, then moved the car seat out of the way, and were now calling for the backboard so they could slide it in through the rear of the vehicle to get the patient out without causing more damage to the spine or neck.

'Easy now!' Tom called as he helped them guide her out.

Thankfully her legs weren't trapped, and they looked in reasonable shape, though there were cuts to her knees. He had to hope there weren't any internal injuries, but he wouldn't find out until later.

Once she was free and on a trolley, he re-checked his primary survey. Her oxygen levels were low and she was at risk of going into serious respiratory arrest.

'Get her to the hospital now!' he instructed the paramedics helping him.

He had to stand back and watch them take her. He'd done all he could, though he felt, as he often did when seeing an asthmatic patient, that he hadn't done enough. He'd given her medication in the oxygen, but that seemed pathetically little help. It always did—especially if the patient was too far gone into their attack and didn't respond to it.

Would she survive? He didn't even know her name. He hated feeling this way.

He felt a hand on his arm. 'Tom? Are you all right?'

Cara. Her soft voice was balm for his soul. He nodded. Smiled.

'Are you sure? I know this must hit home for you. I'm sure she'll be okay.'

'Thanks. I hope so.'

'Hey, do you want me to pop round later? I could bring a takeaway. Your choice.'

'I don't think I'm in the mood for takeout.'

'How about I come round early and take Gage off your hands for a bit? We haven't played footie together for ages.'

'He'd love that. He loves it when you come. Maybe we should all go out? The fresh air will do me good.'

She smiled. 'Okay. I gotta go now, so I'll see you later? About five-thirty?'

'Perfect.'

He watched her return to her team. They had work to clear up. Their job wasn't over just because the patients were all out.

He was thankful for Cara. Thankful for her friendship. Her insights into his emotional wellbeing. She'd realised how treating an asthmatic would affect him. How the sound of an asthmatic wheeze often chilled his blood, because it reminded him of Victoria's battles with the condition.

He headed back to his car, exchanged his empty oxygen tank for a full one from an ambulance that had not yet left the scene, and then sank into his vehicle to write up his notes.

But as he sat in the car he tried to remember the last time he'd spoken to Victoria. What had their last words to each other been? He couldn't remember. *Why* couldn't he remember? Was his brain trying to protect him from something? Or was it something mundane? He felt their last words ought to have been important. *I love you. I'll miss you. Get well soon.* Only he had a sneaking suspicion it hadn't been those. He'd been panicking over her worsening breathing. Insisting she call a doctor. But she'd refused, saying it wasn't that bad, and had isolated herself in their bedroom whilst suggesting he slept on the couch—so he didn't get sick, so he could take care of Gage.

By the time he'd got an ambulance and the crew had assessed her, she'd barely been able to talk. Her eyes had been wide with fear from the strain of breathing and trying to get desperately needed oxygen into her lungs. The paramedics had talked to her as they'd carried her down the stairs in a portable chair. Reassuring her. Telling her she was doing fine. Not much further to go. Then Gage had begun to cry, frightened by these strange men in his home, no doubt sensing the tension and upset, and Tom had been trying to soothe their son. Holding him tight, stroking his hair, telling him to say goodbye to Mummy.

Had he said anything important to Victoria? Or had he missed the opportunity, believing that he would be able to speak to her later, on the phone? An occasion that had never materialised, because when they'd got her to the hospital they'd anaesthetised her and put her on a ventilator and she'd never come off it.

So their last words to each other must have been before that. They could have been anything!

'I'd better sleep downstairs, then, so I can look after Gage.'

'Do you need anything? A cup of tea?'

'I'll leave your plate just outside the door. Try and eat.'

Maybe those words said *I love you*, only in a different manner?

He hoped so. He hoped she'd interpreted

them in that way. Because he knew that when he *had* told her that he loved her she hadn't been able to hear him. Because she'd been unconscious, with a tube down her throat, and dying. He'd had to say it over the phone, with a nurse holding the handset to her ear. But by then it had been too late.

He hoped the lady today had someone who would sit by her bedside. Someone who loved her. That they would get the chance to say to each other all the things they wanted to say.

Because it was awful when you couldn't tell someone how you really felt.

Cara rang the doorbell, smiling in anticipation of hearing Gage race his father to the door, so that he could greet their guest first.

She saw his little figure through the glass and felt her heart swell. Gage was a wonderful little boy, delightfully happy and curious and funny, despite all that he had gone through.

He stretched to reach the door handle and finally swung the door open. 'Cara!' He leapt up at her and she caught him in her arms, swinging him up high, easily, and whirling him around.

'Hello, you! Are you ticklish today? Let me see!' And she put him down on the ground and began to tickle him under his arms, causing him to giggle and laugh and collapse on the doormat hysterically. 'Hmm... Maybe... What about here? Or here?'

Gage laughed and laughed, squirming, enjoying the game, and then suddenly Tom was there, looking great in dark jeans and a white tee, and she felt the usual wave of heat and awareness wash over her, taking her breath away.

She released Gage and stood up straight. 'Hey.'

'Hey.' He smiled back, and she was glad to see he seemed a little brighter than earlier at the accident.

'Want to come out and play?' she joked.

'Let me just grab our jackets.'

'And a ball?'

'Ah, yes. Of course. Gage? Go and fetch your football from the box by the back door, please.'

'Yes, Daddy.'

Tom ruffled his son's hair as he ran past.

'He's getting big,' said Cara. 'What are you feeding him?'

'He'll eat anything. The boy's not picky. Must be a growth spurt.'

Gage came back, ball tucked under his arm. 'Are we going to the park?'

'We certainly are,' she answered. 'Come on, you. I need you to show me your moves and what you've learned since I saw you last.'

As they walked down the street to the park, Gage in the middle, holding Cara's hand on the left and Tom's hand on the right, Gage talked non-stop. About keepy-uppies, how many goals he'd scored against his dad at the weekend, how he was going to be a pro footballer when he was older.

Cara looked over his head at Tom to smile and share in the wonder of this little boy. She loved little Gage. He was perfect. Just the kind of kid she'd wish to have herself, if she was ever lucky enough to have a family of her own. Not that that was looking likely. Men didn't seem to notice her, which only reinforced her doubts about her own attractiveness.

Besides, she was always at work, her body and face hidden behind her firefighter's uniform and helmet. The only men who did notice her were her crew, and none of them were single. They were all married or in long-term relationships, apart from Reed, and they only saw her as a friend and colleague. Someone they could trust with their lives. Who had their backs. They didn't see her as potential love interest. Did they even think she was pretty?

They were protective of her, though. Like extra big brothers. Which was kind of nice, but could be scary for guys who did take an interest. Like Leo, for example. Her crew mates hadn't been fond of him. *Suspicious* might be a better word for how they'd felt about Cara's ex. And when Leo had ripped out her heart and walked away without so much as a backward glance, they'd been queueing up to go visit him and *'have a word'*.

She'd appreciated the offer, and the sentiment...but by then she'd felt so humiliated, she'd wanted nothing further to do with him.

Cara stole glances at Tom as they chatted with Gage and wished that he saw her as more than a friend. There'd been moments where her hopes had been raised. Once, she'd caught him looking at her oddly as she'd helped him put together a treehouse in the back garden. The way he'd been looking at her had made her feel self-conscious.

'What?' she'd asked.

'Oh...nothing. I was just daydreaming.'

'About what?'

He'd shaken his head. *'Nothing.'*

She'd returned to hammering in nails, holding two of them in her mouth, but it had been enough to make her feel that she'd been assessed and found wanting.

Would Victoria have helped him build a treehouse? No. She'd have left him to it. Brought out the occasional cup of tea and told him how good it was looking, but that would have been all. And yet there she'd been, in the scruffy tee shirt she used when she was decorating and some cargo pants, covered in sawdust and sweat!

Hardly attractive!

Tom was so handsome and so deserving of some happiness and she felt she could provide it. But she didn't have many friends outside of the fire service, and she didn't want to ruin the friendship she had with Tom by complicating it. Besides, he probably wasn't ready to date yet. He was too busy being a father to Gage and he would *never* be interested in her. No matter how much she wished he would.

The park wasn't that busy, and they managed to find a space where they could kick around the ball. Gage and Tom used their discarded jackets as goal posts and Tom went into goal, leaving Cara and Gage as opposing team members, desperate to score. Around them, birds sang in the trees and squirrels searched the ground for acorns or whatever it was that squirrels searched for. Gage sent one shot wide, the ball flying over to a bunch of oaks, and a grey squirrel shot halfway up a tree trunk and peered at them as if in reproach.

'I'll get it!' Gage said, running after it, his little legs pumping hard. He picked up the ball and came back, throwing it past her to take a shot at goal.

'Hey!' Cara laughed and let him take his shot.

Tom paused and let the ball roll past him and score, pretending he'd been too slow to stop it.

'Yay! One nil to me!' Gage lifted his tee shirt above his head, like footballers did on television, and ran around until he fell over, collapsing with laughter.

Cara scooped him up, righted his tee and then tried to dribble the ball past him. Gage tackled her. She let him have it and he scored again.

'Oh, you're too good for me!' she said, hands thrown in the air, and then she, too, collapsed onto the grass.

Gage jumped on her and she scooped him up above her, whirling him around like an airplane. Eventually Tom took him from her arms and whirled him to his feet.

'I'm exhausted. Who fancies ice cream?'

'Me, me, me!' Gage said.

Tom raised an eyebrow at Cara. 'Fancy a mint choc chip?'

'You know the way to my heart!' she joked, wishing that he really would find the way.

Maybe he would one day. Maybe she was wrong to think he would never see her in that way. One thing she knew for sure was that Tom was worth waiting for...and if it was meant to take some time, then she was okay with that. Being his friend for now would have to be enough. She just hoped he wouldn't do something stupid, like fall in love with someone else, so she'd have to stand there on the sidelines and watch him with another woman.

Tom held out his hand, which she took, and he hauled her to his feet.

They gathered the jackets and headed towards the ice cream van at the other end of the park. One mint choc chip, one strawberry and one chocolate ice cream later, they were sitting on the benches by the public aviary cages, watching the budgies flit from perch to perch as they licked their ice creams.

'So, have you decided what you're going to wear yet for the ball?' Tom asked.

She sighed. 'No. I keep trying to ignore it.'

'You've only got to the end of the month.'

She changed the subject. 'What are *you* going to wear?'

'I have a tux tucked away somewhere. All I have to do is find a mask.'

She stared at him for a moment as an idea formed. Was she brave enough to ask? Would this be expecting their friendship to go to places it wasn't ready to go?

'Would you help me?'

'With what?'

She blushed. She didn't normally ask for help, and for some reason this seemed like a really big thing to ask of him. It seemed... intimate.

'Help me find a dress? I have no idea what type of thing to look for and I'm just not used to going into those types of places.'

He laughed nervously. 'You mean shops?'

'Girly places.'

'You think *I am*?'

'Well, you must have sat around waiting for Victoria to shop sometimes? Offered an opinion on an outfit? I would like a male opinion.'

She honestly thought he was going to say no. He seemed to think about it for an inordinate amount of time. Looked as if he was going to turn her down. As if he was trying to think of an excuse without hurting her feelings. Maybe she should just let him off the

hook? Tell him she was being silly? Of course
he didn't have to go shopping with her! What
kind of man enjoyed going clothes-shopping
with a girlfriend? None that she knew.

'Okay.'

'You will?' She brightened. At the fact that
he'd said yes and the fact that it meant spending a lot more time with Tom.

'Sure. Why not?'

Cara flung her arms around him and kissed
him on the cheek. 'Thanks!'

She released him to lick her ice cream, her
body thrumming with excitement. One question down. Now to ask the next.

Gage got up and idly dawdled over to the
bird cages for a closer look.

Cara lowered her voice. 'Could I ask you
one more thing?'

'Sure. Go for it.'

She hoped she wouldn't blush. She failed.
Miserably. 'Would you come as my date?'
Her cheeks bloomed with heat and she almost
couldn't make eye contact with him. 'Only
my dad will try to pair me off with someone
if I turn up alone. Last time it was with this
dimwit called Hugo. The son of one of his
best friends. All he could talk about all night
was stocks and shares. I was bored rigid and

totally embarrassed. With you there… I could avoid that.'

'You mean you don't want to hear my scintillating take on the stock market?' he teased.

He could read her the phone book and she wouldn't mind.

'No, thanks.'

They both laughed, tension released, but she crunched into her waffle cone, painfully aware that he hadn't said yes yet.

'So…you want me to pretend to be your boyfriend?'

She checked to make sure Gage couldn't hear what they were saying, but he appeared to be enamoured of the brightly coloured birds flitting from perch to perch. 'Yes. I know it's asking a lot, and if it makes you uncomfortable then please feel free to say no. I'd totally understand. I'd—'

'I'd be honoured.'

Cara stared at him, fighting the impulse to drop her ice cream cone and plant her lips directly on Tom's. Her heart pounded in her chest.

'Thanks.' she said, instead. 'That means a lot to me.'

Tom shrugged. 'It's no big deal. It's just pretend, right?'

She nodded. 'Right.'

* * *

'It's just pretend, right?'

That sentence kept repeating over and over in Tom's mind all night. Condemning him and teasing him in one stroke.

Cara was amazing. Beautiful, clever—and she loved Gage almost as much as he did! But...what would people say? It hadn't been two years since he'd lost Victoria, and everyone had assumed everything was great between them. Childhood sweethearts? What could possibly go wrong?

People had fallen in love with that idea. They'd thought it was sweet and romantic and perfect. How would they react if they knew what had truly been going on?

He'd believed at the time that marrying Victoria when she discovered she was pregnant was the right thing to do. And it had been! It had allowed him to watch Gage grow up in the same house as him every day. To experience his milestones first-hand. He'd been there for his first word—*Dada*. His first faltering steps. But he'd also seen Victoria change. Almost as if she'd resented having become a mother so soon.

She would palm Gage off on him the second he walked through the door, so she could go off and have 'girl time' with her friends.

They'd argue over simple things Her appearance had mattered to her more than anything else sometimes. She'd spent crazy amounts of money on hair extensions and dresses and heels she never wore, when he'd given her that money for the things Gage needed.

He'd tried so hard to be the best partner he could, but it had never seemed to be enough. She'd always found him wanting, no matter what he did to try and make her happy, and so he'd given up trying. Working long hours. Taking extra shifts. He'd told himself he was doing it for his boy, so they could afford everything he wanted in life, but really he'd been doing it because it was easier to be at work.

What would people think if he started to show that he had feelings for someone else so soon? He didn't want to dishonour Victoria's memory. And Cara? She'd think badly of him for fancying her, surely.

Maybe he was reading more into his feelings for her than he should? Maybe he just *thought* he had feelings for her because she was such a good friend? Because she was so supportive and kind and enjoyed spending time with him and Gage?

I'm just misreading the situation. Grateful for her kindness, that's all.

That was why he hadn't turned down her offer to go dress-shopping with her. He'd thought about it! Going dress-shopping with Victoria had been downright exhausting! Sitting in chairs, watching her go in and out of changing rooms, hearing her asking him if he preferred the scarlet or the crimson...

'They're both red, Vic. Just pick one!'

He had been going to say no. Initially. Watching the woman he had strong feelings for putting on pretty dresses? What if he slipped up and said something incriminating?

And then he'd thought about that idiot ex-boyfriend of hers—Leo. The one who had said all those horrible things about her. About how she wasn't feminine enough. Wasn't woman enough to hold a man. And he'd just known he wanted to go, so that he could see her in all those pretty dresses and build up her confidence a little. If she needed it.

She didn't really want to go out with him. It was just to stop her father interfering again and trying to matchmake.

No. They were just friends. Even if his feelings for her were confusing. He loved Cara, yes—as he loved all of his friends. But he wasn't *in love* with her. At least, he didn't think so. It was just confusing because of how good they were together. How Cara reminded him of who he'd used to be.

So he'd agreed to go shopping with her. Find her a dress. Pretend to be her date at the ball. Maybe as long as they arrived together and were seen together by her father that would be enough. He could leave her to do her thing, and he would go and do his thing. Chat to whoever he knew there. The word about the ball had been spreading, and most of the paramedics who were going to be off duty had agreed to go. Why wouldn't they? They didn't very often get invited to a posh manor house and have the chance to get dressed up, all in the name of a good cause.

He was intrigued himself about the idea of going to Cara's family home. She didn't often talk about her childhood, and he wondered if, by going, he would understand her more. Cara had no airs and graces. She didn't expect to be treated differently because she was the daughter of an earl. She was just one of the guys to most people.

To him... She was that and more.

Tom gave Gage a bath and then read him a bedtime story. His son nodded off halfway through, no doubt exhausted by the football, so Tom left the book on his son's bedside cabinet so they could finish it off tomorrow. He

switched off his lamp and crept back downstairs and sat in his lounge alone.

These were the moments he hated. When
his son was asleep and it was late at night he
felt more alone than he ever did at any other
time.

He missed the simple act of sitting on the
couch with someone, watching a movie,
maybe having a nice glass of wine… He
missed that feeling of connection, of having
someone stroke his arm absently, or someone
resting their head upon his shoulder. He hated
going to bed alone. The bed seemed so big
without anyone else in it. So empty.

Later Tom lay in his bed and stared up at
the ceiling. He thought about Cara. About
the way she'd looked playing football with
his son. Her smile. Her laughter. The way the
sun had caught the auburn tones of her hair,
flashing fire. The way she'd looked at him,
her eyes aglow, brightly gleaming with happiness. The way she'd made Gage laugh. The
way she'd brightened his son's world.

And his.

*What am I doing? I'm reading more into
this than I should. She's just a friend. That's
all she will ever be.*

CHAPTER FOUR

'DAD, NO.' CARA had been hanging her things in her locker at work when her mobile phone had rung.

'Why not? Carenza can fit you in this weekend—she's already told me. All she needs are your measurements and she can whip you up something special for the ball.'

'I don't need a designer to make me a bespoke dress. I'll buy one from a shop. In fact, Tom is taking me out to find a dress later on today.'

Her father sounded doubtful. 'The *paramedic*?'

'Yes.'

A pause. 'You two an item, then?'

'Yes,' she lied, gritting her teeth, wishing she could be saying it with a smile, as if it were actually real.

'Oh, that's a shame. I'd rather told Henry

that you're single. He's bringing along his son Xander to meet you.'

She rolled her eyes. 'Well, Xander can say hello, but that's all he'll get from me. I'm with Tom.' She glanced around to make sure none of her crew mates from Green Watch were within hearing. There'd be no end of questions if they heard that. Not to mention the teasing she'd get. And if they found out it was fake…? It didn't bear thinking about.

Her father sighed. 'All right. But make sure the dress is something special. There's going to be a photographer, and I'm going to want official pictures of the only time my daughter wore a dress.'

'You're getting a photographer for *that*?'

'Not just for you, darling, don't worry. It's good publicity, what we're doing for the Werther family.'

'The Websters.'

'Ah, yes. Well, I've got to go. Do ring me and let me know when you've found something.'

'Fine.'

'And, darling?'

'Yes?'

'Just be careful. With Tom. A lot of men might be interested in you for reasons you don't suspect.'

Poor Dad. He thought lots of men were interested in her because she was a Lady! If only he knew that men didn't see her that way.

'He's not with me because of money, Dad.'

She sighed, wishing she could end this call, because it was becoming awful, and she hated lying to him, even if he was the one who had put her in this position in the first place.

'Just make sure—that's all.'

He said goodbye and ended the call.

Cara stood there, feeling an anger that boiled inside. It was so unfair! Her father was interfering in her life again. As she passed through the gym she gave the punchbag a thump, sending it swinging one way, then the other, before she headed to the canteen to make herself a drink before parade.

Reed and the others were already there, propping up the kitchen counters, slurping their tea from mugs.

'Morning, Cara,' said Reed.

'Morning.'

'Ready for another day?'

She nodded, smiled. 'Absolutely.' She filled the kettle with water, but before she could reach for a mug the station bell sounded. They had a shout.

They headed for the fire engine as Hodge

collected the call report. He met them as they dressed themselves in their uniforms.

'Male trapped in an industrial machine. That's all we have.'

Cara grimaced. That didn't sound good. But she switched herself into work mode and the fire engine, with sirens blaring, pulled out of the station, stopping the traffic, and went roaring in the direction of town.

As they passed the park that she and Tom and Gage had played football in she glanced out of the window, remembering the previous night. It had all been a little awkward after she'd asked Tom to accompany her to the ball as her date. Though she'd made it quite clear it was a fake date, she'd hated lying to Tom.

Why couldn't she just be brave enough to tell him the truth?

Because Victoria was an Amazonian goddess, that's why.

She'd distracted herself from her self-loathing and asked Gage to point out his favourite budgies in the aviary. She'd walked over to the birdcages, embarrassed to turn around and look at Tom. What on earth was he thinking? But eventually they had walked home, neither she nor Tom being overly chatty. Perhaps he was already regretting saying yes? Perhaps she was just being overly sensitive over this issue? Perhaps it was abundantly clear to Tom that this could never be anything but a fake date and so he wasn't worried at all? Because clearly he had no idea about her hidden feelings for him.

Which was just the way she wanted to keep it, thank you very much.

In a strange way she was looking forward to the dress-shopping tonight. Not because of the dresses. No. That part she was dreading. But spending time with Tom was always her favourite thing to do, and tonight he had a babysitter for Gage.

The fire engine sped through the traffic.

Hodge turned. 'Ambulance crew and rapid response are also on their way.'

Reed nudged her. 'Maybe lover-boy will be there.'

She glared at him.

They pulled into an industrialised area. Lots of lorries and vans loading up. A man in a bright yellow high vis jacket stood in the road, directing them to the place they needed to be, which was very much appreciated. He ran to greet them as they pulled up.

'Hi. I'm John—the manager. We've got one of our workers with his arm trapped in an industrial printing machine. It became jammed, and he was trying to clear the blockage, but got his arm trapped inside when it started up again. He's lost a lot of blood and is barely conscious.'

At that moment the rapid response vehicle turned up, with an ambulance and a police car following quickly behind. Tom got out, and he and the other medics were quickly filled in on what had happened.

John led them to the site of the accident.

'Has all this been turned off?' Hodge asked.

'Not all of it.'

'I want everything shut down whilst my crew are here. We don't need any further accidents as they try to help your man here. What's his name?'

'Pete.'

'Okay.' Hodge went over to the man, who was trapped in the machine up to his mid-upper arm and looking pale and weak. 'Pete? We're going to get you out of there, okay?' Hodge turned to John. 'Any chance you can get him a chair or something to sit on? If he passes out he's going to pull on that arm and maybe make his injury worse.'

John nodded and disappeared to get a chair.

Hodge took the opportunity to look at the machinery intently. To see where the arm was caught and if there was any easy way they could extract him.

'Okay, the machine's off Tom, do you want to take a look? It's safe for you to approach now.'

Hodge stepped back and Tom stepped forward. He'd already got an oxygen mask prepped and ready and he secured it to Pete's face.

Cara watched. The poor man! This was going to be a life-changing injury. He'd probably come to work this morning, thinking it was just going to be another ordinary day, but this had happened.

As Tom did his assessment, John came back with the chair.

'Where are your engineers?' asked Hodge. 'We're going to need people who can dismantle this machine, because I don't think you want us just cutting our way through it.'

'Er...no. We don't. I can call Carlos, but he's at home.'

'Anyone else?'

'The business down the road has the same machine as us. I can call them and ask if their engineer is on site? He'd get here quicker than Carlos would, as he doesn't have his own car and would have to rely on public transport.'

Hodge nodded. 'Call them.'

Tom was inserting a cannula for an IV into

Pete's arm. 'I'm giving you fluids and a pain-killer, okay?'

Pete nodded, his eyes barely open. Was he shutting down?

Tom grabbed his mobile. 'Control? I'm at the entrapment call. We need a doctor on site. This guy's going to want stronger painkillers than I can give him.'

'Confirmed. Heli-med en route.'

'Thank you, Control.' He turned to Hodge and the team. 'I can't do anything more until we get him clear of this machine.' He lowered his voice. 'Looking at the arm, I'm thinking we're looking at a possible amputation.'

Cara's heart sank. Pete was young. He had a wedding ring on his finger. She stepped forward. 'Pete? Can you open your eyes for me? Is there anyone we can call for you?'

Pete blinked, bleary-eyed, then nodded. With his free hand he pulled the oxygen mask away from his face. 'Sal. Call Sal. My wife.'

'Give me her number.'

Once he had, Tom put the oxygen mask back onto the man's face and checked his pressures and his pulse. 'He's going into shock.'

At that moment they heard running, and Cara turned to see a guy in dirty navy over-alls appear, puffing, out of breath, his eyes widening at the sight before him. 'You need an engineer?'

Hodge stepped up. 'Yes. We need this machine dismantled so we can free this man. What's your name?'

'Charlie.'

'Okay, Charlie. We need this done quick.'

'I've put on a tourniquet,' said Tom.

'Okay...' Charlie paused.

'Problem?' asked Cara.

'I'm just not very good with blood, and there's...um...a lot of it.' Charlie was starting to turn pale.

'Try not to look at that. Focus on what you need to do. I can help you.' Cara guided him forward with his toolbox and they set to work. They'd been working on the machine for maybe five minutes when a doctor arrived in an orange Heli-med jumpsuit.

'Can everyone just stand back so I can assess the patient, please?'

They all did, waiting and watching.

The doctor listened to the patient's chest, checked his pressures and examined the arm, which was still firmly trapped in the machine.

Pete was nearly completely unconscious.

'How long is it going to take to dismantle this machine?' he asked Charlie.

'Two hours, maybe?'

The doctor shook his head. 'The longer he stays trapped in that machine, the worse this is going to get. He's really struggling. His condition is deteriorating. I think we need to do an upper arm amputation and get him out. That arm is pretty mangled. I don't think there's any chance of saving it, and every second he's in there the more chance there is that infection will complicate matters.'

Tom nodded. 'Agreed.'

'Okay—let's do this.'

Charlie and the others backed off, and Tom and the Heli-med doctor set about preparing for amputation. They injected anaesthetic into Pete, so that he wouldn't feel anything, and began to manage his airway.

The doctor and Tom worked fast. Cara watched them. They moved as a perfect team. The doctor in charge, Tom assisting. This wasn't her first amputation, and she could remember being surprised at how fast someone could remove an arm or a leg. In her head, she'd always imagined it would take time. Carefully cutting through bone and muscle and sinew. Tying off blood vessels. Surely that should take hours? But, no. A couple of minutes and it was done.

Soon Pete was freed from the machine and lowered onto a trolley, where Tom and the other paramedics swarmed around him, getting his pressure back up and stabilising him for the trip to hospital via helicopter.

As Tom led Pete off on the trolley, Hodge got back to asking Charlie to open up the machine, so that they could still remove the mangled amputated arm.

Cara wished she'd had more of an opportunity to talk to Tom, but it had been all hands on deck. She would just have to wait to speak to him later that evening.

Tom knocked on Cara's door, trying not to feel as if he was picking her up for a date. Seriously, when had things changed? Because something had and he wasn't sure when. His feelings for her had crept up upon him, lurking like a shadow, always there but not always noticed. But now that he was *aware*, it was as if he couldn't stop noticing them.

He'd taken great care not to dress like a man going on a date. He wore dark jeans, a black tee, and a flannel shirt over the top. He'd not checked his hair before leaving, despite the almost unstoppable urge to comb it before leaving the house, because he needed this to just be another night out with a mate.

Dress-shopping.

Hmm…

He'd only ever gone dress-shopping before with Victoria, and that had never gone well *at all*. Commenting on the first two outfits had been fine, but after that… He'd always tried his hardest to not seem bored. Once, when one of his friends had passed by, Victoria had let him off the hook and told him he could go. And he had. But when he'd got home she'd called him out on it.

Now, it was a memory that made him cringe. He knew he should have cherished every moment with her. But the truth of the matter was that they'd often let each other down. He wished he'd paid her more attention, but that particular dress-shopping outing had been the day after a huge fight they'd had, and the worse thing was he couldn't even remember what the fight had been about. Maybe work. By then Tom had been working long hours. Picking up extra shifts. Telling himself he was working hard to provide for his family—which he was. He just wasn't always there to enjoy the fruits of his labours. Which Victoria would often complain about.

She'd said she felt like a single mother half the time. And she'd been right. But it had been easier to work than to argue, and he hadn't wanted to argue. They'd had a lovely baby boy together and he'd wanted he and Victoria to work *so much*!

Tom had had dreams of the future in which they were all together. Going on holidays. Getting close again. Finding the first flush of love that had brought them together in the early days. The feelings would still be there. They just needed rekindling. Somehow they'd both lost their way. Allowed the small things to become big things.

And he didn't ever want to make such a mistake again.

Maybe he wasn't cut out to be anyone's partner if he could screw up something that had once been so perfect? And Cara deserved someone who would put in one hundred per-cent. All the time. She had got him through his grief at the loss of his wife. Cara had be-come his rock and he couldn't lose her friend-ship. He needed her the way he needed air.

But he had to hold back. Not act on the strange feelings and thoughts about her that had often kept him awake at night lately. Wondering what she was doing. Who she might be with. There hadn't been a boy-friend since Leo, and he knew how much of a knock to her confidence Leo had given her. He wanted to be Cara's rock, too.

When she opened the door he smiled and

said hello, pushing back the reaction he really wanted to show.

She looked simply and stunningly beautiful. And Cara didn't know she was beautiful, which made her even more so. She was oblivious to how she made him feel. Her hair, usually up in a bun for work, was free and flowing. The orange-red flecks were catching the low evening light. The cool blue of her eyes, sparkling with happiness at seeing him, her friend, warmed his heart and stirred his blood. Deliberately, he stood back, casually turning around to look at the road, as if the traffic or the way the cars were parked were interesting, as he waited for her to grab her keys and phone.

She wore light blue skinny jeans, white trainers and a baggy crimson-coloured tee. Something Victoria would never have been caught wearing to go out. But the colour showed off Cara's pale, creamy skin to perfection, and as she locked her door the loose sleeve slipped down one arm to reveal a shoulder, smooth and toned. Her trapezius muscle, sculpted by many hours spent in the gym, showed the gorgeous slope of her neck.

'Ready?' she asked, turning to him.

'Yep.'

'I'm not. I figure I'm about to look a whole lot of stupid.'

She grimaced, clearly expecting him to laugh, so he gave a small chuckle and led the way to the car, fighting the urge to open the door for her, as a gentleman would. Instead, he walked round to the driver's side and let her get in the car by herself.

As they drove through the evening traffic, a song came on the radio. 'Ooh, I love this one!' she said, and turned up the volume and began singing, bopping away beside him.

She had a good voice. He loved listening to her sing. And the way she was clicking her fingers to the music and swaying beside him made him want to stop the car, throw off his seatbelt and take her in his arms and kiss her.

What the hell am I doing? I can't have these thoughts about Cara. It's not right.

He pushed those thoughts to the back of his skull and tried to concentrate on the traffic, praying for the song to be over. When it was he was able to relax a little more. He found a parking space near to the shopping centre, despite it being busy on a late-night shopping evening, and they got out, paid for their parking and began walking towards the shops.

He knew from experience that there were plenty of clothes shops there, but only one or two that sold the sort of dresses that Cara would be looking for.

'Let's go to Imagine first,' he suggested.

He remembered it from before, and knew it had a large range of dresses. He hoped that would mean she'd find one straight away and then this torture would be over.

'What's that?'

'It's a shop that sells posh dresses. Evening dresses. Ball gowns, wedding outfits—all of that.'

'How do you know about it?'

'It's right next door to the baby shop where we got Gage's pushchair and Moses basket.'

'OK, she said hesitantly.'

'You seem nervous.'

'I am. What if I look ridiculous in these dresses? I've got muscles, I'm broad-shouldered, with tattoos. I won't look right.'

He disagreed. 'You'll look amazing. We'll find you a beautiful dress.'

She bumped into him, nudging his arm with hers. 'Thanks for doing this. I really appreciate it.'

He smiled at her. 'No problem.'

Of course he was worried, too. Worried that he'd see her in each dress and fall for her just a little bit more with every one. He couldn't imagine her not looking good in anything she chose to wear. Cara could wear a potato sack if she wanted to and she'd look amazing. The fact that she didn't understand that blew him away. She was different from most women. She was happy to be without make-up, without having done her hair. She'd never had a manicure or a pedicure, or spent hours in a hairdressing salon, or a tanning booth, and she was *perfect*.

And although he'd kind of been looking forward to spending this time with Cara, now that it was imminent he found himself fearing the evening. He told himself to create distance, not to pay too much attention to how she looked. He'd look at her briefly, tell her she looked good in something, and then they could go home.

And yet… He didn't want to lie to her. He didn't want to dismiss her. But most of all he didn't want to ruin their friendship. Cara would know. Would sense if he was just giving her lip service. And Leo had ruined her self-esteem, so he was damned well going to tell her how gorgeous she looked and try not to give himself away.

Lip service… That just made him think about kissing her.

They headed into Imagine and he stood back as Cara took the lead, checking out the dresses hanging on the racks. There were dresses of all colours. Dazzling to the eye, some of them. He even saw one in bright neon orange, like a highlighter pen.

Cara looked at him. 'I didn't expect there'd be so many. How am I supposed to choose?'

'Pick ones that catch your eye and then try them on.'

'Hmm. I don't know...' She bit her lip, frowning.

'Can I help you?'

A very, tall, thin woman, dressed in a navy skirt suit and a cream silk blouse, approached them. She had glasses on a chain around her neck and wore an alarming amount of perfume.

'I need a dress. For a ball.'

The woman smiled. 'How lovely. Now, let me see...' She ran her eyes over Cara. 'You look to be about a twelve—am I right?'

'I guess...' Cara shrugged.

'You'll want something like...' The woman turned, casting her knowledgeable gaze over her stock. 'This. Or this.' She selected two dresses on hangers and presented them to Cara.

Cara turned to look at Tom, seeking his opinion.

He gave the usual male response and just shrugged.

'Why not try them on?' the woman suggested. 'The dressing room is over there.'

As Cara disappeared into the changing room Tom settled himself down in a chair and waited, pulling out his mobile phone to double-check that he didn't have any messages from the babysitter looking after Gage. The teenager next door often looked after Gage. She used those evenings to study for her exams, saying it was quieter in his house than in hers, where she had to share a bedroom with her younger sister.

There was no message, so he tried to sit back and relax. Eventually the door to the changing room opened and Cara stepped out wearing the first gown. He almost dropped his phone in shock and surprise.

The dress was a dark midnight-blue and on the hanger had just looked like any other swathe of fabric. Nothing special. But on Cara it looked…magical. As if she was wearing the night sky. It was asymmetrical. One-shouldered. Sweeping down across her chest to cradle and hold curves that he hadn't ever quite seen before. Cara was usually hidden under her firefighter uniform, or in baggy tees and jeans during her off hours. To see something this tight-fitting on her was...

He swallowed, trying to gather his thoughts, looking her up and down as if he were still thinking about what to say—and he was. He wanted to say *You look stunning. Gorgeous.* But he also didn't want her to realise just how affected he was at seeing her like this.

'You look lovely,' he managed, trying to sound normal.

Cara turned this way and that in front of the mirror. 'I don't know... I like the colour.'

The blue showed off her pale, creamy skin to perfection, and the tumble of her fiery hair, which she'd pulled to one side so she could look at the back of the dress, revealed to him her neck, her spine, the sweep of toned muscles beneath her skin.

This was a woman who could carry a grown man out of a burning building!

She had a waist. And curves that revealed hips that somehow pulled his gaze.

'I think I'd better try the other one on. What do you think?'

Tom nodded. 'Sure.'

He cleared his throat and let out a breath when she disappeared back inside the changing room.

What the hell was happening?

This was *Cara*. Cara! She was just his friend. She couldn't be anything else to him. He needed to stop having these thoughts about her. Hadn't she sworn off guys after Leo? Didn't Reed's daily attempts to wind her up remind her every day that guys could be idiots and not worth wasting her time on? Didn't she say that she was happy being single?

And she would never look at him in that way.

So he could never let her know how he was feeling.

It was probably a phase. It would pass! This was silly. He had nothing to worry about, surely? Just a phase...

The next dress was of ivory silk, and when Cara came out she looked like a Grecian goddess.

Tom felt that lump in his throat once again as he saw the draping silk emphasising her breasts, her trim waist, the swell of her hips.

'No, I can't wear this—it's practically indecent!'

Cara crossed her arms over her chest. Clearly it was impossible to wear a bra beneath the dress, and all he could think about were her nipples, which led to him thinking about what he could do to them...

He just nodded and said, 'Yeah, it is a bit…
revealing.'

When she'd disappeared back into the
changing room he let out a huff of air and
got up and paced the shop, trying to make the
part of his body below the waist feel a little
more…relaxed. He shook out his legs, tried
to slow his breathing, and couldn't remember if clothes-shopping with Victoria had ever
been like this.

He didn't think so.

When Cara came back out, dressed in her
baggy tee once again, he smiled and sighed
a sigh of relief.

'Maybe we should try somewhere else?'
she said.

'Sure…er…there's another dress shop at
the end of this road.'

The besuited woman behind the till smiled
as they left, and Tom was glad of the fresh air
and the cool evening wind that was beginning
to blow. It had got rather hot in Imagine. And
now he understood why the shop was called
what it was…because his mind had certainly
imagined all sorts of scenarios.

The next boutique dress shop was smaller
than Imagine, but the assistant was just as
helpful. She helped pick out three dresses for
Cara. The first was fire-engine-red, which

Cara loved, but she really wasn't too keen on the choker neckline as she thought it made her shoulders look too broad. The second was an ombre dress, in seaweed-green, its colour changing to a Mediterranean-blue at the neck, but Cara said she felt like a fairy in it. The third dress was an iridescent black that shimmered and draped her body like an oil slick.

'What do you think?' She turned in front of him, and as she did so revealed a very high split that went almost to the top of her thigh.

He pressed his lips together hard, wondering just what it was that he'd done wrong in this life that he was being punished in such a manner?

Cara grabbed at the fabric to hold it together. 'It's too revealing, huh?' she said, blushing, looking awkward. 'I'll go and change.'

'No. It's…um…lovely.'

Lovely? *Lovely?* Couldn't he think of another adjective? Had he turned into his father? That was what his dad said to things. To a nicely brewed cup of tea. To a nice slice of cake. To a comfy chair.

Cara was beyond *lovely* in these dresses.

'I feel exposed.' She turned to the assistant. 'Have you got anything that doesn't reveal ninety percent of my skin? It's just not me.'

'Let me think…' The assistant turned to survey the shop and then snapped her fingers. 'Do you know? I just might have something in the back. Bear with me for a moment.'

Cara nodded, still clutching the split in the dress to cover her leg.

Tom wished he had a drink to hand. His mouth was so dry! Cara wasn't tall by any means. She was a whole head shorter than him. But that split made it look as if her beautifully toned legs went on for days…

When the assistant came back out, with a dress hidden inside a cover, he found himself hoping and praying that this one would not make him feel as if he wanted to ravish his best friend, as all the others had done.

His right leg was twitching, his foot rapidly tapping the floor in a staccato rhythm as his nerves increased, while he waited for Cara to come out.

When she did he stood up, a smile breaking over his face at the sight of the smile on hers, and he knew she'd found a dress she was happy with.

It was long-sleeved, high-necked and stylishly draped, in a beautiful gold colour. It showed no cleavage. It had no leg-split. But the diamante and sequins that were sewn into the dress in their thousands made her look like a starburst.

'You look...gorgeous,' he said, his breath almost taken from him. She'd looked amazing in everything, but this... This dress made her happy, and that was what counted the most.

She blushed at his praise. 'You think? It's got this at the back, but...'

She turned, and he saw that the dress exposed most of her back, all the way down to the top of her bottom. The gentle swell of her butt cheeks caused the golden shine to blind his eyes. It was just her back, but it seemed to be the most erotic thing he had ever seen and his body stirred in reaction to her.

Tom sat down. Awkwardly. 'It's amazing. What do you think?' He cleared his throat again, trying to regain control of his body. Who knew it could do so many things involuntarily?

'I like it. You don't think the back's too much?' She turned again, giving him another glance of her skin, the curve of her waist...

'No, it's...perfect.'

'It's a good price, too.' Cara admired her reflection in the mirror for a while, before turning to the assistant and saying, 'I'll take it.'

'Fabulous!' the assistant said.

Tom smiled, but inwardly he was telling

himself, *Okay, so she's going to wear that dress. Keep your hands high, and when you get to the party you don't have to stay close. You'll have done your part. You'll have warned off anybody wanting to ask her out. You'll just have to get through one dance with her and that will be—what? Two minutes long? Three, tops? Then it'll be a drive home, a quick peck on the cheek to say goodnight and it'll all be over. Easy, right?*

Then they could go back to normal, and eventually the memory of her in that dress would fade, and they could just be mates. That was all he wanted. He didn't want to get involved with anyone again. Not really. It was horrible when you lost someone, and he didn't want to lose Cara if this all went wrong.

No. He could behave himself. He was a gentleman.

And that was what Cara deserved.

CHAPTER FIVE

CARA HAD A day off. And she was determined to use it to get stuff done that she couldn't when she was at work. There was a wonky cupboard door in her kitchen that needed repairing, and a pipe that needed replacing under the sink. She'd bought the parts ages ago but had just never got round to it. So she pulled up some music on her phone and began clearing out all the cleaning essentials she kept under her sink so she could expose the pipe.

As she worked, her mind kept drifting to the previous evening, dress-shopping with Tom.

It had been crazy. Each of those first few dresses had made her feel as if she was naked in front of Tom, and that had done some incredible things to her insides! She'd almost not come out of the changing rooms a couple of times, but she had forced herself, curious as to how he might react. He was her friend, but he was also a red-blooded male, and some of those dresses had been…risqué.

He had looked a little as if he didn't know where to look, and that had embarrassed her to begin with. Clearly he'd believed she looked ridiculous in those exquisitely feminine dresses. Dresses meant for women like Victoria. With long, lean limbs and a flat stomach. Women who were fully in touch with their femininity.

Cara wasn't a girly girl. She didn't get the whole thing about how to be a stereotypical woman, interested in handbags and nails and having her hair done every six weeks. She preferred trimming her own hair in front of her bathroom mirror. Handbags were useless if you had enough pockets. And fake nails? How did anybody do anything with those long claws on? And she bit her nails more than she decorated them.

I was kidding myself if I thought Tom might find me attractive in those dresses.

Cara wasn't a woman who used her womanly wiles. She'd never needed other men to notice her. Tom was the only one who was important. The only one who mattered. And it had mattered what he thought of the dresses—especially when she'd felt so uncomfortable in them.

Except for that last one. The gold one. It had covered all the essentials. The shoulders she thought were too broad, the arms that were probably a little too muscly, the cleavage that was too small anyway and the thighs that were thick with muscle and should only be revealed, if at all, to a physiotherapist or a doctor.

She'd felt confident in the gold dress. As if she could carry it off. Because the evening was going to be difficult enough as it was— what with her father being as annoying as always and it being her mother's birthday and the fact that it would be a fake date with Tom. It all made her feel uncomfortable, and she needed a dress to make her feel okay.

Cara would love it to be a real date, but fake would do. They'd walk in together as a couple. Surprise Green Watch. But she would explain it to them later, when the party was over. For a few hours she would pretend and be happy.

Maybe they'd walk in arm in arm? That would be nice. Tom would be attentive and at her side all night, with his arm around her protectively, his hand resting on her hip, her body pressed against his. She would be able to get through the evening like that, no problem. Her heart would probably be racing through it all, but it would be worth it.

And then Tom would take her home and escort her to her door and plant a kiss upon her cheek before saying goodnight. And then she would have to fight the urge to ask him in for coffee, knowing that she wouldn't want the night to end. Because when it did they would go back to being normal friends. Which was great. But when the heart wanted more...

I can't make him love me. I can't make him see me as something else.

Plus, there was Gage to think about. That little boy had been through so much, and although she loved him to bits, loved spending time with him and making him laugh, she would never be able to replace his mother and Tom wasn't the kind of man who entered relationships lightly. He'd only ever been in one and that had been with Victoria. He was no gigolo, no fly-by-night, no *wham, bam, thank you, ma'am* kind of guy. Tom only did serious relationships.

Maybe she could talk to him about that? Ask him gently, as his friend, if he'd ever considered dating again? Test the waters?

What would it feel like to see him with someone else?

She didn't like that thought.

It would be tragic and hurtful. Make her sad.

The pipe came free and some water splashed down upon her, making her splutter and wipe off the excess. She put the new pipe in place and began to fasten it on, making sure there were no leaks by running the tap above.

It worked perfectly.

If only people could be fixed so easily.

'She's dislocated her elbow,' Tom said to the father cradling his daughter in his lap.

The patient was a young child, only two years of age, and the elbow had been dislocated by her father spinning her around in the garden by the arms. The pulling mechanism of the injury was classic.

'I did it. I feel so guilty. Does she need to go to hospital?'

Tom shook his head. 'No. I can fix it here. It's usually an easy fix, but when I put the elbow back into place she might cry out for a moment. Hey, Lacey? I'm going to fix your arm, okay?'

Lacey snuggled further into her father.

That was okay. Tom was a stranger to her and she was in discomfort—it was to be expected. Tom rolled up the girl's sleeve and held her elbow in his right hand, supporting it so that when he performed the manoeuvre he would be able to feel the elbow pop back into place. He took Lacey's hand in his left hand, as if they were shaking hands, then turned her palm upwards towards the ceiling, straightened the arm, pulling outwards, and felt the elbow snap back into place as he folded her arm at the antecubital fold.

Lacey cried out at the click, but when Tom offered her a tongue depressor to hold and she used her left arm for the first time since the dislocation a smile crept onto her face.

'See? All fixed.'

'It's done?' Lacey's dad asked. 'That's amazing.'

'It's one of my favourite things to do.' Tom smiled. 'Make a patient better quickly. If only all my jobs were this easy.'

'Well, I can't thank you enough. I really thought I'd broken her arm.'

'If I could take away your guilt I'd do so, believe me.' Tom smiled at Lacey. 'Maybe Daddy will find a nice treat for you because you were so brave?'

'Ice cream!' Lacey said, looking up at her dad.

Tom laughed, just as his personal mobile rang. He stood up to pull it from his trouser pocket and frowned. Gage's pre-school was calling him.

'Excuse me. I need to take this.' He turned away and walked out into the hall for some privacy. 'Hello?'

'Hello, is that Gage's dad?' asked a female voice.

'Yes.'

'I'm sorry to call you. This is Fiona Goddard from Sunflowers Pre-School.'

'Yes?'

'It seems that Gage isn't feeling very well. He's complaining of a tummy ache and he's not quite himself. Would you be able to pick him up?'

Tom sighed. 'I'm at work.'

'I understand. But we can't keep him here if he's not feeling well. Is there any way you could come? Or a family member who could?'

His mind raced. Who could he call? Who would Gage feel comfortable with? He knew immediately.

'I'll need to check with a friend. I'll call you back and let you know.'

'Thanks.'

He ended the call and dialled Cara's number. When she answered he heard music playing in the background. 'Hey, it's me. Where are you? Sounds like you're in a disco.'

'You're right. It's 1986 in here.' The music went down a notch. 'I'm fixing a kitchen cupboard—what can I do you for?'

He sighed. 'I realise this is an imposition, but I've just been called by Gage's nursery. He's not feeling well and they want him to be collected, and—'

'I'm on my way. Let them know I'm coming. I'll take him back to yours. Is the spare key still in that fake plant pot?'

This was why she was so great. There weren't many people he could rely on like this. He could have called his parents, but they didn't have their own car now and they lived nearly an hour away—probably more if he took into account how long it would take them to get to Gage's nursery by public transport. Cara knew where it was, and she was close, and he trusted her with his son.

'It is—and thanks. I know this is your day off.'

'I've already done what I set out to do today. All I had planned after this was to sit and watch a movie. I can do that with Gage. What's wrong with him?'

'Tummy ache.'

'Ah… I can deal with that—no problem.'

'Thanks, Cara. I don't know what I'd do without you.'

There was a brief silence. 'You'd do fine.'

'I doubt it.'

He really did. He honestly thought that he'd still be wallowing in grief and guilt right now if it hadn't been for her. She brightened his day…gave him the belief that he could do anything he wanted if he just put his mind to it. She was his cheerleader, his rock, and soon she was going to be his date for a ball. A fake date, but he was looking forward to seeing her in that dress again. Just to reassure himself that she had looked that amazing and it wasn't just his imagination that had made the whole thing up. He was going to feel honoured to walk into Higham Manor with Cara on his arm.

'We'll be fine. What's the safe word?'

The nursery had a safe word system, so if a parent couldn't collect a child any other adult would have to use the parent-created safe word before they'd be allowed to walk off with someone else's child.

He grimaced. 'Don't laugh, okay?'

'I promise.'

'It's banana.'

He heard a muffled laugh. 'Banana?' She was trying to sound serious. 'Interesting…'

'I was eating one when I filled in the form. I never thought I'd actually have to use it.'

'Sounds legit. Okay. See you later.'

She rang off and he stood there for a moment, just staring at his phone, before dialling the nursery to let them know that Cara would be collecting Gage.

When he'd put his phone back in his pocket he went into the living room and smiled at Lacey and her father. Lacey was now sitting on the floor, playing with a toy car, using the arm he'd just fixed.

'See how quickly they forget that they used to hurt?'

'You're a miracle worker,' Lacey's father said.

But Tom didn't think so.

Cara was the miracle worker—not him. She'd got him smiling again, laughing again, when after Victoria's death he'd never thought that would ever be possible.

Cara set Gage down by the front door whilst she surreptitiously located the spare key and opened the front door, ushering the little boy into the living room.

Gage sat on the couch, looking solemn.

She knelt in front of him, smiling warmly. 'Okay. Operation Tummy Ache. What are we talking about here? Does it just hurt? Or are we going to need a bucket?'

Gage smiled. 'It just hurts.'

'Show me where.'

He pointed to the middle of his abdomen.

'Okay. I think I may need to operate. Lie back and be brave. I promise to be quick.'

Gage giggled and lay back. He didn't look comfy, so she grabbed a cushion and put it under his head, and then dragged a holey crocheted throw from off the back of the couch and draped it over his little form.

'TV?'

He nodded.

'What do you fancy watching? Politics? The news? Antique-hunting?'

'Cartoons.'

'I think I can manage that.' She turned and pointed the remote at the screen. It came to life and she brought up the menu to find the channel that showed cartoons all day. 'I prescribe three cartoons. Then I'll read you a story and maybe you can try and sleep, okay?'

'Okay.'

'Do you want a drink?'

'Milk!'

'With a bad tummy? Hmm…how about some juice?'

'Okay.'

She laid the back of her hand against his forehead. He didn't feel hot, which was good.

It was probably just a bug, if it was anything at all.

'You watch TV while I make the drinks, and then I'll come back here and sit with you—how about that?'

He nodded.

Cara gave his hair a ruffle, then went to get their drinks. It didn't take long, and she was soon back on the couch with Gage, watching a weird cartoon that she thought was awful but pretended to like. Her gaze kept falling upon the picture of Victoria on the mantelpiece, and all she could think of was how it ought to be Victoria getting the chance to sit with her son. She'd be so proud of him. He was growing into a lovely boy, and Tom was doing remarkable things with him, raising him not to feel out of place because he didn't have a mum, like the other kids did.

What would Victoria do if she was here? Stroke Gage's hair? Keep an eye on him at a distance whilst she got on with some housework? Put Gage in his bedroom?

Tom's wife looked down at Cara on the couch and seemed to say *Well, I'm not there, so do the best for my son. I'm trusting you with him. I'm trusting you with* them.

Cara had become Victoria's friend, however brief that friendship had been. What would she think if she could know that Cara had secret thoughts about her husband? Had *fantasies*? She'd be appalled, that was what. She wouldn't want Cara to be anywhere near them. She'd feel betrayed.

Guilt swallowed her and she looked down at Gage. What was she doing, having these thoughts about Tom?

I can't! I shouldn't!

She sipped at her tea, and when they reached the end of the third cartoon she swallowed hard and switched off the television.

'Aww!' Gage protested.

'Storytime, bucko. I can't have you getting square eyes as well as a tummy ache.'

Gage touched his face. 'Are my eyes going square?'

She laughed. 'It's just a saying. Your eyes don't actually change shape.'

'That would look funny.'

'It would. So! Storytime…' Underneath the coffee table was a small pile of children's books. She scooped them out and presented them to him like a magician, saying, 'Pick a card…any card.'

Gage pursed his lips, then pointed at a book.

'Excellent choice, *monsieur*.' She put the others down and then sat back on the couch, draping some of the crocheted throw over her own legs, and settled down and began to read.

As she spoke she held the book to one side, so that Gage could see the pictures. He lay there, listening intently, his eyes growing heavy, until eventually, about three pages from the end, he nodded off and his little cherub face grew soft in repose.

Cara closed the book with a smile and snuggled down on the couch next to him, watching him sleep, thinking how wonderful it would be to have her own little family. What she wouldn't give to have a little boy like Gage. He was perfect and she loved him a lot.

The warmth of the blanket and the softness of the couch soon had their effect on Cara, too, and she fell fast asleep, the book slipping from her grasp and falling to the floor.

Tom's shift finished at midday. He'd been on since seven a.m., just five hours, but when he'd told Control he had a sick little boy at home they'd told him to go home early, which he was really grateful for. Obviously they knew he was a single dad, and they had been brilliant at accommodating him when life got tough. Like today.

He knew he could have stayed, finished

his shift in its entirety, but he didn't want to take advantage of Cara's good nature. Despite her protest that picking up Gage from pre-school was just fine by her, he was very much aware that this was a precious day off for Cara and he'd hijacked it. With his family and his problems. That was why he was happy to help Cara out with this ball thing... being her fake boyfriend. Anything to make her life a little bit easier, the way she did so often for him.

Not sure if Gage would be sleeping, he quietly turned his key in the lock and opened the door. The house was pretty silent. Fighting the urge to call out either of their names, he tiptoed down the hall after discarding his work shoes and popped his head through the living room door.

And felt his heart melt with adoration.

Cara and Gage were both fast asleep on the couch, covered in the raggedy blanket that Victoria had made in an attempt to learn something new. It had huge gaps between the stitches. Some of the squares were smaller than the others. The colours clashed. But it had been made with love, and after his wife had died he'd not been able to bear parting with something that had been made by her hand.

For a moment he stood there, gazing down

adoringly at both of them. He grabbed his mobile phone, opened up the camera app and took a photo.

The sound of the camera woke Cara. She blinked her eyes open, then sat up in shock, half of her hair squashed to the side of her head by the cushion she'd been sleeping on. Immediately she blushed, then looked down at Gage to check that he was all right.

'Oh, my gosh. I'm so sorry. I must have fallen asleep.'

He smiled at her. 'You did,' he whispered, turning the phone so she could see the picture.

'I must have been more tired than I thought.' She cocked her head to one side and ruffled her hair. 'Do I really look like that when I'm asleep?'

'Apparently.'

'I hope I didn't drool.' She wiped her mouth.

Tom used the zoom function on the photo. 'No drool. How's the patient?'

She smiled. 'Good. Centralised tummy pain, no temperature, no vomiting. He's kept down his juice and…' she checked the time '… I was going to see if he wanted some toast for his lunch.'

'You go. I'll do all that. Enjoy what's left of your day off.'

'Oh, it's no problem. I've enjoyed myself.'

'I can see that.' He grinned. 'I'm going to take this one up to bed. Give me a minute.' Gently, he scooped up his son, who barely woke except to snuggle in closer to his dad's chest as Tom carried him up the stairs.

This was what being a parent was all about, Tom thought. These moments when your kid snuggled into you. When he was dopey with sleep. When he reached for you to provide comfort and love.

'Hello, Daddy.' Gage mumbled.

'Hey, you. How are you feeling?'

His son nuzzled his nose into Tom's top. 'Fine.'

'That must be because you had a good nurse looking after you, hey?'

Gage smiled. 'Can she stay?'

Tom felt an ache in his heart, but he was almost at the top of the stairs and heading towards Gage's bedroom, so he felt it was safe to whisper. 'Not today.'

'You could ask her for a sleepover.'

'Maybe.'

'It doesn't matter that it's not night-time. We had a pretend sleepover at pre-school last week. We told stories and had hot chocolate.'

'Sounds good.'

'She could sleep in my bed with me.'

He smiled, loving the innocence of a three-year-old boy. 'Well, maybe when you're better.'

'And we could look after Cara when she has a tummy ache.'

'We could.'

'You make people feel better all the time, Daddy.'

Tom laid his son in bed and pulled his football duvet cover over him. 'Rest and I'll bring you up something to eat. What do you fancy?'

'Hot dogs.'

'Let's start with something plain, huh? How about some delicious toast?'

Gage nodded from beneath the quilt.

'Okay. Back in a bit.'

Tom trotted downstairs to find Cara folding the crocheted blanket and draping it into position on the back of the couch.

'I remember Victoria making this,' she said, stroking the blanket.

He nodded. 'Me too.'

'She swore a lot.' Cara looked up at him and smiled.

'She was never very good at making things. Except Gage. He's pretty perfect.'

'Well, you had something to do with that, too.'

'I'm going to make him some toast. Fancy

staying for lunch?' he asked, feeling nervous that she'd say no. Feeling nervous that she'd say yes.

'I'd love to.'

The next day, Cara was four hours into her shift when a call came through for a cyclist versus bus. She clambered into her uniform with the rest of Green Watch and got into the appliance, and with sirens and lights blazing they made their way through town, towards the co-ordinates they'd been given.

It was a busy high street, and the traffic had come to a standstill because of the accident. Reed, who was driving, had to sound his horn to get people to move, so they could make their way through. Eventually they got as close as they could and Cara clambered from the truck, hearing sirens in the distance as police and ambulances made their way to the accident.

Hodge led the way towards the bus, which was stopped at a weird angle just past its last stop. It must have been pulling away after picking up its latest passengers and collided with the cyclist. But…where was the cyclist?

Cara got down on her hands and knees and saw a bike and a body beneath the bus. The front wheel of the vehicle was half resting on the cyclist's leg. The cyclist was crying quietly.

'Let's get some stabilisers!' Cara called out, lying down on her stomach and trying to make eye contact with the cyclist, who was just out of reach. Otherwise Cara would have reached for her hand.

As the others placed wheel chocks down, to stabilise the vehicle, Tom arrived alongside her.

'What have we got?'

'Leg entrapment, as far as I can see, but I have no idea if the wheel went over her chest or her pelvis first.'

'She's conscious?'

Cara nodded. 'We'll need to use inflation devices to lift the bus, so that we can pull her out from under there.'

'Okay. I'll get painkillers ready for injection.'

Cara looked back at the cyclist. 'We're going to get you out of there soon, okay? What's your name, love?'

'Penny.'

'Okay, Penny. That's it…just focus on me. There's going to be a lot going on around you, but I don't want you to worry about that. Just keep talking to me. What hurts the most?'

'I—I don't know. My stomach…'

That didn't bode well.

'Can you feel your legs?'

Penny paused, then shook her head, terrified. 'No!'

'Okay. I need you to stay calm. You may
just have spinal shock. We won't know until
we get you to the hospital, so stay positive.'

Penny sniffed and nodded. 'Okay…'

'Where were you going today, Penny?'

'The bank and the p-post office.'

'Paying bills or taking money out?'

'Taking out. For a h-holiday.'

'Fantastic! Where are you thinking of
going?'

As Cara kept Penny occupied the rest of
Green Watch did their thing, finding the correct placement for the inflation devices that
would slowly lift the bus from the patient.

'Crete. I have family over there.'

'Parents?'

Penny nodded. 'I haven't seen them since
before the pandemic. I've been saving so I
can go. Will I be able to go now?'

'Maybe not tomorrow, but let's say yes—
you're going to go to Crete.'

'I'm going to go…' Penny looked about her.
'What's your name?'

'Cara.'

'That's pretty. I knew a Cara once…when I was little.'

'Yeah?'

'She went to my school. It was a boarding school. Monrose…'

Cara frowned. She'd gone to Monrose! Wait… Penny… Was this…?

'Penelope Moorcroft?'

Penny blinked. 'Cara Maddox? *Lady* Cara Maddox?'

Cara smiled. 'It's me.'

'But…you're a fireman. I mean, a fire p-person.'

She nodded. 'Yes, I am. I never expected to meet you again like this.'

'You were such a nice girl at school. I remember being f-frightened on my first day, and you took me to the nurse when I got a headache.'

Cara remembered. 'Looks like I'm going to be delivering you to medics again. Maybe we should stop meeting like this?'

'Maybe.' Penny gave a small laugh. Then, 'Why can't I feel my legs, Cara?'

Cara kept her voice calm. 'The doctors won't know until they scan you.'

'Am I going to die? I'm getting cold…'

'She's in shock,' whispered Tom. 'We need to get her out fast.'

'I know.'

'Why are you whispering?' Penny called.

'We're not. Just working out how best to get you out quick.'

'Ideally, I'd like to get some pain meds into her before we lift this bus,' said Tom. 'Let me shimmy under there. You've secured the vehicle—it won't move.'

'Tom—'

'If we lift this bus from her leg it's going to be agony. She could have compartment syndrome and all the toxins will go straight to her heart, putting her into arrest. I need to be under there with her.'

'I can't put you at risk, Tom.'

'I won't be.' He smiled. 'Not with Green Watch's finest looking after me.'

'I'll need to check with Hodge,' Cara told him. 'Penny? I'll be back in just a second.'

But as she got up and turned her back she saw a movement out of the corner of her eye, and when she turned back she saw the toe ends of Tom's boots as he shimmied underneath the bus, dragging his kitbag with him.

'Tom!'

She couldn't believe he'd done that! It was dangerous. If anyone should have gone underneath, it should have been her. Now Tom could get hurt, and the idea of that happening made her feel sick. Sweat bloomed in her armpits and down her back.

'Hodge! Tom's gone under.' Cara hated hearing the panic in her voice. The fear.

Hodge got down on his hands and knees and spoke to Tom. 'What are you playing at?'

'Keeping my patient alive and pain-free!' Tom's disembodied voice came back.

Cara lay flat on her stomach again, to see what was happening, but Tom was in front of the patient now and she couldn't see what was going on.

'When you get those pain meds on board, you come right back out—you hear me, Tom Roker?'

'Yes, ma'am.'

She cursed silently and looked over at Reed and Garrett and beyond him David Garcia. They all gave a thumbs-up. They were ready to inflate the blocks.

'We're all set out here. Are you done yet, Tom?'

'Nearly… Okay, I'm coming back out.'

Her heart began to slow down as more and more of Tom's body came safely out from underneath the bus. His uniform had oil on it, and he was scuffed and dirty, but he gave her a grin that stopped her from being angry. *He was safe*. That was what mattered.

She turned her attention back to her patient. 'Penny? We're going to inflate now, and we'll have you out in a jiffy.'

'She won't answer you. I've given her some ketamine, so she's woozy.'

'Okay, let's get this bus off this poor woman,' said Hodge, signalling the lift to begin.

The machines started up, slowly inflating the concertinaed blocks that had been placed at strategic points underneath the bus. It seemed to take ages, but eventually the bus was lifted clear of Penny's legs.

Both Tom, Hodge and Cara helped pull her out, and once she was clear Tom began working on her quickly, alongside the other paramedics who swarmed in from nowhere, along with a doctor who must have arrived in a helicopter, judging by his bright orange jumpsuit.

Cara, Garrett and Reed deflated the blocks and the bus sank back down to the road.

The police had created a barrier around the accident site and were marking the road and taking witness statements. Tom and the others got Penny onto a backboard and whisked her over to an ambulance, so she could be kept warm whilst the doctor oversaw her care.

Cara looked at the giant wheels of the bus and imagined the weight of that vehicle going over a pelvis or a spine. Unless Penny was extremely lucky, her outlook might not be all that great. The likelihood was that there was going to be a lot of surgery and physiotherapy in the months to come.

As the helicopter rose into the air with its patient onboard Cara found Tom, grabbing his arm and making him turn forcibly. 'Don't you *ever* do that to me *ever* again!'

CHAPTER SIX

HE'D NEVER SEEN such anger and fear in her eyes. Cara had been *furious* with him. It was an emotion he wasn't used to from her. In the entire time he'd known her she'd only ever been calm, funny, happy, supportive and caring.

But anger? And fear?

He'd tried to apologise, but he really felt he'd done the right thing. If he hadn't, Penny would have been in a whole world of pain when that bus had been lifted.

Once they'd got her out, they'd discovered she had an unstable pelvic fracture, two broken femurs and a suspected lower spine fracture. That was a lot of injury to one body, and without pain meds it would have been horrific. Penny had been numb from the waist down, but that might have been shock, or her mind protecting her from her horrific injury, but once the adrenaline had worn off she would have felt everything if he hadn't gone under the bus.

It had been safe. The bus had been stabilised. There had been no other traffic flowing around them and he had made a judgement call.

But Cara's response had him flummoxed. Was it more than the response of just a friend? Or was he trying to read too much into this?

Now, as he drove them both to the shopping centre once again, to help Cara find shoes to go with her golden dress, Cara sat in silence, staring out of the window. It was an awkward silence and one he wasn't sure how to navigate. He didn't want to make things worse, but he really hated not being able to talk to her. And having her angry with him like this made him feel repentant.

'So…are we not going to talk to each other this evening or…?' He let the question hang.

Cara sighed. 'We can talk. So long as you admit you were reckless.'

'I don't think I was.'

She glared at him. 'Silence it is, then.'

'I'm sorry if I scared you by going under that bus. That wasn't my intention.'

'We hadn't had confirmation it was fully stable, Tom! What if the bus had come down on you? You could have been hurt! You could have been injured. Badly. And then what would Gage do, huh? Without his mother *and* his father?'

Tom got what she was saying, but he was also hearing what she *wasn't* saying out loud. Clearly she was worried about how his getting hurt would affect *her*. Wasn't she? And if she was, what did *that* mean? And if it did mean something...if it did mean that Cara had feelings for him that went beyond friendship, then...

No. He was being ridiculous. She was probably worried that if he got hurt she'd have to rescue him too. That she'd have to take on too much with Gage, or something.

He thought for a moment, trying to think of ways to lighten the mood and take his mind off his quandary. 'Well, I don't have much experience in shoe-shopping with women, but from what I do know it's meant to be a happy experience.'

'Maybe. You could always drop me off. I can go alone.'

'Cara, please. I'm trying to say sorry, here.'

She looked at him. 'You scared me, Tom. Going under that bus like that. It made me feel helpless. That if something were to happen to you I wouldn't be able to protect you.'

So he was right, then. She was just worried

about having to rescue two people instead of one. It was nothing to do with her having feelings for him. It was a realisation that made him feel glum.

'I was fine.'

'Luckily. Aren't you guys taught not to rush to a patient without checking the scene is safe for you first?'

He nodded. 'It *was* safe. You'd stabilised the bus.'

'But I needed to check with Hodge first. He was in charge of everyone's safety at the scene—not you.'

'I get it. And I'm sorry I scared you.'

He liked it that she cared so much. Just not in the way that he'd hoped for. But he was her friend—maybe her best friend. Either way, it felt good to know that someone cared and worried about him. His parents did, obviously, but it wasn't the same as having Cara care. Knowing that she was thinking about him, worrying about him... What had she said? It had made her feel *helpless*.

He reached over and laid his hand on hers. Her skin was smooth and warm. 'I'm sorry,' he said, and he meant it. It wasn't a half-baked apology just to stop the awkward silence. He really meant it. He didn't want her to worry about him. He knew how it felt to worry over

someone you couldn't help. And that helpless feeling…? He was intimately aware of it.
'I promise to never make you feel that way
again.'

'And you'll wait for me to say something is
safe before you go charging in on your white
horse?'

'I will wait.'

She gave him a small smile. 'Good. I hate
being angry with you. I'm not used to it.'

'Me neither.'

He drove, still holding her hand, enjoying
the way it made him feel, trying not to read
too much into it but not keen on letting go,
either. If he could hold Cara's hand for evermore, he would. But it seemed they were
doomed to be nothing more than friends.

'How's Gage today?' she asked.

'His normal self, thankfully. Back at pre-
school.'

'I'm glad.'

'He wanted to know if you were going to
come round again soon, to teach him how to
do keepy-uppies?'

'Can't you show him?'

'I can't do them.' He squeezed her hand.
'And he wants to learn from the best.'

She laughed. 'Tell him I'll see him at the
weekend.'

He had to slow his car as they reached the traffic lights near to the shopping centre, and he had to let go of her hand to operate the gears. His own hand suddenly felt so empty, and he yearned to reach out and take her hand again. But he knew that would seem odd. That was a boyfriend gesture, and he was not Cara's boyfriend.

The moment was over.

They were back to being best friends again.

And even though he feared it would never seem enough, he was willing to take it.

Some of Cara was better than no Cara at all.

The first shoe shop had a display of trainers at the front, and Cara *oohed* and went over to take a look at a black pair that had a flash of neon green near the toe.

'These are awesome,' she said, taking in the neat construction, the multi-coloured laces and the supportive reinforced heel.

But Tom took them from her hands and placed them back down on the stand. 'We're here for something that will match your dress, and I don't think that these will do.'

'Not fair...' she protested, as he led her towards the other side of the shop, where there was a more dazzling array of strappy shoes with heels.

Cara gazed at them, feeling utterly lost. What was she meant to do? She knew nothing about shoes. Was she meant to wear gold shoes with a gold dress? Did they have to match? Or could she wear a neutral colour? A nude? Something contrasting?

'I fail miserably at being a girl.'

Tom laughed. 'You're perfect.'

'Am I? What do I know about shoes? Apart from the fact that they go on your feet and that I'll always choose comfort over style.'

'Last I heard, being a girl didn't mean passing any shoe exams.'

She picked up a pair of pale pink ballet shoes. 'Thankfully. I'd definitely fail. Are these any good?'

Tom shook his head. 'Not with that dress. That dress is…something special. You want a shoe that reflects that.' He picked up a high-heeled strappy shoe in gold. 'What about these?'

Cara turned the shoe over in her hands. 'How are you supposed to walk in these?'

'Gracefully?'

She laughed. 'Have you ever seen me in a heel?'

He shook his head. 'No. I don't think I ever have.'

'Well, there's a reason for that. I look like a toddler who's just found her mummy's shoes. I either look ridiculous or I fall over. These look like they'd break my ankles.'

'Try them on and see.'

'Let's leave them in reserve. What else is there?'

She cast her gaze over the racks. There seemed to be shoes in most colours. There was a lot of black, but she felt pretty sure a black shoe wouldn't look great with the gold dress. She saw a pair that had a small chunky heel. A kitten heel? Was that what it was called? Bubblegum-pink and kind of cute.

'These?'

Tom shrugged. 'Try it on.'

She sat down, pulled off one trainer and a short sock and slid her foot into the shoe. She wondered if she was meant to have painted her toenails. Did Tom think she had ugly feet?

Cara was happy they were talking again. Being angry with him had been incredibly distressing to her. She'd not wanted to fall out with him, but he had scared her so much! If she'd lost him...

Fastening the buckle, she stood up and tried to walk. But it was odd, because she still had a trainer on the other foot. So she sat back down and got rid of that, as well as the other sock, and put on the other pink shoe. She could barely walk. She wobbled a bit, and had to put her hand out to grab the rack and steady herself.

'Whoa! You okay?' Tom asked, smiling.

'It's like learning to walk again.'

'How do they feel?'

'Awful.'

'I'm not sure that colour would go with the dress.'

'Maybe they have them in gold? I could ask.'

'I think you should try a different heel. You don't look right in those.'

Oh. He didn't think she looked good. And nor did she feel good in them. Not really. They were uncomfortable, and they pinched, and the heel was doing something strenuous to her calf muscles.

Cara sat down to take them off.

'Try on the gold pair,' Tom said. 'What have you got to lose?'

'My ability to walk?'

She grabbed the high-heeled golden pair with reluctance, even though she could see they were beautiful shoes. Elegant...stylish... She just wished they weren't so high!

She tried standing and wobbled.

Tom took hold of her arm briefly, then let go.

Cara stood there, trying to keep her balance, but her centre of gravity seemed way off, all of a sudden, and she was afraid to move.

'They look great.'

'Of course you're going to say that. You're a man.'

'You don't think they look great?'

'I do. It's just… I'm not sure I can move. They're perfect if you plan on carrying me into the ball and then plonking me down by the bar, so I don't have to move all night.'

She blushed at the thought of him carrying her over his shoulder, fireman-style. Caveman-style? As if he'd chosen his woman and now she was his.

'Just try and move,' he said.

'Okay…'

Cara looked about her. No one was watching, so she wasn't about to make a colossal ass of herself. They were all too busy shopping for their own shoes, lost in their own little worlds. It was just her and Tom, and he stood in front of her like a proud parent, waiting for his toddler to take its first steps.

She took an awkward step, but it felt as if

she might snap the heel. She was so used to putting her heel down first, then her toe, but that just wasn't going to work. Not for her. Maybe she needed to somehow put the heel and toe down together?

She took another awkward step, and then another, but then her ankle wobbled, and her balance went, and she was suddenly falling forward into Tom's arms.

He caught her, saving her from faceplanting down on the floor. But now she found herself in another strange predicament.

She was in his arms, her head against his chest, hearing his heart pound inside his ribcage. And it was beating fast. Probably from the shock of her falling, that was all. She could feel the muscles in his body…could smell his body spray—something masculine and earthy that performed wonders on her senses. Her cheeks flushed and she looked up into his eyes. Something strange passed through them, and she was so caught in his magnetism she forgot to pull away. Forgot to try and move. Forgot to try and operate her feet.

Because being in his arms like this…so close she could feel every breath…it was a heady place to be.

'Thanks, I…'

His lips were parted and his eyes were large as he stared down at her, but eventually common sense kicked in. He didn't feel anything for her! That was nonsense! He'd just caught her because she'd tripped—that was all!

She coloured and pushed away from him, let go. And somehow, awkwardly, she made her way back to her seat, bending over to slowly undo the buckles, so that her hair would hide her face, her blushing cheeks, the pounding of her own heart.

I wanted to kiss him.

Had he been able to see that? Had she given her feelings away?

She'd wanted it so much. How romantic would that have been? But romance never found Cara. It never had—why would now be any different? Especially with someone who was so off-limits? Her best friend.

Victoria would have been able to handle these heels. She'd have glided down a red carpet. She'd have made her father proud. Tom must think that she was an absolute idiot. Trying to be something that she was not.

'Ankles okay?' he asked, his voice sounding deep and breathy.

'Yeah. They're…they're good, thanks.' She sat up, not sure where to look. She picked up the strappy gold sandals and placed them back on the shelf. 'Maybe we should keep looking?'

He nodded. 'Yeah. I'm parched. Are you parched? Should I fetch us a coffee?'

And he got up and left the shop.

Odd... But maybe he'd seen something in her gaze when he'd caught her, and now he felt awkward because he was going to have to say something about it? Tell her that he'd seen that look in her eyes and it could never happen? They were just friends?

Because it would be so embarrassing if he did. She'd have to protest and lie to him. Say, *Don't be silly! I just fell. Nothing happened... let's move on*.

There was no way she wanted to have *that chat* with him. But clearly he'd felt something, because he'd looked incredibly uncomfortable just now. Probably trying to work out just how he'd tell his friend that he didn't think of her in that way.

Oh, God. This is mortifying.

Tom stood waiting in the queue by the coffee cart, trying to calm his racing heart. Something weird had just happened with Cara. She'd tripped, and he'd caught her...but when he'd held her in his arms she'd looked up into his eyes and...

He swallowed hard. Had he been wrong? He'd thought he'd seen something written across her face—but he had to be imagining things, right? Because this was Cara! She didn't have any romantic feelings for him. And yet he could have sworn that he'd seen something in her eyes. Seen want. Seen desire. Seen...feelings.

But we're just friends.

Those were the parameters of their relationship and that was why they worked together so well. They both knew where they stood, and there was nothing romantic between them—there couldn't be. Maybe he was just being sensitive because they'd had that falling out earlier and emotions had been running high.

He'd reached the front of the queue. 'Two lattes, please.'

Should he say something when he got back to the shoe shop? Should he just pretend that nothing had happened? That seemed cowardly, but he really didn't want to run the risk of making their relationship awkward. He'd hate that. He needed to be able to see her. Needed to have her in his life. If he ruined it he'd never forgive himself.

He headed back to the shop, determined to act as if nothing untoward had ever happened between them.

Cara knew she couldn't risk anything like that happening again, and she kind of wanted the evening to be over—so she could get home and take a bath, or something, pretend that everything was normal. So what if the shoes were too high? All she needed was practice walking in them, and she could do that at home. There was still a week or two before the ball.

So she took the high-heeled shoes to the till to pay for them, and rummaged for her phone when it began to ring.

She had a sudden fear that the caller might be Tom. That he'd gone home, too embarrassed to face her. But when she pulled the phone from her pocket she saw that it was her father.

Great. Just what I need right now.

'Hello?'

'Cara, darling! How are you? Have I caught you at a good time?'

'Sure. I'm just out shoe-shopping.'

'For the ball? Marvellous. I'm so looking forward to it. Seeing you there with all your brothers. The whole family back together again.'

'Is there anything in particular I can help you with?' She didn't mean to sound so sharp with him.

'No, no… I just thought I'd let you know about the latest arrangements. I've been speaking with Hodge, your boss. I know he suggested a deejay or something for the evening, but due to the ball being at the manor I thought a deejay might be a bit tacky, so I've organised an orchestra to come instead.'

She blinked. An *orchestra*? 'Dad…'

'Oh, it was no bother. Nothing fancy—just a local group. But I thought I'd let you know so that you could practise your dancing.'

'Dancing?' She looked down at the heels in her hands. She could barely *walk*.

'You know…waltzes and things. Your mother loved all of that—it will be a fitting tribute. Plus, it will be lovely for people to get on the dance floor and enjoy themselves… not feel like they're only there to open their wallets.'

'Right. Dancing.'

She looked up. She could see Tom coming her way, holding two coffee cups. Dancing. In that dress. With those heels? She'd be clutching onto Tom all night! A few seconds had been awkward enough. How would she ever hide how she felt all night?

Was it too late to get out of going altogether?

The fire engine raced through the dark streets, lighting up houses in flashes of red and blue. They were heading to an industrial estate behind the one where that guy had caught his arm in the printing press. Ahead of them they could see the night sky lit up by orange flames, with plumes of thick black smoke billowing upwards.

Cara hoped it wasn't the paper factory, because if it was then the fire was going to be intense, with all that flammable material around it, fuelling the flames.

Originally, she hadn't been meant to work this night shift, but she'd offered to work overtime as one of Blue Watch was off sick and Cara didn't feel she wanted to be sitting at home worrying about Tom and the upcoming ball. The whole situation was driving her crazy, and she'd had a headache all day. Every time she thought she'd got on top of her racing thoughts and sorted out how she was meant to be feeling, another thing came along and shook the ground beneath her feet.

When Tom had got back to the shoe shop with the coffees he'd seemed surprised that she was buying the gold shoes that she'd just fallen over in, but he'd said okay when she'd told him that practice would make perfect, and then she'd said she was tired and could they go home?

They'd driven home in silence—a comfortable silence that time—but still her heart had been racing and she hadn't told him about the dancing. He'd barely been able to hold her for a few seconds without looking alarmed. If he heard that her father was meddling again and now wanted them to learn how to dance… Well, she didn't want to see Tom trying to get out of their fake date. It would be embarrassing. Better to just turn up on the night and act surprised, suffer through one dance with him and then go home.

She'd have done her duty to her father and her mother and to the Websters, whose night it actually was going to be. They deserved help to find the best home they could afford. She would do it for them. And if she ended up with a twisted ankle at the end of the night because of it…? Well, fine.

As the appliance pulled up at the fire, another two fire engines that had been called from neighbouring stations arrived, and Hodge leapt out to co-ordinate with the other chief fire officers as Cara and the others began to prepare the hoses.

Hodge came back and gave them their instructions. 'Okay, I want you two over here, taking the east corner of the building. Garrett? They're a man down on Red Watch—can you help them on the west corner?'

Garrett ran over to help the others.

Cara felt the surge of the water as it ran through the pipe and aimed it at the flames, feeling the heat from the fire as it roared high into the sky. The ceiling of the industrial unit already had holes in where the flames had burnt through.

Hodge was yelling. 'Looks like we have a missing night guard! Cara? You're with me. We're going to head round the back and start our search at the guard box.'

Cara passed the hose to Reed and set off at a run with Hodge. They had to give the building a wide berth, mindful of the danger of collapse, and when they got to the guard box it was empty. A half-drunk cup of coffee was cooling on the table inside.

'Damn. Where is he?' Hodge grabbed a timesheet off the wall. 'Looks like he makes laps of the building at midnight, three and five a.m.'

She checked her watch. A quarter past midnight. 'Think he's inside?' she asked.

They both looked to the building, almost consumed in flames.

'I sincerely hope not,' said Hodge.

By the time they got back to the front of the building, several ambulances and Tom in his rapid response car had arrived.

Her stomach turned at the thought of facing him again, so she went to help with the hoses. The water was having some effect, and they were able to move forward to beat back some of the flames.

As she watched, one of Red Watch came out of the building, carrying someone over his shoulder. The missing night guard? She hoped so. As she moved forward a few more steps she glanced over briefly. Saw Tom ministering to the unconscious patient, placing an oxygen mask over his nose.

I can't concentrate on Tom. I need to focus on what I'm doing.

It felt like a sucker punch to the gut when Tom saw Cara look his way and then turn without acknowledging him at all. He tried to tell himself it was because she was concentrating on her job. Not to read anything into it. But things had been strange between them ever since her fall in the shoe shop.

And that niggled—because he'd spent the entire night tossing and turning in his bed, telling himself that he'd somehow made up the whole thing. But if she *was* avoiding him... Maybe she was embarrassed. Had she seen the look in his eyes when he'd caught her? Maybe she was *appalled*?

There's a fire that needs putting out. She's not going to stop and come over and talk to me.

But a smile might have been nice. A nod of the head.

Something was up. He could feel it.

He turned his mind to his patient. He had some mild burns to his hands, and his respirations were extremely low due to smoke inhalation. He had soot in his throat and up his nostrils. God only knew what sort of chemicals he might have breathed in through the smoke. It all depended upon what was burning.

He helped get the man onto a trolley and whisked off into an ambulance, which roared away from him to get him to an Accident and Emergency department.

He hoped the man would live. It seemed

they'd got to him in time. But life could be a fragile thing. Tom knew the truth of that better than most.

The fire was extinguished. Only smoke continued to fill the sky. Cara finally had a moment to shuck off her helmet, unzip her coat and allow some of the cool night air to flow in around her body.

She loved her job. She loved to battle against the flames. And although this fire had taken a few hours it was all under control now. The fire investigation team would soon arrive, but Hodge had already come out and said it looked as if some kind of accelerant had deliberately been spilled in the warehouse. He'd found the flashpoint of the fire and the night guard had been found near that.

Whether the guard had started the fire, or someone else had, she didn't know, but the report from the hospital had already told them that the guard was alive but refusing to talk to the police. So…

'Hey.'

She turned. It was Tom. Her heart instantly began to thud again.

'Hey.' She looked away from him awkwardly, back at the blackened building that was now mostly in disarray.

'That was a tough one,' he said.

'It was.'

'I'm exhausted. Looking forward to going home and getting a shower.'

She nodded. A shower sounded great. A shower with Tom would be even better. But that wasn't going to happen anytime soon, so she said nothing about it.

'Gage away?'

'At my parents.' They're going on a cruise tomorrow and taking him with them. They'll be gone for three days.'

'You'll miss him.'

He nodded.

'So will I.'

Another nod.

'Are we okay?' Tom asked.

Her heart leapt into her throat, then began to thump against her ribs. 'Yeah! Of course we are!'

'Good. It's just things have seemed a little funny after...' He tailed off.

'I tripped. That's all. I've just got some other stuff on my mind.'

'Anything I can help with?'

She smiled. Despite it all, he was still willing to help her out. And she couldn't hold it in any longer. 'My father wants me to practise my waltz. He's organised an orchestra for the ball.'

'You know how to dance?'

She laughed. 'Oh, of course! I can cha-cha-cha with the best of them!'

'Really?'

Cara groaned. 'No. I have two left feet. Two left feet that are going to be in vertiginous heels. What do you think?'

Tom seemed to think for a moment. 'That I'm going to need steel-capped shoes.'

'And then some.'

She paused. She wanted to give him an out. Rather than hear him try to worm his way out of his obligation, it would be kinder to just let the man off the hook herself.

'You don't have to do this, you know... I can go alone. You can dance with someone who won't break every bone in your feet, and I will weather the storm with Xander, or Peregrine, or whoever my father tries to set me up with.'

'Are you kidding? I gave you my word. And I don't back out of any promises I make.'

'You sure? I'm not sure our relationship will survive my trying to dance with you.'

She couldn't tell him the real reason. That she wasn't sure *she'd* survive being in his arms all night and not being able to kiss him, or touch him the way that she'd want to, or whisper sweet nothings into his ear.

Tom thought for a moment, then smiled. 'I have an idea.'

'Ditch the night entirely? I can't.' She grimaced.

'No, not that. Daphne—my sister-in-law. She can be our secret weapon.'

'And Daphne will be our secret weapon *how*, exactly?'

'She's a dance instructor. She owns Mango Dance Studio. She could teach you how to waltz.'

A dance instructor? Hmm…

'I know that place. It always looks busy. You think she'll have time to help me?'

'I can but ask.'

'Okay, but be realistic with her, okay? Don't tell her I have promise, or anything. Tell her she's getting a complete newbie, with no sense of rhythm or grace. Tell her I'm like a baby elephant. Or a hippo. Or some other animal that wouldn't be able to dance well but could break her partner's toes.'

He gave her a playful nudge. 'You're not a hippo. Or an elephant. A few hours with Daphne and you'll be as graceful as a swan.'

'You remember me in those heels, though, right?'

'I do.'

'I guess it's too late to find a stunt double?'

He laughed, and she loved the sound of it. Loved how they were talking normally again.

'Much too late. Besides...' He looked directly into her eyes, his voice softening, 'I'm looking forward to dancing with you.'

Her breath caught in her throat. 'You are?'

Did he mean that? And *how* did he mean that? As friends? Or...?

No, it can never be as something more. This man has danced with Victoria. I've seen the wedding video! They were perfect. Graceful.

'Are you kidding me? You'll be the belle of the ball.'

She liked it that he was trying to build up her confidence. He was a good man.

'And you'll stay by my side all night? Because I'm not sure I'll be able to stand upright after dancing in those heels.'

'Always.'

She smiled back at him, then looked away. Because looking into his eyes right now was making all those other thoughts come back. The thoughts she shouldn't be having about Tom. He truly was a gentleman. Her knight in shining armour. But he was also a grieving widower, and she was a very bad person for even entertaining these thoughts about him right now.

'You can dance,' she said. 'I've seen you.'

He shrugged. 'I think I've got some moves.'

Cara nodded. Yes, he had. But even if he hadn't he'd still be a better dancer than her. If the worst came to the worst, she'd throw off her heels and dance with him barefoot, if need be.

Anything to be in his arms a moment longer.

CHAPTER SEVEN

THE MANGO DANCE STUDIO was just off the high street, situated above a Turkish supermarket and a pawn shop.

Cara hadn't been sure what to wear for a practice dance session. The only dance movies she'd seen were set in the past, where leotards and leg warmers were all the rage, but she was pretty sure they weren't in the eighties any more, so she'd decided her usual gym gear would have to do. A sports bra under a baggy long-sleeved tee shirt and some tracksuit bottoms, with trainers.

In a bag, she carried the vertiginous golden heels, in case this Daphne told her that she needed to practise in those, but she really hoped that wasn't the case. Every time she put them on she could feel blisters wanting to make their appearance on her little toes, and her ankles ached in wary anticipation.

And she was also anxious about meeting Daphne. If she was Tom's sister-in-law, that meant she was Victoria's sister, and that meant Daphne would no doubt be curious about this woman Tom was bringing and what their relationship was. She didn't want Daphne to hate her, or to see something that Cara was desperately trying to hide.

As time ticked on she knew she couldn't leave it any longer, so Cara opened the door that had Mango Dance Studio blazoned across it and headed up a narrow set of stairs.

Once inside, she was amazed. The stairwell was painted in a light grey, and as she took the stairs she saw framed photo after framed photo of dancers in various shows. Ballet, tap…something from the West End, by the looks of it. An entire cast taking a bow in front of a standing ovation, and at the top of the stairs a few dancers standing with celebrities, the photos autographed.

Daphne was serious about her business, clearly. She had ambitions for her dancers, and this exhibition of photos let everyone know that.

At the top of the stairs was a glass door. Cara pulled it open and walked straight into a reception area, where a petite blonde sat behind a desk adorned with orchids.

'Can I help you?'

'I'm here to see Daphne. I have a private session with her.'

'Name?'

'Cara Maddox.'

'Oh, they're waiting for you! Go through the door on the right there and to the end of the corridor.'

Tom must have already arrived. She smiled her thanks to the receptionist and headed down the corridor. Again, there were pictures on the walls. Large poster-sized, this time. Dancers in a production of *Swan Lake*. A line of female dancers all on tippy-toes, arms gracefully arced overhead. Something Christmassy that she didn't know. And another that looked as if it was set in the nineteen-twenties. The costumes were amazing, and all the dancers looked happy and proud.

Could Daphne make Cara look that good?

But as she got closer to the studio door her nerves kicked in big-time, and she froze, her hand on the handle, ready to push the door open but worrying about who and what waited for her on the other side. Tom had a relationship with this woman. She was his sister-in-law. Would Daphne hate her? Think she was replacing her beloved Victoria?

She almost turned back. This whole event was crazy enough as it was! But, unwilling to let her father get any satisfaction from Cara failing them all yet again, she yanked the door open, lifted her chin and went in.

Tom was at the far end of the room, in a pair of dark tracksuit bottoms and a tee shirt, laughing with a tall, svelte, Amazonian woman who was the spitting image of Victoria.

Cara felt a jolt to her system, her mouth went dry, and she suddenly needed a drink very, very badly.

Daphne was the perfect embodiment of Victoria. Every reminder of why Tom had married his wife. She was tall and beautiful and slim. Perky and graceful and stylish. She wore a leotard top that moulded her perfect breasts and showed off her slim waist, attached to which was a diaphanous black skirt that just covered her bottom and hips. And below that were long, slim but strong legs.

'Cara! You made it!'

Tom came over to give her a hug and a quick peck on the cheek, but she was too nervous to enjoy it, her eyes clamped onto Daphne, who was watching the entire thing curiously. She was so keen to give the right impression Tom's kiss hardly registered.

'Wouldn't miss it. Hello, Daphne. I'm Cara!' she blurted, holding out her hand for

Daphne to shake. 'Are you sure you can teach this old dog some new tricks?'

Why was she being so self-deprecating? Was she trying to tell to Daphne that she was nothing special? That Victoria's memory would never be threatened by her?

Perhaps I ought to have completed the image by tripping over my own feet walking in?

'Of course. Cara. Tom's told me so much about you.'

'All good, I hope.' She couldn't stop smiling. She felt like one of those ventriloquist's dummies, her face etched with a permanent rictus grin.

'Tom never speaks badly about anybody.'

Good. That was good. And of course she was right. He didn't. She couldn't recall him badmouthing anyone.

'Great.' She glanced at Tom and could see he was looking at her with amusement.

'So, shall we get started?' Daphne asked.

'Let's do that,' Cara agreed.

'Have you ever danced before?'

Cara set the bag of heels down on the floor by the piano. 'No. Well, I had to do a show once at school, but I'm not sure that counts.'

'Do you ever dance when you're alone?'

'No. I'd rather go to the gym and lift some weights.'

'How much can you bench press?'

'About a hundred kilos.'

'Impressive! You're strong. Tom tells me you're a firefighter, so I guess you have to be?'

'Yes, but I enjoy it. It's not a chore for me, going to the gym.'

'Good. So you're not afraid of hard work?'

Cara shook her head. 'No.'

'Excellent. Because that is what's ahead of you. So! Let's get started. Tom says you need to know how to waltz, so before we can get into how to do box steps and fleckerls and spin turns we need to perfect the hold. Tom, would you join us?'

Box steps? Fleck-what? Perfect the hold?

That meant being up close and personal with Tom. In front of Daphne! What had she and Victoria been? Twins, or something? Surely she'd remember if Victoria had had a twin? She couldn't remember such a fact, but maybe she'd forgotten?

And right now it very much felt as if Victoria herself was standing there, asking Cara to get into 'hold' with Tom.

'For a standard waltz we need you in a closed frame hold, like this.'

Daphne began positioning them like mannequins. Pushing her and Tom closer together, linking their hands, adjusting elbows, straightening backs, shifting hips, until she felt they were perfect.

Cara couldn't recall ever being this close to Tom.

Daphne stood back, like a sculptor admiring her handiwork. 'Perfect. Now, you'll need to hold this frame throughout.'

Cara glanced at Tom and smiled nervously before looking away. She was up close and personal with Tom. Tom's right hand was under her left shoulder blade. Her left hand rested on top of Tom's shoulder blade. Their bodies were in contact, though they were both slightly off to the right of each other.

'Stop looking at one another. In this dance you both look off to the left,' Daphne said firmly.

Okay. That made it a bit easier. It would have been hard to have her body pressed against his and look at him, too. Thank God her father had told her she'd need to know a waltz, and not a tango or a rumba. She'd seen those on that television show, and there was no way she'd have been able to do either of those with Tom without becoming a gibbering mess.

'You neck looks broken, Cara. Tom doesn't want to look like he's dancing with a zombie. Do it like this.' Daphne tweaked her neck, elongating it. 'This is a dance of grace and softness. Imagine you're exposing your neck so that a man may plant a kiss there.'

Cara flushed, imagining Tom doing just that. Could he feel the heat radiating from her cheeks? She must have squeezed him with her fingers, because Tom squeezed back, as if to say, *You've got this...don't worry.*

'Right, so now I'm going to teach you the left closed change and the right closed change. These are your most basic steps, all right?'

What followed next was the most gruelling thirty-minute session, during which Cara felt less and less that she was learning to dance, but more that she was against an army drill instructor. Daphne was kind and encouraging to Tom, complimenting him on his form and technique, whereas to Cara it seemed she was less accepting. Everything Cara did was wrong, or out of time, and she kept losing the basic form of their hold.

When she did that Daphne would step forward, pull Cara out of hold and insert herself into Tom's arms and say, 'Like this!'

Cara was beginning to feel like a little girl being told off by a strict headmistress, and inside her rage was beginning to build. She was trying her best! She'd never danced before! Couldn't this Daphne give her a *little* credit?

Cara was sweaty, and tired, and her arms ached from holding them in the correct position. She was tired of counting *one-two-three, one-two-three*, and thinking about how to place her feet, and maintain hold, and look to her left whilst going right, and holding her neck. And Daphne scolding her all the time implied that Tom's last dance partner—Victoria—had been a much better student.

'Can we take a break?'

Cara broke hold and walked away to the piano, where there was some water, and poured herself a drink. She knocked back the entire glass in one go and stood there, hands on hips, breathing hard. She hadn't known what to expect from this session, but she'd expected more enjoyment than this! She was dancing with Tom! Spending time with him up close and personal. And it was being ruined by his harsh task mistress of a sister-in-law!

'You'll never improve if you keep taking breaks,' admonished Daphne, smiling a perfect, un-sweaty smile.

'Yeah? Well, I'll never learn anything the way *you're* teaching me.'

Daphne looked to Tom, as if she couldn't quite believe the impudence. 'I'm sorry?'

'I'm not trying to be a professional dancer! I appreciate your time, Daphne, but you're teaching me like you're trying to get me into a top dance school or a show in the West End! It's just a ball at my father's home. It's meant to be fun!'

'You're not having fun?'

'No! I just want to learn the basics of the waltz, so that I don't fall over my feet in front of my family and friends. No one's going to be scoring me, and no one's going to kick me out of a competition if I accidentally step on Tom's toes! I just want...'

They were both staring at her.

'What?' asked Daphne.

'I want to dance with Tom and I want it to be fun.'

Cara looked to Tom and he gazed back at her with a smile, as if he was proud of her, and in that moment that was all that mattered. When Cara glanced at Daphne, her face said something different.

'I don't need you constantly shoving in my face the fact that Victoria could pick up dance steps easily. I don't need you telling me that I'm not as good as her. I'm not trying to replace Victoria!'

'I'm sorry. I'm not used to teaching for anything but competitions and getting people ready for auditions. Maybe I have been a little...harsh?'

Cara shook her head, wiping the sweat from her forehead with her forearm. 'I need the loo. Excuse me.' And she headed off to find a toilet, feeling humiliated and ashamed.

Had Daphne deliberately been trying to make Cara feel she wasn't good enough? Comparing her to her sister to show her that she could never have Tom, if that was her plan?

She hoped that in her absence Tom would stick up for her and fight her side.

Tom watched Cara go, and when the door closed he turned around and faced Daphne. 'She's right. You were being harsh.'

Daphne had the decency to look shamefaced. 'I'm sorry. It's just...when you said you were bringing this woman I felt like you were leaving my sister behind.'

'I will never forget my wife, Daphne. Never. But life moves on. I've moved on. And Cara is my best friend. She was there for me when no one else could be. She got me through those dark months and she still does it today.'

'You like her?'

'Of course I do! She's my best friend.' He stared at his sister-in-law, hoping that his other thoughts about Cara wouldn't give him away, but he wasn't sure he was that good an actor.

Dancing with Cara had been nerve-racking. A delight. Excitement overdrive. His pulse had been thrumming in the hundreds, without a doubt, and he'd kept sneaking glances at her, even though he'd been meant to look left, away from her. And some of those stumbles had been his fault, not hers.

'I kind of got the feeling she was more than a best friend and that scared me,' said Daphne.

'She's not,' he said, feeling his cheeks flush with the lie.

'Well, if there is ever a chance that you could be something more with this girl, then… you should take it. I want you to be happy, Tom. Victoria would want you and Gage to be happy, too.'

Tom stared at her. He was glad of her kind words, but still all he could feel was doubt. Doubt that he should be moving on already… doubt that he should put his friendship with Cara at risk. What if they did try going out with each other and it all fell apart because he wasn't good enough for her? He'd failed at being with Victoria. Who was to say being with Cara would be any better? He'd been a bad partner.

And why was he even thinking about any of this when he had no idea how Cara felt anyway? She might laugh in his face at the suggestion that they be more than friends, and he wasn't sure he could stand the rejection. And, maybe it was cowardly of him, but he liked how they were right now. He liked seeing her most days, being able to talk to her and share his life with her. And all those secret feelings…? Well, they felt good, too. He could carry on like this even if it did torture him day after day.

Cara was great. Not only with him, but with his son, too. Gage loved Cara. Adored her. She would fit into his little family easily if she was given the opportunity.

Listen to me! I haven't even asked her out and I'm already imagining us as a family!

But that was a good thing, right? That he could visualise it?

'Thanks. I appreciate it,' he said now.

'She's different,' said Daphne.

'Yes, she is.' He smiled, thinking of how different Cara was. Cara was…unique. And quirky. Not your typical girly girl. But he loved that. Loved her strength. Loved the fact that she had no idea how beautiful she actually was. Her innocence on that matter was engaging.

'And maybe different is what you need?' Daphne suggested. 'I know you and Vic had your problems.'

But what someone needed and what they wanted were two different things. Did he have all these feelings for Cara because he needed her? Was he using her to make himself feel good about the fact that he could help her when he hadn't been able to help his own wife?

Normally when he was having doubts about something he would talk to Cara and get her opinion, but on this he couldn't.

Why do I have such trouble telling the women who are important to me how I really feel?

Cara had splashed her face with water and was now standing in the studio bathroom, staring at her reflection in the mirror and wishing she'd never had that outburst with Daphne. She'd been trying to help, teaching in the only way she knew how. It wasn't her fault that Cara couldn't dance and was having difficulty picking up form and rhythm.

I'll go back in there and apologise.

She patted her face with a paper towel, gave herself one last stern look in the mirror and readied herself for delivering a heartfelt apology. She'd not only embarrassed herself, she'd also put Tom in an awkward position with his sister-in-law. Cara had never meant to cause trouble. That wasn't who she was.

When she reopened the door to the studio music was playing. She recognised the music and could even—miracle upon miracle— count the three-beat, as if her brain had somehow been switched on after Daphne's instruction.

Tom and Daphne were dancing the waltz in the middle of the room and she stood watching them, a smile on her face, wishing she could be as graceful.

When they saw her they broke apart and Tom walked over to her with a smile. 'You okay?'

'I'm fine. And I'm sorry. I didn't mean to raise my voice back there.'

'Don't worry about it. Daphne has something she wants to say.'

'Oh?' She turned to Daphne, who was walking towards her like a dancer, all long-limbed and flowy. Graceful, like a swan. It was in her bearing and her stature, after years upon years of knowing how to make her body move in an attractive way.

'Cara. I want to apologise one last time.'

'Oh, there's no need for you to—'

'There's every need. I was unnecessarily harsh towards you and that was wrong. I want to help you and Tom learn to dance so that it's fun.' She smiled. 'Take Tom's hand.'

Cara couldn't believe it! Flushing, she stepped into hold with Tom, feeling the strength and kindness of his grip, the press of his firm body against hers, seeing the reassuring look he gave her. Her back protested a little. Her neck ached and her arms felt heavy from all the practice.

But Daphne stepped back and said, 'Listen to the music. Just go with the flow. See what happens.'

So they began to dance.

It was awkward to begin with. Cara stepped on Tom's toes twice. Grimacing, apologising, her cheeks going red every time. But Daphne and Tom both encouraged her to continue, and eventually she began to get the basic box step.

'We're doing it!' she said. 'We're actually bloody doing it!'

Daphne clapped, then strode over to the

piano when a trill came from her bag. Cara and Tom stopped dancing.

Daphne looked at her phone. 'Ah, sorry, guys. I've got to go. My husband is not so politely reminding me we have tickets to see a show tonight.'

'Oh!' Cara went to get her own bag, with the heels in it. 'We'll let you lock up, then.'

'No, no! Both of you continue! Naomi doesn't lock up the studio until eight. You've plenty of time to practice.'

'Oh, well… If you're sure?'

'Absolutely! It's been a pleasure to meet you, Cara.'

And Daphne kissed her on both cheeks and rushed from the studio, her diaphanous skirt billowing behind her.

Alone with Tom in the studio, Cara turned to look at him and laughed nervously. 'You want to continue?'

'I don't see why not.'

'All right…'

She nervously stepped forward to take Tom's hand and get into hold. Now they were alone together it all seemed so different from when they'd had a chaperone in Daphne. It felt more intimate, his hand in hers… More personal, her body against his.

Forbidden.

Her heart pounded in her chest—so much so, she was convinced he'd be able to feel it, reverberating through his ribcage, and she didn't dare look at him. It was easier to pretend that he wasn't there, to look off to the left and try to remember her steps.

The music continued to play. They stepped forward, right, together. Left, forward, together. She muffled an apology for stepping on his toes once again, but then they began to get the hang of it. Cara was beginning to remember the flow, now, and feeling more comfortable, more able. And when Tom began to make a turn, going in a different direction, she followed easily, happy to be led.

The music was bright and happy, and it made her think of sunshine, and fields full of wildflowers, dancing in a soft breeze. She and Tom were the wildflowers. She became comfortable in his hold, laughed when they turned, began to feel the joy of being at one in partnership with him.

If only life could stay like this for ever.

They began to find an easy sway, moving with the music as it built. They were both smiling and laughing at how easy they were finding it in each other's arms.

'We're doing it!' she said.

'We certainly are.'

'Think we should try it with me in the heels?'

She didn't want to break contact with him. She didn't want to stop at all. But dancing in trainers must be easier than it would be in the heels, and although she felt she'd got a good grip on the dance so far, it needed to be rooted in reality.

'Let's give it a go.'

They broke apart, Cara feeling breathless, but full of excitement and drive. She quickly put on the heels, grimacing at the way they made her feet feel. She'd been practising wearing them. Wanted to show Tom she could walk in them now—even if they did make her feel as if she was about to have the worst blisters in the world.

'Wow! Look at you!'

She liked the way he looked her up and down. He was looking at her as if she was a woman, not just his best friend. She saw appreciation in his eyes. Saw...*want*? That made her heart palpitate!

Cara stepped forward and into his arms once again. Her centre of gravity was off, but it didn't take her long to adjust. In Tom's

arms, she felt she could do anything. Be anyone. Even a graceful dancer. They swayed
and danced, bodies pressed close, enjoying
the rhythm of the music, enjoying the feel of
being in each other's arms. And as the music
came to a crescendo Tom twirled her round
and pulled her close, smiling at her, and the
intensity of his eyes, so close to her own,
caused her heart to pitter-patter.

They stood staring at each other, mere
inches apart, but their bodies pressed close.
She couldn't help herself. She looked down at
his lips. They were parted. He was breathless.
And the way he was looking back at her…
as if he wanted her… It did strange things to
her insides. She reached up, stroked the side
of his face, trailed her fingers over his square
jaw, and suddenly, somehow, they were kissing.

Her mind was going crazy at what was
happening. Disbelief. Surprise. Awe. Terror.
Kissing Tom was everything she'd imagined it
would be. His lips were soft, his kiss passionate, as if he'd been keeping a secret desire for
her hidden and it was now being unleashed,
and he was taking every moment of the kiss
to enjoy it, in case it ended too soon.

She knew how he felt. She didn't want it to end, either.

Her fingers went into his hair, and he growled deep in his throat, and the sound just turned her on even more. The rest of the world disappeared with the intensity of their kiss. All that existed, all that mattered, was the fact that they were together and that somehow this magical moment was happening. She didn't stop to think of the consequences. She didn't stop to think of what would happen *after* the kiss. All she could think of was his lips on hers, his tongue in her mouth and the way he felt in her arms.

That was enough.

That was all she needed and would ever need in that singular moment.

And then…they both came up for air.

Breathing heavily, Cara stared into Tom's eyes, seeing the want and the need. The real world came crashing back in. The dance studio. Who they were and what they were doing. How they had just changed things between them for evermore.

'What does this mean?' Tom asked, gazing back into her eyes, his hands sitting on her waist.

'I think it means…that maybe we are something more than friends.'

Tom looked down at the ground. 'Is that possible?'

Cara gave a hesitant smile. 'Let's find out.'

It was the day of Gage's birthday party. His grandparents had just brought him back from their three-day cruise to Bruges, and he had returned with a dazzling array of different types of chocolate that he'd bought from the chocolate shops in the Belgian city.

Tom was so glad to have him back. He'd missed him incredibly. Without Gage at home, it had been as if he was living a different life lately. That of a single guy. He'd gone out dancing. Kissed a girl. And now he thought that he might be in a relationship of some kind. His life had gone off in a direction he wasn't sure of.

After he'd kissed Cara, the receptionist had opened the door to the studio and reminded them that she'd be closing up soon. So they'd both very quickly separated and nodded and begun packing up. He'd kept looking at Cara, his heart pounding, his head spinning with possibilities. He'd wanted to say more, to ask her questions, but he'd known it couldn't be a late night—and did he really want to send this blossoming *something* into a downward spiral so soon?

He didn't think they'd ended it awkwardly, but his head was full of questions. What did this mean? Had they stepped over a line that neither of them should have crossed? Could they ever go back to just being friends if this went south somehow?

He didn't want to think it would go bad, but he had no other point of reference. He'd only ever been in a relationship with Victoria and he'd lost her. Their romance had soured soon after the rings had gone on each other's fingers. But that was just life, right? It couldn't be sunshine and roses every day.

Or could it? Maybe it was possible—if you found the right person? His grandparents had never had a cross word between them, and they'd held hands right up until the end of their days. When his nan had left this world his grandfather had pined so much he'd died of a broken heart just weeks later.

That was the kind of love Tom wanted.

But right now he was in his worst nightmare. A soft play centre. He'd tried to steer Gage away from the idea, but when he had asked his son where he wanted the party Gage had said here, so… He was willing to grit his teeth and get through it.

Gage had invited his entire class from preschool, so there were about twenty-five chil-

dren. He'd had to sit and make up party bags
for them all, and most seemed to have arrived. The play centre was filled with noise
and that odd smell of sweat and plastic as
children whizzed down slides or swung Tar-
zan-style into a deep ball pit.

Gage himself had just come down a slide.
'Did you see me, Daddy?'

'I did.'

'I did it head-first!'

He smiled. 'I saw.'

And then he sensed more than saw Cara's
arrival. As if his body was attuned, he felt
her coming through the swing doors, holding a brightly wrapped parcel that she passed
to him.

'Hey.'

'Hey, yourself.'

'Cara!' Gage barrelled into her arms and
Cara swung him up and around easily, making him laugh.

'Hey, squirt!'

'You came!'

Cara put him down on the ground. 'You bet
I did! I wouldn't miss this, would I?'

'Are you coming in? I want to show you
my secret hidey spot!'

She nodded. Glanced at Tom. 'Lead the way.'

Gage ran off into the netted maze, bounding up some soft rubber steps before turning to see that she was following. 'You coming?'

'Yep!' Cara turned and looked shyly at Tom. 'You okay?'

'More than okay.'

He smiled. Things were still good with them. She didn't seem to have had any second thoughts. No one had put any doubts into her head. He was both glad and scared. It meant that they were going to go somewhere with this thing they were building between them.

'I'd better go.'

He nodded. 'Yes, you should.'

He watched her scramble away after his son, loving how Gage took her hand and began to drag her deeper into the maze until he lost sight of them both.

Could he ask for anything more right now?

They were both good. Neither had regrets. And his son *adored* Cara.

So why did he feel as if he was standing on the edge of an abyss?

Cara offered to carry an exhausted Gage up to bed.

'Oh, you don't need to do that,' Tom protested.

'It's my pleasure. I haven't read to him in ages.'

She'd missed the little squirt, knowing he was away for a few days, and that she couldn't see him. But it had been nice too. It had enabled her and Tom to get close. That kiss had been... Well... She kept replaying it in her head. Over and over.

Tom had kissed her back!

She hadn't imagined that part. She hadn't dreamed it. It had been *real*, and he'd seemed to want her as much as she had been wanting him. Which was crazy and wild and...

Part of her had worried that when she turned up for Gage's party Tom might be awkward with her, might have had second thoughts, and would take her to one side and tell her that the kiss could never happen again. Only he hadn't.

She'd played with Gage for a bit, then stood with the parents. And when no one had been watching she'd brushed the side of her hand up against Tom's. It had been exciting, feeling that secret contact, knowing that no one else knew what was going on. It had been their own private thing. And when the children had all sat down to eat their chicken nuggets, or their burger and chips, Tom had squeezed past her in the party room, and the feel of his hand brushing over her hip had been electrifying.

In the car on their way home Gage had babbled away non-stop about what a great party it had been, and how much he had enjoyed his birthday, and Cara had felt glad. He'd not been a sad little boy who missed his mum. He'd been happy and bright and he'd enjoyed himself, and that had been a delight for her, too.

As she laid Gage down in his bed he yawned, and grabbed his teddy bear for a snuggle. Cara sat beside him and began to read him a story. It was often the highlight of her day, reading to Gage at night. She'd not realised how much she enjoyed it until he'd gone away and she hadn't been able to do it. Not realised how often she actually did it.

It didn't take too long for the little boy's eyes to grow heavy, and when his breathing became steady and his eyelids flickered with delightful dreams she crept off his bed, laid the book down on his bedside table and silently left his room, pulling the door almost shut, so that a sliver of light from the hall would show in his room.

When she turned round, Tom was waiting for her, smiling, and he reached up to tuck some of her hair behind her ear.

'He's had a great birthday, thanks to you.'

'It wasn't anything to do with me. You organised everything. I just showed up.'

'Showed up and managed to chase him around that massive jungle gym for almost two hours. Honestly, I don't know where you find the energy.'

'There's always energy if it's something you enjoy.'

She was finding it difficult to concentrate right now. Tom kept touching her. Her hair, her ear, her neck... Now his hand dropped to her waist and pulled her closer, and she almost stopped breathing. How often had she dreamed of this? Wanted this? What was going to happen?

Because if he was going to kiss her again, then maybe they should take this downstairs. Kissing, she could cope with. Kissing Tom had been wonderful the last time, and her lips burned to feel his upon hers again. But if it was going to be something else...

Cara hadn't been with anyone since Leo, and Leo had said some pretty hurtful things about her physical appearance. Things she knew she ought not to let affect her, but they did. Of course they did. How could they not? Tom might like kissing her, and dancing with her, but if he saw her naked would *he* think she looked too masculine, too?

She had short arms, short, stocky legs, almost no boobs to speak of, and muscles aplenty. Her body was solid. Not much wobbled or was soft. Leo had said to her that no straight man would want to be with a woman who looked like a guy. That she wasn't as feminine as she should be. That she wasn't as graceful. And Tom had been with Victoria his entire life, and she had been an elegant, tall Amazon. Blonde and sylph-like. If she'd had pointed ears she might have been an elf. Beautiful. Ethereal. Cara had muscles and tattoos and abs...

What if I'm not woman enough for him?

Tom reached out and pulled Gage's door closed properly.

'What are you doing?'

'I don't want him to hear us.'

'Hear us doing what?'

Tom smiled and pulled her closer, his lips nuzzling her neck, sending delicious shivers down her body.

She closed her eyes in bliss, wanting to give herself up to it, wanting to feel she could be confident in her own body. But she'd always let people down in that way. Her mum had wanted her to be more of a girl, to dress in pink and enjoy the things she did, and she'd gone against that. Playing with her brothers, going hunting, making dens and playing soldiers. Most of her friends were guys and now she was a firefighter, pumping iron in the gym, happy in jeans and trainers or combat boots rather than being the lady her mother had wanted. Leo had said she'd looked like more of a man than he did.

I can't compare to Victoria. I can't!

And so, although it pained her, although it ripped her in two, she pressed her hands against his chest and pushed him away.

'No. Stop. I'm sorry. I can't.'

'What is it?'

'I just… I can't.'

She turned from him and began to run down the stairs, heading for the front door.

CHAPTER EIGHT

TOM LAY IN bed alone, staring at the ceiling, wondering just what the hell had happened? They'd had such a great time at Gage's party. There'd been fun, and laughter, and Cara had been there, looking after his son as if it was her favourite job in the world, happily chasing him around the soft play area, joining in his games, never getting tired.

It had warmed his heart, the way the two of them got on, and it had left him free to socialise with the other parents—chat to them, share stories, and basically talk to other adults for an hour or two. About normal adult things.

He'd noticed the way one of the single mums looked at him. And that was nice, and all, but he'd only had eyes for one woman at the party. And there'd been moments when his arm had brushed Cara's, or their fingers had entwined, just briefly, and they'd shared a secret smile, when he'd felt whatever they had *building.* That build-up—the excitement, the anticipation of waiting to be alone with her—had been intoxicating.

They'd driven home, Cara had carried Gage up the stairs and read him a story, and he'd stood outside his son's bedroom door, listening to Cara doing all the voices for the characters and Gage's little chuckles. Cara made Gage happy. And she made *him* happy, too. He couldn't believe he'd fought this for so long, when clearly there was an attraction between them both. It had been exposed now, through that electrifying kiss, and he wanted more.

When Cara had crept from his son's bedroom, a smile upon her face, he'd just known he had to have her. The idea of spending some quality time in his own bedroom with her, slowly exploring her body and discovering what brought her pleasure, had given him so much excitement he'd thought he wouldn't be able to stand it.

That was why he'd had to touch her. Why he'd had to have contact. And he'd thought that she was enjoying it too. As he'd kissed her neck she had let out a little purr...or had it been a growl of pleasure? He'd exposed her neck even more, so that he could kiss her and taste her and imagine all the wonderfully naughty things he could do to her, and then…

Something had suddenly changed. She'd stiffened. Frozen. Placed her hands upon his chest and pushed him gently away. She'd looked…terrified!

'No. Stop. I'm sorry. I can't.'

Six words that had puzzled him, before she'd stepped past him, hurried down the stairs and disappeared out through the front door!

He'd gone after her. Of course he had.

'Cara!' he'd called.

How was she going to get home?

He'd texted her.

Come back. Please. Let's talk.

But there'd been no answer. No response. So all night he'd lain there, wondering what he'd done wrong. If he'd said something wrong. Or whether she'd simply got cold feet and maybe they were moving too fast.

That had to be it, right? All this time they'd been friends, and then they'd shared one kiss and suddenly he'd been doing things to her that he'd hoped would lead to sex. Perhaps she'd felt that too? Perhaps she'd panicked? Perhaps she feared taking that next step with him—because if they slept together and it wasn't great then there'd be no going back to their friendship.

He couldn't imagine that sex with Cara would be disappointing. His desire for her was almost overwhelming. Sometimes he felt he couldn't breathe. He wanted her so badly.

Or maybe it's that bastard Leo's fault? Those things he said to her. The way he made her feel about herself afterwards. Like she isn't woman enough.

Tom had done his best to build her up, build her confidence and self-esteem, but perhaps she still felt scared? He could only reassure her so much, Cara had to take that final step herself, and believe that she was woman enough for anyone.

Tom hoped that she'd had a good night's sleep and that maybe, just maybe, he'd get the chance to see her today and talk things over. Make her feel a little easier about things. Let her dictate the pace.

Feeling more optimistic, he managed an hour's sleep before his alarm woke him up for work.

Cara kept stirring her tea. Standing in the small kitchen of the fire station, she stared at the hot drink, her mind a thousand miles away.

'Earth to Cara?'

Reed's voice finally cut into her reverie. 'What?'

He laughed. 'You've been stirring that drink for about four minutes now. Something you want to talk about?'

There was. But not to him. Never to a man like him. She trusted Reed, in that he was her colleague and a damned fine firefighter. She would happily place her life in his hands and know that he had her back in such a situation. But as a friend? A *confidante*? No chance.

She put down the spoon and picked up the mug, carrying it over to the table. 'Not really. Not to you, anyway.'

He mimed being stabbed in the chest. 'Oof! That hurts.'

She smiled and sipped at her drink.

'Problems with *Daddy*?'

Cara ignored him.

'Too many Lords chasing after our fair Lady?'

'Shut up, Reed.'

'Or is it lover-boy causing all your problems?'

'I don't have a lover-boy.'

'Because you're too busy fawning over a paramedic.'

'I'm not fawning!'

'No?'

Reed sipped from a big red mug and raised an eyebrow at her, and in that moment she hated him with a passion. Why was he always there? Why was he always pushing her buttons? What did he get from that? Well, if it was a reaction he was chasing, she wasn't going to give him the satisfaction of getting one.

She sipped her own drink. Calmly. 'No.'

'Things are good between you and Tom?'

'Of course.'

'Hah! You paused!'

'I did not!' she protested.

Reed laughed, settling back in his seat. 'Oh, but you did! Something's going on. Come on, you can tell your Uncle Reed.'

'And have my personal life gossiped about throughout the station? Even more than it already is? No, thanks.'

'So there *is* something. You've just confirmed it. Hmm, what could it be?' He seemed to think for a bit. 'You finally told him you fancied him and he turned you down?'

So Reed thought it too? That she was too manly for any man to want her?

Only Tom seemed to fancy her no problem... This was *her* issue. Not Tom's.

Feeling humiliated, she turned away from Reed.

'Was I right?' Reed asked, looking shocked. 'Wow, I can't believe it. I really thought he liked you, too. Would have put money on it. I guess you can't always know a person, can you? Want me to kick his arse for you?'

She turned to look at him, tears in her eyes, grateful, suddenly, for his support. He might rub her up the wrong way most days, and he'd got this totally wrong, but he was there for her. She was part of his team and they were a family.

'Thanks, but, no. It's not like that and I need to handle this on my own.'

'All right. But if you want me to stand in the background—all menacing, like... I could hold an axe and everything. Just say the word.'

Cara didn't get time to laugh. The station bell began to ring and they both leapt up to respond, running from the kitchen, down the stairs and into their firefighter uniforms. They got into the fire engine just as Hodge arrived with a slip of paper from the printer, outlining the job.

'House fire.'

Cara nodded, strapping herself in, switching from personal mode to work mode. No matter what was happening between her and Tom, she had to forget it for now. Somewhere out there, someone might be about to lose everything.

And she knew how that felt.

Tom had been dispatched to a house fire on a busy council estate. The area, he knew, was compacted. Lots of high-rise council flats, all packed tightly together, with the exception of a few terraces of two-bedroomed houses, built in the Victorian era. If it was one of those, then there would be the possibility of multiple casualties, as a fire in one of them would spread easily to the homes either side.

He was glad to have some work to do. So far, it had been a quiet shift. Not that he liked to use the Q word. There was a superstition amongst health workers that you never said it out loud. Like actors didn't like to say *Macbeth*. It tempted fate and fate wasn't something you wanted to play around with.

As he came roaring into Gardenia Street he realised he was behind Cara's fire engine. He had no idea if she was on today, but he hoped so. It would be nice just to speak to her and reassure her that everything was fine, that nothing had to change yet if she didn't want it to.

They were getting close to their destination, and thankfully he couldn't see any plumes of smoke billowing into the air. Maybe it was a small fire? Maybe the residents had already contained it?

But when he pulled up at the address and they all got out of their vehicles they saw a bunch of teenagers at the end of the street on their bikes, laughing and catcalling and whooping it up.

Malicious call? He knew they couldn't just assume that. They still had to check.

He saw Hodge in his white helmet, going over to the house in question and knocking on the door. He hung back, waiting, aware that Cara stood off to one side, beside Reed, who was looking at him strangely. He tried to send a smile to say hello, but Reed just stared back.

Odd...

The door was opened by a woman in a dirty bathrobe, a cigarette held between her fingers. She looked surprised to see Hodge, almost taking a step back when she saw the array of emergency vehicles parked outside her home.

'Yeah?

'Madam, we've received a call that there is a fire in this property,' Hodge said.

'What? No!' She took a step outside, saw the kids at the end of the street. 'Those little bleeders! Wait till I get my hands around their scrawny necks!'

'Am I to understand that everything is fine?'

'Course it is!'

'Can we come in to check?'

'What for? I told ya! It's them kids! They've been winding me up all week. I've had it up to here…' She raised her hand above her head, before backing away and slamming the door shut.

Tom let out a sigh. It was a malicious call, by all accounts. Why did people do this? It was such a waste of resources, and whilst they were driving to a fake emergency it was taking the services away from someone who might desperately need a fire engine or an ambulance. Timewasters could kill someone, and when this sort of things happened it infuriated him.

He glanced over at Cara, caught her eye. He saw her look away briefly, then she took off her helmet and walked towards him. He saw Reed grab her arm and say something in a low voice to her, but she shook her head.

'I'll be fine,' she said.

What was that about? Had she told Reed what had happened? Why would she do that?

As Cara came towards him he felt his heart begin to race. He didn't want to mess this up. 'You all right?'

She nodded, not making eye contact. 'I'm fine.'

'Everything okay between you and Reed?' The firefighter was still glaring at him for some reason.

'He just wants to protect me.'

Understanding came. 'From me?'

'He could see that I was distracted this morning.'

Tom sighed. 'Look… I'm sorry about last night. I pushed. I pushed too fast and you weren't ready. I didn't mean to upset you and I don't want things to be awkward between us. You mean too much to me. Can we go back to the way things were before that?'

Now she looked at him. 'I'd like that.'

'I care a lot for you, Cara. I need you to know that.'

Her cheeks flushed and he liked how it made her look.

'Are we still on to meet at Mango tonight?' she asked uncertainly.

'Dance practice? Sure.'

That made him happy. He'd thought she might cancel. This way they could spend some more time together. It would give them time to talk about what had happened. Or what hadn't happened. If she wanted to. He was wary of pushing her. Wary of scaring her. That Leo must really have done a number on her.

'Okay. Well, good... I guess I'll see you later, then.' She smiled hesitantly and went to walk away.

He watched her clamber back into the fire engine. Watched the fire engine drive away. He called into Control. Reported it as a malicious call and notified them that he was ready and open for anything else.

He'd not been driving for more than two minutes, when a report of a suspected cardiac arrest came through, and he turned on the sirens and raced to his next call.

She almost cancelled. Nerves had got the better of her. Did she really want to see Tom again so soon? Did she really want to see Daphne? But this was their last session. They were meant to be learning turns and fleckerls and transitions, so that their changes of direction looked smooth.

She was beginning to doubt if she could go

through with this. Beginning to think she'd made a huge mistake in allowing something to happen between them. Because although she wanted to be with Tom more than anything, she was scared that at the last moment he wouldn't be physically attracted to her— even though he'd told her so many times that she was beautiful, and that what Leo had said had been more about him being a lousy, stupid idiot than it had been about her.

She wanted to believe that. She'd tried to believe that. But…the sting was still there. The doubt.

Cara craved love. Love for who she was. What she was. Love. Acceptance. Pure and simple.

Her father's love was so overbearing it was suffocating, so she ran from it. Her mother's love had been conditional, and so she'd run from it. Leo's love—though you could hardly even call it that—had been critical, and so she'd run from it.

Tom? Tom was meant to be different. He wasn't meant to be like the others. But would Tom always judge her against Victoria? The perfect, slender, soft, feminine Victoria.

Why was finding love so difficult? Why was it this hard?

Could she really afford to risk losing the

man she thought of as her best friend, and probably Gage, too? She wanted to punch something because she felt it was so unfair! If she were at the gym she'd tape up her knuckles and go at the punchbag for a few rounds, that was for sure!

She looked up at the windows of the Mango Dance Studio. She could hear music playing. Something hip-hop...the steady drive of a resounding bass note that practically made the windows reverberate.

I can back out of this. I can walk away. I don't have to go to the ball—I'll just make a donation to the Websters.

But something pushed her onwards and she opened the door, walked slowly up the stairs as if she was a guilty person on her way to the gallows, and entered the studio.

Naomi, the same receptionist was on, and she greeted her kindly and told her to go straight through. That Tom and Daphne were already there.

Oh, God! Tom and Daphne know each other well. Has Tom told Daphne what happened?

Because Daphne would surely hate her, then.

Her steps faltered, but then a small voice

in her head said, *No. You've done nothing wrong. Yet.*

So she pushed open the studio door and walked in, smiling, and sent a wave over to Tom, who stood with Daphne by the piano.

Tom's face broke into a smile and he trotted over to her. 'Hey, glad you made it. I was beginning to think you weren't coming.'

'I said I would,' she said, accepting the kiss that he planted on her cheek.

'Good, good... Okay, let's get started. I hope you two have been practising your steps?' Daphne asked, pointing a remote at the sound system, which began to play a classical waltz. 'Let's get you into hold. Show me what you remember.'

Cara hesitantly took Tom's hand and tried to get into position, looking away, over her left shoulder. She didn't want to think of elongating her neck *'as if a man is kissing it'*, as Daphne had said, because when she'd actually done that it had led to her fleeing Tom's home in shame.

'What's this gap?' Daphne protested, pushing Cara's body closer to Tom's. 'I could drive a lorry through there!'

It was hard holding Tom's hand, being pressed against him, when it was both all she'd ever wanted and also the one thing that she couldn't bear right now. With Daphne watching, the whole thing felt excruciating.

Daphne stood in Cara's eyeline and frowned. 'You had this so perfectly the other day! Have you forgotten everything?'

No. I've just got scared.

'Okay, let's see those box steps. And…*go!*'

Cara tried to remember her steps, tried to use the grace that she'd developed in the last lesson, but it was like starting anew. She felt so awkward and uncomfortable in Tom's arms that she immediately stepped on his toes and broke hold to step back and say sorry.

'Back in hold!' Daphne ordered.

She took his hand again, tried the steps, stepped on his toes again, flushed, felt heat rise all over her. Felt as if she might cry.

'What is going on? You had this the other day? What has changed?' Daphne frowned.

'It's okay. We've got this,' Tom tried to re-assure her. 'Cara? Look at me.'

She did so, feeling it was almost unbear-able. To look at the man she loved and to know that he might yet reject her, and then she'd lose everything.

'Feel the music. Forget the steps. Let's just try going with the flow,' said Daphne.

She went back into hold and tried, making mistake after mistake, but gritted her teeth and pushed through. This was meant to be enjoyable! This was meant to be fun! Once upon a time the idea of dancing with Tom had been exciting! Being in his arms… Pressed up close… Only now it was like a nightmare and…

Her nose twitched. Could she smell *smoke*?

She broke hold and stepped back, sniffing the air.

'No, no, no! Back into hold,' ordered Daphne. 'You were getting there!'

'I can smell smoke,' she said.

'What?'

She wasn't imagining things. There was definitely a smell of something burning. She was attuned to it. Knew something wasn't right.

At that moment, the receptionist ran into the room. 'There's a fire next door!'

'Call the fire brigade,' Cara ordered, turning to usher Tom and Daphne from the room. 'Exit the building. Let's make sure everybody's out. Do you have a headcount?'

Daphne seemed to hesitate. 'There's a register for each class.'

'I'll need them. Get everyone out.'

Cara rushed from the studio, grabbing the clipboards with a class register on each. She ordered Tom to get Daphne out, whilst she went from studio to studio to make sure everyone else was out. It didn't take long. The three studios had already been alerted and everyone had left the building. Cara went outside and told them all to line up on the opposite side of the street, so they could take a headcount. No one was missing.

She turned to look at the fire. It had broken out in the empty building next door and looked to be on the first floor, flames already billowing at the windows...

Oh, my God...

It wasn't empty. There were people in those windows, banging on the glass. Were they trapped?

'Stay here!' she ordered everyone, then ran across the road and used a chair from outside a café to break the glass of the building's door.

'Cara!' Tom shouted. 'Wait for the fire brigade!'

But she couldn't wait. Those people didn't have time and there still might be a way to get them out.

She knew fire. She knew how to read it. She understood about flashpoints and backdraughts and all the dangers inherent in running into a burning building.

Only this time she wasn't wearing her

flame-retardant kit. This time she didn't have breathing apparatus strapped to her back, an oxygen mask upon her face. She could feel the smoke already getting into her lungs and throat and she coughed, looking for a staircase. There was one right at the back of the building. Cement, so it wouldn't burn or collapse. She ran up the stairs, pulling her shirt over her mouth to help filter the air. At the top was a door and it was locked.

Damn!

She looked about her, saw a fire extinguisher on the wall. It was probably out of date, but it would do. She hefted it in her hands and used it to bash open the lock, kicking the door open with her foot.

Flames billowed from each side of her. There were rags and bags on the floor. And what looked like a camping gas tank. Squatters? Had they been using it? It hadn't blown up, but there was a danger of that. She used the fire extinguisher to try and put out some of the flames and fought past them to get to the people at the window.

'Hey! This way!'

'Oh, my God! I thought we were going to die!'

Some of the people rushed past her, leaving behind a woman who was coughing so badly she could barely stand. Cara rushed over to her and hefted her easily over one shoulder, then began heading back the way she had come.

As she made her way down the stone steps she heard a fire crew arriving and saw the familiar sight of an appliance screeching to a halt outside. Tom was there too.

'I'm a paramedic,' he explained to the unknown fire crew.

Cara was coughing madly—could feel the smoke and the soot lining her throat, her eyes burning and watering madly.

'Cara? Are you okay?' Tom asked.

'I'm fine,' she managed to get out, coughing more and more, knowing her lungs needed to try and expel the deadly carcinogens that she'd breathed in during the rescue.

'You need to be checked out.'

'I'm fine. Just look after her.' She indicated the woman.

It was odd to stand back and watch the fire crew work. Despite her almost deadly inability to breathe properly, she yearned to be part of them—running in, dousing the flames, bringing the fire under control. There was something awesome about doing that. Controlling something that was so wild and untameable. Having to stand out here and do nothing made her feel useless.

But I wasn't. I still saved a life.

Paramedics arrived to take the woman away, and another draped a blanket around Cara and steered her towards their ambulance to get some oxygen. She sat there, feeling her breathing get steadily easier, until she no longer needed oxygen therapy.

The fire had been quickly contained and now it was time for the clean-up. She watched as everyone did their job.

Tom finally clambered into the ambulance with her and sat down beside her. He laid his hand on hers and squeezed it before letting go.

'You scared the hell out of me when you ran into that building.'

'I knew what I was doing.'

'Did you? You weren't in your kit. You could have been hurt, or killed.'

'But I wasn't. I'm fine.'

'If you'd have ended up in hospital…hurt… on a ventilator… If I'd had to see you like that…'

She looked at him then. Frowned. 'You didn't. You won't.'

'When I saw you carrying that woman

out...' His voice trailed off and he looked into the distance and grimaced.

Oh. It must have been a stark reminder to him that she was just as Leo said. Too masculine for any man to want her. He'd seen her in her firefighter's outfit often, had seen her fight fires—but had he ever been witness to her physical strength? The woman she'd carried out hadn't been little. It had taken all her strength to lift her over her shoulder.

But perhaps it was easier this way? Because now he wouldn't see her naked, and she wouldn't have to be vulnerable and have her heart torn in two by him.

'It's okay. I understand,' she said, trying to make it easy on him. Trying to give him a way out.

Because she wanted to make this easy on him. Then it would be easier on her. They could still be friends. Forget that kiss. Forget the fact that she felt love for him. Admit that all they ever would be was friends. That way she would still be able to see him. That way she could still see Gage. No reason why that darling little boy should miss out, just because the adults had screwed up.

'We both have such risky jobs, but yours is...' Tom shook his head. 'Dangerous! You run into burning buildings, you risk your life, and I... I need stability. Not just for me, but for Gage. He's already lost his mother. I... I'm meant to protect him. Put my son first. And what have I been doing? Chasing after you...'

'Chasing after you...'

As if she was a terrible choice he had made. She nodded, with tears dripping down her cheeks. She could hear in his voice what he was trying to say. He was ending this. Whatever it was that they had begun. And he was right. Gage had to come first.

'That's fine. I understand. It's probably best. You're right.'

She tried to put on a brave smile, though inside her heart was breaking.

CHAPTER NINE

Apart from an irritating cough, Cara was suffering no ill effects from going into the fire without her equipment. The cough she could deal with. That was fine. If she had to cough for the rest of her life she'd do it. But the feeling she had in her heart at realising that she and Tom could never be was something much more devastating.

She should have realised from the start! Tom could never love her. He was right. He had to put his son first. And she…? She was not good enough for him.

She'd hoped for so much more, but everyone in her life had been right. People had tried to tell her ever since she was a small girl that she didn't act the way a woman should.

Her mother had tried. For years!

'Wear a dress, Cara! Please. For me.'

'No one will notice you if you dress like a boy all the time.'

'Let's do something pretty with your hair.'

Cara had wriggled free of every attempt to make her more feminine.

Then there'd been Leo. He'd liked the novelty of going out with a female firefighter at first. He'd had a few bragging rights. He'd seemed to enjoy that. But when their relationship had become physical he'd not seemed to want her that much.

She'd not understood it. They'd been young. In their twenties. They ought to have been in the prime of their lives. But Leo had begun distancing himself from her after that first time, and she'd wondered if she'd done something wrong. He'd been her first. She'd adored him. She hadn't wanted anything to go wrong between them. And then he'd told her the truth.

'I'm not physically attracted to you.'

'You're too hard.'

'You've got more muscle than me.'

And now Tom. He didn't want her for who she was. Maybe if she'd chosen any other career than firefighter they might be together now.

She was too strong. Too masculine. Too dangerous.

If was off-putting to some—she got that. Had heard it her entire life.

She'd not thought Tom would be like that.

She stared out of the window of the fire engine as it raced to a fire in a block of flats. Normally, with the sirens going, she could block out what was happening in her personal life. She could enter work mode. But today she was considering her choices in life.

Would it have been different if she'd been more girly? If she'd gone into charity work? Worn skirts and dresses? Not gone to the gym and pumped iron? Not got any tattoos? Maybe if she'd paid more attention to being like other women she'd have true love by now? Maybe if she'd become a 'lady who lunched' she'd be with Tom now, because then she wouldn't pose a threat.

Who am I kidding? If I was a lady who lunched Tom and I would never have met.

Ahead of them, thick smoke billowed into the sky. This was a real fire. Not a malicious call. Residents of the block of flats were gathered in front of the burning building, hands over their mouths in disbelief, some crying, some coughing.

Their appliance pulled up and immediately Cara jumped out to provide assistance. She was tasked with finding out how many people—if any—might still be inside the burning flats.

One of the tenants, a middle-aged guy in his forties, ran his hand through his hair. 'I don't know... Er... I don't see Jason from flat ten—that's on the third floor. And the Kimbles? I don't see them. There's Tansy...she's a single mum...got a small boy...only four. They live next door to Jason.'

'What's his name?'

'Khaya.'

'Okay.'

She thought she heard someone call her name, but she forged inside, breathing apparatus on, and began to search the premises methodically.

It could feel claustrophobic, searching for people in a burning building. Vision was often limited by thick, choking smoke, and being clad in heavy kit and breathing apparatus was hard work. And you often didn't fit in small spaces. Ceilings could come crashing down around you, floors could give way, so you had to go at a careful pace, always checking your exit route, inching forward to rescue those who still might be trapped.

'You run into burning buildings...'

Behind her was Reed, and he headed left down a corridor as she headed right. Some people had left their doors open when they'd fled, so she was able to get inside easily, scan the property and then move on to the next. Others had locked their doors, but she managed to open them with a couple of swift kicks, slamming the doors into the walls behind.

She was on the second floor. The missing people were from the third. But she couldn't miss checking this floor in case someone had been missed. She would never forgive herself if someone died because she hadn't done her job.

Tom had called Cara's name as she'd run into the burning building, his heart sinking into his stomach. This was a fierce fire. The building looked as if it could collapse at any moment. A fragile prefabricated building, built in the seventies, it probably hadn't been brought up to code in an age, what with council cutbacks...

He'd arrived right behind Green Watch. Had run over to the residents to see if anyone needed medical help. He'd seen Cara talking to someone and had tried to catch her cye, needing to talk to her. Things had been left pretty awkwardly yesterday, after his outburst, and then he'd had to take Daphne home.

And now she was gone again.

What if something happened to her in that building?

He'd been stupid yesterday. Not thinking about Cara's feelings, only absorbed in his own confusing ones. The guilt he'd been feeling about wanting another woman. The fear he had about ruining his friendship with Cara. The fear of losing her—of having to sit by her bedside if she got injured during a shout.

And then last night he'd been chatting with Gage before bedtime?

'I wish Cara were here all the time, Daddy,' he'd said.

'You do?'

Gage had nodded. Yawned. *'I like playing with her. Do you, Daddy?'*

'Yeah. I do.'

'Good. 'Cos sometimes you're sad and I think Cara makes us better.'

And that had made him think about how much Cara loved his son.

Seeing her carry that unconscious woman out of the building had reminded him of how strong she was. Not just physically, but mentally. Her determination to put others before herself was one of her greatest traits.

If only it was that simple. She runs into burning buildings.

They could collapse. This block of flats could collapse, with her inside, and he would lose everything all over again!

He couldn't do that.

And he certainly wouldn't put Gage through it.

But his heart thudded against his ribcage as he waited for Cara to emerge from the building all the same. His head might be wary of the risks in getting too close to Cara Maddox, but his heart had only ever known how to love her.

Cara paired up with Reed as they took the stairway to the third floor. The stairs were concrete, the only part of the building not on fire, yet still the air billowed with smoke that curled and danced to its own tune.

As they reached the fire door to the third floor they could see flames roaring when they looked through the small window.

'We stay together!' Reed shouted.

She nodded, yanking the door open and hugging the wall that would take them through the flames down to the two flats on the left-hand side.

The heat was fierce. Sweat was pouring down her back, but she barely noticed. They made it to the first door, saw smoke issuing out from behind it, indicating a possible active fire beyond. The door was locked. Reed gave it a hefty kick and they were in.

There was a long corridor, with rooms going off it left and right, thick with black smoke and flashes of orange and red. Cara heard something shatter, off to her left, and entered the first room. Empty. She checked beneath the bed, inside the wardrobes—anywhere someone might think was a good place to hide.

Nothing.

They moved on. Found a bathroom with the door locked. Another kick and it came open easily, and inside was a man, cowering in the bathtub fully clothed, water running over him.

'You Jason?' Cara yelled through her mask.

He nodded.

'Come with me,' Reed said, grabbing his arm and pulling him out. Before he left, he turned back to Cara. 'Be safe!'

'I will!'

With one missing person found, Cara knew they were not going to find the Kimble family in this flat. They were next door, the tenant had said, but she still had to sweep this flat. She entered the room at the end of the hall. A living room, with a small kitchenette off to one side. The ceiling had fallen through here and fire raged above. There were collapsed struts and beams lying haphazardly on the floor, smoking wildly. But there were no other people here.

Cara backed out of the flat and went on to the last one on this floor. The door was closed, but it felt hot. There had to be a fire raging behind it.

She kicked it open and stood back, waiting for the surge of flame, watching as it licked up to the roof beyond. Could she hear something? Screams? Someone crying for help?

She kept low and made her way in, her arm above her head to protect it from any falling debris. It was hard to see in here. The smoke was thick. She got out her torch and switched it on. A television still played in the living room—she could see the flicker of images—and by the window stood a woman, holding a small child in her arms. A child who looked unconscious.

Cara carefully made her way forward, jumping to one side as the ceiling above her collapsed, raining burning plaster and wood down on her. She fell, slamming into the wall, but soon was kicking off the burning joist and getting back to her feet, finally making it to the Kimbles.

'Tansy? Khaya?'

The woman turned, her face filled with fear. 'I can't wake him!'

'It's the smoke.'

Cara took the boy and laid him down, where the smoke was thinnest. She pulled off a flame-retardant glove and touched her fingers to the boy's neck. There was a pulse, thankfully.

Behind them, the ceiling crashed down completely, blocking their exit with a roaring flame. There was no way they could go back the way Cara had come in. They would have to find another way.

The window was slightly ajar, but didn't fully open. Cara looked around, saw a wooden chair, and told Tansy to stand back. She picked up the chair and swung it at the glass, shattering it into a million pieces, then she cleared away the last remaining shards around the frame and peered out to see if the ladders were being sent up.

They were!

Cara flashed her torch and waved to her crew below, indicating that she had two people to rescue.

Hodge was coming up the ladder, with Garrett behind. One for each of them.

Cara dipped back inside and took off her

breathing mask. She secured it to Khaya's face, then double-checked the window frame once again, to make sure that no one would suffer a nasty cut as they were carried out through the window.

'Nearly out,' she reassured Tansy.

'I'm afraid of heights!' she yelled back, coughing.

'You'll be okay. Don't worry.'

Cara covered Tansy's body with her own as the flames continued to get near. Then Hodge was at the window and Cara passed out Khaya. Garrett was there too, and they gently coached the petrified Tansy out onto the ladder. As something exploded behind her Cara ducked, feeling something explode as it flew past her.

What the hell was that?

But then she was up at the window and climbing onto the rescue ladder herself.

It slowly began to lower. And the air became cleaner and easier to breathe. Cara let out a heavy sigh. They'd done it. They'd got everyone out, as far as they knew. If there was anyone else still missing it would be up to the others to find them. She knew Hodge wouldn't let her go in again—not until she'd been checked medically.

She saw Tom at the bottom of the ladder,

waiting for his patients to be brought down. His face was etched in a deep frown. She wished she could run into his arms and just hold him, tell him she was safe and hear him say, *Thank God. I was so worried about you!*

But she knew that was never going to happen. If she wanted someone like Tom then she would have to change who she was, and she wasn't sure she could do that. It would all be pretend. She'd be playing dress-up— something she'd hated ever since she was a child.

No. She would have to look elsewhere for love.

Or maybe she was destined to be alone for ever.

As they reached the ground, Tom set to working on Khaya immediately.

'Is he going to be okay?' she asked, knowing how hard this must be for him. Working on a child the same age as Gage.

Tom looked up at her, his face strained. 'I'm doing my best.'

He was right. He had a job to do. Save the boy, not answer her inane questions! Angry with herself, she walked away, back to the appliance, where her feelings about everything that had happened lately threatened to overwhelm her.

Tears in her eyes, she lashed out, kicking the tyre of the fire engine over and over again.

It was the day of the charity ball for the Websters. Her mother's birthday. Cara's night. She was supposed to be going with Tom on her arm, looking like a lady.

What a joke that was going to be!

They'd both know that she wasn't, and everyone else would too. All her family would be there, no doubt laughing about her behind her back. And all her fire crew family. Reed would no doubt have something to say. And Tom? He would probably feel the most awkward of all.

If he showed up.

She'd not heard from him since he'd called things off between them. This was the longest they'd ever gone without speaking. She'd tried texting, but had got no response. She'd even left a message on his voicemail. Surely he wasn't going to stand her up for this? However wrong things had gone between them romantically, he was still supposed to be her best friend.

She'd hoped for so much more from Tom. That he would *see* her. That he would see the woman she was beneath the firefighter's suit.

Yes. She was totally different from Victoria. They could never be compared. Clearly. But they'd had something…hadn't they? Apparently not.

Maybe she was just terrible at reading men. She'd made a bad choice yet again.

Will I ever learn?

Still, Tom deserved to be with someone who didn't put her life at risk every day. She couldn't expect him to live like that. Wondering if she'd make it home every day. She'd witnessed the trauma he'd gone through after his wife's death, so she understood his reticence as his heart began to get involved.

Cara sighed. It was time to put on the dress. Do her hair. Make-up. Wear those dreaded heels! Instead, she checked her phone again. Surely Tom should have called her by now? Or maybe his silence was telling her all that she needed to know? That he wasn't going to show. That she would have to walk into her childhood home without a date on her arm?

She sat down in front of her mirror and started combing her hair, trying to decide which was the best way to wear it.

If she could get out of this night right now she would. But she'd made a promise and she wouldn't go back on it. And if she turned up alone and anyone had anything to say about it, then she'd just lift her chin, square her shoulders, and walk away.

She decided to wear her hair up. She'd been to the shops and bought some fancy pins. But every time she tried to make her hair stay put, it kept falling down.

How do other girls do this?

In the end she resorted to an instructional video she found online.

Ah. That's how.

She'd been doing it all wrong…she needed to put it up in sections, not all at once.

It looks pretty.

Next, she got out the make-up palette that she'd bought at the same time as the pins, wincing at the extortionate cost, and sought another online tutorial for something called 'a smoky eye'.

The first attempt made her look like a panda, and then she'd begun to cry, so she had to wipe it all off with wet wipes. But the second time was much better.

I'm a quick learner.

She put in some stud earrings she already had, and then slipped out of her robe and put on the dress. It clung to her in all the right places and she sat down to put on the heels. When she looked in the mirror to check out her reflection, she gasped. She'd never seen the entire look put together at the same time! It was astonishing! It was…dizzying! Suddenly she understood why girls did this. They could change who they were. Show different sides of themselves. Looking as if she ought to be walking down a red carpet made her feel…*special*.

Suddenly she wished her mother was there to see it. She would have been proud. She would have cried, without a doubt, and Cara knew that because she felt like crying again, too.

'What do you think, Mum?' she said to the empty room.

Of course there was no answer.

What would Tom do, seeing her look like this? Would he have second thoughts?

No. It takes more than a pretty dress and some heels to change a man's mind.

She checked the time. The car would be here at any moment to collect her. Tom ought to be here, only he wasn't, and the rejection she felt was absolute.

She sniffed, realising that she had to put this disaster with Tom behind her. It hadn't worked. They'd both been stupid to think that they could take their friendship and make it into something more. She could only be a stereotypical woman for this one night, and Tom would want someone who could be beautiful and feminine for ever.

There was a knock at her door.

Cara answered it. Her father's chauffeur, Jamison, was waiting.

'Lady Cara.' He gave a brief nod of his head. 'You look stunning.'

'Thank you, Jamison.'

She closed the door and walked down the path, feeling terribly alone, unaware of the ringing phone in her hallway.

The car carried her up the long driveway and she let out a small sigh at seeing her childhood home once again. She had lots of great happy memories of here. Playing in the stables. Going horse riding. Making dens with her brothers and playing hide and seek in all the attic spaces. Cara could hear her mum's voice now, calling to them all to come down for tea. She missed it. Missed her. Wished she'd had the opportunity to show her how she looked today.

I may have totally ballsed up my love-life, Ma, but look at me in a dress!

She had no doubt her mother would have squealed in delight at seeing her. She would have wanted to take many pictures. Pictures that would have been framed and set in pride of place for everyone to see.

Lady Cara Maddox. How she was supposed to be.

But she'd never fitted into anyone else's mould. Cara had always done her own thing and walked tall, and she would walk tall now, no matter what anyone said. Even if it meant walking in her own lane...even if it meant that she walked alone.

Suddenly the car door was being opened and her father was there. 'Cara! Look at you! Oh, my gosh, you're so beautiful.'

Her father took her by both hands and kissed both cheeks, before stepping back to take another look.

'Stunning. Simply stunning.' He smiled at her, proud, then looked behind her and frowned. 'No gentleman paramedic?'

She shook her head, determined not to cry. 'He couldn't make it.'

She had no idea if it was the right thing to say. Maybe it would have been better to say he was running late? But then when he didn't show at all, she'd get those knowing, pitying looks.

Poor Cara. Lost another guy, huh?

This way, if he did show up—which she

doubted very much now—it would actually be a pleasant surprise.

'That's a pity. Everything all right between you two?' her father pressed.

'It's fine.'

'All right. But I can't have my daughter having no one to dance with tonight. You'll dance with me, and then I think Xander or maybe Tarquin will want to whisk you around the dance floor looking like that.'

'I'm quite happy not being on the dance floor, Dad. These heels aren't best suited to fancy footwork.'

'Nonsense! Your mother danced in heels, and you've been practising, by all accounts!'

He disappeared into the crowd before she could find out who had told him she'd been practising the waltz.

Cara gazed out over the ballroom. It looked magnificent, as always. Tall marble columns stood all around the edge of the room. Long, red velvet curtains hung in between. Beautiful paintings and portraits of Maddox ancestors adorned the walls. The dance floor was filled with couples—men in tuxedos, women in all colours. It was like watching a garden of flowers, dancing in the breeze. To one side was an orchestra, currently playing a gentle number, and in between them all uniformed butlers and waitresses mingled, offering flutes of champagne and trays of hors-d'oeuvres.

She was surrounded by people, but she'd never felt so lonely.

'Can we get there any faster?' asked Tom from the back seat of the cab, trying his best to tie his bow tie, but failing terribly.

'Traffic, my friend. Nothing I can do,' said the cab driver, chewing his gum.

They were in a long stream of cars waiting to go up the long drive to Higham Manor and, unable to wait a moment longer, he flung some notes at the cabbie, darted from the car and began to run—with a large box under his arm.

He'd been a fool. An absolute fool! Thinking that if he removed Cara from his life he wouldn't have to worry about her. Since telling her he couldn't be with her, he'd not been able to get her out of his mind. And then there'd been that conversation with Gage…

'We…er…won't be seeing much of Cara from now on,' he'd told him.

Gage had looked shocked. Then sad. 'Why?'

'Because…'

He'd struggled to think of a way to explain it to his son that he would understand. But that had been hard when he still wasn't sure he understood his own feelings.

'*Because she's busy.*'

'*Has she got a new job?*'

'*No.*'

'*Then why can't she see us? She's always seen us. Always played with me and read me bedtime stories.*'

'*I know. It's just that things happen when you're a grown-up and life gets complicated.*'

'*If she came to live here then it wouldn't matter if she was busy.*'

He'd stared at his son. '*What?*'

Gage had stared up at his father with wide eyes. '*I want to be able to see Cara!*'

'*She has a dangerous job, son. She might...*' His words had got caught in his throat.

'*Might die? Like Mummy did?*'

He'd nodded, barely able to speak at such a thought.

Gage had been quiet for a while, then he'd sat up in bed and said, '*Daddy? If she can be brave, then we can too.*'

He'd stared at his son, surprised at the wisdom that came from a four-year-old boy. He'd been avoiding Cara's calls, sitting on the stairs as his phone rang with her name on the caller ID. He'd hated himself for ignoring them, knowing he needed to keep his commitment to their fake date at the ball but not knowing how he was going to bear the pretence now that things were over between them.

But now Gage had made him think that maybe it could be different.

Cara was a firefighter. She'd always wanted to be a firefighter. That was who she was and he loved her for it. And, yes, she was brave. Perhaps braver than them all. She'd defied everyone who had tried to change her and stuck to her guns. She had been there for him and his son in so many ways and he knew she had strong feelings for him. She had been devastated when he'd said they had to end.

Staying away from Cara for the rest of his life? That wasn't saving his heart—that was killing it! Why stay away when he could be with her? Any time he got to spend with her would be a gift. And if she got injured or, God forbid, something awful happened to her…? That would be terrible, obviously, and he didn't want to think of it happening at all. But if it did then he and Gage would have been blessed by having known her at all. Being part of the love that she gave so willingly.

So, yes. He'd been a fool and he needed to tell her.

She must be thinking he had backed out of their fake date. Well, he wasn't that kind of guy. He'd said he would be there and he was looking forward to dancing with her. Besides, they needed to talk about things.

When he reached the doors to the manor, he stopped, and asked a uniformed butler who was wearing a perfect bow tie if he could help him with his.

'Absolutely, sir.' The butler smiled patiently as he tied the tie, and then he reached into an inside jacket pocket. 'Might I suggest, sir…a comb?'

Tom glanced down at the man's hand and laughed. 'Yeah, thanks.' That was probably a good idea. 'Where's the ballroom?'

'Straight ahead, sir. Just follow the music.'

He nodded and walked towards the ballroom. When he got there someone presented him with a flute of champagne and he took it, downing it in one, before placing his empty glass back onto the tray.

He was looking for the most beautiful woman in the world, who would be wearing a gold dress.

His gaze scanned the walls, where groups of people stood in groups, chatting, but he couldn't see her there. Then he looked on the dance floor, and his eyes caught a glimpse of glittering gold and flaming red hair. She was dancing with her father.

Feeling his heart pound out of his chest, he stepped forward into the dancing throng. 'Excuse me… Sorry, could I just…? Excuse me…thank you.'

And then he was there, right next to her, and she looked stunning, if a little uncomfortable.

'Might I interrupt?'

Cara's head swivelled in his direction at the sound of his voice and she might even have gasped a little.

Her father smiled a greeting and nodded, stepping back. 'Of course. Be my guest.'

He stood in front of her, smiling. 'I'm sorry I missed your calls.'

'Where have you been?'

'Practising being an idiot. You look beautiful.'

She blushed.

'I've brought you a gift. I almost brought you a corsage, but then I saw this, so…' He proffered the large box that was tucked under his arm.

It was wrapped in gold, with a gold ribbon, which she tore open, smiling when she saw inside, nestled in white tissue paper, a sparkly pair of golden trainers.

'I thought these would let me dance with you for longer.'

She bent down to take off her hated heels and slip her feet into the trainers.

Tom took the heels, put them in the now empty box and passed it to a bewildered waitress. 'Could you get rid of these, please?'

The waitress took them and Cara stood up, gazing at him with apprehension. 'I thought you weren't coming.'

'I would never have missed this. I'm sorry I had you worried.'

He stared at her and stepped closer, holding out his hands for her to step into the hold they knew.

She did so.

And as she slipped hand into his he felt that somehow this was all going to be all right.

'I need to tell you how I feel about you,' he said.

She looked apprehensive. 'It's okay. I know. I'm not like Victoria. I never will be. But I am a firefighter and that will never change.'

'I'm not looking for another Victoria and I don't ever want you to change.' Tom waited for her to look at him. 'I've been an utter fool,' he said. 'A coward.'

'And I've been too caught up in myself,' she told him. 'I forgot you needed to think about Gage, too. My job makes me a risky prospect. I get caught up in what I do. I run towards danger. I go into burning buildings and I give up my oxygen and I use my body to protect others. Gage doesn't need someone like that. Neither do you.

'Are you kidding me? That selflessness? That bravery? Both of those things are wonderful! I would never change you. Not in a million years! You're perfect exactly as you are. And when I saw you carrying that woman from the burning building I realised just how much you terrified me.'

She frowned. Puzzled. 'What are you saying?'

'I'm saying that I realised I could have lost you, and that thought was too terrible to contemplate...because I'm in love with you.'

A small smile broke across her face. 'You're in love with me?'

'I am and I always will be. And I'd like to think that you will forgive me for running and being afraid, because I'm not any more, and I'd like to make this a real date between us. Not a fake one. What do you think to that?'

'I don't know what to say...'

She flushed, her cheeks pinker than he'd ever seen them before, and he just wanted to kiss her in front of everyone. Make it real.

Let everyone in this room know that he loved this woman. Because she was all woman. No matter if anyone else had made her feel that she was somehow lacking. She was the best woman. The only woman for him.

'Say you'll be my girlfriend for real?' He smiled, pulling her back into hold and pressing himself up against her, imagining more.

Cara laughed, and looked around her before looking back at him. 'I've loved you since the moment I met you, Tom. Do you know how hard that's been for me?'

He nodded. 'You still haven't answered my question.'

'What was that?'

'Will you be my girlfriend?'

She nodded, beaming. 'I will.'

'Good. Now kiss me. Kiss me before I spontaneously combust.'

Cara laughed, bringing her lips to his, and kissed him as he'd never been kissed before.

EPILOGUE

THE DOUBLE DOORS to her old childhood bedroom opened, and she turned just as her father gasped in surprise.

'Cara…you look beautiful,' he said in awe.

She flushed and turned to check her reflection in the long mirror. She was bedecked in white. A beautiful fishtail wedding gown with a sweetheart neckline, covered in lace and crystals. A diamond tiara and a long, floaty veil.

'Thanks.'

'If your mother were here…' His voice choked in his throat.

Cara reached out a hand to take his, squeezing his fingers in solidarity. She knew what he wanted to say.

If your mother were here, she'd be crying with happiness.

And he was right. She would be. Seeing her daughter like this. About to be married.

Looking like the perfect bride. The fact that her mother would not be with her at her wedding hurt a lot. But Cara knew that wherever she was she would be looking down at her and smiling, full of pride and joy.

'I wish she was here.'

Her father nodded. 'Me, too. You know, I'm very much aware that I've been a bit... *overpowering* at times. What do you call it? Sticking my nose in where it's not wanted?' He smiled.

Cara smiled back. 'A bit. But it doesn't matter today, Dad. Today is for happy memories.'

'You're right. But I wanted to have this moment before I pass your hand over to Tom to try and explain.'

He paused for a moment. Checked his own reflection in the mirror and rearranged his cravat. Plumping it to perfection.

'When your mother died, I was distraught. We all were, I know. But in you I saw your mother. You're so alike in so many ways. The way you smile. The way you tilt your head when you're listening to someone talk the way you're doing now.' He smiled again. 'The way you laugh. And when you moved out I couldn't bear to be separated from you. I still needed that contact with her through you.

I kept trying to mould you to be like her and I should have known better. You're your own woman, just as you should be, and I wanted to tell you today that I've realised what I was doing and it was wrong. So... I apologise.'

'Oh, Dad!' She stepped forward to wrap her arms around him and held him tight.

They stood in an embrace for a while, until the wedding planner, Harriet, came in with her clipboard, clapping her hands.

'Time's tight, people. Ready to go?'

Cara let go of her father and stepped back, just as he reached into his jacket pocket.

'Your something borrowed.' He passed her a velvet box.

She frowned in question, then opened it. Inside, lying on a green velvet cushion, was her mother's diamond necklace. 'Dad...'

'She'd want you to wear it. She wore it on her wedding day. But you know you don't have to, if you think I'm being—'

'Dad, it's perfect. I'd be honoured.' She turned so he could fasten it at the back of her neck.

Cara looked at it in the mirror. Her mother would always be with her, but this was extra-special and made her feel close to her once again.

'Ready to go?'

Her father held out his arm and she slid hers into it.

'I'm ready.'

Harriet left the room and signalled to someone at the bottom of the stairs. Music suddenly bloomed through the high hall and up the stairway of Higham Manor. The 'Wedding March'.

Cara took a brief moment to adjust her veil, so it lay perfectly, and then began the slow walk from her bedroom, all the way down the sweeping, staircase which was adorned with fresh flower garlands.

Beneath them in the grand hall were all their guests. Friends. Family. Work family. Everyone she knew. People whose lives she'd saved and stayed in touch with. Everyone. She saw all their happy faces, all their smiles, and saw how beautiful everyone looked. But there was one person she wanted to see the most.

Tom.

He stood in front of a flowered arch, dressed in a suit like her father's, his lovely face looking up to her as she descended the stairs. Beside him, in a miniature top hat and tails, stood Gage, holding a red cushion with their wedding rings on it.

Her heart pounded with joy as all her dreams began to come true.

People whispered their good wishes and love as she passed them. She met happy gaze after happy gaze. She got a cheeky wink from Reed. A bow of the head from Hodge.

And then she was standing next to Tom and her father was letting go of her and stepping back.

Tom reached for her hand, smiling. 'You look stunning.'

'Thanks,' she answered shyly.

'Are you wearing them?' he whispered.

Cara lifted up her skirt slightly, to reveal the bridal trainers that he'd bought for her. White. Studded with crystals that caught the light.

Tom laughed. 'You look perfect.'

She smiled, covering them up again. 'So do you.'

* * * * *

Keep reading for an excerpt of a new title
from the Desire series,
THE OUTLAW'S CLAIM by Brenda Jackson

ONE

"I NOW PRONOUNCE you husband and wife. You may kiss your bride."

Maverick Outlaw grinned broadly as he watched his brother Jess pull his new wife, the former Paige Novak, into his arms, as if determined to kiss the lips right off her face. None of the onlookers seemed surprised at such a strong display of passion. Not even their father, Bart.

It had shocked the hell out of some when Bartram Outlaw had shown up for the wedding. It really should not have, since it was one of Bart's sons getting married. However, the Outlaw brothers would be the first to admit that their father was ornery as hell and pigheaded to a fault. There were other words that could describe him, but since none of them were nice, Maverick decided not to think about them today.

Maverick was just glad their old man was

here and trying to be friendly and sociable. Maybe that was helped along by the beautiful woman at his side, Claudia Dermotte. She was as friendly, sociable and outgoing as they came.

A few hours later, after all the wedding photos had been taken and the wedding dinner had been served and eaten, Jess and Paige escaped to change into their traveling clothes. They would be leaving to begin their month-long honeymoon, beginning in Dubai.

Maverick swore he'd never seen Jess so happy. There was no doubt in Maverick's mind that although marriage seemed to agree with some people, he was not one of them. He liked his life just the way it was, and he enjoyed being a bachelor. His goal was to remain that way for quite a while. Maybe even forever, since he didn't have to worry about continuing the Outlaw line. His married brothers seemed to be doing a good job of it.

"I noticed you kept your eyes on the old man today like the rest of us."

Maverick glanced over at his brother Sloan and nodded. "I don't know why we even bothered when he's with Claudia. Dad never acts like an ass when he's with her."

"True. That goes to show he can be a decent human being when he wants."

Maverick nodded again, knowing that was true. He wished he could say their father's bark was worse than his bite, but *that* wasn't true. Bart Outlaw was known to take a huge chunk out of a person's ass whenever he was inclined to do so.

Maverick took a sip of his champagne and glanced over at their father. Claudia's hand was firmly in Bart's as she moved toward the newlyweds, who had just reappeared. When they reached Jess and Paige, of course, it was Claudia who made the first move and gave the couple goodbye hugs. Maverick then watched his father give Jess and Paige hugs as well. If he hadn't seen it with his own eyes, he would not have believed it. When did Bart ever hug anyone other than Claudia and their sister, Charm?

"I'd be damned," Sloan said, obviously seeing the exchange as well. "Although he looked stiff as hell doing it, I can't believe the old man actually hugged them."

"I honestly think that stunt he pulled with Cash and Brianna scared the shit out of him," Maverick said, remembering how their father had tried to break up the couple. "He finally realized how close he came to losing one of his sons when Cash was ready to disown the old man."

"I agree with you there," Sloan said. "Maybe that's why he didn't have anything to say when I announced I was marrying Leslie."

Maverick had four brothers, and all were here and accounted for. He also had one sister. He knew some people found it amazing that all six Outlaw siblings were as close as they were, considering each of them had a different mother. Bart had been married to five of the women, and when the divorces became final, his attorneys made sure he was given custody of his five sons. Maverick, at thirty-two, was the youngest son.

Garth, at forty, was the oldest, and he and his wife, Regan, were the proud parents of a seven-month-old son name Garrison. Regan's father had been the corporate pilot for his family's company for over forty years. When he retired, Regan had taken over. Just as Garth had taken over as CEO of their family's multimillion-dollar business, Outlaw Freight Lines, when Bart had retired. Or more specifically, when the company's board threatened to oust Bart if he didn't step down.

Jessup—or Jess, as he preferred to be called—was thirty-eight and became the politician in the family when he went to Washington four years ago as a senator from Alaska. Everyone was happy for him and Paige, who was an actress in Hollywood and sister to their cousin Dillon Westmoreland's wife. Paige had turned twenty-nine today and wanted to get married on her birthday.

Cashen, who preferred being called Cash, was Bart's third-oldest son and at thirty-six was married to Brianna. They were the proud parents of two-year-old twin boys. Cash and his family made their home in Wyoming on a ranch he'd inherited from his mother.

Sloan was brother number four and had gotten married five months ago. He and his wife, Leslie, maintained dual residences in Wasilla and Fairbanks, Alaska. Sloan had had no problem informing the family—the day of his wedding, mind you—that he intended to have his wife pregnant by Christmas. Since that was next month, Maverick could just imagine how the couple spent most of their free time.

Last, but not least, there was his sister, twenty-seven-year-old Charm. She was the youngest of Bart's children, and being the only girl, she was definitely the apple of their father's eye. To this day, Charm's mother, Claudia, was the only woman Bart had ever loved and the one he couldn't handle. And…she'd been the only mother of his children Bart hadn't married, but not for lack of trying.

Hell, their father was still trying. Maverick and his siblings always got a kick out of seeing Bart court Claudia. They figured the reason she hadn't married Bart after all this time was because she needed some sort of affirmation that he had changed his manipulative ways. If that was true, then there would never be a marriage because Maverick and his brothers couldn't see his father turning over a new leaf any time soon, or ever. Just like a leopard couldn't change his spots, they doubted their father could change the ingrained nature of his character.

Sloan walked off, and Maverick was alone again. At least for the time being. There was no way he could ever be totally alone among his Westmoreland cousins. There were too many of them. Besides that, the wedding and the reception had been held in a section of Denver the locals referred to as Westmoreland Country.

Dillon, the oldest of the Denver-based Westmorelands, had built this mega building and named it Westmoreland House. The building, which could hold over three hundred people easily, was meant to be used for special occasions, events and family get-togethers.

Hearing oohs and aahs, he glanced over to where several relatives were admiring his cousin Bane's three-month-old babies. It was the second set of triplets for Bane and his wife, Crystal, and all six kids were a perfect combination of the two of them, though they all had their father's hazel eyes.

Maverick's cell phone vibrated. He had turned off the ringer during the wedding ceremony and now wondered who would be calling him. Most of his female acquaintances only had the number to his burner phone. Anyone he considered important was here, attending his brother's wedding.

Except for Phire.

He felt a slow roll in his stomach after pulling out his phone and seeing it was her, Sapphire Bordella, the woman who'd once been his friend with benefits.

He and Phire had met in Paris three years ago, when he'd been on a business trip. They had been attracted to each other immediately.

He had quickly discovered she was someone he could talk to and enjoyed spending time with—both in and out of the bedroom. They were friends who understood each other, and at the time neither had been looking for anything permanent. One thing they had in common—they both had domineering fathers. Maverick knew how to handle his, but Phire had yet to learn how to handle hers. He was convinced the man was as much of a manipulator as Bart. Possibly even more so.

A year ago, Phire had decided it was time for her to pursue a serious romantic relationship. By mutual agreement they had ended their FWB relationship. However, they had maintained their close friendship and would often call each other to see how things were going. Lately, he'd noticed her calls had become infrequent. He had assumed she'd met someone and things had gotten serious, and he'd been delegated as a part of her past.

"Phire?"

"Yes, it's me."

Maverick heard the strain in her voice. "Is everything alright?"

"No."

That single word stoked his ire at whatever

was bothering her. The one thing Phire would never admit to was not being okay. He walked to an area in Westmoreland House where he could hold a private conversation. When he entered an empty room, he realized it was the huge playroom Dillon had added to the design of the building so the youngsters in the family could have a place to enjoy themselves. This room looked like an indoor playground.

"What's wrong, Phire?" he asked, closing the door behind him.

There was hesitation before she said, "I know we're not together anymore, but I need to see you, Maverick."

He heard the urgency in her voice and glanced at his watch. "I'm at my brother's wedding in Denver, but I can be in Paris in—"

"I'm not in Paris—I'm in Texas."

"You're home?"

"I told you this ranch hasn't been my home in years, Maverick."

Yes, she had told him that a number of times. "Alright. I have my plane. Just give me time to refuel and I'm coming to Texas."

"I hate for you to leave the wedding."

"The reception is about to end, and Jess and

Paige will be leaving for their honeymoon in a little bit, anyway."

"If you're sure it won't inconvenience you."

A part of him knew Phire could never inconvenience him. "It's no problem. I can fly into Austin's airport and—"

"No, I prefer meeting you someplace else."

"Where, then?"

"Dallas. I can leave here for Dallas in a few hours."

"And I'll meet you there. I'll make all the arrangements and text them to you."

"Okay, and thanks, Maverick."

"Don't mention it. I'll see you soon."

After he clicked off the phone, he checked his watch as he left the room. He hoped to have all his questions answered as to what was bothering Phire in a few hours.

"And just where do you think you're going, young lady?"

Phire didn't bother to glance up from tossing items into her overnight bag. The last thing her father needed to know was that she had plans to meet Maverick. The best thing she'd done over the last three years was to keep Maverick's identity shielded from her father.

When he had ordered her home from Paris a couple of days ago, all he'd said was that she should come home immediately. Once she had arrived at the ranch, it didn't take long to find out why she'd been summoned. He had selected the man he wanted her to marry.

Phire's mother had passed away when she was twelve. Less than a year later, her father, Simon Bordella—an attorney turned rancher—sent her to live with his older sister in Paris. He hadn't even sent for her to come home during the holidays or summers. If it hadn't been for her aunt, Phire honestly don't know what she would have done. Lois Priestly had been a godsend for her.

As Phire got older, two things became crystal clear. Although her aunt Lois never had anything bad to say about Phire's father, she'd never said anything good about him, either. There had definitely been a disconnect in the brother-sister relationship. Granted, there was a fourteen-year difference in their ages, but Phire would have thought they'd have a closer sibling bond.

More than once she'd tried getting her aunt to talk about it, but she never would. The only thing Aunt Lois would say, was that whatever was done in the dark would eventually come to light. Phire often wondered what she meant. Another thing her aunt had warned her about was to never to cross him.

When Phire finished high school at seventeen, her father had finally sent for her, saying he wanted her to attend an American university. After college, Phire decided to make her home in Paris, and at the age of twenty-one, nothing her father did or said could make her change her mind. She reminded him that she was now an adult and old enough to make her own decisions. Besides, why would he want her around when he hadn't before?

After she'd been living back in Paris for a year, her aunt had a massive stroke, which left her without speech and paralyzed in the legs. That meant Aunt Lois was in need of constant attention in a long-term care facility. When the funds for Aunt Lois's care ran out, a frantic Phire had no other choice but to reach out to her father, convinced he would come to his sister's aid.

Simon Bordella had agreed to provide the funds for his sister's care, but not out of the goodness of his heart. He'd told Phire that he would only agree to help on one condition—

Phire would agree to marry whatever man he chose for her without any questions asked.

At first, Phire thought he was joking. When she saw he was not, she was appalled. It was only when the doctors stressed what could happen to her aunt without proper long-term care that, out of desperation, Phire agreed to her father's terms.

"I asked, where do you think you're going, Sapphire?"

She turned around. "I need to think, and I can't do it here."

"What is there to think about? I kept my end of the agreement and provided the best care possible for Lois. Now it's time you kept your end of the deal."

Phire narrowed her gaze at him. "I had hoped you wouldn't hold that agreement over my head. I'd begun thinking that you were providing the best of care to Aunt Lois because she is your sister."

"Well, you thought wrong. Lois and I never got along. The only reason I've been paying those exorbitant fees for three years is because of the deal you and I made."

"Why, Dad? Why is it important for you to select the man for me to marry?"

"The reason doesn't matter. All you need to know is that now that you're twenty-five, it's time for you to settle down and Jaxon Ravnell will make the perfect son-in-law."

Phire frowned as she thought of the man she'd been introduced to last night at dinner. "Why? Because he's wealthy and you think he can be easily manipulated?"

Her father smiled as if he found what she'd said amusing. "Jaxon does have more money than he knows what to do with, so what's wrong with me helping him decide the best way to use it?"

Phire didn't say anything. She would admit that thirty-two-year-old Jaxon was definitely a handsome man. He was the CEO of several technology firms in Virginia and was in Texas looking for land to expand. Her father had met him a few weeks ago at one of those Texas business meetings, where the red carpet had practically been rolled out for Jaxon.

Over dinner last night her father had tried his hardest to sell Jaxon on the idea that he needed to invest some of his millions by buying up a lot of the land in the area. Mainly land her father owned that was adjacent to the ranch.

She'd always been good at reading people,

and it had been obvious to her—even if hadn't been to her father—that Jaxon *wasn't* a man who could be easily manipulated. For some reason, she had a feeling Jaxon was actually playing her father by pretending the opposite. That was something she found rather interesting.

What her father had said earlier was true. He had made sure her aunt had the best of care in one of the finest facilities in Paris. He had kept his end of their deal, and whether she wanted to or not, she would keep hers.

"I need you back here in two days, Sapphire. I could tell over dinner that Jaxon was taken with you. He said he'd be in the area for at least six months and you two should spend time together. I want a wedding to take place no later than the spring. Understood?"

When she didn't say anything, he continued, "Just in case you don't understand, maybe now is the time to tell you that I had Lois moved."

"You did what?" she asked furiously, crossing the room to her father.

"You heard me. Just in case you try to wiggle out of our agreement. Don't worry, my sister is still getting the best of care, just in a non-disclosed location. I won't tell you where until *after* you and Jaxon get married."

"You can't do that!"

"As her legal guardian, I can do whatever I want. Don't worry about your aunt. What you need to concern yourself with is getting Jaxon to make you his wife by spring. As far as I'm concerned, there's nothing you need to think about. However, if you feel the need to get away to accept your fate, then by all means, do so. But I expect you back in two days with a smile on your face, ready to convince Jaxon that you are the best thing that could ever happen to him."

When her father walked out the room, Phire sank down on the bed.

Maverick checked his watch as he paced the confines of the hotel room. He hadn't expected to arrive in Dallas before Phire and had texted her all the information she needed, including the fact that a hotel key in her name was at the check-in desk.

He knew everyone was wondering why he'd left Denver unexpectedly, when he and his brothers had planned to remain in Westmoreland Country for another two days. His brother Sloan had made a wisecrack that it must have something to do with a woman. His brother was right on that account. What Sloan was wrong about was in thinking this was a hookup. Maverick considered Phire more than that.

From their first meeting it had been easy to see she was unlike any woman he'd ever known. In addition to her striking beauty, she had wit and a personality that drew him even when he hadn't wanted to be drawn. And the more he had gotten to know her, the more he'd appreciated their friendship. Entering into a FWB relationship had been the first of its kind for him. Before Phire, he would never have considered such a thing.

As he waited for her arrival, he couldn't help but recall when they'd first met. It had been his and Garth's second night in Paris, and Maverick had decided to check out the nightlife at a pub someone had recommended. Since the place was a few blocks away and it had been a beautiful night in April, he'd walked.

As Maverick gazed out the hotel window at downtown Dallas, he let himself remember when he'd met Sapphire Bordella. It was a night he would never forget...